WE THAT ARE YOUNG

WE THAT ARE YOUNG

PRETI TANEJA

ALFRED A. KNOPF

NEW YORK

2018

THIS IS A BORZOI BOOK
PUBLISHED BY ALFRED A. KNOPF

Copyright © 2017, 2018 by Preti Taneja

All rights reserved.
Published in the United States by Alfred A. Knopf,
a division of Penguin Random House LLC, New York,
and distributed in Canada by Random House of Canada, a division of
Penguin Random House Canada Limited, Toronto. Originally published
in paperback, in slightly different form, in Great Britain by
Galley Beggar Press, Norwich, in 2017.

www.aaknopf.com

Knopf, Borzoi Books and the colophon are registered
trademarks of Penguin Random House LLC.

Library of Congress Cataloging-in-Publication Data
Names: Taneja, Preti, author.
Title: We that are young : a novel / Preti Taneja.
Description: New York : Knopf, 2018. | A revised version of the 2017 edition
published by Galley Beggar Press (Norwich, England).
Identifiers: LCCN 2018015399 (print) | LCCN 2018020690 (ebook) |
ISBN 9780525521532 (ebook) | ISBN 9780525521525 (hardcover) |
ISBN 9781524711450 (open market)
Subjects: LCSH: New Delhi (India)—Social life and customs—Fiction. |
Families—India—New Delhi—Fiction. | Interpersonal relations—Fiction. |
Family-owned business enterprises—India—Fiction. | BISAC: FICTION /
Literary. | FICTION / Cultural Heritage. | FICTION / Sagas.
Classification: LCC PR6120.A465 (ebook) | LCC PR6120.A465 W47 2018 (print) |
DDC 823/.92—dc23
LC record available at https://lccn.loc.gov/2018015399

Jacket photograph by John Foxx/Stockbyte/Getty Images
Jacket design by Gabriele Wilson

Manufactured in the United States of America
First Edition

for Meera Taneja   the light

What is this untellable tale about?
The ogress and the dog make bedroom eyes;
The big cat prowls the jungle;
In my family of five, all hell breaks loose.
Led by drum-beating rabbits, a herd
Of antelopes mounts an attack;
The hunter's around, though all he does is watch.
The sea's ablaze, the forest's turned to ash,
But the fish are out looking for game.
The true pundit will get the story, says Kabir.
He's my guru. He'll save himself and save me too.

Songs of Kabir, 138
Translated by Arvind Krishna Mehrotra

I

—.—

JIVAN

i

It's not about land, it's about money. He whispers his mantra as the world drops away, swinging like a pendulum around the plane. The glittering ribbon of the Thames, the official stamps of the Royal parks, a bald white dome spiked with a yellow crown, are swallowed by summer's deep twilight. The plane lifts, the clouds quilt beneath it, tucking England into bed to dream of better times. It is still yesterday, according to his watch. He winds the dial forward. Now it is tomorrow, only eight hours to go.

He's landed the window seat with the broken touchscreen: it's either in-flight information or *Slumdog Millionaire,* the last movie he ever took Ma to. They went on release weekend. The entire line of people had been brown, so for once Ma didn't hunch in his shadow as if his jeans and camel coat would protect her, explain her. Instead they had the same old fight about Iris, and as he bought toffee popcorn she began to sniff: she said she was catching a chill. She kept up the sniffing as the credits rolled over the entire cast line-dancing on the set of an Indian train station. When they got outside, he thought she'd been crying. He put his arms around her: her head was the perfect place for his chin to rest. He asked her if she liked the movie, she said she didn't at all. It was not real India, except for the songs.

It's been a long haul from JFK to the LHR stopover. He's half-shot with the comfort of Johnnie Walker, knows it's not the best but he appreciates the label. It feels bespoke to him, like a child in a gift shop who finds a mug with his own name on it. No gift shop in America has a JIVAN mug so he borrowed JON, and that's been it since he did this trip the other way. Thirteen years old: sold on leaving India by the promise of his first time in the air.

Forward, forward, he wills the plane, drumming his hands on the tray-table, earning himself the side eye from the woman wedged into the seat next to him. She's using her iPhone 4 to photograph the back page of the in-flight magazine: *Ambika Gupta: offering you the miracle of advanced Numerology: a digit for your future.* She pokes the man on her other side: Sardarji in a blue turban, matching jersey stretched over his belly, stitched with a white number 5. Dude looks like he's birthing quintuplets under there. She smiles at him, sits back in her seat. There are thin red lines traced all over her hands in fading bridal henna as if she's been turned inside out, painful, beautiful, the pattern of her is all paisleys. Her ring is a platinum band with a square-cut white diamond and her bag is Longchamps like all the pretty-pretty girls have; navy waterproof with brown leather trim, but small, the cheapest. *Don't you know, pretty girl, that no bag is better than trying too hard?* She's flicking through the magazine: ads for Marc Jacobs, Charlize Theron, flicks to the gadgets, flicks to the movies, *clink-chime-clink* go the red glass bangles stacked up her wrists.

It sounds like the overture to Ma's practice music. Played for her to dance Kathak, with precision, while Jivan kept time. Fist thumping into palm, *Dha-din-din-dha.* His memories are coloured by her last months—Ma, fading from brown to yellow, a bruise that would not heal against the hospital white. *Dha-din-din-dha* became her fingers beating lightly on his temples—blurring into the rattle of her breath toward the end—the background hum of the plane's engine in his ears. They are cruising high over the mountains of who knows where.

He pulls out his own magazine. The cover is a cartoon illustration—a tiny brown body topped with an oversized head. Under a halo of white hair, two puffed cheeks blow out candles on a vast birthday cake the shape of an udder. India, sprouting with the turrets of heritage hotels, factory chimneys. Cars race off its surface, bolts of cloth unfurl, tigers hunt goats through spurting oil rigs. The orange headline shouts: *Happy 75th Birthday Devraj Bapuji!* The spotlight falls on the wily old face. *This* man, on *this* cover, on *this* flight—this is what Ma would have called a sign.

—Sir, beverage?

The airhostess is white bread, plum jam lickable; her smile promises drinks, upgrades, a hand to hold if the plane goes down. Jon wants to show-and-tell the magazine to her, *Hey, my real name is Jivan! When I was a kid, I knew this guy! He is Bapuji, my half brother's Godfather. He's like my uncle, not blood, but you know. I grew up with his daughters Gargi and Radha. I remember when Sita, his youngest, was born.* He might even speak the verboten words: *Have you heard of Ranjit Singh, Bapuji's second in command? He's my actual, like, Pa!* He should just draw her a cast list complete with family trees.

—Nothing, he says. For me.

The plane turns east. On screen its tiny replica inches forward, crossing out half the world. He shifts again, trying to keep his shirt from creasing, his suit from getting crumpled. His tie has a stripe that confirms a certain university (Harvard); his shoes are handmade English (Lobbs). These are the spoils he is returning with. After fifteen years. To Delhi, city of his childhood, a diamond inside a diamond on the map.

The cabin lights fade. The passengers recline, stiff like store dummies, eyes masked against each other. He opens the magazine.

Birthday Greetings, by Barun J. Bharat.

J.J.J. Maybe, Jivan thinks, Barun's one of those guys who needs that extra initial, like some men need a tie-pin, to make him feel safe. Or maybe he has a more famous brother.

The Age of Devraj, writes Barun. *We salute him, founder of The Devraj Company, one of India's most loved tycoons, who has just achieved his Seventy-Fifth year.*

Devraj. Grinning from a double-page spread, dressed in a safari suit and hat. Up to his knees in the watery, fragile Sunderbans, a tiger cub cradled in his arms. *Visionary Businessman, Guru to millions, employer of thousands, head of the hundred-hotel Company, father of three lovely daughters, Gargi, Radha and Sita*, the caption says. *Adoptive father to Tipu Sultan, a two-year-old tiger cub, who was raised by Devraj Bapuji, Animal Lover and Environmental Hero, in the Company private zoo.*

And also—also—Godfather to one lucky bro called Jeet. How could Barun J. Bharat, in-flight journalist, miss that? What about the textile mills from Punjab to Trivandrum, busy spinning silk into gold? Or the cement and brickworks in some serious backwaters? *Huff and puff, said the big, bad wolf, aré, of course the house won't blow down.* Don't forget the transport industry that runs on parts made in Company factories, from steel, mined and smelted in Company concerns—Barun needs a lesson in proper research: the kind of deep Googling a person might do if they were banished to a galaxy far, far away, surviving in exile, waiting.

There is some news. The Company is moving into cars. It will produce, in the name of Devraj's youngest, most precious daughter, Sita, and in recognition of her commitment to many causes, but particularly to Mother Nature, India's first hybrid, the world's smallest vehicle, aimed at the common man. *The Company reach is only growing in these times when India,* Barun writes, *is claiming her rightful place on the global stage. All has been brought into being by Devraj Bapuji's sheer determination, his far-reaching gaze. One of our most venerated business leaders, his spirituality ever feeding his superlative business ethos, his work for the girl-child in education recognised by a special Businesses in Charitable Endeavours Award given to him by the honourable Minister of Human Resource Development and the President of India. A close personal friend of left and right and an adviser on fiscal policy, his skill with a skillet at family barbecues is most appreciated by his friends. He is a man whose fearlessness in business has grown from grassroots to luxury hotels into one of India's leading brands yet he remains humble.*

Wow, could Barun use a class in white writing. His prose is cloying like Diwali sweets, clogging the throat. Jalebi language, made of twists and turns, slick with the street oil it's fried in. Yet Jon can taste his longed-for Delhi in the words. Could he speak Barun, if he tried? He has the core skills. Before he was sent to America, his father would task him to scour the daily national newspapers, to search and cut and read out loud any coverage that mentioned Devraj, Ranjit or the Company concerns. He was an obedient nine years old: he only told the good stories. In those days it seemed that was all there was: it looks as if nothing has changed.

He smiles. Who would guess from this report that Devraj used to wear specially dyed, saffron-coloured Y-fronts every day? That some Guru told the old man he would live past a hundred if he did? Those are true facts. Once when he was still called Jivan, and only about ten, he was playing *The Bold and the Beautiful* with Radha (it was her idea), somewhere they should not have been (Devraj's walk-in closet). In a drawer under the kurta pyjama, the handloom shawls, the ties hanging flaccid from a rack, he saw the stacks of orange underwear for himself. Radha told him what the Guru had said—*for longevity of body and name: saffron must be worn each day, next to the most precious skin.* Was that the first time Radha showed Jivan her own panties? Pink they were, with frills. Then, she cried because he would not show his.

He skims the pages until a smaller headline stops his eye. *Devraj Celebrates as Company forays to Kashmir.* This, he did not know. *Soon,* according to Barun J. Bharat, *the discerning tourist will be able to holiday courtesy of the Company in seven-star luxury in the coolest (literally!) new destination for domestic and international travellers, reclaiming the world's most beautiful memory of love. Where the latest iteration of the iconic Company Mukti Spa,* the article says, *will make you say "Ahh."*

New car launching, new hotel opening. Domestic tourist market growing in a city ripe for takeover. The whole world in recession except at Devraj Company, Main Street, New India. He sits back, the magazine a baton in his hands.

It's not about land, it's about money.

There is a picture of Devraj in a white kurta pyjama and brown shawl. He is looking down at Sita, her back is to the camera—her sari blouse is laced like an old-school corset, pinching her skin to diamonds. *One of Delhi's top young beauties-with-brains: elegant, accomplished, so devoted to Bapuji that since she returned from UK she is at his side for every public engagement. Still single aged 22, she is India's most eligible Bachelorette,* writes Barun. In the final shot they are under a banner: *Green Delhi Clean Delhi!* with the Minister for Tourism, he's having a great trip with his arm around Sita's shoulder. She is holding a hand over her mouth as if yawning or laughing, it's hard to tell which. Jivan examines the picture. There it is, on her third finger—Gargi, Radha and Jeet all have a ring like this—Devraj's initial twinned with theirs carved out in the flat-faced gold.

The caption says *Devrajji, Sita Devrajkumari. Special VVIP guests at the Annual Convention of Indian Tourism and Heritage dinner function, hosted at The Company Delhi Grand Hotel and Mukti Spa.*

Mukti again, mukti. Jivan cannot remember what it means. He closes his eyes. *Liberation.* Sita was tiny when Jivan left. All he remembers is a little princess, attached to her Lottie, who was never allowed to play out. Held in the sky and the world is turning. Perhaps he has always been here, ageing on this plane. Perhaps the last years in America are no more than Disney dreams.

Outside: nothing. He calls for another whisky.

—Sorry, sir, we only serve unlimited drinks in First Class.

The flight attendant walks away, her hair so neat, her makeup so pat she could be Company-made, remote-controlled. She sweeps behind the red curtain that divides the rich from the not-so-much. Beyond that curtain is wonderland. Drinks and legroom; stewardesses who never say *no*.

The captives of economy surround each other. A tangle of saris, plaits, cardigans, high-heeled sandals slung into empty Dunkin' Donuts boxes, torn-up *Glamour* magazines. The men stretch across the seats, the women clutch the children; the children won't let go of their Nintendo DSis even as they sleep. Dinner is given, not served: brown plastic lumps in a makhani sauce, rice and pickles. Or white plastic lumps with herb sauce instead. He chooses Indian, then Western, cannot stomach anything. Next to him, the newlyweds try to keep food, sachets, cutlery on the tray, to eat without elbowing each other. The smells are of rehydrated flesh, the toilets, feet.

Jon's face is reflected in the touchscreen. It looks warped, as if he has become his own old man. *Ranjit Kumar Singh, the Company's Head of New Business, a taste for bright socks and matching breast-pocket handkerchiefs. Suits bespoke from Heritage, fabrics fresh from Company supplies.*

The bride beside him is finishing her food. Her fork breaks; she wipes the plastic tub with her fingers. He shifts to avoid any falling grains of rice. On this journey, it will be impossible to keep clean.

Six weeks ago, he wore this suit for visiting hours. Ma in the bed, getting more quiet and thin. He thought she might dissolve. Slide off the plastic sheet to be mopped away by a hospital orderly. Yet she smiled when she saw her Jivan dressed up. When she was lucid, she said, in her lilting singer's voice:

—Go to your father like this only. He will see that you are my boy. Please water my window boxes in Nizamuddin. Don't forget.

Nizamuddin. The house where he grew up, the son of Ranjit and a Ma so light she seemed to rise from the ground when she danced. She was from a family of Punjabi performers. She always said her distant cousin was Roshan Kumari, who danced for Satyajit Ray. Her skin pale, her head draped with her silken dupatta, her eyes photographed for all the best magazines. She was seventeen when Bapuji and Ranjit saw her dance in Chandigarh. They summoned her to Delhi, to perform exclusively for them. Both men were already married, both *dashing*, Ma said, with gold Ray-Bans and side-parted hair. They wore collar shirts tucked into their pants, creased down the middle, *such style*. And love happened. In the early '80s, sex happened. Unto Ranjit a second son was born.

Tucked away somewhere in Punjab, Ranjit's *real* wife heard all of this in whispers telegraphed across hundreds of miles. She, apparently, did not blame him or Ma, but locked *herself* up in shame. The story was: she went mad in her father's upper storeys. Before she did that, though, she sent Ranjit's *real* son, Jeet, quiet, a gem of a boy, to live with his father in his beautiful house in Nizamuddin. It had once belonged to an army officer: it even had stables, and a yard where iron rings to tie horses still protruded from the walls. That yard was a perfect square, exactly proportioned for marching games, or exercise, for playing Generals and Subalterns when Jeet got home from school. Unless Jeet had extra tuition in Sanskrit or math or whatever Bapuji and Ranjit thought he should have, they would stay out until Jeet's ayah came to get him.

In Jivan's memory, Jeet was always there, a detail of that house like the ring of the doorbell, deep, thrilling, like the clock chimes that came on the stroke of each midnight from the BBC world service radio. The polished floors covered in silk rugs, rolled up all summer, sometimes, with one of them inside. The main part was for Jeet and Ranjit; Jivan lived in the converted stables, with Ma. *One front of house, the other backstage*, Ma said. In Jivan's two rooms, Ma's beauty, the sound of her voice, held his life safe. They also had a small kitchen, with a gas stove and a fridge. Their own squat toilet tiled in white, with a bucket and jug for showers. Two brushes in the toothcup. Living like this, Ma always insisted, was her own choice.

When the '80s gave out, Delhi changed. Tongues started spitting red shame. By the mid-'90s, Devraj decreed enough was enough. Ranjit did not demur: Jivan and Ma had to go. There was an older second cousin in America—a widowed bank manager wanting a wife. A flight to Boston followed: American passport, a house with a double garage, dishwasher, freezer, a square of lawn to strim. Ma, only a little bit older than Jon is now, wrestling every night with an Urdu–English dictionary, Martha Stewart on TV. *In America, language is the power, Jon beta*, Vivek Uncle said. *Mom* and Jon make breakfast, lunch and friends. Do sports, argue, shop. High school diploma, one for Jon, one for Mom, rewards of TV in English only (except on Sundays, when Vivek Uncle played golf). Slowly, Jivan's tongue loosed from his past. Words, never spoken, sank to sediment so easily. Jivan was fourteen, fifteen, sixteen—he did not really notice, nor much care. The old world was sounded in movie phrases— *hum aapke hain koun*—and fragments of songs. Rupees became dollars, earned working service jobs—not because he had to, but because Vivek Uncle said he should. Later, Jon only dated white girls: a choice of which his step-dad approved.

Ma refused to take a job in an estate agency or Visitor Information Centre like the other brown moms. Nor would she become a Yoga instructor or Bollydancerxiser like the white ones. She worked instead as a receptionist for the local water board. After Vivek Uncle died (heart attack, too much golf laced with piña coladas), Ma was promoted to sample collector, pushing her implements deep into designated ground to test for contamination. *Bad water causes breast cancer,* she said.

Jon can still feel her soft, lined hands in his. She always had perfect nails, painted a dark maroon. Five weeks ago, he stood in the Chapel of Peace (a box room attached to the crematorium's oven), trying to recite the only line of prayer he could remember. *Om bhur bhuvah svaha.* The place was lit by a green exit sign, on which a white man was running for the door. He waited alone for the standard-issue urn, then stored Ma in a bank vault in Boston: he did not know what else to do.

A week later, he called Jeet.

Thank God for Jeet, who, in the first year after Jon came to America, answered his Mickey Mouse–embossed letters with notes on Ranjit's thick, Company-headed paper. After the internet happened, there had been emails, sometimes texts, then Viber. In his final year of college, they began to use WhatsApp, with messages months apart. Sometimes, Jon thought about Skyping, but had not mentioned it; neither did Jeet.

Gargi wrote three times in the first year, once in the second. Saying, *Look after Ma, don't forget us!* Nothing ever came from Radha. Once upon a time, Radha's moods, her big feet, her way of kicking the ground to get what she wanted, were more familiar to him than he was to himself. He could not bring himself to ask Jeet about the girls.

His contact with his half brother dwindled to birthdays. Sometimes a song lyric that brought childhood to mind appeared in a text. Selfies of nights out; sent when one was getting up, the other coming down. If they spoke, they stuck to movies and music, dating, financial news, Jon's American life.

Which is over. Ma is in the bank and the house has been sold, the money swallowed up in mortgage and fees. He is here because of Jeet, who promised to get him home.

—What are big brothers for? Jeet said. How long will you stay?

—I'll see. It depends.

—Fine, Jeet said. Wait for me to call you after I have talked to Dad. I'll get Radha to persuade him. Then I'll meet you at Indira Gandhi International with a flower garland, a box of suji ke ladoo and a big old Namaste. We'll give you a traditional VIP Welcome Home.

Jon doesn't eat Indian sweets. He didn't tell Jeet that. When the time came, he would take whatever was offered, he would swallow it down.

It took just three weeks to shut up America. Jon told Iris he loved her, ignoring any hints that she would come with him, if he asked. Iris, his blue-eyed girl. With her lawyer Pop and stay-at-home Mom and just enough security to major in comp lit. Lithe, mocha-loving Iris, always trying to get him to read Orwell or Baldwin or Morrison or Lahiri, names she scattered like birdfeed in the park, talking about *racial prosestyling* and *postpoetic realism* while combing her fingers through her butter-blonde hair. Iris, who thinks Jon will be coming back to her soon. (He won't, he has decided, even if India doesn't work out. It's not a question of her hair, her precious stack of Korla Pandit vinyls—a gift from her mother—or her preference for generic Nina Simone over the *specificity* of the Rolling Stones. Is it her land? No. It is her lack of appreciation for money.)

Another week passed. No call from Jeet. Three more days. Jon had stood in Ma's empty kitchen, barefoot in his shorts and vest, staring into the microwave as it went round and round. Heating up the last of the freezer meals Ma prepared for him before she went into hospital. All his favourites, labelled in capitals. His plan was to spoon up the KAALI DAAL straight from the carton, dredge the Black Label, then curate his résumé for Pierce & Pierce—he had heard they were hiring in the Far East. Then his mobile rang. International call.

It was Ranjit himself. His father's unmistakable cigar-scarred voice, with no preamble, asked:

—Who wants to be a crorepati? Jivan Singh, your number is up. Ticket booked. Time to come home.

It was the first time they had spoken in fifteen years. Mothers, alive or dead, were not mentioned.

The plane dips, the blinds are raised. Sunlight floods the cabin as the whole of Delhi rushes up to meet him. He is caught by the city below. His mantra is right: from the air there is no sight of earth. Instead, miles after miles of corrugated rooftops, unfinished brick buildings and a dump covering the ground as far as he can see.

Picking over it, inside it, giving it life, he imagines all those legs, arms, heads, eyes: with no idea how big the whole is, or care for how little they own of it. All crushed together breathing in, and out, and in. Bodies covering the land, children squatting in the mud: wanting and working to have enough money to survive and then to thrive. Not a patch of dirt left free.

He can make out flyovers strewn like necklaces across the city, jew-elled with billboards promising reincarnation in this life, and ways to afford it, because it must be achieved. There will be ads for new cars, mobiles, modified milk for bachchas' bone strength and protein powder for the boys; ads for Company hotels, for new detergents and washing machines. For flour to make perfect chapatis: pictures of fat young execs and good Indian girls promising hot married sex with their homemade bread.

Now they are cruising over acres of flat white rooftops dotted with satellite dishes, hundreds of ears all listening for his arrival. The bride in the seat next to him puts on her pink lipstick, her mouth a silent O.

—So we return, hamare apne India, says Number 5, smiling.

Is he for real? Right on, man. Then, *Yaar,* Jon corrects himself; he's about to land: talking the talk is a key methodology to winning trust. He considers America where land is king, where everything works to make it pretty or make it yield. In America, the pundits talk about India Rising like they used to talk about the Russians Coming. Here, they talk about India Shining. Come visit Incredible Ind!a. Rising, shining, wak-ing, sleeping. He knows the habits, he really does. In America, he could star as a standard TV Asian in a supporting role: good schools, a sense of humour and a Ma fixation. Here, of course they will see his American smile, his suit and tie, first class, pure gold. The truth is: He is Jivan Singh, half brother to Jeet Singh, son of Ranjit Singh. He was born on this Indian earth, has waited all this time to return.

—Hari Om, Number 5 mutters.

The plane lands with force.

A smile he cannot stop splits his face. Jon has left the building. It is time for Jivan to greet the hordes.

He joins the other passengers swaying down the aisle. It is high noon and a hundred degrees Fahrenheit or more. On the bridge, Jivan can smell his India: fuel, dust, the choking air. This day has waited for him like his mother used to after grade school, arms out to press his face into her damp breasts. He wants to shout (but doesn't) *where's my milky-doodh?*

He is half expecting Jeet to have got past security. To be here, right at the plane. When they were boys, some nights they would be escorted to this point by armed police. They would clutch their bottles of Company Cola, playing with their bendy-straws (red for Jivan, yellow for Jeet) while they waited for the jet to land. Devraj and Ranjit would appear, wearing dark glasses even at night, cradling their briefcases to their chests. He would trail Devraj, Ranjit and Jeet all the way through security and into the Arrivals Hall. Where groups of stick-thin men leaned on each other, eyeing up the white girls and the rich sons of Sahibs as if the girls were marrowbone, the boys were sauce. Through the hall the Company entourage progressed, dripping petals from their welcome-home garlands, bright orange tears on the dirty ground.

No Jeet. Jivan must get through immigration. He might have to dodge the porters and the trolley-boys alone. If Jeet hasn't come (but he will, of course he will), then Jivan will change the last of his dollars to a wad of rupees, go outside and find a black-and-yellow beetle cab with clean-as-possible seats. And then? Home to Nizamuddin, for lunch.

He is inside. Instead of the old, airless immigration hall tiled in speckled grey, a floor that belongs in a Maharaja's palace stretches out for anyone, for everyone to walk on. Enormous bronze sculptures hang above each booth, blessing arrivals as they pass through. It is even air-conditioned.

Only the lines are the same. Emirates slaves hoist their bundles, middle-aged men carrying imitation Samsonites eye up the young bloods with leather weekend bags; there are the Juicy Couture wives, all don't-touch velour and overdone hair. Last come the whiteys, panicking politely as they try to keep some space between themselves and the natives without actually pushing anyone out of the way. He is none of them. He feels himself being checked out; he cannot tell whether it is with admiration, or something else. Is it his suit? Is it too much? He takes off his jacket. He loosens the Harvard tie. In America, he had wanted to take off his skin, just as he peeled onions in his step-dad's friend's restaurant (his first job). When he was young, in India, his illegitimate blood made him an outsider. His blood, which sometimes it seemed everyone could see.

The immigration guard has a full chest of medals and a deep-set frown. He looks exhausted by combat, bored of protecting the border from cut-price bandits and thieves; he flicks through every blank page of Jon's passport until a lonely Indian tourist visa reveals itself. To picture, to visa, to picture.

—Main Jivan hoon, says Jon (and does the guard smile?). Main bahut saal ke baad ghar aaya hoon.

—Good job! Welcome back, Foreign Return, the guard says. He rolls his r's, "foe-reign." Emphasises both syllables, equally.

—Thank you, sir.

Jivan is stamped, and can enter. In Arrivals, the visions duplicate, triplicate: on the walls, ads for HSBC mock him, they show the same stubble-faced guy, hands up and grinning. First in jeans, then a suit, jeans, then a suit. *Leader,* says the caption, *follower,* says the next. Leader/follower/leader/follower: Spot the difference? *Which one, Jivan, are you?* Everything has caught up, grown up, without him.

He fixes on a crowd of men outside. Who can't afford shoes, forget proper suits. They cup their faces to the windows, trying to see into the hall. No matter how much has changed, those poor bastards still hang out here. He catches the desire to bow.

Where is Jeet? There are families spilling over Louis Vuittons to get to each other, drivers holding signs, people at coffee bars and kiosks like at any other international airport in the world. No Jeet. Homecoming. Pah. He wants to spit (but doesn't). His eyes follow a worker, uniform grey as a spent cigarette, using a machine to polish the floor. Standing still, rotating the brush over the same spot again and again and back again.

Move, Jivan!

A thin red carpet leads him out of the terminal, into the glaring day.

For a freak moment, he wonders if he's landed in the right city. The crowd is only one-deep. The honking, bleating black-and-yellow Ambassadors he remembers are gone, replaced by a line of shiny white sedans waiting politely for fares. A few people stand in quiet groups. And Jivan himself is nothing. Just a clean-shaven young man who was teased as a child because his skin was so light. Like a girl, his father used to joke. Before sending him to America, where pale enough cheeks and dark eyes helped him to navigate being the brown one through college and grad school while working every service industry from doorman to tech. Back on demand, with his US accent, his dutiful bottle of Black Label in his Duty Free bag, how should he speak now? Barun would know. He takes a step, feels sweat bathe his sides under his jacket. The attention of the crowd has waned, as if he was the warm-up act and they are restless for the main event.

Then it comes. Beyond the line of cabs, the 4×4s and bags and bodies, a powder-blue Bentley is nosing everything out of its way. He wants to pretend he hasn't seen it—but everyone can see it. The people in the planes circling the sky over the airport can probably see it, even through the smog.

Jeet, he thinks. *What are you playing at?*

Any boy can get a nice suit, a briefcase and a pair of good shoes. Such a boy might indeed ride in a taxi to a hotel in the city. But see the gleaming beauty of the rare, vintage car; see it pull up on the curbside near that tired-looking Foreign Return! See the driver, sharp as if his wife irons him each morning, jump out and salute as he opens the doors. And the two passengers who climb from the back, each a mirror of the other—black linen Nehru-collar suits, silver-plated hair, like two hand-made domino tiles. This you could only be born to, if your past lives decree it and God loves you. And look—one is carrying such a handsome bone-topped cane. What style! This is to be worshipped, and prayed for in the next life. Who are they?

This is not Jeet, playing the fool. Here is his father, Ranjit Singh, Director of the Devraj Group. With a man Jivan has not seen for time. Kritik Sahib, Vice President, Research and Intelligence, shadow wolf from boyhood. The right hand and the left hand, come to meet Jivan, straight off the plane. *Where,* he thinks, *is Barun when you need him? Where the fuck is Jeet?*

—Jivan. Welcome, Ranjit says.

Before America, Jivan had a Kathputli puppet that looked like Ranjit. Wooden face, oval eyes, curling smile. White beard painted close to its chin. He could make it move by putting an arm up its body; make it nod, or make it wave. Shake it and it would blink.

—Wah, Ranjitji, wah, says Kritik Sahib. What a man you have brought from America!

Kritik Sahib has kept himself better than Ranjit over the years. He is bigger: his chest wider, arms thicker. At least five-nine to Ranjit's five-six. His body is more toned, and while Ranjit wears splashes of colour Kritik Sahib has always cultivated a quiet, contained manner, as if he listens without judgement, as if he hears all sound. Looking at him one would think he had a comfortable life, loved his fellows, would do no harm to anyone. But what Jivan remembers clearly about Kritik Sahib is still there: tempered steel around his eyes and mouth. Strangely white teeth. If ever Ma admonished Jivan or even Jeet, Gargi, or Radha, Kritik Sahib was the threat. Now he is smiling. Waiting for Jivan or Ranjit to make the first move.

Ranjit. Cane hooked over his fingers, holding out his arms at a precise forty-five degrees from his body. Not quite high enough for an embrace.

—Jivan beta. Come and greet your father.

Kneel. He wants me to kneel. All of the curious eyes around Jivan focus into one gaze. The heat is fierce. His vision blurs, his upper lip turns to salt water; it is the hours in the plane, it is the lack of food. *My God. No way.* He is an American, he has been in America for fifteen years. Ranjit never came to see him. Or wrote to him. Or called. Or emailed. Or texted. Or thought of him, talked of him, dreamt of him.

Ranjit waits, standing on the curb. Arms stretched, palms upward.

We stay still; it is the world that turns.

Jivan puts down his Duty Free. The driver watches at his window and Kritik Sahib says:

—Yes, just right.

Jivan bends toward the earth, hot as the punishing sun. He reaches, palm down, fingers straight, to touch his father's feet.

—Aré nahin, beta, nahin, says Ranjit. He laughs, cups his shoulders and guides him upright. Come. Car is here. Chalo.

Jivan climbs into the back with Ranjit. Kritik Sahib in front. The doors shut, the driver revs. Without checking his rearview or sides, he pulls into the traffic. The porters and the passengers and all of the families watch them disappear, then go back to their business. Inside the terminal, the floor man keeps shining the floor. *Show is over,* he thinks. He wants to spit (but doesn't). *Time to get back to work.*

The movement of the Bentley: its preserved hush. As if Jivan is back in the crematorium, watching the coffin glide toward the incinerator. He has to have a short, brutal battle with the lump in his throat. The cold air makes him sniff. *Only girls get sick-sick.* The last thing Ranjit said to him before waving him off to America. Jivan sniffs again. His father and Kritik Sahib do not look at him.

The sounds from the road are muted, the car windows frame and colour everything sepia. Scenes from old India reel out before him, comforting things he wants to see. A sabzi wala shambles down the lane, his cart loaded with wrinkled root vegetables dug up from centuries ago, whole families stacked onto mopeds, eight legs dangling over the sides. There are women balancing bricks and bundles, walking barefoot on the broken sidewalks. Half-naked children grin to each other as they clean their teeth with dirty fingers, their hair in helmets of crazy around their heads. All of it seen as if from far, far away. Then punctuated by Mercedes and 4×4s, Toyota, Honda, all the big boys. Jivan takes in these shining beasts as visions from an outrageous future-possible; at the same time, he wants to shout *freeze-frame!* He's thinking, *How long has the party been going on? Why didn't you invite me?* There are even new buses with doors that fully close. But the trucks still say *Horn Please!* in fading yellows and pinks, and everyone still drives as if they don't need sight. There are still a few cows standing dumb as Temple paintings, white against red walls— this, at least, has not changed.

The brightness of July and August, so hot that you could not believe the monsoon once came, is coming, will come again; in summers like this, Jeet and he would wait through all the long days until their excitement broke the sky. The thrill as fat drops began to fall; the painful delight of playing "sink or swim," racing paper boats when rain swallowed the horizon and turned the earth into muddy sea. Once, Ranjit even umpired a game—and for the first time, in that very game, his boat beat Jeet's. The memory douses him like water from the too-hot-too-cold bucket-and-jug baths he has not had since then. He almost says—*Papaji, remember*—but swallows the words and breathes deeply in the conditioned car air.

There might still be scraggy dogs running on the verge, but everywhere there are signs of the future that has happened without him. Apple, Nokia; there is even a metro system like a giant web spun high above the city. The car is caught in it, driving under and alongside it; he is not surprised to see the Company logo, D.C., stamped on the concrete clawing the sky.

He lets his head droop, his eyes focus on the back of Kritik Sahib's neck.

—So, beta ghar aa gaya! This is your son.

Kritik Sahib turns and reaches his arm back. His nails are buffed to shine. His knuckles and age spots are like fine heritage wood, the kind you have to remember not to put your drink on when invited to the offices of Harvard profs. Men who Ma insisted on calling his "dons," even though he explained to her, and sometimes purposely, in public, even though he knew she knew, that *dons* was only used that way in England, that it means *mafia* in America, their country. *So clever you are, beta,* she would say. *And yet I have to spell it out?*

Kritik Sahib smiles, taps Jivan's knee once, twice. Kritik Sahib is the Don.

—I'm sure he is a fine boy, Ranjit. Just like his father.

—Aré nahin, says Ranjit. Kritik Sahib, you're too kind. But nine–ten years he's been gone, a long time, no? His mother wanted him with her, so what could I do?

It has been fifteen years. Jivan keeps quiet, staring out of the window. A young woman alone on a moped overtakes them, her skinny jeans tucked into snakeskin cowboy boots a pale shade of blue. Her hair streams out from under her helmet. Ma would have chi-chi'd at that. Wouldn't she?

—Kritik Sahib, do you remember this one's Ma? Ranjit says. She was a beauty. A young man's heartfelt mistake. But really, I was seduced. My first years with Devraj, I was just an uncouth boy from Amritsar. Such elegance they had, these old performance families. Who could resist? When we are young we are foolish in love. Aré, who can blame a man for falling under the spell of a veshya when she is packaged like a royal princess? And such a voice she had! A rare, beautiful bird. A Bulbul-e-Punjab.

A pause.

Kritik Sahib removes his hand from Jivan's knee, draws his arm back and wipes his palm thoughtfully on his own trouser leg.

—Well, he says. His smile shows his teeth, still so white, as cared-for as his nails. No matter. You've got a fine son out of life, who cares which glass he was mixed in? A man is made by the honour he brings today to his father's name, not by what-all activities his mother indulged in last night! Aré, don't give our Foreign Return the wrong idea. This is New India after all.

—Rightly spoken, of course, says Ranjit.

The two nod together: puppets, pulling each other's strings. Then Ranjit says,

—Jivan, did you greet Kritik Sahib properly? Do you remember him?

He remembers, as a boy, being told to stay out of Kritik Sahib's way. *Devraj's shadow. Don't anger him. Always show respect. Get out of the car, flag down an auto. Take me back to Boston phata-phat,* Jivan thinks. Then he remembers: he has no rupees.

—Kind of, Papaji.

Sorry, Ma. Sorry, he thinks. *I promised myself I would never call him "Papaji." Here I am and you are gone.*

Ranjit frowns.

—Well, Kritik Sahib is a very important man. You should love him like a father only. He might just find a place for you in Research and Intelligence, if he considers you up to the mark.

—Yes, why not, why not? Kritik Sahib's voice is warm. A starter position, we will see how you do. After all, we have plenty of time to get to know each other. Are you interested? Of course. Ranjit's son is absolutely welcome. Company Research and Intelligence always has room for boys with initiative. And you have that. For here you are.

—Thank you, Kritik Sahib. That would be great. But, ah, don't I need some kind of different visa? A permit?

—So upstanding, Kritik Sahib says. Just what I like to see. Don't worry, Jivan, all in good time.

—My friend, says Ranjit. Don't spoil him. He has to earn it. We should send him to the north, he must see the Company properly, get to know the lie of the land. Yeh Foreign Return kuch nahin janta hai.

The two men laugh together, scripted.

Jivan wakes with no sense of how much time has passed. The car is looping around a high, redbrick wall; beyond it he sees the tops of trees, and an ornate tower made of similar rust bricks. They slow for a tourist coach, offloading a cargo of swollen white ladies, Scholl sandals, floral skirts. He watches them turn through an arch, *UNESCO World Heritage site,* says the board overhead.

—*Where are we?* he wants to say.

His mouth is so dry, his lips won't move. He watches the road widen, shaded by more trees, aged by dust. The traffic thins, there are few houses—they are not in South Delhi at all.

—Chalo, says Kritik, we have reached.

They turn off the highway. Clip a tumble of shacks by the side of the road and plunge. Into a maze of high, white walls. No graffiti, no fly-bills: just white gleam, even through the car's tinted windows. The road becomes a potholed track; the Bentley lumbers around as if in some great processional. Every so often a glimpse through a gate: tended grass. A sense of palaces, hidden beyond. *Were there so many walls when I left?* Jivan could only just see out of the windows then: he was short until he was fifteen, only grew after two years of drinking Dairy Pure. Now he knows where they are going: the Farm.

Googling Devraj, the Company, the girls, he has never found a picture of it. He sits forward. They edge around a crater and arrive at a set of ornately carved wooden gates. Lions and tigers and bears. A dark-skinned man in a white-and-gold uniform rests his gun, salutes the car through. Now he opens his window. Sepia gives way to a long shot of heart-lifting technicolour: it is a bright blue day, fresh as if issued to admen for a shoot. Sunken palm trees like giant pineapples frame the pale brick drive, sorbet scoops of lemon and orange marigolds ring the place, a garland for a long-awaited groom. There is a frosting of giant daisies at each corner of the lawn. He faces into the air with his mouth slightly open to see if it will taste as sweet as it smells. A leafy vine curves up the nearest palm, its white flowers like tiny stars scattered all over the trunk. He breathes in.

—Chameli. Jasmine to you, says Kritik Sahib. The Company signature scent. We sell it only in our most exclusive boutiques. Turnover is almost one hundred lakhs a year. Not bad for a perfume made from a climbing weed.

This place was once a wild kingdom, where Radha and Jivan used to dig for treasure, play Hunters and Chirus or whatever game she wanted. Gargi and Jeet let them join in with exploring the land as the pigs were evicted, as the fields were dug up and drained so foundations could be laid. The builders put up bamboo scaffolding and crawled all over it: he remembers the construction of the long, curving façade, the erection of the colonnades. As they reach the top of the drive, the finished house reveals itself: a wide, elegant structure that sucks up all the light and breathes it back out over the lawns.

He gets out of the car. After the stink of the plane, the dust of the airport, the relentless roads, he is washed by a gentle breeze. Lime-green parrots swoosh above, he wants to point (but doesn't) and say *Look! A parrot!* There is even a fat-bodied peacock pecking across the grass to check him out. As he watches, it cocks its head: *Jivan beta! Haven't you grown. How is your Ma? Why didn't you bring her with you?*

—Don't worry, you'll get over it, Kritik Sahib says. Acclimatise toh karna hai. Set your watch. India time.

—I've done it, he says. I'm ready.

Kritik Sahib does not look surprised. He folds his hands under his chin, begins his first lesson: why we call this place the Farm. It is true that Jivan did not know the deeds for the land are only sold on the promise of cultivating at least eighty percent crops from it. What do they produce here? Kritik Sahib invites him to take a guess, then says:

—Base matter into gold. We print money for the rest of the country, I think those government wale can let us off being sabzi wale. *The Farm.* English language, Indian meaning—a bastard word, hey Jivan?

Kritik Sahib laughs. So ends the first lesson.

—Ah, look at his face! says Ranjit. Green is the colour of gullibility, Jivan, not just dollar bills. But say thank you to Kritik Sahib, for his time and insights.

—Thank you, sir, Jivan says. He stretches. Shrugs them off. Kritik Sahib and Ranjit. Wants to run around to the back of the house to find the feral puppies he used to play tag with, their wild, trusting eyes, frantic tails and vivid, twisting bodies; they trembled and tried to bite when they were caught. And even when he was twelve years old, he felt a jumbled longing—love mixed with pain—and understood as he held them that this is what it might feel like one day, to have a child of his own. *Why did Ranjit favour Jeet when he had Jivan?* Thinking this, he would take his shoes and jacket off and roll around with the pups in the mud, and chase after Gargi and Jeet with dirty hands and face. He half expects them to be there: the little dogs and children, warned not to spoil their clothes, unable to obey.

He lets go of the stretch. The ache of travelling settles back into his bones. There are no more wild dogs; instead, another dark-skinned, white-liveried doorman salutes. Ranjit's hand presses lightly on his back, the only touch he ever offers: to push his son forward or hold him. Jivan feels his adulthood evaporating. How to fit in? He will offer the not-so-Duty-Free Black Label to Devraj.

The atrium is so ugly that he almost snorts. Ornate tables in every corner, gold picture frames and carpets hang on the walls; the floor is circular, laid with checked tiles, an infinite game of squares that somehow curves: his dizziness returns, he stretches out an arm and steadies himself against a plinth topped by a vase of laughing pink lilies. They have no scent. He looks up. A chandelier hung with pearls and diamonds drops from a vicious hook above him. A man in a ragged shirt and cut-off pants is splayed flat across the outside of the dome, *Shit, is he dead?* No, there's a rag in his hand; he's polishing the glass. It looks like he's waving. Jivan almost lifts a hand in response. It is only just past noon. *Dude must be getting fried out there.* Jivan's stomach groans.

He clings to the outside world of sun on the lawn, the breeze, the jasmine. He feels again as if something is gathering around him, as if the house *has* been waiting for him—and so have Gargi and Radha—and Jeet, his big brother, all this time. They must be here somewhere. Hiding, seeking. It could be that Ranjit wanted to come to the airport, and asked Jeet to wait for him here. It could be they are all gathered around the table for a welcome-home lunch. He catches the rich nutty scent of daal and ghee undercut by spices, of meat being roasted in a real tandoor. *Thank God.* He shakes his father's hand off.

—Come, Jivan. Want to see the homestead? Kritik Sahib claps him on the shoulder.

—Yes. Go with Kritik Sahib, Jivan, says Ranjit. He flicks his wrist as if he is chasing flies away from his face.

Jivan puts on his shades (Ray-Bans, vintage). He leaves Ranjit to follow Kritik Sahib around banks of lilies, so white, so pointed, the classic offerings for grief. Focus. The positive. Think bright. *Not bad, Jon: a job offer, a private tour and you only touched down three hours ago.* They go through French doors to a garden that stretches the length of the house. The sun beats down. His suit has wilted onto him. Behind Kritik Sahib's back he pulls off his tie, stuffs it in his pocket. He wants to shower, to change before he meets the girls—then his eye is caught by a courtyard to one side, workers are crawling all over a platform, putting up or taking down a childlike banner with the words *Welcome Home* painted on it in red. *Yes,* he thinks. *There it is!*

—It's for Sita, says Kritik Sahib. You know, she just got back from studying economics at Cambridge University in UK. At Trinity College, the same as Pandit Nehruji, as our own Professor Amartya Sen.

Right. Sita. Does anyone speak of him that way now that Ma is gone? Does anyone say, *Jivan Singh, a Harvard graduate, a self-made man has come home?* Where the fuck is Jeet?

—Do you know who Professor Sen is, beta? says Kritik Sahib.

—I went to Harvard, Kritik Sahib. Business School. I saw him give a lecture on welfare economics, right in the middle of the financial crisis. It brought the house down. Must have been about ten years after he won the Nobel Prize.

—Nobel toh achcha hai, but his writing on India lacks a certain . . . what shall I say . . . *love* for our country, says Kritik. Criticism so fine, but at least acknowledge our contribution to progress, no?

—Uh, sure. Even I thought that, at the time.

No response. As they cross the gardens, there is a gap in the neat hedge wall, a glimpse of glinting blue. The pool. He fights the urge to run, get naked, tip sideways, sink to the bottom then let the water lift him so he can play dead while it holds him safe, floating.

They reach an enclosure where pink and red roses stare barefaced at the sun. Not one petal has fallen on the grass; again, the flowers have no scent. He sees workers in stiff white suits and red cotton turbans, clipping the hedges straight, even though each leaf is already standing to attention. More men squat on the paths: for a moment he thinks they are having a crap, Indian style.

—The sight of these guys always arrests the foreign eye, says Kritik Sahib. All they are doing is picking out the weeds from between the stones. Some tasks one has to do by hand.

—Where does this place end, Kritik Sahib?

—If you need a tour, beta, I'll find someone to take you later. Or Gargi will arrange it and you can ask all your questions, OK?

—Is she here? I mean, do you think she'd do that?

—Of course! Now I'll give you lesson number two. This will be all you need. Our Indian women are a special breed in the world. Like beautiful phools they bloom best in beds, when they are well tended. They are strong-willed but only when it comes to three things. One: household politics. I mean, who says what to whom and when. Two: household economics. I mean, husband making money, of which she will save some and always spend the rest wisely. Three: household sustenance. That is, food to feed the family, home-cooked preferable except on Sundays when she likes to go out for whatever outside khaana is currently in style. Right now it is Royal China dim sum and Peking duck, according to our wise Radha beta. These days, India is only hungry for Chinese. And, in exchange? She must be worshipped by the gifting of quality diamonds. Solitaires—a pair at least, no less. Finally: no matter what they say, and this is the most important thing of all, so listen carefully: just tell her what you want, she will never say *no*. At least to your face. (Kritik Sahib grins.) We could all learn from this natural female survival strategy. Come. We are almost there.

Jivan tries to picture Gargi wearing diamonds, eating dim sum, saying *no*, and meaning *yes*, or the other way around. He cannot. To him, she is still twelve years old, all Bapuji Girl Scouts and turtlenecks and long pleated skirts or school uniform tartan salwar kameez. Her hair is always looped in two fat braids garlanded around her ears and tied with bows—or maybe he saw that in a movie. She would not choose meat, she does not eat it because she is sure animals feel pain. She didn't want to drink water because she believed it was too precious to waste; she kept cacti in her room, a whole prickled planet of them—she said she thought she could learn from them. It gave them permission to laugh at her, back then.

They cross a courtyard inlaid with circles of orange, white and green mosaic; at the centre is an enormous sundial set into the ground. Twelve fifteen, two twenty, five forty, nine thirty: their shadows chase each other, the time is impossible to read. He follows Kritik Sahib through an archway of vines covered in thorns and pursed pink flowers, and then they are in the next clearing. Here is a shock of wild grass, a miniature prairie frontier, riven with faint lines where people have walked before them. They wade to the far end where a tired-looking bungalow with a cheap screen door sits sunken, waiting for them.

—Follow me, says Kritik Sahib.

Inside, he must wait for his eyes to adjust. Then feels he is back in the airport, being frisked by security and left with the grimy sense that though nothing is missing, he has been robbed. Sita gets a banner, the works. He gets this. After the whole long journey, Ranjit's appearance, the newness of the old places; his throat closes, he cannot speak. He is standing in a near-perfect reconstruction of his rooms in Nizamuddin. Is this where he is to stay?

Nostalgia is a sickness, he caught it from Ma. He used to wait in a room just like this, for Jeet to get back from school. Then he would cross the courtyard and they would play at being Ranjit, dressing up in his clothes, threatening each other with a bamboo cane they found and kept just for this purpose. In a room just like this, Ranjit would come visit Ma at least once a week. She would tie her heavy, gold ghungroo tight around her ankles and then she would sing and dance. Hiding in the bedroom he shared with her (unless Ranjit was there), he would keep time with his fist thumping into his palm.

There is mustard-coloured paint peeling off the walls, a fan turning sardonically overhead. There is the old wood furniture with the woven wicker covering: tiny diamond peepholes stretched over the chair seats. There is the cupboard: fake walnut, cracking veneer. The faint lemon smell of machar repellent: someone has left a mosquito coil and an incense stick burning to ash on a tin plate alongside a tiny bronze model of the elephant God, Ganesh. The plate sits on a grey metal filing cabinet, covered in a faded block-printed sheet, the kind he used to sleep under until he left India. The small windows are covered with mesh, a broken AC unit is suspended on one wall. In a corner is the final touch: a lacquered hostess trolley with a few dusty, half-finished foreigners: Gordon's Gin and Jack Daniels, an ice bucket and two heavy tumblers. Ma always had these drinks waiting for Ranjit.

You could find a version of such a room in every common home across India, in any office, in any school. He once saw a perfect reconstruction in a New York gallery. Middle-aged brown men in white collars stood three-deep, gazing at it. The mask of assimilation—bland eyes, neutral smile—had dropped from every face. Their mouths were open; their chins trembled. They clutched their sari-clad wives as shields against the mirage, and tried to pretend it did not affect them by whispering, *Hain. This is art?*

Kritik Sahib is watching him. He holds out a pink-striped cake box with curled red writing, *The Company Delhi Deli And Bakery.*

—Croissants, he says. They do them very well in the deli. Want one?

—What is this place, Uncleji? Jivan almost chokes on the word but can't help himself: it's this room, the jetlag, the fucking croissants. This would have been the moment to take off his wilted jacket, his damp shirt: sit down and tell Ma all about his strange day.

Kritik Sahib smirks, dumps the cake box and crosses to the trolley to pour three fingers of whisky into each glass. He takes a sip from one and holds the other out.

—Midday cooler?

The sweat trickles down his neck, his stomach is about to eat itself. He thinks whisky might kill him. Kritik's eyes are on him. He walks forward, takes the glass.

—This is my office. What do you think?

He looks around again. There is even a picture of Sai Baba on the wall, eyes painted wise, lurid orange robes, red dot on his wrinkled forehead.

—There's no desk, he manages.

—What else? Kritik Sahib smiles.

—There's no phone, no fax, no computer even. It doesn't look very secure.

Kritik Sahib laughs.

—Quite right, beta, I knew you were clever. Don't worry. We are never as backward as it appears. Come.

There is an old door behind him. He holds it open.

—After you. He gestures down the staircase.

Jivan can feel Kritik Sahib's breath on his hair, his belly almost in his back as they go down the stairs; he tries not to turn and scrabble his way up to the sunlight. They get to another door: this one thicker, metal. Kritik Sahib enters a code.

The room opens up, much bigger than the box upstairs. Cool air, strip lighting. The plastic scent of everyday offices. Apple logos shine at him like so many forbidden fruits, scattered across eight or so islands of desks. There is a sign hanging over each one with the name of an Indian city on it. *Hyderabad,* Jivan reads. *Mangalore.* Around the walls are framed maps of Company holdings, pictures of Company hotels, photos of storefronts selling Company silks and woollen shawls. Half a dozen young men sit tapping at the screens, their faces uplit, hologramatic flickering. Their shirts are too big on their shoulders, the sleeves balloon on their arms. They all have pens in their top pockets like Indian extras in sci-fi movies. *Central casting Hollywood, Bond in India, Act 1, scene 1,* he thinks, and wants to laugh.

—Kuch funny hain kya? says Kritik Sahib. Upstairs is for relaxing. But if you are interested in working for me, this is where it happens. Come. Observe.

They sit at the central island of desks, in front of a bank of monitors. The sign above them says *Devraj Farm.* Kritik Sahib presses a switch and six screens come to life. Screen 1: a foreshortened view of a soft-looking woman in a dark green sari. She paces between long tables, where about thirty girls in navy-blue Company salwar kameez slide cake boxes into plastic sleeves, stick round, gold stickers, tie red ribbons. She gives instructions to an older man: sharp-faced and concentrating on a clipboard as he ticks down a list. As she leans close to him, they laugh together.

—Gargi, Kritik Sahib says. Remember Gargi? Such a good student before she got married. Such a shame she's getting so plump these days.

Jivan's hand reaches for the screen. Gargi. Who he used to follow around and spy on until she got annoyed. Who he laughed at but always obeyed. Gargi. Life radiates from her like the light from the house over the gardens. He feels it right through the screen. He will not cry. Her hand is on the older man's arm. Her hair is loose and long; she doesn't play with it like some girls might. It is just there, hanging in ripples to her waist. No, he will not cry. What it would be like to press his face into her sari silk, breathe in Chanel No. 5. Feel her hands smooth his hair and her fingers pinch his cheeks as she used to, getting him ready to be seen by his father—or was it Ma who did those things? *Concentrate,* he thinks. *Fucking jetlag.* Gargi. What, he is twenty-eight now, so she must be . . . thirty-two? Thirty-three? Ripe, she looks, like Ma became, in America. (Don't think about it.) *OK: Gargi, you've got a bit heavier over the years. Could afford to lose a few pounds.* She's wearing her glasses on her head; against her hair the lenses stare at him with nothing but black behind. He looks away.

Screen 2: another woman, this one polished to a Delhi-girl shine. He used to see girls like this swarming across Harvard Yard, marinated in money, playing "student" for the summer. Hair, skin, makeup all perfect, getting hysterical in American Apparel, in Armani Exchange, in All Saints: matching bags and shoes and nails and thongs. He looks closer and realises again the limitations of his Googling. He wants to laugh out loud. It's Radha! At her desk in a stiff, candy-coloured dupatta, over a low-necked pink kameez. It should be vulgar, but she looks like those flowers on the vine outside, fragile, delicate, promising. It's the fabric she is wearing: shot silk, handloom. It's her hair, dropping over her breasts in loose curls, the kind that take hours (at least, they did for Iris) to perfect. There is a thickset man leaning over Radha, white collared shirt with a thin gold stripe tucked into his jeans. He is talking, she is smiling, she is flirting: they are stars of the small screen.

—Radha, says Kritik Sahib. Bubu. Her husband. We did the right thing getting her married at eighteen. What was that, five years after you left?

—Ya. We're the same age.

Jivan stares at Bubu. Jeet had told him about Bubu, called him the Brand Manager, for he always had Radha on his arm.

He leans forward. Where is Sita?

—Watch, beta, just watch, says Kritik Sahib.

The central monitor flickers to life. A sunroom full of wild plants and flowers, a deep wicker chair and a man sitting in it, cross-legged like a Buddha. Devraj. The Company himself, the man they call Bapuji: father to the girls, to Kritik Sahib and Ranjit, to every employee in this vast corporation and every shareholding consumer of Company goods. He's there in his white kurta pyjama, with a fine brown shawl over his wide shoulders, his thick white hair gelled close to his head. Liver spots and wrinkles mar his skin and crease his chops, he is fat, with a girth the photos in the in-flight magazine only hinted at. Legs stretched, head back, eyes closed. A business legend. A loving father, a loyal friend and celebrated philanthropist: a man of India. Finally, Jivan sounds like that journalist, Barun J. Bharat.

At Devraj's feet is a barefoot girl in loose, rolled-up jeans. A yellow T-shirt knotted at her waist—Jivan squints at the screen—says *#MakePovertyHis* in red letters. Her hair is shorter than Gargi's or Radha's; it's mussed in a hippie crinkle. She presses Devraj's legs while three yappy dogs tumble about them.

—Look at them, Kritik Sahib says. His tone is a spoonful of ghee sliding onto hot rotis. Look how happy Bapuji is that Sita has come home. He passes Jivan a pair of headphones. Bluetooth. Put them on.

—Hallo Chinku, hallo Rinku, hallo Mr. Stinku! So, so cute.

Sita's voice fills Jivan: strong and light, laughing. Her accent has Indian undertones but something on top—not America, but—

—England, says Kritik Sahib. You know, Jivan, she came home with a double-first-classification result in Social and Political Sciences.

Sita. Jivan sighs. Takes off the headphones. Of course she would get the hero's welcome.

—You're tired, Kritik Sahib says. Hungry. You want to eat something? Then come, lunch must be ready. Gargi is gone from there, see? Screen 1 is dark. Cameras respond to movement only.

Lunch? Like this? With his suit limp, his hair plastered to his head and dried out by air conditioning. The whisky making a comeback in his throat.

—Thank you, Kritik Sahib, he says. I'm OK.

—After all this time, you don't want to meet them? They are expecting you.

—Are they? Wow. But, I mean, I'd like to stay here and get used to all this, you know, if I'm going to work here, to start the job as I mean to go on.

—Come for lunch now, beta, don't be shy.

—I'll stay here, Uncleji. I'd like to get familiar with all this.

Kritik Sahib stands. Over his shoulder he shouts,

—Kashyap? Punj?

—Sir? A skinny youth with spiked short hair appears, offering a glass of water on a steel tray. His ears stick out like the handles on a speech-day cup.

—Thank you, Jivan says. He takes the water, does not drink it.

—My pleasure, sir. I'm Punj at your service. He spins the tray between his hands.

Jivan smiles. He's sitting in a bunker, this close to his childhood and for the first time in his life, someone is calling him *sir*.

—Punj, Kritik Sahib says. Where is Kashyapji?

—Sir, he has gone to pray at the staff mandir. Then to lunch.

—Fine. Jivan, Kashyap is my second in command, you will meet him soon. This young man is Punj, appointed by Kashyap as nominal deputy.

—I'm learning a lot from Kashyapji, Punj says. For example, verses from the Bhagavad Gita: he reads them to us, each day before we begin. He says it creates the right conditions for watching over the Farm.

Kritik Sahib nods.

—Punj, Jivan Sahib is our very special guest. An old friend of Gargi Madam and Radha Madam. Just observing for now. Sit here, but zyada der nahin, five minutes and you take him out, OK? Show him around.

—Yes, sir.

Gargi has appeared on the central screen. Standing at the table in a large dining room, directing servants. Some set plates and spoons, others bring in burners and dishes, place them, step back, wait for her approval. Kritik Sahib's hand squeezes Jivan's shoulder. Then he is gone.

Jivan used to watch these hokey Indian serials on Star Plus TV, sitting with Ma on Sundays. She loved them all: the family dramas with cardboard villains and handsome heroes, non-stop cases of mistaken identity, masters for servants, good girls for bad. Brothers disguised as each other, lovingly beating sisters, wives and mothers-in-law fighting over sons. In the end the good would get rich and the bad were punished. The lovers would be united with parental blessing, kneeling for hands to be raised over their heads in benediction, the parents would kneel and beg their children to bless them right back. It was always happily-ever-after-the-end.

—Hey Punj, he says. You ever see those serials? What were they called . . . *Hum Paanch,* or ah, *Doosra Keval?*

—Sure, sure, those old shows, says Punj. How funny that you know them. One had five sisters—and all dreamed of Shahrukh Khan. The other serial starred him, no? I love Shahrukh. He's the Baadshah of Bollywood.

—No, it was Salman Khan.

—OK, sir, I'm sure Shahrukh, says Punj. King Khan. Salman Sahib is Bigg Boss only.

—No, it's Salman, I'll bet you, Jivan says.

—Yes, sir, says Punj.

It's clear he's just being polite because there's blank fat nothing written through his smile—and doesn't that "sir" sound a bit sarcastic? A bit Apu? As if that's what he thinks Jivan might expect?

—I like TV, says Punj. My favourite is American *Die-Nasty.* I'm watching it these days via reruns.

—*Dynasty,* right, sure.

Jivan turns back to the monitors. One by one, the screens go dark until only the central monitor shows life. Enter Radha and Bubu, his arm around her neck in a buddy grip.

—Radha Madam and Bubu Sahib, says Punj. He's so cool, no? But see how Radha Madam always modifies for Gargi Madam? PDAs not allowed!

He's right: when Radha sees Gargi, she pulls away from Bubu and straightens her dupatta. *Best behaviour for Didi.*

Ranjit comes in. He shakes Bubu's hand and hugs Radha, eyes closed, pressing her into him, *dirty old bastard;* he keeps hold of her hands as they talk.

—Ranjit Sahib, says Punj. I know all sorts of factoids about him.

—Ah, Punj? I'm trying to watch, Jivan says.

—OK, sure, sir. Sorry.

Then comes a man Jivan does not recognise, must be an uncle, or a guest of Devraj's; he's quite old, wearing glasses, a golf shirt and whites. He allows Kritik Sahib and Sita to pass in front of him.

—Sita Madam, she's truly just a Goddess, no? says Punj. So sweet. And so, you know, such zero tolerance about everything. Always fighting. He grins.

—Wow, Punj, tell me what you really think, Jivan says.

—Jivan Sahib, says Punj, shielding himself with the tray. Your disapproval is a wound to my sensibilities. Of course, I'm just kidding. But look at her. Everything just feels so fresh around here since she got back.

Sita is still barefoot. The lettering across her chest now obscured by a scarf. Her arm is linked through Kritik Sahib's. She lets go and takes her place at the foot of the table, her back to the camera.

—Now for the main event, says Punj.

—Punj . . .

—Sorry, sorry, I'll keep silent. But every two weeks, the game, you know? It gets tense, I swear. Watching this, mera toh keema banega, ek din.

Enter Devraj. The white kurta pyjama, the shawl. Jivan puts on the headphones, the chairs scrape his eardrums as the whole family stands up. He remembers doing that! Devraj stands at the top of the table, they all sit, and, at his signal, Gargi picks up his plate. She wipes it, and reaches for the dishes on the table. Devraj gestures that he wants more saag. He wants less daal. He wants chicken, no not that leg piece: a thigh and some tari. Roti, not rice. Raita, no, not on top: put it in a bowl on the side. Everyone is silent for the ritual. All Jivan hears is the scrape of the spoons as Gargi serves her father. Everyone is still except Radha, who folds a chapati into a triangle and lays it carefully on a small plate, next to Devraj's elbow.

—Jivan Sahib, are you married? says Punj. Me, I'm married since ten years. I never go home for lunch. Today she's given me aloo paranthe, as if Sunday brunching came early. Can I offer you some?

He looks up at Punj, finger on his lips.

—You don't want? Fasting? OK, perfect, says Punj.

—No, I— God, never mind, he says.

Gargi finishes with Devraj then turns to her other side, where the old man Jivan did not recognise is waiting. An uncle? A cousin? That cannot be her husband. But something in the way Gargi carefully takes his plate and places small parcels of sabzi, roti, daal on it so they don't touch each other; only someone trained or paid would do that. He looks at Punj.

—Surendra Sahib, Punj says. Such a learned guy.

—Huh.

Gargi, Radha and Sita must help themselves. Sita takes gravy but no meat, rice but not roti—and the smallest amount of pickle.

On Friday evenings, Ranjit would take Jeet and Jivan to Jor Bagh, where the girls lived with Nanu and Devraj in the old Napurthala family townhouse. Ranjit would tell his boys: *Sit straight, finish your plate, chew with your mouths shut, don't forget to thank Nanuji, you especially, Jivan. And you, Jeet. Watch him. Report.*

When they got to Jor Bagh, there would be a children's table set in a corner of the state dining room for Gargi, Radha and Jeet—and Jivan (if he had been good in the car). Sita was nothing but a baby in a high chair. Nanu was always there, crocheting endless forget-me-nots onto handmade lace while she monitored Gargi, and Gargi was Prefect to the rest of them. When she wasn't looking, Jeet would kick Jivan and make him spit out his food. That would mean extra punishment meted out by Ranjit—example: not being allowed to get down from the table while the others went to play; not being allowed to go to the toilet until his thirteen times tables had been recited up to fifty times thirteen.

Now Gargi and Radha are married women, Sita is a fox. There is no children's table.

—Hai Bhagwan. Devraj's voice is deep, his vowels long. His invocation envelops the family, silencing their whispered chatter. He raises his eyes as if God is only up there to help him digest. There is not enough salt in the meat, he says. Kya Sita, ghar kya aa gayi, tum ne angrezi khaana banwa diya? Everyone laughs.

What did Devraj say? What does Jivan catch? Not enough. *Sita, foreign, food.* He shakes his head, as if the meaning of the words will form and fall into place. Then Gargi gestures for the servants to start clearing. Devraj puts his hands flat on the table. Gargi makes another signal: everyone stops. Each member of the family sits up and though they cannot see him, he does too. He feels Punj lean forward, breath on his neck. The silence is waiting to spark.

—Boys and girls, Devraj says. Sita is home, she is about to be married.

The men around the table smile. Spoons go down, clinking on the plates, chairs scrape as everyone shifts about. Radha claps her hands.

On the screen, Sita bows her neck and curls her hands under her chin, acting the demure bride. Jivan stiffens. He pulls the headphones from his ears then settles them back. Sita getting married? Why didn't Barun J. Bharat, or Jeet, or Kritik Sahib say anything?

—We have binders full of boys, Devraj says. We will show you the shortlist later. But pehle, I want to say something important. So please, he points at them. Meri baat dhyaan se suno.

Listen carefully. Jivan watches them all watching Devraj. Only Gargi's husband is still smiling.

—As you all know, I am getting old, says Devraj.

Laughter whispers around the table, up into the headphones and huddles in Jivan's ears.

Devraj holds up his hands.

—Seventy-five is a good age, a fine age, he says. I have seen this Company of ours change with the country; getting better with each year. Two of my daughters are married, although no children, we can pray. He looks at Gargi's stomach, then at Radha's. Sita now is home. Today I have already decided: tumhaare dahej ki baat karne ka waqt aa gaya hai.

What is waqt? *What is* dahej?

—Dahej? Jivan says. Subtitles would really help here.

Punj clears his throat,

—It's dowry, sir. He bangs his palm on his tray as if cheering a dog in a race. Dahej equals dowry. Every Tuesday almost, Devraj Bapuji promises to give dahej, and each time Gargi Madam speaks and Radha Madam follows. It's a game, no? For sport. Both play very well. Sometimes the question that Bapuji asks has to do with the Company, like, *How much do you love the money we make in profits from the Company Delhi?* Or, sometimes, it has to do with staffing, like *How many can we sideline to make way for my real friends?* Or, *Which one of you could find out the most disloyal managers, and how would you punish them?* Whatever he asks, whoever answers right or best gets something added to their chit. And you know, they've both been married for so much time, and in so much time still, there's nothing to give to Bubu and Surendra Sahib. It's too bad. No wonder they both look so pissed.

—O right. Sure, Jivan says. Dowry. *What the fuck is going on here?*

—But, Jivan sir, says Punj. Kritik Sahib wants that I should show you the Farm. Let's go. I have seen this before. I can assure you, nothing will happen now. No dowry. Just desserts.

If Jivan married Iris, what would he get? A handshake from her dad, help with a down payment on a Back Bay townhouse in buggy-walking distance of Commonwealth Mall, and a complete collection of Baz Luhrmann DVDs. The chance to be introduced to the inner circle of a midlevel Boston club, to work all hours in an investment bank, eat macrobiotic meals at home, drink at Harry's on Friday evenings with a group of like-minded psychos. Just to keep Iris in a spa membership to use between her social work stints. Just to provide Vineyard summers for their mixed-race kids for the rest of his days.

Jivan pictures himself at this lunch with her: the Foreign Return and his American wife. He, trading business cards with Bubu, while Iris gamely tries to pull off wearing a sari as a, you know, *gesture.* No thanksji.

Behind him, Punj is waiting.

—Let's go, Jivan says. Maybe we can find me a steak sandwich or something en route. Think you can manage that Punj, my friend?

—As the time is, so shall it be, says Punj.

Outside, the heat is still. Punj is as tall as him, as wide and as snappily dressed in a local kind of way. Long shirt too patterned for Jivan's taste, and sandals instead of shoes on his feet, showing off wide, flat toes like a frog.

—But you know, Jivan Sahib, says Punj. Now we are outside I can say this thing. In any case, dahej is prohibited in India. No dowry, by act of law. I learned this from Mr. Sri *Amir* Khan. On *Satyamev Jayate.* You know that show? Reality talk show format. Very popular.

—No, never seen that one, Jivan says. I'll keep it in mind.

—Very good. Now, what would you like to see? says Punj. That way to Radha Madam's ice-skating house— (his hand glides the air like a plane taking off). Everything in USA, we have here, sir.

No shit. *Where's the zoo? Where are the freaking unicorns?*

Behind the bunker, Punj has a golf cart waiting; he gestures to the backseat. Jivan watches the Farm unfold: the tennis courts, the pitch for cricket and boules; a set of dark globes balancing on a bright, flat rectangle of grass. There's an awning and a small clubhouse and beyond that another prairie: it's like being on set at Universal Studios, coasting through Ye Olde England to find himself back in the Wild West. In a clearing near the pool, workers are sawing, hammering bamboo, the structure half-decked with more bright orange marigolds.

—Miss Sita ki welcome-home-cum-pre-Engagement pavilion, says Punj. Tonight, after the Tuesday Party.

—They still have those?

—Wow. So you really were here before?

—Sure. Tuesday Parties, for the Devraj Hundred.

All of those guys, handpicked by Devraj for a five-year programme of elite training in personal and business development. Money in the bank. Before and after they joined.

—When I was a kid, Ranjit never stopped shoving their brilliance down my throat, Jivan says.

—I'd love to hear more, sir.

Jivan was NFI to those nights when the Hundred would gather, first to listen to the great man lecture on his favourite subject—*the twinned future of India and The Company*—and then to get steaming drunk and wild.

—Will you go tonight? he says.

—No, sir, not for me, says Punj. I was born in Chandigarh to an agricultural family. I graduated in the evening cut-off from GNDU and started with Kritik Sahib's special contingent because I excel in IT. I don't get invited for the Hundred—they're all sons of business, you know? (He grins.) But maybe one day. I'm an entrepreneur. Restaurants. My shares are in up-and-coming Haus Khas Village. Like your Greenwich Village, only ours is better, I am certain. Food is Tibetan–Mexican fusion. You must come try, and tell me what you think.

Jeez, why not just fry some ice cream and serve it with celery soup?

—Can't wait, Jivan says. But, Punj, I've seen the house and the formal gardens. Why don't you show me the rest of this place? Take me to some part where you hang out.

The golf cart veers to the verge and then stops.

—Jivan Sahib, says Punj. I have to confess I was hoping you would ask me this. Today is an auspicious day, a very special day. Miss Sita is home, you know? We are going to have a wedding. Gargi Madam has promised many opportunities for staff to enjoy. In an unprecedented move, Miss Sita asked for this as her wedding request.

—Really? he says.

—I'm serious, says Punj. All the staff. At her planning conference. Gargi Madam promised that Miss Sita said, "No one should be left out. Those who serve should be served on my wedding."

—With her own sweet hands?

Punj gets out of the cart and stands looking at him.

—Sir, this is no joke. Come let me show you what Miss Sita's return means.

Punj drives off the main pathway, turning around raised flower beds, where he points out the places where special shrubs and flowers have been selected and planted by Sita herself. Where she used to gather all the Level 1–3 servants (diggers, waterers, tenderers, wipers, waiters, drivers) and host them for lunch once a month. Where she once—and Punj remembers this with awe in his voice—went against Bapuji when he wanted to install a boating lake, because, she said, it was a waste of India's most sacred life, Ma Ganga, its water. According to Punj, only Miss Sita could stand up and do that.

Then Punj stops the cart. They get out, and go meet and greet. Here Punj works in a special handshake, noticeable because every time it seems to change slightly, as if he has developed this relationship with each manager and wants him, Jivan, to clock it. Punj introduces him as:

—Kritik Sahib's special guest, childhood friend of Gargi Madam, Radha Madam and Miss Sita—

And this is met with smiles and murmurs of, *Miss Sita, she came just this morning to see us.*

They are following the scent, playing a game of *chase Sita through the Farm.* The stories of her beauty and kindness and bravery get bigger and better and the more he hears, the more he believes. There's the old-school manager at the family gym, busting out of his whites (whose handshake with Punj is two palm slaps and a right fist bump). He tells them (his voice choking in his throat):

—I taught Miss Sita her backhand when she was nine, and this morning she came to give me her Cambridge University tennis jacket which she won for her great prowess.

As he speaks, actual tears form in his eyes.

They wait while the manager summons his deputy, who brings the blazer into the light. It seems tiny and sad without its wearer, as if she has shrunk and then disappeared.

—They call this a "Blue," the manager says. They give this instead of a gold statue. She said she owed it to me as the father of her skill.

They all three stand around stroking the soft jacket, imagining it on a podium holding a medal, thanking the sports centre back home with heart on sleeve.

—Sita, says the manager. Only she would do this.

On to the Head Gardener at his greenhouse (handshake: a short grip and thumb turn), who tells them, kasam kha ke, which Punj (unnecessarily—for this phrase is one of the few Hindi movie lines Jivan knows) interrupts to translate as *Truthfully, he eats the truth,* before the Gardener says:

—Miss Sita used to take so much interest in every plant and tree in the Farm. For each and every one, she knew the Latin name, the Sanskrit name and also gave her own trans-planting name. This one: Naomi, this one, Germainey, this one, Sontagi Susisthus. And these plants they were like her dolls. Such love she showed! In fact, she had no fear—even in the wild wood she would always go, first to explore, and then to hide, and then to make her den.

They pause again, to appreciate the nature of such a girl. All around them the emerald tennis courts sparkle, the cobalt sky reflects. Between the two are the men in white uniforms like links in a chain, keeping land and sky connected. It is so lush: Jivan's throat is so dry. He asks for water but no one seems to hear him. There are no sprinklers anywhere.

—Punj, he says, let's go find her den.

Punj looks doubtful.

—She might even be there . . .

—The forest is that way, Jivan sir, says the Gardener. Come, leave the cart, we can walk.

Once upon a time the Farm was covered in trees; and when they were cleared for landscaping, only this part of the forest remained. On weekends, and after school and tutors' hours, and if they had been good, Jeet, Radha, Gargi and he would be granted free time; they would beg to be brought here to play. The ferns were so large, like claws trying to grab them; the trees had a strange, snakeskin bark that peeled into strips like real-life pythons. The place was full of birdsong they never heard in the city; it was the best place for a hideout. After he left for Boston, every park, every copse and clump of trees seemed tame in comparison.

Jivan shares none of this. He follows Punj and the Gardener, moving from the burning sun into the shade of the tallest trees: still those snakeskin ladies keep watch. There are spreading oaks and delicate new saplings, but the ferns have been clipped. Everything looks smaller, less vivid. They walk for what seems like half an hour but can't be more than ten minutes. The place is alive with the sound of cicadas, sawing like a thousand tireless lumberjacks. He stumbles over a root and wants to laugh. *The route to your roots,* he thinks, then, *dammit, where is that slogan from?*

—Here, says the Gardener. And over there, our spy hole. Whenever she was in situ, we kept an eye on her.

In front of them is an ancient banyan tree. This he recognises. Here they would rendezvous and play "house." Mom-and-Pop-and-Sister-Brother, running through the banyan's dangling fingers, using them as whips and ropes, daring each other to steal tin cups from the labourer kitchens and bring them for Radha to make invisible chai and serve it on leaves with sweets made of air. Did he carve his name in its trunk? No—but Jeet did, and so did the girls. He looks for the marks, scratched and gouged, but layers of saucer-shaped fungi have invaded the base.

The Gardener kicks at the growth; rotten wood falls away.

—Poisonous, he spits. An infestation we will get under control.

Now the cicadas sound as if they are calling, *Sita, Sita, Sita, Sita, Sita.* Why didn't she carve her name? Once he climbed up this old banyan and fell asleep, got covered in tick bites, which made Radha laugh. Jivan didn't tell Radha that while he was up there he had spied on Gargi, twelve years old and trying to kiss Jeet. She had begun to cry when he taunted her. *No,* he said. *Your face is too fat. And you should not offer yourself to boys.*

He felt for Gargi, but he had not moved from his hiding place.

The forest is so still around them, as if waiting for all these years for him to act.

—Punj, we should get back, he says.

—OK, great idea. Kritik Sahib will be finished with lunch by now.

They turn. Begin to make their way, single file, through the trees. The birdsong thins. They are almost out of the woods.

—But one more place, Punj says, over his shoulder. Please indulge me, Jivan Sahib, this is my favourite of all.

They reach the golf cart, and Punj starts it up, pressing with his wide, flat foot on the pedal.

They skirt around the perimeter away from the house, then veer left, skidding through a gate which is not guarded or locked. Green grass gives way to a fine white chalk that mists up from the ground and covers their skins, clagging in their throats, in their eyes. It clears to Punj, standing, laughing, one hand on his hip and the other beak-like in front of his mouth, taking the pose of the statue next to him. They are in a graveyard of stone goddesses, handless, armless. Where there are torsos there are no legs, where there are heads there are no noses, some have full lips and almond-shaped eyes stretched back under cones of carved braids, some have pierced navels. All of them are frozen in postures of service or dance.

—What is this?

Punj breaks his pose and takes up another one, arms squaring face.

—*Vogue,* he says, then relaxes. Jivan Sahib, you know *stone cold fox*? You know this American term? They use it to appreciate women.

—Er, kinda . . .

—Actual, you know, stone-cold. But not real foxes, no.

Now Punj laughs: it comes out strange and high as if sprung from his wiry shoulders, his skinny torso and chest.

—This is the only place I've ever been where the girls don't walk away on me.

Punj drapes his arm over a goddess; his fingers graze its breasts, he grins and moves his eyebrows up and down.

—Do you remember Jeet Sahib? Punj says. Did you know him before? This is his storage yard only.

Jivan looks carefully at Punj, wondering if he is for real, whether he's just pretending not to know that Jivan and Jeet are brothers. Sorry, half brothers. He looks around more carefully. On one side of the yard are thirty or so statues; their marble skins have a sheen to them, the carved flowers in their hair, the detailing of muscle around their navels; the fingers and toes decorated with rings and bangles, their ankles entwined with carefully patterned snakes. Facing them, where Punj is standing, are their plasterwork twins: some with no mouths, some missing a snake or a hairpiece; some with bigger breasts, fuller lips and thinner around the waist.

He feels that Punj is studying him, his gestures and expressions. He relaxes his arms from their tight fold. Punj moves into the same stance.

—Sure, Jivan says. I used to know Jeet.

—Jeet Sahib is an entrepreneur and an artist, says Punj. Every piece he collects comes here for repro. All these (Punj indicates the plaster-works) will decorate the wedding garden. Each lady has her special place.

—Punj, Jivan says. Let's go. I gotta getta drink.

Punj drives back to the bunker. Jivan's body flops, mind floats. He knows this feeling well: for days after Ma's funeral he gave in to it, riding troughs of grief, rage, hilarity, hearing her during her chemotherapy saying *khichdi ban gayi* as clumps of her hair, black strands and white, came out in her swollen hand. Laughter in her voice, tears in his eyes. Empty, he felt, without bones.

Since he landed, his eyes have been looking for Ma, or for Gargi. Instead Sita is everywhere, the whole garden springs from her, and Jeet is underneath and behind it all. Eyes sting, every nerve feels pinched and if the only way he could save himself was to lift a glass of water to his lips, he could not do it. *Sita would care,* he thinks, *taught by Gargi: she would care for me as if she was my own.* The image of Sita tending to his thirst will not be banished. She has kind, firm hands. She smells of jasmine and marigolds.

They reach the edge of the prairie. Across the grasses, the bunker sits, hiding its secrets in the earth.

—So, Punj says. I must go. Kashyapji will have returned from prayers, from lunch. He keeps proper time. So, I leave you here.

Jivan gets out of the cart. He raises his arm, a half high five, then drops it. He watches Punj rev up the cart, drive away.

Alone for the first time since Boston. Jivan's suit traps every atom of heat, wet cloth has become his skin. The grasses are still. Above his head no clouds, around him no sound. He walks toward the bunker, climbs the steps slowly. Standing in the upstairs room, eyes closed, he swigs from the bottle of whisky. Looks for the Company Deli croissants—the box has been cleared away. The room presses on him, the incense catching in his throat.

A roar from outside—he almost drops the bottle, as if he's been caught in a thieving lie. He opens the screen door, goes out to the veran-dah; sees Kritik Sahib stumbling through the grasses, his face sheened in sweat. He has a wild startled look, nothing like the man Jivan always feared. He has lost his Nehru jacket; his white shirt is stained with red earth. He trips up the steps, Jivan moves to catch him; they end by almost embracing, the JD held between them. Is that panic or terror in the old man's eyes? Jivan thinks, *He's just a man, after all.*

—Still here? says Kritik. Chal, hat! He grabs the whisky bottle, stumbles onto the verandah and into one of the old split-cane chairs.

—What did you see? Kritik tries to catch his breath; hand to his chest, he presses down, sweat or tears dripping from his chin.

—I should call someone, Jivan says. Punj was just here.

Kritik slumps over, staring into the long grass. Then he clears his throat and spits. Pulls himself upright in the chair. He holds up the bottle.

—So, beta, he says, one hand smoothing his hair. Come, sit, have another drink with me. Now you've seen everything.

—I've had the tour—Punj took me around, Jivan says. What's happened?

—Is that so? Well. Come—be the first to celebrate with me, Kritik says. As of now, I am quitting the Company.

The heat on Jivan's head, the whisky inside him make the words seem songlike, as if Kritik Sahib is inviting him to a party or reading cricket scores. But his face is dripping, it seems almost to be melting. He is ashen. *Quit?* What is going on?

—Ah, I think I'll go and find Ranjit. Get settled in.

—As you like, Kritik says. You must do as you like. Go then, get gone. And Jivan? Don't you breathe a word of what you saw.

Jivan nods; he backs down the steps, into the grass. Turns, keeps moving, walking the path Kritik cut. Then hears him shout:

—Get lost, you bastard! After all these years!

Jivan starts to run, back through the courtyard, where his shadow crosses the sundial; back, he wants to go, to the banyan tree in the forest, and from there find his way to the house in Nizamuddin, where he was a boy with a mother and a brother and some kind of father sometimes. In the garden squares of the East enclave there were crumbling mosques to explore and badminton titles to defend. There was standing on the runner of Jeet's bicycle and swooping around, minding the cobbler on the street corner and the men getting shaved. At home there was his desk, and on it the models of the pyramids and the Empire State Building made by him from chuski sticks licked clean. On the walls, his posters of Bon Jovi, Bruce Springsteen, Samantha Fox tacked underneath. There was Ma, and her music: tabla and sitar. There was always the promise of seeing Gargi for love, and Radha for fun, and water from the nalka and hot cooked food. There was no Sita then.

In the rose garden he bends double, hands on knees, breathing in dust. Sweat drips from his temples to the earth, he drops to a weed-picker's squat. His mouth falls open, he rubs his fists in his sockets, salt and dirt. His vision fills with red dots dancing over each blade of grass, over and under and over each other. Beneath the surface of the garden, thousands of ants are churning the soil, piercing it with tiny holes, working without orders, without mind.

MY NAME IS DEVRAJ. Mine is a simple story, come closer if you can.

The day Ranjit's boy came home from America, I watched him pick about the place, look into the gardens, the sports grounds and the stone yard. It was a time fit. For Kings. What a beautiful place that was!

Months have passed since that hot time. Now, in the death days of autumn, I find myself in Kashmir, the land of milk and honey. Ah, Srinagar, Sringari, City of Wealth! The great Emperor Ashoka named it thus. Life is good: I have brought Sita with me to open my new hotel. The Company Kashmir is my most beautiful property. It sits on a hill-top, waiting for us. We will go there soon.

Sita wanted to see this old house first, and though I once swore I would never come back here, I cannot say no to my daughter. So we find ourselves, wandering through these five storeys of broken, rotting wood.

I can sense the Jhelum, mud-coloured and sluggish below. A snake disguised as a river, changing direction as it wills. There used to be a jetty, where vendors would tie their boats and sell cut-price saffron, tea, bootleg cigarettes. Now the stench of stagnant water rises up. The wooden house is falling down, into its own reflection.

It's very dirty all around. Somewhere outside, the city goes about its business, wrapped in shawls against the biting cold—here the market, there the shrine. The tulip fields are fallow, waiting for spring. While bees make honey and reeds make boats and the world keeps turning, turning. Simplicity is life on the water. No fixed earth.

I cannot remember the last time I was here. These days, I have to work to catch the exact moment, the begetting of forgetting. Forgetting is always there, a slippery fish. Blind, with teeth. Silently it gapes and nibbles.

—Sita?

She does not answer. Dust floats around the place, for there has been a kerfuffle. There is a crater in this floor, and I can see through to the next. My young manservant is down there, lying on his front; his neck is twisted at such a strange angle. I think he must have fallen and be dead.

Maybe Sita went down to fetch the tea. No, of course not, it's not possible. Now I am getting confused. Confusion: the bastard half brother of chaos. Chaos: the torture instrument of forgetting.

Where did she go? For a while she was asleep here, then she ran off. She loves to play hide-and-seek, catch-catch. Now is not the time, I told her. For I am telling my story, and mine is from the heart. It is the most important: through all the ages of my life, the best, most learned men have told me this. Nevertheless, I have learned that all should be judged by their speech acts. So here we are, talking in circles, on floorboards threatening to crack.

I was born in Napurthala, a Kingdom not far from here. To a gambling Maharaja and his fifteen-year-old bride. He died in a shooting accident when she was twenty-five. I was ten years old, her little Prince, growing up under the shadows of Empires. Mughal and British. My widowed mother was strict: always she warned, *If you eat the flesh of an animal, the animal will devour you from within.* Still, she prepared the choicest of meats for me. Stew and dumplings, a sauce with onions, with tomatoes. A dish that she gleaned from the wife of the British Viceroy who also recommended a daily glass of fresh cow's milk, so white it could stain the insides.

I first came to Srinagar in 1957 as a dashing young Maharaja full of desires for life. Accession had gifted Napurthala to our new, independent India, and so I had no city or state. Srinagar had gone the same way. I was a King without a Kingdom, hungry to establish my name. I hankered after this house, and for the secrets of shawl production it held. Luckily for me, a wealthy man lived here, a Kashmiri Pandit of the ruling class, refined in his manners and Hindu enough in the best of ways. Suitable company for a King. His daughter was young and his business was failing, for he was used to fraternising with his Shi'a employees as if they were his family. He did not understand that the modern way was to only favour one's own.

I was virile, with money and connections across our dear country. Quietly I speculated, providing the banks of Srinagar with finance, setting up a few local friends in stock exchange. This was in the days before computerisation, when men were on the trading floor. The Outcry System. It brooked no response. The one who shouts the loudest wins.

Finally, the old Pandit came to me and invited me into this house. In this room we would receive the weavers from one hundred and fifty families, across the Valley. Hand-cleaned, hand-spun wool. Handwoven so both sides of the shawl came out exactly the same. Then carefully patterned and properly hued. We ordered dyed colours, for women did not want a natural look. They wanted Himalayan blue or hot pink like the pursed buds of a bougainvillea. Not to mention rich, royal purple, colours we made from saffron, walnut, pomegranate seed. And then on top, the embroidery! Gold thread spun fine in backwater rooms, glinting like the reeds caught in evening light. These days duns and tans and sage greens are the signal of good breeding, and the less chamki, the better. So does fashion change.

Each piece took one year for one family to make. We paid one thousand rupees each, on top added our margin, and then sold by appointment only, in the best of the Company shops. India exclusive. And ferenghis, Prime Ministers, Princes and their wives came from far and wide to buy them, for no one can deny that they are quality things. Why should a price not be paid for quality things?

Ten years passed. I became restless, for Srinagar was full of honeymoon couples. One could not move without tasting some delicious ware from a hot-chestnut wala, almonds and spice, perambulating down the boulevards, en route to the picture house, perhaps to see the latest films at the Broadway or the Regal, picnicking in the Shalimar gardens in the summer.

Finally the day came when the Pandit's daughter turned fifteen. In this very room, the windows once reflected every angle of the sun. I played my hand and won my bride and every stitch she came with. Her father begged me, *Don't take my daughter! For you take my most precious shawl to keep you warm.*

I promised to take care of both daughter and shawls. And allow her to come back whenever she wanted. It meant she was always half here, half there. When violence began to choke this city, she was here with him. I called from Delhi to insist they leave, but her father said he would not. No one can move a man who wishes to remain stuck in his place. And who can blame him? This house was such a beauty.

It is hard to believe, but rich carpets once adorned these walls. Now they are in tatters, sprouting mould, a breeding ground for moths. A handmade chandelier once hung from the ceiling, pearls and diamonds dropping from it. After my wife and her father were dragged from this room and slaughtered in the streets around, I took that chandelier down and rehung it at the Farm. I shut this place up.

Sita does not remember her mother, or this house at all. But she is such a tender-hearted girl, she was upset to find it so damaged. She cried for what she never knew. She also cried out for her sisters, for reasons I cannot understand.

I tried to distract her, sitting with her, cross-legged on the floor. I said:

—Don't forget Gargi always tried to make you play her games, so I built you a hideout of your own! Don't forget Gargi actually thought you would be safe going to picture houses, but I installed a screening room on the Farm! And don't forget Gargi never wanted you to join the Company, so I gifted you the best share!

None of this seemed to calm Sita. She wrung her hands; she bit her perfect lower lip. She has her mother's delicate bird features, her cocked head, peachy breasts that are almost too big for her frame. I stroked her hair, and told her to speak about her college days, tell me where all she has been. We held hands, and she said, Papa, I love you so much, it is time I told you everything. As you know, I studied for my Bachelor's in the hush of a Cambridge library. How homesick I was, and how free. Experimenting in mind and body, yes, I came naked in so many beds, but no one truly caught my mind's eye. Then, last year, I fell in love with an Indian filmmaker. He stole my heart from the moment I saw him. He distracted me from the life of my mind, and yet he became it. I wanted him. I wanted him. I was ready to betray the calling of my studies. But one night he broke the intensity of my feelings by asking me outright for my body.

Here she paused, and looked at me. I kept my face blank as an unwritten cheque. And then I'll tell you what she said:

—I took the train to meet him. In London. Halfway through dinner, as I was lifting my fork to my mouth, he said, *Will you stay the night with me?*

Here she jumped up and began to pace the room, twisting her dupatta around in her hands. She pulled it off her and let it fall. Without looking at me again, she said that his words shocked her into replying, *No, I cannot,* even though he paid for the dinner. *Papa* (she said, and here she knelt before me), if only he had not asked, I would have let the night unfold and given myself to him. He said it was shame that prompted me to refuse. Fear of what you, my dear Papa, would say. Fear of what people would think. But it was not shame. It was love, for my spirit and self. I wanted him so much, but I knew I would break if he touched me, and that he would just move on. My refusal meant that he did so, anyway. I still regret that decision. I think about him constantly, my body on fire.

As she spoke, the house around us trembled. Yet I could not allow her to see that I was disgusted. I wondered who she thought I was to her—a girlfriend or an aunt? Her sister? Which one? I patted her hands, and gestured to the young manservant who brought us here: though he was over by the door, his ears were like two handles of a speech-day cup. Clearly he was listening to every word.

—Chup-chup, shh, I said. That is over now, Sita, I said. Here we are. No matter. Look at us sitting and telling tales, like two bad sisters together.

This made her laugh, ruefully, I thought. The sound enraged me even more, and I wondered that she couldn't tell. I almost told her that after I spunked to conceive her, I vowed I would never come back to this house again, or to this part of the city. It is a place suitable only for dogs and dead kids.

I must say, I forgot how cold November is in Kashmir. It is almost snowing. When I stick out my tongue, I can taste the ice in the air. The beams creak above my head and pieces of sky bear down. I seem to have lost my shawl.

—Sita?

O Lord, why can't a man just be? Why must he take on a wife, and bear children? More than a woman, a man bears a child. Khaana, daana, dhanda, doodh. So many responsibilities. Where is she? No answer.

ii

There will be no future for Jivan Singh in the Company because looking
stupid is his new career. He has become the official entertainment for the
drivers and garage boys who cannot understand where he wants to go.

—Can you take me to Ranjit's house? In Nizamuddin? Old house?
He mimes a driving motion. Thinks about trying in Hindi, but does not.
Wants to demand the keys for the Ferrari, the Maserati; somewhere in
this garage must be the vintage Rolls that old Nanu was driven around in
when he was a boy. He was not allowed near it, if he even breathed near it
she would threaten to give Gargi a slap. The car belonged to her husband,
the Maharaja of Napurthala. Ma said it was the only thing, alongside
Nanu, to survive the Maharaja's love of dice.

A man in a grey and gold uniform approaches, and the other drivers
let him through. His head is so round, he looks like the letter *i*.

—I am Dipesh Singh. Chief Mechanic here. Ah, Jivan sir, Ranjitji's
bungalow is here on the Farm. Your bag has been delivered. I will request
an escort for you.

—No, I want to go to uska, er, no, unka, ah, ghar. Ranjit's *home*?
Jivan mimes four walls around his face, a roof; he watches closely, does
his rusted Hindi raise the Chief Mechanic's brows? The corner of his
mouth?

—Yes, sir. Praveen!

A boy with hair as shiny as a bowling ball steps forward.

—Chalo, take Mr. Jivan to Ranjit Sahib's bungalow.

Jivan allows them to put him in the back of another golf cart. Thinks he hears sniggering and someone say, "Thank you, come again," as he is taken away.

They pass the bowling green, the pool again. He keeps his eyes closed, head back. It takes around ten minutes. They don't talk.

They come to a gated section, where three discrete bungalows form sides around a well-kept square of grass. Each bungalow has a tidy verandah, complete with a cut-glass table and low beanbags slung around. Each one has flower boxes in the windows. They pull up. The boy hands him an envelope, says,

—Sir, that one. He gestures to the central house. Here, your personalised card key. He starts the cart. He whistles as he steers away.

On the verandah, a wrinkled woman in a mud-coloured sari squats with a long cane brush. She does not look up, just sweeps around Jivan, moving like a crab. *Wild. That's wild,* he thinks.

Inside, the temperature is controlled. Dark wood, glass and porcelain, down-lighting and more lilies. Everything embossed with the Company logo—a shield, two tigers, two snakes. Two mottos, one in Latin and one in Sanskrit or Hindi, he cannot guess language or meaning. The only word he recognises is DEVRAJ.

Ranjit lives in this executive suite. That means there has to be food. He goes to the kitchen: the cupboards are bare. There are only quarter bottles of Tiger in the mini-fridge. The back door opens onto an unloved yard, where the dying sun makes everything look jaundiced. On the laundry step, another woman crouches, slapping wet fabric against stone. Her arms bruised blue with the dye from the clothes. She looks up, her eyes dark and opaque as the bucket of foaming water beside her. She does not smile.

He checks the two bedrooms. In one, the cinnamon stink of his father's Old Spice almost makes him gag. In the other, someone has unpacked his case, laid his things inside the closet. He pulls off his suit jacket. The pockets are empty, his Harvard tie lost somewhere on the Farm. Shoes kicked off and socks discarded, he falls onto the bed. Thinks of Kritik, cameras, microphones—and keeps his boxers on. After the hours in the air and the shocks on the ground, he can hold on to nothing. He sleeps.

. . .

In his dreams, Gargi is waiting for him. Smiling like Ma, smelling of roses, sandalwood, silk. His nose does not register this. He begins to cry as Gargi slowly unwinds her sari, hands definite, eyes steady on his. She comes close in her blouse and petticoat and begins to drape the sari onto him. Her nails catch on his stomach hairs as she tucks it into his belt, sending small shocks to his groin. He can smell the almond oil on her skin. *So pretty,* she says. *Turn,* she tucks it in; *turn,* and again, *turn.* He plays with her hair—like water in his fingers—and feels her breath on his skin as she bends to pleat his sari, he strokes her side as she drapes the pallu across his chest. It makes him hard and hot but wrong-feeling because this is Gargi, who played Ma to his beta. Still she goes on, bending again, lips closer to his belly, fingers in the pleats. He looks around: it's humid in this jungle, the sand beneath his feet is powdery and fine, they are surrounded by date palms, green, luscious, reaching out to caress. There are mirrors rising from the sand; he looks into one—Radha is reflected and reflected—she is so beautiful he wants to touch her too. He stretches out his hand toward her breasts and finds he is wiping tears from his own face. The sari is soaking, heavy all around him. He wants to move. Gargi is gone, the mirror melts into a puddle of silver, and where is Sita? He is looking for her among all the folds of silk between his legs. He needs her to tell him something but she is nowhere. As his hands reach out, fabric begins to knot around his neck then he wakes, choking, caught up in the sticky sheets, strangling Ma's name in his throat before it can come out of his mouth.

For a moment he thinks, *Jon, what did you take?* He does not know where he is, what time it is, what day. His eyes are so dry he thinks they might crumble from their sockets. His legs are heavy. He looks down. The sheets are drenched in his sweat. And, Ma is dead.

Jivan sits on the edge and presses all the switches until there is light. He promises himself that he will stop. Thinking, dreaming. From now, he will live where he is.

Outside the birds are chattering through the pink sunset like first-graders at home time. The sun is melting into the indigo sky.

He takes a shower, then, swaddled in a Company bathrobe, he weaves, light-headed, starving, around the bungalow, wondering if he can order room service. Steak frîtes? He could murder it mid-moo. He tip-toes into Ranjit's study, all wood-panelled, faux college-library. He sits behind the leather-topped desk in his towel and picks up the phone.

—Good evening, Jivan Sahib. Can I help you? A woman: welcoming, hopeful.

—Hello? How do you know I'm me? he hears himself say. Takes a breath. Can I get something to eat?

—Of course. Time is eighteen hundred thirty-five. Would you like a Viceroy Tea? You would get three bite-sized samosas, mini-cucumber, salmon and paneer amuse-bouche, two tikka patties, a selection of finger éclairs, French Fondants and a pot of Assam or Darjeeling. Or Earl Grey. Ranjit Sahib always takes Assam around now if he is at home. Coffee we can also do—Company Cappuccino?

—No. I think, I mean, yes, he says.

—Tea-coffee?

—Coffee. Can I get some fries?

She is gone. He puts the phone down. He doesn't know what a French Fondant is. Does anyone? Jeet would; he cares about stuff like that.

Across the desk, the silver-framed photos document the life he has missed. Jeet age nine or ten at India Gate: Kwality ice-cream tub clutched in his hand. Jeet again: at five-star establishments, restaurants, picnics, parties, getting older, fatter, graduating school, off to college. Standing at the doorway of the Nizamuddin house and looking pretty pleased with life. Jeet in a candy-striped shirt and dark suit, standing by an uplit swimming pool with Devraj, Gargi, Sita, Radha and Ranjit. Sita, who looks way too young for it, is holding a glass of champagne. There's a banner: *Happy 21st Jeet*. In pink.

Jeet, Jeet, Jeet, he thinks. *Where were you today? You promised you would come.*

In the kitchenette, Jivan struggles with the wall-mounted bottle opener, spilling beer on himself. He wipes his hands, downs one small bottle. He opens two more, and takes them out to the verandah. The air has cooled.

Crickets have replaced the birds and there are stars in the sky, so many stars. *What kind of man is Devraj that in this smog-filled city, stars shine over his farm? To you, Devraj sir!* And Kritik, and whatever went down today. He finishes the bottles in six gulps, head lightly spinning. *I am here!* he wants to shout (but doesn't). The stars don't seem that far away. He could reach them, easy, he is just as bright, as shining as them. He is about to stretch his arms out wide and whistle, but here comes a golf cart, *put-put-put,* his father in the back. Quick—hide the bottles; fold the shirt collar down.

—Jivan! Aré, beta, you are here? Good, good. Got a drink? Yes. Very good. Did you see much of the Farm?

Ranjit takes a red-gold pack of cigarillos from his top pocket, taps to release one, picks it out with his teeth.

Jivan doesn't smoke but he takes one when it's offered. It's worth it: Ranjit actually leans in to light it for him, holding the flame close to his face.

—Good evening, Ranjit Sahib.

A young, pretty woman, uniformed grey and gold, appears from the second bungalow. She's carrying a tray with an ashtray and two glasses (a tall and a squat), a bottle of Tanqueray Gin and one of Company tonic, a bowl of ice, an uncut lemon, a knife. She stops with the wide-legged stance, the fixed smile of the airhostess bracing for turbulence. Ranjit reaches behind her and places his hand in the small of her back. The tray wobbles slightly.

—Vanita, says Ranjit. Here is my young friend Jivan. He's staying just for a week or so. Make sure he doesn't get in your way, haan?

—Good to meet you, Jivan. Let me know if you need anything. You just pick up your room phone and I'll answer.

They watch her leave, the father and the unmentionable son, sitting together on a porch in the Company Farm, waiting it out with a drink and a smoke with crickets in the background and stars overhead. A Hindi song crackles between them, Jivan does not know the words but the tune is pure old Bollywood. From his inside pocket, Ranjit pulls out his phone. The tune soars louder, then stops.

—Hello, hello? Ranjit says. His voice loops upwards, goes taut. Jeet? Did Gargi call you? No? Are you nearly here? I can't tell you—just come now, only.

Jivan flushes at his brother's name. He checks his own phone; there is nothing from Jeet, although there are five new texts. Iris—delete. Iris—delete. Iris—delete. *Love Iris.* He jabs at the phone, delete, delete.

Ranjit is still talking,

—Jeet beta, the girls, well, Sita, I—no, I am OK. But things are shifting here. I want you to come here right now and meet me. Don't get late, OK? Have you met Gargi-Radha today? Seen anyone else? This is what happens when—OK, OK. OK, bye. Ranjit snaps the phone shut. He takes a breath and smiles at Jivan.

—So, beta. Obama in America, he says. Three years of black in the White House. This world is a strange place. Truly, we could not envision this thing in India. But, years pass. Things turn about. This new kind of openness, it cannot continue indefinitely. To what end, I ask?

He does not wait for an answer. He raises his glass to Jivan.

—So, come on, beta, tell me what's new?

What to say? Jivan could tell his dad that he graduated with honours. That he fenced in his first year, that he sucks the salt-caramel from Hershey's Kisses. That his favourite season is fall, which they don't have in Delhi.

—Not much, he shrugs. Except I saw Kritik Sahib after lunch today. He was pretty upset.

Ranjit looks at him,

—Relax, beta, just relax. What did you see?

—Nothing. I went on a tour of the Farm. When I got back, Kritik was a mess. He said he was leaving. Like he really meant it.

—Ha ha. Jivan, you must wait, and learn how things work. There is a lot you can be involved with, in time. You might spend a few weeks with Devrajji's Hundred, all fine young men. Handpicked from the best families to train for a future in businesses, in media, in government. Across India they will work, some also within the Company.

Jivan imagines a Devraj army, white kurtas, brown shawls, dark glasses, marching over the Farm to get him. He really needs that food.

—You should also come north, see how we do things in Amritsar, Ranjit says. And if it works out, you can also come to the new site in Srinagar.

—I read about it. The new hotel. I love the idea of the lakes and boathouses. War-zone lux. Very cool.

—Good, you already know about it. The army is there but this last few years it has been decommissioning. This year Diwali will take place in public for the first time in years. Yes, this hotel is Devraj Bapuji's vision and methodology. Unless our young generations can go to Kashmir and fully enjoy its great beauty, how else can they understand what it means?

—Means? Like, as a place? Jivan says.

—Ah, Jivan. So much you have to learn. For our guests, the Company Srinagar hotel gardens, in the City of Gardens, will be stunning. Yes. I will have Jeet take you to Srinagar. He's been doing great work, sourcing antiques for the family collection, such priceless pieces. We have some here, but the main store is at the Nizamuddin house. Such arty things he likes.

—Jeet is living in Nizamuddin?

—Converted it into a gallery. I gifted the deeds to him, when he turned twenty-one. A hint, you know, he should start thinking about doing his duty. Now he is thirty-three years old and still he insists on remaining a bachelor. What does he have to prove?

Wait, Jivan wants to say. *You gave him my house? Ma's rooms?* He shuts his eyes. Ranjit's cigarillo smoke seeps into his nostrils, catching in his throat.

The sound of china: he opens his eyes to see Vanita, hands full with another tray. This time a coffee pot, a three-tier cake stand arranged with wilting bites of sandwich, pert samosas and pretty cakes, more food than Jivan has seen for days.

—This is your order? says Ranjit. Nahin, we don't have time. Go and get ready now.

—But I haven't eaten since Boston.

He reaches for an éclair, but Vanita is already turning back, taking the tray with her.

—Let her go, Ranjit says. There will come a time for this tea party business. Go change. Jeet will be at the party, and so will Gargi-Radha.

Will there be food? All he has to swallow is the old, clear-eyed rage against Jeet, who gets the blood, the family, the house. *What about me?* He could ask the stars—but what is the point? He used to watch Jeet get all dressed up in a short-sleeved shirt and bow tie and disappear into the Bentley for Tuesday Parties. The next day Jeet wouldn't talk to anyone, as if being around the older men made him too good to play out in the yard. On the nights that Ma was performing, he would beg her to take him as well. She made him promise to stay out of sight. When they reached the Jor Bagh house, he would hunt down Radha in her bedroom, make her disguise him with her chunnis by promising to play dolls the next day. As the men drank and the women joined in, Radha would pull him around behind her; introduce him as her girlfriend. There was nothing weird about it; it was F.U.N.: Radha's special subject.

His spare suit is Hugo Boss wool. The summer one stinks of the plane. He puts on the woven trousers, tucks in his city shirt and carries his jacket. He doesn't have another tie. Here he is: broad-shouldered, strong-armed, brown skin, white accent. Starving.

When he comes out, Ranjit is already in the back of the golf cart, éclair in one hand, licking crumbs off his fingers.

—Don't get too carried away, he says. You're here. I want to see you can behave. Shadow Jeet and you'll be fine.

—Great, Jivan says. But first there is this yogic ashram place he wants to take me to—you know the kind of thing he likes. Silence, meditation, no girls. I texted with him about it, a month or so ago, he seems pretty serious about his religious studies.

Ranjit raises his eyebrows, shakes his head.

—Jeet's got these *issues,* you know, Jivan says. He takes out his phone, starts scrolling. He finds the message Jeet sent after Ma died. *All this shall pass. We look after our parents, we take over their dreams. Don't forget, work isn't everything. Take care, and when you come, maybe we can leave it all behind. Start up some new vibe, outside Company life. Even get holy on their asses. Love you, Jeet.*

He keeps his voice Kritik Sahib–light and his face turned toward the gardens.

—Maybe Jeet thought a bit of time out would help, he says.

—Jivan, says Ranjit. Just pass your phone here.

The message came when Jivan was on his way to the bank vault, Ma in his holdall. There was an Indian accent in Jeet's English. It made Jivan feel less alone. It was written recognition that they are brothers, not just one who has and one who has not.

Jivan keeps his mouth shut and watches Ranjit's face. Eyes all slitty, lips brown and puckered as if he's about to kiss the air goodbye.

—Wah, what fine words! Start-up ka bachcha. Start-ups, what, what? Upstarts, Ranjit says.

See? Jivan thinks. *It's that easy.*

Now comes the beauty of the grounds at night. The temperature has dropped to bearable. Clay lamps cast moon shapes along the paths. Banks of flowers wilt and wave like teen fans on MTV. As they reach the house, Jeet's goddesses form a walkway, offering them stone fruits, stone pitchers tipped, their white nipples eternally pert. He cannot tell if these are the real ones or the fakes. He sees a long, curved bar, around fifty or sixty men in suits and ties grouped around. Thank God, there are at least three long tables loaded with burners and covered steel dishes, chefs in tall hats standing to attention behind them.

They get out of the golf cart. Ranjit raises an arm; Jivan flinches, but it comes down around his back. It stays there as they turn, even as they join the party.

Jivan lets himself be pushed through the crowds of young men, slim-cut suits (from no label he can name), pink shirts, floral-patterned ties. He spots some heavy wrist jewellery; he slides his watch into his pocket. It's easy to imagine these young men graduating to boardrooms in New York or London or Dubai, dark chess pieces being moved around by some invisible force. He smoothes his hair, heads turn as he passes—the suit is too warm, but at least it is Boss. It's not so bad walking in Ranjit's wake, being introduced as:

—Jivan, my younger son, home from Harvard, America.

How about that?

Almost every other step, someone asks, *How do you like India?* And the next one, *So, what do you think of India?* Then again, *How are you finding India?* Each time he likes India more, replies that it's even more awesome, that he found it with a map, a plane, his feet (a depleted arsenal of half-remembered words and a motherlode of memories). So it goes on, and when he has found and loved India more than anyone ever has, they reach the heart of the inner circle: three men standing at the bar.

Now he is face to baldspot with Gargi's husband, Surendra, in thick-rimmed glasses, an embroidered silk kurta.

—So, you're here, says Surendra. Gargi mentioned, in passing. His handshake is damp and limp.

Then Ranjit gestures at Bubu.

—Who has our dearest Radha to manage, he says. Poor Bubu.

Up close, Bubu is a beautiful specimen getting spoiled. He has the cheekbones and the stubble and the firm grip, but the whites of his eyes are yellowing and his skin has the same sallow tinge, a hint of Bourbon after lunch. He is also the only man there wearing jeans.

—Whassup, Gee-van? Isn't that how you say it in Amer-i-can? Bubu grins. Jeet's long-lost half brother. Well, well, well. Good job, Ranjitji. Great suit. What is that, Autumn 2010?

All around them men are drinking, talking, backslapping. No Kritik Sahib in sight, and no Devraj. If Kritik Sahib is here, then what Jivan saw was just an old guy having a moment. He keeps smiling as Bubu and Ranjit toast his return; they shoot their JD, as they order more and keep their backs to the rest of the party. Bubu invites him to a polo match (to watch, not play), to swim tomorrow, early morning in the pool, to breakfast with him and Radha, to come shop at DLF Emporio, which is—no shit—a mall owned by the *other* real estate family. You want to go check out Hermès or Gucci? And you must come to the Company store too, it's out of this world.

—Delhi has a mall? Jivan says.

—Yeah, and we eat with knives and forks. Jeez, how long have you been gone? Do we all look the same to you? And talk like Apu from *The Simpsons*?

Bubu's thick eyebrows, plucked where they should meet, rise. So Jivan changes to sport, gets Bubu into a conversation about the manners of Indian cricket versus those of American football, which, Bubu says, he totally loves (to watch, not play). Jivan cannot concentrate, the chefs are taking decades to start service; by now he's so hungry that he's staring at Bubu's lips dragging on a Marlboro Red, while behind him, Ranjit and Surendra are muttering invocations like Aunties at a wedding.

—Hai Bhagwan, says Ranjit. What is happening, see: he's not coming, what is going on? Is this the kismet of a man who has worked so hard, to be reprimanded by this arrogant ladki? Gargi should have given better example. I mean, what kind of world is this? Everywhere the same thing, communal protests, bad governance, new generation don't care. I mean, what is this, yaar?

—Ranjitji, Surendra says. Don't worry. Bapuji is born under a lucky star, all will be OK. I will personally make sure Gargi does not do anything without Bapuji's sign-off; being so busy with running the Farm, how can she?

Gargi's name is scant nourishment. There are no women, not even her, anywhere in the crowd.

Bubu, Ranjit and Surendra peel away from the bar, Jivan stands watching the ebb and flow of suits. Feedback shrieks from the sound system, there is a heartbeat sound, a skid: Surendra reappears on the low stage, stroking and tapping a microphone.

Will there be live music, like the old days when his mother and Gargi danced?

No, the men around him are taking off their shoes and putting them neatly in lines and pulling up their trouser legs to sit on the sheet-covered grass. *Are we all going to pray?* He is almost the only one left standing. He drops to his knees.

Strained excitement presses around him; it's like watching a sports game with the volume turned low. Devraj steps onto the terrace; he's in a white kurta pyjama and the same brown shawl from the magazine pictures, he is flanked by Bubu then Surendra, tall as the first, towering over the second. The waiting men slap their hands against the earth, rumbling distant thunder across the clear night. Devraj stretches his arms out, then seems to fade backward and stumble, to be caught by Surendra and Bubu. He grips their arms; they lower him to sit cross-legged on the stage. He raises his hands, palms upwards over the heads of the crowd, then grasps his own feet, fingers lacing his toes. He rocks back and forth, his body trembling. When he speaks, his finger points straight to the sky, his voice is strong, as if stolen from someone much younger.

—Hello, good evening, Bapuji says.

His voice has that same deep tone that could bring comfort after a beating, or announce some new surprise; even though as a boy, Jivan was not meant to be in Devraj's presence, still there were a few times it happened. The men murmur and signal their greetings.

—So, thank you all for coming to listen tonight, Devraj says.

There is a smattering of warm laughter; then it dies down.

—Tuesday Parties have been continuing for many years. Some of you have been coming for so long and some of you are here for the first time. And what a time!

Across all of the men, their hands in namaste, their heads nodding and bowing, Devraj seems to look directly at Jivan.

—Tonight I wish to talk to you about something very close to my heart, Devraj says. The last few years have been sometimes challenging, but, as great God has been kind to us, Ram, Lakshman (*Go on,* Jivan thinks, *say "Sita"*), nature has taught us how to mind our own, our beloved land, and even that is in His hands. Time for each to tend his patch, weed out dissenters and save himself through growth of goods. Though we have always advocated for family, times are changing and we must beware. Each must protect his own: with walls, and clip the wings of those who wish to fly too far. Tend to minds of children and on Wednesdays, ah, eat only mutton. For what else makes us men?

Devraj smiles toward the star-stuffed sky. The crowd clap—but the writer should be fired—it makes no sense. The great man has lost it.

Devraj coughs into the microphone, Surendra pours him a glass of water. They all have to listen while he sips and swallows, wet in their ears. Then he goes on, his voice rising.

—Not only Gandhiji but all the great lines of this country; I am no different to them. Our tradition continues here. We have always concentrated our efforts within our national borders and we will continue to build inwards and upwards. I, of course, am humble in my work, an everyday man; and that is all one can ask, long life, good health from God. We are like Mohammed, we cannot move the mountain, but we are also the mountain, and Mohammed will come to us! When he does, we will make him pay to pass.

Yep, there's definitely a samosa missing from the high tea selection. Jivan checks the rapt faces around him: not a single raised eyebrow or smirk. Look at them, sitting in their socks like good little children, listening to a man who is mad or must think they are all morons, if this is the best he has got. *Get up, Jivan,* he thinks, *this isn't where you're going to find allies.* But his legs are numb, his ass. And Devraj is still talking.

He tries to laugh in the right moments but now he's so hungry he could eat his own arm. He's thinking about Jeet, Nizamuddin, all he has lost, and he repeats under his breath: *It's not about land, it's about money.*

Bubu and Surendra help Devraj back into the house. The men around Jivan wait till they are gone, then turn from the stage to the bar.

—Jivan. You're here.

A voice stops the drink on its way to his lips. Jeet. His half brother. Standing in front of him in a muted silver kurta and black sliders: the first brown man to make it to earth from the moon. There's a diamond stud in one of his ears, his hair is pulled up in a topknot on his head. Muscled but skinny, he is hipster elegant. Jivan feels his own flesh sweating, hulking under his shirt.

—Bro! They knock arms and elbows and shoulders: they grip each other, a drowning man and the one meant to save him.

—I cannot believe you. Jeet steps back, hands on hips. Looks him up and down.

Here he is. Jeet Singh, honest to God son of Ranjit Singh, only Godson of Devraj. Jivan puts his hand on Jeet's topknot, he pulls lightly; he laughs when Jeet ducks away.

—It feels pretty strange. Like I'm going to wake up in the States tomorrow morning on my own, you know?

—That's just jetlag. What's wrong? Are you pissed I wasn't there for the airport? Come on, Jon, you got here! Let's drink to that. Gin and tonic?

The young barman, eyes on Jeet, puts two drinks in front of them before Jeet has finished speaking.

—I'll actually have a JD. Please, Jivan says.

He waits until he is served his own drink.

—You know what? It's all good. Ranjit came to meet me. With Kritik Sahib himself. In the Bentley. He watches Jeet's face—he can see a blink of something—hurt? Surprise?

—Good for you, Jeet says, swirling his ice. You must have been shocked.

—Just my dues. He smiles and shrugs. A little pride enters his voice. And Kritik offered me a job. Working for him in intelligence. He showed me the bunker—do you know about that?

Jeet raises his eyebrows.

—And then I went for this crazy tour of the Farm, with this guy, Punj, big ears, seems to know you, seems to know everyone—he took me to the repro yard. Jeet, tell me about that—your own business, bro—congratulations. It's the best thing about this place. The only thing that gives it any class.

Now Jeet looks pleased and shy, like an insecure girl who's been told she's got game. He's off; talking about his marbles, the sandstone and terracotta he is saving from states that Jivan has never been to. Hyderabad, Gandhara, Uttar Pradesh, where Jeet says he discovered fragments of a terracotta army of female farmers from the Shunga dynasty, decorating the local head honcho's backyard.

—That's first century BC, Jivan. Can you imagine?

—Amazing, says Jivan. Must cost you a lot, getting it all.

—You have no idea, says Jeet. It's not easy. Dad and Bapuji don't know half the price or value, but they love the results. I'm blessed, you know?

—I know, says Jivan. I am too. You didn't come to the airport—I got a ride in the Bentley—and you know what else? When I got back to the bunker, Kritik was there, kind of having a seizure. He told me he quit.

—Quit, says Jeet. Are you joking?

—No. Why would I be?

—So the job he offered you might not even exist. I mean, people say a lot of things, come to my house, sleep in my bed, marry my beti if you have enough collateral. He could have just been, you know, saying.

—He meant it. He could see—I don't want to be some kind of *tourist* here.

He is the whitest on the Farm, but he sounds like he is begging. Jeet is looking at him, head on one side, a small smile as if he knows everything that cannot be said. He hasn't changed.

—Jivan, he says. Do you really want all this? Being under the thumb—yes Dad, no Dad, how high, Dad? He swallows, waves his glass toward the party.

—It's better than nothing.

—I guess. Jeet smiles at him. I thought you would never come back.

—Me too. I'm going to get my own place, a job, who knows?

—Hey, slow. You've only been back half a day. I was betting on you having second thoughts, Jeet says. He shifts from foot to foot. His pupils are huge and dark.

Waves of men crash against the bar, get their drinks, retreat, repeat. Friends grip each other, toast each other, trade stories and cigarettes, compare who has the best business card, the best phone.

—Is that why you didn't come meet me?

—Enough with the airport, Jeet says. I had to work—things are a mess right now. It's all trips to get artefacts, transport them through customs, state borders, and so on and over. I told Pa, you don't find treasure in the godforsaken city, you got to go to the village, deep-dish Bharat, that's *rural* India, where the good stuff is. People don't even realise what they are sitting on.

—So what's wrong?

—Where shall I start? First of all, there's the Department for Archaeology, full of old-school pen-pushers with their Art Treasures Act. Then there are the Survey curators, who I have to get around. Then there's the state border guys—customs—ha ha, who don't realise what is precious, but constantly open the boxes, impound the art for being "obscene"—it all costs.

Jeet makes a fist and moves it up and down, milking dollars from the air.

—I mostly do it all in Dad's name. For the Company. Only an insider could trace it back to me. Smuggling is a serious charge here.

—I believe that. And he's given you the Nizamuddin house, Jivan says.

—What's this got to do with the house? That was some time back. It's worth five million or more now, and I converted it into a gallery but, you know, I use it as a go-down. You don't remember what a go-down is, do you? Forgotten more than you ever knew. It's where I can, ah—go down . . .

Jeet's teeth chatter and he lets out his high-pitched laugh.

He sounds exactly like Punj, Jivan thinks. *Him and Punj could start a double act.* Jivan tugs his half brother's topknot again. He laughs when Jeet pulls away, his thin frame shaking. Perfect. One of them is high and the other hungry.

—Go down. Jeez. Are you sure everything is OK? Ranjit seems kind of pissed at you.

Jeet shrugs.

—Dad's got a control issue, you know that. He laughs again: jittery, nervous.

—How many lines have you had, bro?

—Not that many, you know, not enough to do any, ah, real *damage,* says Jeet. This whole scene. It's so fucking haute bourgeois. I can't handle it. All these guys, the wives inside, the kids with the ayahs waiting upstairs or at home, the hair, the nails, the unwaxed *vaginas*—

—Whoa—enough . . . Jivan holds up his hands.

Time to lighten the tone.

—Speaking of which, Jivan says. What about our future generations? Love and marriage, it must be on the cards.

—Very funny. O God, Dad keeps introducing me to suitable girls. There's no real problem, except when the party gets in the papers, you know, says Jeet. Truth is, there is someone. I can't wait for you to meet him.

Jivan watches his brother smile as he fishes for the ice in the bottom of his glass, picks it out, crunches on it. He thinks of the last six weeks; propelled through the funeral and all of the rest by the sense that if he came back to India, Jeet would be waiting. Brothers, moving forward as if home could change but they would not, because they shared a yard, some games, a few made-up words he's forgotten now of a language only they could speak. He watches Jeet take the lemon from his drink, suck the flesh, drop the rind back into the glass. He seems to be shivering, even in the warm night.

—O, Jivan says. That's what Kritik was telling Dad about. In the car. Kritik gave Dad an envelope and they talked about you: the Company, the company you keep. It was all in Hindi. I guess they didn't think I would understand.

Jeet takes a step closer to him, his face like a cardplayer's with a bad hand.

—Kritik? Jeet says. Thought you said he was out.

—Thought you said I didn't know what I saw. So there's me, Ranjit and Kritik: dude, when we were kids he was one scary dude.

—What did you hear? Has Kritik put some kind of tail on me? Is it one of these guys? Which one do you think it is?

Jeet's face is gaunt, he gestures to the party, swarming with men. Jivan sees Ranjit at the far fringes, scouting.

—Dad knows about your, ah, *preferences* already, right?

Jeet grips his arm, leans forward. As if he's been waiting to voice this name for all the days of his life, he says,

—Vikram. He's my—Vikram. Jivan, Vik's my . . . go-down. You know. He's my lover. He's Kashmiri. He's from a modest background, he's seen some bad times. Jivan, he's so different. Just the most intelligent guy. I met him getting finds out from a forest site near Anantnag; it's near his home village—no one knows about it. Iron age. Fifth century—we're saving *art*, you know, from the *conflict*. Dad doesn't know about him, or me, or any of it.

Vikram. Right. Jivan takes a deep breath.

—Would it really matter? I mean, you could be riding a cow called Vincent butt-naked round the Farm; as long as you're making money, making a name and keeping everything else quiet, Jivan says.

Jeet swallows. —If you're going to stay here, you can't talk like that, Jivan.

—Sorry? Jivan says. He puts his hand on Jeet's shoulder. It's a tough world for your kind everywhere. Trust me, no matter how much pride there is.

Jeet looks terrified. As if he wants a trap door to open just for him.

—Yes, but it's not illegal. Not right now. Just, if Dad knew, if Bapuji heard . . . O God. I've got to get out of here, says Jeet. Tell Gargi, when you see her.

—That you're gay?

Jeet laughs, then his smile drops.

—Don't be stupid, I told her when we were sixteen. You were still playing dress-up with Radha. Just say that—o, kuch nahin. I'll be in touch.

—You better go, Jivan says. While these guys are all busy worshipping at the shrine of Devraj. Or the bar.

Still Jeet hesitates. Typical. Even as a child he could never make up his mind to act. Cowboy or Indian? Police or thief? Soldier, dakoit, boy or *girl*?

—Come on, man. I'll message you, Jivan says. I'll let you know what's up. You know whatever Ranjit wants, Devraj will give him. Devraj might be your Godfather, but he's Dad's closest friend. Like brothers. Or half brothers. Like you and me, he says.

—I'll go, Jeet finally says. Be good, OK? And take care. I'll see you.

—Watch your body, OK?

They embrace. Then Jeet moves to the edges of the crowd; from the back his shoulders droop, a sad clown in a kurta, leaving the ring. He stumbles and disappears beyond the lights. Jivan thinks, *And that's all, folks*. Fifteen years of exile, Ma's death and it's: *Hey, what's up, I'm in love and in trouble, catch you later, bye. And also, I got the house. Turned it into a fucking gallery. For my art.*

Jivan counts a slow hundred. Then he gets out his phone. *Don't go to Nizamuddin*, he texts Jeet. *If you're in serious trouble, that's the first place anyone will look*. Done. Bad brothers make you do mad things. Jeet Singh is gay, and stupid.

. . .

A Bollywood beat with an R&B mix rises around him, a group of men near him punch the air, taking off their jackets and making kiss-faces at each other, shouting "Chammak Challo!" Across the terrace, the French doors slide open; high-cut sari blouses and low-slung petticoats, glitter-tube dresses and bandage-silks spill out, tickertape parade. Pink, red, deep blue and purple: more fit, bare, brown-girl flesh than Jivan has ever seen in real life. Dinner. He has to eat. He takes off his jacket, loops it around the milky shoulders of one of Jeet's stone goddesses. Top button open, sleeves rolled up, Jivan pushes though the crowd, jumps the queue at the buffet then goes around the world, cramming as much food as he can onto his plate. Herb roast lamb with gravy potatoes, cheese and tomato slice, daal makhani, prawn-battered potstickers, stir-fry vegetables, kofte, tabouleh, pilau rice, salmon sashimi, pasta arrabiata, chaat, chopped salad, coronation chicken and five-spiced ribs with corn. Only thing missing is some drumsticks, southern-fried, but maybe they don't do black food here. He fills his belly, standing up in the centre of the garden, planning his assault on the sweets.

If you asked him what happened for the next two hours, what he saw, whom he talked to and what he did, he would not have been able to say. More than once when the men are piggy-backing and thumping each other to the beats with their drinks raised high, as the women bend backward in unison, he hears person after person ask where Sita is, and someone always replies, *She's over there somewhere and looking so lovely, and shouldn't her dad be proud?* Every time that happens, Jivan wants to get up on the bar and proclaim himself arrived—that Jeet is a faggot but also a thief—he steals artefacts from the poor and houses from his half brother and who knows what else? Added to that, Devraj Bapuji is clearly cracked in the head, that speech was a little bit crazy, wasn't it? Come on, wasn't it? And where *is* Sita, exactly, could someone please point her out? Thinking all of this, standing at the bar, he puts down his glass with so much force that a woman in a French Fondant–yellow dress turns around to stare at him.

He stares back. There are diamonds in her ears, single solitaires like two shining eyes; the type of jewels his mother always yearned for. From the front, the dress has a high neck, and capped sleeves. From the back, it plunges in a deep V. It's a little too avant-garde for her figure, the softness of her skin.

—Gargi, he says. He counts the seconds. Five, four, three, two.

—Jivan? she says. Her hand goes up to her neck; her rings catch the light and cast tiny rainbows across her cheekbones, her chin. O. My. God.

—I'm back, he says, at the same time as she says,

—You're home.

She is shorter than he remembers. Her skin is still smooth, and although her eyes seem swollen, they are wide and full of delight to see him, as if the years of no contact were no more than a summer holiday apart. He wants to ask why she didn't try to keep hold of him (but doesn't), because now she puts her left hand on his arm; on her middle finger he sees the Devraj family signet ring, on her third finger, a fat, square-cut ruby, and a thin gold band. Yes. That's right—she got engaged and married at eighteen, just after he, Jivan, left. Although she looks soft, the women around her seem less than her—they look at her as they talk, checking for her response.

She takes him a little to one side.

—I looked for you before lunch, but your dad said you went off to rest, Gargi says. Did you eat anything?

Her voice, trained by his own Ma to *emote, with elegant suggestiveness* when needed, has deepened with age—and, he guesses, playing the Memsahib for so long. He puts his plate down on the bar. It is smeared with the remnants of his dinner.

—Gargi, he says. You haven't changed. Still worrying about my stomach. It is so good to see you.

He waits for her to step forward. To hug him, just like she used to when he did something good, that pleased her. She does not move, just stands looking at him, her eyes on him, in his woollen suit.

—I only brought two. The linen one got itself filthy in the plane, he says. Her gaze drifts down to his belt.

—Coach, he says. A gift from Ma, when I turned twenty-one.

Gargi's eyes finish on his Lobbs, then her gaze travels all the way back to his face.

—Jivan, she says. She reaches up; her palms open on either side of his temples. She does not touch him. You're home.

The music starts again. Will she take him to some corner to talk? Will she come dance? She can't disappear, she says, she is meant to be hosting. She can't dance with him, it doesn't look right.

—Come on, he argues, all the old men, even your husband, must have gone to bed.

—Still the same naughty boy? she says. Let's just be here, you can tell me all of your news. Start with now, go backward. No, of course, you don't want to do that. First you should come meet Radha.

The girls around her murmur approval, *ya-ya-meet-her*. Now Gargi links her arm through his. They walk the party together. Eyes still clock them: this time it's the wives, more than the men. By the time they reach the edge of the dance floor, she has pulled her arm away.

Another scoop of women, all younger, thinner, more toned than Gargi. In the centre, a killer black dress, slashed and ruffled almost to the waist. Radha, his old playmate. Favourite colour: naughty pink; favourite food: golgappa, secretly bought from a street café in Sunder Nagar while Nanu went antiquing. Buying back her past. Radha. She's a cut-out-and-keep princess now—her hair is braided into a crown around her head, her face is made up: red lips, black kohl and mascara that emphasises her pony lashes.

—Radha, says Gargi. Look what I found!
—Jivan! O My God!

Radha glances at Gargi, standing a pace away. Then she steps forward and throws her arms around Jivan, pressing him into her, he smells roses, lemon musk, underneath it all, the sour scent of her childhood excitement.

The Good Witch and Wicked Witch pull him onto the dance floor to find Bubu and his friends busting some bad hiphop moves together. One of them gets Jivan more drinks, another tells him *how great it is to meet him, man; how much he looks like Ranjit;* another slaps his back and says, *How come Radha never mentioned her best friend in the world?* He answers this to himself with, *So what? I'm here now. Ready to party where the party is at? Absolutely.*

Jivan stands in the centre of them, all shooting their whisky and backslapping him, forming a circle around him, cheering. He grabs Radha and Gargi, gets them both in the middle, and twirls one, then the other, watching them dance around him, three together, *home at last.*

Gargi lets go first. She laughs and breaks through the group of men; he follows, but can't make her stay. She leaves the dance floor without turning; he watches as the groups re-form around him. She walks straight through the crowd and into the house. When the loops of "Chammak Challo" have pierced his eardrums into pure white noise, he goes inside to find her, and also to piss.

Through the atrium, pick a corridor, follow the diyas burning at intervals, turn left, turn left, he tries a few doors but all seem locked, he follows the smell of sandalwood and cinnamon to a carved window, lace as wood, giving him a kaleidoscopic view of a plush white sitting room, iced in gold. Fendi, he registers. All the furniture. Jeet must have chosen it. A giant TV is suspended on a wall, paused halfway through an Indian game show, Q and A.

He knows he should keep walking. Almost he turns to leave, but then comes a shout. A skittle-shaped man in a Company uniform is being pushed and stopped and pushed by two of the Devraj Hundred. A sculpture sits on the sofa wrapped in a shroud; no, that is a real woman in a cobweb sari, white with pale blue stitching matching the veins on her neck, her silver bun coming loose at her nape. Nanu.

—Get me another plate, she orders. I wanted daal-chawal only. And you bring me this from those goondas outside? Chi! Chi!

It's Nanu! She never spoke to him when he was little—only about him and only when he could hear. She is the only living proof that Devraj didn't spring as a fully formed businessman straight from the Goddess Lakshmi's big toe. Nanu, Devraj's beloved mother. The last Maharani of Napurthala, in the over-preserved skin.

—But, Nanuji, the servant bows. Gargi Madam wanted you to have the best only.

—Gargi? says Nanu.

Her permanently outraged tone hasn't changed, the vowels are refined, the *r*'s roll, the consonants over-emphasised as if each one is there to salute on parade. "The Imperial croak," Jivan used to call Nanu's voice (and sometimes, Nanu herself); it would earn him a twisting pinch on the back of his upper arm from Jeet.

—Don't you take the name of that arrogant ladki in front of me,

Nanu says. What has she done right? All these years I've been trying to teach her? Nothing. Till today we are still waiting for her to do her duty. You don't even think her name in front of me, OK?

—But, Nanuji, says the servant. This is what Gargi Madam ordered.

Across the room a door opens, Devraj strides in, no help needed. The servant sees an exit route, tries to escape. Devraj blocks him, he looks at Nanu—she makes a face, as if to say—*he makes me sick.*

Devraj picks up a gold candlestick and hits the servant with it full in the chest. He drops to his knees, Devraj kicks him in the stomach. He falls on his back, spilling white-and-brown mush across the floor. Devraj brings the candlestick down again, it cuts into his cheek and he comes up splattering red blood, dark food across the white furniture, gristle mixing with flesh as if the man's face has been cooked on high pressure in sauce. He's crying out but Devraj does not stop, arm up, arm down, arm up and down. An animal sound comes from the man, he holds up a hand, his blood staining the carpet, spattered across the floor. No one moves. Jivan, watching through the lattice, sees fierce glee on Devraj's face, it is mirrored on Nanu's. The old woman claps her hands, the other servants in the room stand stiff while Devraj goes on and on. The beaten man whimpers; he stops moving.

—No? Speak! No? Speak! No? Speak! Devraj shouts.

Move, Jon, move, he thinks.

There is a burst of laughter from the sofa: the candlestick strikes bone. The crack sends Jivan stumbling back down the corridor, turning handles until he finds a jasmine-scented bathroom, with gold taps and a wall of mirrors that reflect him in fives, flushed, dripping, fish with no water, beast with no oxygen, human with no value here.

Hugging the toilet bowl, he vomits JD, makhani, JD, mango kulfi, JD, rice, salmon sashimi, coronation chicken, brownie and five-spiced ribs with corn. *It was Devraj, with a candlestick, in the bedroom!* He makes himself sick again, head bathed in sweat, resting his cheek where his ass should be, the face of the beaten man swimming in front of his eyes. He retches on his own laughter, his tears, on half-digested chunks of whisky-soaked food, until all that comes out is clear, bitter bile.

WHEN SITA WAS A CHILD, she would beg me to let her stay up for Tuesday Parties. She called herself the hundredth and one knight. Of course, I could not allow her to mingle alone with my boys. Instead I devised a game. *Gargi-Radha, stand in line. What is two times two? What is two to the power of five? Subtract thirteen times nineteen from twenty times two hundred and fifty-one.* Whoever answered first, correctly and could show their workings, won the right to take Sita to the party. How this game delighted them! Then, *How much do I love you?* I would ask.

This much, they would reply, holding their arms out, wide as their smiles. And so, I allowed one of them to take Sita to the party, for one hour only, and on the promise they would not speak to anyone. If Gargi took her, the extra instruction was no dancing. If Radha took her: no eating. For Sita, nothing was out of bounds.

It is getting dark outside. The scent in the air is of smoke. From burning coal-pots perhaps. I'm cold and tired. Am I seeing things? Above my head an angel is floating. If I reach, I can almost touch its feet. I wonder if it is male or female. I could check its parts but I suppose it does not matter.

I wonder why no one comes to serve me. Perhaps they know I am beginning to tell my story, and they do not want to interrupt.

Now, the most winning stories always have the same cast of characters in one form or another. There is a set of twins, or double-beings, a trainee architect, a father, or uncle, or brother, a desirable sister with no self-control, and of course, incestuous love. There is always a narrator:

an old man in a pickle factory, sitting on his chutpoy reading Dickens in the old English language, framed by a picture of the Taj Mahal. The settings are new worlds, the language tricksy. Pah. Making up words and full of side-splitting doubt. What is the value of such stories? Expensive paper and lies.

My story is a simple one, come closer if you can. The language you understand it in is not the one I am speaking. It contains elements of truth, the genius of ancients, and some more modern influences. It is priceless, and therefore free for all.

As a young man, I used to travel all over the country, gaining support and strength. I used to take my Godson, Jeet Singh, Ranjit's real boy, with me, for I wanted him to learn. Sometimes I took my Hundred as companions and guards. But always I was surrounded by stupid fools and sideways types. Government chor wale, Company thieves. Always trying to take something, always wanting something. Always I was giving away something. This is a man's lot. And what did I get? An embarrassment of daughters. A shame of sisters.

I admonished them to get up early, sharpen their pencils, wear shined shoes. For the elder two, morning exercise and critical studies: See how the other behaves, watch and report to me. Did they both greet their elders with respect? Did they serve lunch politely and tirelessly? Did they both show modesty and dignity? Girls these days think it's modern to show their legs, to have sex on movie screens. To shuck off their fertility as if someone else will do the needful. They want to live like men. But what do they know or care for my responsibilities? I warned my girls: Above all, remain pure. Do not attempt translation, the most dangerous of all acts.

While the girls were being schooled, my boys would come to me and say, *Bapuji, we worship you. Teach us to become rich in bank and body.* They all would say that. And I imparted everything I knew to them. I didn't have such support when I started out. My father was the Laughing Maharaja of Napurthala, loved his wine and dice, and look what happened? Left me with nothing and from that I made all this. And who am I? Gandhiji, Churchill, Reagan, all these men, they are no different from me. My country in my hands.

There are very few men who can deal with such pressure, such responsibility. That dead fellow down there, he could not fulfil his task without falling. The Company I built sprung from my brain, my heart, my limbs. I took what I learned at my father's knee, and won myself a string of palaces and car collection to boot. A wife, a shawls business, the threads that weave a myth. There are many ways to occupy. Kashmir. Me, my Company, mine.

iii

Vomiting freshens his head. Gold tap running, Jivan splashes his face and rinses his mouth, careful not to swallow. He needs a way out. He tries not to walk in circles, turning, turning until he reaches the chessboard atrium. Through the long windows he can see men swaying to the music, arms around each other, ties loose on their necks. There are crates overflowing with empty bottles and smeared china, towers of used glasses waiting to crash to earth.

He turns around to see Gargi. Jivan notes the fine lines around her eyes and mouth, the beauty spot high up on her left cheekbone, punctuating her eye. Her arms are full of small, silver boxes. There is a man behind her.

—Are you OK? Gargi says. You look a bit, I don't know, vague.

—Jetlag and partying don't mix, maybe. I could use a time-out.

She peers at him.

—Maybe you should go back to Ranjit Uncle's bungalow. Or I can have something brought for you from there. Although—you didn't travel with much.

—That was you? The unpacking?

She nods like a Girl Guide winning a badge.

—Of course. Well, I arranged it. Jeet told me you were coming. I could not believe it. I feel so bad that all these years—I wanted to call you and your Ma for my wedding but my husband, Surendra, he's super conservative. Super.

She shifts the boxes in her arms, they knock together, remind him she is busy doing, not just being.

—You're a doll, he says.

She snorts.

—You are, he says. But I'm interrupting something.

—Ah no, Uppal and I were just organising some tasks for the Engagement Packing Committee. Uppal?

The man behind her gives a small bow.

—He's my right hand, Gargi says. She pauses, looking at him with that kind, appraising smile of hers, as if judging how good he has been. Jivan, she says. You definitely need a drink. I mean of water. Uppal, let Jivan help me with the boxes. You go check in on Radha and report. Jivan, come.

When Gargi says *come,* he will. In the gloom, the smooth brown piste of her back is the only clean thing he has seen all night. At every corner she turns and smiles, all he does is follow. The junglewhoops of Devraj's boys recede as they plunge into the house.

—It's good to get out of the scrum, Jivan says.

—O, they're just messing about, Gargi says. You must have got up to all sorts of bad behaviour in US, no? Little Jivan all at college. What was it like? Girls and partying and all that. You must have some secrets?

—Sure, he says. My secret is . . . I don't have any secrets.

They reach a door, Gargi opens it. The dark hallway surrenders to a brightly white foyer. Five doors lead from it.

—Where to now? he says.

—Jivan, just hold these for a second.

He finds his arms full of boxes. Papier-mâché, painted silver and traced with delicate flowers and vines, with leaves and tiny birds of paradise. The kind they sell in the white hippie shops on the outskirts of campus, burning incense among the purple bruises of tie-dye sarongs.

—Careful, the insides are gold-plated.

He struggles not to drop any.

She punches a code into one of the doors. It opens to a scene from the monitors in the bunker: a studio space full of Company women, busy packing golden ladoos into more boxes. And over there, putting the boxes into plastic sleeves, and over there, tying each one with a Company ribbon and finishing with a deep red seal stuck on. Sita's name embossed on them.

He is relieved of his boxes, given a bottle of Company water and a misshapen ladoo from the reject pile; he walks with Gargi down the rows as she explains each step in the production line.

—Just one question, teacher-Ma'am.

—Yes? Gargi says, hands on her hips.

—Where is Sita, exactly? Jivan says.

—Come.

Now he follows her back to the foyer, through another white door and into dark. She claps her hands once, twice. Lights rise on a red velvet screening room, seating only about fifteen in plush chairs. Gargi flops into one, the yellow dress frothing around her. He sits next to her, arms draped over the seat, hands nearly touching hers.

—It's soundproof, she replies. No one can hear you scream. Don't worry, I'm joking.

—Are you? he says.

—I just wanted to, you know, catch up a bit. We can do that, can't we? She smiles.

—Jeet told me about your Ma. I'm so sorry. She was always full of stories. Like the Arabian Nights.

He wants to crawl into her lap and weep. She is the only person who has said this to him since it happened. Would she let him?

—She would have loved seeing you like this, he says. Boss lady.

Gargi's head goes down.

—Jivan, I got married. I don't dance and sing anymore.

Saturday afternoons in the old Company house, watching Gargi and Radha learn with Ma to sing notes and scales; mouth work, throat work, breath work. The sound they produced, Ma said, would begin with release, pass by imitation and move toward art. He and Radha never got past screaming before Ma would send them both away. They would leave Gargi practising, controlling the climb up the ladder of her own voice until she was sweating and hoarse and Ma let her go—to her next tutor, linguistics or accounts or whatever.

—Ma gave up singing too, when we went to the States, he says. She never publicly performed again.

—Jivan, that is so sad, she had such a beautiful voice. It was so unfair that you got sent away. But perhaps better for you, no?

—Gargi, do you really want to talk about this?

—Sorry, she says. She rests her head back on her seat but her fingers pleat her dress. You know how I spent my day? Packing ladoos. For Sita's engagement: we are meant to be announcing soon. Fifteen thousand gold-plated Company-embossed Kashmiri jewel boxes made by Shi'a artisans, the finest painters and craftsmen, last of their kind. Each box lined with velvet, six perfect sweets in each. All for family pride. That's one thing I thought we would always have.

An image of the servant's battered face blooms in his mind and he almost retches again. Nanu on the sofa. Gold hitting bone. Should he spill that he saw Devraj, her father, beating a servant to a blood-spitting mess just because he felt like it?

—Do you ever get time to watch movies? he says. Shouldn't you be outside at the kitty party?

—Ha ha. It's not a kitty party, dummy. Those are for girls' afternoons. You want to go back outside, just tell me.

He shakes his head.

—No, sir. Those guys are animals.

She shrugs.

—Like I said, it's normal Tuesday stuff, Bapuji's chosen ones. But what about the girls these days, all Radha's friends? All they do is go gymming, go to the parlour, get makeup, hair and all done, I mean, how do they do that? How do they look like, you know, movie stars all the time? Her hands go to her face and stretch the skin, her eyes become slits and her mouth all teeth. Unaware how graceful her movements are, even doing this.

He takes her wrists and lowers her arms. She looks like herself again.

—You aren't old. Gargi, come on. I know I've been gone for years, but even I can tell something is up.

Will she speak? She looks at her wrists. His hands as her bracelets. Then back up at him. Her eye makeup is a touch crooked.

—I should get back outside, she says. Party-party, no?

—Sita's welcome home party, he says. So I hear. But I haven't seen her since she was little.

Gargi slumps in her seat.

—Right.

—Is this something to do with Kritik? I was in the security bunker.

This afternoon. I saw him after lunch. He shouted at me. Said he was quitting.

Gargi twists her hands out of his grip and stands up.

—One afternoon and you think you know everything?

—No, of course not, he says. Just seems like things aren't all party-party . . .

—OK, fine, Gargi says. Sita's gone. Her own path, like the liberated woman she should be. But this is India. We don't go about any which way, even less so if your family name is Devraj.

—Slow down, he says.

—Jivan, did your mother never use the word "sharam" to you? Of course not, why would she? We girls are stalked by shame from the moment we are born. We cry to escape it. Then we are caught.

—I know "sharam." I am it. Remember? "Jivan the backyard boy."

—I never called you that, she says.

She sits again, puts her palms up on her knees. Her voice becomes soft—almost, he thinks, with defeat.

—It's different. You got sent away by default. Sita has gone. By choice.

—I keep hearing people saying they've seen her.

—Perfect. All these people, they're talking absolute bakwaas. Didn't you hear me? She left this afternoon. Gargi begins to laugh.

—Shh. Gargi. It's OK. You don't have to tell me anything, he says.

She wipes her eyes.

—I'd have to go back years. No time.

—I can see that, he says.

—Everything changed when you left.

She drops forward until her head rests on arms folded across her knees, her hair almost sweeping the carpet. The gap between them narrows, the deep room swallows them. He is not a poet. But the air is so still around them. The velvet interior so thick. He feels they are inside the belly of some red-blooded beast, they are its lungs, inhaling, exhaling together.

She looks up. Mascara on her cheekbones.

—How do you think Ranjit Uncle is doing? How are you? What are your plans? she says.

—Remember all those times you tried to get me to stand straight, sit nicely, be good?

He slips off his seat to kneel in front of her, a strange kind of Romeo.

—Gargi, please let me and Radha make noise, Gargi, please can you tell Radha to stop chasing me, Gargi.

—Don't play stupid, she says. Come, sit back again.

—This was supposed to be a celebration for Sita, wasn't it? he asks.

She looks down at him. Her fingers reach toward his eyes. She makes two clawing motions at his temples and completes the circle by bringing her fists to the sides of her own face.

—It is so great to have you back, she says.

He wants to take her wrists again. He wants to pull her down to his mouth. She is Gargi. He does not move.

She gets up; sweeps past him to the wall and presses one of the panels. It opens to display a DVD library. To Jivan it seems all the discs look the same.

—The family treasure, she says. Our whole childhood is on these discs. Since Jor Bagh, and before this place was even built. I had everything digitised: all the official tapes from our birthdays, Diwalis, Tuesdays, remember the time they closed Jantar Mantar so we could play hide-and-seek? And none of us could find Jeet, and Nanu nearly called the police?

—Jesus, he says, sitting back in his seat. This is what you do in here? With popcorn? Watch it all back?

She laughs and presses another panel. The minibar. She throws him a foil bag of toffee Butterkist.

—My Ma's favourite, he says.

—We aim to please. So, what do you want to see? How about you and Raddy, trying to bake your first cake? She runs her fingers across the DVDs. Or, the four of us when Sita was born? She pauses. I might even have one of your Ma, dancing at the Company Delhi hotel opening. You were in that cute pink cap you used to love, remember that cap? Playing harmonium, such a good boy. Or was that Jeet?

She carries on, running her finger over the DVD spines.

—What about after you left—let's see. My wedding, Radha's wedding, all the Company openings from Amritsar to Zebulon, every single one of Sita's birthdays till she left for London. All of her crazy pickets and protests—trying to get Dad to go green in all the hotels, all her practice Cambridge talks, on and on about saving the world one leaf at a time. Less water, more recycling: as if the people who actually sweat blood in this Company don't matter, as if my work for women means nothing, as if settling down, helping me—all that matters is her . . . world.

She runs out of breath. Has to stop.

Jivan thinks of Punj, telling him he wouldn't miss anything as they drove around in a golf cart, meeting the *staff*. All the while something was actually happening in the house, probably at the lunch he could have been at. He was *invited*.

—Sorry, Gargi says. She is holding a stack of DVDs; she bangs herself gently on the forehead with them. I sound hysterical. Sita's gone, OK? Off with a boy. Not even engaged. We don't know his caste, his family, none of us have even met him. Nanu has taken sick. Bapuji blames me. He is right to. I should never have fought for Sita to go study in UK. Now, God knows where she is.

—Why? Is she in some kind of—ah— he hesitates —trouble?

Gargi's look almost skins him.

—You mean is she going to be a *mother*? Of course not. Don't be crude. How could she be? I would know. This isn't some Bhagat-based TV movie, she says.

—What?

—Never mind. She slots the DVDs back onto the shelf.

A sucking noise—the door opens at the back. Uppal slides into the screening room, he comes down the aisle.

—Uppal, says Gargi. Report.

—Radha Madam is taking the jet and eight friends to Goa for dawn swims and poolside nashta, Uppal says. I am still working on Miss Sita's activities. Earlier this evening, she checked into Company Gurgaon. He hands Gargi a file.

—Alone? she asks.

—No, Ma'am, says Uppal. He only looks at Gargi. He has a balding head on a short neck; his hands, Jivan notices, are thick, the knuckles knotted like old trees. He must be sixty at least.

—As you thought, Uppal says. With the young man. The one with the movie camera.

—Same room? Gargi says.

Now Uppal looks at Jivan. Then he says,

—Minor Rani Suite. Queen bed, lounge with sofa bed, one rainforest bathroom with Jacuzzi bath. Ordered couples Aurvedic room massage and in-room dining at twenty-one forty-five.

—Thank you, Uppal, that's enough.

—What about Kritik Sahib? Jivan says.

—That chamcha, Uppal says.

—Uppal! says Gargi. Enough. It's late. Go sleep. Come, Jivan.

He has to follow. He brings the popcorn. Thinks about leaving a trail so he can find his way back here, one day.

Jivan walks in Gargi's shadow, Uppal behind him, twisting and turning through the house until he realises Uppal is no longer there. The noise from the party reaches them, the DJ playing "Chammak Challo" again. He tries to count the guards as they pass but loses track. Gargi marches ahead, tying her hair into a knot he wants to undo.

Outside, the bar is still serving. The dance floor is empty but for a few women, swaying around each other. The men are mostly playing chase, or standing in close groups. Gargi, looking at the scene, takes a step back into the house.

—Now you come with me, Jivan says. I do have some things, so many things to tell you.

He does not want to let her go.

They walk loosely, shoulders touching, away from the crowd on the dance floor, the bar. They end by the turquoise pool. She tilts her head so it comes to rest on his shoulder. The knot releases, her hair falls across him like the sari in his dream. The night garden sighs as the chords of "Chammak Challo" fade and are replaced by "Kissing You," as if Iris has tipped off the DJ, and sent Baz Luhrmann to haunt him.

—If it's such a big deal, let's just go get her, he says. I mean, is Gurgaon far from here?

—No. It's not just Sita, Gargi says into his shirt. Apparently, my dad, the revered Devraj Bapuji, quit his own Company today.

—Say *what* now? Is that even possible?

—Ya. At lunchtime. After he finished dessert. Which essentially might make me queen of all you can see.

The top of her head. Her back. Her toes, red-painted at the hem of her dress. The still waters of the pool, the strange plants around, all the stars above. He pulls on her hair, lifting her face up to his. She twitches at the gesture. She allows it.

—Are you for real? he says.

—I hope not, she says. I'm praying my dad might have been just, overreacting, maybe. To Sita's drama.

—Jesus. I do not believe this day. This is going to be headline news, surely.

—We can't let it be—please don't say anything, don't tell anyone for now. I can't get near my dad tonight. Everything must be as normal until I do, she says. I'm going to make this thing stop. No matter how much I've dreamed of being Chairman of the Company one day, I have to make this stop. Now.

—Chill out. If Devraj really quit, he wouldn't have been up there on the stage tonight. With Bubu and Surendra and Ranjit. That would have been you. (He pauses.) I'd love to see you with a hundred guys sitting at your feet.

Gargi does not laugh; he cannot see if she is smiling.

—I could never do that to my dad, she says. He was there because that's what he does. It's his thing. Even if he actually did mean this stupidity, no one can take that away from him, especially not me.

—Why not? Jivan says. Because you're too pretty?

Gargi thumps him gently. The weight of her head. Her fist on his chest is delicious. He tries not to move.

—Jivan, please don't be smart. I can't take your chien-chien American compliments. They wouldn't because they have too much respect for my dad.

He says,

—You just need the kurta pyjama, the shawl, you know, the short hair.

Now he takes the whole mass of her hair, piles it up to his chin, making it his beard.

—I don't wear our Shahtoosh, it's not allowed. Don't you remember that game? Where you were the chiru and we were the hunters for skin? she says.

—No, he says. He lets her hair drop. He moves so she has to sit up, away from him.

—Anyway. She catches her balance, coming upright. I don't wear it. It's illegal and it's cruel. It looks arrogant to flaunt the rules like that. I've tried to tell Dad, but when would he ever take advice from me?

—Devraj is a legend. But you? He smiles at her. You're a wonder woman. The first of your kind.

—Hardly. I'm old. She sweeps her hair up, releases it. I've been married since you left India. And now you're back. All fine and ready for life.

—Stay here, he says. We need to drink.

In the pool house he finds a stash of red wine and Indian champagne. *Sula,* the sun. Looks potable. In the back room are two used glasses and an empty bottle on the floor. He washes out the glasses and goes back to Gargi. With a high, pure chime, he proposes:

—To the Rule of Gargi, the most beautiful, old-married-businesswoman I've ever met.

—The Rule of Gargi! she laughs. Then, in a low voice: Jivan, even if one day I do want to be Chair of the whole Company, he'd never allow it. Not even if he meant today. O, I don't know. Let's drink.

They down the golden fizz, then another and more until the bottle is empty. As he swallows he feels his American life being scoured from him. He is a kid again, playing in the hosepipe fountain in Nizamuddin, then running around the wild wood and all over this land before the Farm was built. This is how they used to play, even Gargi with her studies and her duties, even he, the bastard son of Ranjit Singh. *This is it!* he thinks. This is how we used to be when we were young. He feels it gathering around them, every plant, each leaf standing up to wave and cheer. Finally: a hero's welcome home. He persuades Gargi to drink with him, to her future and his, to India, to popcorn, to the night. While she giggles and gets loose, he says,

—Drink! To the Gargi Company brickworks!

She drinks.

He says,

—Drink! To the Gargi Company carworks!

She drinks.

He says,

—Drink! To the Gargi Company eco-technologies, future laboratories, all-India concrete!

He says,

—Drink! To the Gargi Company factories which make every part of every cooker in this country!

—How do you know all this? she says.

—Drink!

She drinks.

He lifts the bottle and fills her glass one last time. Then promises to get Sita back for her, as soon as the sun rises.

—No, Gargi says. Let her come back on her own. She also needs to learn.

These are the lessons he thinks that every woman after Gargi should note: be brave but also fragile, be available but do not call, come home early, speak the language of eyes against mouth. Sit always with your legs crossed and do not mind any messing around. He bets Bubu does it. Does Radha? Jivan raises his empty glass and salutes that, silently. Does Gargi? Watching her, head back on his lap, eyes closed, hair covering him, he salutes all of the other things, the ones he cannot voice. The hopeful yellow of her dress, her capable hands, the softness of her skin. Her spontaneous, wide-open smile.

Five days pass; he finds it hard to believe that this moment ever happened. First, he has to tell himself the story of the night's events, then the day before, then the plane journey and all the way back to America. His Ma, her cold, limp hand, the hair that kept growing on her face. The alkaline tang of hair removal cream. The resistant tenderness of flesh after breath has gone. Then play it forward again—to work out how he got to the Farm, who he met, what was said, what his next move should be.

Jivan cannot reach Gargi. Every morning, before he's even awake, she apparently travels from the Farm to the Company head office in downtown Delhi, and does not return for lunch. He has to ask Ranjit to intervene with Kashyap, Kritik's second, an old guy, a less fit version of Kritik himself, even down to the pointed white teeth. Kashyap has taken charge of the bunker since Kritik Sahib left. Every morning he blesses the workers, with Punj standing smirking behind him. Every lunchtime he goes to say prayers. Now Kashyap shakes Ranjit's hand, and promises to look after Jivan. Then shows him a chair at a desk and leaves him to Punj.

They sit, sharing homemade aloo paranthe in the bunker, Jivan listening as Punj confides that Kritik Sahib has always told him that should he disappear for a while, Punj, not old Kashyap, should take interim charge. Until such time as is reversible. Kritik also left a note with Punj, who passed it to Kashyap, who (with some reluctance, Punj says, as if he didn't want Gargi Madam to have it) passed it to Uppal. From there it will have been given to Gargi and passed around the family. *Gone to my wife's place. Do not disturb.* No one actually knew the wife existed, or where her place might be.

They dip the paranthe in homemade yoghurt; they lick their fingers while watching the Farm on the bunker screens. Devraj and a fraction of his Hundred ripping the marigolds from Sita's engagement pavilion to drape them in strands around their necks. Radha and Bubu fighting over breakfast. Ranjit pacing back and forth on the Farm's terrace: always on his phone.

In exchange for Jivan teaching Punj Harvard Business 101, Punj promises to give Jivan the *absolute first lowdown* of any sightings of Sita across the Company. He also agrees to train Jivan in all aspects of Research and Intelligence. But only, he says, if Kashyap*ji* will allow him the time.

In the dry afternoons, Punj drives him to the graveyard of stone goddesses. They shoot blanks at the plaster repro girls. Arms and legs and heads roll, Jivan wonders where in heaven Sita is, when on earth he's going to get an audience with Devraj, where the hell Jeet has disappeared to, run away, it seems, butt-naked: Ranjit found his clothes, his phone and his kara in a pile on the bathroom floor of the bungalow the night of the first Tuesday Party. The contents of the bathroom cabinet were scattered into the sink, a favourite pair of Ranjit's chappals were gone.

Life on the Farm absorbs Jivan, his plan to reclaim the Nizamuddin house gets tomorrowed and tomorrowed; he justifies this by telling himself it's only a day away. Each night he goes with Ranjit to eat in the house with Gargi and Surendra, Bubu and Radha. Half the Company board around the dinner table.

Devraj does not appear. Jivan waits for the meal when he might re-introduce himself properly. He wants to be ready with something about the Company, America, what potential there might be, if Bapuji was interested in such plans. Every day Gargi apologises—Bapuji is enjoying the Hundred, enjoying the gardens, he will not join them to eat. Nanu is resting, says Gargi. She has been since the day Jivan arrived.

He feels Nanu's presence around them: in the way Gargi and Radha start each meal, with a whispered *Hari Om;* by their serving Ranjit, then their husbands, then themselves. Where is Sita? The morning after the party, Uppal reported that she had left the Company hotel in Gurgaon, and gone, Gargi tells them, *who knows where with a boy.*

—You should have let us go get her that night, says Bubu. Gargi, this one is on you.

—Noted, Gargi says. Thanks. And where is Jeet? We need him here.

Jivan shrugs, looks at Ranjit.

—On a buying trip, Ranjit says. In Bihar. I've told him to check in as soon as he can.

So. Those who are missing in action are not recalled. Instead Gargi commands the others, *business as usual:* all of them agree.

Five more days pass. Around them the heat drains rasping cries from the peacocks; the marigolds wilt in the grounds and shrivel on Sita's home-coming pavilion. One afternoon, Gargi comes home early. She calls Jivan to her private study. He stands, looking at the art on the walls, huge canvases painted with one black spot, or a square of scorching red, while Gargi bundles bricks of fresh rupees into a bag for him.

—Just until you can bank here, she says. Go, get out of the bunker.

He rides with Bubu and Radha to the edges of the city to make obeisance to the gods: Bajaj, Tahiliani, Rohit Bal. And for the accessories, Gucci and Tod's. He takes note that the cheap-ass mall is right next door to the high-street one, which leads, via a fountain courtyard, some armed security, bomb check gates and a steak house called Smoke House, to Emporio Mall, where the players roll. This is the natural progression of man.

—Hey, Radha jokes. Have you ever watched *Pimp My Ride?* I'm gonna pimp my Jivan!

Radha, always in the right clothes for the weather, always with the hair and the nails and the shoes, and a skin bag the size and softness of a small piglet. She takes Jivan for a wet shave, a manicure, a pedicure, a head massage. With Gargi's money, he buys himself a new watch, an 88 Rue du Rhone chronograph Double 8 Origin. From this montage he emerges, shopping bags held high, costumed and ready for the new life.

Outside the mall, they sit in Radha's armoured, bullet-proof 4×4, stuck in the traffic, punching the touchscreen to make the seatback player work so she can watch the end of *Slumdog Millionaire* again. She confides her first crush was Anil Kapoor in *Mr. India,* a film Jivan has never seen, or if he has, does not remember, until Radha makes Bubu waggle his eyebrows and say "Mogambo khush hua" in a deep, cartoon villain voice. Jivan laughs, swallowing a sudden surfacing fear. He looks up to see a hillside covered in shacks: the fires burning, the dark-bodied silhouettes blending into the night. He does not mention this, even when a child's mud-cast body taps a finger on his window and brings its blackened hand to its mouth. To even see it would be to confirm the tourist stamp in his American passport.

Over family dinner he is silent while they all talk state of the nation: Gargi says the country is an heirloom silk carpet, moth-eaten, fraying— intricately woven patches of beauty still just about visible. She uses words like *hope, femmeability, common, market,* she eats one roti then disappears into her rooms to work. He wants to follow, but is not asked.

The others exchange looks. When they speak in Hindi, he finds he can catch more and more, linking the normal words like *person, tender.* He rises to leave the table, they look up—and smile—and the talk switches back to Radha, in English, her hands orchestrating the air, telling tales of Bollywood stars, and who-all she's rocked with at Cannes.

Two weeks are gone. Another Tuesday Party takes place. This one sees Devraj back on the stage, Bubu at the bar. It is a clockwork night, almost down to the same speech. Jivan listens to his father; he lurks at the fringes of the crowd, because Ranjit has told him he must wait just a little longer before Bapuji will meet him. Later, Jivan wanders through the chatter, hearing a few women ask Radha or Gargi after Sita, and the answer quickly comes—*she's off on a final pre-Engagement trip. To have some fun, before she joins the Company.*

This time the party dissolves into Wednesday afternoon. Various of the Hundred, who should be working at their futures, still taking up the Farm's space, sunlight, air. Jivan comes across twenty of them playing a slow game of "dead" in the pool. Holding each other down until mercy is begged by hands beating the surface. *Maaf.* Jivan wants to swim, alone. He decides to persuade them to leave. He does this by making it clear that Gargi has requested it, as lady of the house and her father's eldest daughter, as Executive Director of the Company's resources, human and otherwise. They do not argue, just get out of the water, drip away across the tiles to find Devraj, spending his days in "prayer," somewhere in the grounds. All of this is watched, he knows, by Kashyap in the bunker, and by Uppal, who is, of course, reporting on him to Gargi.

At dinner that night, Gargi is late. They get started without her; but when she comes into the room with Uppal, they fall silent.

—We are lucky to welcome Jivan, as if gifted to us by God, she says, her eyes, her voice full of delight. Ranjit Uncle, I know that before he took leave, Kritikji offered Jivan bhaiyya a place in Company security. With little guidance, he is already making such a difference. Well, I have a return gift for him.

Uppal steps forward, he hands Gargi an envelope. She pulls out a hard document. Dark blue, embossed in gold.

—Passport ki-Ma! whistles Bubu. Jivan, bro, you're legit!

—I think we should celebrate this by making you official, says Gargi. Vice President for Research and Intelligence North, liaising on the South, East and West with the existing guys there. For is it not our way that the Devraj family protects its own from outsiders? Our trust has always remained within. Kritik Sahib has chosen this moment to take recess. So.

—Hear, hear! shout the others.

—What about that guy, Kashyap? Surendra says. He was hand-picked by Kritik Sahib, wasn't he? Gargi—you cannot do this—Bapuji also trusts him.

—How do you know? Gargi says. In any case, Kashyap can't take Kritik Sahib's place. He is sixty this year. He'll get an excellent retirement package. Dear Surendra, don't get involved—or do you want to take my job as head of HR? Please do so—then I can get on with running the Company.

A small silence. Surendra lifts his cloth napkin to his mouth. He belches softly into it then places it on the table.

—Excuse me, he says. I have writing to attend to.

Whisky is poured, and that night, with Radha and Bubu cheering him on, Jivan cuts his American IDs into confetti, he dances with his shadow around Bubu's private bar. He lets himself drink until he cannot count his own five fingers in front of his face.

· · ·

The following afternoon, Gargi herself comes in a cart to seek Jivan out at Ranjit's bungalow. She waits for him on the porch. It takes longer than it should to get ready. Then he goes out to her.

—Come.

He follows. Silently, she put-puts back to the main house. He has learned enough about the architecture of this place to know where she is taking him. Back to the white curve, with five doors leading from it. Her private rooms and overstuffed study, her pristine personal training zone, her studio, where the girls are reworking the Kashmiri boxes, replacing each "Sita" sticker with a standard Company seal.

The screening room. This time, the popcorn is fresh-made and waiting. Gargi sits in the front row.

On the screen is the family dining room, table unset, place empty.

—Home movie time, he says. What is this?

The lights fade. An earlier Gargi appears on the screen—happy, purposeful. Next to him, his own Gargi's eyes are closed. The control is loose in her hands.

—You should know what really happened the day you came home, she says. The reason why everything around here is falling apart.

Then begins the lunch Jivan missed on that day. The parts he has already seen repeat: Gargi, robotically ordering servants to lay the table, the food mechanically set and served, rice, daal, meat, no meat, chapati. Gargi, filling Devraj's plate and then Surendra's, Radha serving Bubu. Ranjit and Kritik and Sita, serving themselves. Sita. The back of her head seems so small, her neck exposed. Her plate, empty except for vegetables and half a roti. Arm up, arm down, drink water.

He remembers that day as one of thirst. Tracking Sita across the Farm. His eyes fix on the screen. The camera has captured it all. How young they all look. It is a scene from another life, many years ago.

Then Gargi says,

—This is what happened. All of us were there.

—There's no sound, he says.

—Allow me, she says. She stands. This is me, telling my father for the hundredth time how much I love him, she says. —O Daddy, I love you so much, more than all the light in the sky, the water in the ocean, the cars on the road. O Daddy, without you life would be nothing, she mimics herself.

She times it perfectly: on the big screen her image looms upright at the table making some kind of speech, and finishes just as Gargi, in the screening room, falls silent.

He looks at her, amazed. She is tense, as if tears are gathering in the base of her body; rising through her, threatening to spill.

Screen Gargi sits down, holding a large white envelope. Next, Radha stands up.

—Watch this, Gargi says.

Jivan stares at Radha, smallscreen goddess promoted to the bigtime. Her body is tighter than Gargi's, more curved than Sita's. She is so fucking polished, beautiful in a girls-magazine kind of way, just asking for the page to be ripped out and pinned. But there it flashes: the old insecurity, her eyebrows go up and her eyes become squits, breath held like a jumper on a ledge. Jivan remembers her like this, when he was dressed as a girl, hiding behind the door with her at Devraj's old house during Company soirées. She, pressed against him; her dress scratchy—it tickled his arms. They watched as first his own mother, then Gargi, performed for the guests. Fingers stiff, elbows out, head moving, neck still: *Dha* went the beat, *dha-din-dha*. Little Gargi was graceful, her eyes speaking, her movements witty, controlled. Jeet was there with a Masterji, showing off his tabla skills. Jivan's own role was to keep out of the way, and keep Radha from being sick before she had to perform. She can't dance, she can't sing; she can only copy. *No one likes a pitti-parrotter;* so Nanu said. The grownups clapped Radha anyway; she was all cute cheeks and smiles.

Gargi turns up the volume, sits back down next to him. He wants to take her hand (but doesn't).

On screen, Radha is ready, Bubu is smiling, leaning back in his chair with one hand behind his head and the other probably resting on Radha's ass.

Radha says,

—Really, Daddy! Husband? She gestures at Bubu. Do you actually think I care about this one? He pouts, *hands up!* and laughs.

—Bapuji, you know husbands are nothing when daddies are around, Radha says.

For that she gets a clap, and when she sits down, an envelope that she gives to Bubu, with a kiss.

—Now watch, Gargi says, her voice almost breaking.

—Chalo, Sita, you're last but not least, says Devraj.

In the screening room, on the screen, they all look at Sita. Gargi is fiddling with the corner of her envelope; Surendra is scraping his dessert bowl. Bubu and Radha are waiting.

—Come on, Jivan whispers to the screen. Makhan lagao. The childhood phrase tastes good in his mouth.

Gargi looks at him, then back to herself at the table. Smiles. Shrugs.

—Too late, she says. Look.

Sita does not stand. She stretches her arms above her head, signet ring glinting on her finger; her body arcs forward at her father. Then she straightens.

—Papaji, mujhe kuch nahin bolna hain, she says. She holds up her empty hands: there is nothing but air in between.

Father (respectfully), *I don't want to say anything.* The words form in his brain like a poem learned in fifth standard, translation/recitation/ explanation class. From nowhere, Jivan thinks, *"Transplaination" class— take that, Barun J. Bharat.*

Kritik told him that day: Indian girls never say *no.* And Punj said the family play this game once a month. It was hard for Jivan to see how this time was different, but each face around the table was changing at Sita's words. Laughter giving way to wariness, Gargi, sitting up straighter, Surendra, slowly putting down his bowl and spoon. Radha looking from Bubu to Gargi to Ranjit, her hands flat on the table, fingers spread out stiff over her envelope.

—Come on, don't be shy! Be strong, stand up. Be a soldier, says Devraj.

—Papa, says Sita. I love doing whatever you ask and need. But I'm an economist. And an environmentalist.

No one laughs.

—And then there's "Future Husband." Sita makes the quotation marks around her own head. I have to supply his demand also. Follow the example set, she says.

—She has always been like this, says Gargi. Afraid of the people who love her the most. Not caring that pain inflicted on others also hurts the self.

Screen Gargi is staring at Sita, the fingers of her left hand crossed against her mouth: her old sign for "shut up." Radha's eyes are fixed low, Bubu staring straight at Sita.

—You don't say "no" to me, says Devraj. Madam, kuch toh sewa karo. Are you sure you have nothing to say? Your wedding gift is in my hands. Speak! No? Speak! No?

—Daddy, Sita says. You should know better. How can you even call it "dowry"? It's illegal, it's outdated. Don't you know me at all?

Damn if Punj wasn't telling the truth. *Satyamev Jayate.* Unable to look away from the screen, Jivan waits for Devraj to break the standoff. To laugh and give in. But Surendra's shoulders are shaking, as if his knee is going fast under the table. Radha is perfectly still. Bubu's grimace says, *Who do you think you are?* And look at Gargi on the screen, and at his Gargi, living, breathing, here. Four eyes wide, two faces rigid, smiling without showing teeth.

Devraj says,

—Fine, beta, fine. What's in a name? Call it inheritance if it makes you feel better. Or nothing at all. Chalo, all good. You go, do as you like. If you don't need what I have worked for all of these years, let us see who wants you.

His voice is light, so light. His arm rises and his hand floats as if scattering her ashes over them.

—If you don't want my Company, you won't get it. So what?

He rests his fists on the table, wrecking balls ready to swing. He leans forward, his body stiff.

—Where did you learn such talk? he says. From your sisters? From Gargi Madam?

In the screening room next to him, Gargi's body seems to shiver. The first tears fall.

—What are you? Devraj asks Sita. His voice drops to the register of shocked news announcers, struggling to report: *Lives have been lost in this terrorist attack. The country is at war.* It pins Jivan to his seat. He keeps absolutely still. This is the God of his bastard childhood, invoking all the sacred books that none of them—not even Jeet—could ever memorise properly.

—Rg Veda, verse ten, one hundred and twenty-one. Can any of you tell me? No?

Devraj waits but no one speaks.

—Look it up, Sita, and learn this by heart: "He who by the awesome sky and the earth were made firm, by whom the dome of the sky was propped up, and the sun, who measured out the middle realm of space, this world which we live in, who is the God we should worship with sacrifice," I swear to you now, you will not get a jot more from me.

As if she's been thumped in the belly, Sita sits down.

Jivan feels the breath leave him, as if he, not she, has lost. He thinks back over the night of that party. The last time he sat here. This all happened the day he came home. *The wool suit,* he thinks. *My city shirt. Where did they even go?*

On the screen, Kritik Sahib bends and murmurs something into Devraj's ear.

Devraj's head snaps up. He says,

—Don't you roll your dice for her. You are a deer provoking a tiger! You also should know better than to talk like this. Aré, Kritik, harami, after all these years, learn something from this one, and just keep quiet.

Harami. Jivan can transplain this word himself. *Bastard.*

—As you wish, Devraj, Kritik Sahib says. There is rage in the set of his shoulders, shock in his tone. A silence stretches out—no one defends him, not even Sita.

—Out! shouts Bapuji.

Kritik Sahib walks off the screen.

—Jesus, Jivan says. His own voice sounds tiny in the realtime dark. That was when Kritik came back to the bunker. In that heat. I was there, so jetlagged, drinking his whisky.

—Ssh, says Gargi. Watch.

—Hai Bhagwan, meri Ma! Devraj mutters, clutching and pressing his left arm with his right, rocking back and forth like old Nanu at her prayers.

—Hai Ram!

Devraj stands up; he pushes back his chair. He points at Sita.

—Fine. Sita has decided she wants nothing. Let her future mother-in-law take her just like that, he says.

In three steps, he leaves the room. Ranjit following, Surendra following, Bubu pushed after by Radha.

The women are alone. Sita has her knees pulled into her chest, feet on the edge of her chair. The others do not comfort her.

—You should have just humoured him, says Radha.

—She's right, says Gargi, taking Radha's hand.

She reaches for Sita, who starts to uncurl herself. Stops.

—No.

—He is giving you this enormous gift, the best part of everything we have all worked for, Gargi says. It's your heritage. Your future. Don't make me sound like some kind of school ma'am. Come on, Sita, it's the *Company*. Even if he hadn't asked you to speak, he would be giving it to you.

—I don't want it, Sita says.

She is shaking her head at Gargi. She wipes her nose with the back of her hand. She points at her sisters. Her tears have rinsed her English accent from her mouth: when she speaks, she sounds as if she has never left home.

—Why is he even still asking us this question? Why are you still humouring him? I can't act to please, I never could.

She steps toward her sisters. All wait for the other to speak.

In the screening room, Gargi wipes her eyes.

—I tried to reason with her, she says to Jivan. Why doesn't she understand? It's a game, sure. But one day she is going to be *married*. She has to learn to look after her husband, his family. It's not easy. Husband, in-laws, running a house and doing a job. Daddy. She has no idea what this all entails. I said, *Please, go to him and tell him* sorry. *Tell him what he wants to hear.*

—What did she say?

—She said *no*.

—Sita, Gargi says. Please, listen to me.

—Promise you won't track me, Gargi di, OK?

Next to Jivan, Gargi presses PAUSE.

What is worse? Jivan wonders. *To lose a mother, or to lose a child?* Ask the loser, you will get the same response. Then he remembers that Gargi has neither mother nor child, anymore. Was never even really a mother, just the understudy, shoved into the lead.

—You know, Jivan, Gargi says. Her voice is low and steady. You know what is at the core of this?

—What?

—The Company Kashmir. The new hotel.

—Sure, he says. Will it have a Mukti Spa? That will make you say *Ahh.*

Gargi looks confused. Then her face becomes sad.

—Sita doesn't think it's right for us to be expanding there. It's a place so fragile. Not ours to brand. In my heart, I have to tell you—

—What?

—I know she is right.

Uppal coughs quietly, a few rows behind.

—Gargi Madam, is there anything more you need? Can I get you some chai or some hot chocomilk? he says.

He comes down the aisle. From his pocket he gives Gargi a white handkerchief folded into a triangle.

—No, thank you, Uppalji, that's kind. She wipes her eyes. Shakes out the handkerchief, blows her nose into it, gives it back to Uppal.

—I didn't even finish her trousseau planning, she says. I let my little sister leave without putting sugar in her mouth.

Now, with Uppal watching, Jivan reaches for Gargi. Her tears spill onto his hands.

—Where is she? he says. After that night, where did she go?

—She told me I should leave her alone. She didn't think twice about what she was leaving me to reckon with. That's my fault, no? Her attitude.

—She must be traceable, he says. If you really want her to get back here.

—Of course I do. But then, there's the rest.

—What do you mean?

—Don't you want to know what we won?

He waits.

From a pocket she pulls an envelope, Company-headed. The same creamy grain as the ones Jeet used to send him so many years ago. Gargi unfans the letter. The script is handwritten in dark blue ink, wide looping rounds and squirls. Jivan has to squint through the backlit glow to read it.

LETTER OF INTENT (POSTDATED)—

I, Chairman of The Devraj Group
(holding company of The Devraj Company)
Hereby divide my 60 per cent holding

Between my two sons-in-law and my three daughters
And divest of all interest in subsidiaries for which I am also Chair
For Surendra, in lieu my eldest daughter, Shares
of Materials, listed overleaf.
Transport—going forward.
From my private holdings: the Farm. With the expectation of due care
    to my person, the 100 Programme and said property—
In perpetuity.
In tender name of my future generations.
For such is my stage of life.
Yeh hai:
Mann ki baat.

Jivan turns over the paper. More dark blue scrawl; he cannot make sense of it. Gargi takes it from him.

—Materials listed: bricks and steel, she reads. The car production. All the bits I like least, all that need the most work.

—What about Bubu and Radha?

—Some of Services: the malls. Some of Engineering. The rest of Consumer Products. As if Radha gives a shit about *bathrooms*.

She holds up her hands, counts down her fingers:

—And for Sita, twenty percent of the Devraj Group. From the subsidiaries, Directorships of Services, which includes the deeds for most of the hotels. From Consumer Products, the best parts—i.e., the shawls. And from Materials (and now she takes a breath), Bapuji wanted Sita, my baby sister, to have the concrete plants. My plants. In her own name.

Voice low, she tells Jivan that Bapuji has promised to divide Sita's share between Surendra and Bubu, but has not told them the lines he will draw. She says they will finish with thirty percent each of the Devraj Group, with Ranjit still holding twelve percent (Jivan thought he had some, but never knew how much). The final twenty-eight percent is split. Half ringfenced in performance-related shares for A–E level employees, the other half held by private individuals who invested way back in the beginning, when Bapuji was raising the capital for his first batch plant. Crorepatis all.

—Between us, Gargi says, I'm having the concrete, whatever happens. And Radha *is* the shawls. If Sita doesn't come home, she'll officially forfeit every once and future brick and thread.

Jivan looks at the screen. The three girls framed by red curtains, in the heart of their family home.

—Maybe it's fairer this way, he says. A slice for each of you . . . but honestly I can't see Radha running a huge company. With Bubu.

—My dad isn't doing it to be fair, Gargi says. Her voice cracks again. Fear, sorrow, Jivan cannot tell.

—He's doing it so we can't ever hold a match to him.

—Candle, Jivan says, gently.

—Gargi Madam, Uppal says.

—So much for *Gargi, Queen of All You See,* Jivan says.

She sighs.

—Will you settle for *Queen of Half You See*? Bubu and I have agreed. I'm going to take the lead on things for now. Business as usual, till after the Kashmir opening.

—Gargi Madam, Uppal says again.

—Ask Ranjit Uncle if you don't believe me. I'm surprised you haven't heard it all from him already.

—He hasn't said a word. I promise. Hope to die, Jivan says.

She shifts away.

—My dad, behaving as if he's on a permanent holiday, won't speak, except to berate me. I am thirty-three years old. The Company, my dreams—Surendra doesn't know the first thing about it, nor does he care.

Her hands, clasping and unclasping, now clutch Jivan's arm. Behind them, he hears a small sound: Uppal getting up, slipping out of the room.

—Jivan, Gargi says. I am going to take legal counsel. Sita *will* come home. Anyway, it's more *complex* than this. Constructed for confusion, to hide and keep safe. What if Bubu decided to build Company malls without Company concrete? It doesn't make *sense.* The Kashmir hotel was meant to go to Sita. That's one thing, but Bapuji marked the Delhi townhouse to Radha and Bubu. That was my maternal grandfather's town palace. It is worth at least as much as this Farm, if not more. By *crores.*

—Is that so? Jivan says.

Gargi slumps in her seat.

—After all, blood matters. It's on me.

She looks up at Jivan, full in the face. Her eyes glitter.

—Jivan?

—Yes, Gargi *Madam*?

—Don't. Please. We cannot let a soul outside know what is going on. Not a whisper, not a single sound. Until I can fix it. Or it is done.

All these days of shopping, eating, talking, learning, shooting. The hours of smiling chat and the end of *Slumdog* on repeat. Not Radha or Bubu or Ranjit has told him any of this. Not even Punj. All this time they've let him tourist around, believing this was just about Sita.

It's not about her. It's about money.

—OK, he says. Soft, so Gargi might only catch a light sense of hurt, hear no hint of his rage.

—I could not tell you until now, she says. I had to wait. And see.

On the screen, the pause times out. They are left in the half dark, staring at each other, faces cast against a storm of digital snow.

Jivan escorts his father back to the bungalow. As with each night since the party, he sits with Ranjit on the porch. Nursing drinks, spearing cocktail olives with toothpicks, spitting the stones into the grass. As with each night, he watches Ranjit perform his rituals, walking around the square in front of the bungalow, seven times forward, seven times backward to ward off the evil eye, reading his online horoscope, checking Ambika Gupta for his lucky numbers on his phone.

He listens as Ranjit starts blubbing after Sita, after Kritik, and finally, for Jeet. He comforts his father, promising that whatever trouble Jeet is in, he, Jivan, will not allow the family name to be soiled. With this new word in his mouth, he also declares that Jeet has wounded him deeply, with his disappearance, his lying, *his ways.*

Unhearing, downing whisky after beer, Ranjit blames not Jeet, but the blood-red moon that rose over India for a hundred minutes in June.

—An eclipse so long and so deep, Jivan beta, that it was talked about across the world.

Ranjit produces his iPad. He uses it to compare maps of the country against star charts from his astrologers in Amritsar. Two weeks before Jivan returned, the red moon rose. The sun, the earth, the moon aligned straight, exactly straight, as should not be.

—When our shadow eclipses the heavens, the body cannot but be harmed, Ranjit says. We fasted here; all stayed inside except of course Bubu, naughty boy. The Parliament closed and Sonia Gandhiji and her ministers continued to work from home; even Gargi did this thing. The moon's face turned red with shame; no wonder Gargi after all these years of marriage is still not yet a mother. Now the monsoon is late, strikes are choking us, the tax inspectors are baying for our records and the Company Srinagar hotel, Bapuji's dream, is running too high over cost.

Jivan learns that the eclipse before this was ten years ago, the week that Radha got married. But it could not be seen in India—or they never would have taken that date. After the wedding, the astrologer himself was in a car accident. He was left unable to use his arms. The eclipse before that was in '71. And then, for the love of God, Ranjit starts on the subject of war and atrocities and the looting of land and the repeated fracturing of hamare apne India to give birth to Bangladesh. So much land lost, so much potential for growth cut short. For what?

—Cloth mills, textiles, cheap labour. This we benefitted from. But, Jivan, Ranjit warns. When the shadow of the chandra graham descends gently, we are all inside it. And now, the worst, the darkness that came from that moment, the longest eclipse we have known, what happens? People disappear. When earth's triumphant shadow thinks it can cross the moon, no wonder that the world has gone fruit salad. This Gargi with her women's projects, what does she really know of business? O for the star charts that were prepared when she was a babe!

He jabs his stick like a snooker cue, trying to pocket all the problems away.

—But these charts are in storage in the Napurthala Palace, where Gargi was born. Only those charts, Ranjit says, could possibly explain what has transpired here.

Jivan himself was made under Rahu and Ketu, a two-headed demon who can swallow the sun and whose body can swallow the moon. His chart, stored somewhere in Nizamuddin, Ranjit thinks, shows he was born under the shadow planet. The stain of his conception, the astrologers had said, cast his skin darker than his brother's, though his mother was fair.

So now what should Jivan do?

His father orders him to track all incoming video, to use his name and call in favours with police he does not know, to marshal the spies, to look for Sita and Jeet—which he of course promises to (but doesn't). His brain feels smoked by cigarillos; he rolls his eyes then reminds himself who he is becoming and how fast. He remembers Gargi's tears, and agrees that *the red moon in June is a sign of chaos coming soon,* a phrase, he thinks, that Barun *J.* Bharat would envy. He agrees that they must beware, and he promises on Ma's ashes, because seriously, that is what Ranjit asks of him with his eyes; that he, Jivan, will work to make it all right.

After all of this, when the goddamn burning day is done, Jivan stands out on his porch while the whole Farm is asleep. He has a smoke of his own, and a last Company beer. The night is a bowl of planets, satellites tipped up, pouring to earth. He takes position, ready for his inaugural address.

—Jai ho, he whistles. OK, Rahu and Ketu: it's just you, me, us. I have a hunger for the moon and the sun. I'm going to eat it all.

I WAS GIVEN THE NAME "Devraj Bapuji" the day I shot my first gun. It was ten o'clock in the morning. My target was a tile wala who decorated my Palace at Napurthala. He refused to complete the mosaic, he demanded his payment. It was in the spring of 1947, I have not forgotten that time. The tile wala was a dissenter. I missed my shot. Just. Went limping to Pakistan. The other. Side of the line is. Remembering?

Now the evening is approaching, and after that the night will freeze us. If I had matches, I could spark the fire—we had one before, started by that young manservant before he fell down the hole. It has gone out now and no one has come to see to it. And I am hungry, I wish someone would bring me something to eat. It must be almost six o'clock. I like to have my dinner at this hour. Starting with a teaspoon of turmeric, dissolved in hot water. My doctor says that this will allow me to live until I am 120 years old at least.

Sita always found this funny. She asked me what I thought I was going to do if I lived that long—go to the moon? She said that turmeric was an overrated plant. She said that its overharvesting was contributing to the falling earth, the rising sea levels.

I wanted to prove her wrong. I took her on a trip with me, once. I asked her where she wanted to go, and she said the Sunderbans, in the tiger-infested mangrove forests and mudflats of west Bengal. We took security, for pirates operate there. I told her we would eat nothing that did not contain haldi, then no mosquito would bite or plague us, we would not get upset by the food. I was right—although our tongues turned orange, we did not get sick. I showed her that we are not sinking, by putting pressure on a surface that will hold.

Still, she refused to wave, or take part in the press shots. She spent all of her time collecting samples of weeds, and telling me off with her eyes for my clothes, my shoes, the amount of kit and the number of media and crew. And that I brought Tipu, my tiger cub, along for the ride. Why not? I thought the beast would like to see its origins and natural habitat. When we returned to Delhi, Sita didn't speak to me for days. And who financed for that trip?

—Do you know that this particular plant is unique to our Indian ecosystem? she asked me. She stated these opinions from time to time. I indulged her earnest assertions, while she pressed my feet. Then she traced a shape in the dust: bulbous leaves, spiked tongues, drooping petals.

—This plant, she said, is perfectly balanced to survive both flood and drought. Its roots grow part on soil and part on water. Not marsh. Just exactly divided, a genetic mix of male and female in one. Or, a child with one Indian parent and one other. Isn't it beautiful? It's hardy too. Even though the world is heating from the core, upsetting its doshas and the balance of its food, it adapts with such passion for survival. And these flowers bloom emerald green, sapphire blue and pure white. All the peacock colours. Its name is *Githalonius androgynata*. Meeraka, in Sanskrit.

—So what? I asked. Can you eat it?

She smiled her mother's smile. She told me that the little plant holds the secrets to eternal life. Then she blew on the dust, and the drawing was gone. She looked sad, she said something romantic; like the earth is getting too old, too tired to fight.

—Look, I said. Look up! I went to her and fell on my knees and put my head in her lap, pressing into her. I turned onto my back and put my hand to her mouth. Through the broken roof, pockmarked with bullets, we watched flocks of birds go racing across the sky. I could feel the pulse in her thighs as she inhaled, exhaled. Sita was always convinced the world was ending, breath by human breath.

Can you sing? Sita is full of songs. So many songs. I cannot make her focus on my hands, though she knows I want her to. A line of red-breasted sparrows is perched on the beams: tiny bodies and inquisitive eyes. Still they come to rest here, where there should be a ceiling and a ceiling fan. There are other birds. I know their names. Black-Throated Accenture. European Bee Eater. The staring, long-tailed Eurasian Cuckoo. The Lesser Cuckoo hides behind. They come and perch in the beams. And if I should see a Kashmiri Flycatcher, that will be the day. They chittered for joy and trilled in the sunset. I along with them. For what else could I do? Shoot them?

II

—.—

GARGI

i

She is glad to get out, though it is already so hot that the air has turned liquid and the earth seems to waver, as if the world cannot decide what to be.

She is Gargi Devraj Grover, granddaughter, daughter, wife, sister. She is Gargi Devraj Grover, Acting Chairman of the Devraj Company, custodian of the key to her father's office. A polygonal space on the eighteenth floor of a gleaming obsidian shard-like building, a space to which she, this bright, early morning, is going, alone, and for the first time, with the key in her hand. She is custodian—the word fits—for though Company Headquarters was built in the 1970s, the key is satisfyingly long, heavy, ornate; it might have fallen straight out of one of the classics Gargi read as a girl. *David Copperfield. Vanity Fair.* Under the covers with a torch at night, in the morning when she should have been going for a bath, she stole time for herself, disguised by the sound of water splashing from the nalka onto the tiles. Sitting on the pot, she would read; her smell—a slight tang from between her legs, the overripe sweetness of her sweat—rising around her while she put off the shame of touching her body to clean it, of allowing her dirtiness to wash down the drain to the street, spewing into the poor, stinking Yamuna, mixing with the dirt of millions. Back then, she had wanted to be the heroine of those books, what pretty names they had, evoking their pale fresh skins. Dora. Amelia. Like flowers, she had thought—and asked her grandmother and sisters to only call her Rosa—since *The Mystery of Edwin Drood* was her favourite book, once.

She reflects on that time as she stands on the steps of the Farmhouse, conscious of what she is leaving inside, alive to the early morning rush hour of sparrows chittering above her. Her eye falls on the sleepy gardener at the far end of the lawn. He is wheeling a barrow to pick up—what *is* he picking up? She cannot tell—in any case, as she waits for Satwant, her driver, to bring around the car—*he is late, he is new, it is not his fault*—she thinks about those heroines of her girlhood books, the straight lines of their lives from birth, through school, to some stumble of fate and finally fortune in finding love and marriage. Only Rosa did not have that—her story remained unfinished—and this mystery suited Gargi, for although her reading had given her, as a girl, a trust in the turning of pages, the sense that someone—possibly Nanu—might be writing *her* story, too, with a sure hand towards the promised end—she had never been sure she wanted that end at all.

As Gargi's birthdays had come around each year, as her desires had swirled inside her—simple things, like wearing jeans, leading her school debate team, winning her father's set tasks—her body grew soft, and she moved through crowds with eyes downcast, smiling in a way that Nanu approved of. Around her the talk was always of love-marriage-children, the excited, pre-wedding—*how many do you want?*—became, after Surendra—*are you eating right, are you pleasing him, are you trying every month?*—then—*something is wrong. Here is the doctor*—and finally—*you should see the Ayurved, herbal remedies are best.* Gargi had listened, nodding, answering; her thoughts escape artists she did not control. The memorising of ratios—water:gravel:sand, for the different kinds of concrete the Company makes. The nurturing of her cacti: how to coax them to bloom. As she grew, she retreated into her plans for a free-shoe scheme, at X–Z staff level, Company-wide. For a crèche for the women of P–Z levels (in the hotels, offices, the cloth factories), caste-no-bar. And from B–Z a women's management training programme inclusive of a college bursary, again, caste-no-bar. How to get this done despite Bapuji's echoing dictates—*the natural order of the world sustains itself—workers hungry in body in mind do a better job overall—the smell of stagnation is a full belly of food*—was the problem that vexed her most. How to get this done, through her puberty and into her marriage, the cyclical weeks of the month when Nanu inspected her bedsheets? Her clothes, her bras, her panties, each size change mulled over and measured. Ayurvedic remedies offered, bitterly taken. Every pimple on her face considered a sign. Years pass, duty undone, never, never, no.

Now, as she waits on the low steps of the Farmhouse, on her way to Head Office, she breathes in jasmine—her shoulders relax—for this morning, a rare, fresh, liquid morning in New Delhi, she thinks there might be a time when Gargi Devraj Grover comes to live as she believes. A possibility that seems, on this day, when, as she waits for Satwant, her soft leather briefcase in one hand, to have become—as astonishingly as the fact there are marigolds still blooming (in August!) all the way down the drive of the Farm—an increment more real. For a chance has opened up that she never expected would come so soon.

To take the Company forward. Her own way.

Where is Satwant? She must wait for the car, then wait again for him to get out and open the back door and shut it behind her and climb into the front. Although she has *told* the drivers that this is not necessary for the younger members of the family, they never seem to remember her words.

The Farmhouse recedes, and, though Gargi loves her grandmother, her father, her sisters every day, she feels this drive to the city as a slow, rising euphoria, the sensation that Radha says is to be had from taking selected illegal substances while trancing in hotel clubs. For Gargi, it is enough to be on her way to Company Headquarters, as close to the centre of national government as commerce is allowed to be, a secretly longed-for key in her hand and without her father. Hasn't she just left him, choosing to stay home and reorganise his almari, instead of coming to office? In his white singlet, in his saffron underpants, *like a hardboiled egg cut in half,* she had thought, he stood among the rails of his shirts and suits and ties and shoes, ordering his houseboy to pack them all up and get fresh ones, while telling Gargi (as if his mouth was full of acid and nails) that he had heard all about the moment, almost two weeks ago, when, as the Tuesday Party fell over into morning, she had sat on the pool deck with *that boy, Ranjit's returnee. Gargi, you were drinking alcohol. And touching him, and inviting him to touch you. I heard about what you did, all you said.* His words had landed on her skin, she felt them burning around her mouth, her nipples and chuchi. The houseboy had scuttled around, she could see he was terrified but also scandalised, his face the colour of her father's Y-fronts. *Every passing pool boy and member of the Hundred saw you both together.* He would not look at Gargi, kept on with his toilet, slapping lemon-scented cologne into the white hair on his chest and his head, rubbing it, pinching it onto his ears. *His hands are enormous,* she has always thought, all the better for silencing crowds, or raining down thapars onto bare skin. *Slap, slap,* the hands, the cologne—*How fat he has become.* Gargi had stood, watching but trying not to look, the sight of Bapuji like this soiled the memory of that night with Jivan, the Tuesday Party when she had sat by the pool and he had toasted her, and she—drinking more than she had allowed herself for years—had shouted *The Gargi Company!* as she did it.

Bapuji had heard about that. From whom, it does not matter. She, Gargi, should have been more careful—for hasn't she been watched on and off, every minute of her life? *Shame, Gargi, shame,* said Bapuji. *Get out. Go see to your grandmother.*

Gargi was there, clear-eyed this morning in Bapuji's rooms. To try to talk about why Sita left. The weight of that is on her, setting like concrete around steel. She did not bring up the splitting of the Company. She had decided business as usual: she would take it day by day. But Bapuji had seen her open her mouth. As he buttoned his kurta he said,

—I have set the tasks in motion. Minutes have been drawn up. All you have to do is sign the board papers. It is past time.

Behind him on the flatscreen, the latest Company advert was on, for a sound system called REVERBOT. REVERBOT responds to hand claps and obeys voice commands such as "PLAY." Bapuji turned up the volume. He watched and clapped. Gargi said *please*—but her father could not hear her. She was dismissed, as a difficult book is shut and pushed to one side.

She had left her father's rooms (for she is nothing if not obedient, and it is this knowledge of her own nature that has made her so good at HR), feeling full of secrets and tears. Her heart pounding—*hehas setthe tasksin motion*—in a way it has not since before she got engaged. She felt released. Almost. Free. Perhaps to make up her own story as she goes along.

She is Gargi, the key is in her hand. How good it will feel to put it in, turn it, open Bapuji's office door. She will lock herself inside. Alone.

The silence. She had not imagined this—it was Radha (backed by Ranjit Uncle, over dinner last week) who suggested Gargi take the office for now. He could see, he said, that Bapuji's actions were testing. *But, Ranjit Uncle,* Gargi said, *don't you think this is all too extreme? Even for Bapuji?* He looked at her, and for once did not resort to star charts or prayers. In a steady voice, he said, *Let him be. You forget. Your father has always been a master of the long game. He has given you this gift. You must play along, for now.*

Before she left for Goa, Radha said: *I am Executive Director with responsibility for Public Relations. For now, we must introduce you properly to the outside world, while showing them no change.*

—*Radha is right today,* Ranjit had said. *Gargi beta, all you have to do is steer the ship.* A day later, on a rare, fresh morning, she had the key.

She will order the blooms for her father's Mughal desk herself. Swollen, pink-scaled Gingers, bright orange Birds of Paradise with thirsting beaks and spiked blue tongues that pierce the air. They will become Gargi's audience; their shadows will be her chorus. She might order a REVERBOT, so she too can play music with a clap of her hands. Her own selection, gathered over years of daydreaming about what it might be like to travel to the furthest curves of the world: Cuba and the Buena Vista Social Club, the American South and Nina Simone, Mali with her favourite—Rokia Traoré. *Blackie songs* to her father, to Ranjit Uncle and Kritik Sahib. In the hour between work and drinks, she will put one of these tracks on loud, and when Jeet returns from wherever he has gone, ear pierced, his throat full of stories, that engraved silver kara she gave him when they were sixteen—*Jeet Singh with love from Gargi*—still circling his wrist, she will ask him to gift her a sculpture. Some elegant, fierce Durga—*from the fourth century, Gupta period*—as he would tell her, with one bare breast, to witness Gargi's private dancing, to wrong-foot unwanted visitors and to glare at the secretaries for her.

Though she is, she reminds herself, only the *custodian* of this key, as the car speeds up the flyover (Company high-performance concrete, here), ahead of the smog and the punishing traffic, Gargi will set up camp in Bapuji's office. And wait to see what comes.

. . .

When the lift doors open on the Bapuji floor, Uppal is waiting. His bald head in furrows, his palms up, as if to push Gargi's plans to ground. Behind him is not an empty corridor but a total, actual carnival of people in black T-shirts and black pants, all making hungama. There are three-legged stage lights and rails of clothes; makeup-stands, a mirror framed with bulbs. Everyone seems to be rushing—although for what she cannot tell.

—Photoshoot, interview, Uppal says.

—Isn't that next week? she says.

—Next week, Gargi Ma'am, has already come.

The key hangs flaccid in her hand. She is supposed to be in charge, but in fact she's only the performing elephant for Radha's PR team. As ever. And there is the journalist, already inside Bapuji's office, sitting before the vast, carved Mughal desk—*younger than Sita,* Gargi guesses—in faded skinny jeans and leopard-print flats, a white shirt buttoned to her throat, a dark blazer hanging open, the sleeves rolled up. Her hair is in a kachcha bun, lose entrails fall around her face. Her glasses are thick-rimmed and square, as if she is the model on a shoot for "reporter: lifestyle magazine."

—Hi, says the woman. Nina Sengupta, *Perspectives.*

Nina does not get up, or hold out a hand, just ticktocks her pencil on the desk.

—Congratulations, Mrs. Grover, she carries on. How does it feel to be, albeit temporarily, in the driving seat? Is that the key to the office? Wow. Looks heavy.

Gargi Devraj Grover looks down at the key drooping from her fingers. She decides she will do a Nanu on this girl. She sits in her father's chair, powers the computer.

—Welcome, she says, not looking up. Can we offer you something to drink? Are you tired? You seem a little dehydrated. Uppal?

—Yes, Ma'am?

—Please organise Rina a Coke or whatever. Now, Gargi says. Are your questions about the Company? Or me? Not that there is any separation.

She waits.

Nina Sengupta stands up, she pulls at her shirt, tucks a strand of her hair back, out of her face.

—Thank you so much for your time, Ma'am, she says. We want our readers to get to know your softie side. We want to emphasise that aspect.

Look at that! Gargi feels a piercing pleasure to see young Nina, still standing. Now she's chewing the end of her pencil, flipping the white pages of her notebook.

—O God. Where to start? Gargi smiles. Please sit, Rina, sit.

Nina sits.

—So, says Gargi. Why don't I begin by telling you about our new eco-car. We are really excited about the upcoming launch. After that, you can ask me whatever you like, OK?

—Great, thank you, Ma'am. Your school days. And then, your beginning in the Company. How did you come to be here in this office?

Gargi looks around—the leather armchair in the corner—this is not real—the carved wooden elephants holding up lampshades on their trunks—none of this is real—and back to Nina, sitting, waiting, almost on the very spot where Gargi, when she was young, was called by Bapuji to stand every Friday after school. Riding in the car with her Lottie, stuck together in the jams. On the way to this place, Gargi would want to talk to her, would want to know about her, because the Lottie had looked young in the body but old in the face, and could not remember her own age. Gargi had wanted to ask about her village, whether she ever had to go to school, *and why did she not speak good English?* But Nanu had instructed the Lottie not to answer any questions, just to keep Gargi clean, her hair tight in her plaits. The Lottie used to say, *Chup chaap baitho,* or threaten to tell Nanu, and the fear of her kept both of them silent, Gargi, with her school uniform and the Lottie in her dark blue salwar kameez, the Company logo stitched over the heart.

—School was school, you know? Gargi, now sitting in the office, for the first time *behind* her father's vast Mughal desk, says to Nina. Tell me, Rina, where did you study?

This response is a Bapuji tactic, cultivated over years of milking con-tacts and contracts from little men and large ones. *Take the question with a question and listen while the other person shares. Let them finish with nothing you have given: yet feeling so good and understood. Next time you see them, watch as they fall over themselves to adore you.*

—DPS, R.K. Puram, Ma'am, says Nina. Then Hindu College, En-glish Hons. I wanted to go into financial journalism. But I got assigned to lifestyle. Yet I love writing about details of, you know, deals and so on. I'd love to do in-house work like that one day.

Nina looks around the office. Though Gargi has not spoken, she scribbles intensely. Her pencil nib breaks.

—You don't use a pen? Gargi says. Here, take this. She passes Nina a black-ink Company Executive Rollerball from her father's stash.

—Keep it.

Gargi watches Nina look at the logo and smile. She, as a child, had loved those damn pens. She had polished her shoes to prepare each Friday in the hope Bapuji would reward her with one or two extra for her pen-case. Sat, on the way to Head Office after school, legs swinging in the back of the white Ambassador, counting her pens, or watching as the city sprung its elegant surprises: an arrangement of gerberas sprouting bamboos on the phool wala stand—now vanished, for the new city rules have clumped all the flower sellers in a market outside the ring road—and she had waited to snatch glimpses of the crumbling mosques, blushing to be caught by the sunset. In Lutyens' Delhi she had loved the roundabouts best; they showed off their plantings like the English women, the Doras, Amelias, Rosas in hats who, she imagined, used to trot around the circles in their carriages—would they have had carriages, or open-top cars? Her grip on time and its details is hazy. Today is not real. She was not allowed to wind down the window; but had spent the journey counting the Company ads on boards by the side. Daddy's toothpaste, *whiter than white,* bathrooms, tiles *moulded, for the clean of tomorrow,* hot tawas and happy children—*that's a Company non-stick smile,* all her father's goods on display from home to school to office and all the way back. *Chhi chhi chhi chhi,* the Lottie would say if the street vendors tried to hawk them a magazine or a coconut or a balloon—two bucks, what was it to Gargi— but the Lottie always said no.

Nina twists the pen. Says,

—What is the cause closest to your heart?

—I personally sponsor several charitable initiatives, including education for girl children. I have projects in almost every state, training women to become schoolteachers. We focus on local languages and Hindi, and run sponsorship programmes to get them into English medium schools. We also teach core subjects—mathematics, so they can account for their households. Geography, so they understand the scale of the world we are in. Governance structures, so they can challenge any official. And in some places we run the schools, for a closed system of supply and demand inspires loyalty, impact and longevity.

Gargi watches Nina's hand—is she writing, or doodling? Making circles, circles, eyes, nose, mouth. A monstrous face with long dark hair.

—Our next aim is to start a water salvation programme. We in this country are facing a crisis. Hence, the new Company Eco-Car.

In the car every Friday since she was seven, Gargi never drank water because then, she knew, she would need to do susu. She did not listen to her own music, because Nanu had told the driver he should only play Krishnamantras. Even when a girl in her batch had lent Gargi a cassette tape of Alisha singing Madonna, she was not allowed to put it on.

Looking out of the car window, she had seen the old green-line buses spilling men into the road, the boys on their scooters out-racing her car. She wanted to be cheating the traffic, even with such a big bundle on her bike. She wanted to balance like that and go fast on two wheels, not be stuck inside four.

—Water, she says again.

—Right. What is your one secret for absolute well-being? Nina sucks on the Company pen.

God, what crap this woman is asking.

—I compile lists, Gargi answers. Any busy woman who also runs a household does the same.

Those Friday car journeys were Gargi's chance to list everything that had happened that week. All the things that Radha had done wrong: Bapuji particularly wanted a report on those. A full account of what Cheti the gardener said to Topu the cook. And all the shlokas and asanas she, Gargi, had been given by Nanu that week: seventeen different Vedic ways to say prayers for Bapuji's good health. Then there was Sita. Her first words—*Aape-aape*—her first step, her many first-division marks at school. Whatever masti she was getting up to—letting loose the house goldfish into the outside pond, cancelling the mutton order behind Gargi's back—Gargi always told Bapuji that Sita was perfect. She saved all her points about her youngest sister until last, to put Bapuji in the best mood.

—Do you have a favourite place? says Nina, leaning in. Somewhere, you know, that inspires you?

—Here, of course, Gargi says.

—Right behind Bapuji's desk? asks Nina. She looks surprised, as if Gargi has said some bad word in public.

—I mean, in the Company.

Not this office, where Bapuji had waited for her each Friday, where, when she arrived, she had to knock and wait, and was never able to sit down. Why not? Because Bapuji never invited her to.

Nina is chewing the pen.

—Was Bapuji the kind of father you could goof about with? He's such an amazing role model for all of us, she says.

—Naturally, Gargi says. He has a great sense of humour. He loves Chaplin, Laurel and Hardy, Mr. Bean. All the practical jokers. And memory games. That is how he keeps his mind sharp.

His favourite game was played for exactly one hour, every Friday without fail—Gargi—stand, memorise, repeat—what he told her about the things he had eaten outside that week and with whom. Bapuji counted all the most prominent political families, especially Sanjay and Ranjiv Gandhi, among his best buddies. He told Gargi all about what was served at this or that lunch with them; it was in their home that he first tasted Italian wine and olives. Focaccia bread so rich and tasty, he said. It was up to Gargi to teach Topu these recipes, or source those same things through Company contacts and present them also at home.

—How do you think a woman's touch has helped the Company thrive for all of these years? says Nina. Her voice is eager, as if there is a secret to female success that Gargi will freely share.

—You can read our history on the website, you know? Gargi says. But really, it is simple. Everyone loves Bapuji. He does everything by the book. This is the reason for our success. Just straight talking, no backhanders. What you see now is the result of that ethos, that ethic.

—Yes, says Nina. I've brought a printout.

She pulls a paper from the back of her notebook, and reads,

—Beginning with nothing but the palace in Napurthala and the state townhouse in Delhi, the shawls business, then the first hotels, la la la, and into concrete production, *to build the India of tomorrow,* great strapline, I love those 1960s ads.

—Yes, says Gargi. The Company mix was poured into every grainstore and dam of the third five-year plan. All across the country. And in the years of the License Raj, when Bapuji's hands were tied like everyone else's; he couldn't employ more than three hundred workers without the government getting involved. Luckily, we have always kept cordial relations with those in power. By our very honest ethos we ensure this.

Nina pauses, keeps writing, not asking, no, *Do not ask, Nina*—Gargi thinks—*what-all Bapuji did in those years,* Gargi thinks, for he always stayed on top.

—When you were growing up—how fantastic life must have been! Nina says. (She looks like she wants to kiss the desk.) Eldest daughter of one of the most important, respected and successful men in the country . . .

In the early '90s, Delhi was dry: there were no English wine shops in the markets, no drive-up car-o-bar. The Devraj family had alcohol: an extra-special case of wine or spirits gifted to the family by a supplier to the Company five-stars. Crates would arrive and bypass the customs, from NRI mothers in Dubai or Sharjah, trying to charm Nanu into allowing them to look at Gargi or Radha for future reference. Whenever someone wanted something, there was always down payment. All the real business was done in the evenings: over whisky and ice cubes made with filtered water, melting in the glasses. Sometimes, Gargi had served. Sometimes, especially in the year after Jivan and his Ma went away, she had sung some classic song, accompanied by—yes of course, it was Jeet, on harmonium.

Now Nina leans in.

—What do you see for India's future, our next decade?

—A good question, Gargi says. Of course we welcome the international competition from foreign companies, India needs investment, we need training and jobs for all our graduates at every level, so they don't simply go into call-centre work, or exit for the US. And our customers are loyal. But we also need to pay attention to our resources, and I don't only mean human. Water, minerals, solar, I cannot emphasise this enough.

—But in terms of competition from multinationals?

The answer to this one has been drummed into her. By Nanu, Bapuji, Radha and Bubu. She takes a deep breath and smiles.

—At heart the Company is a traditional family business. This is why we have always remained within the nation's borders. Though we do invest outside, our vision is focused here, on the Indian people. And perhaps we *do* have a secret weapon.

—What is it? Nina says.

—*Jugaad,* says Gargi. This is the Indian way. My grandmother is an example; I take my notes from her. She could make anything out of nothing. This comes from our indigenous, pre-"India" nature, before the British, or any of that. *This is why we call it?* she emphasises the question, the answer, trying to believe in it. *Jugaad.*

Nina nods so hard, her bun lurches sideways. Then she frowns,

—Yet even today not so many women are business leaders.

—No, that is not correct. There are many, many strong women in this country. Do your research, you will see. My grandmother is a case in point. We just know it is best to maintain a low profile, for that is how we can operate effectively. As Bapuji always reminds me, *Don't think too highly of yourself, let others do that for you.*

So Gargi was told, at the end of each Friday, when her legs ached and even if she had not drunk water at all before the meeting, she still needed to do susu. Before she was allowed to leave, Bapuji would shake her hand. Then watch her back out of the office. *Goodbye, Gargi,* he would say. *Report back sharp next Friday.* O wow, she felt she was the apple of his eye when he said that. The apple! Then she raced her shadow back down to the lobby where the Lottie was waiting, keeping the ladies' bathroom door open. The Lottie stayed outside so no one else could come in; she hummed so that no one could hear the boss's daughter sitting on the pot.

—And how did you meet Surendra Sahib? Such a sweet man. So gentle. I've met him before, at the polo ground, Nina says.

Nina, she wants to beg, *ask me something that matters, ask me where my little sister is and doing what-all with whom. Ask me how it feels to be looked at properly, by a man who is not my husband. Ask me, even, what it is like to be sitting on this side of the desk. Or even about the Company Kashmir hotel. I dare you.*

—You've met Surendra? Gargi says. I am so glad. Yes, we sponsor part of that Cup. Surendra and I were introduced here in my father's office. We liked each other, it was agreed, we got engaged, we got married. Just like millions of couples across the country. Our story is just like theirs.

Except of course that day, just after her eighteenth birthday—there was still a sense of excitement in her, as if her present was still to come. Nanu, not the Lottie, came in her Rolls-Royce to collect Gargi from school. She even came up to the office with Gargi, then, at the door, she said she would wait outside. Gargi went in. Bapuji and Surendra were sitting—one behind the desk, one in the armchair, behind where Nina is now. Gargi stood in the middle. She did not know which one to look at. Surendra seemed to blend into the leather: she kept her gaze on Bapuji.

Gargi, what have you been doing today? Tell us, Bapuji had said.

Morning: I got up, got Radha up, made sure Sita had her bath and they both were ready for school. Made them come to breakfast and eat, they had a boiled egg each, and soldiers. Swamiji read the Bhagavad Gita to us. I looked through the business pages. Then I made sure that both girls had done their homework and got their snack, and Lottie no. 4 had tied their hair properly. Ordered the cars to come, made sure Nanu took her breakfast and also swallowed all pills. I gave the lunch order to Topuji, we also arranged dinner; bachchon ke bhoot, milky sweet, Sita's favourite. Sita went with Nanu. Radha and I and the Lottie went together in my car. I sat in class, gave a presentation on multinational accounting practices in three selected Forbes 400 companies. I got full marks, then had games: because it is a Friday, it is hockey. This evening, I will teach Radha and Sita to tie French plaits and practice their grammar, eat dinner, do computing, recite prayers, go to bed.

Then Bapuji had asked a question he had never asked before. *And, Gargi, what do you want to do with your future?*

His words had risen around Gargi in whole, shining cities that stretched from the Kashmiri carpet to the mural of Bhishma, painted flat and fat and furious on the ceiling. Gargi's eyes went up to him, fallen hero of the Mahabharata—still he lies on his bed of arrows, dying on the field at Kurukshetra, his tongue lolling sideways from his mouth as if he wants to lick her, endlessly. She had spotted and named the five Pandava Princes, their consorts and all their children (even the ones who should have been dead, in the battle, days before) gathered round, before she had answered, *Bapuji, I have topped my batch in Commerce and I want to come and work with you. In Mergers and Acquisitions.*

He laughed. *Good idea. You can come and work for me.* For a moment, Gargi's heart stopped beating in her chest. Then came the bargain. *After you get married. Then, you can take your place here as one of the deputy managers in Human Resources.*

Gargi: hot from her knees all the way to her face-cheeks, as if someone had stripped her naked and painted her red. Nanu, in her head, telling her to say *thank you* to her father.

Gargi had whispered it: *Thank you, Bapuji.* Then watched Daddy lean towards Surendra and say, *You know Gargi is in charge of my house. Of course mistakes get made, but she does a good job.*

Then he had turned to her. *Gargi, today I am giving you a great gift.* He had waved at Surendra. *Gargi, this is Surendra Sahib. Say* hello, *nicely. Hello.*

The first time Gargi had ever sat down in this building was the day she was given her own desk, in her own office, on the tenth floor. She became Mrs. Gargi Devraj Grover, Executive Director of the Devraj Company, with overall responsibility for Human Resources. That was her final title—until two weeks ago.

What should she call herself today?

From the ceiling, Bhishma still glowers. Tongue still reaching to swallow her.

—What do you think is *your* contribution to the Company so far? I mean, in terms of your ideas and so on? Nina asks.

—Believe it or not, Gargi says, I introduced cappuccino to the Company coffee shops. I had it in the Hyatt in the mid-nineties. I insisted we serve it too. Guess what? Now, it is our bestselling beverage. We have added Valrhona chocolate dust, of course.

—Seriously? I love that cappuccino. The best in the city. I stop for one every morning on my way to work.

Nina's life. Maybe she keeps her room at her parents' in the respectable parts of Punjabi Bagh, but has her own exit and key. Perhaps she rents in a shared house, with her brother and cousins in Noida. Or with her college friends, or even alone. Shopping at Zara, stopping once a month for Italian food at La Vie. Does she drink domestic gin or green-tea cocktails in rooftop bars, with new money as her friends? Does she risk driving herself home late, alone, paying no heed to the men who wait to give chase?

—It's my indulgence, Nina says. It's worth it.

—Thank you, Gargi says. Plus tax, every 170-rupee cup adds up to an extremely lucrative product. It is the small things that yield the most.

Gargi's first cappuccino was bought by Surendra on their first date— the first time she, at eighteen years old, had ever been alone with a man who was not Jeet, Ranjit Uncle, Kritik Sahib or Bapuji. It was an early spring afternoon. They went to the Hyatt Regency hotel coffee shop—Surendra did not want to go to the Company Delhi hotel; had said too many staff would recognise her. He ordered Gargi a vanilla-chocolate ice-cream sundae, fudge sauce dripping off. Then ate it himself, twisting the spoon in the soft ice cream; licking while Gargi watched him. Surendra had a thin face with neat eyebrows. They almost looked parlour threaded. She stared at them, then at his thin lips. Nanu's voice raged in her head: *Make your bed neat and tidy, fold the corners, plump the pillows, be always fresh, make it welcoming, soft when needed, hard will come, be happy and fruitful and obey your husband, and that way you will get whatever you deserve.*

The waiter came over, straining in whites that seemed to wear him. *Are you satisfied, sir?* he had asked, looking at Gargi. She picked up her menu and ordered *Cappuccino* because she did not recognise the word. It took time, but when it came, she sipped it, savouring it, *Cappuccino*. Trying not to give herself a milk-mouchie while Surendra talked and talked. He told her he was twenty-eight years old (a lie, he was thirty-three, the age—Gargi realises, sitting with Nina in the very spot where she first met her husband—that she, Gargi, is now). He told her that he *loved* his roti to come with ghee, he *loved* having his feet pressed before bed, and every six months he *loved* to do a cleanse of his gunas using a nose flute that was passed down to him by his be-*loved* grandfather. He did not ask, *Gargi, what do you love?* Lucky (or unlucky) since she would have answered, *The beautiful horizon of the production possibility frontier. The maximum possible output combinations of two goods or services an economy can achieve, when all resources are fully and efficiently employed.* If she had said that, he might have changed his mind.

A month later, Gargi was dressed in a cutwork pink lehenga bordered with gold thread. The choli was tied tight behind her neck. The fabric left a circle of her back exposed. For the first time in her life her shoulders went naked in public. So smooth. The dupatta was almost three metres of stiff tissue silk, almost see-through, not quite. She stood in her sandals, trying not to move while the dresser wrapped her in it.

She had been persuaded by Nanu that this colour, this style was *the in-thing*. But standing in front of her mirror before her sagai began, she saw that her outfit did not say *elegant, eighteen, about to be engaged.* The dupatta made her look like boodhi amma ke baal, she said, and Nanu, patting her hair, agreed. Candyfloss. On a stick. *Cho chweet.* She walked down to the party—which Radha nearly spoiled with a sulk because she also wanted to get a pink lehenga, and go outside to eat with boys—and heard one uncle look straight through to her blouse and say, *Aré wah! Target on her back, missiles on her front.*

She pulled herself up straight as she passed through the crowds, and realised Bapuji had cheated her. That she should have negotiated. She is Gargi Devraj Kumari, daughter of a family dharma that turns back to the beginning. Surendra Grover was banking. His paternal uncle Lal Sahib had held a powerful place within Indira Aunty's government. With Lal Sahib's help, the Company changed its name and went to ground for a year or two, avoiding the taxation and curtailments of the Emergency years. As the worst of times ended, the Company re-emerged. Its holding group was now called The Devraj Company, with Devraj and Ranjit and a few choice other families holding shares. Then, there were the subsidiaries, also privately owned—except for Consumer Goods, which they listed on the stock market for the benefit of millions to buy into. They launched a new line of food products, Pot Daal and Pot Chawal—*just like Mummyji's*—that could be rehydrated with hot water, *just add instant love.* Gargi, sitting on a golden chair on a flower-filled stage, bored, had listed in her head the entire structure. The Company, the three main subsidiaries and forty-five companies they owned or co-owned then—some listed, some not—then their partners, their turnover, their share value, their debt—then their directors, their wives, their children, their pets. She watched the line of people queue up to offer respects to her father, then to Lal Sahib, then Surendra's father, then Surendra himself.

As Gargi swallowed the pieces of ladoo—pressed into her mouth, hand after hand—she wondered if she was the investment, the interest or the bonus reward. Her dahej was three cars, a small raise in her end-of-year package, a tea-chest of saris to wear and linens for her bed, a promise of her (married) name on the deeds to the Napurthala Palace (which even then needed lakhs of renovation) and a furnished wing at the Farm for her and Surendra to live in. She was very lucky. She was grateful. She was. No more than a deposit against future dividends.

—Can you tell me a bit about your wedding? Nina asks.

—Really? Gargi says. It's so long ago now.

—I was seven, Nina says.

—It was the early years of economic liberalisation. We were going through some painful restructuring then. You can't appreciate this, but my wedding was a landmark event. Such food we had! Everything from French crepes to hakka noodles, never-seen-before dishes here. It was the first eighty-crore wedding in India, according to *Business Day*. At the Company Nilchamand Hills hotel, our beautiful hundred-acre heritage estate. We stayed there for the honeymoon also; it used to be the shooting lodge of the Maharaja of Golkattapur.

She watches Nina write *shooting lodge* and draw a box around the words. Hearts appear, on stalks.

—It has its own jheel, Gargi says.

After thousands of hours and faces and sweetmeats and lakhs of gold and jewellery and songs, Gargi and Surendra, newlywed, had retired to the Maharani Bridal Suite. Rose petals lying all over the bed, the floor. Waiting to be crushed by the weight of their bodies, or under their feet. Then to remain untouched—as Gargi spent her suhag raat weeping in the bathroom, a Company hand towel stuffed in her mouth so that he would not hear. Thinking of how Surendra's head jerked back when she tried to kiss by inserting her tongue. His mouth tasted like broiled liver with no masala. She did not gag. She had undressed herself. Stood in front of him naked—something she had never done in all her years of life, not for any person, including a Lottie—and felt that just having Surendra look at her made the lips between her legs become engorged, her body turn to pure, hot ras, enough to burst all over the room. Despite all of that, Surendra did something that set the tone for the rest of her marriage. He let her stand. Naked. While he turned his back and took his time selecting, for the background music, Raag Chaundrakauns: slow tabla and mournful sitar like a river tumbling over rocks. Gargi had stared at him, ras crystallising to goosebumps all over her skin. Surendra had lain back on the bed. He told her to dance for him. To music one should only listen to alone—music that makes one weep and then find solace in its movements. This was not music to perform to. On such a night.

She can still hear the drone of the strings, replacing her heat with duty. She can still see Surendra, leaning back on the bolsters, the stiff silk of his wedding pyjama flat against his crotch. This was not what Gargi, at eighteen, had been told to expect. Even Nanu had whispered to her that it would be pleasurable for her, and might take her breath with its power. But though his mouth was smiling, her new husband's eyes were closed.

She keeps her voice steady, her mouth firm. Her gaze on Nina direct.

—Fifteen years ago, I got married, I took my first step on the Company ladder, and now, here I am.

—Do you know how many people you employ? asks Nina.

—You want numbers? No, it's not nice to talk about people in those terms. I prefer to think of us as one big happy family. The whole Company has this ethos top to bottom. I have a thousand children to look after.

She smiles. And counts down in her head to the next question, wondering how Nina will pitch it. Five, four, three, two . . .

—And yet no babies of your own, Nina says.

The statement gambit! So predictable, so easy to respond.

—O my God, I knew I had forgotten something! Stupid Gargi.

She laughs, leans forward; looks through her papers and under the desk.

Nina laughs with her. She waves the Company pen in a circle, like a magic wand.

—What would you like to achieve next? she says.

Abracadabra. Bring Sita home.

—And where, ah, is Bapuji, exactly?

Gargi raises her eyebrows.

—I know this interview is meant to be focused on you, Nina says. But Barun, my editor, asked me to put this to you.

—As he already knows, Rina, directly from my sister Radha, Bapuji is currently at home, enjoying the Farm, taking a well-earned rest. Do not be concerned; we have a very experienced board to hold the fort here. Everyone doing their bit.

—Great, says Nina. Thank you. So Bapuji is well. He's not, ah, retiring . . .

—We will carry on working for the good of the people, as we always have. Anyone who thinks that just because he is seventy-five, Bapuji has had it, better check their backsides. He is as vital as always, and we have so many plans. We are a very close family. Nothing can change that. You have a father, I'm sure you feel the same.

Nina smiles, she agrees, she shuts her notebook. Gargi waits for her to put it away. Then she calls for Uppal: he brings in a sugar-free Company Cola in a glass bottle, a quarter of lime wedged in its throat. A touch of nostalgenticity, a strategy for which Radha spent lakhs of her PR budget on a boutique consultancy: not a Western one, but homegrown—design newbies, straight out of Bengaluru. *How to coin the current trend.* Gargi watches Nina smile at the bottle, stroke it, poke down the lime, insert the bendy straw. Suck it up. She allows Nina to finish, then to summon the makeup artists, the lights and the wardrobe girls, the photographer. The photoshoot begins.

The article is published the next day. *Meet Mrs. Devraj Grover, a woman guarding the top: a dynamo dedicated to her country's growth, to her family and to the Company, hoping one day for a family of her own.* The picture shows Gargi sitting behind the Mughal desk, smiling over paperwork, wearing her glasses (she insisted). She is dressed in a gold-and-black kameez and block-print silk churidaar, an olive-green dupatta, hand-embroidered with yellow sprigs. The caption reads: *Mrs. Devraj Grover, at work. Churidaar-kameez—Ritu Kumar, Kunti collection. Estée Lauder Malabar Spring eye-palette, MAC Lipglass (clear), Mikimoto pearls (gifted by Mrs. Devraj Grover's husband, Surendra Grover, on the advent of their ten-year wedding anniversary).*

—You had the picture taken in Bapuji's office. Sitting in his chair, Surendra says.

He pauses, eyebrows raised, fingers hovering over his breakfast white moons of idli. He picks one out, breaks it in half, uses it to scoop yellow sambar into his mouth.

—Don't tell me. It was Radha's idea, he says.

Mistakes get made, Gargi tells herself. She takes her magazine and leaves Surendra to his dosa, which he always has on Saturdays.

She allows her feet to carry her through the parched gardens towards the glittering pool. The plants must wait for water. Every evening when the sprinklers are activated, each flower takes on an expectant freshness, a bride before her ceremony. *The heat,* Gargi thinks, *inflames the desire, melts the will.*

She has not come to the pool since the night Sita left. *Drink,* she remembers. *To Gargi Company!* She feels red upon red burn through her veins, invisible on the surface of her skin.

. . .

Jivan lies on a sun lounger, eyes closed, arm over face. His chest hair is tightly curled, dark. His black swimming shorts have bunched between his legs, catching the drops of water trailing the curve of his thighs. His mouth is open.

Surendra, Gargi thinks. *Brunching.*

She stands at the lounger, casting her shadow over Jivan. He moves his arm. Looks up. She passes him the magazine.

—Pretty cool!

He smiles at her, and flicks to the article in the centrefold.

—You look like you were born to it, babe. Which you were. You look *damn hot.*

He mimics a cartoon Indian accent like the ones they do in the West, as if he is mocking her, her father and his own. Is this how she sounds to him? It hurts to hear it. She tells herself he is only joking, like a loving younger brother or a best friend might.

At this point of time, Gargi tells herself, *we are nothing more than old friends.* Jivan was her sister's playmate, he is Jeet's half brother, he is the son of unmarried parents. One of them is Ranjit Uncle, as close as a father to her.

And Jivan is also the naughty bachcha who was always getting into trouble with Radha: not big things, but enough to get Gargi scolded by Nanu for not watching over them properly. Weird obsession they had with dress-up. Always a Lottie would find Radha's oversized dolls wearing Jivan's T-shirts in Bapuji's rooms. Or Radha's party lehengas missing from her closet, later smuggled back from Nizamuddin by Jeet. Ranjit Uncle used to tease Jivan for being dark, and short. If Jivan stood up now, he would easily look over her head.

She watches him, the grown-up Jivan. Water droplets trickle and sparkle. He is staring at her picture, as if he can see the fears that run like mountain chiru through her, replacing her breath with their bleats.

—What's wrong? he says. The pic is fantastic. You'll be every Mumbai banker's pinup.

—Thanks, that's why I went into business, she says.

—Gargi, come on. You look great. What's the issue?

She has a sense that if she speaks, she would crack the perfect shimmer of this moment. Her body would be exposed, its weight-loss-weight-gain stretch marks on her hips, the self-made scars from the compass point of her school days, criss-crossing up her thighs. The triangular forest of her own dark, curled hairs between.

The research that has just come in—almost one year late—on the new car says that the common man does not want zippy, affordable eco-friendly. The common man wants beasts like hers: oxcart wheels, fenders to break walls, cars that could ram (if you so pleased) every other idiot off the road. But the production funds have already been spent; every delay means they are losing crores. In addition to this, a tools-down strike is brewing in the Ghaziabad construction plant, potentially three thousand workers demanding what? Bapuji says all they want is more holiday time and paid leave, as if even the state would gift them such things.

She has also been drawn into a bakwaas administrative nightmare with some government eco-depot over the sand mining they have been doing in Puri beach: it's a question of religious sanctity— (Uppal should have sorted this out) —and the sea turtles are suffering. What about her beloved concrete: self-consolidating, high-performance, ultra-micro-reinforced, all Company-stamped, needed to pour on the earth for the new metro extensions, the housing blocks, the hotel expansions the government praises her so much for? As if that is not enough, they're about to be hit by a tax inspection across the hotels, all the key staff have to work day and night to prepare the right papers—and get rid of the wrong ones. The Kashmir hotel is not even finished; the delicate negotiations need more grease; the contractors are eating their high-performance grit weight in bribes to get the plans realised in time for Diwali. There are new terrorist threats in the Valley, there is still no real news from Sita. It is almost four o'clock and she does not know what Bapuji and Nanu want to eat for tonight's dinner.

Silence seems to rise like smoke from the scorched grass. The blue of the pool answers the sky.

—I don't come down here enough, she says. It's relaxing.

—Come on, then, says Jivan. I dare you. Blow it all off, no one will say anything. Radha is in Goa. She's got some UK magazine people with her, so technically it's work. I think Bubu is in Gurgaon, at Utopicity. Three hundred units of luxury apartments complete with concierge, gym, golf membership and club, a mini-mall and deli-cum-supermarket, and a special touch: private tutors supplied on demand for pre-school kids. All of it Vastu-compliant, with extra charge for Feng Shui.

—Very good, she says. You've been studying. Did you know Radha loves to spa in the rain? If it *is* raining down there. Not like you, roasting here. And Ranjit Uncle is in Mumbai meeting with the banks; no one else can reassure them by saying nothing in exactly the right way. Surendra is busy eating idli-dosa. Then a nap, then he has cocktails and golf this evening.

—Gocktails, Jivan says. He grins.

—What? Hey, one thing I wanted to ask you—have you seen Jeet since you got back? I'm missing him. We need him for board stuff. Your dad said a trip, but no one in the office knows where. Which isn't unusual. But I could use his head right now.

—He's taken off, Jivan says. He told me the night I got back that he was going on a "pilgrimage," know what I mean? To pray at the shrine of some poor bastard, who hasn't got a clue that Jeet's going to rob him of his family treasures.

—Jeet doesn't do that, Gargi says.

—Of course not, I'm joking. He'll be back soon, I guess. Anyway, good job, Gargi Madam. Jivan smiles at her. Fans her with the magazine.

—Time for a swim, he says. The water is fine.

She thinks about taking off her clothes, getting in the pool. She wants to feel her hair like reeds in the water, her limbs held as they will never be allowed to drop. She thinks of her body, encased in its one-piece. Her swimming style, which Radha calls *Aunty in the kuaan*: chin raised, hands paddling, hardly moving as she tries to keep her head above the surface. Her body its own lifebuoy.

—I can't, she says. Tomorrow maybe.

To Gargi this feels like the first calm moment since that night, when, after they sat by this pool and toasted to her future, she and Jivan stayed up almost until dawn, walking in diminishing circles, she showing him the places on the Farm which she loved and which he had never seen built: the duck pond, the sundial courtyard. The ornate jhoola, cocooned in its orange blossom bower. There they had sat, swinging gently together. He'd pulled her head onto his shoulder. She told him it was her mother's own swing, which Bapuji had ordered to be left to age, become overgrown.

—After your mother died, Jivan had said, my dad banned Jeet or me from talking about her. Bapuji's orders, apparently.

—You remember that. You can't have been more than, what? Eleven? Same as Radha.

—Ranjit told us your Ma had gone to Srinagar, and she wasn't coming back. Jeet had to explain to me she was dead. He wouldn't say how.

Gargi's own recall of this time is laden. Expectations on her, elbowing out grief. Nanu had told her at breakfast that her Mama had gone to Srinagar, was not coming back. Sita was only ten months old. She needed feeding. The Lottie was making a mess, so Gargi sent her away. As she listened to Nanu, she spooned food into her sister's mouth. Then went to check Radha was ready for school.

Sitting on the swing, she remembered Nanu telling her that there had been a fire at the Srinagar house. She was thirteen—still she didn't believe it. How could a house, with everyone and all the things in it, burn down?

—I thought maybe Mummy had got so tired of being with us that she left us for the next life, she said. Why am I telling you this? I never think about it now.

Except every birthday, when she feels the age of her mother's death getting closer. Making tiny, insistent holes in her hopes, as moths devour shawls. Except every time she does something, for Bapuji, for Nanu, for Radha or Sita, that her mother should have been there to do.

—Do you really believe in all that reincarnation stuff? Jivan had asked.

She hadn't known why—it might have been his American accent— but his voice seemed to dilute her faith. Just for one moment, she had tasted that doubt. Then swallowed. Why not? she had said. It can't all be mumbo-jumbo.

—Mumbo-jumbo, he had repeated, and laughed.

—Don't you believe in God? Gargi had asked. And had wondered how he could live like that.

—Nanu is a very dedicated Hindu, she's very spiritual, never even touches eggs, she had said.

—Nanu doesn't eat eggs, so that means there is a God?

—Do you really want to know how my mother died? Don't you know anything about Kashmir? Her voice had risen. Jivan stayed still, eyes on hers.

—I'm Indian again, he'd reminded her. You have to educate me. That's always been your job.

Google it, she had wanted to say. I'm not here to tell you what you should know. The words came out of her slowly—the story of how her Nanaji was sick, so her Mama went back to Srinagar to look after him. She was always going back there, always worrying about him, even though Bapuji didn't like it. There was unrest in the streets, her mother's Pandit community under siege.

—She was killed, and so was my grandfather, in the street outside their own house, Gargi said.

—In the case against religion, the prosecution rests. Jivan sat back on the bench and folded his arms.

—Bapuji went mad. We lost all that land.

Jivan's face had remained in the shadows. The jhoola had rocked them. He whispered something, it sounded like *land, honey.*

—Yes, they call Kashmir the "Land of Milk and Honey," she replied. So much for that.

Then Jivan put his hands on hers. His were warm, bigger than Surendra's, the palms rougher, though the nails were buffed. She had looked at the knots their fingers made together. If hands could speak, would they answer her question—*Who am I to you?*

—If I had been allowed to stay in India, Jivan had said, I would have been able to help you.

—How? What would you have done?

—I would have made sure you didn't have ladoo in your hair!

—O no, do I? O God, like a small kid!

She pulled her hands away but he was laughing. He asked her to sit with her back to him and she, conscious of her naked spine, her bare shoulders in the bright yellow dress, had obeyed.

—Canary, he said. Your hair is so long.

She felt his breath on her back, a shade warmer than the pre-dawn air. Had shut her eyes to welcome an old memory of her mother doing this. Fingers combing through her hair, slow rocking under the bougainvillea's puckered lips. She could hear grasshoppers singing and the sounds of men cheering and splashing; it had been that time of night: the Drunken Dip. She let Jivan play with her hair. Her anger and hurt drained from her shoulders, her neck and out of her mouth in a slow sigh.

· · ·

Then a peacock had cried, high and harsh. Her eyes had opened. She must go and organise the buffet breakfast. People would be cold after the swim, be expecting garam garam paranthe. Croissants.

For many years, the Tuesday Parties had only been held once every two months and always finished at midnight, on the stroke. It had been a point of honour that each man in the Hundred would be at his desk the next day: *No shirking on Company time.* Slowly the parties became monthly, then every fortnight. Since Bapuji turned seventy-five, the nights have got more and more wild, lasting into Wednesday morning, even afternoon. Bapuji's temper is a rakshas, but since Sita left, he has been playing the sprite, lighting pockets of chaos flash fires across the Farm. Gargi never knows what mischief will ignite next.

The day before Gargi's interview and photoshoot, the noise from the party humped through the house. Gargi went looking for Bapuji as various members of the Hundred ignored her or tried to persuade her to join in their games. The house-servants kept serving Bapuji all he wanted; they were scared of him—even more than she was, or she would have closed the kitchen down, full stop.

Nanu has been no help. Refusing to get up until Sita comes home again, until wedding preparations are underway. Nanu does not want to hear stories, does not want to bathe. Yet she is full of happy predictions. Yesterday evening Gargi had gone to tend to her. Nanu lay on her bed, she seemed to be shrinking, pickling herself from within. Her body looked frail but her grip was steel. She wanted the lights and the covers and the air temperature adjusted; she wanted some music. She refused to eat, but would take liquid food. *Will you talk to Bapuji, to bring Sita home?* Gargi wanted to beg Nanu's advice—but all she got was her grandmother, ninety years old in full rhetorical flow, quoting from some scripture—the name and section of which Gargi, if she was any shade of good—should have known.

—*Crack,* says Vishnu, *and half the egg becomes heaven, half is hell. If the gold is all we can see, the shell will be empty of both,* Nanu said, and coughed as she finished, and rolled over on her bed, turning her face to the wall. After some time, she began to snore in soft shudders, as if weeping in her dreams.

Gargi had left her. Gone back through the house to bursts of cheering—the men watching sports in the central living room. The noise became a metal band around her head, so tight. In the games room, she had discovered Jivan playing poker with a few of the quieter men, three from this batch that Gargi knows by name. Rahul, Shiv, Manoj. She stood a step or two behind Jivan, while he said things that she didn't understand: *Straight-up flush, he's going to bet the farm.* Later, Jivan found her lying in the darkened Red Room, a mask over her eyes. He left—she thought he'd gone back to his game. But as the house became quiet, that evening before dinner, Uppal informed her that Jivan had kicked at least half of the Tuesday boys out of the house, told them not to come back. Until they were invited by Gargi herself.

It is hard to believe, now, in the smothering heat of midmorning, next to the still pool. That all of this had raged.

—Jivan, she says, thank you again for the other night.

—No problem, he says. It is my job now. I better show I can do it.

Snip, snip, snitch. The sound of shears at the hedge beyond the water. Gargi moves away from Jivan. She shades her eyes with her hand.

—I have to find my dad, she says. I have to tell him we voted for you to replace Kritik Uncle, at least for now. He's not avoiding you, it's just—he's doing his own thing. I'm sure he will want to meet you again. I'm so sorry he hasn't yet.

—It's OK. It's been so many years, I can wait a bit longer. Jivan frowns. Then he waves the magazine at her. I'm keeping this. You know where I am if you need me.

If Gargi had three wishes, the first two would be to have her sisters' abilities: Radha's to attract and Sita's to speak out. The third would be: the ability not to look back. She gives Jivan a last smile. She walks away, wondering if he is still watching her.

Daddy could be anywhere. On the bowling green or on the driving range. In the ice-room where real snow can be made to fall. At the bird tower with his peacocks and his pigeons, cooing and pouting at the southernmost tip of the Farm. She must make him sit down with her, and listen.

He will want to know about the strike. He must have more directives for her on the Kashmir hotel. She feels she has become heavy as the key to his office door. Keep out, keep in, keep turning.

Her kurta sucks at her skin; her thighs bloating, her cheeks must be two red plums. Her middle puffing upwards: a puri in hot fat. She reaches the duck pond. On a stone bench she takes rest, sheltered by the kindness of willows. The stone's warmth seeps upwards, into her. The bench is scarred by stubbed-out cigarettes. She fingers each dark burn.

Sita has always been—wayward and forward. Too outspoken. Too tall. Bapuji believes her disobedience has been caused by her time in the UK. *At least,* Gargi thinks, *girls over there take the family's blessing before they go off to do what-all.* She knows her father is wounded by Sita's self-ishness. So must he punish everyone?

Radha says Sita is answering her texts. Just with a *hey-ho I'm OK, I'm with my friends, don't worry.* Gargi never thought that Sita could lie—and this pains her most of all. Sita writes *friends,* says nothing about *a boy.* But Uppal's full report, gathered the days after the party when she had already left the Company Gurgaon, said that one of the suite's beds was not slept in. Sita had ordered room service but nothing was consumed. Ten green bottles of Cristal had been opened—and left to go flat. Nine bottles of Sula Dindori white wine—emptied into the bath. Eight fresh limes had been quartered—and left floating on top. Seven Diet Cokes and six butterscotch sundaes with extra dark chocolate shavings had been mixed together—and left to melt in the bidet. Meanwhile, five rounds of Char Sui Bau—pork sticky buns, she is told—were found cut open, the insides gouged out and rearranged into tiny, perfect models of pigs. At Uppal's request, housekeeping provided photographs: four little caviar whales were found, diving over the pillows. Sita must have spent hours hunched on the bed with a bowl and a tiny silver spoon, moulding the black eggs into shape. Two dozen oysters were discovered stinking in the double sink; their innards had been picked off and strung into a necklace with the complimentary sewing kit—and left on the mirror as garland to a lipsticked message the concierge did not understand.

No Sorry—In bourgeoIs socI-ety capItal Is Independent and has In—dIvId—dualIty, whIle the lIvIng person is dependent and has no IndIvIdualIty—No Thankyou. Save the monkeys.

There was one red dot, the height of a bindi, on only one *i*. Gargi notices. The word "is."

Sita Madam also had some tattoo done. This last was according to a maid, called to hold her hand for the duration. Where did Sita mark herself? The maid indicated, her left side. Why? With what design? Of course the mute maid has no idea.

Sita and the boy had left the suite the following morning. The concierge saw them walk, actually walk, with no security down the sweeping drive of the hotel, past the drivers waiting to drop off their employees, past the gate police doing bomb checks, into the street. He didn't stop them, he said, how should he? Two weeks have gone by. Sita has bought nothing with her cards. It seems that the city has swallowed her. She is either dead in a ditch or indulging in the height of selfishness with that boy. Gargi had promised not to track her. She must obey herself.

She leaves the shade of the willow; its branches trail over her shoulders, trying to persuade her to stay. Whispering into her, *Could it be that Sita knew that Daddy would turn his back?* Gargi's hand smoothes the length of her plait, bringing it around her neck. Worry is weaving grey strands through it; she must get it dyed. She wraps it tight around her throat. *Girls these days have no respect.* Gargi says this out loud:

—Girls these days have no respect.

It makes her feel strong, as if she comes from a line of powerful women: a sisterhood who say such things about their children because they have such things to bear. The air around her is stiff with the effort of plants trying to survive. Sita's betrayal is paining as an ulcer might. If her guts were rotting, would they smell?

She wonders for a moment if one of the dogs has done toilet here, and no one has cleaned it up. No, it is not that. Something nearby is stinking like sickness—just like when Sita, at four years old, caught typhoid. Gargi had missed over a week of class, holding her little sister's hand, not letting anyone else feed her or sponge her. She cried over Sita and slept by her through the nights. The doctors had praised her care, saying, *Gargi, you are so dedicated, you will heal her.* What would their mother have done? This only. And so Gargi did it too. She found herself curled on her knees, her forehead pressed to the ground: the only way she could show she meant her prayers. She promised Lord Krishna she would always do what her father told her. She promised she would never curse Nanu in secret again. She promised she would make sure Radha started behaving. She would give up chicken and meat and eggs and stop playing her music for a whole year—if only she did not have to tell Bapuji that Sita was dead.

After Sita recovered, Gargi had made sure she had everything she wanted. She even signed her a birthday card especially from Bapuji and wrapped her a gift from him every year. Something precious—once, a plant book, once a botany set—in addition to whatever finery her father actually bought.

Now the sun falls on Gargi's dark head and on her body, swelling her ankles and wrists. Every pore of her skin is weeping. *Sita,* she thinks. *Come home.*

The stench spikes the hot summer air as if a sewer pipe has burst. In the rose garden, Gargi covers her mouth and nose with her dupatta. Expecting the comforting nod of the roses—their quiet approval—she finds the stems have been stripped naked. The whole garden is a tangle of thorns piercing the sky. Where are the petals? What is that stink? She forces herself to inhale. On the other side of the yew hedge a shock of colour. There are peacock feathers, bright turquoise, deep blue eyes wide on the bloodstained grass.

Wild dogs? It cannot be. There is a concrete wall and a barbed-wire fence protecting the Farm's backside. There are garden boys. She crawls along the hedge, almost strangling herself as she kneels on her dupatta, sees more dark eyes—sapphire ringed with turquoise, beige, emerald green staring up at her—each quill writing a fat, closely feathered body, white legs splayed—the feet are scaled, like Nanu's old fingers encased in her lizard-skin gloves. Gargi has to reach under the yew, and pull. The peacock's talons scratch her as if it is still alive.

Struggling with the branches, trying not to rip the tail from the mass of flesh, she waves away a swarm of flies, to pull the peacock's body into her arms. A dry lake of blood stains the earth. There is more dry blood, crusted around a hole in the breast. The stomach is sliced open—pale guts spill from it—the creature's juice seeps onto her, sticky, unctuous, the wet earth smell of a child unable to hold her toilet. Gargi tastes ulti rising in her throat, and swallows. She cradles the peacock in her lap: yes, it is the size, the weight of a small child.

She rocks the bird in her arms. She turns it over as best she can: the blue neck, which she always thought so elegant, is broken. She strokes it with a finger: rough like raw silk. The jet-black eye stares up at her. The points of its crown are bent; the tiny razor teeth exposed as if trying to bite the air.

Sweat pours down Gargi's neck. It drenches her underarms, her breasts. Her head feels so light it could float from her body. Around her the stripped rose bushes entreat the heavens. There is no reply.

She has to find Bapuji. Her arms are numb; she eases them out from under the peacock. Trying to place it back on the grass without twisting it more, as if it was only hurting. Not dead, not yet. She wipes her hands on the grass, fumbles in her pocket, pulls out her phone, presses 1.

—Uppal, she says. Her throat is parched. Her voice shakes. Rose garden phata-phat aao, mali ko lekar. Mali ko lekar aao, someone good. Get him to bring a wheelbarrow, a shovel. When you are done here, go round the whole Farm, check for more. I don't care if you are still disposing of the ladoos. Do this now. And, Uppal . . . don't bring any peacock feathers into the house.

Gargi gets up and begins to jog, not towards the bunker but away, across the estate. To the bird tower.

On the way, she sees more feathers, more tails fanned out over bodies across the grass, legs sticking out stupidly like drunken girls in lehengas, falling over their skirts. Do they have no shame?

She keeps on, barely stopping when her phone rings. It is her grandmother.

—What is it, Nanuji?

—What are you doing in this leaky balloon? This world is a gambling den, Gargi, you cannot be too carefreefull. There has been an outbreak of Avian Flu in Golkattapur. Government is killing all chickens. I called to order—evening meal. Aaj raat ke khaane ke liye, saag banwana.

—Yes, Nanuji, Gargi says. *Khaana, birds, killing.* Gargi goes as quickly as she can across the Farm, propelled by a memory of herself at eight years old—the year that Bapuji had almost lost the Company to the Bank of India. An income tax raid had shut him down for weeks; every part of the business was put under surveillance, all offices occupied by state officials. Bapuji took down the gun from his study wall, loaded it up and went hunting on the roof garden at the old Jor Bagh house. Gargi had crouched with Radha in the music room, listening to the shotgun fire—and watched as feathers rained down on the front lawn. A pink flamingo, flapping towards the Lodhi lake. A huge black kite, the biggest she had ever seen. It tumbled from the sky as if Lord Krishna had kicked it from heaven. It landed right outside their window, making little Radha howl.

When the shooting had finally stopped, Gargi left Radha with the Lottie, and crept upstairs. A group of police had arrived, they were pacing the rooftop garden, she could see their boots moving between Nanu's precious flower pots (which were full of pinks with English names). The men were asking Bapuji about the size of his gun, the range it could fire and the cost of each cartridge. They congratulated him on his aim.

When she showed her presence, boldly she thought, like a lady of the house come to quell a commotion, Bapuji told her to get back downstairs and organise tea.

She ordered the tea. Went back upstairs with Nanu, and was allowed to stay. Sitting under a canopy as the sun bled through the smog, Nanu informed the police that the gun was gifted by a Major General of the British Army to Nanu's own father, the Maharaja of Lutchapur in 1903. Then it became part of Nanu's own dahej when she married at eight years old. Her husband, the Maharaja of Napurthala, tried to give it back to the British as a parting gift, but the gesture was taken as a bribe and refused. Nanu described to the policemen how her husband, the Maharaja, then took the gun and ordered his servant to shoot him just weeks after he acceded his land to India. His death had left Nanu and a boy-king with no kingdom to rule.

—*Look,* said Nanu. *How my son has used his money and built this India into a rival for any country on this earth! Look how he can buy any Westerner a hundred times over! That is a real Maharaja. One who knows the value of the mother country can never forgo his bright future.*

The Inspector Sahibs had agreed, and congratulated Nanu for bearing the kind of son they wanted their own future boys to emulate. Before they left, they sat, legs spread on the roof terrace swing, and toasted her with bone china cups of the finest Company own-brand tea.

Lies, lies: her paternal grandfather died broke, yellow from gambling and wine. Even as a girl, Gargi had known that.

·   ·   ·

Gargi must get to the bird tower. Save at least one peacock. Even one pigeon will do. She will go through the forest, around the domestics' quarters. She runs, walks, bounces, runs—it is hard—until she almost reaches the edge of the grass, where the manicured Farm meets the outer ring road. There is not even a tarmac here, just a kachcha path, yellow earth hard and cracked.

This is the line they were told as children never to cross. If they did, Nanu warned, they might get stolen, or swapped for some low-caste child, and never find their way back home. Jeet and Gargi used to dare each other: up to here, a toe over the line, a leg, and arm, Radha and Jivan watching, too little to join in and too scared. Too late to think about it: she has to save the birds.

She forces herself away from the gardens and up the small rise. Ahead is a pine grove, deep and densely planted, carpeted with ferns, sweet, strange flowers and long grass; sharp, slicing her arms. A sudden chill and an alpine scent like the Pahalgam of her earliest memories, summers spent high in the mountains of Kashmir before it became dangerous, before her sisters were born.

She reaches the far side of the pines. Through the clearing she can see the white concrete boxes of the day-servants' quarters planted in orderly rows. It looks peaceful, empty, like the graveyard of headstones in the old cantonment in West Delhi—she used to go there with Radha and a Lottie, for Sunday walks. A place of strange nomenclature, Westerners mostly; the Gloucestershire Rifles, Machine Gun corps, the fallen commonwealth soldiers of undivided India who fought alongside her grandfather's men. When she was young, she felt safe among the dead.

She crosses another dirt track. No one is here. The silence is watching her as she walks through the blocks, waiting to jump on her, take her inside one of these white boxes and brick up the cavities. In this heat, all the liquid would be sucked from her body; eventually her flesh would tandoor, peel from her bones. Behind each clean hut, rubbish fills the gully, baking in the sun. *Who is supposed to be taking care of this?* Are all the servants who live here hiding, waiting to mob her?

Don't be stupid; all are working at the house.

As she walks deeper into the compound, she sees a group of black children squatting in the dirt near the old water pump, skittling pine-cones along the ground. She catches her breath. Servants are not permitted to have their wives or families here.

A voice calls,

—Madamji?

Gargi looks up, forced to squint through her own sweat. A dark-skinned woman in a print cotton sari stands on the steps of a concrete dwelling; her shape cut out against the whitewashed walls.

The woman's eyes do not waver as they take in the bloodstains on Gargi's kurta, her torn chunni, the contrast of gold bangles, diamond studs. Gargi's hair is heavy and caked with sweat. *I am thirty-three, I am thirty-three, I oversee thousands of people,* she thinks. She has not felt like this since she was thirteen: Nanu caught her sleeping in the afternoon, the chaadar rucked up around her waist. She had no panty on. Nanu had slapped Gargi's naked cheeks with her hard, flat hand.

Gargi pulls herself straight, the pose she uses to toast her father.

—What are you doing here? she says. Who are you with? Who are you to these children?

The woman draws her sari over her head as if she is going to pray, still it does not cover her eyes. Her face is full of a hangdog pleading, mixed with an insolence that, Gargi thinks, would make any sane person want to scream.

—Paanchopi din ki baad, the woman says. Gargi Madam. Now, you come.

Her language is crusted in some thick local accent; its origins lost, here.

—Come, she says again.

Gargi follows her. Up the steps and into the concrete dwelling. Carbolic soap, sandalwood smoke, and sour, male sweat hang in the airless room. Wires twist out from the ceiling where the fan should be. There is an empty tin thali and cup by the bed. On the wall, a 2009 Company Resorts of India calendar secured with a rusty thumbtack shows the month of November: Radha and Bubu in their most formal Indian wear, silk encrusted with gold, grinning as they light candles with a long taper at Diwali. That calendar. They give them to the G-level staff every New Year.

In the grey room, a man is curled on the low cane bed. He is wearing a dirty singlet and pyjama; his head and chest are covered in strips of cloth, stained with turmeric and dried blood. The woman peels back the sheet. On his ribcage, sour bruises; green, yellow, purple, spread from under bandages made from torn-up sheets.

Gargi looks away. A Company Server's uniform, bloodstains rinsed out but still visible, hangs from a hook near the bed.

She blinks. The room feels choked with despair. The dust presses on her. She tries not to inhale.

—What happened—did he get in a fight?

—No, Madam. No fight, Madam. After the Mangalvar party. Sita-Ma'am ki welcome-home. Farmhouse wale ne asahu bheja inko. Put-put mein.

The woman wipes her face with her own dupatta. She squats down by the bed.

Gargi understands—something about Sita, the Tuesday Party two weeks ago. The *put-put*—the woman is telling her that this man was brought here, like this, in a cart from the house, has suffered here all this time.

She takes out her phone, dials 1.

—Uppal. Get the Company doctor down to the day-servants' village. She turns to the woman.

—Sector? Unit?

—G-Teen-panch, Madam.

—G level, sector three, unit five, she says to Uppal. Come now with the doctor. Bring two thousand, no, bring five thousand cash.

Then she says to the kneeling woman,

—Doctor Sahib aa rahe hain, Uppalji ke saath. Aap yahan par unka intezaar karo, aur unko batao ki kya hua hain.

The woman makes a hissing noise. She does not look at Gargi. Eyes on her man, she slides her hand under his. She begins to sing as if to a child, lori, soft and low.

—*Nanhi kali, sone chali, hawa dheere aana.*

Gargi's own mother sang her this lullaby. And Jivan's mother used to sing it to Radha, and she, Gargi, sang it to Sita, tucking her up into bed for afternoon nap. Gargi watches. Limbs too heavy to take another step.

Behind the kneeling woman, Gargi stands, tears sliding down her cheeks. There is comfort here, a dissolving language of sounds she cannot let herself recall. She is watching a woman turn into a mother, a man back into a boy.

She reaches out and places her hand on the woman's shoulder. The cheap print fabric is rough against her palm, the bones sharp beneath. She wants to kiss the wavering line parting this woman's hair. She stares down at her own hand: her dated, round-cut diamond engagement ring winks back at her. Nanu would never touch a servant's wife. And neither would Bapuji, Ranjit Uncle, Kritik Sahib, Jeet, Surendra, Bubu, Radha, Jivan—only Sita would do this. What will become of her now?

The woman tenses but does not turn. The song stops.

The man on the bed sighs.

Gargi becomes aware again of the smells of blood on her kurta, the weight of herself. Sweat drying. She turns away from the bed and walks from the room, into the evening light. The children have abandoned their game and vanished. She crosses the pine grove and the road. She begins the long trek back. The Farm is waiting: her place.

Keep walking, Gargi, just keep walking.

No more waiting for Sita. No more running after Daddy. No time to monitor Nanu, or cry for dead peacocks. Kings and courtiers once ate them stuffed with rice or baked in pies. If that is what her father wants, that is what he should get. What would happen if she took the bad-luck feathers into the kitchens, and served Peacock Pie for his dinner?

She reaches a circle imprinted on the grass. A bare, bald patch where Sita's engagement canopy has been taken down, every marigold and ribbon removed. She steps into it. One day songs will be written about what Sita sacrificed, from the raw concrete to the built hotels, yes, but also every tiny stitched diamond within a diamond, each chashm-e-Bulbul, every precious strand of toosh. The shawls business that was their mother's own offering when she married Bapuji, and which Bapuji wanted to give to Sita, in her own right, her own name.

Now, from this scarred place she will announce that this land and all the land beyond it—all the people who work on it, everyone who is invested in it—everything belongs to Gargi and Radha. They will not sign Bapuji's plan to divide. They will work together to make the Company *sing.* They will found a trust. Perhaps build a small town, its programmes to educate girl children will birth poets, scholars, journalists better than Nina, editors, future songmakers, and translators of stories, in every language there is. She will offer her classes in Malayalam and Kannada, Gujarati and Punjabi—and back again, and back again and again—so that every woman can talk to the other without division of borders or minds. Tamil to Telugu, no one will be silenced.

Thank you, thank you, she thinks, and feels she is a girl again, six years old. Dressed in her precious hand-loomed Kashmiri salwar kameez, brought back from Srinagar by her Mama. How she had loved that loose pyjama, that peasant-girl kurta. It was black velvet, with gold work on the bib. It had a yellow dupatta to tie around her head, fringed like the fortune-tellers in the lobbies of the Company hotels. The kurta was cut on the bias, it swung around her body when she wore it, and she had danced the Rouf dance dressed in that, the steps learned from her very first Lottie, a woman she remembers for her agility and aged skin, wrinkled, beautiful like an elephant's around the eye. She came with Gargi's mother from Srinagar when she was a bride. She died when Gargi was six.

Standing in the circle, Gargi crosses her arms over her body, hands held out either side, imagining Radha's hands taking hers, then another Gargi, another Radha, a Sita, a Nina and the wife of the G.3.5. They step forward and back, a chain of paper dolls, welcoming the seasons as they come. Gargi steps the dance until she is out of breath, her hair in tangles, dirt encrusted on her skin. Then she bows, and carries on marching, marching, marching, unseeing of the garden wale and pool boys, their sideways glancing eyes.

She cannot go straight into the house. Instead, she stops in the spa behind the pool and orders a jug of nimboo pani, squeezed from Farm lemons. Glass after glass, she drinks the bittersweet juice until she has finished it. Then orders another jug, this time with vodka, made strong. She sheds her ruined clothes, wraps herself in a robe. Drinking time in the steam room, where every part of her body can now weep in peace.

Lying on the massage table, she sees herself reflected in the mirrored ceiling—her flesh like a mudflat—riddled with pale dried rivulets of stretch marks; the earth photographed from the air. The massage woman enters. She holds a towel and looks away as Gargi turns onto her front. Her hands begin: a sound between a moan and a sigh comes from Gargi's lips.

—Hurting you, Madam? says the masseuse. Turn, please.

The woman is large, she leans over, her belly rests on Gargi's. There is no sound in the room except grunting effort. Fingers press the day through Gargi's muscles, they rub the feeling of dead birds, the beaten man from her skin. Gargi hears the servant woman's lullaby, she thinks about her own marriage. The tender knot of what it means to be a wife. She lies on the massage table, understanding she was bartered before she could value herself. Yet Surendra has never been bad to her or raised his voice; he rarely shows any interest at all. She has never told him what she wants or does not want. She wants the whole world, except one thing. One, natural thing.

This is Gargi's secret, released from her body by Sita's absence, by the cradling of a dead bird in her arms. By a beaten man, lulled to sleep in his wife's song.

Gargi Devraj Grover does not want to bear children. She will not. She realised this promise after her wedding night. Has shared it only with Radha, who once, before she herself got married, begged to know what a blowjob was (Gargi couldn't say), what squirting was (Gargi couldn't say), why Bapuji's friends gesticulated around her, brushing her here, or there (because men's arms are so much longer than women's they have to, an answer that Radha had laughed at until she cried, cried—and then said, *No,* it's because they *can*). Finally, she wanted to know why Nanu kept saying that sex was a *duty of women after marriage,* when Radha wanted it to be fun.

—*Sex is for making babies,* Gargi had said. *You have it, and them. They can inherit this earth. I don't want a single one.*

In the quiet room, the masseuse's hands press down on Gargi, as if to test her womb for truth.

She goes back to the house. The pool lights are off, no music comes from the house or grounds. The night is warm; its deep gloom casts her into relief—a walking white towel robe and slippers—she cannot see her own skin. She goes to her study, she spends some time. Working on the Srinagar staffing plans. She texts Jivan a hello-what's-up (no reply). She calls Radha and talks only about her sister's day. Then she orders one last person to come to her.

Hair unbound, she sits facing herself in the mirror. The hairdresser stands behind her. He has tiny silver scissors in his ear lobes, a bandana round his head; he stands with the rope weight of her plait in his hand as if he is about to jump ship and use it as his swing.

—Cut it, she says. Short all over my head.

—Gargi Madam, he says. It will not look nice. I will do a Rachel. Just below your shoulders, with bangs. Very flirty-pretty-modern. Yes, I'll do that.

He begins by unwinding the plait, washing the hair. Then cutting one handful. She tells him,

—Shorter. Shorter.

He does it in lines. Cutting, cutting, then snipping, then shaving her neck. The snarls of hair turn the floor around them into a sea of black.

When he is gone, she unties her robe and stretches in front of her mirrors. Five of her gaze back. She raises her arms. Her breasts are heavy. Her nipples seem bigger, more pointed and full, trying to peek upwards at her hair. She feels so light: if she leapt into the air, it would hold her, suspended before she came down. All creatures rush to their destruction, like snowflakes on the breeze. There is a soft part on her neck that she has never felt before.

For the first time in her life, she goes naked to bed. Surendra never comes to her. So, in the night, if her hands reach up to stroke her hair, to cup her full breast and pinch at her nipples; or travel downwards below her belly to press a finger between her lips, there is no one to see, no one to know, or tell. She herself might not be aware, if, in the hot night, she spreads across the bed on her back, arms and legs wide open. Arching up: one of her hands spans the flesh below her navel, the other underneath her back, tracing down and down, meeting the fingers of her other hand inside the delicate parts of herself. No word in her language. For delicate bone. For sliding, for wetness, front and back she caresses, her fingers patter on her insides —*Ram, Ram, Ram, Ram,* she whispers, for the first time summoning a flood.

She bears down. Into her own hands, then up, her cheeks an offering to the air, mouth gasping, sucking on the night. She sees herself, as if from the vantage point of the camera that scans her dressing room, crawling there on all fours, mounting the chaise longue, knees splayed, fingers inside, eyes closed, head back, ass up, fingers inside, from both sides, spread open, she does it on the bed, kneels, nipples, belly, hanging down, head full of mirrors, the eye of the camera, the wire to the screens; Jivan's face, watching, Jivan, no one else, ever, watching until he must come. Heat rises, her own voice fills her, repeating his name, only hearing herself, and there is the core of the heat, there, through the folds and layers; pure, she hears her own voice whisper,

—*Gargi, Gargi, Gargi*—

She obeys. She is the only one there to hear her wish, or grant that it will come true.

I WANT, I WANT, I want to go hunting. Legs astride a horse, we shall ride. A shooting party. Shh, don't tell I said that. Sita wouldn't like it, I know. She has got to learn, though, that guns protect. Straddling time, I have seen this thing.

Sita was always the quiet one, so good at listening. But when we got to this house, she began talking, talking, and I, her father, could not make her stop. She was full of sentiments that I cannot abide. Desire, charity, her sisters. Instead of focusing on her country, she wants to think about herself in the world. She accused me of pollution. Me! She said that for every centimetre the sea levels rise by, one million species of plant are lost. So Gargi and I have a plan.

—Really, I said, do tell.

Sita smiled as she does when she wants to say something she thinks that I must hear. Her eyes, green and blue and ringed with a smudged brown line, were wild and wide.

—Sita, I said, my hands on her pretty little face. Have you ever lied to me?

She did not lower her eyes or hang her head. Straight to my eyes, I think she said,

—Gargi and I went together to the Valley of Flowers. Bhyundar, high in the Western Himalayas, where Lord Hanuman found the herbs that brought Lakshman back from the edge of death. Gargi and I sat in the back of the Land Rover and ate kathi rolls. We drank tea from a flask. Gargi always thinks of everything, she even brought brownies she baked herself. She knows I love to taste. Eating her food is like being warmed by the new summer sun.

—Why are you telling me this, Sita? I said. Don't say your sister's name.

And her reply was cryptic I remember and perhaps she said,

—But, Papa, I want to start an institute to study this warming effect and save our precious species from destruction. I could live there in the Valley, while it gets established. Gargi said she would support it, if you would.

Over by the door, the young manservant cleared his throat. I looked at him and together we shared our sense of wonder at the female imagination. Gargi and Sita wanted my money and my blessings so Sita could live in the middle of nowhere and tend plants!

This was Gargi's way of stealing her from my sight. Of preventing Sita from managing my line and my legacy, of fulfilling her function, her destiny as it has always been written. I will not allow Gargi to win.

Then I asked, as gently as I could,

—Sita, in all of this time, where have you been?

Smiling as if tasting some memory of love, I tell you she confessed that she went to Sri Lanka, alone. Without me, or anyone she knew, she went about with monkeys and insects, the only girl of the group. I heard the manservant suck in his breath, and both of us waited for her answer. I can tell you it, since she is not here.

—Father (I think she said, or maybe she said *Pa*), in Sri Lanka, the forests chatter with monkeys, and strange flora and fauna bloom. Spiders make webs that span the gap between trees. I stepped from the loving circle of my family to learn how to save creatures and their world from human destruction. To me this seemed the highest calling. Can you understand that? All we can breathe is air.

—I know why you really went: to follow that boy who enslaved you.

—No (I think she said, lying again). Not at all. It was my desire to go there alone, to recapture that love for the forest that he forced me to abdicate. I wandered, seeking rare plants. I wore my vest and shorts, and went sandy-footed on the beach. My body lithe and gold, my hair wild, I swam in the warm waters of the deep blue ocean, wearing a two-piece tied with no more than string. Barely covering my breasts and cunt, I was able to live as I please. But, though it was paradise, I missed you too much. After a while, all I wanted was to come home.

That is what she said.

As she spoke, I writhed in her lap, waiting for her to notice how her words disgusted me. I asked her with my eyes to stop talking, to allow me the purity of silence. She would not listen. She never listened. But she is not the only storyteller here. I taught her everything she knows, after all, didn't I pay for her to be educated? Thus I am the source. Of her. Knowledge. Am I not? I got up, and stood behind her in this dusty room and I put my hands lovingly about her neck. The manservant started from his post by the door, but did not intervene.

—Of course you cannot stay alone in Uttarakhand, or go gallivanting in Sri Lanka, I said. Your roots are here. For why else are we building a new hotel? Only in such a way can we balance the books. You were born in 1989, on the cusp of civil war. A year later your mother was dead, pulled from this house into the street. Who knows what she did next? Spread and begged. Reports vary. Some said she promised her body in exchange for her life. Some said she offered money and the house. Some said they took what they wanted from her and left her to die. I heard they threw the bodies of her people and all those who died into the Jhelum. I heard that some got eaten. Even the elite of this town, the ruling class! That such a boundary could be breached is inconceivable to me. Now their houses are broken, their storeys are tinder sticks, rubbing against each other. That is the way of this world. So it keeps turning. The lesson is: keep your wives, your daughters close. Make return with interest.

And Sita said, I recall, as if talking to the birds,

—Must generation after generation be punished for history's crimes? This earth does not belong to us.

She moved away from me, her body so lithe, she could have been an actress, in another life.

And, O how wrong she is. It is this territory, here, which should matter most to anyone of our blood. This is not about the women. In times of war, land endures and lays claim to us. It is our duty to obey.

The manservant was watching her from the door: I signalled to him to come over.

—Come here, I said. Come help me with this daughter, so I can make you both understand. I gripped Sita's arm, and held her.

—Papa, she said, and this rings clear in my mind. I want to get out of this house, this state. Let me go.

ii

The only thing Gargi keeps is the Mughal desk. The bar is dismantled, the armchair exiled, the antique guns discharged and the hunting heads sent to storage on the Farm. The photographs of Bapuji which line the wall behind the desk—as a ten-year-old boy in knee-length shorts and a shirt standing with Pandit Nehru on the steps of the Napurthala Palace, Nanu in the background in Jackie-O dark glasses and a heavy bordered sari; as a young man shaking hands with Mrs. Thatcher; then Indira Gandhi at Rashtrapati Bhavan, smiling with one of the Georges Bush; and most recently, in a fine silk kurta with Sita on his arm, at the Durbar Restaurant in the Company Delhi hotel for the state visit of the Chinese Prime Minister: Gargi banishes all of them. Has them remounted and rehung in a discreet area of the lobby marked with a short red carpet and a velvet rope, just to the left of the revolving doors. Everyone has told her it looks *totally awesome, too good, just beautiful,* guarded by a selection she has made herself, of winter-flowering cacti.

She replaces Bapuji's photographs with an Indian city on fire. A print taken from above, a nightscape of deep blues and blacks. Three fingers of flame captured racing through urban streets—up, up, into the sky. Yes, Gargi has acquired her first Dayanita Singh, an artist whose work in light she has followed for years, and whose other photographs are of an old hijra called Mona, reclining on a day bed, eyes burdened with the blessing of seeing both sides. She could fall into this image of the city. It would be like becoming. *Where fear and pain are exhilarating, and sorrows dissolve in flight. The streets endlessly renew.*

She has invested in art, on Uppal's advising (*this on trend, this show in London, all the arty-parties love this one's work these days*). Never has she bought for herself, until now. She thinks that the image is of Mumbai. She can almost make out the Company hotel in the far, far away. *My hotel,* she tells herself. *My Company. Me.*

She allows herself to swivel in her chair. Faces the inside wall of the office, made completely of glass—an atrium which, when she was first married and new to this building, she filled with trees and flowers from all of the gardens of India and Arabia. The species number over three hundred, she had learned them all for college admittance tests: she got into St. Stephens, though she was married before she could attend. A *Syzgium cumini* presses its canopy close to her window—she knows it from her *Trees of Delhi*—"a beautiful, large jamun tree, more or less evergreen. Bark is a pale brown, flaky and rough, especially on the lower trunk. Leaves with numerous secondary veins, running parallel and united with a marginal vein. Flowers in dense clusters . . . white to creamish. Fruit is a round or oblong berry, deep purple. Sweet or tart to the tongue. It is used in folk medicines for diabetes, dysentery and diseases of spleen." "Spleen," a word she associates with laughter and bursting. This *bursting* goes together so naturally with the Latin name for the tree, it pleases her. The top of the atrium is open—and bright green parrots swoosh in, swoosh out. Sometimes a stray pigeon comes and sits on a branch, head cocked towards the glass with a beady eye. She runs her hand up and through her short hair. After ten days, the softness of her neck still surprises her.

She has kept one photograph for her desk. The groundbreaking ceremony for the Company Delhi hotel. Foundations had not even been laid. There was mud, and squares cut into it, as if an ancient city had been dug up. Nanu wore a printed silk sari, Bapuji was in his toosh and cap. Gargi herself was five years old, a plumpy peach with ribbons in her hair and socks with a frill. It had been Gargi's job to garland the guest of honour, Madam Indira Gandhiji. She remembers the stomach-churning feeling of grown-ups crowding around. The pressure of Indira Aunty's hand, terrifying on her shoulder—and the words she had said: *Never forget whose daughter you are.*

Gargi had declined her head and stepped back. The adults around her applauded. Then she watched, holding Nanu's fingers as the Swamiji blessed the earth. In his saffron robes, she had thought him the brightest colour on the barren land. But his smell, she remembers, was almond oil; she didn't like it when he came close to her and put his wrinkled palm on her head.

—Thank Swamiji for his blessing, Nanu had told her.

—He smells like the bath salts.

For that, she got one tight slap.

—Bhagwan sab kuch dekh rahe hain. Papaji sab kuch dekh rahe hain. Don't ask questions, do as I say.

Nanu filled her fist with earth. Gargi threw it into the fire. She felt she was marrying the land. So it would provide for her always. (But, she had wondered, if the land was a husband, why was it always called *Ma*?)

Gargi remembers asking this question and getting no reply, just a hand held up as if to slap again. She remembers the day ending, Radha crying in a Lottie's arms. Where had their mother been? Probably away: it was that time of year. Spring in Srinagar. She always went back for the flowering of tulips.

Now Gargi sits at the Mughal desk. She stares through the glass wall, into the jungle. The trees need spraying, the leaves are grey with city dust. A small bird, not a sparrow or pigeon, lands on a Jamun branch, close to the glass. Monochrome, slim, with a forked tail—a Black Drongo— Gargi thinks, so elegant, though people think it's a bad kind. For a second it observes her, head on one side. Then it flies away.

Dhanya, her father's secretary, knocks on the open door.

—Gargi Madam, can I get you anything? The Director Sahibs are on their way up.

Dhanya is from Cochin. She reports back to Gargi on life in the female staff hostel, a new build in Paschim Vihar, telling stories about the other secretaries she lives with. All from every part of the country, all working in Head Office. Dhanya sniffs at the Bengali girls, who think they are *all that*. She struggles to cook home food (fresh fish is hard for her to get). She eats with one or two girls from Trivandrum, as if her city and theirs are close as first cousins, not ten hours distant by bus. She has bought earplugs, since her roommate Aarti either snores or sings all the time, mostly Kannada songs that Dhanya cannot understand. Dhanya cannot get the coffee she likes in Paschim Vihar. Nor do the market men open early enough. She rides to office each day in the metro. On a good day it takes seventy-five minutes, half the time of the staff bus; she sits in the main carriage so she can watch boys squirm. But her year in Delhi, so she tells Gargi, has given her nosebleeds and asthma. She cannot go out alone, and how is she to meet a man while living only with women, especially since Delhi is so big? She is thinking of returning home—if a place could be found for her in the Company hotel there, she would like to retrain for management. Gargi has told her, *We'll see.*

Dhanya, one hand on her chunni, now flattens herself against the doorframe to let three men in.

—Kishoreji, Deepakji, Sunilji. To see you, Gargi Madam, she says. She shuts the door softly as she leaves.

Gargi observes them, the three independent directors of the Devraj Group; the first meeting Gargi has called here since the paint on the ceiling dried. Sama, dama, bheda, danda. Engraved on her heart is this Vedic lesson, which Nanu and Bapuji schooled her in. Make friends, give gifts, divide the parts and use the stick. These men, pulling up their chairs, getting out their papers, each of them like a thick jar of Company pickle; *mangoes,* she thinks, *no, amla, the round, brown fruits. Gym jao,* she wants to order them, *and stop stuffing paranthe.*

She pictures them as characters from her childhood books as a way of tempering her fear. They are Serious Men—each of them with his story. And degrees. So many—learning gathered from Princeton, Harvard, IIT. If Jivan were here, Gargi thinks, he would read these men in a way I cannot—all I see is the same face, repeated. When I was young, I thought these men were the three bears, or sometimes, the three little p's.

No, she decides now, they are the three monkeys—see no, speak no, hear no. It is easy, on the basis of appearance, to write them off: so bland in their uniform shirts, plain ties and grey suits. Same. Old. Between them, they can spend half a lakh on a five-star dinner, then take a frugal breakfast: perhaps one (or two) ajwain ke paranthe, a little homemade dahi. They could do this and call themselves moderates. All would agree.

Always they back one another (though in private they diverge, she thinks, but only late at night when they count their sons and maybe they whisper, *The Company is waiting for you*). She watches them look around the office. Take in the city on fire. Now the men look straight at Gargi's shorn hair, she should have worn salwar kameez, the suit is too harsh, makes her look top-heavy. Stop.

—Come sit, Kishoreji, Deepakji, Sunilji. Welcome.

Scenes like this do not belong in books, she thinks, in which little people reflect without pause on art and violence, the big questions through the worship of everyday things. The colour of her lipstick (Plum Dynasty), or the deep, sideways part in her fringe. Jivan does not read fiction, she knows. Do these men? They are listed on the "Real-world giants" page of the Company website. They are here to give wisdom and get answers. They demand answers. First and foremost to the all-important questions:

—Gargi beta, what new ideas is Bapuji experimenting with in office design?

—Gargi beta, you cut your hair? Looking very professional?

—Gargi beta, I have brought the papers of divestiture. Will Surendraji be joining us to sign?

The final speaker is Kishoreji, an independent director of the Devraj Group for just five years, but Bapuji's legal counsel for forty at least. He got into college on the archery quota, played for India in the Olympics, then became a lawyer in his uncle's firm. Kishoreji, who wears a cravat whatever the weather; today's is a plain, dark blue.

—Gargi beti, is there a problem in progressing your Bapuji's desires? he asks. Ranjitji tells us you are somewhat reluctant. But may I remind you: delay causes doubt, the most dangerous disease.

Kishoreji likes his coffee with pista burfi, he likes that Gargi always supplies this. Does he remember every time she has sat, listening to him talk about the implications of new laws, how to thread the Company through loop after hole—two words, she thinks, she has always associated with going fast and being crazy? Cartoons again—a wedge of Swiss cheese with big eyes and wild arms, waving from a roller-coaster carriage. There's a mouse chasing the cheese, a cat chasing the mouse, not catching up, never catching up, for roller coasters run on rails, like at Apu Ghar, the first-ever theme park opened in Delhi, where she went with Jeet as a young girl. He had fed her ice cream from a paper tub with a small plastic spoon (she always chose green) as they sat waiting for the ride to take them up, up, up! Gargi, with mehndi drying on her hands (done by a woman the Lottie had not wanted her to touch), had tasted the air, flavoured with vanilla, hands stretched out as the cart rose higher—higher—higher—and plunged, all the moments of childhood passing in a blur while the young Kishoreji loopholed the Company with his fine legal brain. Money and land and pleasure, tangled in the steel of a helter-skelter track.

—Every day you wait puts lakhs at stake, Kishoreji sings. He hands her a brick of Company papers.

—These are for you. Please, take them to Surendraji for reading. But as the eldest biological child, it is you who must sign.

Gargi thinks about all the lakhs, tied to the stake like witches from white fairytales, burning, burning, burning. *Money is not real, it only exists in the mind of a computer.* Jeet—*where is he?*—had laughed so much when she, as a girl, asked him where the bank vault was, the one that stored all the rupees for every person in the world. How did the bank know what size safe each person would need? Jeet—with his precious hardback Sanskrit–English dictionary—bought by Bapuji in London, from Sotheby's when Jeet was seven years old. Jeet loved that book so much he would fall asleep over it some nights; was bullied for that from tenth standard onwards—but he used it to teach eight-year-old Gargi the language of money; that the word "lakh," with its one and five zeros, comes from either the Pali (masculine, noun) for "stake in a gamble," or the Sanskrit "laksa," "a target," "a sign."

The three men do not yet understand. She will not take from Sita. Nor will she be responsible for splitting the Devraj Group. *The future, the market, the Country,* she thinks. *What will people say?*

This is a question which Deepakji could answer as a media man—before he joined the board he was one of a conclave of graduates from the Bapuji Hundreds of years gone by, who work across the papers and TV stations as proprietors, editors, reporters, as advertising salesguys—*isn't Barun one of them also?*—Gargi cannot remember—*must be,* she thinks—it is not like her to forget such details, but Deepakji is talking, his voice riding over her thoughts.

—Gargi beti—your sister Radha and Bubuji take their lead from Surendraji and from you. Please, set the example. Let Bubuji manage his share, and let us call Surendra Sahib to talk over the next stage. When the details are worked out, we would all three stay with him. And you.

He waits for her to thank him. She does not blink.

—Sunilji, as Financial Oversight expert, will you not agree that split-ting the Company is absurd at this stage? she says.

—Absurd is as absurd does, says Sunilji. Nothing is absurd here.

—Get me all figures for the Kashmir hotel, she says. It is already over budget and invoices are not being monitored correctly. The news around this construction has always been against us, and I am concerned about its legality. This is on your watch, all three.

Kishoreji wants to explain it to her, she can see in his face. He wants to tell her that in the year 2000, the state law was changed so that Kash-miri women who married outside, for example as her dear Mama married Bapuji, would still be able to buy land inside the state. Where before this had been prohibited under Dogra laws of 1846, when the Hindu Maha-rajas bought the territory and its people "direct" from the British with the Treaty of Amritsar. Gargi has Jeet to thank again for this knowledge, and she trusts it—Jeet, who used to pretend he was a distant descendant of those Dogras—their rule lasted for one hundred years, until the begin-ning of "India." Jeet, who has gone on a bloody trip just at the moment he is most needed—nevertheless Gargi thanks him, silently, while she watches Kishoreji's mouth moving, explaining what she already knows. In any case, his answer is incomplete, because the real question is: *What is the case if the law changed when that woman was ten years dead already?* This is what Gargi does not ask, what Kishoreji does not explain. It is too late. The hotel is only months from being finished. Bapuji wanted a November opening, to make the most of the drama of snow.

—Perhaps we should halt all construction, Gargi says. We should wait. I am sure Bapuji will reverse his decision. Something might give.

No one mentions Sita. *What do they know?*

Three pairs of eyes on her, behind her father's desk. She smiles her best smile and says,

—Sunilji, please share your thoughts.

—Ah, Madam, says Sunilji. The opening of the Company Srinagar hotel—it cannot be halted now. The financing chain is finer than the filigree on a bridal nath from nose to hair. We cannot pull it, for fear of drawing blood.

What it would take to stop this business—too late—she knows—for it is not just financing, but staffing too. Company policy has seen hundreds of workers shipped into Kashmir from Maharashtra. A whole new town has sprung up for them. Informal shops selling their songs and their Gods. Schools in Hindi and Marathi; restaurants serving their food. There have been local protests and some bad press. But all men love a dhaba, whoever is the cook.

Now a question hangs over Gargi, like the mountains above the city where her Mama died. Does she love her country? No one has ever convinced her that they know what her country is, or could be. Does she love the Company? Her sisters? Both.

She reaches across the table. Pulls the papers towards her. Holds them in a vertical stack.

What will happen if I sign? All will fall.

—I want to know, she says. Every link in that money chain. Make me a full report. Show me how delaying on the Kashmir hotel is more complicated than splitting the whole Company between—

She stops herself from saying *two* or *three*. She catches the men's eyes and the thought comes again. *What do they know?* In Srinagar this question is debated over kahwa and cigarettes. Jeet goes there, he knows what they talk about in the coffee houses, where a girl walking by might taste tobacco just by breathing through her mouth. Gargi does not smoke, she never has, though Radha once dared her to try. Once, before Sita left for Cambridge, she found the two of them together, Sita and Radha, on Radha's small terrace at the Farm, sitting and smoking and laughing together. They stopped when she appeared.

—The Farm, she says. What about the family-owned properties, apart from the hotels? Where do we stand on those?

Kishoreji says that though she might successfully stall the generous *sharing* of the Company that Bapuji has mapped out, she cannot stop the gifts of his personal wealth from being distributed. The Company Kashmir hotel, the Farm, Delhi townhouse, and the Napurthala Palace (under renovations since the last seven years) shall go to their named beneficiaries according to Bapuji's design.

—With due respect, says Kishoreji. Bapuji is both wise and good, avoiding conflict by deciding now. Hindu Undivided Family law would do so equally between you and your sisters, married or unmarried, if ever your father should expire. But with no son to be the karta, and sons-in-law not counted, there would naturally be a difficulty between you girls in trying to share.

Karta. The law of inheritance and power of authority passed to the eldest male in a family. *In my lifetime this may change,* Gargi thinks. As the eldest, why shouldn't she be the karta and decide who gets what and how much and when, and not have to consult with anyone? This future imaginable would mean Bapuji gone. She looks up to the ceiling. Bhishma, now hidden behind a white emulsion, is still dying, after all these years.

From the dark of the office, she steps into the slanted sun. Satwant is already waiting, holding the car door open for her. He chooses the Parliament route, they get traffucked by the metro construction. It will take over an hour to reach home. She takes a can of Coke from the car fridge, presses it to her forehead. A man on a scooter pulls up alongside the car. He raises his visor and stares in through her window. She stares back until the jam starts moving and leaves him behind. She shuts her eyes as they cross Rajpath, Rashtrapati Bhavan just over the hill. As they inch towards the artery roads, she slides the car window down. The sun is a golden gulab jamun sinking in a syrupy sky, the smell of sweat and traffic fumes deep-frying under the smog. It coats her skin, a layer of dirt made from the breath of thousands of striving humans. There are the college boys in their knock-off Nikes, standing ten-deep at the side of the road, waiting to catch the bus home to the outer colonies of the city. There are the college girls, Fab India block-print kameez and jeans, heading for wood-fired pizza in Khan Market, maybe smoked salmon bagels in Haus Khas Village; perhaps crowding into the ladies' carriage of the metro, hungry at the end of the day.

She puts the window up again. Her dream of a city is no more than this: New Delhi in its sunken layers, every roundabout and enclave, every scooter and auto and bike. She wants to say to the swarms, *Tell me your story and I'll tell you mine: I am the reason you are riding that bike—we make the parts. I am the reason your truck is running so smoothly—we designed the engines. I am the reason you can dream of your perfect wedding venue, your honeymoon destination—because my hotels are the best. Whose story is whose? Mine is yours and yours, mine.*

The Coke goes down in gulps. Sugar and guilt. It tastes so good, even without lemon and ice.

—Make sure there is ice and lemon in the car next time, Satwant, Gargi says.

She presses 1 on her phone.

—Uppal?

—Gargi Ma'am, are you on your way?

—Kyun? What's wrong? Nanu?

—No, although she is still not eating. Both breakfast and lunch she refused. It is your father, Gargi Ma'am.

O God. What now?

—He went to your studio. He ordered the women to stop packing. Ten of the Hundred came with him, and they took Sita Ma'am's wedding ladoos. For cricket.

She lets out a bark of shocked laughter. Drops of Coke spill and settle on her hands like Bapuji's liver spots. She licks them.

—What? Why are you not making sure he's not doing any nautanki?

—Gargi Ma'am, this is not that. There are ladoos all over the lawn, all over the jubilee garden. Stuck on the rose bushes also. You know this time I think he has truly gone mad.

—Uppal. Since when do you speak like this of Bapuji?

Silence, weighted and waiting. Uppal came from Kashmir with her mother. He wears his story as a warrior's shawl. He was a boy then, and a young man when he joined the Company. He was placed in a general assistant manager role, to watch over her mother's interests, he told her, as a requirement of the marriage bargain. He was old before Gargi married. He was there to guide her from the first day of work. It is thanks to Uppal that Gargi knows the Company from back page to front.

—Where is my husband? Gargi says.

Uppal snorts.

—Call him, she says. Tell him I want him to come to dinner. And tell him what Bapuji is doing, if he has not already noticed for himself.

—Ma'am, I gave Satwant a file for you to look at. Did you see it?

She raps on the safety glass. Satwant, keeping his eyes on the road, lowers it and hands her a yellow folder full of papers.

—Satwant, next time, papers pehle dena chahiye, she says.

She ends the call. The traffic lights change, the car horns honk, the traffic does not move. A hawker smacks a picture of Bapuji's face against her window. *TIME: The Kashmir Issue.* Gargi stares at the photo. She would never buy the magazine off the street. Does not have to read the article to know it will tell of the suffering in Srinagar under Indian barricades, checkpoints and roadblocks probably cast in Company factories while the Company hotel rises above them. In their decimated city, the girls who were born in the same year as her, as Radha, as Sita, are now grown women. The piece will not tell of the Srinagar Gargi loves, where she first learned to disappear, to go through the perforated streets wrapped in layers that hid her, for in Srinagar people can walk (though they cannot stop. To gather.). Past the coffee houses where old boys meet to remember, or try not to. Past the long-closed cinemas, showing only sandbags and barbed wire. Through the market, around the lake, to the crumbling museums that Jeet used to take her into, full of found coins and fine swords, guarded by old women younger than her. Their bodies written with the stories that end in fire and tears.

Satwant edges forward, the hawker moves on. Gargi's eyes throb. She dredges the Coke. The car seems to rock slightly: thunder, calm, thunder again. Outside is a crush of men, voices are being raised. An accident? There are hundreds of people walking in the road, stopping the traffic. They are all moving in the same direction, the opposite of hers. So many heads, so many eyes, mouths, noses, men and women going together on foot.

—What is it, Satwant? she says.

—Ma'am, anti-corruption protest, I believe.

Her view is blocked by someone's back, pressing against the car window. On the other side, there is a crush of college boys and girls, office workers, even domestics on the streets, shoulders against each other, some are protecting fragile flames, some carry printed banners and signboards on sticks. A man in a shirt and chinos is wearing an Indian flag as a superhero cape; another drapes his flag like a chunni over his head. Gargi sees maids carrying ruffled babies, there are even men with tired suits, hair combed over like her three directors, every building in the city seems to have turned itself inside out and onto the street. Her hand goes to the door, then she pulls back. She cannot get out. *Sita would.* Sita might actually be in this crowd—in a new family of shouting, marching, slogan boards. Allowing bodies to rub against her, hands reaching, salwar-top tearing, what if then—what if—what then?

Gargi sees a bunch of girls, dark-skinned, in bright colours, clips in their hair and adorned with beaded jewellery—walking, draped all over each other as they claim the road. A lighter-skinned woman is holding hands with one of the dark ones, her long hair is loose—she is in jeans and pinstripe shirt. How fierce they look, how free. Is it Sita? Gargi presses her hands against the glass—she wants to order Satwant to press his foot down, to drive away from the crowd and the Farm, on a different direction—say, to the Ridge—from there to the river, to the parts that are clogged with the city's effluence, disturbing the rats and rag pickers. She cannot imagine what voices she would hear. How those peoples' eyes might see her.

Sita has been down there, to the water that can kill. She has tried to describe it to her sisters, begged them at least to sit together and watch *Salaam Bombay!* But she is Gargi Devraj Grover. She has no time.

Wait, is that Sita? No.

Gargi sits back. She sees a handpainted sign, red in letters and numbers: *SMS NO on 555 to support the movement!* She texts her NO to the number, almost hiding the phone from herself.

The car inches forward. Gargi sighs, and opens the file Uppal has sent. A few clipped pages, topped with a photograph of a man in a singlet and dhoti, covered in purple-and-green bruises, all the peacock colours. He is curled up on a split-cane bed. Gargi's eyes skim the typed note: *Night of July 15 Tuesday Party, trying to give daal makhani and chawal to Nanuji when khichdi was ordered. The manservant G.3.5 given name Bilal Kakri was beaten with a gold Napurthala Palace candlestick c. 1925 belonging to Nanu suite. Witnesses: Three (Nanuji, B.1.4 and A.5.2), who say Devraj Bapuji was not the perpetrator. Injuries: three broken ribs, cheekbone, collarbone. Severe bruising on the back and shoulders and behind the knees.*

Date of injuries: 28 June. Compensation finalised: 25 July: agreed one-off payment and additional relocation funds. Further actions: none needed, servant has left Company employ for home village (Jharkhand state) as per contract agreement. (Appendix A: signed gagging agreement note marked with G.3.5 fingerprint, left hand third digit ineradicable ink.)

Outside, the protest has moved on, leaving a broken jigsaw of cars on the road.

What is the difference between daal-chawal and khichdi? Grain size. Texture. Pressure and steam.

—Satwant, I'm getting too late now. Use the horn sometimes.

Satwant steers the car through a tiny gap. He mounts the curb past a coconut-stand, its round fruits so many severed monkey heads. She sees the seller, caught in mid-action, eyes wide, arm strained, hammer raised above his head.

So. Bapuji struck one of her men. G.3s are employed directly by Gargi for special tasks: serving Nanu, giving her a bath and so on. Gargi touches the bruises on the photo. Presses 1. She covers the mouthpiece with one hand, speaks into it, low.

—What should I do? Uppalji, please advise me. I don't want to see Bapuji right now. Just tell him I'm down. O God. If you don't want to speak about women's things that way, just tell him a cow has jumped over the moon.

—Please don't take it too hard, Uppal says. So much has gone under your father's watch. What is one more life, here?

They turn off the highway. She kicks the front seat. Satwant's eyes flick up to the rearview mirror; blank as if he is watching TV in a language he does not understand. Gargi forces herself to stop. She gets out her compact and lipsticks a smile firmly back onto her face. Yes, it is true. There have been protests against the Company over the years. In Orissa, sorry, Odisha, when the first cement factories were established. *Locals against progress,* said Bapuji, said Ranjit Uncle. *Yes,* Gargi thinks. *People have died, it is true.* Swamps have been drained, rare species lost, children uprooted from their ancestral homes. The Company has done these things—her father always told her to think more of how communities relocate and eventually flourish thanks to them. But this one man, this Bilal Kakri. This was Gargi's man.

They crawl past Dilli Haat: it is Nagaland week for the tourists to shop. Her phone in her hand. One last call. It rings, twice, four times, five. Then Radha answers.

—Hi, Big Sis! What's up?

—Hey, Gargi says. She sucks in her stomach. Goa party starting or finishing? OK, don't answer that.

You could have called, Gargi thinks. And then, *Go on. Ask me how I am.*

Laughter, the sounds of other people talking: Radha is at the end of a long lunch—or maybe just starting on evening drinks. She sounds breathless.

—Things are pretty good, she says. I'm working on the guests for the Kashmir opening. We're using the same gold-edged cards we ordered for Sita's engagement to invite the A-list.

—And the gift boxes? Gargi says.

—Yes, all done. Titanium for the VVIPs getting thank-you suites in

Goa, Mumbai and Delhi. That was Dad's express wish. White gold for the A-list, they're so cute, Gargi, you should see them. About pinkie size, and set with the semi-precious stones. Silver for the B-list: Srinagar VIPs and that level. All those joining us by satellite from the Mumbai, Delhi, Goa and Amritsar hotels on opening night get gold- or silver-plated, some will get bronze.

—What about staff?

—I thought we agreed we would use the ladoo for the staff. They'll be fresh enough.

Gargi can hear the sound of a piano down the line, a deep trill of notes, the kind used for the break-ups and make-ups in the boy–girl movies she loves—and she watches—alone, and only on Sundays, when work can be done from home. She imagines her sister at the pool bar, baring her teeth over a cosmopolitan so she does not smudge her lipstick.

—Radha, she says, we can't. Daddy's not coping. He's batting the ladoo all over the Farm.

—Batting what? Aw, silly Daddy. Don't worry, I'll call him up.

—I can't monitor him. And there's something else—the birds, the tower—do you want to hear this? Because I really can't tell you how bad I am feeling.

—Gargi, if you can't cope, you need to get more staff.

—It's not that. You're not here, you can't see.

—I do see, though. You should give him a break. He's bound to be upset right now. Does he know we haven't signed the papers yet? Have you even tried to talk to him?

—Please listen, Rads. I don't have a lot of time. I'm trying to get to grips with the office. I can't be at home every day for lunch.

—And I can? I'm working here too, you know.

—I didn't mean that. But Nanu is also not eating, I'm fighting with the board. And I'm worried about Sita.

—Chill out about Sita, Radha says. Her tone softens. Gargi, I've said this to Bubu and I'll say it to you. She just wants to prove a point. I've SMS'd her a bunch of times in the last month, she just texts back —*No reception*. I'm like, thanks, we already got that message. She is fine.

—O God, Gargi sighs. At least she is answering you. You're right. She will come back. And Radha—when she does, we will sort out Dad's mess, between us.

—Yes, Ma'am. Whatever you say.

There is a pause.

—So, how's Jivan *bhaiyya*? Radha says.

The way her voice sounds on the word "brother." Suggestive, sly. Gargi's hand tightens on her phone. Glad that Radha cannot see her.

—Also fine, she says. I'll catch him later.

—You do that, Big Sis, Radha laughs. Got to go, OK? More soon.

Gargi sits in the back of the car. Watching the light falter through the plane trees, fracture on the road. As they pass the Qutb complex, she notices that the boundary wall is crumbling. She curls her feet under her and leans against the window. Here the city widens into the outer reaches: where there used to be desert, irrigation pipes were laid and houses sprang up. Around the minar itself was the space where ruler after ruler added his mark. A Temple, a pillar. An ornate doorway. To praise God, or to make the commissioner immortal, Gargi cannot tell.

The car slows as they pass a modest Gurdwara. The women are preparing to pray. They roll up their salwars to wash their feet, then their faces, their movements economical, a dance of bending, slinging water, rubbing down, standing up. How they smile and talk, help each other straighten chunnis and hair. As she is carried past them, Gargi looks back. She sees the evening sun set the golden dome aflame. All around it, the crows stretch their wings. They float slowly downwards, pieces of ash from a pyre.

When they reach the Farm, Gargi does not go to her rooms. Instead, she walks through the garage. She takes a cart. Drives around the Farm perimeter until she gets to the rose garden. She wants to see the crumbs of ladoo strewn all over the grass, the sweet globes speared on thorns. What a mess. She resists picking one up and stuffing it into her mouth. She carries on, past the sundial courtyard, the cart taking her to Jivan.

In the bunker, Sai Baba has abdicated to a flatscreen TV, set to *Star-Sports:* tiny men, padded and caged, run at each other, lobbing a white ball across a pitch. She knows she should stop to see who is winning. She has never cared about fucking cricket. Still, when the crowd cheers, for a moment it feels as if the day is just starting. Nothing has happened: no meetings, no ladoo, no traffic or evidence files. There is nothing coming next. Her smile widens. *Like a clown,* she thinks. *I must look like a clown.* On a low table there is a picture of a bloated woman in a polished silver frame. Jivan's mother—ill, unrecognisable. She picks it up carefully, then puts it back.

Downstairs she punches in the code for the basement door. The light flashes red: No Entry. She presses 2 on her phone and hears Jivan's mobile ringing on the other side.

—Open sesame!

And there he is.

—You've changed the door code, she says.

—Haye-haye! You cut your hair! Jivan puts his hands to either side of his face, pretending shock at her audacity, again with that fake funny-Indian accent.

Gargi's hand goes to her nape.

—It was your idea, she says.

—OK, peace, you know I like it.

She follows him inside. At this hour, the bunker is almost empty, the night shift not yet started. Jivan walks between the desks, sleeves rolled up and collar loose, hands in pockets as if they are resting on guns in their holsters. He's the baddie in *Unforgiven*—the last movie she actually went to see in a public cinema hall, when she was about sixteen. She notes the muscles of Jivan's forearms. She forces her eyes back to his face.

—Come on, spill, she says. What is going on that could be worse than this? She waves Uppal's file at him.

—All right, Jivan says. Let's work. Come over here, you're gonna wanna see this.

They sit in front of the central screen bank. Sita's room is dark. Radha's rooms are being cleaned; there is the maid, pulling dirty polka-dot underwear out of the bedsheets. Gargi cannot look at Jivan. In the dining room, tables are being set for dinner. She looks at her watch: six o'clock. Dinner is usually served at six thirty sharp for her father. Who gave him lunch? She realises she does not know, or what he had, or how much.

Jivan turns towards Gargi. The day has left her skin dry, her head paining. *Kiss me,* she thinks. She crosses her legs. Her eyes fix on a postcard of a snow scene, a Swiss chalet on a mountain tucked in a work-station corner.

Jivan gestures to the TV on the far right.

There is Bapuji, made shorter and fatter by the camera angle, march-ing to and fro across the screen. His shirt hanging from his pants, his chest smeared in a sticky yellow paste that must actually, she realises, be ladoo. He paces up and down the Old Drawing Room spouting some nonsense to twenty of his Tuesday boys. She identifies the worst of them—Kishan, with the heiress wife and seventy branches of the family shoe franchise going bust, who feels he must always act up. Wady, eldest son of Wadra Sahib, CEO of Indiatechnow: when he chews, he does a good impression of a sheep eating grass, it always makes Bapuji laugh. She watches one of them, Akash, she thinks—*isn't he a particular friend of Jeet's?*—lean on a seventeenth-century Gujarati wood sculpture of a woman hung with necklaces and with wide almond eyes, balancing on one leg while playing a dhol. Akash has his jacket off, his shirt half-open, although the evening is only just beginning. He strokes the round cheek of the statue and the others, predictably, laugh.

With a shock Gargi realises. It is Tuesday. Today. They are waiting for the party to begin. No one has given the word for the music, the food, the stage to be set. They are all waiting—for her.

Her eyes meet Jivan's; they are flecked with green and fringed with dark lashes. They still have the same naughty twinkle as when he and Radha used to play bat and ball or skip-rope contest, and she would come to umpire. She wants to sink into the stories of those days, the deep end of the pool. Hear how he thought about her then. She wants to grow gills, never have to come up for air.

—Look at them. She watches Bapuji, his arm deformed by the cam-era angle into a truncated instrument that shakes as he points. His voice rises as he dispatches one of the boys to hunt for food: the house phone sits on a table next to him, sulking with lack of use.

—What a *cock* my dad can be, she says, and giggles; then she begins to laugh properly at Jivan's shocked face. What? Good girls can say bad words, you know.

—When was the last time you laughed? he says.

—It has been reported to happen, yaar.

—I'm not your "yaar."

He pronounces it *yare,* as if the long "ah" would give too much away.

—Then what are you? My yeah? It is fun to talk with him like this—to play, almost, at being Radha.

—I feel like you have never been away, she says. And as if you have been gone forever. Too long, yaar.

For her, the long *a* is a slow, sliding acquiescence, as the sound of the word "ya."

—Don't get all serious. Gargi, come on. You know our dads are like—

Jivan puts his palms together like a Christian praying, then laces his fingers into one big fist.

—I'm just glad you are here, she says.

He swivels in his chair. Towards her, away. He frowns.

—My dad wants me to go up to join him. Learn about the Company in the north. Would that be OK with you?

Gargi thinks of Jivan working from Amritsar. Perhaps helping to get the new Srinagar hotel ready from there. She thinks of herself staying in Delhi, working alone.

—Can't we put Ranjit Uncle off a while? she says. I would like, I mean, the Company needs you here.

—He's my dad. Then, this thing with Jeet . . . He's actually in deep shit.

Jeet. It has been weeks since the night Sita left. She has called Jeet—no answer. And texted—no answer. The day of the peacocks, she remembers—since that she has stopped—hurt that he hadn't called back.

—I *knew* something was wrong, she says. Is he OK? If he is back in Delhi, he should be here with us.

—He's fine, as far as I know. But, Gargi, I think, he's been . . . I don't know how to tell you this. Stealing.

—*What?*

Shock after shock today might turn her hair completely white. Like Nanu. She will be known as the grandmother of all sorrows.

Jivan's laced fingers open and shut like some kind of deep-sea creature, mouthing water to breathe. His face a mask of concern, he tells her that Jeet has gone. That, according to Kritik Uncle's files, Jeet has been smuggling artefacts and antiques without a license, offering far more than the correct level of bribe. He has been using Company channels and Ranjit Uncle's personal savings. On the night of Sita's Tuesday Party,

Jivan says, Jeet had wanted him to join in—and when he refused, Jeet had taken off.

Jivan's dark-lashed, green eyes narrow, his lips tremble as the story spills out.

Gargi has known Jeet every day of her life. For God's sake, her own father named him. She has been tying handmade rakhi on him since they were small, binding him to her as her brother—in the promise to protect her from all rakshas—that part of the ceremony always made them laugh. She would wind her threads—*No glitter—I hate it,* Jeet always said, around his skinny wrist, watched by Nanu, and then they would have to sit through the story of the ritual before she could open Jeet's gift to her, which was of course—year after year—jewellery—including all she is wearing now, except for her wedding ring. The gold hummingbird pendant. The pearl earrings set in platinum, *so unusual.* She once even dreamed she might be married to him, even as she knew it couldn't happen. She is proud that she was among the first to know about his other life. He told her when they were sixteen, in the dark of Priya cinema hall, pushing her off him, wiping his cheek of her saliva. Whispering, *Fucking stop it, Gargi, have some self-respect. I don't like you* that *way. You stupid idiot, don't you get it?* At first she thought he had only said it to make her stop mooning over him. Then he said he would never even *practice* French-kissing with her, and, tears dripping down both their faces while the bad guy told the good guy (who was about to shoot him), *I'll see you in hell,* Jeet spelled out to her why. Yes, that was the *Unforgiven* day. Jeet's choice of film.

Jeet. In trouble. Stealing from the Company. How can she have been so blind all this time? She thinks again of Sita, walking out of the house. Of Bapuji, using a candlestick to beat a man almost dead. Did any of them love anyone at all?

—You have to go to your father, she says.

Jivan smiles at her, head on one side.

You don't pity me, she thinks. *No.*

—You should get to Ranjit Uncle as soon as you can. I'll send Radha up to Amritsar. She can carry on the prep for Srinagar from there. Talk to Bubu, he'll work out a strategy. No wonder my Finance guy was looking so shifty all day. He must know Amritsar is bleeding money.

—What are you going to do? Jivan says.

—Don't you concern about it. I'll have to think about how to handle it. Maybe through the Assistant Secretary for Heritage—I know his daughter. Bubu can put checks on the airports and borders, if Jeet hasn't gone abroad already. We can't let this turn official.

—You guys really are the dons, he grins. Would you do that to find Sita?

—Of course not, Gargi says. She hasn't committed a crime. Radha is in touch with her. She is OK. Probably still in Delhi or Mumbai, hopefully with some school friend. She will return when she is ready. But Jeet—he could have gone anywhere. He's better travelled than all of us.

—Thanks, Jivan says.

—I'm just doing my best to keep my family together. Keep the Company tickety-boo.

Tickety-boo, she thinks, *who says that?*

—Gargi Ma, he says. Come here.

She lets him pull her up. Put his arm around her shoulders. She feels him pressing her into his side. His ribs through the shirt, his chest. She could turn her face to him, stand on tiptoe, they would be eye to eye.

—O shit, he says. Look!

He points behind her.

On screen Uppal sprawls on the floor. Above him stands an older man in a dirty kurta, a battered topi, his face wrapped in a shawl like a chaukidar in winter. Have the seasons changed while Gargi has been underground with Jivan? Will she walk outside to see her own breath in the air?

—Who is that? Jivan says. Punj's old *boss*?

—*Kashyap?* O my God, everything is going to hell, Gargi says. I let him go—he's come back again. Why don't these people take me seriously?

—Stop. Don't worry about him. He can't get re-employed without your agreement, or mine. Why is he dressed like that, though?

—Probably drunk. Who knows?

Uppal. Get up now, Gargi thinks. They watch Uppal get to his feet. They watch Bapuji shaking with laughter. Kashyap and other men are clearly laughing with him.

Uppal stumbles out of the room. He pushes past Nanu. Watching, Gargi puts her hand over her mouth. Nanu. *But*—she reminds herself— her grandmother has a habit of looking as frail or strong as she wishes. Was there ever a time when she did not have white hair? Nanu is one of the last of a species, forever trembling on the brink of extinction. *Yet Nanu is more likely to live longer than any of us,* Gargi thinks. Even without Bapuji she will endure.

Gargi cannot look at Jivan. She slides her hand into his. She ignores the rub of her wedding ring. They watch. Nanu is like wire, bending into her seat, helped by one of the boys—Gargi thinks perhaps Ritesh, who likes to bait the younger members of the Hundred, she has heard, with any weak point he can find (a fat sister-in-law, a divorced aunt). Ritesh settles Nanu in an armchair, her white sari so thin against the silk brocade. *At least she is up, and that means she might want food.* Nanu raises her arms as if to cue an orchestra. Gargi wonders what lesson her grandmother is giving. Maybe one of the boys has come to her with some wedding hope. In such a case, Nanu would speak the words of her favourite warning, which Gargi knows by rote. *The dog has a human heart, she must not be allowed to get ideas above her station. The mongoose eats mice, just as the cat eats the mongoose; the dog devours the cat, and wild beasts eat the dog.*

Nanu sits back in the armchair. The boys, about twenty of them sitting around her feet, clap. Nanu smiles and raises her palms, gesturing, *Enough, enough.*

—Enough. I can't watch anymore, Gargi says. I have to get rid of them. She stands up.

—Do you want me to come?

She looks down at Jivan. Feels faintly surprised that there were years when she did not have him in front of her. But no, she decides. This she must do herself.

—I've even wondered how much cash it would take, she says. To make them stay away. Hundreds times hundreds maybe.

—You can buy anything, can't you? Jivan says lightly.

Gargi pulls herself as tall as she can, away from him.

—Listen to me, Jivan, don't act surprised now. You were born here, you lived here before. This is your country too. Fast-forward every day— and going nowhere. We talk about the government being corrupt here, and we ourselves are forced to bribe each other for everything. To get contracts, we pay. To get paid, we pay. Fake invoices at the bottom, empty partner companies listed trading shares in the middle, untouchable at the top. Even in billion-dollar multinationals it happens like this. There isn't a VP of finance across the board without dirty hands. You should meet the three fakirs I had to deal with today. You think this is the only secret bunker on the Farm? My God, the whole of the ballroom floor slides back. Built on bricks of gold. You ever need cash quickly, I'll give you the codes for that. You know we have an entertainment farm, right? West Gurgaon? That's where your dad takes the CEOs to relax. Models, drugs, blue movies on the big screen: whatever they want. Sorry, but it's true. The pile-ons come here for Tuesday talks and mingling, but they go there, to Gurgaon, for "elite Company training." Tax law, industrial statutes, you think that's what they learn? Not at Devraj's special school for turning good boys into future leaders. Here we say *Aise hi chalta hain!* So what? It's all good! This is India, Jivan, try to understand.

She crosses her hands over her throat. Rests her chin on them, stopping her own voice. Starts again.

—Sorry. I'm very tired. You should go to Amritsar, and sort out the mess with Jeet. He at least needs to answer for what he has done. When Radha reaches there, tell her and Bubu all of it, including what's going on here. Even better, take digital files, they need to see for themselves.

She gathers her jacket and bag and tries to smile. It is almost too much to ask of the muscles in her face.

—What are you going to do? Jivan says.

—What else? she says. Go make sure dinner is organised. Tend to my father and see that Nanuji is not getting tired out. It's Tuesday.

She laughs.

—My God, I just want—I just wish he would be a father, for once.

—Why do you care about his approval so much? Jivan says. Gargi, I bet you know the names of ninety percent of the employees down to middle management across every hotel, parts factory and shop that you own. That's more than your father could say. You're a beautiful, wealthy grown-up woman. Not some shit-for-brains, sorry, heiress; a real businesswoman, in charge of something important. You could've done anything you want in the world. Shopped at Barney's. Partied in Dubai. Got a summer tan in the Maldives and a winter one on the slopes. Gone for the culture or the couture in Paris or London or Milan. But you want nothing more than to carry on the family business. In the States, you'd be on the cover of *Newsweek* by now. Real estate moguls would be kissing your ass.

Don't stop, she thinks. *Talk more than you should, talk more than is*

*decent, talk and talk until it seems you are talking to tell the world what it
should see just by looking.*

—You wanted the Company: you've got it. So make the most of it.
You don't need your father, or Nanu's blessing, he says.

—They've always been like this. Old guard, you know? And they've
also been through a lot.

—Don't make excuses, Jivan says. Not for that.

He gestures at the screen. Nanu is doing her best impression of
Pinku, Sita's little dog, pretending to pant after Ritesh.

—I better go, Gargi says.

She is not like Sita: brave enough or stupid enough to let her heart
spill out of her mouth. She is Gargi, and that means she should not say
any more.

—Fine. But don't let them bully you.

She went to Mumbai after bombs ripped the Company hotel to Lego
bricks and dust. When they were rebuilding, she stood on the scaffolding
high above the city, like the bad big brother from *Slumdog Millionaire.*
Wind, and the view, and the silence: *surely from this height,* she'd thought,
she could fly.

—I won't, she says.

—I'll be watching. Go Gargi, Go Gargi Go!

He pummels the air, an American cheer. One arm around her shoulders, he walks her to the door.

—I'll meet you in Amritsar, she says. Give my *hi* to your dad.

The bunker door swings shut between them. Gargi kisses her palm;
gently presses it to the frame. As she walks upstairs, the warm night air
meets her skin. Outside, a breeze ruffles the prairie grass. She can hear
the frogs croaking on their way to the pond.

She is alone. The quiet dark calms her. When she reaches the house,
she calls Uppal. Checks he is not hurt. Tells him not to begin the party
set-up, that there will be no party tonight. She follows the corridors to
the room where Nanu is singing: an old, old ghazal in a voice smooth
and harsh as incense smoke, silvering through the cracks in the door. It
catches in Gargi's throat.

It is almost at the end. She cannot go in. Hasn't she sat so often at the close of the evening, caught in her grandmother's song? Finding it more and more difficult to sit and listen: less and less able to get up and leave with every year Nanu ages. Wanting to print each verse onto a sari—wrap it around her body—never take it off.

Ye ishq kii kahaaniyaan,	*These are stories of love,*
Ye ras bharii javaaniyaan	*Tales of youth, drunk in pleasure,*
Udhar se meharabaaniyaan,	*Some filled with clemency, endurance.*
Idhar se lantaraaniyaan	*Others coloured with vanity, arrogance.*
Abhii to main javaan hoon	*I am young,*
Abhii to main javaan hoon	*I am still young.*
Ye aasmaan ye zamiin,	*These skies, this earth,*
Nazzaraahaa-e-dilanashiin	*These sights so close to the heart,*
Une hayaat aafariin,	*This beautiful life—*
Bhalaa main chhod duun yahiin?	*How can I leave behind all this art?*
Hai maut is qadar qariin,	*I shall never believe*
Mujhe na aaegaa yaqiin	*That death can be so near.*
Nahiin-nahiin abhii nahiin,	*Not now, not so soon,*
Nahiin nahiin abhii nahiin	*Never, not here!*
Abhii to main javaan hoon	*I am young,*
Abhii to main javaan hoon	*I am still young,*
Abhii to main javaan hoon	*I am still young,*
Abhii to main javaan hoon	*I am still so young.*
Gham kushuud-o-bast kaa,	*I sorrow neither about distance, nor proximity,*
Baland kaa na past ka	*Neither about the nadir, nor the zenith.*
Na buud kaa na hast kaa,	*I fret not about my life, its status, or my existence,*
Na vaadaa-e-alast kaa	*Or even about promises of future creations.*

Ummiid aur yaas gum,	*I neither hope, nor despair.*
Havaas gum qayaas gum	*I have lost both logic and intuition.*
Nazar se aas-paas gum,	*I see nothing, near nor far—I'm*
	blinded,
Hamaan bajuz gilaas gum	*I see nothing save that goblet.*
Na may mein kuchh kamii	*Let this liquor never fail me,*
rahe,	
Kadaa se hamadamii rahe	*Let my bonds with this bar forever*
	remain,
Nishast ye jamii rahe,	*Let this party never end,*
Yahii hamaan hamiin rahe	*Let us gather here again and again.*
Vo raag chhed mutaribaa,	*That song, Madame, sing that song*
	once more,
Tarab-fizaa, alam-rubaa	*Which exhilarates my being,*
Asar sadaa-e-saaz kaa,	*Drowns the woes from my core.*
Jigar men aag de lagaa	*Music and rhythm have always been*
	the coal
	That sparks the fire in my soul.
Na haath rok saaqiyaa	*Do not stop, bar-tender,*
Pilaae jaa pilaae jaa,	*Let the drinks overflow,*
Pilaae jaa pilaae jaa	*Let me drink some more, oh,*
Abhii to main javaan hoon	*For, I am young,*
Abhii to main javaan hoon	*I am young,*
Abhii to main javaan hoon	*I am still young,*
Abhii to main javaan hoon	*I am still so young.*

The song fades. A breath, then the roars begin. *Move, Gargi.* She swallows her memories of sitting at Nanu's feet learning these precious words, when she had imagined a time when she might sit, her own family around her, and sing them herself. Back then, Bapuji used to call her his *Gargi, Precious Canary.* Never again.

.   .   .

She pushes open the door.

Though it is not yet dark outside, the red brocade curtains in the room have been drawn. Lamplight casts gold bangles carelessly around, leaving deep shadows. Diyas burn on the sideboards, the walls flicker with dying flames. Framed in gilt, Gargi's paternal grandfather glowers above the stone fireplace, dark skin offset by the crown on his head, blue silk robe falling open to show off his tweed three-piece, his Imperial sash, his sword at his belt. His moustache is waxed; the expression on his face just like Bapuji's after a good dinner. His right foot rests on a dead English bird, like a peacock but red-breasted, with red flopping over its eyes. His chocolate spaniel pants at his heels. In one corner stands his inlaid grandfather clock with its Westminster chime, made by master-craftsmen in England in 1830 with techniques, according to Jeet, borrowed from the Taj Mahal. On a low table his favourite music box; a golden treasure chest with a soldier-monkey perched on the top. When wound by a small jewelled key, the little monkey arms bang cymbals together.

Men sprawl on the chaise longues and on the floor cushions, one smoking a shisha, something never before seen in this house. With the sound of each sucking inhalation, Gargi feels her rage bubble up. A group of three or four sit at her grandmother's feet. She looks for Kashyap, but cannot see him. No one notices her with her new short hair. Then Nanu looks up and raises her hands. The men sit alert, alive to new game.

—Welcome, welcome, look who is here, rasps Nanu. Gargi the Great! Gargi the Magnificent has arrived, let us pay our respects!

She presses her palms together.

—You are truly a great woman, Gargi.

The men at her feet raise their glasses.

—Namaste, namaste, they laugh.

Gargi. Breathe. She turns to her father, watching her by the fireplace. There is no fire, nor has there been for years—the chimney cavity is hung instead with strings of dried chillies like shrivelled tongues. Radha's design, *for fusion,* she said.

—Bapuji, Gargi says. Daddy, please don't let Nanu say these things to me.

—It's a joke, Bapuji says. Come. Sit and tell me all about your day in my office and the progress of our Srinagar campaigns. Don't look like that, you will spoil your face. Face value shouldn't fall even if market value plummets. Book value should remain. O dear, you're going to tell me off! Women with short hair are susceptible to hysterical outbursts, sudden dramatic impulses, all kinds of base thoughts that should not come. Be careful, Gargi.

He cowers behind his hands, as if she, not he, holds power over every body in this room.

—Bapuji, Gargi says. Clearly, Nanu is not well. And all these boys are making a mess. Come on, Daddy, please?

Radha is so much better at this. She starts again.

—I heard today about my manservant.

Bapuji shrugs.

—No idea. What is the problem, Gargi?

—You. What was *your* problem? With my G.3.5? Please send these men away so we can talk.

Bapuji stares at her. Eyebrows raised, one hand goes to his head.

—Like this you talk to your father? Nanu says. Chi!

The men around Nanu shake their heads. She is sure she hears a high-pitched *meow* come from one of them.

—Bapuji, she says, this is my home, also.

—Home-tome, hum-tum, what is that? Yours? My daughter cannot talk like this. Kya tum office mein aise karti ho? Go, change your clothes, wash your face. Then you can speak. And serve dinner. Have you forgotten today is Tuesday? Party will be starting.

Gargi thinks about the wife of the G.3.5. Her song, her hands. Her jutting collarbone: the feel of it under her palm.

—No, she says. Enough. I can't stomach any more. Years this is going on—can't we finally stop? It's getting unseemly, Bapuji.

—Aré gadhi, chal hat! Go rinse your mouth with soap, says Nanu.

The men shift around Nanu's feet. Her grandmother is calling her a donkey. Gargi sees a couple of them drink, trying to hide their smiles.

Bapuji plants his feet in their chappals on the carpet and heaves himself to standing. In his kurta pyjama, his brown Shahtoosh, his hair white, he reminds her of the snow-capped Kashmiri mountains: impenetrable, forever. Her legs feel weak. The men fall silent.

—Main kaun hoon? Bapuji says. I am a father, am I not?

—Yes, sir!

—But can a father be blind? Can a father be deaf? Can a father be dumb?

No one moves; there is no sound but the grandfather clock. Gargi thinks, *That clock must go.*

—I think I must be. I am the ghost of a father who has worked for all time for his daughters.

—Yes, and now they are trying to replace your mother, Nanu says. Instead of bearing their children themselves. Gargi, are you sick? Gargi, are you overeating? Were you dizzy this morning?

The old woman will talk about her periods to anyone who will listen. It is a matter of national concern, it seems, whether or not Gargi conceives. All the men in the room stare at her belly, as if just by looking they can see through her skin to her womb, could plant a seed in there.

—Now, says Bapuji. If I am Devraj the father, then who are you? Come, tell me, tell me.

It is a question she has answered almost every Friday of her childhood.

—You are Devraj. Father to me, to Radha, to—to all of us. Senior of this family. Head of the Company. With all my heart I appreciate you. But, Daddy, I am asking you to send these men home. I need your help. Why are you playing with these boys when you should be living up to your name? Don't laugh—tell me, where did you get this shisha? You turn this place into some kind of dirty—I don't know—cesspit.

She slaps a hand over her mouth. She wants to force the words back in. Her heart rises in her chest, sticks in her throat. Tears trip over her fingers, she rubs her eyes, they sting with mascara but she carries on, rubbing black makeup all over her face. She looks at her father. How ugly she must be.

—You cannot stop lying, can you? he says. All of your life, you can't control your servants, and now you're blaming it on my boys. All of these young men are handpicked from St. Stephen's College. From Hindu College, IIT. Deepak here— (and Deepak grins from his place on the floor, though Gargi knows he is spending every paise his wife will give him on bad investments in tech start-ups) —Deepak attended Doon School. What are you talking, Gargi? Don't make a pasha out of me. All these men are the future captains of this country, here to learn better than you ever have what it takes to run a company. All you are concerned with are your programmes. "Gargi for women," as if this will steady the ship and manage the balance sheet. My God. Are you a daughter or a snake?

She sits down heavily in her father's chair. She watches him stride to the door.

—You beat a man senseless just for doing his job. And those boys try to make *me* serve *them*? she says.

He turns to the men.

—Chalo. Let's go. The Tuesday Party is waiting, others must have come.

Satisfaction floods Gargi's mouth. Its taste is so unusual—nimboo pani, extra salt. Bapuji will go outside and find the unlit burners and empty dishes. There will be no golf carts, no drivers. The lights remain unlit in the courtyard, the stage is not set up. The microphone and speakers are not plugged in. Darkness, silence—nothing more.

—Daddyji, what is going on?

It is Surendra. Gargi's dear husband, just finished with his evening raag. He stoops slightly, his face concerned. Under his arm is *The Hindu*, which he gets each day and reads to guide his writing style. Endless compositions of letters to the editor, practice columns on every topic from liver-cleansing diets to the correct way to wear a starched kurta.

—Surendraji, please let me pass.

—Wait, Papaji, wait. At least tell me what is happening? Surendra's voice is soft, so low that Gargi can hardly hear him. He has always hated any kind of argument: it upsets his digestion.

She wipes her eyes, watching her husband flap his paper, and make Os with his mouth as if blowing bubbles into the air.

—I don't understand, says Surendra.

Bapuji ignores him. He turns to Gargi. His eyes go soft, his face drops. He does not need to speak, for she can hear him without words. *I am very disappointed in you.*

Here they are, her father, her grandmother. Their skin rubbed smooth with years, their hands clenching and unclenching the air. Bapuji's silence around her, heavy as fallen snow. She licks her lips.

Bapuji walks back across the room, towards her.

—You are the one whose name is evil, the one who lies with disease upon your womb, who kills the embryo as it settles, as it rests, as it stirs, who wishes to kill it before it is born; you hunger for the one who spreads apart your two thighs, who lies between the married pair, who licks inside your womb, all for your own unnatural pleasure. And if you think you are going to be the great Mother of my whole company, you are wrong. You cannot be a mother to anyone.

His words are so extreme, the quotation so out of place, Gargi almost starts to laugh. She sucks in her cheeks, she chews them.

Bapuji sees it. He stops in front of her, his shawl across his shoulder. The Shahtoosh she has begged him not to wear, so fine it can be pulled through the O of a woman's wedding ring.

—Everything you touch will turn bad while you continue to refuse your duty, he says. To fulfil what you were put on this earth to do. Gargi, you will never know how much you've hurt me tonight. No barren woman can know how ungrateful children can wound. So much we do for you. Nahin, beti, nahin.

He sniffs as if Chinku the pup has circled, sniffing at the ground then gone to toilet carefully, specifically at his feet.

Daddy, she thinks. *Bitches bare their teeth and bite their own babies to death. What will you do now?*

But the feeling of Sita as a toddler still sits on her chest, clutching her throat, sleepy heavy. Story, story, story she had wanted. She had always wanted. At bedtime, she would only ever let Gargi touch her. And so it follows that Bapuji is right: Sita is Gargi's own fault. She looks at Nanu. *Let it be her fault too, then,* she thinks. And Bapuji's: she looks at her father. *He divided us for his own pleasure. Like meat torn from bone.*

Her father spits,

—Pah! I will first have my party. Then I will leave. I will go to Goa, to Radha. Spend some time in meditation there.

He ignores Surendra as he leaves the room. In ones and twos and threes, the boys in the room arise and follow after.

—Beta, wait toh karo! Nanu calls.

Bapuji does not answer; he leaves her, sitting in the armchair, reaching for him to come back.

—What have you done? Surendra says. What has she done, Nanuji?

—Don't trouble yourself, Surendra*ji.* Gargi links her hands behind her neck. Pressing the tension out of her voice. Let Daddy go to Radha and make a fool of himself. That's his job now.

—Did you sign the paperwork? Surendra asks.

He walks around the drawing room, picking up glasses, putting them down. His living quarters are opposite hers: his bedroom, closet, golf practice area—the outside shower and toilet he prefers, because he likes to see the sky while he sits on the pot. On her wedding night, she had stood naked while Surendra informed her that it was her duty to keep herself clean at all times. He took her to the bathroom and watched while she washed herself according to his directions. He checked her chikkis, where none but she had ever touched. His fingers were hard and matter-of-fact. Her heat quickly faded and turned into her old enemy, the need to do susu came on her. And then Surendra undressed, and made her kneel to wash him in return. Eyes to his *dick*—how foreign she feels when she thinks of that word—but "lund" she called it back then, learned from her Lottie—so soft, so hidden, like a little finger twirled in hair—still she had felt her throat open and close. She had wanted to take it in her mouth and suck it, but also to put her fingers inside herself: her own excitement had risen again.

Then he had led her from the bathroom and made her lie, face down, on the bed. She felt his hip bones press into her thighs. She had spread her legs wider, and waited for the pain Nanu told her to report back on, and waited for the pleasure she had been promised by her Lottie. A hot feeling. She had pressed her face into the pillow; she had chewed it. She had twisted the bedsheets up in her fists.

His lund, when he put it in her, was no more than a little caterpillar that tickled her insides. She had felt like bearing down, like doing susu and laughing at the same time. Then his body had bumped against her bums until he gave a cry and collapsed on top of her, smothering her into softness. Her mouth full of pillow, breasts flattened against the sheets, a dribble of something sticky on her thigh, she had thought: *Honeymoon suites should have firmer mattresses. Complimentary chocolate. Scented candles, a hardback Kama Sutra and massage oils. A sex counsellor for the morning.*

She called it the *Bridal Extra* package. It was rolled out three months later Company-wide, charged at Rs 2500 per unit, and had become one of their bestselling staples, particularly in the northern states.

For seven years she allowed Surendra to bump at her once a month. Every three months she went to the dermatologist—a kind man, the best—who prescribed her the Pill (for her acne, of course.) Then, she turned twenty-five. On that very night, as she blew out her candles, she decided she would never have sex with Surendra again, even if they were the last married couple left at the end of time. With no mother and no child she would be, simply, sister to her sisters. Herself to herself.

—Let him go, Surendra, Gargi says.

He doesn't answer her, or look at her. He leaves the room, his shoes squeaking on the marble floor: eek ek, eek, ek, eeek. Gargi sits in silence. Nanu has her eyes closed, her head back. Minutes pass. Gargi crosses to the long windows. She peers through the red curtains. On the terrace, her father and his boys. Bapuji: waving the very same arms that beat a man black-and-blue, broke his ribs and collarbone. Now he is smacking his hands together, looking to right and left. The boys are spreading out over the terrace, among the stacks of chairs and the unlaid tables, as if they could conjure the party up.

Surendra reaches them. He tries to catch Bapuji's arms in an embrace. Bapuji turns away, and then back, as if he is caught in a skipping rope and someone is pulling each end. He pushes past Surendra, then turns again, he is coming back into the room.

She waits.

He is inside. Coming down the corridor, shouting for everyone to hear.

—Gargi, have you no shame? Cancelling the party—and that saala, Ranjit's boy—now I find you told him to ban fifty of my Hundred— you, a woman with no control. Don't you know whose daughter you are?

She walks out to meet him, tries to take his arm.

—Daddy, she says. The servant's name is Bilal Kakri. He was specially selected for his gentle ways to serve Nanuji. We had to send him back to his village in Jharkhand. What about *his* daughters, hein?

—Don't expect me to cry. I will become blind and sit in the basti, scratching fleas off diseased cats before I cry in front of you.

Now he speaks without a single tremor; he sounds as happy as he does when reporting the Company annual profits to the press.

—I think my name is Devraj, and this Gargi is not my daughter. Chup! Don't speak. Not your turn. Gargi, you have my Farm, my office, my desk, my chair. Now my seminars and my boys. Nahin, beti, nahin. Tum aisa nahin kar sakti ho. Do you think to have the whole Company for yourself? Ungrateful, besharram—

—What? Ungrateful what? she says. She leans towards Bapuji, hands folded across her chest, eyes wide on him, heart almost falling from her mouth.

—Aré chup, randi, chup! he shouts.

Whore. In the deep, wide silence, the word floats down. It comes to rest between Gargi and Bapuji, a peacock feather falling on the grass.

All this while Nanu has been watching from deep in her chair. Now she pushes herself up.

—Gargi, she says. By nature you have always been sly like your mother. Always you speak without respect. You think that boy Jivan, Ranjit's thook, can bar fifty for you and nothing will happen? I know you. Always. So. Let him lick between your thighs and see how you taste. Devraj beta, meri baat toh suno. Let us go to Radha. She at least knows how to serve.

Bapuji crosses to Nanu. With his arm under her back, he helps her rise from her chair. She leans on him, wiping her hand across his face. Together they walk away.

—I will reassign your share to Radha and Bubu, Bapuji says. Let them have it all. Then you will see.

Gargi watches them, her hands over her mouth, body stiff. *Like wire,* she thinks. *I must become like wire.*

Surendra sits on an ottoman, patting his knees, rocking and murmuring,

—Hai Ram! What has happened here? Reassign? Gargi, what is Bapuji saying?

Sita, Gargi thinks. *You have ruined our lives for good.*

She takes out her phone and presses 1.

—Uppal? Please take this down and email it to Radha Madam straightaway, Gargi says. She speaks clearly, loudly. She tells the story of the peacocks, the injuries suffered by Bilal Kakri. It sounds like a list of nothings: she begins to itemise each wound. Fingers broken. Arm, lifted from socket. Ribs cracked, three. Back bruised, side almost pierced. Surendra pushes his palm at her, holds it almost in her face. She covers the phone with her hand.

—What is it?

—Can't you see the mess you're making? he says. Go and say sorry to Bapuji and give the word for the party to set up.

—You want to run after him, she says. You go. But there will be no party tonight.

She waits until he leaves. Then turns back to her call, instructing Uppal to tell Radha and Bubu *to remember, we are strongest when we act together.* Also, to get up earlier and not sleep so late, cut down partying, and most of all, treat Ranjit Uncle tenderly.

—And Uppal? I want you to go up to Amritsar. Tell Radha directly that whatever Daddy says, we are going to announce his retirement at the Srinagar opening. Everyone will hear about it while eating our khaana and drinking our drink. They will see how we do things as a family. Tell Radha to make triple sure the right ministers, judges, writers, cricketers and a good quota of Bollywood types are begging to come. *We've waited long enough.* Tell her to say that to Bapuji, OK?

She shuts the phone. The candles gutter around the room, flames lilting towards the floor. Cushions have been tossed and abandoned; wine glasses lie empty on their sides. Pistachio shells, upturned like tiny boats, lurch over the priceless seas of carpet and cloth. The monkey on his music box stares at her, waiting for permission to clap. She will pack all these relics and hang this room with works by modern masters. She will turn it into a space for her own trainees.

Her arms are limp; her fingers touch a bottle of Company wine by the chair. She picks it up and brings it to her lips, then lets her head fall back, the bottle loose in her hand. Thinks of the brick of papers, waiting for her signature. The red curtains seem to move, to whisper the old warning, "The life of a business house is sixty years." But everything is silenced as Gargi tips the bottle, and drinks. Her eyes go up to the camera in the corner. Who is watching who? *Abhii toh main javaan hoon,* she says. *Now see what I will do.*

— • —

MY STORY IS A SIMPLE ONE, come closer if you can. A story reverber-
ates in the telling, as a blessing, a warning or a curse. It changes shape
and tone, but mine is the voice that will endure, for do not the Vedas say,
"I am not the first of me, and will not be the last"?

I used to have one companion, he was a strong man! Kashyap was
his name, I am surprised I have not forgotten. He was a true man of the
people. Sent by old Kritik, to look after me. He was old and stern, nothing like my boys, but so what? He was from a different side of life, but
he was a good man. No idea what happened to him, but so they come
and go.

The night I left the Farm, I took with me only three things: Nanu,
Kashyap and my good name. We left Delhi and travelled around the
country, checking on our holdings and gathering support. Then we
went north to Amritsar. I had deals to make with associates; I had to
speak to Ranjit about his bastard's place. I wanted Jeet, my Godson, to
come and take up his role, as long as he could behave himself and get
treatment for his illness. I wanted my dear Radha to open her door,
welcome me inside, make good on her promise to secure our dynasty,
even if her sisters so stubbornly refuse to yield.

Middle child, what are you for? I ask myself. Radha eats too much
sweet. She needs to take care not to allow her husband to dominate her.
This I have told her so many times. Told and told and told.

Sometimes I look at her, and feel surprised. She is beautiful, in a
new sort of way. Skin over bone. She is loyal, for her brain is not first

class. She is clever rather than intelligent; this is a strength for her sex. Company shawls are woven for endurance, warmth, finesse and modest beauty. Radha has few of these qualities, not all, though she keeps her husband happy and plays her part. This is why I decided I would gift the shawls business to Sita. I knew little Radha would be hurt, but this was the only way to keep her in line. O, and one more thing—though Radha makes the most noise of my three little birds, remember this: her tweets are empty as air.

III

—·—

RADHA

i

The blinds are down, the slats half-open. The room is a cage of light. She is the bed-cat Radha-baby, purring and kneading her cover. She waits for the happy tinkle-tinkle of silver and china; the butler delivering breakfast. When the smell of pav bhaji reaches her, she can taste the peas and crunchy carrots, the onions and the fluffy potato, the burn of hot spices, the softly fried puri buttered on all sides, *mmm, too good.* She slides out of bed and flexes her toes in the carpet. *Good morning,* says the suite, reflected in her mirror, it looks so jaunty and bright, all decorated in blue for Goa. Such a lovely suite—concept "the beach," bedroom, living room, the sea view; and the ensuite, so lovely, with a colour wall that she can set to suit her mood: Dawn Rise, Rainforest, Ocean Ridge. There are jet showerheads all at different heights, and a bidet as well. A Company suite, still, it's trying to be different from the others. Yes, how special it is.

Radha reaches for her mobile—then a whistle comes from the living room. *Slide out of bed, Radha, leave the mobile, leave it! Pad to the bedroom doorway in your shorties and vest: lean against the frame.*

Bubu stands at the hostess trolley, his paunch nudging through his waffle-cotton robe. Sometimes he pets poor paunchy; today, it has been punished with a morning session in the gym. Bubu does rowing machine, he skippyskips, he lifts weights. Silly Bubu, he is such a cutey-cuddle-bear. He pretends not to notice Radha; he raises his eyebrows, lifting silver domes like a TV chef at the end of the episode. Da—da! There is her pav bhaji! There is her bowl of organic strawberries (grown right here at Company Goa—so she tells the guests who come from outside). Bubu sticks his finger in her green-tea shot, licks and makes a khatta face. He hangs the serving dome over the sofa's corner gargoyle so it goes bald and one-eyed at her—*OMG Bubu is so bad*—that is a hand-carved Jaipuri antique—she had it made especially for him.

What is Bubu having? His coffee, black. His turmeric power smoothie with extra amaranth. And there it is: a plate of three perfect suji ke ladoo dipped in dark chocolate and covered in gold leaf. *O Buji. Mini ladoo.* No matter how much her hubby works out, he cannot resist his breakfast indulgence.

—What are you smiling at? Is it my ass? Dirty girl.

—I'm smiling at your breakfast choice.

Bubu walks towards her, holding the plate low in front of him.

—Don't you want a taste of my golden balls?

The ladoo knock together, alive with the movement in his wrist.

—Filth! I'll call the concierge, she squeaks.

She skitters back into the bedroom. She launches herself face down over the bed, reaching for the hotel phone.

—If you touch that handset, you know what will happen to you, Bubu says.

She rolls over to look at him. Underneath his gown he is wearing his Donald Duck boxers. Quack, quack, quacking—always she has found them just a little unsexy. He chooses a ladoo and drops the plate onto last night's dirty clothes pile. She spreads her legs: the silk of her shorties slides up.

—What? she says.

Bubu stands at the end of the bed, between her feet. Donald Duck catches on her toes, then drops. Bubu's crotch is now striped pale, dark, pale. *A tiger in the cage of light.* Yes. Good. He takes Radha's ankles; he pushes her up the sheets until her head hangs just over the edge of the bed, her hair sweeps the floor. There is dust under the bedside table, and is that the earring she was wearing last night? Blood fills her throat, her temples. She looks up; the ocean swaps places with the sky: slices of infinity, framed in the window. This is the best view to do it in front of, and this is her favourite suite in her favourite of all the hotels.

—Come on, man, don't make idle threats.

She says her lines with feeling; she raises her leg and sticks her toe in his mouth: so cute and pretty her toenail is, a sweet for him to suck. She thinks the ceiling fan behind Bubu's head is ornamental. Is it? Bubu presses his thumb into Radha's instep, spiking her senses to neon. He rubs a ladoo to her crotch; she feels silk inside. The chocolate shell cracks; he brings his cupped hand to his mouth, swallowing the crumbs with a snap of his head, bending over to tongue all the sticky-golden-chocolatey grains onto her belly. The mirror says he is ready, yes, ready, yes. She reaches her arms back over her head to stretch her body out.

Her mobile begins to chant—

Like a G6 like a G6 like a like a G6   Like a G6 like a G6 like a like a G6 Like a G6 like a G6 like a like a G6

Bubu pauses, watching her. For a moment she thinks all will be well. Then he backs off the bed, pulls up his boxers, pats his friend inside.

O Shityaar. So, they will have to get dressed and re-begin the whole game. Call the butler to take the trolley away so Bubu can order breakfast again, so he can serve it, again. That is her signal to get up, go over, watch him, tease him. Again. *Wake up, Radha, smell the pav bhaji, and turn the mobile off.*

—Bubu-bear, don't be like that, she tries.

—Answer it, then. I gotta get on with my day.

He walks away. A chorus of diagonal ducks quacking at her from his butt.

She lies in the bed—*lovely bed. Lovely bed, you like me.* She wants to smoke. She hears the starting of the shower. Then turns onto her stomach, reaches down and cups herself close and cosy between her legs. Sliching begins. Nail pink in pink, feeling so pink, brown ass-cheeks flushing pink, face in the sheets she breathes her own scent: ylang-ylang, bed-sweat, her fingernail catches at her clitchie; it shoots pain, her lungs scream *move.* She comes up gasping for air. Crumbs of ladoo stick to her thighs. She licks her finger and eats some. *Honey and milk.* The bed, the dresser, the robe on the floor, wait to see what she will do next.

Press a switch. Open the blinds. Outside, only a thin, curved line divides the ocean from the midday haze of sky. It is so calm, so clear. She scrolls her mobile: iMessages first: two cute cat pics from friends in Delhi; a shirt-shot, from Jivan, of a full-sleeves Burlington stripe she bought him at the mall. There is the daily message from the Company automated service, Bapuji Bol! It comes with a Temple-bell chime: *Sell your vision, it is the product.* Radha commissioned this service; she selected the dictums. It has at least a million subscribers, which is pretty—ha—very pretty, isn't it?

She listens for a second. Bubu is still in the shower. She has time to open Twitter. Her account, her little secret, @MrGee. He will like today's Bapuji Bol! Will retweet it and comment on it—*Just got this—a great message from Devraj Bapuji, to begin your business day.*

Now she checks her WhatsApps. Gargi. O God. With a message longer than Radha's birthline. She scrolls through it. Has a vision: a dark wall of angry water rising up, crashing through the windows.

—Buji! she shouts. She kicks herself off the bed, goes to the bathroom.

Bubu is in there drying himself, watching cricket and checking his teeth through a cloud of ylang-scented steam. He always uses her shower pearls; he always has the water too hot.

—Bubu, you have to read this, she says.

He snaps his towel at her thighs.

—Besharram!

He snaps at her again, her skin smarts with it.

Her voice becomes the sticky one she uses for foreign journalists, first time out, wanting to go see the *real India* and wannanother lychee-vodka-lassi to cheers while they take in the tour.

—Bubu-bear, seriously, you have to read this now.

—You first clean yourself. Then you can tell me what to do.

He turns back to the cricket.

—Shit, he says. You made me miss that six!

Fucking cricket! She puts the mobile down carefully on the black glass top. She will let her silk vest slither down her body. *Nice,* the mirror says, *but not enough.*

Bubu sticks his finger in his ear and shakes his head sideways: his eyes stay on the screen.

Radha steps into the shower. She chooses Rainforest birdsong for background colour and sound, then immerses her head, drowning out the hollow *pop* of bat hitting ball, men cheering.

Then Bubu opens the cubicle door. He stands fully dressed, staring at her. She turns off the jet. Her arms hang stupidly by her sides, water running off her chin, hair, off her breasts, the bird soundtrack twittering around her,

—Really? Again? she says.

—Don't be a junglee. Also, you need a wax.

—Wax?

One hand moves to her mouchie, the other to her mound. The water drip-drips down her, welling in her navel, weeping between her legs. The steam from her shower clouds the mirror, escapes out of the door.

—Taange bandh. And your mouth. Get dressed in your travel clothes, pitti-parrotter, says Bubu. We're going to Amritsar.

From her room to the lift to the hotel lobby to the car. Doors open and shut. Company walls and doors and chandeliers say *hello* and *welcome; here you are again, OK bye.* Radha keeps her face turned in, her shoulder to the car window: Bubu loves to describe every dirty bhikshu they pass. —*I just saw one crapping on the road!* he says, or, —*I just saw one skinnier than his own cane!* And when he really wants to punish her, it's —*Let's stop and give that one a ride, don't you want to do your bit? Sita would be so proud.*

She used to roll down the car window and stick her nose right into the city air; she used to beg for street food as they passed every cart. Always she wanted to stop for a bite, the men's hands so fast on the atta; kneading it, pinching it, moulding the roti, flipping it, slapping it onto the tawa. Roti, puri, dosa, hot-fried gulab jamun: whatever it was, she wanted to taste.

—Have a peanut, Gargi would say. Radha would take a handful and crack the shells with her teeth, then flick them to see what she could hit. Nanu herself used the road as her rubbish heap. Sweet wrappers, orange peel—it all went out of the window—and put Gargi in an executive sulk that made them poke fun at her until she cried. Then Gargi had said —*Remember, you are Radha Kumari, the daughter of a Kashmiri Pandit and the Maharaja of Napurthala, you are a walking example of cleanliness.*

Nanu had sniffed at Gargi. —*Young girls do not show their faces to the street.* She told Radha that if she looked at a beggar in the eyes, she might be cursed; her face would change and she would age overnight, become a white-haired, skin-like-a-peanut-shell budiya and wake up the next day in Dhimbala basti; some other, prettier girl would be in her bed and no one would believe Radha if she told them her name. It was enough. Even now, the story polices her body, it makes her check her compact; it stops her from looking outside. The only thing that helps is Bubu's game of spot-the-worst.

Radha looks over at Bubu but he does not want to play. He is on his phone, talking about Jeet. Disappeared, money gone, heritage trouble, *should have known.*

Really, what the big fuss is, Radha cannot say. Jeet the Enigmatic, Jeet the Mysterious, Jeet the Peacemaker, the Yogi, the Great Hope. Actually, it's Jeet the Selfish: that is his trademark. Jeet—who always pokes fun at her—but then comes to her to beg and borrow her girlfriends for parties. Jeet, who expects everyone to cover for him while he remains Ranjit's favourite, Nanu's pet. Even Bapuji considers him a young Birbal, *so wise.* Because of Jeet the Selfish, Radha and Bubu are going to back-water Amritsar—where Bubu will moan and she will be diligent, kind and solicitous, all the better to comfort Ranjit Uncle. Always this task falls to her.

—Man, he must have gone mad, she says.

She scrolls her phone. @MrGee has thirty-seven new Twitter followers. Most of them young men, hiding behind eggs.

Bubu looks up, catches her staring at her mobile. She flicks to her video newsfeed so he can't see what she's doing. He leans over her. A mob is marching in Delhi, the ticker runs: *police arrest hundreds in anti-corruption*teargas threatened against action*unions organising across the country*no leader claims mob organisation or message*government buildings attacked*police arrest hundreds in anti-corruption*no leader—*

She turns it off. Bubu sits back, his humped shoulder saying, *Why aren't you working, doing something useful, at least fix your face and your hair.*

—Sooner or later, he says, the media is going to find out what is going on around here.

Sooner or later. Thinking of her jobs, she feels *so tired:* Bubu wants her to call up Barun, her journalist buddy, and all the proprietors who aren't in Bapuji's train. To remind the editors and the distributors of Company advertising spend, which will only increase with the launch of the eco-car.

—Nothing should get out about Jeet. Nothing about Sita, Bubu says. And nothing, I mean absolutely not, about your dad's state of mind. When we get to Srinagar, then we will tell the world.

—So what *shall* I say? she asks.

Now he speaks in his Bubu-bear voice.

—You know what to do, Raddles. Give them some titbit to scoop on. They already have Big Sis. Concentrate on the Srinagar hotel: everyone is bored sick of hearing how bad things are in Kashmir, let's give them instead our fairytale of opportunity—jobs, tourism—opening up. Give them Jivan. Give your Barun an exclusive intro to the NOW generation. He'll love it. *Jivan Singh: Our new right-hand man.* No: *Our fresh eyes.*

—He is not *my* Barun, she says, but Bubu is no longer listening to her.

Press. Release. Jivan Singh. *Ranjitji's beloved son.* The story of his mother, a world-class singer, who gave everything up for love. (It was the '70s— The Beatles—Ravi Shankar—Norah Jones—it was a different time; such things were less fixed.) They can bring in Jivan's *Harvard* education, before the real killer: his decision to leave America and return home to India, to be with the family he loves so much. She imagines the cover: Jivan in a dark suit (or maybe a handloom kurta and jeans?). And the headline: *Jivan naya jeevan hain.*

They have left the hotel for the tatty beach road, lined with foreigner stalls. Here Radha can look out of the window; she is on safari, spotting the white girls in bikini tops and denim hot pants, skin like razor shells discarded on the beach, hair sand-blasted or twisted into long, dead snakes. She watches them bargain for cheap churidar to wear with tube tops, for chemical incense, for pirate DVDs from the bootleggers who have annexed the old Hindi music stalls Ranjit Uncle used to take her to. How plump they are, these women; even the rich ones, she can never understand them sleeping in shacks like unwashed bums, getting high on home-grown ganja, riding on the backs of motorcycles with shirtless, muscled Goan boys. And why do they wear all those tie-dye sarongs? God, the market stinks. Raw fish and old fruit. Thank God for the high-way, the flat blue water stretching out on either side.

MrGee writes a tweet: *Goa getting spoiled by white girls with no style. Media calls for appropriate Indian beachwear rules.* She posts it, with a picture of Priyanka Chopra in a string bikini. Like like like like like like like: she watches the Twitter feed.

She is so eager to leave the public parts of the city behind that she almost trips as she climbs the plane steps. Company doors shut, seatbelt clips, blinds go down. They race towards the ocean, bank and turn north: at last they are free of it all.

Up in the clouds, Radha unclips her seatbelt. The interior of the little jet is camel leather. She likes it, so soft: skin on skin. She calls the airhostess, to order their lunch. Cholay-puri and saag-meat for Bubu. He eats like a starving bachcha, using his hand to tear bits of soft puri and scoop cholay into his mouth. He picks a piece of marrowbone from the saag, he sucks the inside clean.

—Equal share, family bond, he says through his food. Future proof the trust.

Radha feathers her sprout salad with her fork. She eats a pea shoot. She thinks about pav bhaji. You can't get street food in the plane. She wants a cold glass of Sancerre, and presses the button to call the hostess.

—*All in good time,* Bubu says. Your dad's favourite pill. In ten years since I married you, I have worked like a donkey for the Company. Have I ever asked for anything in return?

He does not wait for Radha to answer.

—When we get to Amritsar, make sure you take care of Ranjit.

Why he has to tell her this, she has no idea.

—We have so much work to do, to get ready for the Srinagar opening, now we are taking time for this.

Who is he actually talking to? She counts her finished olive stones. One (for sorrow), two (for joy), three (for a girl), four (for a boy), five (for a King). She scrapes her teeth over one more.

—When we get the Srinagar hotel open, you'll see what we can really do. I mean, giving our business to *Sita*? Hotel and shawls? What was your dad thinking? All I can say is, thank God she left. The whole Northern network is dependent on that trade.

Yes, Bubu, yes it is. The little plane dips and rises. *The Kashmir Corridor.* Radha taps her nails on her knee. *A dark place, a thin place, a no place on the map.* Here come the arms and there go the drugs, liquid, solid, gas. Through hallways and in corners, through doors into rooms, light weapons, they call them, though they are heavy and hard. All wrapped in high class and soft fabric. Hush–hush—the move of things—slipping through men's hands like a beautiful shawl over skin. In a blessed communal of

Allah and Shiv. A deep state. Of grace. No crackdown. Consignments are increasing. Nothing so romantic. The store must be ready before winter comes, deep in the cellars of the new Company Kashmir hotel.

Bapuji has named Bubu for this business. Outright. The shawls, made from the tums of protected little chiru, are a different matter. They happen, despite the wild-lifers, the media, and Gargi's legal objections. But still, all because of Bubu. He says he keeps the bribes down to workable strata right from the guys who pick the fluff off the tum of the damn hoofy goat, up to the stores on Sansad Marg. And the Kashmir Corridor stays open. In all conditions, it is open for free trade.

Bubu takes another puri and scrapes it around his bowl, chasing the last shreds of meat in the sauce.

—I cannot wait until we get the Kashmir hotel done, he says. If your sister doesn't sabotage it somehow. Why do you both have to be so senti*mental*?

Srinagar, Srinagar, late summer on the lake. Lying in a hammock in a garden in the hills, looking up through the branches of some wide, spreading tree. Her slim waist. Her long legs. The responsibility of her own beauty against violence in the streets. Thirteen mosquito-bite marks on her ankles, one for each year of life. Big Sis somewhere around. Jivan left behind. Radha had felt so aloof and lovely up there. Lonely, in the singular way of mountain flowers. Even though there was table tennis. She was the red paddle and Ranjit Uncle was the blue. And of course, there was the petting farm, with real live chickens and goats.

Now Bubu points his food-covered fingers in a gun at her. He shoots at her face then licks them.

—When we get into the new hotel, Gargi Madam will know for sure that she cannot strut around pretending she's the boss.

—Gargi just wants whatever is right.

—You need to stop defending her. Radha, you are twenty-eight years old. You need to start thinking for yourself. Stop worrying about what Big Sis will say. Don't ever forget—you're my wife. And head of Company PR.

Perfect Radha, Pretty Radha, Pukka Radha. Bubu is stuck on his favourite topic now: How Gargi Thinks She's God. Radha does not want to listen to this again. Yet she *chose* Bubu, she knows that—it wasn't as if she had been wrapped in a bow and just gifted away. Bubu's gotra was excellent, a Rajput pedigree going back in the male line right to the source. His parents were in town planning, his wider family in politics. They were new money, but it was the late 1990s, the country was opening up. Though Radha had to have it coaxed from her by Ranjit Uncle one night, she finally confessed that out of all the guys who offered for her, she was crushing on Bubu. Cosmological charts were made. Their stars matched and the family Swamiji was consulted about the date. Radha thought Gargi might disapprove, but she had only said —*Don't you think he's a bit fast?*

—I'm going to use this time in Amritsar to head up to Srinagar once or twice, Bubu says. Contractors need to know I am there. You come, be the good cop. OK? Or I'll take Jivan, not a bad idea. Yes, Jivan with the Amer-i-can accent. Do you *dig* his accent, Raddles? Lick-lick-like it?

Has Radha ever been glad Bubu talks so much? The little plane shudders around her. On early dates, she had thought it was sweet, that Bubu wanted her to understand him. He took her to the Habitat Centre because she liked its fortress style, and he liked the English pub there— they served these salty-spicy nuts with the drinks—he could not find them anywhere else in Delhi, he said, not even in her daddy's hotel. She sat and listened as he told her of his childhood, Dad and Mom building the business together; going to office then coming home for lunch; taking keep-fit strolls in the evening around the colony square while Bubu learned fractional math with a tutor. Two Mercs in the driveway and ten-plus help: driver and chaukidar, cook, maid, safai wale. And so on. Happy little Bubu had been sent to St. Columba's with the sons of his parents' friends; he had sat with his family over dinner each night being fed, and fed, and fed at his mom's own direction. Uncles in the police and in the civil service, rising like English bread. Lunch on Sundays at the Lodhi restaurant, parties at the Gymkhana club, an MBA from MIT Sloan, a year or so working for Pierce & Pierce in London. He came home, he said, after 9/11 shut down the office. Anyway, the job didn't like him; and it is true, Radha thinks, he is better, in charge of his own thing. At eighteen she had been desperate to get married. Bubu was The One: she had decided when, for their fourth or fifth date, he made Bapuji laugh with his impressions of London, then got his permission to take Radha out to dinner alone. He chose biryani at Delhi O' Delhi, though she wanted shakes and burgers in the American Diner. It was too full of kids, he had said, and bad lighting (and if she thought the place was damn cool then—well, she was only eighteen).

A jolt of turbulence—Bubu puts his arms out—then stretches his hands behind his head.

—For now, all conditions of our cooperation will be based on Gargi's behaviour, he says. Let's see if she can hack it at the top.

As a bride, Radha had no bargaining chips. But she would not go and live with Bubu's parents in his new-build city. Even though Bubu told her that Paradise Park was *the place of the future,* even though he *promised* he would build her a mall there. So she could go from bedroom, to car, to covered shopping. Buy her favourite brands without even feeling she had left the house.

—*I don't want to,* she had said. *I like going to London; they have the best clubs, and street food you can eat until three in the morning.*

She wondered that he had never been to that road near Selfridges, near Marble Arch, so like a miniature India Gate? Such succulent shawarma they have there, and fresh-fresh juice. On her first trip to London when she was seventeen, she ate there every night after dancing at Opium: she and her school friends, allowed to go to UK together since the other girls had brothers to come too. It felt wild to go with bare legs in the street, high heels and tight dresses, sleeping on the floor all jumbled up close, fingers and hair, and hot breath, kissing cousins and what-all else in the night. Not rising each day until noon.

Bubu hadn't answered; just asked if she never felt it was unfair that she had more money than any Britisher, yet couldn't get the latest fashions unless she got on a plane. Why, he said, shouldn't India compete? He told her it was all the fault of a closed financial system based on a mirage, an endless cycle of government dreams locked up in five-year plans. Till now. *You can blame the late eighties,* he had said. *And the early nineties. My uncles in Congress, your dad and Ranjit.*

No one had ever said such things to her about Bapuji before. She liked the certainty in Bubu's voice. She only had a loose idea of what he was talking about. She had footsied him under the table and said,

—*But it's the Naughties.* She expected him to laugh.

—*Right,* he had said, holding out a bite of tender lamb for her. *And what happened in the last decade? Bailout. Hello international money. Lak-*

shmi Devi has blessed our generation with a liberalised economy; it is our duty to make the most of each rupee. It is our time, Radha, we cannot waste it; the begging bowl is going to change hands, you watch.

He had been right. Bubu, she thought, was something of a Business Guru, just like Bapuji. Still, she refused to go and live in Paradise Park. Some of the enclaves were only half-finished; the rest were full of retired uncles and aunties in tower blocks, their kids in neat bungalows set around their feet. It was no country for old money to live in. She put it like this to Ranjit Uncle, of course he had agreed. He spoke to Bubu, and for ten years they have lived, instead, on the Farm with Gargi and Surendra, Bapuji and Nanu. Ranjit Uncle.

Radha turns to look out of the airplane window; all she can see are a few wispy clouds; white hairs trailing across the bald, scorched earth. She thinks about Amritsar, where Ranjit Uncle is. And Jivan.

Press. Release. She takes a gulp of her wine. Once, when Jivan's Ma was trying to teach her the basics of Bharatnatyam—araimandi, *half-sitting,* samapadam, *legs together*—Radha confessed she wanted to be Jivan's rishta. *Stiff body, soft face.* To get engaged in the gardens of the Company Delhi hotel, where the terrace would heave under the weight of all of her school friends' envy, and her sisters would look on, and her father and Ranjit Uncle would bless them with more sweets and money than she could even eat or count. *Arm out, foot stretch.* Would they agree? Better not to think of that, or Ranjit Uncle's hand in the small of her back, guiding her in the right direction, all of her life it seems.

—*Chi,* Jivan's Ma had said. Take a note of your elders, your sister. Learn well your steps for the dance.

She had called Radha a pagal, said that Lord Shiva would come disguised as an unwashed gopi and milk cows for her morning doodh before Bapuji would allow his middle daughter to marry Jivan. *Why not?* Nice girls do not ask. *Why not?* Such a match would be as unwanted as the noon sun shining on freshly made curd.

No one had told Radha that Jivan was being sent to America until after he had gone. It was October. The Farm was being finished for Gargi's wedding. Everyone was obsessed with each detail of Gargi's jewellery, her clothes, even her underwear was going to be new. Ranjit Uncle had come to the Jor Bagh house and found Radha alone, smoking on the roof. He did not seem to see her cigarette. He bowed to her, and invited her for tea in the Palm Court of the Company Delhi hotel, just her, on her own. He took her in the Bentley: it smelled of leather polish and Old Spice cologne. *Well hello,* said the seats, *how are you, pretty Radha? So elegant at just fifteen, still practicing your makeup.*

Her kameez that day was stitched with tiny mirrors. She could see herself reflected in parts. She sat in the backseat with Ranjit Uncle, his ebony stick between his knees. He told her that Bapuji had just gifted him a beautiful thing. She was confused. Watching her, he had laughed, said —*It is the Company Amritsar hotel, to mark so many years of loyalty and friendship.* He asked her opinion on his new suit. Radha said she liked it, and he took her hand and used it to stroke the fabric over his leg.

—*See?* he had said. *Brushed cotton. Almost as soft as your skin.*

When they reached the Palm Court, Ranjit Uncle let her choose wherever she wanted to sit. He asked the pianist to play her favourite tune: back then it was "Memory" from *Cats.*

She had cried when he explained, so gently, that Jivan's Ma had demanded to leave India, and have her own new house. She had felt a bit better when Ranjit Uncle shifted his chair to put his arm around her, and said that Jivan had chosen to go with his Ma, of course that was the case. He pulled her head into his shoulder, and the handkerchief from his top pocket. She blew her nose in it, and gave it back. He had held it up for a moment, then folded it tenderly, like a letter, and put it in his trousers. He had stroked her hair. He told her he had a present for her.

From his briefcase he produced a stack of old photos of himself with Bapuji. She gazed at them, the heroes of back-then cinema, in flares, waistcoats and Ray-Bans—she thought Ranjit Uncle a little more dashing of the two. There they were in the pictures, leaning on balustrades all over Europe, in Switzerland, by the Lac de Genève. (When Radha got home, she showed them to Gargi, who had told her the background was Srinagar, not Switzerland. Radha had checked up with Nanu, but her grandmother took the pictures from her, and sent her away with a stinging cheek.)

By the end of that first tea, Ranjit Uncle had promised to make it up to Radha. He said —*Haven't I always been your playmate, since you were a little girl?* It was true, he had always been there, whenever Jivan was not allowed to come out to play.

Ranjit Uncle promised he would take her to tea *re-ligious-ly* once a month. He promised he would be Radha's special friend. She was so hip-hip-happy. Jivan had left her for good, she thought, without even saying goodbye.

—Stop dreaming, Radha, Bubu says. I might have a tenth-anniversary surprise for you. What would you say if we moved to our own Farm?

Right, Radha thinks. With space for his parents, his sister and her kids, Bubu's whole buddy crew.

—Running around after Daddy is an elder daughter's job, Bubu says.

—Yah, but I don't want to leave Gargi alone with all of that.

—Did Gargi think about you when she got married? Lucky for her Surendraji has no family. Lucky for us, as well. Don't worry, we will invite them sometimes. And you will keep your place as the fourth of Bapuji's five loves, Bubu says.

First: the Company. Second, it's Nanu. Third—Sita. She—Radha comes fourth. At least she isn't last.

Bubu reaches forward to pinch Radha's cheek. His fingers smell of cholay.

—Don't worry, he says. You are always my Number One. Do you want to spend your life working the crowd for Gargi's parties? More tea-ji and how about a burfi or two? Or do you want to host your own? No more speeches . . . just party, party, party!

Bubu jabs the air towards her as if she is the party, three times around.

Stop dreaming, Radha, stop dreaming. She pours herself more wine. *When we get to Srinagar . . .* After the Srinagar hotel opening, she should take a cruise. Or maybe a trip to the Maldives? Or she could start a new project, like her own shawls line. Future-modern or old-colonial? Heritage or avant-garde? She will order some Mumbai design magazines and have them delivered to Amritsar.

Gargi would not approve. Unless—Radha could have a baby. She thinks she might like a real live baby.

—Bubu-bu? she says. Her arm snakes across the table, around the dirty plates.

—Want to be my baby-daddy?

Bubu puts his work to one side. His eyes narrow.

—Get up, he says. We've got time. Before we come into land.

He signals to the airhostesses to get into the cockpit. At eighteen thousand feet he unbuttons his fly. Then he invites Radha over to his side of the table and asks her to lift up her skirt. He pulls down her panty and sits her on his lap, facing forward so that his fingers can pinch at her nipples. His chin presses into her back. She stares at the dishes. There is still some puri left in the basket. She braces: her knees are trapped under the edge of the table. Bubu bends her forward, starts his familiar rhythm. She cries out, so loud that she is sure that far below, every man from Goa to Amritsar can hear her: a beautiful, wild mynah swooping in the sky.

The heat in Amritsar. A fierce thirty-eight degrees. It burns through the soles of her sandals. Their car edges out of the airport, away from the old walled city. Radha is full of sex and pastis; she feels safe, so safe, enough to let her eyes look up from her phone, skim over the ragged women squatting in the dirt. She tells herself the old curse is stupid. *I'm research-ing*, she thinks. Looking for the money shot. That her magazine ladies pretend they do not come to see. *We should get some of these rope makers, these mattress weavers. Hang some large portraits of them in the hotel, taste-ful, looking into the lens, so their heads fill the frame and their eyes look like owls'.*

—Feeling good? she asks Bubu.

She cannot see his eyes behind his shades.

—Feeling great.

He reaches over and tugs on the ends of her hair.

—Hey, look! There's one with no shoes, see? Making a tandoor with her bare hands. You want one? A tandoor maker? We could buy her and all of her pots. Let's stop! he says.

They pass a parantha stand, a crowd of men around it; she can smell the hot ghee, thick like a fur lining her throat. If only she could have one—*no*, she cannot. Bubu hates her street food habit. He has banned her from eating carbs after breakfast. It is for her own well-being.

—Look! There's some kids, trying to eat chapati off the mitti! Bubu says. You want one mud chapati? Do you?

—No!

—Come on, babe, you gotta play.

The car is too small, the road broken.

—What are their names? she asks.

—Ummm, Chinku, Rinku, Mr. Stinku! He laughs. Like Sita's dogs.

—Don't be a meany, she says. They're cute puppos. It's not their fault Sita has left them without their mommy.

—Hello? Since Sita Madam went to college, your dad spent more time with them than he does with you. They aren't cute; they're vicious. Particularly Mr. Stinku. He's really on his last legs.

Just like that, she thinks. One should not get fat, sick or old.

—Poor Mr. Stinku, she says. He's such a cute pooch.

—Nasty yappy mutt. Don't get ideas. We are not getting a dog. If you wanna be licked so bad, ask that one!

Bubu points to a thin old man on a tired bicycle, piled high in the front with a vast cloth bundle that could contain half her hundred-piece wardrobe. His feet are in broken chappals, his face twists as he bears down on the pedals. *As if grieving for his legs.* She can see the veins on his neck standing out, like the rivers on an ancient map. His eyes bulging, his tongue clenched between his teeth.

—OK, you win, you always win! she says.

Bubu laughs. The car slows; it turns through the pink stone gateposts of the Company Amritsar hotel. *Salute, salute,* the doormen recognise them. Radha smoothes her hair. She arranges her dupatta into a perfect smile across her breasts. Radha Kumari. Radha Kumari Devraj Balraj has arrived at her Ranjit Uncle's hotel.

You, again! the lobby says. *Welcome, your regular rooms are waiting. Indian fruit basket (lychees, satsumas, jackfruits, banana—pineapple optional); champagne on ice.* There is the atrium to pass through, and lifts to go up and corridors to walk down, and rooms. Rooms for eating and some for sleeping; rooms for being pretty in, and some for drinking in. All the Company rooms. Some with connecting doors for suites done in business traveller–gothic style: clear plastic chairs, black-and-purple candelabra, laser-cut and cast as antiques. Velvet fruits and paisleys covering the walls. Amritsar is a boutique hotel: there are only thirteen floors, stacked one on top of the other like a giant tiffin box. The internal corridors have no windows, just soft, low lighting. You can go around in circles, up and down, and never know where you are until you get to the top. On the eighth floor the schema changes; half of it is rooms, half is cut away. One half is Ranjit Uncle's suite and the offices of the Company North, the other his private terrace. It is full of Jeet's statues. The precious and the fake. All together, posing: Radha calls this the terrace of standing still. On the hotel's roof is a deck, a bar, a pool and hot tub which, when Radha and Bubu come to stay, becomes exclusive for their use. The hotel sits in five acres of tended gardens, watered every day. All of it bordered by a yellow brick wall. At the back of the hotel, south-eastwards (she thinks), is the stinking Dhimbala basti: the hotel kitchen gives food to the children on festival days. Beyond that is the Kingdom of Napurthala, where Gargi and Radha were born. *A place for the sweetest of times: the tale of a mother and two Little Princesses playing together happily, all day long.* Stop. Outside, the highway leads south, into the city; and north, towards Kashmir.

When they get into the Srinagar hotel . . . Doors open and close.

Dinner tonight will be in the public restaurant, among the aam janta. In the fifth year of her marriage, Ranjit Uncle had told Radha (over tea) that he had made some bad investment decisions. Sole ownership of the hotel was at risk. Outsiders might become involved . . . he held her hand, and wept. Now it was Radha who plucked out his handkerchief from his top pocket and used it to wipe his poor sad eyes for him. Thank God Bubu came to the rescue, and bought out three-fifths of the place (without a word to Bapuji). Still, they observe the protocol: Ranjit Uncle will invite Bubu and Radha to join him for dinner, and Bubu will accept.

In Radha's room there is a present waiting. A soft cloth bag with a brand-new toosh inside. The shawl is creamy white, scattered with hand-embroidered butterflies. Such fine zardozi work. Radha touches a wing with her finger. The creature looks almost alive. *With love, Ranjit Uncle.*

Radha wraps herself in her butterflies, over her bra and panties. She wanders around her room, she hops to the mirror like a chiru; long-legged antelope of the high snowcaps. It takes three chiru to make a woman's toosh and five to make a man's. A Gargi, a Radha and a Sita chiru, a Jeet and a Jivan too. Ranjit Uncle taught them this process when they were kids, after-lunch lecture in the library. Then Jivan was the baby chiru, hopping through the forests in the mountains above India, almost in Tibet. *One of the harshest environments in the world,* Ranjit Uncle had said. This was demarcated by a stern ridge of books, pulled from the shelves of Bapuji's library, it was not as if they were ever used. Light-footed, Jivan the chiru-baby clip-clopped around the parquet of the Jor Bagh house, finding his hiding place. Radha was the hunter with the knife, she had to report to Gargi and Jeet, take instructions on where to seek until the chiru was caught. Or until Nanu would not allow their noise any longer. They would not stop, so Nanu called Ranjit Uncle. Jivan had been taken into the garden and beaten, in such a way that his soft underbelly did not get bruised. Little Radha kept her part, holding the stick with Ranjit Uncle's hand over hers for a few good whacks; he said she had to learn how to teach animals a lesson.

Then the chiru would start to die. Before it did, the fur would be taken from its softest parts, tuft by tuft, and handwoven by nimble-fingered women and children, squinting over the work in their huts. They would lay Jivan down on his back, tickling his tum, pinching until he stopped crying and played dead. After that, Jivan became the poor Kashmiri woman, carding the wool, weaving the fine shawl for a year or more (five minutes), and then he was the Shi'a man who did the embroidery: another year or so (five minutes) for that. Gargi was the distributor, Jeet was the chief buyer, and Radha was the English lady customer at the end. Compare and try, free to say no or buy.

Then the three of them were called to dinner. Ranjit Uncle finished the story with the words —*Those who wear the Shahtoosh are the Kings and Queens of this life.* If she and Gargi and Jeet ate all that they were given, they washed hands and were allowed to touch a Shahtoosh, maybe even tuck it over baby Sita in her crib.

Radha twirls in the mirror. The sequins catch the light, they cast shadows, glitter ball. She pinches her fingers together: the lotus flower, the wolf. *Very nice,* says the mirror, *just right.* The mirror is repro-vintage, fake-spotted to look aged. An older Radha gazes out at her, like a movie star from back then, considering her youth. *This lovely girl will never grow old or die.* The mirror keeps silent on that.

She dresses herself: a green silk sari, a blouse held up by two strings:

one across her back, the other around her neck. She ties the sari as low as possible: her navel stares out so brazenly. It winks at itself in the mirror. She pokes it with her finger, *naughty naabhi!* Then dusts it with bronze powder. She calls for a set from the hotel jewellers—a collar of antique gold, crusted with diamonds; a pair of earrings like tiny chandeliers. Now the room says, *Ah, pretty Radha—so like a bride!* Ranjit Uncle will appreciate her adorned in the wares from his shop. *Yes, so he will. And Jivan?*

Strange, how she wears a touch extra scent. Is this for the rate-paying public? Come get your tickets to see the Goddess, extra to ask her your fate!

There is no mirror in the elevator; it has been replaced with a video of a goldfish, eyes rotating, mouth gaping as it flickers from side to side. Bubu stares at the doors; Radha at her toes. The fish swims behind them. They reach the Lagoon Bar (members only). The maître d' greets them; Radha follows Bubu, *now the night begins.*

Hours of Fashion TV before she got married have taught her to straighten her back, drop her shoulders and stick out her hips as she walks. Everything in here is deep sea: cold light on blue velvet. The bar watches Radha pass by, the backlit bottles a rainbow regiment; they stand to attention and say, *Good evening, Radha Rani, so lovely you look. How about a cocktail tonight?* Strings of clear glass beads cascade from the ceiling: tiny waterfalls hiding each clamshell booth. Radha carries her new shawl, butterflies flitting through aquamarine.

The music is jazz. Not, for once, Ranjit Uncle's old filmy favourites.

—Bubu, Radha! Welcome, good to see you.

Jivan. Waiting at their table, in jeans and dark shirt. His eyebrows have been trimmed. It makes his face look sharper, his cheekbones more pronounced. He always looks as if a joke is coming and it is going to be dirty. Radha's smile spreads down her body, warm like Goan sun.

—Hey, look who is here, says Bubu.

They do the boy-sniff-boy: grip, pull, backslap, press, release. They seem genuinely pleased to see each other. Bubu likes the corner position of the booth, but raises his eyebrows at the waiting bottle of Veuve Clicquot. He waves it away. He always drinks Indian (there is no import tax). It is his father's habit, to care about such things.

The maître d' clutches the ice bucket; he shakes it as if it put itself there on purpose. It sounds Radha's nerves as she leans towards Jivan, feels his hand on her back; she kisses him once on each cheek, European style. His stubble grazes: she thinks of herself as a long, slim match striking against him. He smells of citrus and almost, perhaps, of jasmine. He pulls her lightly into the velvet clamshell.

Under the table, she presses Jivan's palm with her thumb.

—Sirs? What can I get? A young waiter. His uniform is too big: it sits on him as if expecting him to instant-grow, *just add water*. His trainers are luminous under the ultramarine light. *Drink, drink,* chime the glass beads behind him. *Drink? Why yes, I will.*

—Tiger? Bud? Jivan says to Bubu.

—He'll have a Tiger, says Radha. Vodka tonic for me.

—Ek dum thanda, OK? Jivan snaps at the boy. Aur glass nahin chahiye. Bhoolna nahin, OK? And one JD for me, one vodka tonic for Radha Madam, ice and lemon. Bring Mr. and Mrs. Balraj some snacks. What will you have? Spicy nachos? Finger chips? Or shall we start with some of the hot specialities?

Bubu raises his eyebrows.

—Wah, wah. Not bad Hindi, Mr. Head of Intelligence. Man, you only just landed and you can talk the talk already. Pretty impressive, my friend, he says.

—Yah, well, you know . . . I grew up with it. And Gargi Madam said I should practice my language. What Gargi Madam wants, Gargi Madam gets, Jivan replies.

Bubu laughs, so Radha laughs as well. So funny, it all suddenly seems. *Her and he and he and where is Ranjit Uncle?* Jivan's face does not register when Radha lets go of his hand; she places both of hers on the table. Wedding ring, engagement ring, eternity ring. They wink at her, Bubu's co-conspirators. She wants to crawl inside Jivan's head and pick through his memories, see which Radha he remembers: Is the one who used to dress him up and play hunter hunts chiru still there?

The drinks are served: she watches the men, the whisky and the beer. Bubu dismisses the *nachos-katchos,* so she orders hot samosa, *the good stuff.* She sips at her vodka then rolls her finger around the top of her glass, trying to make it sing.

.   .   .

Three little vodkas and the room has warmed to her: how cosy it is in Amritsar. She loves the bar, the sense of blue; the talk about this and about that swirls around. Bubu scoops up a fist full of peanuts and shoots them into his mouth. Jivan smiles at her every now and then, lazily. As if time slows for him. She watches them. Bubu loves home cooking, loves going shopping. He takes an interest in her clothes and hair. Jivan, she thinks, is younger, more fresh. A thought snakes into her with her vodka and tonic; it wants to rise with the bubbles and come out as laughter —*Bubu and Jivan, perfect for each other. They could get married, go honeymoon in Srinagar, go boating on the lake.*

She drinks and scrolls her mobile. MrGee has fifteen new followers. She taps out a tweet. *Pre-launch buzz on the new Company Eco-Car is hot! Advise getting an order in soon—I've got mine already!* She watches her two men; catch up, catch up. Drink down. They start to talk about Jeet. Jivan actually seems very upset.

—Seriously, where could he have gone? he says. Naturally, my dad is devastated.

—Damage is done, Bubu shrugs. Jeet has always been flaky. I've got the Delhi and Amritsar police working together. If they catch him, I've told them not to hurt him. Those guys can be pretty easy with the sticks, know what I mean?

—Are you joking? Jivan says.

Now he just looks scared. Or is it excited? In the pale blue, Radha sips her vodka, she watches little dots of light dance all over him.

—Why would I be? says Bubu. Jeet's picture is with all the international and domestic airports, the train and bigger bus stations. We've got some plainclothes on it as well. Just in case he's still hiding out in Delhi. In the *old town.*

—Wait, you mean, like your own Secret Service? Jesus. Isn't that my job? asks Jivan.

—Huh. Kritik and Kashyap. As intelligent as monkeys trying to write. Look, we don't even know what Jeet is involved with. It could be some terrorist group, some communals, could just be he's got some gandu blackmailing him. Either way, we've got to protect the assets.

—From Jeet? Jivan says. Really?

—He knows a lot of characters. It's how he does his work. Tribals, Tamils, crazy Sikhs wanting a separate state. Kashmiri fanatics. We've already been hit by them once, Bubu says. He better not have been stealing from them—with Jeet you just never know, and I've tended not to ask.

The music becomes a frantic piano, undercut with drums. The rhythm beats, *Where is that boy?* Radha's glass is empty.

—OK, back up, says Jivan. Where the hell has all this come from? This is some heavy shit. Kashmiri *fanatics*? You mean, like terrorism? Jeet couldn't be involved in anything like that. I can't believe he even knows the right end of a gun.

Yes! Finally, something only Radha can answer.

—Bapuji taught him to shoot for his eighteenth birthday, she says. They set up paper targets in the wild wood—all these cutouts of industrialists Bapuji was feeling mad at—Jeet actually kind of enjoyed it. He told me.

—But terrorists? Jivan says.

—Trying to get us to quit Kashmir, says Bubu. You Americans aren't the only ones who have to deal with this stuff. There have been attacks on Parliament in Delhi. Four years back there were bombings in Mumbai— our Company hotel and a bunch of others. Last year there were more. Don't you know about it?

—That was crazy, Radha says. I was there that day—out at meetings with this fantastic young director, Amit Khanna—we were talking about web serials and we had just ordered matcha tea. I remember it so clearly.

Bubu reaches over the table. He puts his finger to her lips. He strokes her cheek. She moves against him. Wants to bite, but doesn't.

—I remember that Mumbai thing. Forgot you guys got hit, says Jivan.

—Yah, terrible, Radha says. Terrorible.

Jivan and Bubu look at each other. Neither of them laugh.

You here, at this public hour? The lobby is so bright, it is too full of strangers. Radha puts her shawl on. She holds her phone in front of her face. Snap, snap, snap. For MrGee to tweet, later on. The restaurant is full of families eating from the buffet, so many dishes on burners and on ice. Perfect for having a private conversation—*a tête-à-tête*—where no one but the person next to you can hear what you say, not even the wine- or the water-waiter. Every place is set with five knives and five forks; a stack of three plates crowned with a napkin in a peacock fan.

Ranjit Uncle is already at the table, waiting for Radha to *come sit by him.* He stands to greet them; his eyes are a little bloodshot. He looks a little old: even his beard is a little untrimmed. Ranjit Uncle: who taught her to mix an Old Fashioned before her wedding—*survival skills,* he said. Who took her to Dubai for her twenty-first birthday because Bubu was too busy with his mall. From whom Radha learned the art of get-what-you-want-without-losing-any-friends.

—You like the shawl? It is so *you.* His palm is damp. His voice, his breath are whisky over ice.

They take their seats, Radha, then Ranjit Uncle, then Jivan, then Bubu. One is her husband, one is her mentor, the other her oldest friend. She cannot tell which is the honest one, which is the naïve one, which is the monster under the bed.

—I must tell you all, I cannot believe Jeet could behave with such callousness. From where did he learn this? Ranjit says. Usne mera dil chir diya.

How strange it is that he says his heart is ripped, not broken. Is that because he now has Jivan? She smiles at the son, across his father.

—We can't believe it either, she says. Your own precious Jeet.

—Aré, Radha beti, I wish I could forget this thing. How can I face your Bapuji?

Chef Mistry comes to the table. His hat stands like a pillar of icing on his milk-chocolate face. He wants to know what delicacies he can make for Radha, then tells her what he likes best.

—Bring a selection, she says, as she always does. And another round of drinks.

And now, she must turn to Ranjit Uncle, must soften her voice, old style.

—Dear Ranjit Uncle, I know you love Jeet, but sometimes he does misbehave. With Bapuji's Hundred. Gargi tells me they have been going wild on the Farm, encouraging all sorts of pranks. It is so bad for Bapuji's health. Did you know Jeet is close with them?

—I don't seem to know, beti, what-all Jeet does.

—It's true, Dad, says Jivan. Jeet has always been into those guys. And their scene isn't exactly veg, you know?

Check it out! Jivan is using old slang, the kind Gargi used as a teen-ager. "Veg," "non-veg." Don't they say—what is it? "Savoury" and "unsa-voury" in the West? Even more interesting: Jivan is backing her, Radha, up on something that, after all his years in America, he cannot know is true. And is he trying to hint that Jeet is gay? *To his own dad?*

—Yet Srinagar hotel is about to open. How could Jeet have gone off? says Ranjit Uncle.

Like milk, she thinks. *Jeet the Doodh.* She drowns her laugh in her wine.

—I thought Bapuji might even bring his boys to Goa, and expect me to play host. It's too much, she says.

Eyes all wide and mouth open, her dismay tugs at her cheeks, as if Ranjit Uncle himself is pinching them.

Ranjit Uncle shakes his head. *Yes, dear Radha, too much.*

—Don't worry, Bubu says. We'll find that bad boy Jeet. And then you can decide his punishment.

Bubu looks from Ranjit Uncle to Jivan; puts one hand on each of their shoulders.

Ranjit Uncle picks up his drink. For years Radha has watched him do exactly this: swirl the liquid, knock it back. He puts the glass down but does not let go. His eyes stay on his hand; his expression is impossible to read. His skin is pocked like the cutwork on the glass, notches of too many late nights. *Bubu,* she thinks, *is more likely than Jivan to look like Ranjit Uncle one day.*

The food arrives. Butterflied king prawns, split pink and looking so pleased, as if they swam to the pot and sacrificed themselves willingly to the sauce. Roti, a tandoor-baked daal. A jewelled rice, bright with pome-granate seeds, with saffron, the finest from Kashmir.

—Let us eat, Ranjit Uncle says. Come, beta, come. You're welcome to all I have.

After they have eaten, Radha leaves the boys to a game. Poker, with Jivan's self-devised, all-new *American* rules. She accompanies Ranjit Uncle back to his suite. He presses her to stay for one more drink, he wants to show off his new toy: a wood-fired pizza oven he has just had installed on his terrace. He promises a pizza party next weekend, in Radha's honour, and will she just spend some time with a South African business colleague of his, who should not leave without a taste of their proper hospitality?

Clive is over six foot (taller than Bubu); his shoulders are wide as India Gate. He has warm hands, big, with rough palms. He is what Radha would call "hot" if she liked white guys; she does not know what it is about him that makes her feel so relaxed, but she decides that she will stay. He is in India, he says, to buy cigars, direct from Ranjit's own personal Cuban supply, the best he has found for his taste. Radha smiles, yes, yes, Ranjit Uncle has such eclectic habits. Clive pours her two shots and lets her suck his cigar. Ranjit Uncle nods along. After this, she feels absolutely fine. She confesses to Clive (in a low voice) that of course she knows who he really is—the manager of certain factories outside Johannesburg. He looks so surprised that she giggles. He makes small parts that hold tanks, guns and observation devices together. The Company Materials subsidiary (some of which, she supposes, is now hers) has a small, significant share.

—It was this factory that supplied the air-conditioning units to Saddam Hussein's palace in Iraq, Ranjit Uncle says. In the Middle East.

—Did you go there? Radha asks.

—Sure, says Clive. All gold, inside. Even the lift.

Radha has no view on this, what is it to her? It makes a good story. The business brings in several hundred undeclared crores per year. The parts are sold through the Company to governments in Pakistan, Afghanistan and across Iran, Iraq, Syria, Yemen. To UK and America. They come home, as grown-up weapons, through the Kashmir Corridor. *What big arms you have,* Radha wants to laugh. *He he he.* She raises her arm. A small bulge of muscle under smooth skin. The shadow of a dancer is cast on the wall. *Arms and the highest bidder.*

Clive seems excited that Radha drinks—*nice girls do not*—that she tastes cigars—*nice girls would not*—that she knows his profession—*nice girls should not—what? Talk about it.*

Radha says, while Ranjit Uncle looks on, proud of her (a feeling that smarts in her eyes like cigar smoke), that she and her *husband* run the Company Consumer Goods subsidiary, the shawls and extras: she knows exactly what they buy and sell, from whom. And how it comes and goes.

—Peace! says Clive. Women's lib.

Over whisky nightcaps and flambé toffee apples, gold skin crisp and flesh so soft, Radha curls into the sofa, to the left of Ranjit Uncle, *her good side,* her pretty feet near enough for his hand to use as a rest, should it want to. She tells stories of Bollywood stars and their unnatural demands, desperate PRs, working non-stop on the gloss; money goes through this system, getting snorted and smoked; a cash injection of liquid highs, supplied from the most secret of Company sources, *isn't that right, Ranjit Uncle?* He laughs and presses her foot; he remembers the time a Hollywood studio came to Mumbai to meet Radha, wanted her to take them to Dharavi basti, to hear all about Bapuji; yes, and she drinks her shot now, and confesses she supplied them with details—Bapuji's love of antique guns and his fixation on Q&A games—they didn't believe her. They made a biopic (which flopped) in which Bapuji started life in poverty and made it big in the textile trade by never taking a bribe. How Clive laughs at this, his laugh like a rifle shot, *hapaphapahapa.* Radha laughs too, she laughs in the right moments as Ranjit Uncle shares every single detail of a chocolate-making course he has just completed with a Swiss-trained pastry chef called Miles Vertenbaker, a name she thinks is funny, but this time Clive doesn't laugh, maybe he didn't get the joke. As her sari slides off her shoulder, Ranjit Uncle brings a selection of delicate dark truffles wrapped in gold leaf—he made them himself. He and Clive want to feed her them one by one with their sausage fingers; she bites and smiles, and laughs and swallows; small, hard globes with sharp liquid insides that clog her throat. She keeps drinking whisky and air. *So fun, this is, so fun.* When Ranjit Uncle leaves (to go find, he says, more wine from the hotel cellar), it is time. Clive shifts a little closer to her. She allows his hand to rest in hers, among the sari folds.

He can't stop talking about his son, a fifteen-year-old boy called William (after the British Prince).

—Wills doesn't like what I do. He won't talk to me. He loves all the gear it brings him, though, his iPad, his jeep.

She leans back. She strokes her fingers through her hair.

—Ah, life. Would you be doing this job if you had the chance again?

Her legs uncurl. He watches her toes peek out from her sari, but Clive does not move.

—It is too late for me to change now, he says. He tilts his head downwards, towards hers.

God, he looks *too* sad. Why are foreigners always so *serious*?

—Of course it's not, she says.

She jumps up. Steadies herself. Foot in one sandal then the other. A selfie with him and his cigar. For her private album.

—You seem like a good man, she says. Take your boy on a safari, he'll love it. Bubu and I went for our fifth anniversary to Rwanda to see gorillas. It was just awesome. I don't know who was more interested in who, Bubu in the gorilla or vice versa!

Laughter, laughter, before Ranjit Uncle comes back, she says goodnight and leaves.

Days pass like this: Radha in the gym, working out every morning with Jivan or Bubu. Lunch. Mould creeps over the fruit in the basket, white-speckled green over orange. It starts to collapse and smell; she has to ask for it to be replaced, wondering if the service in this city will ever catch up with Delhi. Afternoons working on the details for the Srinagar opening parties. The pool gets cleaned each day, the water drained out via a sluice pipe which ends—where? Radha does not know. She likes the way the tiled sides are scrubbed; ready for her evening swim when she goes lengths, then into the dipping bubbles while Ranjit Uncle sits by her; he goes through her plans, adding names to the list, taking some off, who is in, who is out. *Never outsource your initial sales. Acquire your first hundred customers yourself,* chimes the Bapuji Bol! Drinks. Dinner. Morning: *An educated child is a future tycoon.* Tea, cakes, there are no macarons. Bubu calls on friends from Amritsar to play Jivan's poker game each night—the rules become more and more complex. No one can quite make all of them out—though Jivan himself says they are simple as snap for children.

Radha spirals through the hotel corridors, she goes up and down in the lift; gym in the basement, lunch in the restaurant, tea in Ranjit Uncle's suite. Working in the hotel's offices, to the rooftop bar and back down to her bed. At night, thoughts of Jivan make her press against Bubu, which earns her one tight slap after another on her cheeks. She feels chased by boredom, *thank God for MrGee.* Tweet this, tweet that, about all things Company. And the automated service chimes the passing of the days. *Our dreams have to be bigger. Our spirits deeper. Travel further: together we can make new.*

One evening Bubu takes her back to the airport and up in the little plane. They fly towards the sunset: half an hour later they are over

Srinagar; they do not land, but loop high around. From the window Bubu points out mountains turning red in the sinking sun; bouncing light off the snow. There are the passes through which money melts, into the river that flows through Company taps. Down there somewhere is the high place where chirus are hunted. Radha tucks her shawl into her jacket, though it is not cold. On the way back there is turbulence; it only makes Bubu excited, and more energetic. The little plane tosses against his rhythm and she, face in a backrest, hips in his hands, knees lifting off the seat with movement and countermovement, grips on to the thought of Jivan. His hand reaches forward into her mouth, the finest fresh snow from the Kashmiri mountains rubbed onto her gums. Then it feels good. She shrieks like a chiru, feeling split in half by her husband.

Three nights later, after drinks, dinner, drinks, and a shot-by-shot game of jubaan twisters with Ranjit Uncle in his suite, Radha goes up to the roof. Night rules. The palms loom over the pool as if the trees themselves have drowned and left their ghosts behind. Jivan and Bubu are playing the card game with two of Bubu's Amritsar friends—Pankaj and Rahul Singh, both tall and broad-turbaned, with family in local sweets. A box of jalebi is open on the card table. She looks at it, full of gooey, twisty, gold. *Bad jalebi. Bad sweets. No, Radha, no.*

Jivan has added in dice: the Indians are non-stop losing. Radha is in a mood that wants their attention, will sing and dance to get it. She stalks around the deck. She leans over the balustrade to watch the trucks playing chicken on the highway. If she raised her hand, she could pick them up from here, pull off their wheels, watch them try to keep running. When she was nine, Jeet used to make her do this to cockroaches, wiggle-wiggle if you catch them, then crack as you squish, brown blood on Radha-baby's hand. Screaming tears, she would hold out her arm, five fingers spread. Jeet used to tease her, force her to lick them.

It must be two in the morning at least. She never goes into the city here, it would take at least an hour—in the daytime Amritsar is a simpleton, Delhi's big, fat Auntyji squatting in the corner of the party. Yet at night it is held in a wired kind of peace, fuelled, she supposes, by the chanting from the Golden Temple, non-stop, non-stop. Her class of tourists *love* this monument so much *more* than the Taj Mahal, *it's so clean, so quiet, no one bothers you there. And have you seen the langar cooked to feed hundreds of the poor each day?* So strong the Sikh faith is, so beautiful, so honourable. Ranjit Uncle's faith. A breeze rises in the treetops but the hotel is too far away to catch the chanting. Still, there is *something,* like a snatch of music in the air, which Radha cannot identify. A whistle, perhaps, just the trees.

Radha wanders back to the card table; Jivan has a pile of chips in front of him, he is leaning back in his chair, grinning. Bubu has lost his tie, his top shirt buttons are undone; his face like a sulky schoolboy's. The men look up to greet her cocktail dress and legs, her Louboutins. *Yes,* say the trees, *you are pretty;* the night sky seems to agree. Bubu holds his arm out and she stands behind him, resting her glass on his head. He twists his arm around her waist, pressing her sequins into her skin. He's got shitty cards.

—Babe, he says. This madarchod foreigner is whipping my ass.

—Aw, it's such a cute ass. Come on, you can't let this American beat you.

—Hey friend, says Jivan. I've known you since you were in poopy nappies, I've got the Indian chips *and* the foreigner chips.

—Not possible, dude, says Bubu. You gotta choose. And you didn't properly grow up here. How can you know what's up? We like to party hard, we like our women sexy, we like our spirits neat. And we don't play by anyone's rules but our own. That's the Indian way!

Jivan tips his glass to Bubu.

—And yet here you are, he says. You think I can't beat you?

—Don't worry, your day will get over. You know what I say to the US of A?

—What? Tell us, O Bubu, O Sage! Radha says.

—This is India, man! Anything they can do, we can do better. And we'll have theirs as well.

—Amen, says Jivan.

They all raise their glasses and drain them; they order more bourbon to be poured.

—Just don't lose too much, she says to Bubu. It's my birthday soon.

Jivan looks up at her.

—Hey, yours too, she says. November. God—do you remember Gargi and her cakes? Me, then you. Yours was always nicer. You used to come to our house all dressed up for an official birthday visit. Wasn't there even a bow tie one year?

—OK, Miss Piggy, says Jivan.

—Wasn't she your favourite toy? Piggy, piggy, chants Bubu. Don't disrespect your sister. It's too bad for Gargi that she doesn't get any. Blow on my hand, Raddy. Be lucky, or I'll lose everything and I'll have to bet you.

She sits on Bubu's knee. He has to put his arms around her.

—And what will happen if Jivan wins me, and I protest? she asks. Will he pull on my sequins? I don't think Lord Krishna is going to appear and replace them with Prada after Prada.

Bubu drums his hands on the table as if she is the singer of profound ghazals, just about to begin.

—Jivan, do you know what she's on about? Look—our Foreign Return doesn't even know his basic *Mahabharat*!

—Kids' stories, says Jivan. Star Plus rubbish. I know how to count what you owe and that's good enough for me.

—But you should know these things, Radha says. According to our resident Sage Bubu, *Hamare apne India mein, yeh chize pata honi chahiye, nahin toh sab toot jayega.* Get it? Poor Jiju. Let me transplain. In our India we should know these things, otherwise everything will be lost. No, "toot jayega" means "it will break." Whatever. Here begins your first scripture lesson.

She gets off Bubu's knee, stands, the stem of her glass falling between her fingers. She shakes out her hair, watched by Bubu and his sugar buddies, she moves so that she is in front of Jivan, hand on jutting hip bone, wine raised high like one of the Sisters from her convent school, about to baptise him in the name of the Lord.

—Let me play, and I'll tell you, she says.

—Tell me, and I'll let you play, says Jivan.

—Promise?

—I cross my heart. Isn't that right? Cross my heart, hope to die, he says.

—Never, ever speak a lie, she continues, then together, faster and faster, If you do I'll tell Nanu and that will be the end of you! One, Two! They reach to slap each other's cheeks; she ducks, he lunges, her wine spills between her legs and she is bent double, hair hanging down, teetering over the dark red mess.

—Radha, come on, get up, says Bubu.

—Whoa, hold on there, sister! Jivan kneels to help her straighten. Come sit down. Want some water? Want to go to bed?

She smirks a little; he does not see.

—She's fine, man! You need more wine, baby? says Bubu. Just get her some more wine.

They sit her up on Bubu's chair. Her glass is full again. Red, *like liquid rubies. Drink up, drink up.* None of the men have noticed that Radha almost puked at their feet. They leave her to go and smoke at the bar. Only Jivan stays. She puts her elbows among the cards and the scattered rupee notes. Zeros swim up at her, a thousand pink faces of Gandhiji. *Laughing, laughing, laughing.*

She wants to know if Jivan remembers how his Ma used to do that dance with the stripping: Draupadi in the gambling hall, *you know,* the wife married to the five brothers. And her husband gambles everything he has to his bad old cousin, until she is the only thing left. And then her husband rolls the dice and loses. He loses everything, and then he loses her.

—Then what happens? Jivan says; he leans forward, stroking her hair back. His hand feels so cool on her face.

—Draupadi comes to the hall and refuses to go with the evil cousin, then one of her uncles tries to take off her sari. She's a pious type, so she prays hard to Lord Krishna; the blue one with the flute? Anyway, as the sari unravels, one more appears, then one more, then one more. You must remember. It was our favourite part of the dance. Your Ma used to spin and spin, she used to flick out her dupatta—

Radha stops. She looks at Jivan and sees the little boy who used to hide behind the door with her, gripping her arms too tightly as his Ma stripped her coverings until there was only one left. Red, a flame. And their relief as she stopped there, and began to circle, her skirts spinning out, her feet going so fast, jewels on her wrists and neck flashing under the chandeliers as if she were the force that made the earth turn.

Jivan gets up from the table.

—You need water, he says.

. . .

Bubu comes back; he pats Radha's head. He reaches into his shirt pocket and takes out a small wrap of coke. He uses his favourite card, the Queen of Diamonds, to cut it into lines; the Jack of Clubs to make them straight. Radha watches Bubu's hands holding the cards. She stands so he can sit on her seat, she takes her place on his knee. He rolls up a pink thousand note and passes it to Radha. He pushes down on the back of her neck, holding her until she is finished. *Flick up your hair now, Radha, and wander past the pool, to the lip of the roof. So high. And your beauty, and your body is the only thing between the drop to the ground and the stars.*

The world is full of glimmering colours and lights. She takes off her heels and begins to trace the steps of the Draupadi dance, slowly beginning to twirl, then faster and faster until she cannot stand anymore. Her dress has no straps and no pleated skirt, her black sequins are sparkling, catching the pool light, making her feel like a comet.

—O my God! she shouts. Awesome! I'm awesome!

Jivan's Ma must have loved this dance. Radha collapses on a lounger, panting. Tries to pick out faces among all the stars.

She leans over the balustrade again. Down below, at the back of the hotel, she can see the back-kitchen courtyard, bright-lit. There's a group of men, a circle around two figures. Wrestling, or waltzing? She cannot tell. She lets out a giggle. Something fun is going on down there.

She picks up her shoes by their heels: her diamond rings flash dark against the patent leather, the red sole. She should just drop one shoe over the balustrade and let it bomb. Behind her, Jivan says,

—Radha? Something's going on downstairs, my dad wants Bubu and me. We're going down.

—Wait for me, she says. I'm coming.

She carries her shoes in her hand. They take the lift. Radha could run down the whole thirteen floors. At eight, the doors open; Ranjit Uncle is standing there. He is in his topi and kurta pyjama, carrying his stick, looking too old. Radha feels her giggle rising, something about nightcaps and nightcaps, get it, *get it?* One for @MrGee.

Radha slides behind Bubu, pulling her sequins up over her breasts and then down again over her thighs. Up, down, up, down, off! Don't speak, Radha, chup-chup, *shh.*

—Bubu! What kind of host am I? Ranjit Uncle says. He is flustered, his pyjama string hangs below his kurta: Radha sees it, tries not to reach, and pull. I'm sorry your game got disturbed, he says.

—Let's see, says Bubu, sounding sober.

How can he be? Radha thinks she wants to poke him with her shoes, they should be on her feet, but she cannot reach down to put them on, she knows she will fall over. O God, giggles are coming again: Bubu's face is so damn straight. The Lobby is on night watch; *service exit this way, dear, this way, not that.* They follow Ranjit Uncle through the restaurant—all the tables are set as if for a party of invisible friends. Through the swing service doors and into the kitchen, where men in white coats endlessly clean a stainless steel world, where the light is too bright and the duty chefs stare at her as if she is next for the chop. Bubu stops. He takes off his jacket. He drapes it around Radha's shoulders. He holds her as she puts her shoes on—one, two—she still wants to laugh. Maybe she should do the Draupadi dance. She begins to wiggle, but that makes her stumble, so she stops.

She follows Bubu outside. Radha has not been outside at ground level since they arrived here one whole week ago. She has never been to the back of the hotel. A floodlit space. Clean, but the smell, she thinks, must be rotting food turning into sludge. She pulls Bubu's sleeve over her hand, presses the hand over her mouth and nose. A group of orderlies, skinny, dark figures in dirty vests and dhotis, smoke bidis and cheer as they watch the fight. Inside their circle are two men, wrestling. One, Radha thinks, is definitely Uppal. It's quite funny, because he's wearing work clothes, the dark jacket and trousers of Company special advisers, all a little too tight. When he stretches one arm, the other jerks up a little. And his opponent—Radha squints—who is he?

—Stop this, shouts Bubu. What is happening here?

The smokers disperse, the acrid smell of bidis lingers. Eyes flick over Radha, elbows nudge sides. Ranjit Uncle waves his stick at them: they scuttle inside. *So they should,* Radha thinks, lazy buggers standing around.

Uppal is bruised, but his opponent is an even older man. Head tied up in a dirty pagri, he is bleeding from his nose into his beard. *Gross.* Ranjit Uncle clasps his stick, he wrings his hands. Jivan crosses to the fight, he grabs the old man by the arms. All of them caught in the lights: eyes bloodshot, skins dusty, pricks of bright, *liquid rubies,* here's a beggar, a madman, a hijra, a bhoot. Radha's skin prickles as if flies are landing on her, landing, leaving, landing, landing, leaving. She shakes her head to clear the dancing colours; an old filmy tune comes to her, becomes the chorus of the night, *Mera joota hai Japani, ye patloon Ingalistaani, sar pe laal topi Rusi, phir bhi dil hai Hindustaani.* Earworm, earworm, she will never be rid of this song.

—You say you have come from my father? Nahin, tum gully ke ho, she says.

She has never heard herself sound like this: like lime and salt in the cut. As if she has lived so long that she is young again and able to say whatever she wants. The old man breaks Jivan's grip and crouches on the ground. Radha really wants to go to him, tickle and pat him. *Nice doggy.*

—Kashyap, he barks. I want to speak to Ranjit here. I have messages from Bapuji.

Ranjit Uncle starts, he holds his hands together over his heart—*who me?* He seems to be saying: *Why should Bapuji send you to me?*

—Kashyap, says Jivan. What are you doing here? You don't work for the Company anymore, or did you forget?

—He is Kashyap, Radha dear. He followed Kritik Sahib for many years, says Ranjit.

Kashyap. Is Radha meant to know him? She will call him Ketchup and order French Fries. Now he is shadow boxing: a grizzled contender refusing to retire. *Fight! Fight! Come on,* Radha whispers, fists clenched. Almost, she wants to cheer.

—I was dismissed before my time, but I will never leave Bapuji's side. I've been his man and Kritik Sahib's deputy for thirty-plus years— I am not going to give up now.

—I am sorry, Bubuji, Radha Madam, Ranjitji, Mr. Jivan, says Uppal. I am here from Gargi Madam, she has sent me to help you. With the Srinagar hotel opening plans. I was just collecting my thoughts out here when this filth showed up. Last time in Delhi he humiliated me in front of Bapuji and Nanuji. He pushed me, then he punched me. For no reason. Just now, he kicked me again.

Kashyap balances on his toes, fists up. He pulls up his dirty banyan and wipes his face on it, showing his belly. It is covered in grey hair, like an old doggy should have.

—Uppal, he barks. You have really strained yourself, fighting your betters.

Ha ha, funny man, Radha thinks, *to think he can be so familiar. Familiar man,* she thinks, *they say he has been around for years. Watching.*

—This is Amritsar, the sacred city of peace, Kashyap says. But Waheguru is not within any of you. He points at Uppal, his finger seems so long.

—Even Allah is not in you, he says to Uppal. Aré nahin. Tum toh pathar ke bane ho.

—What absolute crap, says Bubu. Come here.

Kashyap salutes. He wipes his face again. Sweat and blood come off. He smiles, and his teeth are so white and clean. They bloom out of his face like jasmine flowers from rock. *Sharp,* Radha thinks, *like Kritik Sahib's.*

—Hanji, Bubu Sahib! Maybe you were painted by Mr. M.F. Husain, come back among us! Art for the people! Or, an untrained darji made you—no reputable tailor would stitch such a poor fit of a man. Ha ha ha!

Is this funny? Radha tries to be quiet and keep still. Uppal says,

—Apparently he is now one of Bapuji's men. But why should Bapuji send this man, when he could call you up directly? Or communicate any issue through Gargi Madam via me?

—Suar ke bachche! Don't open your mouth, Kashyap spits at Uppal. White foam lands on the ground. Radha stares at it dissolving, leaving nothing but a stain on the earth.

He said his name was Kashyap and he comes from Bapuji. He said he worked for Kritik Sahib. His teeth are white, so white, so pointed. *Bubu, Ranjit Uncle, Jivan—Kashyap is just like Kritik Sahib.* Has she spoken? Perhaps not? No one is looking at her. Ranjit Uncle and Bubu and Jivan are standing arms out, forming a fence around the two fighters. There is nothing beyond but the yellow brick wall. Then there is the sky and the same sky is over Dhimbala basti—from there to Napurthala, where— stop.

Radha is actually outside. No rooms, no walls, no doors. She is out-side. She is outside Bubu's or Ranjit Uncle's view. Now all that comes out are giggles. Such a pretty night to be. So many colours in this stink of a place. *Kashyap is Kritik Sahib's man, he is Bapuji's man—O shit.*

—Bubu sir, Kashyap says. I know you are a great being, and your family is involved in the construction of our beloved country. It is com-mon knowledge that you have the prospect of following your respected uncle into political life. You are married to this fine lady here (*me, that's me,* Radha thinks) who has grown from excellent seed.

Almost, she bows. Instead she teeters towards Bubu, she tries to catch his arm. Now the Kashyap–Kritik–Bapuji man is pointing at her, his voice rising,

—Yet she is the wife of a flesh-eating ghoul, she covers the sacred fire and sits on it, he says. Just let me take care of this Uppal. Then I will show what this elder can do.

—Bubu, Radha says. She tugs his arm. He shrugs her off.

—Chup! snaps Bubu. Don't you know when to say "enough is enough"?

Kashyap smiles.

—I know this well enough. But enough isn't yet, sir, enough is when one is dead. When we are righteous, we cannot say enough.

Now Radha's giggle can come out, now is the time to let it.

—Radha, I mean it, enough! Bubu says. Ranjit, can you take her inside?

—Come, Radha beti, Ranjit Uncle says. Just wait in the kitchen, at least. Jivan, please take her inside.

—I'll be quiet, she says. Look! She retreats to the wall, she puts both Bubu's jacket sleeves over her mouth. *Kashyap is just like Kritik Sahib,* the wall agrees. *He is Bapuji's man.*

—Tell me this. Years I have watched you, I know what you are. I know you value men like this Uppal with his Gargi, Kashyap says.

His face is now blocked by Bubu's back, Radha can only hear him. She moves, but now Jivan is in the way, then Ranjit Uncle. At the kitchen door, there's a security guard, *give me a leg up?* She wants to say: *Be my piggy or my horsey, let me see what's going on.* All she can do is listen.

—This Uppal who says *Yes, Gargi Ma'am* to everything, never speaks the truth to those he is meant to serve. Has he not ruined his Gargi Madam? Caused her to steal from the Company for herself? Spied for her on our dear Sita, our dear Bapuji? says Kashyap.

His question crashes behind Radha's eyes, causing stars, such pretty stars, to jump. Bubu is angry, she can tell, even the back of his neck seems enraged. This man better shut up soon.

—Actually, it is not Uppal's fault, Kashyap says. *Still talking, he's still talking!* He is a dog begging for treats. Typical smiling, as if nothing can matter. Chi! he says. Out, you, go back to your Farm with your Gargi Madam. Come, let me beat you back there!

—Enough, says Bubu. Uppalji, get inside. Get cleaned up, we will sort out this business in the morning.

Uppal retreats into the kitchen. Bubu signals, Jivan moves; now Radha can finally see. Jivan pins Kashyap's arms behind his back. There is a short struggle—but Jivan is strong enough, he is so strong—*and cleaner too*—then Kashyap stops. There are only his words, which fall from his mouth as fast as if someone were sucking them from him; Radha licks her sleeve—if this Kashyap can speak, then Radha can too—she opens her mouth—but Kashyap gets there first.

—He is a liar, I am honest. He is a lizard, I am a man. What else do you need, sir? He follows the leader, these days I lead the followers. I don't like his face.

—So what? says Jivan. He hands Kashyap to the security guard. He wipes his arm across his forehead.

—Come on, man, apologise, or things will get bad.

Kashyap's eyes flick over Bubu, over Ranjit Uncle. Over Radha's legs and her Louboutins. He seems to edge towards her.

—What is it this Madam does? Blowing garam hawa in a hot country. I have travelled all over India and seen better faces licking out the village latrine than any I can see now.

—Aré wah! says Bubu. Big words. Salah chut! He raises a hand. Radha knows what is coming, she cannot watch. She hears Bubu strike, the old man cry,

—Pah!

Radha sucks her cheeks, her lips, into her mouth. She bites. Tastes her own blood. Swallows.

—Bhagwan jo hum ko dekhta hain, Bhagwan jo paani hum ko pilata hain, tat tvam asi, Sasri Akal. I thought you, being from such a fine upstarting family and married to this Goddess, would appreciate me speaking in the language of the Brahmins. I speak as the common man. I am as honest, cries Kashyap.

Radha peers through her splayed fingers; Jivan has his knee on Kashyap's back, Ranjit Uncle seems frozen, like one of Jeet's statues.

—Tie him up, says Bubu. At the back gate.

—O Krishna! says Kashyap. This lot would make a fool out of Yudishthira, a servant out of Bhim!

—Get the handcuffs, Ranjit, Bubu says. He bends close. Maybe this can teach you a lesson in manners, since you didn't learn it in school, he says.

—I'm too old, Sahib, for foreigners' teaching. Ranjit Sahib, fetch your iron choodiya and let Madam Radha put them on me to wed me to her; maybe I can please her tonight, heh heh?

—We will cuff you to the back gate, and you sit there until tomorrow midday, or until you can say *sorry*, Bubu says.

He spits into the dirt.

—Come, Madam! Kashyap holds out his hands, beckons with his fingers. Embrace me, since I come directly from your Bapuji. You might know him: Mr. Devraj, Maharaja of Napurthala. Your shame has no bounds if you insult the man who has given you . . . shall we calculate? O everything.

Now tears prick her, not fair, no, a drink, a little song, that is all; Kashyap's face is ugly, he is her old Masterji, threatening her bad report. The lights are so bright here, why are they, what for?

—Don't you address me, she says. You can sit until tomorrow night. Until the day after morning. I am Radha Devraj Kumari Balraj, I say so.

She twists away from Bubu and kicks at old Kashyap. Catching his knee with her shoe's pointed toe.

—Madam! You would not do this to your sister's dog, Kashyap gasps. His voice is pained and full of sadness, as if he knows her (*of course he does*) and she has proved him right. As if she is the biggest disappointment of his entire age.

Ranjit Uncle comes with the handcuffs. Radha has never seen real ones before. She wants to feel their weight. How shiny they are.

She gives the man one more kick in the side of his thigh.

—Bubuji? Radha beti? Ranjit Uncle looks at her as if he cannot imagine that his sweet Radha could hurt a man like that.

—Please think again, Ranjit Uncle says. Kashyap is rude beyond all reason, but he has not done anything wrong. If he has, then let Bapuji deal with it, OK? This, this handcuffs business—this is how we punish boys who steal from the kitchen.

—Ranjit Uncleji, don't worry, she says. We must teach as we have learned. Why don't you go up. I'll order some tea for you and some rice khir to come to your room, OK?

—It is my duty to advise but ultimately to obey.

Ranjit Uncle shakes the handcuffs. *What a clink chime clink.* He says,

—I will make sure it is done.

. . .

Tired, so tired, it must be time for Radha-baby to go to the roof and finish her wine and play some cards. Or get a foot massage and order hot milk and go to bed. She does not want Bubu near her, he looks too rabid tonight.

—Hungry? she asks him.

—Rumali roti, tandoori chicken kebab. Make sure it's hot, OK?

—Go finish your cards. I'll just give the kitchen the order.

The night-duty chef must be told how charred and how tender to roast Bubu's kebab. Radha stands in the kitchen among sacks of rice, flour, sugar; she repeats the order till the chef can say it back to her. Then she returns outside, scuffing her shoes across the kitchen courtyard and down through the gardens towards the back gate. Strange night, strange path she has never been down before. She still has Bubu's jacket on. In his pocket she finds his Camels and his gold Company Zippo; she offers herself a cigarette and takes one. Feels the smoke calm her; inhale and exhale: *smoke, Radha-baby, smoke.*

Lotus-shaped light bulbs are planted along the path. Sprinklers hiss. Bats cut the sky above Radha's head. She can see the gate, and a group of men around it. She treads so softly in heels.

Halfway there, the path goes kachcha, the lighting stops. The night freshness of wet foliage is undercut by the stink of rotting food; *must be coming from the basti just beyond the back gate.* Radha ducks into the trees. She watches the group of men; she sees Kashyap cuffed to the chaukidar's post. Hands behind his back. She sees Ranjit Uncle commiserate with him, but the chained man just shakes his head and laughs.

What will her father say when he hears about this? Doubt licks at Radha. She creeps closer. Hears Ranjit Uncle and this man sigh together. Thinks she can hear them: *Sita.*

Radha cups her cigarette to contain it. Squats down as Ranjit Uncle and his security begin to walk back towards the hotel.

The chained man calls out,

—Don't worry, Ranjitji. Sacrifice creates the heat that keeps the world turning. If no one sacrifices, the sun will not rise.

Ranjit Uncle laughs. He salutes a goodnight without looking back. He passes so close that Radha is sure he can see her, or at least smell her smoke.

She needs to pee. No one is watching, no one in the world knows where she is. Above her head the sky is pierced with stars, Swarovskis hand-stitched over a deep black shawl. She crouches on her heels, bites down on her cigarette and hikes up her dress. Pulls her panties down to her ankles and strains until susu comes. She can hear her heart competing with the crickets. She holds her breath then slowly exhales. It streams out, it spreads around her feet—and she cannot stop it touching her shoes. She tosses the cigarette into the puddle. It hisses out. There is a skitter of gravel from somewhere behind her, then silence. Can the chained man see her? She wriggles back into her panties, pulls down her dress, *fucking sequins, stupid dress,* and tries to stand.

—Hai Ram! says the chained man. Time cooks all beings. Smile on your servant, Lord Shiva. So does the wheel of dharma turn: Come then, what will come, and Indra take pity on me.

He begins to whistle, "Memory."

Radha takes a breath. Feet slipping on the wet grass, she turns back. Onto the path. The lotus lights wink and follow her; the captive's whistle fingers her inner ear, all the way up to the roof.

———•———

WANT TO KNOW MY SECRET to business success? Sell your vision, not just the product. Not many people know I can be poetical. A statesman must be many things. First, he must tell a good story so you fall for his dreams. Second, he understands the power of repeating, until his stories transcend to the level of mantra and myth, become the truth of what has passed, a blueprint for the future. Third, a statesman is a statesman.

These days modern women profit from all we have worked for. They work for themselves and this we also support. Many give up their work after marriage, some don't, and this we think is right, particularly in certain sectors of the family business. Soft management, for example, which they so appropriately undertake. Public relations, which Radha is quite good at, and which is necessary for today's world. I thought that after her marriage, Sita could take over, and Radha could get on with the business of motherhood.

But Sita just told me that she does not want to marry.

—Until the law changes for the rights of women, and all are protected, from eyes, from the streets, from brothers, uncles, from husbands.

—And from fathers, I suppose? I said. Sita, what is this legality? I laughed. What price tradition?

—To say *no,* and be heard! she said. That is a freedom some will only dream of.

—Should I beg you for kindness? Will you please spare me this? I said.

Above my head the angel turns, so sad at my tears.

—Come down now, I ask it, but there is no reply. Don't you want to come? Answer me. No? Still refusing to speak? Fine, I said. Listen, little bird, and I will tell you another story.

When I was on the road, I met a beggar boy named Rudra, who was pretending to be a girl. He was always cold, so I gave him my best shawl. It was an act of love. Rudra was a kind boy, and reminded me of myself at his age. Funny and honest, with the ability to move a crowd in his favour. He had a peculiar way of talking, mixing his words in many tongues as if it didn't matter what language he was speaking, as if from the mountains of this place to the jungles of Sri Lanka, anyone would be able to understand. On the night I was caught in a terrible storm, he sang these words to me:

When the King does not wield the punishment justly, a dog will lick the offering. Then every thing will be turned upside down.

ii

In the morning they flock to berate her: Kritik Sahib, Ranjit Uncle, Nanu, Sita and Bapuji. They stand at the foot of the bed: a five-headed fury. *Radha, nice girls do not! Nice girls could not!* She hugs her pillow and wails to the faces gathered around her. *Why are you persecuting me only? Bubu was there, and Jivan. Ranjit Uncle, you were there too.* Kritik, Nanu, Sita and Bapuji fade away, but Ranjit Uncle stays; his eyes are so eager but so disappointed in her. The same look he gave when she was too tired for tongue-twist-finger-kiss, blindman's touch: it gives her that fly-crawl-on-skin feeling.

A mellow light hints through the curtains. The room is shadowed and chill. Bubu has left her wrapped in the sheets, a body waiting for burning. Where are the servants? Where is her breakfast? Around her the wallpaper's vines of cherries creep, its leaves and apples dangle, looking so juicy and ripe. *Stop dreaming, Radha, stop dreaming.* Do the dead eat? What do they eat? Do the dead order room service? Can they read today's papers? Radha is thirsty. *If I eat and drink and look pretty, Ranjit Uncle, will you please go away?*

Do chained men deserve water? He shakes his head. So sad, he is. So gentle.

Stop dreaming. Radha opens her eyes. The phone is a solid reality: that is good. She sits up in the bed. The stern hands on the old carriage clock point straight up. Noon. The room shrinks back from her; last night's cigarette smoke lingers in her clothes. Using the bedside phone, she asks the chef what the specials are.

—Ranjit Sahib has organised a rare Wagyu beef burger for you, Radha Ma'am, he says. I can make it with bacon, cheese, and smoky sauce.

Radha should not eat this. In Amritsar. She knows Gargi wouldn't like it. Neither would Nanu. But Ranjit Uncle would be disappointed. She cannot decide.

—I'll have it, she says. With a side of stringy fries, a katori of mayonnaise, and one of ketchup. Ketchup. She rubs her head. A soft bun.

—Make sure it is soft, she says. And the sauce should come in a chilled silver dish with its own tiny spoon.

To drink: a chocolate milkshake. And to finish: a fruit cup with raspberry ripple ice cream. No, a rasgullah. No, ice cream. Perhaps what she actually wants is hot, fresh cholay, piled high on a puri and squeezed with lime, black from a street vendor's hands. She will have the burger, and a Bloody Mary with extra spice to start.

In the bathroom, Radha splashes her face and arranges her hair. She puts on her base, her foundation, her powder, it makes her feel so natural and fresh. She does not bathe, just runs and jumps back into bed, settling herself with her mobile to wait for her food.

By the time the butler has knocked to say her cocktail is mixed, her burger is assembled, and would she like salt and pepper on her fries—by the time she has scrolled MrGee and tweeted, *Did you know the Company Srinagar hotel is bringing jobs and hope to over 100 impoverished local women* (not true) and *Bubu Balraj works out every day—he's a role model for young entrepreneurs* (could be true) and *Cigar smoking is the new pastime of wealth and cool* (as of now, true)—her food has been served on a bed tray, with the day's press cuttings on the side. Radha dips a fry in mayonnaise. Almost eats it. But is caught by a snap of Bapuji in Goa, doing Yoga on the beach. Bent into positions Radha has never seen him in. Niralambha: shoulder pose (unsupported): pyjama rolled up, toosh around his neck, bums in the air. Pasasana: squatting, arms twisted around legs, hands joined in a noose. *Morning prayers, evening prayers,* she reads. Then, Bapuji went to Ghaziabad, where he met with the strikers. *He shook their hands,* the cutting says, and promised to address their demands. After that, in Mumbai, he held a vegetarian lunch for all the key religio-politicos in their saffron and khadi. Which ended in a rendition of "Jana Gana Mana," led by Nanu, apparently exchanging the word "Sindh" for "Sindhu." *Can you exchange a province in Pakistan for a river in India?* Radha thinks. MrGee goes online, finds the story and retweets it: *Check it—Jana Gana Mana: the Bapuji mix.*

La la la, Bloody Mary and a burger. Bapuji cannot action any of his plans. He can promise nothing to the workers but his words. Whatever he wants to do with that Goa land—retirement villas for foreigners, hundred-hole golf courses, whatever—Bubu and Gargi will not allow it. The Yoga and the sing-song—maybe that is just age. Older men cultivate their spiritual intensity; *India Today* said so, only last week. *Huh,* she thinks. *Yoga is a philosophy, not just a pose.*

Her mobile chimes: *God watches over those who watch over themselves— Bapuji.* Radha thinks of Bapuji's subscribers, all reading this text right now. She bites into the burger, tasting cheese, pickle, the tang of raw onion and a tomato slice that seems to have been cooked (why do they never get that right?), as she checks through the faxes brought up from reception: every single one is from Gargi. She has seen the cuttings and thinks Radha has authorised these stories. She pulls a sliver of tomato skin off her tongue and wipes it on the bedsheets. It seems as if Bapuji is en route to Amritsar. Radha tries to visualise a *What Would Gargi Do?* scenario; instead she can only think, with some surprise, about Sita.

—Sita, she says, to her burger. What would you do now? Be honest. O? You would tell Dad, when he shows up, what you really feel. Very good! What do I really feel? That's an interesting question for a girl like me. Chalo, let's think.

Radha picks up a French fry—it is her father. *Good PR is the future of this Company. Bapuji, you are mad if you don't realise this. I am a wife, and since Gargi has abdicated that responsibility I will also be a mother. Now that Sita has gone, it is up to me to supply the future of this family. Yes?* She bites the top off the fry.

Enough thinking. Time for her daily dose of weird and wondrous, though the file is slim pickings today. *Two-headed cow born in Chandigarh as full moon rises on consecutive days* (the picture almost makes her spit out her burger). *Freak gale brings Calcutta to a standstill:* this one with a picture of the normal choked traffic lanes, the normal standstill—not that funny. *Delhi's INA vegetable market covered in filth and flies—source for all households and five-star hotels.* Why is that even news? The next one is better: *Five-limbed baby needs immediate surgery, angry villagers call her Goddess, want extra arm to stay.* The parents are trying to get admission to hospital. Radha will get someone to call them up and offer to pay the fees. A little job she can do.

Now to the columns, and the *Speaking Tree,* where her dear brother-in-law has failed once again to be published. Poor Surendraji, always scribbling away. Penning his mind for anyone to read. He keeps trying to get a slot; yet it seems all the kickbacks in the world cannot make the editor print him. Today is for Swami Vivekananda: you have to respect a Guru who reached thousands of followers before mobile phones even happened. *The path of non-resistance,* his message for today. Surendraji should take it as a sign and give up.

Now to the horoscopes: all agree—this is the time for stinging Scorpio to find love and adventure. The advertisements endorse this: again and again Radha sees a picture of a brown Penelope Pitstop astride her pink scooter, her hair blowing out under her helmet, her legs in high-heeled pink boots. *You, as a woman, love to revel in every sensation, and express every emotion. Here is a feeling you have never touched before. Just mount your new scooter and kick off: become one with the universe, your karma complete, your chic intact. Come into a new world you never dreamed of. Now cherish your engine power*—Does she want a scooter? Is she too old? This thing is for college girls from the outskirts of the cities: good families, but even so. Or girls who, for the first time, are making their own money; who don't yet have husbands to think about. Where would Radha even ride? She never goes out in the city. Not to markets or to restaurants where everyday girls go. Still, she might get one scooter. To scoot around the Farm. She could use it as a prop in the ads for the new Company engagement and honeymoon brochures: *Come awaken your senses. Begin your new life in the most elegant Company.* Leather chairs, old movie posters: *Mother India* or *Sholay,* "entry from the backside only" signs, and in the ads, a young couple in formalwear (or maybe lux-Western?) sipping chai (or champagne, she has not decided) on a terrace. Nostalgenticity shabby-chic circa 1950s to the '70s: this is the romance of now.

Her bedside phone rings—her hand hovers over it and she prays, *Not Gargi, not Bubu, not Daddy. Let it be . . . Jivan.* And then she answers.

—Hello?

—Radha beti, are you OK?

—Ranjit Uncle. I'm just, you know, catching up with work. I wanted to stay in the room; it's so quiet, so nice here.

She hears the chained man's whistle. She curls her toes in the bed.

—Is your food OK, Radha dear? How was your burger?

The remains are congealing on the plate; the sheets are stained with streaks of red. *Radha is eating beef! Radha is eating street food again! Radha-baby is putting on weight!* And so on, up and across the family. Blood on the sheets! *Radha-baby ke Aunty aa gayi hain? Is she down?* Why not call Barun and get it on the front page? *Times of India* of course, after all, it's got the biggest circulation of any newspaper in the English-speaking world. Fact.

—Thank you, Ranjit Uncle, very nice, she says. The chef is really too good. You have done such an outstanding job with this place.

—He can cook anything you want. You want to eat sushi? That he can also make. When you are here, this is your home. I got this meat only for you, air freight.

—Did you try it?

—This is a holy city, beta, he says. Aur waise bhi, as you know, beef main nahin khata.

She knows. The whole business world does: Ranjit Singh, Company Director. So devout, he is famous for it. Moo. Radha picks up the rest of the burger. Stuffs as much as she can in her mouth.

—I hope you find the bed to your comfort, Ranjit Uncle says.

She almost chokes, chews fast and swallows. The whole room stinks of barbecued flesh.

—Ranjit Uncle, she says. I think Bapuji is coming to Amritsar. Did you know about this?

She realises she sounds . . . exclamatory, as her English tutor used to say. With her fetish for glass bangles and market-bought jutti, her printed tea dresses from Liberty London and Scottish cashmere *cardigans*—a word Radha found so alien it always made her think of old white men. *Alicia, not Alice,* had come out to Delhi with her husband, a property developer who Bapuji was using for deals. *Alicia* said she used to work in UK publishing; was always correcting Radha's sentences, trying to iron Radha's accent, until she gave up, and moved on to groom Sita for Cambridge entrance. Now look. Ranjit Uncle thinks Gargi can oversee

70,000 members of staff, even head the Company for now. And Sita can go hang out wherever. But Radha, wife and PR expert, is still his Little Firebrand, running about, begging for a lollipop from his special stash. Still making up stories about the others to enchant him and pressing his feet while she does so.

—Listen, Little Firebrand, Ranjit says. I am going to send some paani to the back gate. Last night Bubu was very upset, but you know your Papa wouldn't like Kashyap treated so badly. Such uncouth brutality should be left to police or the Company gundas. He should be released, at least we should give him one roti and a glass of water.

—No, Radha says.

She hears Ranjit Uncle take a sharp breath.

—It was Bubu's decision, not mine. And Gargi wouldn't like it. Please don't ask me to go against my sister and my husband. I agree with you, you know I do.

Bapuji glares up at her from the cuttings.

—You know I can't say *yes*. Imagine if Mummy had done something Daddy didn't want? My hands are also tied.

—Ah! Your mother, Ranjit Uncle says.

Radha takes one more bite of the burger, ketchup and meat juice squirts out of the bun; it lands across her father's face. She picks up the magazine and licks it. *Chill pill,* she thinks. *Ranjit Uncle cannot actually see.*

—Radha? Ranjit says. You should get up, get ready, come down. Let's at least have tea together, before you have to go.

She won! She cannot quite believe it. Pieces of her fruit cup, the mango and pineapple, are now drowning in a melted sea of pinky ice cream. So much for silver service—they can't even bring the dessert after the main. Giving it all together as if they trained in some two-star opposite a train station. She almost picks up the bowl and drinks the juice, then decides that a first-flush Assam served in bone china is more her mood now.

—Yes, Ranjit Uncle, she says. But have you seen the press today? People are wondering more than ever what is going on in this big old Company of ours. You have to talk to Daddy. Only you can do it, before he does something crazy stupid.

—Don't talk about your Bapuji like that, naughty girl.

She hears a sniff. And another.

—I'll wait for you in the members' lounge, says Ranjit Uncle. Ninth floor.

Good, she thinks. *At least there will be cake.*

The glass door opens and shuts. *Yes,* sings the water, *time to be clean.* Under the shower she feels soft and slippery, she whistles, *no, Radha do not whistle.* Hand over mouth: the chained man is still outside. What talk can she take to tea with Ranjit Uncle? It must distract, delight. Radha steps out of the shower and begins to dry herself. How about her own special plan as a joint shareholder, a very special plan indeed? (What should she wear for tea? Salwar kameez, this red one.) So.

This is the plan. Mrs. Radha Balraj is going to rebrand the Company. No more Devraj Company—Sindh to Sindhu. It's going to be . . . Radha poses bare with her tongs in one hand, the other behind her head, stomach sucked even further inside. —*It's going to be . . . "The India Company! Yes, all you Cosmo-Metro guys and gals, all you newbies to the minted classes, here comes InCo.* Or maybe she should make it IndiCo? No—InCo sounds better. *It is fresh, it is now, it is a new India Company—for the twenty-first century and beyond!*

Radha stretches her arms to the mirror, let the legions of shoppers and shopkeepers come to her mall. Bubu will build it in Paradise Park (and she will not let him call it Radha Mall; God, he is so clueless). No. It will be: The InCo Mall. Short for the India Company but also—*InCo*—she puts on her salwar, she ties the string—this little word sounds street to her: *Inko—they, them*—the InCo Mall for the in-crowd. An ad with a group of girls in acid-brights. Tummy tops and tight jeans and bindis and bangles. Caps back to front, desi-cool, like the girls MrGee eggs on Twitter.

Inko InCo Mall pasand hai!
They love the InCo Mall!

Are you sure, Radha-baby? InCo, or IndiCo? IndiCo sounds too much like IndiGo—which she does consider the best of the country's domestic budget airlines—in branding terms at least. Maybe they could do a tie-up. She would give special airfares to customers travelling between InCo hotels and malls across India. *IndiGo.* Such a great name. She wishes she had thought of it first. Maybe the Company could buy the airline. India: Go go go!

InCo IndiGo pasand hai! InCo loves IndiGo!

No, the other way round:

IndiGo InCo pasand hai! IndiGo loves InCo!

Yes—and the in-crowd—setting off from a Company hotel. All the colours blinding. Or maybe she could use a picture of herself in a business suit, waving from the steps of an InCo–IndiGo plane. It might be good to position herself as the face of the Company—a family touch. Or maybe not. Would she actually have to fly with them?

—I'm in the in-crowd! Kaun? Tu? Haan main! she sings.

Now she flips her head over and begins to blow dry. *Wear your hair straight today.* Spritz your face, Radha, makeup needs fixing. These are serious times. Done. Ready. Tea-time Radha, going down.

She is still whistling as she puts on her rings, her sandals, her beautiful butterfly shawl. She picks up her bag and her shades; she clickclacks to the lift, deciding that—yes—Ranjit Uncle will be first to hear about *InCo.* If he and Bubu like it, Gargi will agree.

When the pianist sees Radha, he begins to play. *La lo la lo,* "Latika's Theme." The lounge has no mirrors, the dark wood and potted palms are anonymous, she ignores them, and the clusters of dimly lit globes. The place is empty except for Ranjit Uncle, sitting at the table in yellow socks and a dark linen suit. *How bald he has become, a Fabergé egg.* She bends to kiss his cheek; soft, wrinkled like the handmade paper in the Company hotel shop. He keeps hold of her hand, he presses her, he has sharp nails and it hurts. She used to massage his hands, rubbing rich cream into his skin. Fixate on them, stroking her knees. Such smooth hands, in the space between. Her school socks and her skirt. Now the skin is scaling, she notices, and peeling around his fingernails.

—You know? he says. I think they should make one musical of *Slumdog Millionaire.* Now, that would be an interesting thing to see.

—Ya, that would be awesome! You should fund it only.

She pulls her hand away, waits while he rises and seats her.

—Can we have macarons? she says. We have started serving these with afternoon tea in the Company Goa hotel and in Mumbai. Really excellent, different-different flavours, liquorice and lychee, massala chai even. Let's order them, please?

Smiling, Ranjit Uncle taps his stick on her shoulder.

—Radha, go easy on me. In Amritsar we like to keep things simple. See? We have excellent choux pastries here.

On the cake stand are five profiteroles. She slides one onto her plate and presses her spoon into it. Cream oozes out of the sides. She scoops a tiny bit up. Vanilla. Ranjit Uncle is watching her, the lines under his eyes fine spokes on a wheel.

—Thank you, Ranjit Uncle, she says.

—Come, come, he says. Have more.

He pushes the profiteroles towards her.

Come, Radha-baby, just one more. Three little profiteroles. She takes one more. Just one more. You and me, together at tea. *A profit of roles,* she wants to say. Ranjit Uncle would not get the joke.

Their heads are so close she can smell him. Cloves, and musk. He is the uncle with the tickly beard: there is still some black in it. He balances his stick by the table. His hands cover hers, and the look he gives her! So kind. She feels tears prick, and swallows.

—Radha, I know you are feeling bad. About the terrible acts of last night. It is thirty-nine degrees today. We cannot leave a man like that. We should go outside together.

—You know, Ranjit Uncle, she says. It was you who taught us kids about how our finest luxuries get made. Remember?

—My sweet Radha.

He moves away from her: his hand twists the air, plucking memory like an apple from the tree. He strokes her, on her shawl, near her collarbone.

—Don't talk about when you were a child. Let us not have tea, let us have a drink, no? Ranjit Uncle says. I'm not so old that I can't have a cocktail with you?

—Of course! You are so young, you could still play dande padenge. Hunter-chiru with the stick. What a harsh game that was, she says.

He smiles at her. His eyes so kind, so calm.

—Two whisky sodas, he says to the waiter.

Radha leans over, and kisses him on the cheek.

—O no, you have a lipstick mark!

Her finger sinks into his cheek; she can feel teeth. She leaves a red smudge as she rubs.

—O now you look as if you've been bitten, O God, what did I do?"

—Don't worry, don't worry.

She straightens but he catches at her shawl, pulling her close again.

—Fine. Just make sure Bubu is in a calm mood from now on. Give him some of those kisses, he says.

Ranjit Uncle tugs. His lips catch hers, a dart of tongue inside her mouth, *less deep*, she thinks, *than he used to go. Maybe I am getting old.*

As she pulls away, her shawl feeds through the loop of Ranjit Uncle's fingers, she feels the pressure of his hand on hers. The stick beneath. Training her to beat her victim, almost until he bled.

In the evening, there is no rest: Bubu has called friends to come from Delhi, nearly fifteen people gather to play in the gold-panelled games room. The two sweets brothers, some more of their local friends. Everyone smoking, getting high in the bathroom. Wine glasses, whisky and shot glasses form towers and condos, they cover every surface, a fragile future city where wood can no longer be found.

Jivan's poker game has been abandoned; the rules were impossible, even he had forgotten, or had never understood. Now Bubu and Jivan are locked in a top-trumps match that has Bubu down to his shirt and underpants while everyone else gets to watch, place bets, drink, smoke, gossip, SMS, drink more, listen to Bubu scream *Trump!* and Jivan *Top Trump!* Jivan still has his pants on. *Trump!* He has the better body, built up and smooth. She already knows what he might feel like beneath her hands: Didn't he act as her horse when they were children? Touching him would fill her with life, and tenderness, and excitement and maybe even she would get pregnant and live happily ever after. She looks at Bubu. Whose body she knows better than any other man's—right down to the hairs in his butt crack.

Radha has a black dog on her shoulder. She lurks on her cell: scrolls through Ambika Gupta, looking for lucky numbers. Around the table she goes, Jivan, Bubu, Jivan, Bubu—her husband is losing again. The stakes are in lakhs today, bricks of paper notes that Jivan likes to move straight from their safe to his; *the building blocks of our economy,* he calls them. *Thank you very much to the National Bank of Bubu.*

—Come on, Bubuji, you're getting thrashed here. This guy has his ass in your face, Radha says.

—So what? Bubu says, Jivan isn't shy. Don't worry, Memsahib, we won't shame you—we probably couldn't, even if we tried.

—*Trump!* shouts Jivan, he smacks the cards down.

—*Trump, shot!* shouts Bubu. Jivan bends down to pull off a sock.

She turns her back on the room and stands at the window, forehead against the glass. The air outside seems choked with dust. Down below, she can almost see through the smog to the back gate, the crumbling yellow brick wall. Dhimbala basti stretches out from here, all the way to Napurthala. The chained man's whistle creeps over her skin. Deep between her legs, it squats like an alien baby, eating her insides.

Her mobile chants in her hand, a message from the doorman, waiting in the hall: she must come, Madam, urgently. His words kick her black dog in the muzzle, she yelps, takes the message to Bubu (his back is oily, the hairs matted, he has not showered since morning), and whispers it in his ear.

—O man, whatthefuck? Radha babe, we're busy, Bubu says.

She steadies herself, her hand on his shoulder. His focus is all on his cards.

—But it's Ranjit Uncle, she says. Bapuji is here. I'm telling you, we have to go down.

—*Telling me, telling you—there is nothing we can do,* sings Bubu. *ABBA. Get it?* Bapuji will just have to wait.

Back to the mirrored hallway, where she sees herself: a hundred arms, a hundred legs and heads. A hundred strapless nude bandage dresses, tight from bust to mid-thigh, as if she has been cut open and bound back together like this. So many high-high Miu Miu platforms, in patent black. A diamond drop on a jet stone necklace, worn in strings for her hands to play with. *See, a legion of us!* There are a hundred doormen watching.

—Ma'am? Will you come now? says the doorman.

Is his voice sharp or normal? She wants to drink, she cannot tell.

—Who is with Bapuji? she says.

—They say he has come with the Maharani of Napurthala, his dear mother, your grandmother. First to the back chaukidar's gate. Then to the hotel front lobby. Ranjitji will bring them to the eighth floor.

A day has passed. The chained man is still at the gateposts, his skin might be burned, peeling in strips off his face. When she looked outside, she saw the heat had tinted the sky a jaundiced yellow, the air itself seemed to be on fire. It was not Radha's place to free him.

—Ma'am, excuse me? They are saying that Bapuji has walked here from the train station. He went to Golden Temple first, and now he has come here. He is a great man, Radha Madam, a great man.

Ha! The Radhas toss their heads. Bapuji's feet have not touched common dirt in this country since before she and her selves were born. What does this servant know about greatness? Kuch nahin. She almost opens her mouth to demand he stop looking at them, or speaking about Bapuji, but then remembers it is better to say nothing. Right now, she thinks, Bapuji is downstairs, he has found them out. O God, where is Bubu?

Radha goes back into the golden room. Bubu is still sitting at his cards. He has lost his tie; he is down to his boxers and one green spotted sock. She approaches the table, gingerly. Jivan looks up, encouraging her to speak.

—Bubu, come on, please, let's go down.

Bubu scowls: Radha tries again.

—Bapuji is here, Ranjit Uncle is panicking. That guy you chained outside could be seriously ill. We have to go down, she looks at Jivan. All of us.

Jivan and Bubu grin at each other. Bubu starts to laugh—to whip his thigh with the flat of his hand.

—All of us? On each other? *Get down, get down!* he sings. No. It's not even seven p.m. I'm high, I'm naked, and, Madam Radha, you still have fewer clothes on than me. No. The big bad Bapuji will have to wait. Let Ranjit see to him. I want to party. I want, I want to party. *We like to party, we like, we like to party.* Know that tune?

—You're disgusting, Radha says. I'm going. The guy outside said Bapuji walked from the train station. Walked—Bubu—something is seriously wrong.

Jivan tilts back on his seat. Bubu stops shuffling the pack.

—Radha, he says. It is simple. All you have to do is what I'm saying, OK? He deals the cards and looks up at her with sad-dog eyes.

—Where's your F.U.N.? he says. Stay. Play.

She looks at Jivan. She could, for a while, sit with him and play a hand against Bubu . . .

—O God, she says. I'm going. I'll say you are sleeping, Bubuji.

—Say what you like, say I am sick, yeah, that's right: sick of being disturbed.

He raises a hand to get his high five from Jivan; palm to palm and a matching grin. Yet see how Jivan looks at Radha? *Stay*, his face says. *Play*.

She knows she should leave them to each other. She calls the doorman on her mobile.

—Tell Ranjitji I am tending to Bubu Sahib. And ask Chef to make some chicken dippers. And keema paranthe also. Don't forget the nimboo and the curd. Make it kheere ka raita, she says. And a hot chocolate volcano. Three spoons.

Now the games room wants to punish her: See how the lamps gutter and flicker, the chair feels so hard? The boys slap cards onto the table, the sound like doors, shutting and shut. The hotel manager, R. Sethi Singh (a dark-skinned, Gargi-quota local hire with a stooping sort of smile), comes in, all the way to the table. To tell them in person that Ranjit Uncle is waiting for Radha Madam, that Sri Bapuji wants her now.

She gets up.

—Where are you going? says Bubu.

There is a fire in Radha's head, behind her eyes, scorching her tongue. She feels she might start shaking.

—Daddy has been travelling all day, Bubu. And Jivan—Ranjit Uncle is depending on you. You think he will support us, against Bapuji? No question.

—I don't think so, says Jivan, then Bubu cuts him off.

—Well, well, Madam Radha Devraj Balraj. Insubordination! What do you think, Jivan? Shall we punish her?

Bubu slaps his hand on his own thigh, he leaves a red mark. He has passed through drunk and wild to drunk and calm, so calm, Radha thinks, that anything could happen next.

Jivan puts down his cards. He finds his shirt from the floor, puts it on.

—She's right. I just got back in my dad's good books after fifteen years. I'm going down. Anyway, Gargi wouldn't want Devraj and my dad plotting without us there, would she? And I've kind of had enough of this.

He gestures to the room. One of their friends, her ruby sandals winking under the jumble of shawls and coats, has passed out on the bed. She's clutching her Toto bucket-bag as if she might be sick into it. *A sick-bucket-bag,* Radha thinks. *Ho ho.*

—Good advice, very wise, says Bubu. You're pretty usefulji. But let's eat, then go. No? OK, fine. Come on!

He pulls on his jeans, his shirt. He grabs Radha's wrist, drags tens of her down the mirrored hallway, a brace of Jivans following after.

—Bubuji, let me at least get my shawl, she says.

—No. You want to go, chalo—let's go.

He pushes the doorman aside and calls the lift himself.

—You look fine, baby, very sexy. Right? he says to Jivan.

Jivan ducks back into the suite. In a few seconds he reappears, waving a yellow pashmina: it is not Radha's. She wraps it around herself: it gives her borrowed gold.

They take the lift down. In the background, the fish gapes and swims. *Level 8,* the doors announce: Ranjit Uncle's floor. He greets them himself, still in his daytime suit, his stick in a hand that is trembling.

—Bubuji, Radha, where have you been? I've been calling and calling upstairs. Bapuji is here. I told him what happened last night. He saw that man. Kashyap. I have had him released. Just now, the lockup. His face is burned. He is covered in open sores—he needs medical care—dehydration—I had him taken to the hospital in a local taxi. All of us understand the need for punishment, but this . . . Bapuji is not happy. No.

—What did you tell him, Ranjit? says Bubu.

He-is not-ha ppy-no. It sets up a rhythm; Radha feels it from her feet to her skull. Wishing for a drink, now, to smooth the words through her, reverse them and absorb them.

—I just want everything to be peaceful between you, Ranjit Uncle says.

From the terrace Radha can hear her father's deep voice shouting,

—Aré chup kar mere dil, bohut hogaya.

Then, Nanu:

—Dekh teri beti kya ban gayi hai? Bakri ko shaheed hone ke baad chup hone ko kyon bol raha hai?

—What's she saying, Rads? whispers Jivan. Radha takes his arm.

—When the goat has already been sacrificed, why tell it to be quiet and stop bleating? she whispers.

—Stop bleating, Radha, stop bleating.

Jivan laughs, and pokes her.

She twists away. He is not really like them, she realises. She crosses her arms around herself; in a huddle she walks with Jivan through the suite, they step across the threshold into night.

There are no flowers here; just stone troughs filled with smooth white pebbles, spiked with ferns. *Jeet,* Radha thinks, *is everywhere here*—in the terracotta benches with clawed feet, in the pieces of broken sculpture. Torsos in grey stone, with no heads or mouths, no tongues or lips, loom through the trees. No eyes. So plump. Radha's skin creeps cold.

In the near corner of the garden is an ebony two-seater bar inlaid with silver tiles; a servant stands behind it, preparing two tumblers of liquid gold. At the centre is a circular clearing surrounded by skeleton palms. Nanu sits to one side on a low stone bench. Her legs are wide apart, her white chiffon sari sags between her knees. From her bag an orange is produced. She digs her nails into it, ripping the skin, throwing the peel on the ground. She curls her lips and slurps at the segments. Radha goes to greet her grandmother, bending, inhaling the fine powder on her cheeks. Nanu catches her shoulders; she plants a wet kiss on Radha's head. Lets her go.

—Now, Radha, come greet me. Bapuji stands by the small pond, holding out his arms.

—Yes Daddy, she says. Yes Daddy yes. And isn't that everything she has to say? Hanji. Can this scene be over now, among the cold white pebbles and the skeleton ferns—she has not been drinking, a mistake, she thinks: this night might be brighter and easier—even a glass of water—the only water here is in the small ornate pond. She has never properly noticed the bust of Gandhi standing guard there—an eye for an eye—what was it he said? A world in which everyone goes blind. Now Daddy is watching, waiting for Radha, his kurta is dusty, his feet in their chappals—did he walk here from the train station? A thing never done. From a place she has not been to since she was a child. Before they started to drive, or fly, there was lunch service in first class and boys selling water balloons on the platforms they stopped at. *Stop dreaming*, Radha, for Daddy is greeting you, his grip is so tight on your shoulders and shawl; *don't slip, shawl*, a breeze is picking up, it is setting all the ferns at her, stupid green plants, she hates ferns. Daddy smells of something sharp: yoghurt just about to turn. She does not pull away: for here they all are, in the garden of standing still.

—Radha, beti, you are glad I am here; you don't forget your priorities.

—Yes, Daddy.

Now she is so close; his body close against hers, squeezing all thought from her head. She blinks into his face, it seems about to dissolve. Wait—this is his cue to cry? No. Stop. The shawl is slipping but she cannot pull it up, so she stands in her bandages, half-mummified, half-bronze—then Daddy takes the ends and wraps them around her neck.

—I have told your sister she can do as she likes. For years she has behaved as a vulture with its prey. She has no thought for myself.

Now on the word, he collapses, his head on her shoulder. Her knees buckle; she has never carried more than a crocodile bag—and now she must kneel with the sack of him in her arms—where is Bubu, where is Jivan—where is Ranjit Uncle now? Picking them up, Bubu on one side and Jivan on the other, they form a cradle; they lead her and Bapuji to the bench across from Nanu. Ranjit Uncle is sitting with her; now he is also peeling an orange.

Now Radha licks her lips. Her mouth is too dry—and Bapuji has never looked like this: not even when the Company Mumbai was bombed. Overnight, so much lost. The hotel name, the family stock. Radha took him sweetened chai and badam ki burfi, then was too frightened to give it, so ate it herself while standing at his door, until she felt sick. Had she not been first on the scene in Mumbai, and stayed? Why is it always left to her, to write all the scripts for sorrow and grief?

Now Radha wants to run. But the shoes, the dress, the shawl.

—You won't believe it, Radha. Your sister is a junglee. What do you say about that? Speak, then, Bapuji says.

Now Radha watches Gargi. Every time they are set a test, Gargi always wins. Gargi gets more praise, more fondants and finger chips for Sunday tea. Gargi got the nicest new clothes and Gargi was allowed to ride up front in the car. Gargi was so good: at listening, repeating, under-standing. There was always someone to tell Gargi every shitput that came out of Radha's mouth.

Now Bapuji presses his hand on her forehead. Tender and firm, as if to hold her down and take her temperature. She goes limp, as a trusting child. Convinced for a moment she is actually suffering a fever. Next to the bench is a female torso, its belly low and round; it has no naabhi, Radha realises, none of these torsos do. The rest of your life will be spent here, Radha, under Bapuji's hand.

Now she tells him she knows he's disappointed. But Gargi is not *ambitious,* just conscientious. That she is not *too independent*—she wants to do her best. That maybe the Tuesday Parties were getting too much, that Gargi herself could not cope.

—She can go to hell, Bapuji says.

—Ah no, Bapuji, you are so very tired. Naturally you feel you want to keep working but now is the time to rest. Go back to Delhi, Radha says. Take Gargi some Amritsari sweets. Mitha is her favourite thing. Tell her *sorry.*

Now Radha slides off the bench and kneels, feeling the bandage dress catch, hoping it will not unravel, revealing her anatomy; Ranjit Uncle over there nodding and smiling, and Nanu eating her orange—Bubu, with only one dotty sock on, pouring Jivan a drink at the bar—is her father's tone all in her head? He gets off the bench and he kneels with her—facing her—as if he wants to play clap-hands like schoolgirls in the yard. Now stand up, Radha, yes, that's what she'll do—so she does, then realises her mistake.

Now Bapuji leans forward to touch her feet.

In his best English accent he says,

—Dear daughter, I am going spare. I beg, give me room here with you. Only you can feed me and give me my clothes. At least—he grips her ankles—you could offer me one drink.

Now he looks up, his eyes hard, his lips pucker as if to blow a dry kiss to her knees. She clamps them together and takes a breath, swallowing, she sits on the bench with him there on the floor. She kisses his head.

—Daddy, she says in her softest voice. Family bond bhi toh hai. Please. Don't play the clown. Go back to the Farm, to Gargi.

Now she could pinch his nose, maybe make him smile. Lean and kiss him, yes? *No,* say the statues around them. Stay still to survive. Bubu and Jivan are somewhere behind her, not moving. The sky has a reddish tinge. There is sand in the air, she can taste it.

—Gargi has cut the Tuesday Parties, says Bapuji. The one thing that brought me some joy. My legacy, my reputation, my learning and name. Passed down through them. What: you think that is nothing? Gargi wants to take everything.

Everything? Right down to your entire collection of saffron underpants?

Now, as if he has read her mind, Bapuji's face clouds, he yanks her arms, pulls himself, then her, up to standing—then he shakes her fists at the sky.

—I ask Lord Vishnu to snap her bones and play sticks with them! he cries.

—Devraj, Bubu says. Let her go.

Now *finally!* Bubu is here, he pulls Radha from Bapuji. She stands, rubbing poor wristos: they hurt. Knees and ankles, shoulders—to be treated like this is harder than sitting and whistling all day, under the sun's glare. Still, she wants to be good; being good means doing well. *Am I doing well?* No answer, from any of the beings, men or stone, here.

—Daddy, your words will kill me, I swear, she says. She puts out her arms, she tries to embrace him.

Now Bapuji catches her, holds her face to his shoulder; his body feels damp, her mouth fills with cloth. The world around her goes dark.

—Chup, beti. Nahin, don't cry. I will never say these things about you. He takes her chin and tilts her head up to his.

—You have my eyes, he says. You see with my vision and would never stop me from having my fun. Above all you know how to respect your elders. You at least understand that half of my share of the Devraj Company is now yours. Tell me, don't be shy. Who locked up my man outside? Come now, tell your Bapuji.

Now a birdcall sounds and then exactly again, again. Bapuji lets Radha go. She turns, with Bapuji and Bubu, to see Uppal stepping onto the terrace, holding up his hands. His mobile flashes, chirping like some deranged sparrow, as if it is morning, not night.

Now Bapuji grips Radha's shoulder. One of Nanu's pips hits Radha's arm as if spat from the window of a car.

—Get lost! Bapuji shouts. Radha, this bhenchod should have been beaten for the way he talked to me. Just because that woman Gargi has forgotten her duties—just because she turns to him for every little thing—he thinks he is the puppet master.

—No, he doesn't, sir, Uppal says.

Now, a movement behind him. *Shit. Gargi.* She emerges from the suite; she's in a shot-silk sapphire salwar kameez. *She's cut her hair off.* She looks fifteen years younger. *Shit.*

Now Bapuji starts; a lock of white hair falls over one eye. Radha thinks of Popeye. *Stop.* Gargi looks so determined, like Olive when she's mad. *Stop!* She is smiling, she says something to Uppal. *Look, how he just retreats back inside.*

—Hey Radha. Hey Bubu. And dear Ranjit Uncle. Then, her voice—*a shade warmer?*—says,

—Hey Jivan.

Now Gargi is waiting, now Bapuji is waiting, now Bubu is pulling at Radha again, pinching an instruction into her arm. Bubu has a twisting pinch, practised on his sister when he was young, perfected on Radha in the first years of their marriage. She knows what he is telling Radha-baby to do: it is what she herself *wants* to do.

—Radha! Stay! says Bapuji.

Now she means only to give the lightest of air kisses. But the smell of her sister is always the same: her dear sweat, laced with old-fashioned Company jasmine. Radha wants to press herself into Gargi's body, she never wants to come out.

—Love your hair, Sis. You should have sent me a snap, she says. Gargi slumps, just the tiniest slump. *What did I say?*

Now Radha stays beside her sister, holding hands.

—Jesus Christ, Bapuji says.

—Why shouldn't Raddy stand with me? She leans forward, squeezing Radha's hand. She keeps squeezing. It hurts, her rings are hurting. Then Gargi, her face pointed at Bapuji, says,

—Just because you're old does not mean you automatically get my respect.

Now the night seems to clench every muscle. Radha can see red tinge the sky. Bapuji's eyes widen; *he's going to have a heart attack,* Radha thinks, *right here on this terrace, before the Srinagar opening.* Shit—he can't speak. Shit—he's actually going to cry. *Radha Devraj Kumari Balraj—you are about to have your first major PR disaster.*

—Come, Radha, tame this Queen Cobra, show her what respect is. Gargi, sharam nahin aati kya? Bapuji cries.

—Sir, Bubu says. If you want to know who locked up your man, I did it. He's lucky I didn't do worse.

Now Radha must let go of Gargi. She must go between the men. *Cross the ten paces, count them down, Radha,* she must try one more time to calm Daddy down. Nanu claps again as she passes, she is on to her second orange, scattering the peel around her and kicking it under the bench.

Now the others just watch, even Ranjit Uncle, who is staring at Gargi's haircut as if it just spit on his shoes.

—Daddy, Radha says. *Curl your voice, volumise your hair.* You know you aren't as strong as you think you are. Here is Gargi, she is sorry, she has come to take you home.

Now Bubu is nodding—yes, good idea. Gargi is shaking her head—no.

—Phir wohi baat? Bapuji says. *No.* I will not set one foot in her territory. I will take my cap and go begging in the street rather than spend any time with *her.* I'll go like a dog, make friends with the rag pickers and rats. After this, my Radha tells me to go back with *her*?

Now Gargi's hands are on her hips—her look is hard—Bapuji tries to glare back at her but he cannot hold it. He falters. He actually turns away. Radha looks around—Jivan's eyebrows are raised, even Bubu seems surprised. Nanu is eating her orange, Gargi has not moved. Ranjit Uncle almost gets up but Bapuji halts him.

—No, he says. I'll go beg in the street for some khaana, one anna. Go back with this one? He gestures to Gargi. I'd rather tag behind, and keep the chappals of this Uppal from getting in the mud.

—Up to you, Ji.

Now Gargi actually *shrugs.* This is Big Sis, her life is Bapuji's pleasure. This same Gargi, who never even looked at a boy before she got married, is smiling at Jivan. He is giving her a thumbs-up. And Bapuji is going on,

—Chup, beta. Don't trouble yourself to understand me, and I won't trouble you. We won't meet anymore, so what?

Now he waits. Radha watches. Gargi keeps silent. How can she not speak? Radha opens her mouth—she must say something—then Bapuji says,

—Magar tum mera hi khoon ho, mera hi hissa ho. I have to own up to that. I can't cut you out. You are me: a disease in my veins. Ab aage jo bhi hoga, woh tumhare upar hai. Shame will come in its own time. I will stay with my Radha, and we will hold our Tuesday Parties wherever she is.

Now. It goes like this. Why didn't Radha listen to Bubu, or see for herself what Gargi was doing? Hasn't Bapuji always warned that Gargi only works for herself? Now she, Radha, will be forced to play grandma to her own elders. She waits for someone, Nanu or Bubu, even Ranjit Uncle, to remind Gargi of her duty. She waits. She waits.

—Daddy, you know the Srinagar hotel isn't ready yet. There is still so much to do. How can I look after you here? All is fully booked for months. There is no space for your boys; they would have to stay outside.

—Were you there when your husband locked up my man, Radha? Yes. I know you were. Everything you have, I have given. All.

Now his voice is so flat—as if everything was nothing but something to say *thank you* for.

Now Radha thinks of Bubu, working with only a salary as his reward. Marrying her on a promise of more. She knows he never listens to her. Does not see her, walking in circles, talking to the walls. The games she has had to play with him, morning, noon and night, almost for ten years, the God help her Donald Duck sex.

Now everyone is waiting for Radha again. What a night! What an audience. What did Gargi tell her to say, what should she say, what was it?

—Well (it comes out), you made us wait long enough.

There is a pause, then,

—Ungrateful little chut! Bapuji says.

Now *Cunt* bubbles up in Radha's mouth. *Say Cunt, Daddy. That's the English way.* Maybe Radha will adopt this as her brand. Cunt. *What would be the slogan?* She swallows a laugh and a sob.

—I have put you in charge of the Company, invested so much in you—and all I ask is that I can still keep the Devraj Hundred. And you are telling me twenty-five? Is that what you are saying? You think this is

the moment to show weakness by cutting numbers? You don't understand the first thing about business. You disgust me, Radha. You make
your sister look good. Chalo— (He looks at Gargi.) We will go back to
Delhi with half the party.

—You know what we could do? Gargi says. We could set up a satellite link. You could give the podium without even having the party.
It could be wonderful, like an exclusive TED talk. We could run it on
a loop in the hotel TVs. Others have been doing this for some time.
Radha, why are we not already doing this? And Twitter, Daddy, Twitter.
You could gain fifty thousand followers! Maybe fifty million! You should
see this one account even I have heard of, all the younger staff love it—
a guy called MrGee—it's about business life, so funny, so clever. You
could do better than that . . .

Now Gargi's face; alight. Nanu laughs, and Bubu and Jivan are
smiling—at Gargi talking Twitter, and telling them about MrGee—no
one knows Radha started it, that it's her inside the egg—if Bapuji likes
this idea, will anyone believe it after this? Not fair. No.

—Bapuji? she says. Searches for her phone, to show him, to tell him.
But look at Bapuji's face. He does not like it. There will be no tweeting here. Who needs to drink? Not Radha, now—for nothing is funnier
than his face, and Gargi's and Bubu's all frozen as if someone shouted,
STATUES!

—Is this all of me? Bapuji gestures to his chin.

Now Radha thinks, *Yes, Daddy, that is all you are, your own chin.*

—Am I only a voice, a head on a screen that can be turned up,
turned down, turned off at will? By any and all of the masses? No. Once
upon a time we had a good strong form of government here, working to
industrialise so each would have enough. You girls have no culture, no
history, you do not remember these things; those were the times when
each man and each woman knew their place.

—Daddy, don't start this good-old-days nonsense, says Gargi. We
do know, because now we have to deal with those cards that you played.

—Gargi means that we are building the best on what you left,
Bapuji, Bubu says.

Now Bubu defending Gargi? Radha wants to laugh.

Now Gargi widens her eyes at Bubu: her *shut up, asshole* face. *Ha! Big
Sis is great.* No one ever looks at Bubu like that. He retreats to the bar.

—I only want to produce the effective way forward for all of us.

TED is wonderful, Gargi says. You don't need to be so exclusive, after all, Devraj—let everyone see you and hear your wisdom, why not?

—Devraj? says Bapuji. Need? Look at you, Gargi, a fountain run dry. You cannot serve a man's needs. Radha, as for you? So fine, so fine. My God, as if fine cloth can cover your true nature. You girls are like two diseased owls, unnaturally taloned, freakishly beaked with your face and your nails all painted. These things you think so beautiful do not cover your stink. Nari nari bohut hogaya, Sarkar mat bano.

Now Bapuji takes three paces, he pulls at Radha's yellow shawl; she must spin around, or choke and be left in her bandage dress: waving head, cleavage, arms and legs: the missing parts of the statues, living, breathing.

—Dear God, Bapuji says. He wrings the shawl in his hands. I am full of sadness that my life has come to this. If you are punishing me through these daughters then also give me the strength to bear their disrespect. Let me be fair, and if I am angry, let me be justified. But don't allow me to cry, like this girl here, who cries on demand. Yes, Radha, I know you. Both of you. You— (he points at Gargi) —Radha has told me you refuse to bear children to this family.

—What? Gargi says.

—And you, he points at Radha. Gargi has told me that all day long, you fill your body with food from the gutter.

—What? Radha says.

—And both of you, I know you tattoo yourselves like two lowborn Naphs on all those parts of your unseen flesh, buttocks, thighs, who knows where else, what for?

—That's Sita! Gargi cries, and claps her hands over her mouth.

—Chup! Inside women is a long-tongued demon, just waiting to come out. Look at this one, bandaged here. Under your wraps is a body covered in open lips, the lips you hide between your legs, waiting to suck a man dry. If we engage with those lips, we are stuck to you, and we cannot escape. Down! I will not submit to this. Down, you kama, rajas and tamas! Tamas, the very nature of prakriti, women infecting all men. One day you will wish, as I do, that you had never been born.

Stop, Radha wants to beg him, *please, Bapuji, stop.* He will not stop. Pacing, shouting, arms now waving; casting back and forward. He goes from Gargi to Radha, to Bubu, to Gargi. Ranjit Uncle and Nanu on the bench, Jivan at the bar. Dispensing drinks.

—You treat me as if I am going senile, watch and your wish will come true. Don't you cry, that's my role but I will not play it, not for you, not now, not here.

Nanu has finished her oranges. When Bapuji falls silent, she claps, sings—

Me shogun,
Me bigwig.
Me the chief's son.
I make the rules here.
It's a load of crap.
                (Ha ha, that is your word—)
Laughing, skipping,
Tumbling, they're all
Headed for Deathville.
In the blink
Of an eye,
The king will be
Separated from his kingdom.

—Chup chup, shh, Bapuji says. He puts an arm around Nanu. He grits his teeth and helps her rise.
—Mama.

Now this is his last word. Radha watches them walk through the garden, the ferns bow to them, the sky is red, it tastes of dust. Where are they going? Ranjit Uncle follows, does not look back. Bubu has replaced Jivan at the bar. Jivan is kissing Gargi hello: one cheek, two cheeks, three cheeks, four! Why not five, or six?

Radha is standing on her own.

Now what should she do?

One by one, they go inside. The wind has picked up, whorls of sand caress the windows. They move away from each other, finding the corners, the other rooms. There are doors to shut. Locks to turn and taps to run. Radha snakes around, wishing for a smoke. She follows Gargi to the bathroom; she waits outside. What is the price of water when it comes from a golden tap? *Leave it running, Gargi.* Radha goes back to the sofa:

here she sat with South African Clive. That first night in Amritsar, when she tried to convince him there were ways in which life could be different. Around this very glass table, held up by a sculpted stand of formless silver. She watches Jivan standing at the door to the terrace. Bubu himself brings a tray from the terrace bar, cut-crystal glasses, fingers of whisky, ice.

Jivan takes it from him. He brings it to the table, places it down. He sits on the sofa next to Radha, hands looped over his knees. He has such long fingers, such buffed nails.

—Where is Ranjit? says Gargi. Her suit a little too tight, her makeup slipping off her face. She sits alone in the single armchair.

—I'm here, he says from the interior door. I went to see if I could calm your Bapuji, but he is so very upset. He refused all help. I have never seen him like this.

Ranjit clutches his cane; he wipes his forehead with his free hand. He looks small, a bit apart.

—Don't trouble yourself, Ranjit. You know he will be fine, says Bubu. Right, guys? He drains his whisky. He gestures to Jivan to pour him another.

Someone has closed the doors to the terrace. Radha can see the five of them reflected, warped and widened, the night a backdrop for their ghosts. *It may never be morning.* Alcohol burns her insides. *Look, this is you as a fatty,* says the Radha in the window. Tomorrow, she will get some assistant to call up her favourite designers; come bring her fresh dresses to try in her room. And the bright cherries on the walls of her suite will beam at her, she thinks, and advise on what is modest, what is daring for this place. Maxi, maybe—she should start a new trend.

What is this warmth? The yellow shawl has found its way back to her shoulders, it's slightly damp; it smells of Bapuji.

—Bapuji cannot leave just like that, Ranjit Uncle says.

Well, has he not been sitting for the last half an hour, sucking Nanu's oranges?

—Gargi, he didn't take a car, Nanuji is with him only, no one else. How will he manage? Does he even carry cash or cards or his own cell phone?

—Don't worry, Ranjit Uncle, Radha says. There are plenty of places from here to Goa where he can make a visit. Any of his friends will welcome him, since he does not want us.

—Right on, Rads, right on, says Bubu.

She will never get used to him, standing behind her, kneading her neck with his thumbs. It hurts. He always does it when he wants to de-stress.

Radha glances at Jivan. He is looking at Gargi.

—Jivan, Radha says. It is up to you. You want to take on the Company security full-time? Then make sure Bapuji stays away from me. Don't let him cause any mischief I have to fix in the press. There is too much at stake now.

Jivan's smile warms her skin, the yellow shawl slips.

—Yes, Radha. He rolls her name on his tongue.

—Right, she says. Am I right, Ranjit Uncle?

Ranjit Uncle gives a small sniff, he smoothes the top of his cane with his hand. *His cravat needs retying, he should take more care.*

—You know best, beta, he says. I can no longer comment. But remember, your father has seen the British quit India. He built this Company from nothing. He raised you, educated you, married you. He is older than this India herself! Without him none of us have any future. Let him keep his Hundred, so what? Over such small moments more will be lost, so the flood will come.

Bubu laughs.

—Don't worry, Ranjitji. We will be lucky if the rains even give us one drop this year. Jivan, Gargi, one more drink?

—I think I'll say goodnight, says Ranjit.

Radha watches Ranjit Uncle stand. When she was young, she loved him. She saw him always surrounded by women, having F.U.N. He used to call her over, to sit with them. He was so smart and fresh-smelling, he brought her new T-shirts and jeans, whenever he came back from America or UK or anywhere outside. She looks back to Jivan, they have the same skin colour, the same head. Jivan, she thinks, probably has better teeth.

—Goodnight, Ranjit Uncle, thank you for all of the lovely tea, she calls.

He walks to his bedroom as if age is guiding him tenderly towards his pyre. He closes the door behind him.

All of them sit back. Although they are still in Ranjit Uncle's suite, now Radha wants to take off her shoes, to pummel the cushions and stretch her feet into Jivan's leg. He is smiling; he even raises his glass to her.

—Right, he says. I'm going to take a dip. Who's in?

—Great idea. Jacuzzi time. Bubu stretches his arms, flashing his Rolex.

—I'll come!

—Atta Radha! Gargi, you won't join? Jivan mimes a doggy-paddle, panting and grinning.

Look at Gargi, sitting like Queen Elizabeth on the sofa. Pinks and purples don't suit her. And someone has plucked her eyebrows into a permanent question—*she looks like a Russian doll.*

—I can't, Gargi says. We have to talk about how we are going to deal with Dad and the next stage. Rads, I want you to put together an internal brochure. There is no point waiting. We will let the heads of all subsidiaries know that we are taking over now. There are also quite a lot of problems I am dealing with that we all need to talk about. Tax inspections on the hotels and malls, Bubu. The feedback from the eco-car . . .

—Come on, Big Sis, let's do this tomorrow, says Bubu. He picks up his drink. Twists his mouth around a sip of whisky; it ages his face. Shutting his eyes, he drains his glass.

—This morning's coverage, of Bapuji in Ghaziabad, Gargi says. Radha, any corrective action yet? Or should we just focus on all the leaking holes and shell companies washing cash through the new Bubu Balraj building projects? I know exactly how much each contract is worth, what gets spent, what goes into your personal accounts and what percentage should come to the family.

Bubu does the graft, Radha thinks, *so why not?*

—O Sisterji, she says to Gargi. Don't frown so much, your face will stick.

It works. Bubu snorts, Jivan sits back, Gargi gives a small, tight smile.

—Let's get some rest and have a power breakfast in the morning. We will order you some oatmeal and fruits. I promise we will talk, all of us, together. Even you need to unwind, Radha says.

—Jivan? Gargi says.

How sweet his smile is, so apologetic, so helpless! He lifts one shoulder at Gargi.

Ha! *One in the eye for Big Sis.* Good. Let her sit with her work, it is her true love. Radha will go to the roof with Jivan. Because Gargi or no Gargi, Dad or no Dad, and Bubu can point her six ways to the sky, but Jivan does something else. Look at him, so relaxed in this drama. He makes Radha laugh. Without thinking first. He calls back leela to her eyes. Bubu does not even guess she has this thing. Now Jivan is here, she feels it again. Life.

That night she decides to stop thinking about the past. No more remembering that little Radha and little Jivan were bachchas together. Or trying to copy Gargi, or do only what Bubu wants. And—maybe—no more tea with Ranjit Uncle. Gargi he always ignored. With Sita—Radha will not think about Sita. Sita should be home keeping Dad happy, at least looking after her dogs.

From now on, all of Radha's memories will begin here, on the roof of the Company Amritsar. The plunge pool! What a name for this thing. A shallow circle of water, a stone seat inside. It is still early, before midnight. Two or three staff shuffle around, so slow. Pouring drinks, fetching towels. Finally, they leave. Twenty minutes, half an hour. No Bubu. He said he wanted to powder his nose and would join them—she found him two hours later, passed out on the floor of his own dressing room, hugging his Kashmiri box, among the hanging suits and folded shirts. She left him there.

Turquoise shimmers its reflection against her skin, turning her amphibious. She peels off her bandage dress. Bodice tight. Anatomy released. Her swimsuit has a cutout: an iris around her navel. She strokes it and pokes it with her finger. *Nice naabhi.* The scent is of chlorine with roses. It eases her. She holds on to the curved rim of the pool and floats, waiting for Jivan.

—Are you OK? Jivan says. He climbs in; two arms' lengths away, asking that simple question. Tears begin to slide down her cheeks. She dips her face and comes up. Smelling of roses.

—You should come to Goa, she says. It's the most beautiful hotel in the country. Until the Kashmir one is finished. We're actually creating fake lakes in the grounds, so people can have their own houseboat suites.

Full service, all the treatments; an outdoor screening room in summer, an autumn lakeside lit-fest—books and all that are so hot right now. Maybe even a theatre where we can do English puppet shows. Whatever we like we will do it. Live local music each night. Ski passes in winter with private tuition from Swiss pros. It's going to be awesome!

—Radha. Stop. What's up?

The water reflects ripples onto his face and onto the windows behind him. A strange feeling, as if they are walking the ocean floor, but are still able to breathe.

—You must think we are savages, after all that.

Jivan moves; his legs touch hers. The texture of wet tongues slipping against each other.

—Wait, she says. Bubu might come.

—What do you think I'm gonna do? he asks.

He reaches under the surface. Takes her foot in his hand, strokes her calf with his fingertips. It feels as if a thousand small sea creatures are brushing over her. Radha's mouth drops open. Turquoise floods through her. She becomes Ganga Ma. She tries not to let Jivan see.

—You didn't shock me, he says. The only thing that has shocked me since I got here is the state of the roads near the Farm.

He lets go of her foot and pushes towards her. Her back is against the side. He traps her between his arms.

—Still the same crowd-pleasing girl. Come on, he gives a laugh. Tell me. Who is Radha? What does she love to do?

A dry wind catches the tops of the palms. It sets everything whispering around them. The starting of the jets, the motor hums: bubbles press up between her legs, on her stomach. Between Jivan's body and hers. It feels good. Jivan pushes back, away from her. She thinks that she could ask him to do anything at all, and no one would blame her or talk badly about her, no paps would point the finger, because there would be nothing to point at. To be Radha with Jivan is the most natural state of being in the world.

—I've never handcuffed anyone like that. But Bubu . . . he likes to play rough, she says.

She sinks down and lets the water lift her hair. Her words drift towards him, spreading out. She waits. He will comfort her—he knows how it feels to be caused bruising, bleeding pain to the most tender parts of one's self, pain at the hands of someone you only want to please.

He stretches his arms out and grips the sides of the pool.

—Radha, what do you think I am? You remember me as a child—half in your house, half to my brother, half allowed to play, half left out. I'm Indian, I'm American. Half this, half that, always the other. My mother used to sing America's praises. At least everyone here knows the score. *Come and live in Dream Town, built on favours and bribes.* And shrug it off and say *so what? Aise hi hota hai!* Great, just get on with it, live your life. No one has the guts to be the whistleblower. Why should they? Even the whistleblower is probably getting some on the side. Money. Fluid as water, nowhere more than here.

She floats to him and puts her hands on his knees. She has no idea how she looks, mascara probably running, eyelashes stuck together. She puts her face near his, lips almost on his.

—Of course. You are right, it's always like this. And we are in it.

She skates her hand across the water—up to the top. We work very hard for every paise we spend.

—Dude, are you for real?

Is he laughing at her? She sits herself back on the seat.

—I mean, poverty, of course it's there, she says. But we create so much employment, what else can we do? We live in a young country, Jivan. Five years ago you couldn't even get Coca-Cola in a can here. The kids who are making money now, like all the upper-level staff we employ, the girls and the boys who didn't grow up travelling abroad, they just want to make money, be cool. They know what stuff they want; the great thing is, they don't know why. No context! My God, they are the ideal customer! They didn't have access to anything, and now look—everything. All at once. Now, now, now!

She laughs, beats her palms, sending drops flying around them.

—And what is my place in it? What is yours? he says. Aren't we just the big fish, waiting to be eaten by the small?

Now Radha moves towards him again, she balances on him, a circus act of hands on shoulders, legs floating behind. He takes her arms and pulls her onto his lap. Stubble and skin, wet, hard, muscle. Bone. Ranjit Uncle's cheekbones and his full, sensuous mouth. Between his legs, ah God, she thinks: it feels good to be so close to him. Bubu (who still hasn't shown: *O please stay passed out, o please*) would be sucking on her by now, biting, hurting, not like this. Then she thinks, *Ha. Let him come find them. Let him see.*

—Radha, lovely Radha. Haven't you learned that you have to be brutal to survive in this world? Don't be fake, don't pretend. Why can't you just say it if you feel it? Jivan says.

Radha stares at him. Faces close together as they haven't been for years. She wants to pinch his cheeks and twist them. *Did you really miss me? Don't you think of what might have been? Do you want to fuck me?* If she said such things, she would risk becoming Sita: she would find herself. Nothing but herself.

—Do you like it here at all? she asks.

Jivan's arms pull around her waist, she is on his lap. His lips rest on her shoulder. When he speaks, his teeth graze her as much as his words.

—What, you think I'm homesick? I'm not homesick. For the first time in fifteen years. I was born here. When I'm around you and Gargi, I feel like I've come home.

The shadows from the candles and the light from the pool seem to gather around him, framing him in a luminescent glow. A blue God, Krishna, churning the ocean around her at the creation of the world.

—Jivan, I wish, she begins.

His head is so solid, a coconut under her hands.

—I wish you had never gone.

Then she is limbs and hair all around him, arms, legs, his naked chest, his crotch. He stays completely still beneath her; it is exciting to move against him. Heat burns through her to the ends of her hair, and still he does not move. His eyes are closed and his head thrown back, she can feel him pushing between her legs. She pulls her swimsuit down to her waist and brushes her nipples side to side, over his mouth. Then one arm around his neck, she kisses him. Wet skin, lips as full as hers. His tongue is warm and thick, he tastes of the plunge pool—

—Jivan, she says. *Home.*

He lifts her, turns and places her down on the seat. She is confused then realises he is taking off his shorts. Before she can speak, he lifts her again, onto him. Water makes it easy; they are returning to their element.

It has been so long since she saw a man's face like this, close, beneath her. He is so still: his eyes are all she can see, he strips off her costume; he lunges forward and bites her nipple, sucking first one, the other, one, the other, one, the other, one, the other, one, the other, she sees his dark head bent over her and the pleasure sends her whispered *yes* high into the night, it is snatched away by the wind.

Her hands grip his hair. She pulls his head back so she can see his face, stretched and grinning.

—Love, she says.

There is no going back, after that.

They lie together on a lounger, wrapped under one towel. An hour or more has passed. *No Bubu,* she thinks, *ever again.* Her cheek feels the bones of Jivan's shoulder, her ear to his heartbeat. Once or twice she raises her head to look at him: he is smiling but his eyes are closed. Years have gone by. She counts them: Gargi and she, performing with dances for Bapuji. Growing, staying still, trying to twist away from the uncles who always kiss you on the lips no matter how old you get; fixed interest that gets harder to pay the more the years pass. Then Surendra, her big brother-in-law, policing her always until Bubu came along to open her to more, more, more.

Now her skin prickles in the rising breeze, it fans old daydreams to life. She will have Jivan, and Gargi will have Jeet, and Bubu and Surendra will somehow be gone. The four will live untroubled on some sandy beach with nothing to sell or buy. She and her sister will dive naked each day in clear blue waters for strange-shaped fish, which they'll bring home to Jeet and Jivan to gut and cook. Sun will warm, sand blast their features and bodies to abstract bronze. They'll squat and eat with their hands, sharing morsels between the four, waiting for Sita, who is coming. But then the daydream breaks: Gargi kisses Jivan, Jeet looks on smiling— Radha opens her eyes and speaks.

—I thought you liked Gargi more than me.

Jivan pulls on her hair, says,

—Some women you want to marry. Some are just meant to be adored.

She is not sure who is who, and tries not to ask him. Lazily she tells him,

—Gargi doesn't want children. Did you know that? I mean, how could she not?

A short silence, then,

—Is that for real?

—Maybe she had enough, playing Mummy to you and me.

—And Sita, he says.

—Mmm, and look how she grew up. Jivan?

—What is it, Mrs. Radha Devraj Balraj? Which, by the way, is a crazy big name for such a skinny girl.

—Thanks, she says, and sucks in her stomach. You know Gargi has a massive mummy crush on you?

He rolls to face her. He slaps her lightly on her cheek.

—Don't be mean.

—Ask her yourself, see what response you get. You think she has control. She doesn't know what she is doing.

—Do you? Jivan asks her.

—Do you?

—Always. But I do have one question. What is a chut?

She grins. This, she won't translate. Not even for him. She takes his hand and pulls it between her legs.

—O right. I guess I should have realised. What do you call it? Come on, you can say "cunt."

Yes, she can. But she won't in this moment, wanting everything to be soft around her.

—Come on, you can say it! Cunt, cunt, cunt, cunt, cunt. His lips against her ear. If you say a word enough times, it empties to nothing.

—I don't want to.

—Just once.

—No.

—Cunt.

—No.

—Cunt.

—No.

—Cunt.

—Stop! OK. Cunt. Cunt cunt cunt. Happy now?

He grins.

—Nanu always called it *yoni,* she says.

—Yoni. New age, man, I like that. He kisses her on her neck, her arms, her hands. And your dad seems to think you've got them all over your body. Mmm. Sexy.

She laughs as the wind gets stronger, the trees around them lilting, the sky tinged red. Is it dawn? No—something else—it's like the night of her wedding moon. Sand rises in gusts around them, forcing them inside. Only one manservant remains, wrapped in a rug under the pool bar.

She goes to her room with the imprint of Jivan's body on hers. She whispers her sister's names as she does each night to bless them. Then sinks into bed. Does not want dawn to come.

Eyes heavy, she thinks she can hear thunder cracking over the city plains and distant mountains, all the way to the border. Somewhere, she senses that rain has begun to fall. *Sweet dreams,* she whispers, and sleeps.

A freak storm comes that night. It spins around the Amritsar hotel, whips out across Dhimbala basti; it reaches the derelict grounds of the Company Napurthala, tearing up the earth and pulling down the trees. The Mughal gardens that Radha's mother once lovingly planted to her own, specific catalogue of memories are scoured with sand and falling stone. Gargi comes to wake Radha with this news.

—Come see the damage, she begs, let us see what there is to salvage.

But Radha cannot leave the hotel. She cannot take breakfast until Jivan comes to sit with her. The Bapuji Bol! text service chimes crypticisms she did not choose and cannot make sense of: *None can destroy iron, except its own rust . . . A sadhu's shack is a haven for Kings . . . New India is new tourism.*

In the afternoons, an unbearable game of watching and being watched begins; Radha circles the corridors, scrolling on her mobile till Jivan catches her. In the stairwells or storerooms or sometimes in his bed. At night she avoids dinners and drinks; sleep is swallowed by the news on repeat: Radha follows the cycle and reports back to Gargi: no sight of Bapuji.

Three days pass.

It is a Tuesday. Bapuji resurfaces where they least expect him: on every front page across the country. An image of him in the ruins of the Napurthala Palace, not more than fifteen kilometres away. He has crossed the stinking Dhimbala basti to the other side.

Radha stays in her bed, reading the English cuttings. Sending the local-language ones to a service to be made comprehensible. There is international coverage too, the *FT,* the *Times,* the *Telegraph,* the *New York Times, Wall Street Journal, Asian Age* and *Sydney Morning Herald,* even *Dawn,* for God's sake, *Dawn.* Syndicated by Barun J. Bharat, exclusive to the world: The great Devraj with hollow eyes and sagging skin, wearing a kurta and dhoti, a Nehru cap on his tamed hair, he stands at the podium, finger pointed up at the sky, addressing a crowd of men. These look like factory workers, locals, picking over the ruins of Radha's childhood. The kind of people her father never usually sees. The kind who serve his servants, if that. She knows that a man does not need violence to make a crowd love him. All he needs is a stage, a pointing finger, a few well-chosen words. *I gave them my Company, and they kicked me out. I return to my people, to lead them to truth.*

At Bapuji's elbow is a half-naked holy man, all eyes—maybe some Sant picked up from the road. Wrapped in Bapuji's priceless toosh as a covering for his shame. Unbelievable. Where is Nanu? Radha squints through the pictures, but cannot see her. She wants to find Barun, and kill him.

Ranjit Uncle advises them—*keep calm, wait and watch. Your Bapuji will burn himself out and come home.* He does not call Radha in her rooms in the morning: he does not invite her to tea. She notices this but there is so much else to concern her. The corridors are circular, she touches Jivan, she ignores the curved walls —*Gargi, Bubu, married, slut, sex, shame.* With Jivan, Radha can be happy. In his room, she hears nothing but his voice.

Another week. A blistering, dry heat locks the city inside. Gargi and Bubu now plan for the Srinagar hotel opening all day; and at night they leave Gargi on the roof, scouring the stars through a telescope. Ranjit Uncle commissions Oxford astronomers to measure the distance of India from moon and sun, then he sends Bubu and Radha their horoscopes each day, via internal post. He excuses himself from dinner: he says he is working, trying to make progress in his attempts to communicate with Bapuji.

At 3 a.m., before the crush of the day, Gargi now waits for Radha in the hotel lobby. Together they go to the Golden Temple. Across the marble platforms, their bare feet make no noise; the chanting wraps around them like the most delicate of fabrics, they are left alone, to walk and whisper plans for the coming days. They sit for a while by the sarovar; Radha watches Gargi's reflection and wonders if she should confess. Her sister will tell her that adultery is a crime. Jivan could go to jail for five years if Bubu were to sue. What about her reputation? What will people say? Around them the chanting swells: they are blessed as they bow their heads.

Bapuji begins to cross the country. The people host him wherever he goes. Idiots, don't they realise he is going out of his mind? That he has never—not once in his life—given something for nothing, or anything back? Every time Gargi and Sita wanted to start some poverty-pleasing venture, they were told *no*. Even that one time when Radha thought she and Bubu could maybe adopt, she was told *no way.* Now look at him. One day he's in Madhya Pradesh, the next in Maharastra; never in Company hotels. Instead, this new Bapuji seems not to sleep, or tire of finding new ways to disparage the Company that he founded, built, directed. He spends his time in the bastis of wherever he visits; he seems to take delight in pulling some filthy child or other out of some godforsaken factory. —*Look! This one should be in school, not working! See what the Company is really built on!*

Most of the blame is reserved for Gargi, some of it spills over. Bapuji's supporters talk badly about Bubu: all those government contracts he milks for five times their worth. Nothing is ever levelled against the three wise men: Bapuji himself, Kritik or Ranjit. No one is interested in the past. All they remember is what they see: a great man who built the Company from his father's ashes, and now wants to help them. Gargi is called to defend herself, she appears on television and in the papers. There are allegations the Company concrete is mixed to crack; there are rumours it is laid too thin on the roads, the unpoured extra inches become money in the bank—the balance so healthy, the accountants happy. To Radha, everyone seems happy these days. Then costings are released of the light bulbs in the Company hotels—each one far more than a worker's daily wage. A montage is run of Radha at parties; the cost of her dresses—*why is this news?* Her phone becomes her second hand—each moment a new call from a reporter, an editor, or worse, a shareholder wanting to be reassured. No matter how many freebies Radha can arrange, still the men turn out for Bapuji: how they love to march for a cause!

Radha stays inside. She feels punished by the silence of corridors and lifts. It falls to her to manage the shouting in the press. Words and facts and other truths come out of her father's mouth: *Did you know that in each brickworks, Bapuji tried to set up a school? But Gargi Madam said the children could not be spared from work! Shame!* Wherever he goes, the crowds get bigger, the podiums swathed in khadi and white, adorned in marigold garlands. Amritsar seems a place where Radha should stay. As long as she is under Ranjit Uncle's roof, nothing can happen to her. The days pass. It is getting to October. She might have been wedding planning, if Sita had stayed.

Gargi gives interviews: talks about her women programmes, the new eco-car. No one will listen. Paper after paper prints lines of truths Radha cannot verify. That Gargi is corrupt: she bribed a woman whose husband was beaten in Company employ. That Gargi is unstable: this summer, she went mad and shot all of Bapuji's lovingly tended peacocks and pigeons on the Delhi Farm. Radha advises Gargi to swathe herself in nothing but saris, to stick to homespun and saffron borders; when she wears blouses, they should have high backs and elbow-length sleeves.

—You're on fire, Bubu tells her. "Dress-up Gargi"—this is the best PR work you've ever done.

Radha tries to avoid Bubu: he wakes up in a rage and stays there, until he passes out drunk each night. He flies about, trying to stop his building projects turning to rubble. Mud sticks—and no one in this climate wants to do business with a man responsible for high numbers of publicised worker deaths on-site—whose cement comes from exploitation—who doesn't give back to the local economy, offer jobs in private security or hire local women to comfort him (he brings his own) when he is away from his wife. Who is Bapuji's daughter.

Radha spends an hour with Barun on the phone. She points him to Twitter, where MrGee is full of support for Gargi; MrGee reminds his 28.6K followers (not bad) that Bapuji was in charge only until recently; that Gargi is a good egg; that so many women look up to her. MrGee (so Radha tells Barun) and his 29K followers call Gargi "Devi," for she prays each morning and evening; she knows each member of staff in the Company by name. MrGee tweets all day to his 35K followers with pictures and gifs: *Everything Gargi has learned is from Sri Sri Bapuji (she pays him respect with her whole heart).*

Barun runs his "Gargi Ma" piece with a picture of the sisters in Amritsar, at the Temple, at dawn. Blue light, and Radha has her head covered; Gargi's dupatta is looped around her shoulders. Interest in Bapuji drops; for forty-eight hours, the cognoscenti cognose on That Hair Cut. It is a sign, they say, that Gargi is mimicking the charisma of other strong women, that she is trying to win the respect of the business world. To keep the Devraj Company name from rotting inside out.

Then Bapuji goes on hunger strike. A statement is published. Radha sees it first retweeted by @IndiaBS to @MrGee. Then it comes to the press. *Corruption no more!* The target is not Bapuji's daughters. Now he calls on the poor to be inspired by his work to stage protests against "the terrible conditions of their lives." What? Conditions are of his making only. *Corruption no more!* The pundits state that this is the great repentance, a seismic moment in the history of twenty-first-century India. Change will begin with a fast. It will cleanse Bapuji's body from years of indulgence. Then will come a reckoning against backhanders, manipulation, greed.

It is enough to isolate Bapuji from some important business friends. Some begin to send flowers and presents to Amritsar, addressed to Gargi and Radha. Some try to come; she puts them off. @MrGee carries on, tweeting common sense and facts; citing the many initiatives Gargi was prevented from implementing—the provision of shoes for the workers, the crèche for the secretaries. The Company women tweet and retweet; they confirm Gargi is a Ma to them all.

Radha and Gargi stay in Amritsar, putting up with the village-standard service in Ranjit Uncle's hotel—the staff hate her and Bubu, she knows they do—and she tries not to blame Gargi for the bad HR culture here. Details of the business wash over her: Jivan and Bubu reframing the security of the Company, more cameras, more watchers, more alarms. Bubu in Srinagar days and nights, fighting with the contractors, dealing with the local politicians. Gargi, implementing an immediate financial penalty to stop Company workers joining the Devraj Campaign; an army of them is no match for Radha's desire.

It becomes clear that Gargi is not just crushing on Jivan: she thinks she is also in love. How her eyes follow him, how she tries to be with him at every opportunity! But in the late afternoons, when Bubu is away and Gargi must answer call after call, it is Radha who captures the chiru. Sometimes they simply burrow in his bed, turning one way and then the other to press lips, thumbs, knees, elbows, into each other's spines. Sometimes this is the prologue to sex that begins, slowly, gently and always face to face, getting stronger until Jivan makes so much noise that she threatens to put a pillow over his mouth.

She tries not to think about what she is doing and how many people must know. From the basement right up to the thirteenth floor. Even Bubu. Does he know? She tells herself she does not care. Only Gargi cannot know.

When Radha goes outside in the early mornings, she finds the temperature has dropped. She can see her breath. At the Temple, the peace and silence feel almost like a drug. The marble chills her feet as it has not before. She will call for woollens to be sent from Delhi, she thinks. She listens to the chanting, it is still dark. Her stomach churns. As she and Gargi do their round, she counts five black ravens at the side of one of the Temple pools, stark against the early morning gloom. She points them out to Gargi, who shrugs and tells her that the peacock story is true, only it was not her, in the Farm at Delhi: it was Daddy who sliced them all up.

She returns to the hotel, she cannot eat: she wants Jivan but the concierge tells her he has gone out on a drive with his father. All day. This makes her feel slightly sick. *Do they talk about her together?* she thinks. *Does Ranjit Uncle know?*

Radha crawls into her bed. MrGee on her mobile, her cuttings in her hand. She wakes in the dark, a flickering in her head, words, scrolling, words, lines, with no idea what day it is, what time. Bubu is there, he is climbing onto her. He stinks of the office, of sweat: he reaches for the lights.

—Get up, pretty Radha, he says. Why are you sleeping? It's only seven p.m. He wants her to play bosses and secretaries, to smack him hard with a wooden rule.

They lie, the cuttings shredded around them. She, scrolling her mobile while Bubu sleeps beside her. A bell. Bubu opens his eyes. The bell rings again. He gets up to see what's what.

—Stay here, he says.

Where would she go? Radha in the bed, retweeting a pic from the *Mumbai Mirror* (her favourite paper) of Bapuji in Chandigarh (wait, they are covering him from there?) giving a rally—his face in a frown; his finger pointed, always pointed at the sky, the crowd, at anything but himself. She writes—*That finger when your dad doesn't like your skirt length*—and tweets. Thirty hearts instantly respond. The doorway to the living room gapes at her.

Then she hears Jivan's voice, she thinks it is in her head; *is he here? greeting Bubu?* She strains—hum, hum, something about Chandigarh, a drive—then,

—*Sita.*

Radha fights the sheets; she puts on her robe and goes to the living room. Jivan and Bubu are standing still by the dining table; there's an arrangement of dried lavender shedding little flicks, it needs replacing—this whole suite needs updating—*tourism, the foundation of the future*—she stops next to Bubu, trying to read Jivan's face. *Tired, slight panic,* she thinks. Interesting.

—I knew something was up with my dad, he says.

Bubu's body goes slack, he shakes his head. Radha looks from him to Jivan. Is he saying that the money for the Devraj Campaign is coming from Ranjit Uncle? That he, instead of having tea each day with Radha, has been out and about, supporting all of Bapuji's natak, for weeks?

—What else? Bubu says.

Jivan purses his lips. Bubu starts to laugh. A sound worse than he makes when he loses a deal. He doubles over, holding onto Radha's arm. What else? What?

—Do you know the basic structure of the Devraj Group, Radha? The holding company for everything we have? says Jivan.

—Explain it to her, Bubu says. She's never deigned to learn it from Gargi or me.

She shrugs Bubu off. What's to explain? She and Bubu, Gargi and Surendra now hold thirty percent each of the Group. Ranjit Uncle has twelve percent. Fourteen percent shares held for staff on (mostly unattainable) performance-related rewards. All are invested in shell companies registered in the UK, which the Devraj Group has nothing to do with (of course). The shell companies sometimes buy shares in the listed Consumer Goods, which keeps the other subsidiaries happy. So happy—that makes Bubu happy. Then there is fourteen percent between forty or so private individuals, deep, long-standing family friends who bought in the dry years, when capital investment was needed to grow. Some have only one percent, some have six. No one has more than eight. *What else?* MrGee could spit this out in less than ten tweets.

—You and Bubu, Gargi and Surendra now hold thirty percent each of the Group, says Jivan. Sixty percent together. My dad had twelve percent. Fourteen percent was held for staff on a rewards-based scheme. Fourteen percent was with private individuals, all of them from here, in Punjab. So that's forty percent.

Jivan still says Pun-*jab*, like the stick. Radha wants to laugh. Jaab, jaab, jaab, she has tried and tried with his accent. She looks from boy to boy.

Bubu puts his elbow around her neck, catching her hair beneath.

—How many has Ranjit bought out? he says.

—All, says Jivan. He showed me the papers himself. He says he's going to put it all in trust.

—For you? Radha says. Wow.

—For Sita, says Jivan.

—Sita. She'll have twenty-six percent. Radha thinks, *What about my shawls?*

She grips Bubu's arm, tight around her throat.

—Good work, little girl, says Bubu. What else?

—The staff shares—the Company lawyer—what's his name?

—Kishore, says Bubu. Eldest son was in the Devraj Hundred. Batch of '05.

—Right. Kishore has agreed to reconfigure the terms of the staff share allocation to go through Ranjit—on paper, he'll control forty percent. To pass more to Sita, or Bapuji or keep for himself. Who knows what he will do?

Forty percent.

Now Bubu tilts his arm, forcing Radha to face him. Is that sympathy? His grin is wide, splitting his face.

—My intelligence is reporting that this protest-*showtest* is all Sita's idea, says Jivan. Is this the kind of thing she would do?

—Sure, but . . . I can't believe Ranjit Uncle would . . . I mean, Sita wouldn't do that to me. Or Gargi. Especially *Gargi,* says Radha.

—Why not? Bubu says.

Radha pulls herself free. Then feels Bubu's arm around her back, his thumb in the belt-hook of her robe.

—Prove it, she says.

Jivan takes a Company envelope from his pocket. Inside is a paper, covered in Ranjit Uncle's handwriting. *Painkiller,* Radha thinks. She takes the paper, and reads.

Sita, you must come meet us in Kashmir. Launch won't take place with-out you. Your father needs you right now and will be happy to see you. I'm sure you are aware of the problems your sisters are causing. I will arrange it, our secret. Yours always, Ranjit Uncle.

She will not cry.

—So what? It's just a letter. Your dad is on my side. I know he is. I'd bet my butt on it, she says.

Bubu has a jackal smile on his face. As if he could just stand here and smoke, and drink and play cards, and watch all of life fall down. He tugs on the ends of Radha's hair.

—Poor Radha. You know better than anyone that Ranjit will sniff out any chance to protect himself. Looks like your charms wore off, dear wife.

She stands next to Bubu, facing Jivan, the paper limp in her hands. She considers which one she loves—which one she should spend her life with—which one would be a better father—which she makes happy. Is Bubu, she wonders, ever happy?

—Gargi's on her way, Jivan says, pressing buttons on his mobile.

Bubu pulls out his Camel Golds, his lighter. Gives a smoke to Jivan, who lights it and gives it to Radha. Bubu shrugs. Smirks some more. Gives Jivan another. How Radha hates that smirk.

—What I want to know, Jivan, is why you didn't catch this earlier. Bubu drags on his cigarette, exhales. His smoke hangs, then disperses.

—You're right. I've just been distracted, that's all I can say. And you?

—Guys, Radha says. Enough.

Neither responds: both of them concentrated on each other. The room; the room is no help, it is nothing but sharp corners and hard angled light—everything fractures and rearranges through smoke—the space in between Bubu and Jivan narrows. Radha says, to separate them,

—There's only one person who might fix this. Jeet. Where the fuck is Jeet?

Now Bubu leans forward with his cigarette, the red eye pointing at Jivan's sweet face.

—Good question, he says. Where is Jeet? Weren't you supposed to find him, Jivan Singh, son of Ranjit Singh, bastard half brother of Jeet Singh?

Before Jivan can answer, the main door opens: the sound of Gargi talking to Uppal. Radha sees: Jivan and Bubu straighten themselves and move apart as Gargi comes into the room.

—I'm going back to Delhi right now, says Gargi. I'm going to sack Kishore. All in favour? Put your hand up, Jivan, you can be Ranjit's proxy.

Bubu raises his hand. So does Jivan. Radha can only nod.

—I am working for the good of all of us. I know what I'm doing. So do you three, most of the time. Someone talk to Ranjit. Tell him we will give Sita her half share if she comes back. Fifteen percent minus the concrete and— (she looks at Radha) —the shawls. Ranjit should give his to you, Jivan, if he is so eager to rid himself of it. Agreed?

Gargi smiles, her eyes light up with it. *She is excited. This is what she loves.* But in fact, her smile is all for Jivan, *and that,* Radha thinks— inhaling smoke into her dry mouth, ignoring Gargi's sideways look— exhaling away from the others—isn't *right.*

—Do you think my dad takes you seriously, Gargs? Jivan says. I mean, he still talks to me as if he can tell me to stand straight, pull up my socks, or dande padenge. (Jivan beats the air with an imaginary cane.) No. I think it needs more than talk.

He seems so buzzed, and so does Gargi; Radha wonders if they have been somewhere, drinking together.

—Gargi, Jivan says, you told me the night Bapuji left the Farm that this is our time. Don't we have "the youngest population, the fastest-growing democracy" in the world? Everyone says so. Come on. Don't you want to grab it all and hold tight for the sake of the—you know, sisterhood?

Now he looks at Bubu, waves his hand to clear the smoke:

—Bubu, you've been going on about those hungry middle incomes waiting for your apartments to get built, your malls to open up, your fashion to trade, your hotels to serve them dim sum with dipping sauce at Hakkasan Delhi. This Company doesn't need old men, still living in the glory days of the eighties and nineties. It's *now,* guys. *Our time.*

Jivan says, *Our time.* Radha notices, and she notices Gargi's quick smile. Her sister and her lover, a natural pair. She bites the tip of her tongue. Pulls it between her teeth.

—So what do you think we should do? Bubu says, slowly.

—We should fire Ranjit Uncle, to start, Radha says.

Gargi snorts.

—I could take out his eyes for the trouble he's causing.

—Madam-Gargi-Directorji. Your wish is my command, Bubu grins. Meeting adjourned. Get back to Delhi, Gargi, and fix your side of it. I will take care of Ranjit.

Radha has to watch them go. Her bones hurt, her eyes hurt, her stomach feels hollow. Bubu gets out his Kashmiri box and cuts her lines for the evening. She wants to see Ranjit Uncle this second now.

—Let's go find him, she says.

—No, says Bubu, snorting the drug, rubbing his gums, putting on his pants.

Silly pants, he cannot manage, and for a moment hops around the room, shouting *fuck, fuck, fuck.* Now come Radha's giggles, mixing with the anger in her belly, means the snow is melting into her veins, turning her blood to ice.

—We've had our orders from Gargi *Ma,* Bubu says. He calls out to the doorman,

—Get Ranjit down to the kitchen. A problem I need to speak to him about there.

He keeps hold of her elbow as they take the lift down. When the doors open, the lobby is empty, there is no whisper of greeting from anyplace. What time is it? Surely only 10 p.m. There should be people, and service, and bags, and guests. But no. The floor shiner has started his rounds. Bubu gestures to front desk security, two of the men fall in behind. He drags Radha through the restaurant, still waiting for the ghostly party, *where is everyone?* There is no answer. Into the kitchen, the spiced air chokes her: the scent is garam massala, onions, raw meat. The fridges and ovens and mixers and mashers, shiny, so shiny. Service is ending (this is Amritsar) but Radha's mouth starts to water, her nostrils sting. Bubu pulls her into the wash-up, more steel and steam—they pass a pot wala, arms in the sink as if chopped off by water and foam; she recoils at his dirty toenails, black skin pricked with wiry hairs, tiny matchstick legs. The man stares at her, a cockroach caught in the light; she wants to crush him but not touch him, she holds her body as tight as she can, this is how a nice girl stops any part of herself coming too near any part of his. Through the kachra room Bubu pulls Radha, piles of onion peel and scraps of fat, pink and white skin; bits of bone mixed with vegetable choppings waiting to be thrown to the Dhimbala basti kids. Is that a rat? Bubu pulls her onwards: outside again, ground level turn, around the curve of the hotel, turn, away from the lights, and turn again, into an alleyway she never knew existed. She slips on the wet floor, dragging something with her on the soles of her chappal. God, she is hungry. Bubu stops. She almost puts a hand out to steady herself against the wall. She puts her shawl over her mouth instead. Lips to butterfly wings.

A narrow passage lit by a few strip lights. At the far end, a vast tandoor is still belching out heat, the smell of the night's service: chicken, lamb, all the marinades Bubu loves. It is hot, so hot down here. Radha cannot lean back; the walls are dank, it smells of susu and blood, sharp vinegar, soy piss. She wants someone to lift her up so her feet do not touch the filthy ground.

Ranjit Uncle rounds the corner. He's wearing a jaunty peach cravat, a beautifully cut black suit. Ranjit Uncle, who she thought loved her better than the whole world. There is that smile on his face, his glee for her discomfort. She forces her body to stay, though the years have trained her to spring forward, give him a kiss, let her breasts brush his shoulder and her hair tickle his cheeks. Behind him, a group of orderlies melt out of the walls, and she is blocked: tandoor on one side, workers on the other, in the back kitchen alley. They stand and look at her. Like city cows dreaming of grass. To be invisible among them she would have to be dirty, naked, dark-skinned and poor. The feeling creeps over her. It is not the potwashers. It is Ranjit Uncle.

Radha looks up, tries to see the night sky, she wonders where Gargi and Jivan have got to, if they have passed the state boundary. Tears trickle down the sides of her face, catch in her ears and hair. She straightens her head. She says,

—How could you turn your back like this? You heard how Bapuji spoke to me, Ranjit Uncle.

Ranjit Uncle only wrinkles his nose and licks his lips. He keeps his eyes on Bubu. All of his body seems to shrink. He grips his stick.

—Let's meet like civilised men, Bubu. What do we need to come down to the bowels for?

Ranjit Uncle's face is like a dog's, denied its bone. Radha knows this look too: Did he not teach it to her? Does she not use it, time after time, to get whatever she wants from Gargi, from Bapuji? *My little Firebrand,* Ranjit Uncle calls her. And now, here they are. *Yes,* she thinks, *now you'll see.* She wants to press against him like she did when she was a girl, the smell of cologne, the scratch of his beard, his tongue in her mouth, his hands, his stick, his fingers, his tickly beard. His beard. Now she wants to rip the hairs out of his chin. *See what you have done,* she will say. And send the torn parts to Sita.

—Ranjit ko pakado, says Bubu.

The security men step forward, they grab Ranjit Uncle, he struggles but Bubu slaps him. Radha stuffs her shawl into her mouth; she wants to scream, but cannot.

—Tie him up, says Bubu.

He pulls his own tie loose. *Don't use that, it's Armani,* Radha thinks. He signals for the security guards to do the same. They push Ranjit around so he is facing the workers, his fingers wriggle at Radha—five or ten fingers—seem to grow towards her, to want to touch, in her—she watches Bubu fumble. *God, so incompetent.* She pushes him out of the way and snatches the ties; she begins to bind Ranjit Uncle's wrists; Bubu knows nothing about real knots. Radha does, though, for didn't Ranjit Uncle teach her himself how to bind Jivan the chiru? And didn't he impress upon her how important it is to beat but not kill? The bonds are fast: he struggles and tries to twist, almost he wants to bite at her, though he is stronger than he looks, of course so is she, from boxing and Yoga and abs and bends and spreading her legs above her head and working her core and all she does to keep her figure, to not become a fatty, or get sick, or old, to make sure the walls and the doors and the floors and the bars and the fucking press, the mirrors and the doormen and the public and Bubu and Ranjit have something pretty to feast their eyes on—she binds Ranjit more tightly; she turns him to face her; he cracks his head on the wall. The shock on his face delights her. He tries to get free. Then realises he cannot. Radha's arms are loose, her hands reach out: she takes the beard she used to stroke and pulls as hard as she can.

—Radha! he cries out, her Ranjit Uncle.

A puddle begins to form around his feet. His susu runs down the

alley, mingling with what is already there. Grease, dark mud. His stick
drops, he falls on his knees.

—Bravo! Bubu claps.

Behind Ranjit Uncle, the onion peelers and whatever else they are
swarm up against the two security guards. The alleyway is so narrow,
so lucky to be so thin. Arms loom towards Radha, over Ranjit Uncle's
head—someone's fingers almost grasp her. Bubu pulls her behind him.
The security push the servants back towards the alley's neck. This is all
Ranjit Uncle's fault. When she was little, he promised to love her always,
and protect her; he said he would keep all her secrets and pat her and pet
her and gift her and treat her. She pushes past Bubu, she shouts in his
face, barely aware of what she's saying: Pissing in the gully, talking to Sita,
lying, cheating Ranjit Uncle. *You promised you would look after me and
this is what you meant?* The hurt is sharper than the vinegar smell around
her, it takes her body to those hot afternoons, dizzy with champagne;
missing Jivan, riding in the Bentley, home from tea with Ranjit Uncle,
head in his lap, taken to Nizamuddin for naps to get sober—he would
stay with her, stroking her, stroking her, there, one hand on his stick,
one, two, three, four, five fingers in her. Waking up with blood on the
sheets. His tickly beard. Ranjit Uncle's chin drips crimson onto white:
such a bright, hurt red under the strip lights. Dead flies caught in them;
still bodies above their heads. The blood is beautiful, it makes her own
eyes burn, her skin, her insides; she wants to pull again, see that red come
out. *And is Sita next? Is she?*

Ranjit Uncle swallows. Radha wipes her palms on his cheeks. A
shock to feel Jivan's bone structure, Jivan's flesh, hard under her hands,
now turned to stale papad that no one will eat.

—Sita wanted me to help her reconcile—she wanted the lie of the
land—I gave her the truth, that is all.

His old play-time voice. His *our-keeping-secrets* voice. Now Radha
hears it differently: cowardice, cunning. Fear.

—Ranjit Uncle, please sach batao. Who am I? she shouts in his face.

She starts to weep. She can feel Bubu behind her, pushing her out of
the way. She holds up her arm.

—Stop.

The softness in her voice raises Ranjit Uncle's head. There is blood
all over his lips like a liquid lipstick. He is crying. His nosey is running
into the blood.

—Radha, he whispers. He sounds so serious and so hurt.

—I have known you and your sisters since before you were born. I have seen you fight and play. I have watched you take on life's challenges. I watched you become a wife to this idiot, and tried to guide you. But I cannot stand to see you and Gargi take everything from your father. His titles, his houses, the eyes in his head? You cannot imagine and you don't care.

Ranjit stops. Splutters on his own blood.

Radha takes her white shawl, she tries to wipe his cheeks. Ranjit Uncle turns his head from her.

—You are not the Radha I tutored and loved. Even if some pagal kutta had barked outside in that storm you would have let him in. God will show us what happens to delinquents like you, who make such great men into slaves.

—God will show you nothing, says Bubu.

He pushes Radha out of the way; she sprawls in the alleyway then gets on her knees. She touches cold stone, dark matter, the taste of earth and filth. The orderlies shout out—that sound, what is that sound? *Crack,* as the snapping of a cane. *Thump,* as a body falls down. She looks up. Bubu is standing over Ranjit Uncle, the splintered cane in his hand. He raises his arm; he pushes the end into Ranjit Uncle's eye, he twists the stick and turns it.

Blood spurts all over Bubu, all over Radha. She screams, and beneath it, hears a deeper note: Ranjit Uncle. A sound so like Jivan, in the bed, under her—and all she can see around her is red; all she can feel is the slip of flesh between flesh. Wet like the night in the dipping pool, heat as he sucked on her breasts one by one, one by one, so fast. One, the other, one, the other. It fizzes in her mouth and she says the words that will change her story forever—says them in a haze of red, the sentence from which she will never be free, no, never, never, no—

—The other one too, the other one too! Or one will taunt the other—take the other one too!

Bubu takes her hand, he wrenches her shoulder, but she cannot get free. His palm on hers, the stick in her hand. He raises their arms: *Bleed little chiru, but do not die.* They give a sharp twist. Seconds. Slow, a breath, or two. It is done.

—*Ayeee, ayeee!* The servants break past the security, Radha sees them stumbling towards her.

—Bus karo! One, no more than a child, barefoot and slipping on the blood, tries to climb Bubu's body, get the stick. *Ayeee, ayeee!* Bubu shakes him off; he falls on the floor. Smack: his little head. Radha tries to kick him; Bubu kneels over him—then someone—a guard—hits Bubu on the temple with a tandoor brick: he thuds to the ground, he lies still.

The guard hits again. Radha cannot get close enough to make him stop. She is covered in blood. This is her youth: she is meant to be in Switzerland or Paris or London; she can feel the cool of the fresh snow, the blinding white of the Alps. It is so far from the piss in the alley, from the blood, from the stick now flailing in the guard's hands, trying to school her husband. The tandoor's mouth, a dark hole: *It is our time. Now, Radha, now!*

She scrabbles towards the guard; finds his knife in his belt. He does not see her. She pulls it out, she stabs the man in his side.

—Don't touch your betters, you disgusting Jhimba!

She has to pull the knife out. It is harder than putting it in. Meat on the bone, torn with teeth. It takes all her strength, then the man collapses.

Around her: men. Stop. Eyes wide. At her feet, Bubu gapes, staring. He grabs at her. There is so much blood. The whole right side of his head is mashed. She wants to leave him in the alley. Three bodies and a half. Ranjit, Bubu, the security man. The whimpering child.

A groan comes from the red wash.

—Jivan, where are you?

Ranjit or Radha? No one there could tell.

The orderlies huddle around Ranjit Uncle. Some melt back against the walls. Some help. She heaves Bubu out of the alleyway, lays him down among the five-kilo bags of Company flour. He is bloodless, it seems. As if stunned only, not dead. As if dead only, about to wake. When the car comes, she climbs in also, holding his hand. She does not cry. When they get to the hospital, she does not go in. She will not be seen in this back-water, covered in blood. She is folded in hospital blankets; she is returned to the hotel. Through the back gate. Up in the lift, the goldfish gapes and flickers, the light strobes her stained clothes. In her suite, she begins to sob, so hard, choking: someone, she does not care who it is, slaps her. Then pats her and wraps her up again, and puts her to bed, her cherry room, with something milky to drink. How red and bright are the fruits on the vine. She closes her eyes. No, keep them open. A silence descends: so complete it is as if Sita has come home, and filled every corner of the whole deep world with her nothing.

She wakes, she sleeps. She wakes. The clouds roll towards her in shadows of grey, pale silver, deep blue. Fissures of light slice through the blinds, glittering gold like that day in Goa. There are waves of dark purple, then flicks of yellow again. A sky so bruised, it covers the city, swallowing the earth.

Gargi texts her, *Don't worry*. She hates Gargi for making her hurt Ranjit Uncle, and for having Surendra. For being older, for taking Jivan back to Delhi with her. She hates Jivan for going. She hates Bubu, and she hates Ranjit Uncle. For leaving her alone. And she cannot explain this to anyone, because the only man who might understand, Radha thinks, and here, she stops: Bapuji. He is not speaking to her either: she hates him most of all. Too busy getting the whole nation against her. She is alone. She has always been so, since she was young.

The cushions of the suite watch her and whisper, so does the sofa, the antimacassars. Pieces of her own skin, stripped from her. The carpet smothers her steps. She does not remember what she should say or care about. From the bar she takes the bottle of scotch, the vermouth, the cognac, the vodka, good bottles all, she lines them up and begins. A toast to Bubu! Shot. A toast to Jivan, now rich as a king! Shot. A toast to Sita, wherever she is! Double shot. To Gargi! Shot. To Nanu! Shot. And, to her mother, long burned and scattered. Shot.

Where is Nanu? In the room, here surely, her mutterings jangle with the shadows, a skeleton of words. *All this shall pass, as it has passed, as it is passing, and come again. And every wife whose husband is a bear shall bear no children, but the children of owls. Twit TWOO!* The glasses on the bar take up her refrain, as clear as if she were in the room. Radha chants the words herself and toasts to the windows, to her own translucent self. *To Radha!*—Shot.

Radha writes her own eulogy on Company paper, she will send it to Barun J. Bharat, recently promoted Senior Happenings Editor at the *Times of India*. *Here lies Mrs. R. Devraj Balraj: a widow aged twenty-eight, a living death for a motherless girl. Mrs. R. Devraj Balraj, abandoned by her father, a blinder of men, murderer of a servant in the name of honour. Who cannot do a wife's basic duty and keep her husband alive.*

Rampaging, marauding, she drinks the gold liquid and the clear, the white wine, the red cherry liquor, the disgusting sweet kahlua lurid blue on her lips, Shiv's poison she cannot hold in her throat, see, see? All downed, all drowned. She paces as she drinks and chants like a Yogi, invoking the Book According to Nanu, to shut out the sound of men dying. Then she opens Bubu's Kashmiri box. There is no Queen of Diamonds to cut the lines. She dips her finger and licks and licks; a meal made of pure white snow.

Shh, say the sofa cushions, *hush,* says the bed. *Calm,* say the curtains, you must try to be calm. She cannot listen to them; eyes blazing and blood red from tears, she forgets she is human, turns jackal. Naked, breasts swinging, hair wild, she finds a pair of scissors and goes to hunt, slashing at every soft thing in the room. Catch the chiru! The blades shred the chaise longue, the curtains, the pillows. *Ayee, ayee,* she thrusts, she rips; nothing has the same give, nothing makes the same soft slurp of eyes giving way to the splintered end of a bone-topped cane—only the thrill as the blades plunge in: then the floating softness of feather and down.

When she is spent, she sits on the floor in the fluttering ruins. Sweating and bleeding from tiny gashes where the scissors have caught her, she crawls into the gutted remains of the bed and picks up the phone. To whoever answers in the kitchen she croaks,

—Bring me a pot of first-flush tea. And a plate of rose macarons.

The next morning, the papers report the great rally at Chandigarh Bapuji held, where he announced a vow of silence. In the far western state of Odisha, they give thanks: rain has come; there is relief for the farmers thirsting, although there is a risk of some dams breaking (Company concrete—again). They say that Shilpa Shetty, the sylphlike Bollywood star, the heartbeat of millions, is offering Vastu-checked apartments off-plan in Gurgaon. Parents are outsourcing homework and science projects to IIT grads so their children can get ahead, and this is a well-known, multi-lakh scam, while on Page Three, Radha's friends are partying in

Mumbai and Delhi without her. There is nothing about Bubu, or about the man Radha killed. Days pass; by Sunday, there is still nothing at all. Monday's news has something, though: Bubu is dead.

An urn was delivered to Radha twenty-four hours later. Radha stayed locked in her room. Its mother and father, its sister, arrived in Amritsar—Radha said she could not see them, she was just too devastated. She sent the urn down in the lift to its mother.

Every day Radha expects a knock on her door. Why is the hotel still running? How come the servants aren't talking? Why hasn't anyone come to question her about Ranjit Uncle, or Bubu—or even come to sit with her, to ask her how she is? Where is Gargi? The walls do not answer. *Jivan,* she thinks. *Maybe he, too, is dead.*

A week, or three days—no, a week later, as Bapuji's silence resonates across the nation—the paper reports that a man has been caught and charged for the murder of Devraj Bapuji's second son-in-law, Bubu, son of Manpreet and Nalini, the town planners and mall investors, brother and sister-in-law to the MP for Commerce and Industry. Who are suffering so much at the loss of their only son. Radha watches on TV as the case grips the country: a servant who thought he could tell his boss where he was going wrong, a man of the people, from a rough area, left behind from prosperity, seemingly loyal, but who had a history of violence of course, a poor family. The accused was also fingered as one who was in the Company under Gargi Devi's special quotas for Muslims to find jobs. Those *in the know* say the culprit will rot in jail for the rest of his life, and that life will be short, if God (or the police, where Bubuji had great friends) have anything to do with it.

Yes! The lowborn man who killed Our Beloved Bubuji will go swiftly to justice—for that is the penalty for murder. A good man has fallen, a man who was building a future for the country beyond anything his grandfathers could have dreamed. And his wife! Radha Devraj Balraj, such an icon of loveliness. Yes. A beautiful girl has been left bereaved. Too young, too young, the media agree. But she is an heiress to an empire's fortune. Aré, who knows, in time, what will happen? Widow remarriage is not so unheard of these days, and she too has charms. It was not a divorce. And she is still so pretty. Yes, thank God, they all agree: at least she is still quite young.

ALL YOUNG GIRLS SHOULD be like Sita. Penitent, studious and kind. Out of the five of them, my three girls and Ranjit's two boys, it was Jeet and Sita I thought would make a good match. Everything about him is exactly as a man should be. Just one flaw, he has. I won't say what it was, because in the polite society of fallen manservants, dogs and birds, angels and dust that I find myself in, such things should not be mentioned. But let it be placed on record that I valued him despite that. And how he believed in the Company dreams! I built the hotels, and Jeet made them beautiful. Such taste, he had. I wonder where he is now, why he does not come. He loved me. He will come again, I am sure of it.

I once asked Sita to prove her love for me. But now I realise that even if she had spoken, I would not have been told the truth. Because Sita's love was not really for me, it was for nothing human.

—What is the most important thing in the world to you? I asked her.

—Photosynthesis, she said, the coming into being of breathable air.

So much she feels, for my life's work.

There was a night when Sita was still missing, and I stood on the eighth-floor terrace at the Company Amritsar. When you are on that plateau, you can see the city stretching out beneath, as if on fire. You can imagine all the men roaming around, there are hardly any women at that time of night. In any case, women are fewer there. And all of them seemed to be gathered on the terrace to speak, speak, speak, speak, speak at me. Only the sky was dumb.

It seems a small step between Amritsar and Srinagar, but much happened in between. That night I decided I would ignite the country for my cause. I knew I could do this, for people love me blindly. It might be because of the things I have experienced, it might be because I am so generous with my resources and forward-thinking with ideas. I invoke India, I call for a new order. The country should be wiped clean and we can start again without that Muslim-loving Gargi or that bad apple Radha to stop us.

Sita used to say that if she could start a movement, she would feed and educate every girl child and grow crops without chemical intervention. Hers was an economics of love. Nevertheless, I used this ambition of hers to invite her home. We promised her:

(1) Her own apartment in the city of her choice. She wanted Mumbai. She told me it would have a sea view, and room for me. She wants to live there because she loves the water. We will do this, but maybe on the Farm we could build it. Brick against brick. Story against story. Will it have a glass house? She wants to write and research and publish her findings. On plants of all kinds; indigenous, strange and native. The ones that flower between the cracks of brick buildings and in the cisterns of the Mughal gardens. To show the world that beneath the surface, all creatures are of the same matter. I said, of course, just come home, Sita, and all this will I give you.

(2) A campaign of her designing. This on the condition she would come home, and release her shares back to me. She could have her nothing and get everything she wanted in one go. Yes, yes, yes, (no).

She came home.

How simple are her desires!

When she raised the issue of the Kashmir hotel, I took a fasting vow of silence, until she promised she would protest no more. When I began to speak again, I told her this story, to make her understand why we had to come back to Srinagar and build.

—Once upon a time, there was a King with many lands. Who answered to no one lower than him, but only to one very demanding God called Kalki. Kalki was embodied as a warrior on a flying white horse, whose wings needed storm winds to move them. Kalki waited always for the King to make war, which would be a mistake so bad it would ignite a storm for Kalki's flaming sword. But the King was clever. Instead of waging war, he found a plot of landlocked land and built on it.

The problem was, the people on this landlocked land had suffered for many years under the King's family's rule. Still the King would not stop. He had to build on that land. From there, he would win the hearts of the whole kingdom. And open that place to the world, through a tunnel, cut through rock. The more that people came in the name of beauty, the more the whole world applauded; for they were only there to be entertained, to spend their money, to create a service economy and build a newfound prosperity; of course there would be approval and gratitude from all. And the people of that place were glad. All of this was done over decades. Kalki, waiting, got bored and was asleep.

And so did Sita, her head in my lap. Darkness and chill all around us. The manservant was back in his place at the door. He watched as I tried to move without waking her, his eyes shining, his ears two jug handles, like that chap from *Slumdog Millionaire*. Was that Radha's favourite or Gargi's?

—Then what happened? he asked me. His face was eager, like a boy's with a gun.

—I forget how, I said. It ends.

IV

—.—

JEET

i

—Rudra bhai, can you swim and can you fly?

This from Felix, a basti boy, seven years old, in a faded *Coke is*it* T-shirt and cut-off pants.

—Rudra bhai, do you remember everything about your past life?

This from another boy: Akul, about thirteen, but short, with no Pa, always begging for stories of drinking, ganja, and the ability to blow rings from a pipe (as unimaginable girls, fishing, fishy, tried to hook Jeet with their made-up smiles and their sighs).

—Rudra bhai, what is the worst thing you have ever done?

This from Nakul, his identical twin, who came out second (he tells them each time), as if this makes him more willing to believe that Rudra the Sage was once a Babu named Jeet Singh.

—Rudra bhai, what does it take to kill a man?

Silence. The boys look up at Samir, their fourteen-year-old leader, who always seems to find the treasure in the rubbish pile; a gold pendant, a half bottle of hot-pink nail polish, a silk Heritage label tie around his dear head. Samir, whose father wears a Company uniform to guard the back gate of the Amritsar hotel, and who has a pair of proper shoes; flat leather lace-ups with scratched red soles, too big, a found pair, but his own.

The day before the storm breaks over Dhimbala, Jeet will sit under his tree, watching the boys through half-closed eyes. He wonders what Samir had to do to get those shoes. Is he a con artist? A spy? No. Jeet must not suspect Samir's sweet smile. This is the path he has chosen: to try to be clean, to be good, to think only pure thoughts, and set himself towards salvation. To remember that he is: Rudra, Rudra, Rudra. A Naph Sage.

Dhimbala lies in a scoop of land formed by an ancient lake bed, long dry. It is at least two kilometres wide, maybe three. But how would Jeet know this or count? All he knows is that it begins at the feet of his father's Amritsar hotel, and that its shacks have spread like fungus in a bowl, taking no heed of the state border—spreading, spreading—until they stop at the high stone walls of the old Napurthala Palace, where Bapuji was born.

Each day, the hour comes when the basti boys will climb off the dump. They will gather around Jeet at the foot of the tree. Dark skins covered in scraps of fluttering white plastic, as if they are mosaics of themselves. Overlooked by the back of the Company Amritsar, its white façade pocked with air-conditioning units, the walls stained with blue streaks (the windows are weeping mascara tears), they will pick and pull the scraps off each other. Pester him with questions such as

What does it take?

and ask for stories before they go home to their mothers. They demand these stories straight: beginning–middle–end. But Jeet's calling is not to simplify these boys' lives (nor is it to listen to their sorry tales)—

so he tells his stories in vernacular circles, backwards and around: for his own sanity, to stay here, he must teach the boys that life is not lived in linear fashion. They must learn what it means to be the future of those ancient tongues that count no time but today.

.   .   .

Half the rim of the basti is edged by a cracked plain, where stilted, rusted advertising hoardings show washing machines, dishwashers, pictures of the beach, peeling in strips to reveal Bapuji's face—and Nanu's—their hands in namastes battered from years of monsoons and harsh, dry heat. The slogan in patches across each board reads: *Company City—coming soon!*

I can't go on, Jeet thinks, sitting under his tree. *I will go on. I will join the pilgrim's route to Amarnath. I will get the blessing of Lord Shiv and see for myself the lingham formed of ice. That waxes and wanes. Amongst so many pilgrims of all purses, I will walk; all of my sins will be absolved.* Yet, even on the day before the storm, when his mind will reach this freewheeling point, when the tiny scars all over his arms have faded to thin white lines and he counts the weeks he has been here, *is it four? five? six?* he will not leave. Instead, he concentrates on the boys, on how he has come to this.

What does it take to kill a man? That Tuesday when Jivan came home. That night. Jeet spoke to Jivan; then walked away from all he knew. He reached this square in Dhimbala in an open-backed lorry—driven, it seemed, from the core of the earth by a white-haired, white-robed Sardarji whose patta snapped through the carriage window, clapping against the sky, an Asura being chased by God. The truck had no number plate, no markings on its side.

Jeet had clung on, bleeding from so many small cuts, shivering between the jute sacks stuffed with maize, chanting his new name: *Rudra, Rudra, Rudra.* As dawn broke, he was dropped on the highway somewhere outside Amritsar. He walked from there, parched, freezing, early cars rushing past him, until he reached his father's hotel.

This was the first test.

Rudra, he told himself that morning—*Rudra is a Naph Sage.* He must fight against desire, of the body and mind. Still, it was difficult not to run inside, to be greeted by faces who knew and loved Jeet Singh. To bathe, and eat, and change his clothes, and sleep, and eat, and bathe and order. Instead—reciting the Gita under his breath, *strengthen the self by means of the self*—he limped off the highway, then followed the yellow brick wall, until he came to a space big enough for a family of elephants to turn full circle in.

There was a beast called Haathi, who used to live here. She was used for the hotel weddings and tourist rides; she was hired out to grooms in downtown Amritsar. She was fed leftovers from the Company kitchens and her dung provided her keeper's sons with a side business in fertiliser for the local farms; it was made into paper by the keeper's daughters to sell in the Company shop; it provided mosquito repellent when rubbed on children's skin. They even squeezed that shit for water in times of drought, which came, increasingly regularly, as the beast grew old. After Haathi died, the Amritsar side of the basti had to *diversify* to replace her. According to Samir, the competition for slices of the dump became fierce.

Jeet walked down the kachcha path made by many, many feet over years. He was pulled by the sound of men singing. He reached a block of unpainted concrete stores. First, he came to JAB WE MET PAN, a mobile top-up shack, closed because it was so early. The place has a fridge selling chuski and drinks; local newspapers, cheap magazines for lifestyle, homes and soft-focus girl porn. Plastic jars of candy line the shelves; silver-wrapped packets of paan dangle in streams at the entrance like strings of individually wrapped condoms. Jeet has since found that Kal and Dodal, the two muscled brothers who work in the shop, do not live in the basti; they live downtown, they ride pillion on their motorbike to the store. They never give anything free, not even one sucking sweet, even to Rudra, the Naph.

Second, there is the swap shop moneylender run by Mr. Kataria Senior, a man with five sons the basti women call 1, 2, 3, 4 and 5, since they all dress the same, are the same height and build—except number 4, who has the longest nails Jeet has ever seen on a man, and 5, who is missing a finger. He has been told that these five slice up the basti between them, collecting rent once a month, monitoring the distribution of tokens to use the first-circle toilets, keeping an eye on what the boys find on the rubbish pile, which might be more valuable than they could know.

Third is the dhaba, run by a short, taciturn man with a clipped moustache and clean-shaven cheeks who Jeet now knows as Feroze Shah, son of Charan Shah, who makes the kind of dark, burned aloo paranthe tourists dream of tasting but would order only if a guide book recommended them to do so. Tastes of charred atta and green chilli—so hot—eyes water if you eat them without curd. Shah was there, that morning Jeet arrived; he was just setting up outside for the morning clientele. His small TV, rigged up over his counter, was already streaming live from the Golden Temple, the rhythmic tabla overlaid with men singing *Shabad* from the Guru Granth Sahib. It washed over Jeet—as if this place, with its wooden tables and benches, the plastic ketchup and chilli sauce squeezers, the faded posters of '8os starlets were the inner rooms of the Gurdwara itself.

Shabad—for Ranjit's faith buried in Jeet through years of Catholic school with prayers to Jesus (who died bleeding on the cross, and was reborn each Sunday). *Shabad*—for Jeet's precious Sanskrit–English dictionary, its delicate pages listing an almost infinite variety of meanings; words beget words as leaves from a branch. *Shabad*—for *speech-sounds*—to perform speech. School was spent singing of the omniscience and omnipotence and omnipresence and the dilemma *therein* of the omni-beneficence of God.

The Christian Brothers were not kind. They brooked no deviance, not an inch. They taught Jeet denial. For Lent each year he fasted, he prayed. Later, these rituals made him want to compete with Vik at Eid, but Vik did not keep the fast. He was Kashmiri, he said he knew already what it was to starve.

Until you might eat rats? Jeet asked him once.

Shabad.

When he heard the Temple chanting from the dhaba TV, the morning he arrived in Dhimbala basti, Jeet faltered.

.   .   .

He wants to go back. To that morning with the voices pulling him in. He had approached Feroze Shah, who was lighting the burners. And told him what his name was: Rudra, the Naph, on his way to Kashmir, to join the pilgrimage of thousands to the Amarnath shrine. For this, he got to wash his face with carbolic soap at the dhaba sink, he was served hot water in a tin cup; he tried to sip it, but it was gone in one gulp. He got an aloo parantha too, pat with butter; he paused when Feroze passed it to him, dammit, for a moment in the dawn—*Jeet—dhaba food—never, never, eat it*—then he rolled it up and swallowed it in three bites.

The light sprang into full sun. Feroze Shah took back the plate and cup, he nodded to wish Rudra on his way. Where should Jeet go? He did not return to the road. He stumbled across the square, avoiding the hotel back gate. The guard box, the CCTV camera attached to it seemed to follow him, but its wires had been cut and were dangling.

Jeet saw the neem tree (now his): a good tree, offering some meagre shade.

He saw seven water pumps; he went to one; he was so thirsty—he tried it, but it did not work.

He thought his eyes were failing: in the lightening sky, a mountain range appeared, covered in snow.

Jeet blinked.

A slapping noise made him turn. Behind him, black slumwomen in chappals were coming out of a stone archway called (he has since learned) the Amritsar Gate; some were carrying cheerful plastic buckets to the water pumps.

. . .

And now he knows that the pumps give liquid between the hours of dawn and 8 a.m., the people of the basti pay Kataria 1 for individual, couple or family tokens that can only be bought a month in advance.

He tried to hide by squatting under the tree; looking up, up, at the mountain—which he thought he could scale—but how was it there—

and realising it is not snow-capped.

It is a slope of rubbish, at least five metres high (but again, how would Jeet know?) stretching around the curve as far as he could see.

Dhimbala is embraced by the city's dump.

It begins at the skips outside the Amritsar hotel, it rises up and around in a stinking half circle until it meets Napurthala. The wild dogs and rats and the people of the basti live on all it provides: everything they have to feed on, to shelter them. From precious plastic bags and wrapping for their houses, to the freshest cementing excrement that humans eating food waste can produce. Jeet has walked on it; there is a softness to some parts of it—gelatinous black liquid bubbles up, gasping for air or desperate to suck him down. A monster of the deep waits for those who work and play on the rubbish; they know she is there, they can smell her breath.

That first morning, Jeet sat on the earth under his neem tree, head pounding, mouth dry. Eyes heavy, as the weight of hot sun on his shoulders. His arms wrapped around his knees, he watched the basti begin the day.

The boys preparing to climb the pile.

Jeet wept. For them (but more for himself), sweat trickling salt into his mouth as the sun reached midday and the shadow of the tree carried on its rotation across the ground. After they had used the pumps, the women departed. He took off his singlet and soaked it on the ground, then put it back on. Telling himself he is Rudra not Jeet, that Jeet would never do this; Jeet loved beauty, he was raised by a man with a bone-topped cane, who always matched his ties with his socks and pocket handkerchiefs.

Singlet wet, cooling a little, he had watched the boys, their mahogany hides, their hair matted, faces dusty, as they climbed, and picked, and found. By the end of that morning, he had identified the leader, who he now knows as Samir—watched him show his finds to the Company guard in the guard box, then spit at the gates of the Amritsar hotel. Jeet sat under the neem tree, eyes closing, spirits sinking. Waiting for what? He did not know.

The day before the storm is a Friday. Some of the boys should be washing for afternoon prayers. Others should be working in the rubbish. Yet they crowd to Rudra under his tree; they are almost close enough to touch. The whites of their eyes are the only clean things about them. There is no breeze. The weeks of heat now seem ineffable but the boys never seem bothered by the sun. They want to know stories of Jeet's old world, where there are squares and gardens just for walking in; where the houses are made of concrete or brick, bank vaults for human lives. Where the terraces have plants growing in pots just to look at, and birds are fed from wire bags full of nuts and seeds that cost no more than 50 anna—a whole meal for a family of five in the basti or some similar conversion. Jeet has never bought bird food, so this number is a guess.

Dhimbala has nine circles. As all civilised men discovering new lands, Jeet has mapped it, and marked his favourite routes.

The first circle smells, he thinks, of rotting food. This is because it is reserved for those lucky enough to work in the Amritsar hotel kitchens (though none of them higher than pot-washing level). The first circle also has a block of its own squat toilets—token-operated, again; some families even have electricity, sluiced from the Company wires to the dhaba, then out to their shacks.

In the second circle, Jeet counts five generations of men who carve soapstone Temples to sell in the old city; the shavings from their work collect in the drains, turning the black sludge grey. He counts rope makers: boys hoarding plastic bags and bottles, cutting them with rusty scissors and blades, sitting, plaiting, learned from mothers, sisters, little girls. Their huts are brick and tin; they too share some electric light.

After that the structures change, to three, two and one storeys built of found-brick in the third and fourth, where, on the first day, Jeet sees a real prostitute for the first time in his life—he has only read about such women in the stories of Saadat Hasan Manto. She is a Madam called Madam; her building is a faltering three-storey brick house, leaning onto the one next to it. He expects Madam to be sassy and savvy. To greet Rudra the Naph with sly respect, which he would of course ignore. But she doesn't look up when he passes. She sits in her courtyard each morning, her pale blue pallu over her head, she's not even chewing pan or smoking a bidi. She has a newspaper in her lap: she's reading it, Jeet realises, shocked. Beside her is a huge brass bell suspended over an old bore hole, and in the opposite corner, a deep, rusted brazier.

Jeet walks by that place almost every day. Propelled by his own sense of yearning: only to connect, for a second, not with Madam or her girls, but with the small group of hijras who come and go quietly through the lanes; they sit on a mat in the whores' courtyard sometimes, in the evenings they oil each other's hair. Their hands are quick and capable. Jeet wants to see more. Rudra goes near but never gets close; he is sick, jealous of the band wale who live in this circle and will perform for grooms' processions when October comes. He hears them practising some nights. He imagines their crimson jackets and gold epaulets; they are friends of the hijras and live alongside the brothel, they are welcome in the courtyard, they store their instruments in the basement, where it is warm and dry— and Jeet wishes he could play an instrument, the drum or the trumpet or even the pipe; then he would have been able to go inside. To prove he isn't afraid of the way women touch, and what they touch or how.

He has come to know the fourth circle by its painted shutters. Here, Samir says, once lived a white woman, Anya. She came for months, before Samir was born; she had a stills camera with Kodak film and one with pictures that developed when you shook them. She took snaps of all the young basti girls, their jewellery and clothes. When Samir's mother was a sixteen-year-old bride, she helped Anya to live. Here, in a small brick room. The tin shutters are now pulled down and locked, painted with a woman; her face brown-pink, her dark hair flowing, held back from her face with a chequered scarf; some scratched Hindi lettering on her curled bicep spells *Dhimbala Women's press: an independent project of the All India Women's Commission on Women's Rights.*

There is money hiding in the fifth, Jeet can smell it. The Muslim lanes are scrubbed clean. The shacks are small, set out in a chain with connecting doors between families. Rudra spits whenever he passes through the fifth. The Muslims also, Jeet has noticed, have a Hindi-medium school; the murals are of happy children sitting under a painted tree, listening to Krishna as a teacher. A speech bubble over his head says that their hands, hearts, minds and mouths are as offerings to the Ministry of Human Resource Development. According to Samir—who shrugs as he says it— no one goes to school there, only the Muslim boys and even some of the girls; the building was put up by Kataria Senior; it only opens for a month or two, around election time.

In the sixth and seventh, the structures are made of jute sacks, soaked with urine to stiffen them, then packed and bound with plastic rope against bamboo. They are sturdy, though they crawl with lice and stink in the heat, on days when rain is a memory from years ago. Here live the Christians making moonshine. In the eighth, the structures are made of cardboard, plastic sheeting and found things, old suitcases and clothes; this is the circle of the workers at the burial sites and cremation grounds, the men and women and children who clean the open toilets on the farms across the state, whose life's work is to handle every dead thing in the basti and the town drains, from rabid dogs biting each other to death, to the ragdolly foetuses spat from waste pipes in the back lanes of the city, which wash up in the Dhimbala scrap.

The lanes between the circles are no more than two metres wide. From the first to the fifth they are rough mud. From the sixth onwards, wooden planks are balanced over rancid black water; *the blood of the beast,* so the basti boys call it—even as they scare each other with the threat of a push off the boards. A foot goes in, a shoe is sucked off; it will sink or get stuck in the drain that leads to the next alleyway. If it is a small shoe, it will travel through the gap to the ninth circle of Dhimbala, where those who have nothing do something like living—and from there to the pit, ten men deep and twenty wide, so the basti dwellers say, filling slowly with rubbish to be burned; a pupil in denial at the centre of the eye.

The hair on his face has grown. He claws at it in his sleep. For the first week he could not wash it, it got in his mouth and nose as if a heavy-bodied girl was sitting on his face. He knows he must look wild—not the picture of himself he had seen that night of the party, when he left Jivan at the bar and went to Ranjit's bungalow. He stood in his father's room and looked in the cupboard mirror—his own long hair, unbound, over his artful stubble. The layers of skin and fat that marked him out as a stranger here when he first arrived. That night of the Tuesday Party, Jeet had taken off his silver kurta, and squatted. His balls ached slightly with the movement, he banged a knee on the bathroom cabinet when he opened it to rummage amongst old medicines and cotton balls. Hidden at the back was a small baggy containing three pills engraved with some primitive beast, maybe a cow or a yak. He took one with a tall glass of Company sparkling water.

Naked, he went back to his father's room. Shivering in the air-conditioning, not caring about being watched, Jeet opened the wardrobe: Ranjit still slept in white cotton kurta pyjama with a singlet underneath, bought from the same tailor for years. He would not miss one from the many; he does not count them. Jeet took one. It was too big but he put it on. He drew the string of the pyjama tight: it bunched around his waist.

After this, Jeet folded his clothes. He left them on top of his shoes. He removed his piercings: one ear, both nipples. There was blood; he washed it. Then he paused. Placed his kara, then his mobile phone, then his wallet on top of the pile. He took one more round of the bungalow. He tried on a pair of old chappals, then decided against them.

Pilgrimages must be taken barefoot.

After ten minutes walking across the Farm grass, he had to stop, sit on the ground. He held his feet as if they were babies, surprised by the pain. Then hobbled back to the bungalow, to get the chappals and put them on. He tried not to hate this false start.

. . .

The smell of rain was on the wind, teasing the dry ground. The monsoon was late then (it still has not come). The outer reaches of the Farm land were parched and burnt. The night embraced him, and as he felt the buzz of drugs through his blood, in his cheeks, behind his eyes, he began to jog.

At the perimeter fence, his journey proper began. He climbed through the barbed wire. It tore; he bled from tens of tiny cuts and scratches. Stuck halfway, he could not go back. He was afraid it would only be worse. So he pushed on, feeling the scrapes begin to swell, knowing he might get an infection—and thinking, *So what?* The pain felt sweet, it had certainty. Christ. It hurt. Worse than the burns he used to make with cigarettes on the parts of his skin that no one could see. Could anything hurt more? The Brothers' stories were of monks who would mortify themselves with nails, with pins, with wooden pricks.

Jeet howled. When he scraped through the wire to the other side, he had to roll in the dirt until his hair was matted, the white pyjama stained with mud. He lay flat on the ground, staring up into the sky. There were so many stars—it was summer—tears ran down the sides of his face; he didn't wipe them. He set his teeth on the pain. He wanted to prove he could pass, and live amongst the hundreds, thousands, millions of nobodies that shadow the land. Where no one would stop him—or believe, even if he told them—that once he had been Jeet Singh, son of Ranjit, Godson of Devraj Bapuji, one of the richest men in India. He thought of the men he had left at the party. What would they say if they saw him now?

They might kick him, ask:
—What is your name?
To which he would answer:
—Rudra the Naph, keeper of the sacred rites.
They might wonder: *Why?*
He would tell them, in a voice more bleating, more guttural than

Jeet's, that it was his dharma to take on a disguise; it was the purpose of his birth.

—Where will you go, you ugly pagal? Rudra, scum–pilgrim–saint? Where will you go? they might ask.

—I will turn my face to the longed-for rains of the north, to the winds. I will make my way to Amritsar and from there to Amarnath.

—What tongue will you take?

To which he would say:

—That of the ancient Sages and BlackBerry texters: all those who hear it will call me mad. My name is Rudra, I will beg for food and rely on the earth to provide. My mind will be free of Jeet.

Then the drugs gripped him, the words found his mouth, and he began to chant, lying there on the ground, on the other side of the Farm—

—*Long Hair holds fire, holds the drug, holds sky and earth . . . These ascetics swathed in wind put dirty saffron rags on. Our bodies are all that mere mortals can see. Long hair drinks from the cup, sharing the drug with Rudra.*

Ignoring the pain in his feet and all over his body as much as he could, Jeet swallowed his dry fears. He mouthed goodbye to Gargi, to Bapuji, to his father, the tap-tap-point of the bone-topped cane. Clean and unclean. He set his face towards the road.

At night the circles of the basti turn to the sound of Madam's bell. It rings once for the Hindus on the Amritsar side, who come at half-hour intervals as far as Jeet can count it, in order of employment, circle or family near the brothel, though sometimes this seems reversed. It rings once for the Muslims, who come in order of age and sometimes wealth, though Jeet has seen the less well-off boys go before their uncles. Every fourth day of the month, between the hours of 3 a.m. and 4 a.m., it rings for the Napurthali men of any age, who come for the left-over girls. Jeet hears the bell. He creeps to the fourth circle to watch Madam in the courtyard, taking money from the clients before they pass into her house. It is impossible to know who is visiting the whores, one way in, one way out. Jeet thinks Madam knows he is there: the next morning when she sees him under his tree, she raises an eyebrow and shakes her head, she smirks, bitch smirks at him—even he, who is meant to be Rudra the Naph, and without desire—even he can see her teeth bared, lips curling, pulling every last drop from a man. The night cries sink into his body. *Why do women,* he thinks, *always scream?* He cannot hear the men. They say nothing as they arrive, as they leave. They sound nothing inside.

Under his tree, all he has are questions to dwell on. His own sins come back to him. *To kill a man—*

Rudra tells the boys—*Once, late at night when his driver was dismissed, Jeet was sixteen. He was drunk on his moonshine, high and speeding between parties in his white Mercedes jeep. Then a swerve for a dog—only to mount the curb—or was that a sleeper on the pavement?* He watches the boys: they bite their little lips, they look at each other to check everybody is accounted for. *What happened next?* Nothing. Jeet kept driving. At home, Jeet's father took Jeet to his Sarkar. The two men sat him down. They told him that such accidents do not count. It is simply one of those things—a shame—that so many pups get run over by cars.

Everyone imagines his own death. All of us wonder what it is to die. But to *kill*—and then to live? *Gargi knows,* Jeet thinks. He had watched her circle the fire, tied to Surendra. She killed something that day, voluntarily, without thinking twice. Jeet was a jungli at his best friend's wedding; it was nothing like that Julia Roberts movie where the gay gets the girl, and they waltz.

Jeet knew his Gargi was gone. A week later, when he saw her again, she refused to talk about Surendra, or her wedding night. Not even one detail, as if she now knew more than Jeet ever would about sex with men. All she would say was, *he's very spiritual*—as if Jeet wasn't; as if he hadn't always made Gargi the heroine of his life. Gargi, who he told every secret to, the only person who said,

—*Don't cry, have some popcorn, the movie will be over soon.*

.   .   .

Sitting under the neem tree, Rudra tells his basti boys that Once Upon a Time Jeet Singh died at a glittering party, even bigger than the ones that take place behind the yellow brick wall of the Amritsar hotel. That Jeet committed a sin so bad he has been reborn to this life to make amends. That his karma has rebirthed him, as Rudra, and brought him to Dhimbala basti, to this moment beneath the neem tree. By Rudra's third week, the boys want the full story of Jeet's life.

—*Please, Baba, please.*

He makes them all do adho mukha svanasana, three times each. Then tells them that Jeet was a man who loved wealth and parties and being pampered: that in his world (he points to the Amritsar hotel), even the dogs had baths and doctors to attend to them. That Jeet was beloved by a very rich man, and he had a wise teacher—she taught him the Bhagavad Gita, the Vedas, the Upanisads, the first nineteen laws of Manu from Chapter Nine of the Manusmṛti (translated by George Bühler in 1886, with the patronage of the Rani of Napurthala, which Jeet made his own interpretations of when he was twelve). This text, he tells the boys, is the foundation of all society, the living code of the Naphs. All boys should learn it if they want to be grown men, particularly the first four rules:

(1) Day and night woman must be kept in dependence by the males (of) their (families), and, if they attach themselves to sensual enjoyments, they must be kept under a boy's control.

(2) Her father guards her innocence, her husband guards her flowering, and her sons guard her hunger when she is old; a woman is never fit for independence.

(3) Bad is the father who does not give his daughter in marriage when she is ripe; worse is the husband who doesn't get on his wife when she is clean; worst is the son who does not keep his mother from the world after his father has died.

(4) Women must be guarded against evil inclinations of every kind, including eating sweets and wearing paint. If they are not guarded, they will bring sorrow on two families.

Jeet looks around his small class. The boys have stopped listening. They are knee-twitching, dirt-scratching, peeling and sticking flutters of plastic onto each other's eyes and ears. So he will not disclose that as a boy, Jeet learned the grammar of the old Napurthali language from Nanu, who spoke it with all the precocious entitlement of a child schooled in performance from the moment she was born. Sitting in her inner room. A special time. No Gargi or Radha there. She told Jeet tale after tale of the Naph sect: how they were the sacred warriors of governance, advisers to kings; how they worshipped Lord Shiv—and in later days knew how to mix a perfect martini while quoting the sonnets and Kabir.

Rudra makes his eyes wide. His shadow grows over the boys. He tells them that in a land Far Far Away, he was a Bengal Tiger of rare type, hunting only when he was hungry and to maintain the balance of life in the forest, for that is the dharma of such animals. Then the slippage, and he became human: he was called Jeet Singh, a name given to millions across our great land. Now they listen: they are absolutely still.

He does not say he was the son of their own Ranjit Singh (drug of choice: Ecstasy); favourite Godchild of Devraj Bapuji (half brother of Jivan Singh); rakhi brother to Gargi, Radha and Sita (first kiss: Gargi, aged eight, on a joint family holiday in Pahalgam in the Kashmiri mountains, which was also the first time they experienced snow); dater of some of the richest girls in the city (lover of a Muslim boy); heir to his father's fortune (smuggler of antiques for the greater good); Sikh (wearer of kajal); scholar of *D* Catholic Convent for Boys, St. Stephens College and IIT (pierced in three places); brilliant debater, class orator, prodigious economist (secret poet), scholar of the sacred texts (the Napurthala tattoo on his left butt cheek—a lotus and a snake); eligible bachelor (penchant for receiving blowjobs from bourgeois Jat boys met at certain clubs); speaker of three living Indian languages and two European, reader of one that is "dead"; thinker, ghazal and opera buff (lover, liar and dirty cheater at cards or dice); owner of some of the finest handmade shoes known to man (an in-and-out gandu) who thought that fulfilling his duty would only mean attending the parties, squeezing the cheeks of the girls, telling them they are *looking so tired,* a little *plump,* should not wear *this or that* label (he would still pick out one or two females to be his pets for the evening while he assessed the men). He was ready to do his duty always, even if it led to marrying a woman; giving his dad a couple of kids. This, surely, would be enough, he thought. The taste in his mouth is of tamarind, like new-moneyed semen after too much rich food.

The basti boys are afraid. They believe that Jeet actually died and was reborn as Rudra, who somehow remembers that life. They make a new game: "What I was in my past lives." Some choose a movie star and some decide a rich man, and some say a politician with a five-door jeep and four shining wheels. Each evening before they run home, they play at being hotel guests with shopping bags and flower garlands and taxi-carriers bigger than their own shacks, and Rudra schools their manners. He thinks all of them dream of attaining the life Jeet once had, even if it leads back to this.

—Wake up! What are you doing here? My Samir says you have been sitting since morning, watching our boys work.

The first day. He was woken by a woman, demanding answers. Her voice, her foot kicked him. She stood over him, a bundle of her kind behind her, holding their dupattas over their foreheads. From under his tree Jeet blinked up: at a thin face, black-skinned, kohl-rimmed, gold ring pierced through her nostril. Her pink cotton sari was bandini-printed—it had a parrot motif with black sequins for eyes; there was one, at his eyeline, right over her teats. She looked young but her arm on his shoulder was wrinkled, he smiled, as if she were wearing opera gloves.

Jeet shook her off; with difficulty, he stood. A voice was shouting from a loudspeaker attached to the dhaba post,

—TEMPLE BUS, LANGAR BUS, DEPARTING FIVE MIN-UTES!

Men, women and children poured from the slum through the Amrit-sar Gate. Some ran, some walked quickly across the square to the lane that led to the highway. Jeet wanted to go with them, he had to: at the Golden Temple, he could wash his face, cool his broken feet; he could sit for a while in its sacred grounds, would be served a fresh, hot meal with the thousands of others who feed at the Temple each day. He might rest, undisturbed, in its merciful calm. He watched Samir run for the bus; he tried to push past the woman. She tripped him, he stumbled and turned on her.

—I am Rudra the Naph, he said. En route to join the pilgrimage to Amarnath.

—Naph? She turned to the other women. He says he is a Naph! Come with us, we will see if you are telling the truth. Don't think to get out on the langar bus; first you follow me. I will give you rice, just come.

He obeyed; he followed her feet, smack smack smack in black plastic flipflops, through the Amritsar Gate, the taste of burnt aloo parantha rising to his throat as he passed cages of diseased fowl, as Madam, reading, ignored him, as the sudden, strange cleanliness of the fifth circle made him stumble. He tried not to gag or show any fear as the houses sank lower; he took his first steps onto the boards. Ta da! He almost slipped, blackening, he cried out—the women laughed—then he had to walk behind them, all the way to the ninth.

An hour or more on his swollen feet. For some of it he was back at school, being led to the boiler room for a round of Midnight Martyrs (*You're such a fucking wimp, you little gay asshole*); at other moments he was back in the lanes of Old Delhi, where he used to go, to go, to go to heaven via the stench of sewage, of stagnant drains, skirting the dippers with their steaming vats of dye, the hung carcasses of goats skinned raw, the beings thin as dandas who smiled despite their dusty hair and blackened eyes; the flea-bitten dogs—still cleaner than the girls. He went—he went there in the old life, as Jeet. He tried not to think of it, but how could he not? Or wonder whether his Old Delhi was simply rehearsal for this.

Then, on the other side of the pit, Samir's mother stopped so suddenly, Jeet almost slipped into sludge.

—Here we are, at the Napurthala mandir, she said. If you are a Naph, show us.

The shrine's plasterwork façade was pink, once. Its three alcoves held chipped, painted icons: a five-headed Shiva for the five elements, his two eyes the sun and moon, his third eye for the fire that destroys the universe for rebuilding in future forms. Jeet reached up. He pointed to the snake around the God's hips—then to the tiger skin, painted with bright orange oils and dark black spots, for desire, for craving that covers the surface of the world. He mimed this to the women—hands, teeth, tongue—a gesture that sent them retreating.

The second statue was a lemon, cut open, its seeds representing the atoms that constitute the universe; he cannot express this to the women. And finally: Saraswati for the once-great rivers and lakes of the lost Indus civilisation, from whom the Naph are descended.

Jeet felt the women watching him. The shrine was so crude; he waited to feel God around him, to feel transformed. It had to come—he was born a Sikh and schooled as a Catholic but this was his true form; Nanu promised him so, when he was no more than five years old.

On a low shelf, an oil wick diya in a terracotta pot burned a steady flame. A real snakeskin was looped around a garland of fresh blue flowers, the pale colour of sky. Flowers! Here! An incense stick, stuck in the cracks, was burning; the smoke smelled of amla oil, bitter and sweet. Jeet's eyes filled with tears. He joined his palms; he intoned the first words of Napurthali he ever learned. The Naph prayer—which was only told to very special boys, those destined to be the Birbals of the Napurthala court:

Na tuevahaparam jatunusam   *Never was a time when I did not exist*
na tuenemek janadhipahra   *nor you, nor all these kings*

—What are you gibbering, fakir? said Samir's mother. You are no more a Naph than I am.

Jeet looked at her. He untied the cord of his pyjama. Then he turned, and bent over, and exposed his left butt cheek, adorned with the Napurthala tattoo.

Which was how Rudra the Naph came to be given a shelter near the shrine. It is a patch of mud (he can lie down, either curled or diagonally) facing the tail end of the dump.

It belongs to a family of nine, who pay the highest rates of rent in Dhimbala: Rs 185 per month, decided by ratio of boys and men to women and square meterage. Because he is a Naph, they partition it for him with whatever stackable material they have. There, he huddles at night, listening as the men on the other side, all different ages, take turns to sleep, to eat, to have sex. Jeet stops his ears, repeating his new name: *Rudra, Rudra, Rudra.*

.　.　.

Soon, I will go to the pilgrimage, and join the brothers on the way to Amar-nath. Soon, soon, soon.

His body is ash. He has scavenged for cardboard to line his walls; he has found, to the muttering jealousy of the basti boys, a blue plastic sheet for a roof cover. That first night, his nose wept for the stink. He was ter-rified of himself, of what he had done.

He could not sleep, of course, and stumbled around the ninth circle in the dark, trying to get to the Napurthala Minar. A strange, square, half-finished brick tower that stood glaring across the pit at its Amritsar twin. Three storeys each, no windows, no doors, only empty rooms and a flat roof, where Jeet thought he might be able to shelter—to imagine himself in something like a house, and sleep.

Who built them? Samir tells him, *Kataria 5.* It was before local elec-tions took place—Samir was six. He could not remember what they were voting for. But he knows that as part of his campaign Kataria 5 prom-ised the Napurthali Jhimbas, the untattooed scavengers and those on the Amritsar side, these minars for their weddings—at last, proper spaces for the community—not just one, but one for each side. No. 5 chose the sites, though Samir believes that he was warned: Jhimbas only marry in their own villages on the far side of the state, where they return to get their brides. *In any case,* said Samir, *who would want to marry at the edge of the stinking pit?* The boy had fallen about laughing: imagine the stink-ing wedding, the miserable, stinking bride! Needless to say, the election bid failed; construction stopped.

Kataria 5 lost a finger when he tried to stop sixth-circlers moving into the buildings. Blood was spilled for the sake of inanimate bricks: of all things the Napurthali Jhimbas consider this the worst stain a man's dharma can accrue. When he hears this, Jeet realises why no one lives there, why he cannot make the minar his.

Down and out, his space stinks: his body cannot easily take the scraps he can scavenge. His bowels churn endlessly. Shit runs from him as sweat. In the first week, he could not make it to the field on the far side of the dump, where each morning, the men of working age take the first turn to squat under the sky. Rudra finds a patch on the edge, almost shel-tered by the dump. He feels that his hide has never been clean. He holds the memory of Paris and London, and the Farm, white tiled bathrooms, genuine artefacts, the feeling of scented soap lathering. Water. Dhimbala has strict rules on the rationing of water from the pumps—water he cannot afford. *Then leave. Go inside, Jeet—go knock on the door of the Amritsar hotel and find softness and rest in those safe walls.* He squats, looking anywhere but below the waist. The other men don't consider him, they are too busy on their mobiles. They all have phones except him.

Jeet learns how to avoid his eyes turning red with infection. That first week, they oozed and then they wept. He crawled through the lanes of the Napurthala side of the basti, directed by Samir to a woman called Mumtaz, who was born without a fully formed tongue. She is known for her skill with herbs. Mumtaz treated his eyes, his belly. He let her touch him.

The Napurthala side—it is darker than the Amritsar side. After a certain hour, only men walk the lanes. The boys all carry sharpened sticks at night. The Napurthali women are rarely seen outside their hovels, the girls do not undertake paid work. They are busy all day doing what Jeet does not imagine. *Bleeding somewhere,* he thinks, *some girl is always bleeding.* He asks around, and finds they mostly stay inside until the bi-annual market when Kataria Senior comes with job *possibilities* from states across the country. What pride to send a girl to work in Mumbai, Delhi, Kolkata—names, Jeet thinks, that evoke what their lives could become.

Ha, remember when Gargi got her first period? She didn't leave her room for a week. Jeet had roamed the Farm without her. Sat under the willow and smoked cigarettes, stubbing them out on the bench and flicking the butts into the duck pond. He was glad she was not there.

On the Napurthali side, Devraj Bapuji might be king, but he is also a constant subject. Men sit through the days, discussing what they would ask him if they had the chance. The Dadajis, the Taojis and Chachajis and the boys who worked for the Napurthala Royal family are all tattooed on their upper left biceps. When Bapuji was young, they were the masters of the basti: raiding the invisible lines into Amritsar land. There are hundreds of children in the slum named Dev, or Devi, or Raj. Then Bapuji relocated to Delhi, and the Palace became a hotel.

There was hope for new jobs for some of the Napurthali boys, the ones in the first three circles. But not all of them can be gardeners and bearers. Not all can work as kitchen staff or earn paltry tips from crude puppet shows. It became clear that Gargi Madam's policy was to bring in staff from outside (she hates her own and does not hire locals; has become famous for this thing). Then the hotel closed; they said it was for renovation. There has been no hope of work for more than five years. And this year, again, there will be no work leading up to Diwali for the men who can cook, the boys who pot wash and sweep. When the rats go hungry, so do the babies. No one can pay for the girls. The boys must learn a new trade.

Some of the men travel out to find labour on the farms. Jeet knows what they will witness: for twenty years the Company seeds have not flourished. All that the land yields is widows and daughters whose fathers and brothers have taken their own lives. That crop of women is growing, bringing more females to the basti on both sides—Amritsar and Napurthali—and what are they now to do?

Loans against seeds must be paid with interest even if nothing thrives. Drought began last year; it yawned across the state, it cracked the earth's skin and lay still. In the Napurthali circles of Dhimbala, the people hate Gargi, and blame her even for this. If she thinks she can bend nature to her will, the men of Dhimbala believe it. The drought was preceded by a storm of ice chips falling from the sky. This had never happened before in their state. After that, more basti girls than usual were born deformed; they had to be put down. They say Gargi is starving them out because Devraj Bapuji and Ranjit Sahib will not allow her to move them from the dry earth bed of their sacred, ancestral lake. Some say if she moves them, she will expand the hotel. There, according to her warning, she will build a cold, cold room where dikhata will fall, white as it does in the mountains. Others say a vast expanse of swakachcha will be imported from Goa and arranged around a man-made pool, where girls will go naked at all hours for anyone to see.

More rumours have it that Gargi Madam is turning the Palace into her private residence. That there will be no more work at all, because she surrounds herself with Muslims from her mother-state of Jammu and Kashmir; or with educated girls from South Indian Brahmin families only. That no, actually she is selling the Palace to a short man from far, far away, who will turn it into a factory staffed only by Chini-workers. All will be given houses: the slum will be cleared for this purpose. They say that Devraj Bapuji is no longer in charge, and when he is gone the people will lose their place for good. Only Bapuji can help them. If only he would come, he would see for himself. He will come, one day—they are sure of it.

The day before the storm is the same as each day before. Dawn springs the basti awake. The sharp smell of open drains is refreshed by the sun's hopeful efforts. Jeet curls from his sleep; crouches in the field with his hand over his mouth and nose, looking at the others, yearning for a phone. He has learned how to shit without soiling his pyjama, his feet. After this, he makes his way around the pit, through the lanes of the basti towards the square. He sits beneath his tree, to watch the morning routine. First, the matriarchs come with their buckets. One runs a cutting salon in the first circle for girls coming of age. Her sister is the basti matchmaker—she chaperones the new brides, jasmine wilting in their hair. Then there are Madam's girls, putting on their free show just by walking. Jeet watches the boys at the dhaba watch them. Then come the acid-attacked runaways; they form a curtain of saris around the pumps, so eyes can only see feet, hair and hands. They carry their water in buckets to their shacks to wash their daughters, to make fresh chai. They help each other and watch each other. They are careful with each drop.

The boys come, minutes later, the older ones pushing the young. They scatter through the gate, cluster at the pumps; splashing and soaping themselves white, down and up; then they stand as close as they can to each other, to rinse it all off.

Then comes the hour for swachh basti, when the women fold the night into piles of cloth and store them away, when the square inches of floor space are sprinkled and swept, when every female tidies her family's corner, empties her toilet into the lanes and begins her next task—to sort plastic, to weave blankets, to cut rubber nuggets, or turf, to wash kapde, to service the men. Observing each woman as he takes his morning circular, Rudra learns the art of work. The dogs, even the mangy dogs, even the flies on the dogs have place and purpose here.

The rest of Jeet's morning is spent under the tree. The men slink about; others sit under corrugated awnings to begin the day's philosophising.

· · ·

Once a week, three buses take the basti dwellers to langar at the Temple. There have been four trips since Jeet arrived at Dhimbala, if he counts the first day it would be five. Since then he has learned to climb the rubbish heap, trying to avoid the soft sinking parts, the places where fires begin and go out as if to reheat the waste from the Company kitchens. He has learned this is a shortcut to the square, quicker than going around the pit and taking the lanes to the Amritsar gate, where people always push and shove to pass each other. Four meals, four blessings in the cool white spaces. The chance to see water for its own sake.

August passes in heat. Rudra possesses Jeet; he purges his body. Jeet rises in him; he craves the sensation of water on his skin; food, a phone; the play of credit cards stacked in a wallet, the smell of new shoes. His hands never feel clean.

On the second week he takes the bus. He eats in the clanging hall, sitting on the floor alongside hundreds. He watches the door for dignitaries and white boys careless with their mobile phones. To steal? From here?

He cannot—then he does—it's only a cheap old handset stuffed with spam messages and three saved contacts:

Aunt June
Driver Narain
Jaipur Hilton.

Before taking the bus back to Dhimbala, Jeet allows himself one short forage in the back alleys of Amritsar. Why is he walking the back lanes? The city makes him do it. Rudra would not do this—would not take a small baggy with one last pill engraved with a cow and go hunting for a couple of middle-class chumchas with poetic sunglasses and tight ripped jeans—Delhi-ites, he thinks—but who cares? He sells them the pill for 300 rupees when it should have cost 1500 but they laugh in his face, they won't pay it—1000 he says, 500. They walk away—300 is an amount for kings in the basti—so he submits, thinking *Yes! Yes!* Only first- and fifth-circlers have this kind of cash.

That evening Jeet waits until after the story hour. Then he climbs with Samir around the dump, to a hollow place, which they use as a kind of store. He gives one note to the boy and tells him to take it and change it with Kataria 1; they get 75 rupees back. They split this in half and half again. They call it the *aloo parantha ration*. Samir buys ten paranthe, for him and for Rudra; they climb to the top of the heap between prayers and eat half and discuss how best to save half for the next day. With another bill, he pays Samir to buy Coca-Cola, watches him go, wonders why the boy must be so dark-skinned.

Now Rudra can pay Samir to charge his new phone in the mobile top-up shack. Now he can pay Samir to buy tokens and fetch him water. Now he can pay Samir to stay off the dump for half the day, and stand guard as he meditates under his tree.

It is during one such meditation that Jeet has an idea, such a simple idea, an idea to be proud of. He begins to collect the plastic bags that blow from the dump into the lanes; he chooses three boys who wash with tokens—Little Amar, Akul and Nakul—and tells them to fill these bags of water if they want his stories. How they love the story hour. Enough to risk Kataria's rage and do as Rudra desires; to form a chain through the circles, which Rudra oversees. All the way to the Napurthala side of the basti. He sells their water for coins from those who can pay, and collects empty bags on his way back through the lanes.

—Rudra bhai, have you been inside the Company Napurthala? Samir asks one evening, after they have eaten, settling his jeans on his nagin hips.

Aré, basti hipster, knowing what style is! What line shall Jeet spin for this boy who performs, as part of his many tasks, what it is to be a man? He licks his lips.

—Mujhe ek glass pani milega? Phir main tumhe ek kahani suna-onga. He waits until Samir brings the water in a tin cup, warm and bitter, making a man sick when it should keep him well.

—Samir, Jeet says. The Napurthala Palace is the first, the eldest, the most exclusive of all Company hotels. It was the childhood home of Bapuji, and belonged to his father before him. How can I explain to you the priceless art, the silver artefacts, the four-room suites, each with their own English butler? What an honour! The memory of that place is a dream of silence and meditation, a life lived in the softest of clouds. As far away from here as London, or the moon.

—No it's not, says Samir. The Company Napurthala is on the other side of the basti. You know that, Rudra bhai.

—OK, it's the speech police! You are right. Now, what else do you want to know?

—Make me the Napurthala tattoo? Samir sticks out his arm and the ball of his shoulder rotates all the way around. The boy is a natural Yogi. He shakes his hand, a dog wagging a wet paw: the day is too hot for sweat to dry.

—No, Samir, I will not give you the tattoo. You should be grateful— you live in the first circle, on the winning curve, where business is good.

—Please, Samir says.

—Don't you understand there is nothing for you in this? You will belong to a dying brand. Chal. Go do your work and bring me what you find. The poor man who lives on rich people's garbage also lives on their pleasure! Next life toh achi banegi teri.

Jeet was once possessed of the five demon consorts of Ravan, to fuck, to thieve, to drink wine and play cards; he disobeyed his father and cheated his so-called friends. When the dark mood took him, he remained so quiet, and then he would rise and dance and play Gameboy. Instead of studying maths, he wanted to be a rockstar poet—not a good business boy, made to run after whores whose daddies pay them to be perfect in public and bad as bitches in heat in the dark.

—What's the worst thing Jeet ever did, Rudra bhai? Motu, the only fat boy in the whole basti, says.

—Can you think of nothing better you want to learn? Jeet says. Ask instead, the best. For example, that there is nothing more beautiful in the world than Temple flowers: the saffron of fresh marigolds mixed with red rose petals, a diya placed in the heart. That with the correct approach a simple steel thali can be transformed. The ancient Naphs believed that the divine was a cow, taking many forms, bringing pleasure in each. (And now Jeet has a new idea for business—that every Amritsar cow wandering the back lanes should be brought to this square, a sort of cow museum.)

The boys look at him, faces dropping. This one sniggering. That one rolling his eyes at Rudra's teacher-tone. They want their stories served with blood, but if they want epics he will give them his versions, himself as the centre of the story. For Jeet, too, has done great things. He has saved art from destruction. As his beloved country minted more and more millionaires, it became Jeet's business to show them the way. Most of them were pleased to have a genuine artefact in the corner of the living room, some precious iconography in the household mandir (after, of course, the installation of the Company-inspired home cinema in the illegally converted basement). If it took a few extra thousand rupees of cash to smooth official egos, what was wrong with that? Who else could identify a priceless antique amidst a pile of rubble and—what is more— not show any reaction until it was safely in his possession? Who else knew where to find such things in Assam, Odisha, Uttarakhand and Himachal Pradesh? All those villages—places his father and Godfather would never go unless the Company was starting a mine.

Jeet does not know that tomorrow, the sand will reach him, and so will the rain. Today is still for the fight against desire, to love his poor neighbours, to accept he is one of them, to accede, to try not to dream of meat in this place where most people eat no more than rice mashed with whey—and whatever leavings the Company kitchens discard. To count the sightless windows of the Amritsar hotel, concentrating on the daily rhythm of the basti, trying not to think of the life inside that clean, soft place.

He ponders the questions the basti boys have asked him.
  He teaches them Suryanamaskar, down-facing dog.

—Rudra bhai, says Samir. You have to tell us now. What was the sin that cast Jeet Singh from that highlife to this?

The sin was not hate, but love, for a boy called Vik.

. . .

Their year together was marked by the butcher's cleaver: chop skin, chop flesh, chop gristle, chop bone, coming from the stall underneath Vik's rooms. It was a strange thing to be lulled by. The memory of that sound and the feeling of Vik's fine-planed body against his remains imprinted upon Jeet, inside and out, the skin, the muscle of him meeting his, cheek to heartbeat to hip and hip bone, ribcages cleaving to each other: a pair of eyes looking into its mirror while a voice smoked smooth as a high after drinks sings in Kashmiri at night.

Vik's laugh, when he said: *Society is sleepwalking through despair, this world is a pill called Soma.*

Love. Teeth on lips, biting just enough.

Vik came from a village outside Anantnag. His family were apple farmers, with a small orchard always under siege from one blight or another. Vik's mother had sent him to Delhi to study, then to find work—he said he wanted to write. He had been in Delhi for two years when the spring turned to blood in the Kashmir Valley. Protests, stone pelters against the Indian Army, bandhs, crackdowns. All Jeet could think of were the treasures he had left, how he had wanted to get them out that summer, but now could not.

He met Vik at a poetry launch in a tiny bookstore in Haus Khas Village. The poetry was in translation—good enough, Jeet thought, still a mockery of the original. Jeet looked around for someone's eyes to meet, so he could ask, silently—*do you agree? That the Urdu version was so much better?* No one responded, then Vik put an elbow in his side.

Jeet remembers smiling. He remembers Vik's eyes, his answering smile. He felt his blood slow. He looked around at the faces in the bookstore; alight, alive with listening. He'd thought of school, where the Christian Brothers were definite about the destructive impulses of self-love and male sex (slippery, remembered, hard, luscious and biting). The brothers lectured on the sanctity of the family, the value of marriage. Jeet knew his own religion would agree; he knew Nanu would agree, despite the fact that once upon a time the Naphs treasured same-sex love between men as golden. So Jeet, as a young schoolboy—before he had ever tasted a tongue (male or female)—knew that when the Brothers said these things they were speaking directly to him, about *him*. The scion of Ranjit Singh, unnatural in his desires.

He knew—because the Company owned the land underneath it—that bookstores such as this one, built on translation, would not survive in bricks and mortar, the cost of rent was rising, would sink them all. Instead, these old and young men, aged, Jeet thought, between twenty-one and fifty (some of whom he recognised from that night in the Union Café, in 2009, when they had celebrated the legalisation of love fiercely—as if such bonds were gold [forgetting that gold can be melted], with coffee and shots and the words of Lalla— [Lal Ded, the wandering Kashmiri, the wild goose of writing, who Vik loved] —singing, *surrender to the soul's light, you too shall be free*) would be forced underground again, when the bookstore closed. Men, and store, would only be able to trade in another, virtual world, a world of sin or hate or pleasure—it would be hard to tell which through the screens of devices.

Vik had driven Jeet's car through the city, around and around the ring road. The night pulled through it: a light, warm shawl. Jeet talked, he could not stop—but Vik had only listened as he drove. *War stops men's tongues.* It had taken his friends and brothers to silence. Vik said he was a coward: he never wanted to throw stones, or join the armed resistance against India. But Jeet knew differently. It must take courage to resist at all.

Months passed before Vik would speak of that time; saying that, as a child, he had taken messages between Anantnag to Srinagar, between this azadi and that. So, Vik *was* brave—but perhaps unaware of it. *Silent dreamers,* Jeet had thought, *never know their own strength.*

Vik had told Jeet he wanted a different kind of azadi. To drink fresh milk every morning, to eat dark chocolate every afternoon and night. To sit and argue in cafés on the comparative literary merits of Manto against those of Manu Joseph, a writer who Vik had discovered only after he moved to Delhi. *You have your Laws of Manu, so do I,* he said.

Vik, whose real name was Nadir. Jeet changed it, sitting in the car that very first night, outside the gallery in Nizamuddin. Before they even kissed.

· · ·

Under the burning sun, Jeet remembers the texture of that night. Trying to persuade Vik to come back to Nizamuddin, Jeet had said, *This is a war.* Vik had looked at him briefly. Then back at the road.

Vik had said it back to him, that last day: *This is a war.* They had fought; words thrown between them to the rhythm of the butcher's cleaver, chop, your *faith,* chop, your *silence,* chop, your *brother,* to the bone, your *father.* They fought with all the words they could think of—shame, prayer, kneel, sin, *bite.*

After months together in the city, Jeet had wanted Vik to come back with him to Kashmir; he wanted them to go together, first to Anantnag—where he would collect the treasures he had left—and then on the pilgrimage to Amarnath. He thought they both should let go of their old lives, that this would bring them full circle. Something about them would feel different and then Jeet might be ready to bring Vik to Gargi, to meet Radha and all his friends. Finally, after all the nights he has spent auditioning females for the part of future wife.

Most in his circle knew Jeet preferred chocolate to khir—and he knew a dozen men the same. They met at parties and in each other's houses, able to live as long as they married. Yet these men were not for him. They were all variations of Radha's Bubu. Uncouth. *Unclean,* Vik called them. And meanwhile all of his closest friends would smile and exclaim, trying to be modern about the ancient forms that love could take.

Vik laughed at Jeet that night. Actually laughed at him—*a Hindu yatra in a German 4×4 over stolen land won't make it better, you idiot. Can't you understand we don't need that shit? We are the new world—just say it and be it, that's all you have to do.*

He can do nothing now. This afternoon. But sit and wait under the neem tree for the basti boys to climb off the dump and begin their flutterpicking. *Flutterpicking.* A good term—one that obeys the rules of Sanskrit, the meshing of two consonants to make a word. Rudra will apply the rules to English if Jeet chooses to now, here, crouched, as the figure of an Ajivikas ascetic from Harwan, curled in a posture reminiscent of the foetal position, the cosmic goose beneath him. Jeet once saw this figure etched on the last surviving terracotta tile from that place—a third- or fourth-century fragment held in the LA County Museum, USA. He wished he had found it himself. It was curved, emaciated, eyes sunken into cavities, its long hair and beard unkempt.

Crouch and meditate: that's all there is left to do in Dhimbala basti, barefoot.

The dhaba TV blares news. Extreme drought. The monsoon is not expected. The office of meteorology is calling this an extreme drought. In the holy cities, cows are being washed with their own milk.

Jeet remembers how he and Vik stood that day, arms crossed, shouting at each other over the bed. They stood for what felt to be hours; it was the afternoon Jivan came home, all afternoon, when Jeet was supposed to be going to the airport. Then Vik said, *Catholic boy of the Sikh religion, wannabe Naph whatever—in any case, you wouldn't last a day without your father's money.* Vik's voice, telling him: *I can't live like this with you.*

Jeet fell face down on the bed, burying his nose in the sheets. He had bought these sheets for Vik from Good Earth. They smelled of Vik's body and his own. He lay there, his hands gripping the pillows, waiting for Vik to come curl around him, to say *sorry* and whisper *love.*

These sheets belonged to Jeet and so do Vik's ID papers. Jeet paid the rent on this property so they could be alone. He enrolled "Vik" in the upcoming term for college in Delhi University, night quota, IT: reservation: Other Backward Classes, to make good his disguise. He breathed in the smell of old love, thinking: *it stinks from Daryaganj to the line of climax, what I have done for Vik.* Under the bed, a locked box held half the income Jeet had not declared from trading in three-headed Goddesses. He gave it to Vik in cash blocks along with his signet ring. Which is on Vik's finger. Vik, who said that Jeet could not survive without his father's money.

He did not take it back.

Jeet sits in the meagre shade, watching the young men pull up on their motorbikes to order at the dhaba: hot-hot parantha, chai and smokes for lunch. The smell of ghee saturates the air—now, as always, it reminds him of those Tuesday Company nights. He hardly ever ate at them.

In the final months, he would leave after Bapuji's speech, before the dancing started, to go to Vik's place. There, they would spark up or take a pill or read out loud to each other from Vik's book of Lalla. Then make love: hands exploring skin between them; they might wander to the roof and lie on their backs, searching the sky to choose the stars they were born under. Then go back down to Vik's bed. He would watch Vik sleeping until his lover turned over, protesting he was being *too weird*. He never left until the dawn summons of the Old Delhi muezzin, when Vik woke up to pray.

His skin is burned dark now. A penance. His toenails have turned black. He watches Madam and four girls pass through the Amritsar Gate, across the square to the dhaba; Jeet gestures the boys to come close around him.

—So! Let me tell you all the times Jeet cheated and lied. He stole possessions from the ignorant aam janta, believing it was for a higher cause.

He watches the boys shuffle forwards and poke each other's ribs, eyes wide, licking lips.

—First I will explain to you the crore value of beauty. What is the most beautiful thing you have ever seen?

The pack is struck dumb. They think for a moment.

—Rani Mukherjee! Preity Zinta, Katrina Kaif!

Little Amar jumps up and mimes a starlet: one hand at his temple, the other on his hip, wiggling and fluttering his eyelashes, sticking out his bums.

—Kissy, kissy!

The boys push each other and laugh, trying to get closer and away.

—The fountains at Company Napurthala, says Akul.

The boys fall silent again, impressed by knowledge from the forbidden place, which lies around the pit, far on the other side of the basti.

—How do you know about them? Jeet says.

—We play in the gardens sometimes. They have monkeys and all kinds of real-life birds, and loose women who have been turned to stone. Once we had a Teacher Madam here—she said they might just be waiting for a prince to come, and kiss them awake, says Nakul. He looks around the other boys, daring them to call him a liar.

—None of you chutiyas has ever kissed any real girl, says Samir.

—Have you ever kissed a woman, Rudra bhai? Little Amar says.

—Chi! You don't ask such things. You should count your luck that from this basti you cannot go lower. The only way you can travel through your lives is up, up, upwards!

—Right, all the way to the thirteenth floor! says Samir.

The boys cheer and jostle each other; they stand with hands on hips and stick their tongues out at the top of the Company Amritsar hotel. Jeet laughs with them, wondering all the time if Jivan or his father might be inside. If Gargi or even Radha is worried for him—or angry. He does not know how to go back. Still, at the least he could answer the basti boys truthfully. He could say that the world of women was wide open to him—that he could have married any girl he wanted and fucked her every Sunday, or never touched her; he could have stayed in his old life and let his father sort out the mess, and lived as a dead man working for the Company. He eyes Samir and Tharu and Amar, these bachche-log who have no clue that the statues they are mocking are some of the finest examples of fourth-century desire, found in the hidden parts of his beloved Kashmir. His first coup. It took stealth and cunning to get those pieces to Jor Bagh for Nanu's birthday celebration. At twenty-one years of age, he had felt his life was beginning at last, although it cost as much in bribes as the amount in his first Company paycheck. Money is fluid, he thinks, the only thing more precious here is water.

Sin comes in many forms, Rudra wants to tell the boys. It can be an act. Or a lack of action. It can be a lie or believing a liar. Doubt is one of the worst sins of all. In his past life, Jeet listened to his half brother—and believed him, too, when he said that Kritik was watching him. It was a possible truth. Kritik *could* have pictures of Jeet with Vikram. Shots of them in Daryaganj or at the Cinnamon Club; even amongst the white sheets in the laundry room of the Imperial hotel, where Vik insisted on working nights.

Jeet remembers his own protest, telling Jivan that India is not so backward. Since 2009, the government has *celebrated* the sex acts of

Indian males; the law is no longer an ass of the British kind. Being Indian and gay is now, legally, natural. He had a sense this could not last, but still he said,

—*Piche se penetration, that's anal sex to you, has not been a criminal offence for three years. Catch up, brother—we are way ahead of you.*

Jivan had only shrugged, said he didn't think Muslim boys could be gay.

Jeet should have known, then. This bastard-caste American: Could he really be so stupid? Could distance and mothers really make Jivan so opposite to Jeet? All he could think of, that night at the party, was Vik. Daryaganj was crawling with plainclothes cops, their white trainers and clean fingernails, their strange, staring poses. If someone in the Company wanted to hurt Vik, Kritik Sahib would only have had to point a finger. Vik could already be dead.

—Tell us about the party, Little Amar says. That's what we want to hear.

Ah yes, that night. It should have been the same as so many others—should have begun eight hours before with a pedicure, a massage, a frankincense facial to keep Jeet's skin light. After that, a little shopping, for this he would go to Chanel and Dior. He describes these temples to the boys by drawing the brand symbols in the sandy mud. The boys twist their tongues around the French words, their eyes widen when he tells them the costs of things in that world. A shawl for 30,000 rupees! The boys check with each other, none of them sure what this amount might actually mean. But when Jeet tells them that one cup of chai sold for 200 rupees plus tax?

—No way! Samir says. You're lying now.

—You can get the best tea right here in Dhimbala for less than twenty annas, Motu says, even the chini is free.

—The evening, Jeet goes on, might begin around ten o'clock with drinks.

—Cocktails? Big Amar says; his cousin serves as glass washer for the Company Amritsar public bar. Whisky soda?

—Yes, and gin lime tonic and vodka too (here, sitting in the dust, he mimes shots and being drunk). Jeet wants them to hear this, for then they might be wary of the basti bhang and petrol sniffers and aspire to spirits that are pure. He explains how he would swallow so much of these liquids that the faces in the crowds would blend into one and the bottoms of pools seem a good place to sleep by dawn.

—Did you meet Rani Mukherjee, did you meet Preity Zinta? This from the younger ones who are allowed to watch the dhaba TV if business is slow and their mothers are working.

—Don't be stupid! This was past life only, not last month, Little Amar laughs.

Jeet looked up from the bed, where he was still face down. Vik had gone. To the roof, with his diary, a sign that he wanted to be left alone. So he did; Jeet left Vik's rooms and made his way through the lanes to the main road, where he went through the auto rank until he found a yellow-and-black that had the words *War chariot* painted in pleasingly correct Hindi on its hide. He felt the city whip around him, the road hard and potholed underneath, bumping as the auto raced along the avenues. The smog caught in his mouth—diesel dhokla. As they drove, the sky turned pink, the rhythm of the traffic sang *shame, puppy, shame, shame, all the monkeys know your name*—as if everyone knew where he had been, but still would keep his lovely secrets. Splayed on the backseat, Jeet had urged the driver to go faster, faster; he loved the feeling it gave him. If only he could live as if there were no destination and nothing to do but ride! Once or twice he *whooped!* and the driver turned to look at him, grinning black gums, teeth missing from bad hygiene or a fight.

Then, just after India Gate, the guy pulled over; he flicked his eyes across Jeet's body.

—Gandu, he spat.

Jeet got out without argument and paid without argument. Skin burning, he watched the man phut-phut away; he vowed again to stop Vikram's essence from clinging to him—he needed a carbolic scrubbing even then.

Standing on the wide pavement under the sheltering trees of Lutyens' Delhi, Jeet called his own driver Balram to come get him. He walked all the way to Mehar Chand Market, where the real estate was about to go through the roof. A new set of expensive kids' clothing stores was reproducing along the strip where customers once came to get all kinds of cloth cut and altered. You wanted a suit to fit or a tent to sleep in? This had been the market to come to.

Jeet walked the high pavement; he almost went into a design boutique which had sets of pink *Delhi 100* anniversary pencils in the window, unsold from the year before. Instead, ignoring the lounging guard's gaze (*no one walks in New Delhi, only white people and the poor, this one is clearly mad*), he went and took refuge on the roof deck of the Habitat Centre. There he ordered nimboo pani, sweet/salty.

The view was of traffic, a tiny army crawling in their tanks up the avenues. Two boys were playing football on the airforce school field, highkicking, goose-stepping miniatures of the Indo/Pak border guards at Wagah. He was too high and the dusk too rich to see the ball. He was higher than even the birds; the rag pickers and street sweepers were less than ants. Parrots sliced and swirled under his nose, chasing the last of the light.

When Jeet reached the Farm, he could not bring himself to go to his father. At the pool, Abhinash was on duty but no one was swimming. They went into the caretaker's room at the back of the pool house and locked the door. Sitting on upturned buckets, they shared a joint. The weed spread up their nostrils, through their heads, took root and bloomed in the crevices of their brains. For a moment it was as if the room, the pool, the Farm, the city outside—everything was dissolving or was never actually there. He heard from Abhi (who heard from Umesh in the kitchens via Satyam, Radha's hairdresser, and Vesh, Sita's personal maid, who was ordered by Uppal to pack and get out with Sita) that Gargi Madam has been crying since lunch, and Surendra Sahib has been chanting in the mandir all that time. Radha Madam ordered her usual cocktail and headache pills in her room at seven, and when Chintu the busboy went to give them to her, she answered the door herself, in her innerwear and only a robe to cover. He saw— (and here Jeet waved his hand, not wanting to hear what Chintu saw; he can well imagine). Anyway—the dear, very dear Radha Madam is apparently leaving at dawn. Suresh, her driver, is on call for the airport. And Nanuji? She has taken to her bed. Juiciest of all: Sita Madam is gone.

Gone? Jeet remembers his mellow high, punctured with this word.

. . .

—Where has she gone?

Abhi did not know. But Umesh, the pastry chef, was devastated. He was in charge of covering the *Congratulations Sita Engagement* cake with a golden crown made of spun sugar, a delicate web that was to be dusted with real gold powder. Umesh had planned to try a fingertip as he prepared it, just so he could report to the others on its taste. But again, Jeet did not want to hear about how Shivji deprived Umesh of this one chance to eat gold. Nor how he wailed in the kitchens (asking what, in his past life, he had done so wrong that this should happen to him). Jeet wanted to hear about Sita—and finally, Abhi got to it: Sita has left, with a boy. The rumour is, she is going with him, to Sri-land. It took Jeet a moment to work out what Abhi was telling him. Sri Lanka. Perfect.

Jeet laughed, and when Abhi looked confused, he called him a dunderhead. *Sita. The Ramayan. Sri Lanka.* When comprehension dawned, Abhi laughed too, so loudly that Jeet had to silence him with a smack.

Feeling in need of some comfort, Jeet let himself be persuaded—by an unbuckling of his belt and the soft pressure of an arm around his shoulder—to sit on the caretaker's ladder and accept a handjob to calm his nerves. After, he cleaned himself with a cream Company pool towel embossed with red lettering. Sitting on Abhi's lap, he called his dad and tried to smoke out his guilt. He leaned back, Abhi's chest hairs tickling him. They shared a bottle of champagne; then, he left Abhi and went back to the house, to the party. Jivan was there with Ranjit. Devraj Bapuji was about to speak.

MY NAME IS DEVRAJ. I sat with my Sita cradled in my lap, singing quietly to her as evening turned to night. The call from the mosques came for me through the gaps in the walls, over the roof beams.

The young manservant said,

—Bapuji, is Sita Madam sleeping?

He asked if he could approach and I gave him permission. He came over and sat down. Sita was sleeping so deeply that when he took her pretty brown ankles in his hands, she only stirred a little.

—What is your name, son? I asked.

—Punj, sir, he said. At your service. For good.

—Then listen, Punj, I said. You better mean that. For everyone else has left me, as the proverbial rats.

—Sir, said Punj, I've been listening carefully to all you have to say. I want to learn from you.

—Can you bring tea? Weave a shawl? Start a fire?

—Sir, the last one is possible, but only in some time. See what I have here.

From his pheran he produced all of the materials we would need: a small can of kerosene, a Company lighter.

—Tell me about your young days, Punj said. Did you have great parties in this room?

I thought for a while, for it is important to me to tell the story the crowd wants to hear.

—When I was a boy, I said, we used to have such gatherings here!

All the great men of Srinagar and Delhi, of Amritsar and Lahore. In this very room, Nehruji promised me he would be a father to me in our new India. I am a simple man with simple needs, and this I learned from him. I believe in ahimsa. I have never wanted to hurt anyone. I have made my name in service to this country. After he died, we gathered here to mourn. It was warmer, and you could not see the sky through the beams. It was a palace!

—Bapuji, said Punj. Did you know that this place has now become a palace for dogs? A kuttamahal. A toothi-phoothi-jhoothi mahal. And did you know that in the basement, a bitch has given birth to a party of pups? I saw them on my rounds. I thought I would bring you one, but look, she bit me!

He held out his arm and I could see the marks. Punj looked worried, but honestly he is here to keep me safe, not the other way round.

—Punj, I said. Don't interrupt. Your language hurts me. Don't speak and you will hear the truth. Listen. Back then there were no dogs on thrones of rubble. I was a King once, and would gallop all over these hills with my dear friend, the Maharaja of Kashmir. We shot and played and he helped me progress in business. In winters, we would ski down the frozen lakes, across the snowy plains before life made me a leader and a role model for the youth.

—Yes, you are my role model, Punj said.

—My daughters could not learn, I said. Always too stubborn. They hurt me so badly, but have I ever cried? No, Punj, I said. I have not. Even when I found myself in the darkest of nights, in the harshest of storms, among people who behaved as demonic ghosts, I did not cry.

—Sita's feet are so beautiful, Bapuji, said Punj. I touch them for mercy. I promise I will not leave.

He stroked Sita's feet. She stirred a little but did not wake up.

—Everyone leaves.

—What do they leave?

—A body, a name. I am Devraj. That I am.

The day of the storm. He is woken early, not by the usual calls of women, the bleating of goats or scratching of pigs, or even the stench of the pots being emptied, but by a boy running through the lanes, shouting,

—A man is chained at the back of the hotel! A man is in chains!

Jeet pushes himself out of his hovel. His feet thump the boards; he will not slip into black: he has learned to avoid this plank and that plank and this one that splinters. On raw feet he runs with the other basti men to the square, where twenty or thirty have gathered, reaching almost to the back gate of the Company Amritsar hotel. Jeet pushes himself to the front.

A man is chained to the back gate. His eyelids are crusted almost shut, his cheeks are swollen; he is covered in bruises from some kind of beating. The chaukidar in his box shakes his head, warning the basti not to come any closer. A few of the boys run up to the fence.

—Kya hua Chachaji? Aap haathi ho kya?

They circle back, daring each other to do it again.

The chained man does not speak, even when the boys shout *Circus haathi,* even when they throw small stones.

—Jitinder, Nalini, Karan, Ranjitarani, Balthazaar, brother of Surmit, Shivan, Garginjali, Rita, Devisitaraj! My daughter, Munni, and my own son, Samir! Chal! Get back to your work, shouts the guard. And the rest of you, get lost, unless you want this man's fate as your own.

Jeet sidles forwards, towards the gate, muttering prayers in Rudra's voice. He feels dizzy with the race, has not eaten this morning, or last night. Water—the chained man needs water. He looks towards the dhaba: the morning service has begun for those who can pay. There will be no help there.

The loudspeaker crackles Feroze Shah's voice across their heads,

—All those for langar today, board the Dhimbala bus!

The basti turns away from the chained man; now begins the familiar race.

—Come on, Rudra bhai! shouts Samir.

They run towards the highway. Jeet overtakes—the bus is almost full—it is starting. Jeet catches a rung of the ladder soldered to the metal body; he climbs, he clings, someone's foot in his face; he holds his hand out to Samir and pulls him up; they grip the rungs while men clamber over them to the roof. Jeet clutches another man's hips as the bus picks up speed, they roar down the highway towards the old city. The hot morning, so bright, passes in a blur of pale sand and blue sky; Samir grinning below Jeet, both of them eating the dust as they go.

On Railway Road, the sun, a traffic jam, turns the bus into a roasting tin. Jeet and Samir climb up to the roof, using their elbows to make others give room. Now Jeet can see: they are nearly at the train station. People are getting out of their cars to walk up the line, men are standing on the roof of the bus in front, as if something is happening in the station courtyard itself.

—Devraj is coming, Bapuji will be here—

—By train, because he is a great, great man—

—He is at the station!

The cries sweep back to them, pulling people from the bus. Jeet and Samir follow them, weaving through traffic.

—Can it be possible? Samir clears his throat, coughs. Says, with excitement, Rudra bhai, I have never seen Bapuji—and now, with open hands, he has come to Amritsar! Maybe he has come to choose the next Hundred from the basti boys! Maybe he will give dan, for is he not a Maharaja, whose dharm it is to ensure that the hungry do not starve? Is that not correct, Rudra bhai?

—Anything, everything is possible. Jeet must shout to be heard. His feet burn on the tarmac but he does not stop. Past the cars and jeeps and buses, the sound of horns. His mood is higher than the 10 a.m.

sun. Samir and he jog towards the station and into the forecourt. There, they see a crowd of ninety or more, the noise blurs into heat—Bapuji has arrived, on the *Mughalpura Shatabdi*. When it runs, it terminates in Amritsar.

At last! Bapuji has come to address the common man!

Men, women and children stand on tiptoes. *I can see, I can see— I can't—lift me!* Now Jeet's stench is an advantage. Starched kurta'd females move aside for him. Some of the men are young, wearing white T-shirts; most look to be middle-rankers—clean turbans, trimmed moustaches, tummies full of proper food. These are the men whose lives Bapuji has transformed—with jobs in his businesses or as links in the supply chain. They have come from office to pay tribute—they shrink from Jeet's approach. He moves forwards, chattering teeth and dirty hands, naked legs. He loses Samir to the crush. He can see stalwart Company support-ers: family types, small shareholders; even the matriarchs, the real house-holders, have come. Jeet feels his body rub against them, his heart swells under his blackened skin, even as the crush around him almost stamps on his feet—even though the people look at him with disgust before they see he is a Rudra, and move to let him pass. He giggles high and sharp; it ends on a spluttering choke.

—*Voo hoo,* he mutters, make way, make way, intermission.

The crowd parts—for a second he sees: his Godfather in an ivory kurta pyjama fastened by tiny diamond-drop studs that catch the light, and wink at the crowd. And his beloved Nanu, flanked by five of the Hundred and two or three local dignitaries—waiting by a makeshift podium draped in saffron and white. Nanu is clasping her—*Jesus, her Kelly bag*—to her chest. Jeet blinks. Her sari is apple green; the pearls around her throat are as big as Jeet's knuckles, *Grandmother, what big pearls you have*—he never noticed before. Her hair is coiffed and held with ivory combs, her eyes hidden behind dark glasses.

—Nanu! Jeet shouts. His voice is drowned by the chattering crowd, who are pointing, waiting for Bapuji to speak.

Barely lifting a hand to them, Bapuji makes for three black Mercedes, parked to one side, clearly waiting for him and Nanu. But Nanu stops. With the help of one of Bapuji's boys, she mounts the five steps to the podium. She reaches for the microphone; she waits while it is adjusted for her; she grips the stand. When she speaks, her voice is stone on stone.

—There was once a man who lost a key in his house, she says.

Jeet smiles; he wipes his eyes. He knows this story—it was her best one for teaching him, as a boy, how to school his will; to achieve his desires.

—And he came to Amritsar to find it, says Nanu. A fox came along who had eaten the key and smiled at the man, who was surrounded by seekers, all looking for the same. In the heat they searched, far from the man's house. The fox asked the man, "Why are you searching here, when you lost your key at home?" The man said, "Because there is more light here."

She finishes her story with hands open to them all.

—If I could exchange a knife for my jewels, I would slaughter that fox as a lamb to the pot.

The crowd cheer as if she has announced a holiday in their honour.

—Nanu, Nanu, Bapuji, Bapuji! Drowning the sound of microphones.

Nanu turns from the podium, giving her arm to the aide. He helps her descend. He shuts her into the car, salutes; the engine starts. Forwards, forwards, forwards; they push against the cars. Jeet pushes too—forwards, forwards; for a second he is pressed to the outside of the car window, he can almost touch his Godfather's face. But Bapuji does not look up. They drive off, leaving the crowd salaaming.

Jeet forgoes the Temple meal. Clinging to the back of a public bus, he returns down the highway to the basti. The excitement of the morning has dissolved in the heat haze, glimmering over the earth. Sitting with his back under the neem tree, he observes the chaukidar come out of his box, to kick the chained man. In the square, a few eager dogs wander around, investigating every little thing for food. The basti men are all gone to the fields or the city, to work or look for work, the others are still at the Temple. There are only four or five women sitting veiled on their charpoys, perfectly still except for hands on makeshift looms, spinning plastic into thin, tense strips. A few drunken kubhatas roam around, shouting every so often. The chained man is slumped, facing the hotel, his fingers burned around the gate; Jeet, his own body a husk, his mouth dry, gives him a brief namaste as he passes.

Jeet sits cross-legged under his tree, sharing its shadow with a few small girls and a boy—Devinder, he thinks, a crippled second cousin of Samir. Devinder crouches in the mud; he has no pants on, he wears only a filthy vest and an adult-sized chappal slotted onto his fingers, as if his hand is his foot. He is using this weapon to squash the lazy flies that land around him. Every time he kills one, the three girls scream and push each other closer to him, unsettling more flies. *Swat* goes the chappal, a cripple's thunder on the ground—and the fly dies—to be flicked into the air by its boy killer. The girls scream again.

Jeet's thoughts sink low. Vik comes to him fleetingly, laughing in a bar full of backlit glass bottles. It feels as if Vik happened to someone else, in some festival film. The sun beats down; Jeet scratches at the earth. The hotel wall hides the gardens, the kitchens, the lobby, the lift where a hologram goldfish swims back and forth. Inside the hotel the air is so cool. In the restaurant, the scents will be cinnamon and clove; titillation for the noses of silk-wrapped women. *Cold coffee, ice cream, make it fast.* On Ranjit's terrace, some of Jeet's most precious Kashmiri pieces are displayed. Relics of his old life. Beauty. A small pond reflects the sky. Tonight, in some room, a game of dice might take place; there will be more money on the table than the boys in Dhimbala will see in any lifetime. Of course, Jeet has always known this. Only now, when his body has become a husk, when it is too hot to even raise a hand to wave the flies away, when the knowledge that such an action is as futile as imagining one of these children a king, does he begin to understand what it means.

Live or do not live. Each person must choose for themselves. This child will sort waste, this one, sell flowers. Each must enhance his parent's pride. Then procreate and multiply. Build a house better than your father's. The ancient order of the universe has its foundations here. Weeks living as Rudra alongside the basti dwellers has brought him the realisation that all of them, fly killers to poker players and the masses in between, are doing nothing more than this; working out life until death. Under the sun's glare, their troubles are merely steps on the road.

The girls get bored of the game of flies. They look to Jeet for entertainment. Their leader looks familiar. She is about seven or maybe eight or nine, Jeet cannot guess; she is too dark, thin as the neem twigs men chew to clean their teeth. Her hair is plaited, held back with pink, polka-dot Minnie Mouse clips. Jeet has noticed her before: a small Gargi, she marshals the females and the younger boys, scolding them this way and that.

—Apka naam kya hai? Jeet asks her.

—I am Munni. The sister of Samir.

That is all they stay for. They move, a flock of ragged peahens to the next game: tag, where one of them, Devinder the runt, of course, ends up standing stock-still. One by one, the little girls take turns to hit him and go. Tears run down the child's cheeks, he lifts his fists to wipe his eyes; his shrivelled penis stares sadly at the ground.

Dazed with hunger and thirst, Jeet feels himself as a brother to the chained man, who at least has the promise of freedom. He watches Samir and Munni's mother cross the square, bringing three glasses of steaming chai in a wire holder. She passes one through the window of the guard box. She gives another but the guard shakes his head, he empties the cup at her feet. As Jeet watches, she clicks her fingers in her husband's face, a gesture of disgust. Then she turns; her face is obscured by her cotton pallu. She reaches Jeet, she stands over him, and hands down the last glass of chai. He can barely thank her. He drinks it; it is too sweet. It could be water mixed with mud. He sits, eyes closed, letting the flies settle on him.

Afternoon creeps into evening. The sun dissolves through the smog, casting a jaundiced light as the wind picks up and eddies of sand lift along the dhaba, skidding loose rubbish into the lanes. The women rise from their charpoys, packing up their work with quick controlled arms.

—A punishment will come tonight, one says.

—Toofan aaraha hain, bohut bada toofan, says another.

Jeet gets to his feet—at the dhaba, men are putting out their bidis, telling each other *Toofan aaraha hain;* they disappear into the gullies to tether their animals, to strengthen the plastic over their shacks. Jeet takes it all in with no sense of its meaning. A storm—they are worried, that is all he can tell.

The working boys climb down from the heap; they come to Rudra under his tree. They don't care about the warnings; they sit, begin to shed their plastic skins; they demand their evening story, though all around them, their parents are rushing, there is a rising sense of something coming.

Jeet raises his arms; he jumps into monkey pose, he roars at the boys the words of the great poet Allama Iqbal—

—Ooo ooo oop! Watan ki fikr kar nadan! Museebat aane wali hai. Teri barbadiyon ke mashware hain asmano mein, tumhare dastan bhi na hogi dastanon mein!

They shriek and scatter—he watches them go—he holds himself— *And whisper it in English, whisper it, Jeet—Worry about the country, O native one, trouble is afoot! The skies foretell your destruction: nobody will remember you, even in stories!*

The boys change direction, swooping away from the basti towards the highway. There are black cars with darkened windows lumbering down the lane, pulling up outside the dhaba.

Jeet goes forwards, to see what-all is happening now.

Three sleek Mercedes, the ones from the train station. Doors open, Bapuji and Nanu are helped out by their men. They do not acknowledge the basti men and boys, the women who have appeared from the lanes as if someone has whistled. The crowd swells; there is murmuring and nudging: Bapuji and Nanu stand before them. On the plain, the hoardings show their own paper faces grinning down in blessing.

Jeet presses forwards with the others. Bapuji's aides, divine monkeys in suits and dark glasses, hold them back. Bapuji picks across the square, Nanu follows, slowly, holding the end of her sari over her mouth and nose. How can Jeet, or any of them from Dhimbala, understand what they are seeing? Though he knows Nanu would trail Bapuji anywhere— still, Jeet wants to go to her, to lead her back to the car. He looks at his hands; they are black with dirt. His kurta streaked with dust, his skin grimed. He touches his beard; it fills his hand. The shape of his chin is lost beneath hair. Bapuji passes close; he does not see Rudra, he cannot see Jeet.

To watch him, Jeet stands on his swollen toes. Look at Bapuji—his beautiful kurta, its diamond fastenings so clean, so bright. His hair is newly greased down on his head. Look at Nanu—the fresh apple of her sari hurts Jeet's mouth. He watches with the crowd, wondering how a group like this, who speak of nothing but Bapuji when they want to admonish their children or encourage their work, can now keep silent.

The guard is waiting inside the gate. He keeps his hands pressed together, the keys between them. He does not unlock until Bapuji and Nanu reach him and the chained man. There is rattle of iron against iron.

—So this is how you spend your time? Have you no shame? Who did this? shouts Bapuji. He kicks the gate.

Ha! Now the guard scrabbles to unlock it.

—Yeh kisne kiya? Bapuji says.

The crowd takes a step back. No answer.

—Ih kaun kiha?

No answer.

—Yehin ke kehin?

Jeet creeps forwards so he can see better. With difficulty, the chained man looks up: through his swollen eyes, he cannot even blink.

—Bubu Bhai Sahib, Radha Madamji, says the guard as he opens the gate.

—Nahin, says Bapuji.

—Hanji, says the chained man.

—Do not lie! Bapuji says. In the still afternoon his voice carries across the square. They would not do such a thing to my property, my person, my self.

Without ordering the man to be released, Bapuji walks through the gate. Nanu follows, gesticulating at him, grabbing at his sleeve. Saying things in a rapid chatter that Jeet can't quite catch—about birds being blind, fathers, safe money, broken roads, daughters, children, daughters—

Bapuji shakes her off.

—Shut up! he shouts. You climb inside me, crazy mother, always clawing at my heart.

Jeet hears this; the guard and the chained man hear it; the basti men standing closest to the gate hear it; they relay it back through the crowd. Is Bapuji drunk? To speak so to *Nanu.* Only women lamenting the deaths of their sons cry out with such sounds here.

The guard locks the gate, he gestures to the crowd—*be patient*—then he hurries behind Bapuji and Nanu. The chained man bangs, iron on iron, out—rage, out—cry, cry, the chains clang against the gate as Jeet watches—they all watch Bapuji and Nanu go up the path towards the hotel—the crowd breaks the line of security; they press forwards. Jeet sees Ranjit—*his own father!*—hurrying from the hotel to welcome Bapuji and Nanu. The guard meets him—and after a moment turns back, brandishing a new set of keys. As he unlocks the chained man, the tight formation of the basti crowd releases. Jeet feels it inside himself—the sense that danger has passed. All can now return to normal; the storm is over, there is nothing more to see.

—Security! Ranjit Sahib gives orders that you should take this one to the hospital! shouts the guard.

He unlocks the gate. The chained man falls sideways, making no sound that Jeet can hear. Two of Bapuji's aides, men Jeet does not recognise, lift the chained man; another beckons to the crowd, holding a ten-rupee note.

—You people. Take him, put him in a taxi. Send him to the hospital. Ten more when you return.

Five or six basti men rush to the highway. In a moment, two come back; they take the chained man from Bapuji's security. There is shouting—there are the basti boys, trying to help—the women talking about Nanu's bearing, her words—strange how no one mentions the jewels they have just seen, or the fine sari and so on (the only concern is for how despite her great age Nanu is still beautiful, and how, after so many years, Bapuji has not changed). The security men watch all of this. When the chained man is taken to the highway, they push the children aside; they get back in their cars, and, with a group from the basti shouting instructions, they make five-point turns, then crawl, back to the front of the hotel.

In minutes, all that is left is a wild-eyed man called Rudra, who was once, and still is, despite all this time, Jeet. He lurks, not wanting to go into the basti; he slumps under his tree. He is hungry, the air is laden with sand particles pushing on his lungs; he feels the basti dwellers could have done more for that man. Why didn't anyone insist he be covered from the sun? Or give him something to eat? Or do anything more than laugh and stare? If he had been one of their own, they would have. Even the children could have begged their mothers to do it. Even if only to be told, *No, this is a matter over your heads, do not bring trouble down on ours.* Exhausted, Jeet leans back against the trunk.

Watan ki fikr ka . . .

An hour passes, or more. In the late evening gloom, thick with dhaba ghee and the smell of rubbish, Jeet becomes aware of a tingling, as of someone picking up the ends of his hair, brushing them across his face. *Vik,* he thinks, waking him to go home.

. . . *aane wali hai* . . .

—Vik? he says.

There is no one in the square; no child on the rubbish heap, no men in the dhaba; the shutters are locked. He gets up; every bone begging him to stay—even the guard box is empty. The lights from the hotel cast everything red, or is that the natural colour of the sky?

Bursts of sand scuttle over the mud, playing timpani on corrugated tin, stinging over Jeet. He wants people—he moves towards the rubbish heap, climbing up and along. He falls into stinking, sweet, rotting scraps; he swims through plastic; he pushes off a goat carcass; he smells his own breath, sour, neem. He tries to reach the fourth circle but cannot map the usual route—when was it ever so dark? It cannot be late—he was not asleep for so long—the wind is vicious, the sand wild—he tries to bury himself lower. An old double mattress, almost hollowed by rats, makes a cover he can use; he hears them scrabble around, so near, *was that one?* He counts seconds to minutes, a time sutra to calm as the wind whips and flips from playful to bully. He peers up, into the sky—high above him, the hotel seems to sway. Jeet waits, eyes wide, trying not to move or breathe. A storm. Ha! After the sacrifices he has made, it cannot bring more than he has already survived.

He is wrong. One moment the sky is red, then almost black, then: dark green. The wind slaps sand across the square; it beats against the hotel walls then comes back at Jeet for more. He struggles; he cannot see his foot, his hand, his fingers. Rubbish flings itself out and up, he is afraid to move: he counts his breaths. He loses count and starts again as sand reaches inside every cranny of the dump; everywhere the wind catches filth and whirls it upwards, strange plastic birds taking flight. Tasting sand, hearing sand, seeing nothing but sand. The earth rises around him; a sepia void—*the skies foretell*—he climbs around the dump, he makes his way, an actual madman, the crazed Rudra, skin rubbing raw and eyes unable to weep—his body so brittle he feels it will snap—*your destruction.* He falls into the third circle of the basti. Lurching into other bodies, black sludge, passing hovels full of eyes, *no one will remember you;*

children crying, sand sweeps up and through the lanes, scouring them; finally it dips, rises, gives a last flourish—*even in stories*—and stops.

A ghost town, bleeding. A glow from the hotel windows through the dust-ridden sky. What is going on up there? Crouched in a broken doorway, squatting on all fours, he would give his next life to know.

In the hut opposite him, a group of women are wiping their children's arms, their buttocks and plaits, pulling at them, muttering, asking each other what they can have done to deserve this. Calling on Shakti to protect them all. One has an oil lamp going. It casts a deep glow down the lane and Jeet can see the children, their sudden whiteness. He wants to laugh. Remembering the beauty of the figures he used to surround himself with, the frankincense facials and creams he used to buy to lighten his skin. Has a storm like this ever been seen? Not by Jeet in his world—but now he knows how this world is going to end. He springs from his doorway, scaring the women; they grip their children to them.

—Rudra bhai, help us, one says.

She holds out her bucket. He stares at it—at her. She puts it down on the ground—and then he takes it. Bright yellow, so beautiful, so deep; it could hold a day of water, or more. He nods. He goes through the circles back to the square—and back—each time bringing water from the pumps to the lanes—the thunder sounds; getting closer, closer—a thousand frogs croaking at the back of the sky's dark throat.

Disbelieving Jeet looks up, but can only see sand. How can thunder follow sand?

On the thin plank over the gully, he does a little jig, whirling the bucket around his knees.

—Basti mein masti hain, bachche kyun ro rahe ho? Voo hooo, voo hoo!

He runs down the gully, crying,

—When will it come, will it come?

In the lanes, the mothers hold their children, waiting.

Walk circles, fetch water. Jeet reaches the sixth circle for the seventh time, a full bucket with him.

Spills not one drop.

Then, the sky breaks.

A tongue, lashing lightning—the rain weeping rage down to the cowering earth—the sky a father disappointed. And they, the people of the basti, do cower: as the sand beneath them turns to swamp and then becomes submerged, as the gutters between their shacks become a river which rises, rises, rises. It takes only minutes before shit floods through their hovels, bringing with it rats, big as baby monkeys, tails propelling them furiously against the night. The rubbish becomes a wave, washing away language, voices, drab stories of past lives, sufferings and hopes. All the circles of the basti turning, turning, counterturning, as people of the ninth, eighth, seventh try to push from the pit to the outer edges, only to be stopped at the fifth by makeshift barricades—and forced to turn, and spiral back from there towards the pit. Screaming to each other: *How unnatural it is for a storm to rise in the ninth month of the year! It is a sign, but of what?* Above their heads all the lights in the hotel go out. The power cuts across the basti. They are left in darkness. Now they walk, as fast as they can, in single file through the lanes—a human chain, not speaking, not screaming. They go deeper into Dhimbala, carrying anything they can grab: a tawa, a bedroll, a water can, making for the pit and the Amritsar Minar at its edge.

Two by two, people shove their pigs, their pups, their goats and kids through the doorway, up the narrow stairs to the first floor. Disbelieving, Jeet sees Kal and Dodal, from JAB WE MET PAN, who never give anything for free. Holding torches in their mouths, they hand out plastic rope, directing animals to the first storey, women, children and elderly to the second—*Don't be scared chotu, be a man, it's only rain,* they joke—*Look at me, I'm not scared,* they grimace, they grin.

Jeet climbs with the men to the roof. Arms slither across each other; they use their ropes to hoist up those left in the lanes. He joins in, heaving, hoeing, heaving, wasted arms screaming while he clenches his teeth. They pull together in torch light, trying to get as many to safety as possible.

Two figures come sliding through the river of sludge. They knock from side to side, pushing others out of the way. No one can hear their cries—Jeet wants to, but any sound is stamped out by thunder. The sky is lit by sheet lightning; everyone pinned between the rain above and the filth below. This is the ninth circle, the water is swirling into the pithole; the figures are at the base of the tower, they reach the rope. Jeet, leaning over the parapet knows these shapes—he knows: Bapuji and Nanu.

Bapuji.

Nanu.

Jeet pushes down the stairs, all the way to the lane. Nanu's skin has turned to scales, water running down every wrinkle—the Goddess Saraswati, of learning and art, enraged, aghast, drowning. She grips Bapuji's arm, she waves her Kelly bag; her chiffon sari is stuck to her, horribly translucent.

Rani Mukherjee, Preity Zinta, this is all Jeet can think.

Bapuji is covered in crud. He has fallen and risen trying to orchestrate the tide streaming around him. He raises his hands and grips the rope. Men try to pull him to safety, to drag Nanu up after him. No one shouts *Bapuji! Nanu!* They do not notice or perhaps they don't care. Jeet jumps into the river: they need to be lifted from below. But he cannot bear the weight of his Godfather. He falls backwards into the muck. His head goes under—he opens his mouth and it fills. Dark, dark, dark, the taste of effluence in his nose—something scrabbles around him—he feels the tight, hairy body of a rat. Jeet wants to scream: he must not open his mouth.

Jeet goes under again; he surfaces, retching, into the water. Bapuji stands above him, waist deep in a tide of Company plastic bottles, flattened cake boxes, shower caps filling, strange bulbous fish. Jeet reaches for his Godfather's hand, misses, and then waits, arms raised to be pulled up. No one is looking for him. He struggles to his knees, he clings to Bapuji's waist and tries to pull himself upright.

—*O Varun!* What was the terrible crime for which you wish to destroy me, I who did nothing but praise you?

Bapuji's voice crashes around, praying hard, fervently.

—Proclaim it so that I might kneel before you, liberate me from my mistakes, for you are hard to deceive and are ruled by yourself alone. Free us from the harmful defects of our fathers and the sins we have committed with our bodies. The boys should beat it! My old friends have become my daughters' monkeys. How could they come against me, I, with my hair so white and getting so tired?

Then: Bapuji, the dark water rising around him, shakes Jeet off. He smacks his palms together as if to crush the world flat between them. He picks up Nanu, and hands her into arms, waiting to pull her inside.

Jeet finds a foothold in the ground-floor window, and he is pulled up in turn. Nanu crouches on the roof, shivering. There is nothing to warm her, nor wipe the sludge from her. Jeet wants to put his arms around her—but even now he does not dare. Nanu shouts:

—I hate to get wet! I want to go back inside, I want him to apologise to his daughters. There is no reason for this! No need!

Jeet looks back over the parapet. Down below, Bapuji is still fighting the sewage. All that Jeet can think is: *Jivan, Bubu, Radha, Sita, what have you done? Gargi. My God, Gargi—what have you done?*

The thunder and lightning, the flood, are siblings of pain that will not stop.

Hands reach and reach from the first-floor windows. They catch Bapuji, they manage to lift him, loop him to the rope; the men on the rooftop drag him up the building. Nanu tries to put her arm around his head but she is shivering too hard. She scolds him for being led with his lower parts instead of his brain, for not listening, never listening to her.

—You are like a man with many wives and nothing left to sustain himself with. You always thought Radha was kind—were you too busy looking in the mirror to see her truly?

Bapuji does not answer Nanu. He stares around, smiling at the men. *Is he smiling?* Jeet thinks. It is impossible to tell.

—All of you who know God, ask yourselves why this storm has come. You know what you have done, as fathers and daughters, uncles and nieces, don't think it goes unseen. You have lied, you have cheated and you lust after what is not yours to touch. Tonight is the night to unburden your selves. Come, tell whatever snakes hide in your hearts. It is their natures only that bring us to this. Come! Bapuji cries.

The other men take no notice. They are too busy winding up the ropes, counting each other, finding a place at Nanu's feet. Jeet crouches with them. Their faces are naturally rapt in the storm—of course they are—she is chanting—Jeet realises—the Naph prayer—*"Never was a time"*—

Bapuji splashes about on the rooftop, smiling like a crafty Buddha, and says nothing.

.   .   .

The thunder finally rolls away, leaving only the whiplash rain. The men squat, staring into the night, a congress of owls. Arms around each other, heads on each other's shoulders. Jeet laughs. It is too, too funny that here in the basti men are allowed to touch. He realises that it's not funny. He must be mad. He can still taste excrement in his throat. The rain drums upon them.

Bapuji is on his knees, crawling about. He reaches Nanu. She puts her hand on his forehead and he raises his eyes to hers.

—Poor Nanu. Poor, poor Nanu, he says.

Nanu begins to croon to him. Stroking his cheek, her face so soft as she looks down at her son—as if she can see through him to the floor, to the mud, to the sewers. All the men lean forwards, to hear her through the rain.

> *How do you,*
> *Asks the chief of police,*
> *Patrol a city*
> *Where the butcher shops*
> *Are guarded by vultures;*
> *Where bulls get pregnant,*
> *Cows are barren,*
> *And calves give milk*
> *Three times a day;*
> *Where mice are boatmen*
> *And tomcats the boats*
> *They row;*
> *When frogs keep snakes*
> *As watchdogs,*
> *And jackals*
> *Go after lions?*
>
> *Does anyone know*
> *What I'm talking about?*

She kisses Bapuji's bare head.

—We will remain babes in the flood.

—Hanji! comes the refrain.

Up on this rooftop, with no shelter, where the night might last for hours more. Tomorrow will bring disease, infection. Nanu is ninety years old, the last Maharani of Napurthala. Is she to die here?

Bapuji begins to cough. He clutches at his mother's lap.

—When the mind is free . . . he mumbles. And the heart . . . no, the head . . . and hand to the mouth. Cry? Who says? Keep trying and I will not . . . Come, my Chachas, bring the rain and the storm, where the heart is kind and the head is held high.

—Let us take them down to the women, someone says.

Jeet hangs back as others help Nanu to her feet. They guide her towards the stairs. Bapuji will not go with them. Jeet can hear him protesting: he has already felt the worst from Radha and Gargi, why should he be scared of rain? They group around him—they force him to walk. They have to save themselves.

Nanu and Jeet stumble down after. On the floor below, the huddled women make room in the stinking water. They do not look to see who has come; they do not reach their arms out or pat the wet floor. Nanu sits, and Bapuji follows. Jeet climbs over the women to a corner near the windows; it is ankle deep in sludge. He sinks into it. The walls are dank: they smell of acceptance.

The rain comes in at the windows; the dark seems to shield a hundred pairs of veiled eyes. Jeet's mouth tastes of the basti, the human meat all around. How has it come to this? With Bapuji and Nanu down amongst the women? With him, here?

They sit, waiting out the rain, listening to the moans of the sick and fevered, the younger children crying.

—Come sleep, come sleep, a mother sings.

Hours pass; they doze, their minds washed blank.

When a gauzy light begins to flit through the windows, Bapuji rouses himself. His hair is wild around his face. Jeet watches him take in the room: see the naked children, the makeshift toilet where they have been forced to squat. Filthy water lies inches deep around them. They have been there for hours, throats parched, legs wet, yet the mothers (or are the white-haired ones grandmothers?) still hold their children above the water's reach. Then Bapuji catches sight of a boy's arm, a faded Napurthala tattoo. He struggles to his knees.

The women start to murmur as they, in turn, wake. Even though Bapuji's kurta is soaking and torn, it remains fastened by diamond studs. His shawl is wound tight around his neck. Nanu's pearls are more luminous than any of the teeth or eyes in the room.

—Devraj Bapuji! The whisper spreads. Nanuji!

They straighten their saris, try to wipe their children. A woman cries out in Napurthali,

—Give my babies your blessing!

The woman holds out her child. Bapuji stops shivering. He kneels, reaches out his hands and rests them on the heads of the two women either side of him. In Hindi he begins to sing that tired old song that every child learns at his first teacher's knee. Bapuji's voice is high; for a fevered moment Jeet thinks Gargi is there. He looks around, expecting to see her smiling at him, her head tilted to one side. But there is only Bapuji and Nanu, and the flood waters lapping at them all.

—*Hum honge kaamyab, hum honge kaamyab, ek din*
O mann mein hai vishwaas, poora hai vishwaas,
Hum honge kaamyab, ek din.

Bapuji waits; the women stay silent, so many of them in the room—how can they all stay so silent? Some of them are still holding out their children. Hushed, to hear more. Bapuji considers them all. He begins again in English, banging time on his knee,

—*We shall overcome, we shall overcome, we shall overcome someday,*
Oh deep in my heart, I do believe,
That we shall overcome someday.

—Now that I have seen you, I will save you, Bapuji says. I will pray you have sons in the next life, and that you are born to an achche din!

The woman nearest Jeet raises her head. She gives a harsh laugh.

—How many times can we sing this song in *this* life? We are sitting in water up to our knees, and still we are waiting for clean stuff to drink, she says.

—Om Shanti Om, intones Bapuji.

The women rock their babies, eyes closed. Bapuji's words fall and scatter, coins cast into a well.

· · ·

A wailing cry reaches them, stirring the women to standing. One goes to the window; the rest watch and wait—to hear—a child has been found floating face down in the water, a boy has drowned in the flood. The women struggle; steadying each other, they move to the window, lean out—*who is it?*

No shirt, jeans. One brown lace-up Babu shoe, with a red sole. *Who is it?*

In his corner, Jeet puts his hands over his mouth. He knows who it is. *Samir.*

A scream. Jeet had not noticed Samir's mother here amongst the poorer women; he sees her faint backwards, she is caught in her sisters' arms. The thunder rolls a final distant *tarrantarra;* the women hold her, framed by the rotten window. Their wails rip through the red curtain of dawn.

Jeet rocks himself, head between his knees. *Samir.* Now is the time for madmen to rise, for Sita to abscond, for Jeet's beloved Gargi to go against her father, for Radha and Bubu to take charge. Then there is Jivan. These are the players—sitting warm and dry, eating samosa with fresh mint chutney, monsoon mangoes and hot khir. What will they do next? No matter how much Jeet prays, curses or hides: Samir is gone. This is the age of Kali.

SITA WAS STILL SLEEPING; it was getting really, unbearably cold. Past hunger and on to pure thirst. Punj said he couldn't leave us, not even to fetch water, that someone is coming to bring us to the party.

—You must be immune to hunger, Punj said. Didn't you fast for days? I read that in the papers, headline news. How did you survive in the basti?

Punj got up and made to light the fire. Sita stirred as he moved and raised her head.

—Papa, she said, what is happening here?

—Shh, I told her, go back to sleep.

—Who is this? she said. It is so dark, I can barely see.

—Don't worry, just that serving man, here to keep company, I said.

She struggled to her feet. Punj tried to stop her. He put his arms around her.

—Punj! I said, just tie her with my shawl. She will stay if we bid it.

—Papa, she said. What are you doing?

—Sit! Sit with Punj, my Sita, and play along, while I ask you a question.

—Don't you tie me, she said to him, just as she should have. I'll give you one tight slap! Leave me alone, I will sit.

—Good girl, I said. So. Both of you tell me, which brand of tomato sauce do you prefer? I like eating finger chips with sauce. I remember when, after years and years, Heinz began to trade in India. Did you know they sell their sauce in two variations? The Standard Tomato and the Chilli Sauce. Who prefers what?

—Standard, said Punj, grinning. All the way.

—No, Sita said. Chilli.

—Wrong, I said. All like all. Caste-no-bar. This is the danger of tomato sauce.

Sita told us that even in the UK she ate Tomato Chilli Sauce. She said she used to put it on her Angrezi breakfast. She said she ate eggs, and pork in rashers and sausages, and even a pudding made of pigs' blood. Now, I am not a Mussulman but this I cannot endure. I willed her to go back to sleep. Even Punj looked shocked. And to think, I was trying to design and develop her a car. So all could ride her dreams!

Whose daughter does she think she is? Time for her history lesson. I drew her a diamond in the dust.

—Here, I said. We have campaigned from Amritsar to Napurthala, Napurthala to Chandigarh. Chandigarh to Delhi and from there to here. Srinagar. Across and back and up and down. The world keeps turning, turning. There are no straight lines but those of lineage, and on maps and spider's webs. This is where you belong. It is written.

iii

The storm becomes a prologue to the scoop on Bapuji, rolling out across the country, felling reputations and raising banners to his newfound cause. The men in the dhaba watch the small TV and read yesterday's newspapers; they quote Barun J. Bharat, who reports exclusively on how Bapuji left the Company Amritsar on the night of the worst rains to lash Punjab since the British left, and then made his way to Dhimbala basti to give succour to the people there. What happened next? In the morning, Barun writes, local men came looking, handing out bottles of Company water, packets of sweet, dry biscuits. They found Nanu and Bapuji on a flood-soaked parapet, Nanu squatting on a small cane stool, reciting shlokas to a rapture of women. Bapuji was in another corner, teaching a song to a group of happy children. The men tried to bring them back to the hotel, but they would not come.

Instead, they insisted on being escorted around the pit to where the untouchables of Napurthala lived, wading through alleyways choked with stagnant sludge, past broken hovels and fearless rats, dispensing blessings and wisdom as they went. Bapuji did namaste to the men, low caste, no caste, sweepers, the untattooed Napurthali Jhimbas who once gutted fish and were now busy clearing the storm's dead, carrying bodies to the basti cremation site in a corner of the pit. Yet Bapuji touched their hands; he invited each and every one of them to be his guests at Napurthala Palace as soon as humanly possible.

That last part of the story (about the invitation) was true. But no one who reads the rest of the article while sipping on bed-tea brought to them late on Sunday morning—who, selecting between the weekend supplement (*Hot now! Saying you're an Artist or a Photographer is the coolest tag to have*), the property ads (*Unitech Nirvana Country—the gateway to Paradise—Gurugram!*) or the matrimonials organised by caste, creed, geography, sex (not gender, never that, no)—will read that the men who came for Bapuji were locals. They were not sent by Gargi or Bubu, but someone else—Ranjit. That the water was in resealed Company bottles, that the biscuits were out-of-date. Or that Bapuji was actually found, after a long hunt-and-seek and numerous cash bribes, not teaching a song to grateful children but raging on the rooftop of Naph Minar with a twenty-pack of sharabis from all nine circles (since intoxication does not discriminate) who had managed to save their moonshine from the storm.

No one passing the time with the papers and cups of first-flush Darjeeling in the hotel lobbies—as the rain freshens gardens and terraces and window boxes—would hear about how, the morning after the storm, Nanu and Bapuji were ignored as they made their way through the circles of the basti. The people were busy with their ruins, their families, their water and food. This was no time to be blessed by a madman or duped like a politician's fool. Their constant work enraged Bapuji: he shut his ears against the women singing to their babies to scare off the dysentery that would wring small bodies dry. In the square, the dhaba and the moneylender reopened: queues began to form—for if anyone had cash in the basti, it had drowned. Madam demanded that Kataria 1 open up the women's press: she wanted to print pictorial pamphlets on how to stay clean without water. He asked her: *What is it worth?*

So, no one had time to stop and listen to Bapuji lecture. Some, out of love or duty, offered food and shelter, but Bapuji only wanted to drink and talk, and for people to sit and listen. Soon even the small children stopped following them.

No one outside Dhimbala knew that after Bapuji and Nanu could not be persuaded to go to safety, the security men simply left. They promised they would come back with aid—that is, if the people remained loyal, and kept their mouths shut about the Maharaja and his mother in that eyesore of a shit heap.

A day passes, and another. A violent seam of mosquitoes invades the lanes, threatening to bring and feed on death. The boys are warned to keep off the most toxic parts of the dump. The more they are warned, the less they listen. They dare each other: *deeper, deeper.* They say they are diving for Samir's other shoe. They hate to go home and they love the dump: it is where they find food and bits of scrap to trade; they play in it and shelter in it; it whispers to them words no one else can catch. It is their motherland.

The storms leave behind a blood-spitting fever. Jeet is ill. He swarms and shivers in the ruins of his hovel; visions appear and dissolve. He sees a man stab another man, and eat him; then a man eats another man, who is screaming; then a man eating another man, who is soundlessly screaming—and he wakes up making the face of someone drowning. His arms are around a puppy, one of the few that survived the storm. Then Nanu (*Nanu?*) appears, a small goddess in his hovel. He hears his own voice, high, gibbering, words spilling out of him until the vision disappears. Then Bapuji (*Bapuji?*) himself is there, and the night seems to rise again behind him.

When Jeet wakes up, he finds that some of it is true, and he has not been dreaming. The storm happened; Bapuji and Nanu were there; he is in Dhimbala basti, still. Above his head the blue sky is flapping—so blue—no—it's his sheet of blue plastic, a corner loose in the wind. The middle sags under the weight of water, it seems to be closing onto his head. Nanu is here, Bapuji is here, crouching with Jeet in his hovel. He feels hands caring for him, cradling him, calling him Radha, then Gargi. Bapuji pinches Jeet's ear and twists it to burning. Through the slow haze of fever, all Jeet can remember are rhymes from his youth. *Ek, do, teen, char, panch; Row, row, row your boat.* He hears himself beg Bapuji to save him from a demon called Vikram who has been chasing him through the rain. High laughter whips around him; his naked body shivers with it, he realises it is his own voice.

—Are you Rudra? Bapuji asks him. Do I know you? I think I know you.

Jeet buries his face in his Godfather's lap. He is Jeet. However much he wants to be Rudra, however much he tries to escape himself, he is Jeet: a man who loved Gucci, and all the things made with money. Jeet: who wore skin-lightening cream and waxed his chest, put kohl in his eyes to make himself beautiful for beautiful boys. Jeet: who was proud to pay for sex, who drank whisky and could match any man at poker. Jeet: who was at his best with high-class women fawning over him; he let them lick his cock and take his money for dinner. No one had ever been able to match Jeet for flirting, except Vik—who follows him, eyes on him, pleading love.

I cannot survive on nothing.

No one can.

However much he tries—he wants, he wants. He begins to sob. Bapuji rocks him gently. *Shh, shh, be a good boy,* Jeet thinks to himself in the basti. *Say nothing, chup chup, let the rain come again. Let it wash all life away.*

Rain falls in a light sheen over everything; it drips through the holes in Jeet's plastic roof; it washes his face as he tries to look up. He sees Bapuji so clearly: every line on his face, every pigment mark. The man he has worshipped all his life is really there, looking at him with pity. Jeet thinks he says *Tat tvam asi,* but he cannot be sure. Then the fever takes over. Jeet remembers little after that. Until night comes, the second after the storm, and Bapuji is in some new sort of frenzy. He tears at his filthy kurta; his diamond studs fall off. Jeet scrabbles for them but Bapuji kicks them into the sewer; he rents at his shawl and drops it in the mud.

Legs tremble, arms ache, but Rudra raises himself up and falls on it; he wraps it between his legs and around his hips. Nanu wakes up from her corner, a bundle of torn chiffon and sodden papier-mâché skin, as if she is waiting to be re-formed. She tries to stop him, calling to Bapuji not to allow a madman to wear his clothes, not to turn the world ulta seedha upar neeche, risk each becoming the other.

He feels Nanu's hands grab at him and slap him; his limbs twist with fever. He retreats to a corner, stroking his new covering, nursing himself.

—We that believe in India Shining—he whispers it into his shawl. We that believe we are better than all others. We that are the youngest, the fastest, the democracy, the economy, the future technology of the world, the global Super Power coming soon to a cinema near you, we, hum panch, that are the five cousins of the five great rivers, everybody our brother-sister-lover, we that are divine: the echo of the ancient heroes of the old times, we that fight, we that love, we that are hungry, so, so hungry, we that are young! We that are jigging on the brink of ruin; we that are washed in the filth of corruption, chal, so what? Aise hi hota hai: we that are a force of all that is natural—slow—death—to Muslims, gays, chi-chi women in their skin-tights, hai! We that sit picnicking on the edge of our crumbling civilisation, we that party with shots and more shots, more shots as the world burns beneath us, as the dogs bark, as the cockroaches crow, as the old eat their young and the young whip their elders all wearing the birth masks of respect, we that present only the shadows of our selves behind our painted smiles, we that protest for the right to drink whisky sours served to our beds at noon, we that eat our beef with chopsticks, we that twist tongues to suit our dear selves, we that worship the ancient religion of Lakshmi, of Shiva, of wealth creation and ultimate destruction, we that will be born strong in the next life and in a party that never ends, we that are the future of this planet, we that begin with this beloved India, will endure, yes it all belongs to us, and we will eat it all. All of it is ours, we that are India and no longer slaves: we that are young!

—Who do you think you are? Nanu says. Where? This is the world where pundits take bribes for blessings. Do not shiver. When thieves don't come to the market, when gandus and hijras get married in Krishna mandirs, then humara apna India will shine, heh? Somewhere it rains every day, whether you feel it in your palace or not.

Na tuevahaparam jatunusam	*Never was a time when I did not exist*
na tuenemek janadhipahra	*nor you, nor all these kings;*
na caiva na bhavisyamahoputra	*nor in the future*
sarve vayam atah param.	*Shall any of us cease to be.*

Midnight comes: almost the third day. Jeet shivers in his hovel, hearing voices, noises. The sun beats down. He crawls outside: in the lane, Devraj and another man—Jeet thinks it is his father (*his father!*)—are together. Arms locked around each other, they are doing ring-a-roses. Why isn't Rudra there? He sees himself hopping about around them—*Voo hoo, Voo hoo!*—he feels the softness of toosh warm his cock. His Godfather's head is lit against the night. The two men roll in the mud and Jeet laughs—he catcalls, he claps from here, from there, bringing the dump sliding down onto their heads—until Ranjit has Bapuji pinned. How the prisoner struggles! A slippery fish, gaping.

Jeet feels cold, although he is wrapped in a fine, forbidden kingly shawl. He slithers through the mud to take his Godfather's hand. He begs to play with them. Hands grip him, pushing him back into his hovel. He buries the piercing confusion that Ranjit doesn't even seem to see him, and touches him with disgust on his face. He wants to say, *Don't you know me? Your only son, Jeet. No—I am Rudra, against desire. No—Jeet.*

Words will not come. Jeet has forgotten how to speak, is afraid that if he opens his mouth, the only sound that will come out will be, *Vik Vik Vik Vik Vik.*

In the morning, local men from outside the basti are led to the ninth circle by those who know where Rudra can be found. They bring clean water and sponges; they give Bapuji and Nanu a new set of clothes each; they want to take them away from the filth. Bapuji keeps tight hold of Rudra's hand—he is a Naph, he is needed. They are escorted around the pit, to the Napurthala Gate on the west highway. A car is waiting. They crawl inside, Bapuji, Nanu, Jeet. Three drenched cats.

The smell is so rich; the deep spice of money. Calfskin leather and walnut trim. Jeet curls inside it, as if returning to the womb. When he closes his eyes and breathes in, it is as if the basti does not exist—has never existed. For a moment he wants to claw at the window: *Let me out!* But no one would hear him, and no one would help. Jeet succumbs to the soft moo of the car, its lovely lullaby. *We that are young.* He rests his head back; he sleeps.

Truth haunts those news reports; it's there between the lines. Three days after the storm, a mela does take place in the abandoned grounds of the Napurthala Palace. As the internet will archive, this mela is the first great spontaneous gathering of the Devraj Campaign, the beginning of Team Devraj and the great fasting protest, the birth of a movement for the common man. The people of Dhimbala basti are there. When Bapuji was amongst them, they had no time for him—they respond only when he is on the stage.

They are in the car for no more than an hour. By the time Jeet—still filthy, his back sticking to the car seat, leaving dark smudges (but wearing a fine shawl, such a fine shawl around his groin)—reaches Napurthala, they are surrounded by droves of ragged men—on foot, on cycles, in auto rickshaws. It is early; a fresh breeze blows away the storm debris, the remnants of disease. As they turn into the grounds of the Napurthala Palace, Jeet sees carts selling snacks, bhel puri and chana. There are water-balloon sellers, popcorn wale, men with pink clouds of candyfloss, toys sold by toy-men skilled at bringing wooden snakes to life with a flick of their wrists, *Yes, dear children, it is so easy: for five rupees, just five rupees, you too can own a mechanical animal and make it dance.*

Behind the chaos, and through his strange fever, Jeet looks for his father. There are Napurthali dignitaries in their conical hats; their tur-baned counterparts from Amritsar, smiles fixed, eyes waiting. Two bus-loads of workers pull through the gates. Someone must have paid for them: all these bodies to make the crowds: farmers, labourers, basti dwellers. Jeet has seen this before at factory meetings and local Company shareholder rallies. This isn't Gargi. Just as the plainclothes men in the basti did not belong to Bubu. The aid and the biscuits and the bottled water: Was it Sita? Jeet sees cardboard boxes from the Amritsar hotel bakery being handed out; tea party pakoras, samosas, white bread sand-wiches with cream cheese inside.

Ranjit, he thinks. *Here you are.*

Jeet walks through the Palace grounds with disbelieving eyes. The peacock-shaped hedges, the yew and rubber trees, the manicured gardens he played Holi in as a boy have become wild. The place is a kingdom of monkeys. Large and small, bare-arsed, hairy-faced, whiskers and beards and bright black eyes, sitting in the trees and under them: long arms dangling, tongues unfurling as they yawn, as they scratch—old men holding court with many wives while their babies chatter and screech around them. It fevers his brain—remember Gargi planning his own twenty-first birthday party and throwing it on these lawns? How the monkeys laughed when Jeet allowed Gargi to organise a cake by the pool, when he agreed to family photographs, as long as Gargi wore the dress of Jeet's choice. A "baby-pink" (if your babies were "white") Tom Ford tube. Meant to suck Gargi in, and promote all of her curves. Jeet bought it in Dubai, where he could see the legs of the city spread wide below him from the lip of a twenty-seventh-storey infinity pool; he gave it to Gargi for rakhi. She protested, she did not want to wear it, he called her *chicken* until she put it on. Then she appeared at the party, the dress underneath a knee-length Kashmiri silk jacket, which she would not remove. She looked so elegant. He was silenced. *Gargi.* Jeet shivers with shame; he is still feverish, still dirty and half-naked. His beard has colonised his mouth, his cheeks.

He stays close to Nanu. They follow a path through the rubble until they reach a low, wide bench in front of an ancient banyan tree. Its dry roots hang from its branches, fingers accusing the earth. Jeet circles it, looking for the rusty sign nailed to the trunk; it used to fascinate him as a boy. *Under this tree in 1947, Gandhiji met with Maharaja Ram Devraj and Maharani Ram Devraj, belovedly known as "Nanu," father and mother to us all. Yuvraj Dev was also in attendance.*

No one here stops for English words. Yet all know the story of how Gandhiji came and blessed the tree, how this has protected the Devraj family all these years. Now, Jeet realises, the tree is dying. *So much for blessings,* he thinks.

The people form a line, pressed close together as if queuing to enter some heritage site; they want to touch Nanu's feet. Their fathers and grandfathers must have done the same years ago. Nanu sits on her bench, her feet stuck out, her dark glasses hiding her eyes. Jeet stands behind her, a Rudra sentinel.

—Ram Ram, Nanuji, Ram Ram, says a young woman, her baby strapped to her back. My husband is a farmer. I am his wife, and a bee-keeper. What shall we do in this time of storm and drought?

—When a deer eats the barley, the farmer does not hope to nourish the animal, Nanu says. She flexes her feet; her chappals are sturdy. For the first time Jeet notices her toenails: they are painted bright pink.

—When a lowborn woman becomes the mistress of a noble man, her husband does not hope to get rich on that nourishment. Now, the barley is the people and the deer is the Royal power, thus the people are food for the Royal power and the one who has the power eats the people.

The farmer's wife moves away, the weight of her baby making her stoop. *Poor thing,* Jeet thinks, *so illiterate that she cannot even be grateful for the lesson told to her.*

Men in cotton shirts and suit trousers, some with dark glasses, some with good watches, are handing out cake boxes to the crowd. Jeet leaves Nanu to walk behind Bapuji—who is changed now, into a clean white kurta pyjama, a bright orange scarf around his neck. His hair is still wild, though it has dried. Someone has given him a loudspeaker; someone has given him a fresh pair of jutti for his feet.

Bapuji's arm is around his Rudra: Rudra is holding Bapuji's hand. The crowds part for them; Jeet will not let go for one second. He can feel the men in the crowds looking at him. To be untouchable in the highest sense and not the lowest! To be a man in the eyes of other men! From beside his Godfather, Jeet decides to address the crowd himself. He will speak as Rudra, and see how they take it. His first lesson to the people must be given in a calm clear voice. He reaches for the loudspeaker in Bapuji's hand.

—Go to the mandir, he says. Pray to God you will be born better tomorrow. Your lives are lived in the fog of kama: we must learn to banish this thing called desire, to act without attachment to the fruits of action.

His voice crackles across the garden. Do the men draw back when he speaks? Is it with awe and admiration?

—Aré, pet! Aré, pagal! Your stars have blessed you to be at Bapuji's side, someone shouts.

Jeet hangs back. Hot all over his body. Despite the catcall, he thinks he can feel awe. Rudra raises his arms to the crowd, strokes his beard. He thinks he can see some nods, some smiles. Bapuji gives him a shake, a nod of the head. Rudra strokes his beard.

Small fires begin to burn all over the lawns, protected from the wind by bricks taken from the crumbling perimeter walls. Jeet teeters on the edge of things, watching people claim the ground and settle. Future generations of their children will play here, he thinks; shoeless, naked, rolling in the earth; they will thrive amongst these ruins as if raised from these tombs.

—Let the Panchayat begin, Bapuji says. He reaches Nanu on her bench. He climbs onto it and stands beside her, beckoning to Rudra to come to his other side.

The men part from the women as naturally as trees in a forest bow to wind. They leave the fires; they surge towards the stage, jostle and sit; a sea of turbaned heads and naked ones, light skins at the front, dark skins behind. Is it Tuesday? Rudra feels so happy. Yes, this is his new life, already come.

—In days gone by, begins Bapuji, pointing at his own feet, I sat here with my father in this very spot, witnessing him administer justice to you, the people of this state, under the watchful whites, eyes making sure that each and everything was weighed, measured, accounted for. By coming close to us, by whispering, they undermined our future. Now we must come together in the great tradition of our faith.

Jeet watches his Godfather pause as if trying to remember the next line.

—Hanji, Devraj Bapuji, he shouts, to help.

—Men of Bharat, says Bapuji, his voice so rich. We are living through a time of crooked despair. O! Our unfortunate country is being overrun by my daughters: a hundred-crore house is more important than your struggles. I understand that you want: everything you see.

Bapuji waves the loudspeaker, then shouts into it again.

—We have to prepare for catastrophe. We cannot continue as we are. I am a father who has given everything to his daughters, and so, my friends, have you. I have been punished in this life: my mother outlived my father, and I have brought only daughters into this world. They are tearing apart my legacy and yours. They are corrupting our beloved country; they are selling you nothings; they are bankrupting your hearts. I am Devraj of Napurthala, Yuvraj then Maharaja. You might call me besotted or mad, but only the clouds understand the earth's anxiety.

Bapuji embraces the men with his words. He knows many of them are farmers, their crops thirsting; many of them have invested in bad seeds formed by scientists from the West—seeds which promised great yields but have failed. Even the monkeys seem to stop on their pillars and walls when Bapuji speaks. Jeet feels the sun on his head, he feels monkeyish watching Bapuji take his place at the head of the people. *What it must be to inspire this kind of love, these faces full of trust.*

—Who do you think has sold you these unnatural pips? Who has starved your sons? Gargi, says Bapuji. Who promised you fertilisers and sold you the chemicals that have caused your crops to fail? Did a Company man do this? If so, he was instructed by Gargi. Bad crops. I see too many dupattas among us. Sisters, if your husbands took their own lives in Napurthala because they could not find work on the farms, ask yourselves what Gargi Madam has done for you in exchange. What kills the poor man is shameless daughters: lament, lament that Gargi Ma should be so callous.

Jeet, standing on the bench, sees some of the women put their hands to their faces; covering yawns or wiping tears—he cannot tell.

—If you have sold what little you had to allow a new development to come up in its place, you have been robbed. I stand here before you, dead. They steal from me before my body has been laid on my bier, says Bapuji.

—For shame! shouts a well-dressed man; Jeet thinks he is one of Ranjit's. The farmers around him cheer.

Now Bapuji sits down cross-legged on the bench. The listeners sit cross-legged with him. An aide in a cotton kurta and jeans brings a plastic stool and places it by Bapuji's elbow with a small bottle of water and a tin cup. He unscrews the cap, he pours the water; he bows and backs away. Jeet sees the bottle. He licks his lips.

—Come, tell me your problems, Bapuji says, and he points his finger up to the sky, keeps it there. Let us discuss here our svadharma. Our duty to society is part of our rule. Do you have daughters? We will judge all rewards.

—On this side, Nanuji, Maharani of Napurthala.

Bapuji gestures to Nanu: she holds up her hand, palm out.

—On this side, he says, this simple Rudra, a rare breed, a last representative of the Napurthali Yogis, who I now keep by me. This Rudra has the qualities all daughters should display: modesty, loyalty, a tongue that speaks when it is spoken to, does it not?

Rudra! Jeet flushes; he puts his hands together and nods, grinning.

—Hanji, hanji piyo aur khauji! he says.

Laughter ripples through the audience. He thinks: *What? What did I say?*

An old man gets to his feet, his shirt ragged and his dhoti stained. His belly hangs low over his legs and his hair wisps around his face. The deep wrinkles around his eyes and mouth lift as he works his lips and swallows. Twisting his scarf, he begins to speak; Jeet can see a dark gap that runs across his gums. The two remaining teeth are square and yellow, ingots of dirty gold.

—Devraj Bapuji, this year the tax has been too much for us to bear, he begins. I had only three goats and none would breed.

—My daughters! cries Bapuji.

The loudspeaker feeds back a screech. Bapuji sips from his tin cup and places it back on the stool.

—I had three goats and last spring, says the old farmer, this man here, who once was my dearest friend— (he points to the ground where

Jeet can see another man, head bowed, bald crown giving nothing away)
—he stole my goat, Bapuji, he stole it and traded it for seeds that will
not grow. We are cursed by God, for our crops continue to perish. I have
contemplated death as many of my fellow farmers have taken their own
lives. We will be food for the unwatered soil; our grandsons will be old
before those seeds will yield.

—Did you do this for your daughters? To buy their wedding night
pleasure? asks Bapuji. Then you are a fool and should weep for shame,
and pray they do not take what little you have left. Sit down.

The poor man sits down. Another rises. In a business shirt and rimless glasses, he is thin and tall; his head seems too heavy for his frame.

—I have worked all my life as a clerk in Napurthala, and my children
are grown up, he says. Bapuji, we have given them everything and now
they will not come home! One is in a call centre and all night she works.
When she brings money, my heart aches to eat the food it buys. And my
son, his wife is a pase wali kaam chor who will turn us out before she will
give us one hot roti in her house. I want to be proud of them, but at least
let them come home or meet us once in a while? We are left wondering
ki what did we sacrifice for? I have borrowed to pay for their studies and
their weddings and now I cannot return. The interest rate is making me
a pauper, country is facing recession, I invested in one of your respected
companies that I prayed would come good. Yet I have less today.

—Daughters! cries Bapuji again. Investments that go down on us
never come up. Take them, beat them, let them die even before they
are born. Do not the ancient texts warn us that it is the very nature of
women to corrupt? For that reason circumspect men should not be careless among women. It is not just an ignorant man; even a man of the
world can be lead astray. Heed the Manusmṛti: "No one should sit in a
deserted place with his mother, sister or daughter, for her base nature will
distract from duty even a learned man."

Fever dries Rudra's mouth and bakes his head from inside. He stands
up on the bench; he jumps up and down, pointing, at the clerk who
asked the question.

—Look at this fool, a daughter begging for more shoe money when
she already has ten pairs. Don't glare, you moon-faced clerk, sit down!

—Rudra, Bapuji says, his tone stern. Why have you come here looking like this? Did my daughters force you to shame?

Rudra puts his arms around himself, teeth chattering. Everyone's eyes are on his ragged Shahtoosh, his chest, the skin broken, cross-hatched with scars.

—Put some clothes on, sir. You are working in my name, you look as poor as a Mussulman who cannot afford Haj.

Jeet sits down. He hangs his head. He watches a line of red ants crawl one after the other across the bench. He hears the crowd clap until Bapuji starts to speak. It's about Gargi—again.

—Do you think she has a heart to see what she has done here? No, she has no heart.

Bapuji points at the tin cup of water, resting on its stool.

—There she sits and says nothing. Speak Gargi: tell the people why your face is so ugly.

Jeet sees how the crowd is caught by Bapuji's joking, how the people smile and nudge each other; a smattering of laughter, a slow clap begins.

—Gargi, Bapuji cries. He kicks the stool, the water spills, the stool rolls towards the first row of men; one stops it. He raises it above his head shakes it, spits on it, passes it back through the lines. Hand to hand on its legs, its seat slapped, hand after hand, it travels over heads until it reaches the edge of the gathering and is flung to the monkeys behind.

Now Bapuji points at Nanu and shouts,

—She takes from you as she has taken from me, and she will sell this earth, just you watch, and her sister will build a mall on it, dig up this sand for oil and make petrol from it, not for you and your children, but for those who have got fat from the corruption souring this government as milk turns to curd in the sun. The dogs shall lick it, Chinku, Rinku, Mr. Stinku. Where are my babies now?

He buries his face in his hands.

Nanu looks at the crowd, her lips pursed as if guilt is a sweet she is sucking on.

—We will go to every town and village, we will stop this Gargi nonsense. Stop them from stealing; stop them from pretending. Stop them, shouts Bapuji.

—Stop Gargi-Radha! Stop the looting thieving ones! shout back the crowd.

The men press towards Bapuji, the women gather their skirts and their children. Rudra bares his teeth; he feels ready to bite if they get too close. He flings his arms out but he cannot stop the crowd kneeling to Bapuji as his voice soars from the loudspeaker's throat.

—Gargi, yes, and Radha too—both are kameeni. They will rip my head from my body and dance while they drink my blood. They will destroy everything around them as they take, take, take. O God, why are they so?

Two sturdy men grasp Bapuji's ankles; they lift him onto their shoulders and bear him away. Rudra tries to follow, but his body feels engulfed in feverish burning. There are too many heads between them; he stands on tiptoe on the bench, he sees Bapuji reach the edges of the gardens borne high on someone's shoulders, then he is lowered to the ground.

Rudra thumps onto the bench. Nanu seems to have wandered from this place; he thinks he should try to find her. He looks up. A woman, her block-print chunni a bright, fresh yellow, approaches him; she offers him a scoop of halva, wrapped in paper tissue. Rudra takes the gift; he presses his cupped hands to her.

Slowly, he eats. Warm, sweet prasad. The crowds begin to disperse. He sits for a while, watching them go. He wanders through the banyan tree's roots. There is Nanu, hobbling towards the doors of the Napurthala Palace. She is going back to the rooms where she once played, an eight-year-old bride. Perhaps her wedding portrait still hangs in its gilded frame, above the vast fireplace in the bridge room. Amongst the antiques and hunting trophies, cobwebbed memories of afternoons spent drinking tea and eating sweetmeats, playing her sitar for her husband. She is going back to the rooms where memories wait, her tender maids, to soothe and bathe and put to bed.

It is almost noon. Jeet watches Nanu make her way inside, and disappear from view.

WHEN MY FATHER DIED, the Palace of Napurthala was mine. I was nine years old. The Viceroy's missive came attached to an arm to tell me my kingdom was now an annexe of the Empire, and then, as the myth has it, Nanu entertained him with wine and stuffed peacock. She gave him boys with the paan course, and he, suffering a colonial hangover and too ashamed of himself to admit it the next morning, went back and revoked the order of possession. To tell the truth, I simply paid him in gold. As much as he could carry: he even filled his mouth. And then, for I was a strong boy, I gave him a kick up the backside and told him to get off my land.

After that I began to build my business and who can say if I did anything wrong? In the years of the License Raj, nothing was possible and everything happened. Some say they never bribed, did not milk connection from Mother India's breast. Good luck to them. The time is past for lies. I learned survival from the look in men's eyes when they came to drink my bootleg whisky, for the country was dry back then, from Napurthala to Delhi. Who could blame them? We all got rich and why not? Cash in hand to be hidden under the bed while who knows what took place on top. Outside world go hang.

But this house. This Srinagar tinderbox house. If only I had known there were angels living here, I would have stayed. How the angel dances, so lightly above us, and the stars twinkle down on this clear, clear night. Today is Diwali, the time for homecoming. The return of Kings and consorts.

—Sita?

Good, she must have gone to bed.

When she was small, she was a Girl Guide. Could have taught a man to make a fire. And when she was in college, she wrote to me each week. Then she came back to the Farm, and it was time for the flower to bear fruit. Where has my jamun gone?

Nanu once said, *Amass your wealth, follow your desires, search for liberation in your own sweet time. It will come,* she promised me. *What you deserve. It will come in some form to us all.*

iv

September is passing; as the hot, clear nights turn cold, the breath of the monster goes from rancid to chilled, the hotel kitchens spew butter chicken, rogan josh, Amritsari spiced fish into the basti bins. The boys won't touch it—they know every dirty tributary of river starts here: they will eat no fish. Nor will they eat discarded club sandwiches—they don't trust the colour of the meat, the taste of white toastbread. They do not complain. From the dhaba TV they digest the news that Bapuji has begun a fast.

They gather for stories, telling and retelling what they saw in the grounds of the Palace: stone peacocks and birds of paradise, real blue flowers growing in every crack. Their own Rudra sitting between Bapuji and Nanu.

Gifts begin to appear at the Napurthala shrine:

A length of saffron fabric to wrap around Rudra's body.

A mala of sandalwood beads.

A packet of dry masoor daal—an aluminium cooking pot—a few dung brickettes like the ones Madam uses for her courtyard brazier.

The boys climb the rubbish pile and watch as the yellow brick wall of the Company Amritsar is fortified and topped with glass shards pressed into wet cement. A new guard comes to sit in the box at the back of the hotel. Samir's father, who used to sit there, can now be found in the ninth circle, singing from the rooftop of the Amritsar Minar. He has joined the drinking club of broken basti men.

His wife is dead. The night after the rally she followed her husband to the rooftop. Grieving for her son, she threw herself into the pit.

Samir.

Jeet heard the shouting from the roof that night. The men were high on moonshine, from inhaling petrol-soaked rags. He could have been up there, telling the drinkers (for Samir is dead) stories of what goes on behind the walls of the Amritsar hotel, where the clever boys who have been gifted tomorrow and all the tomorrows after that—who don't need to worry about food, or water, or where their lives will lead them (protected as they are by their father's money, their mother's creamy, cloudy rasmalai)—will not age. They will pass, comets trailing fire, they will be reborn as their own offspring and continue to dance to top DJs spinning the same songs over and over again, until the earth implodes to dust and becomes a burning star.

The vagrant men of the basti loved these stories almost as much as they love their petrol-soaked rags. They applauded Rudra's wilder anecdotes, as Samir used to do, they saluted him, as the boy did, they encouraged him to tell more. Jeet felt love for them in turn; he felt they were his real brothers. They burned whatever rubbish they could grab; they sang songs to the Company. Jeet danced for one night, or maybe two, through toxic smoke, flourishing imaginary money: O drunken uncle blessing the bride! Remember the bricks of notes Jeet used to trade in? Samir was there, and turned into Vik, who he could buy whatever he wanted. Jeet drank, the men with him, as if he was their Guru, and they were all young.

As for Munni, Samir's sister—Madam has taken her in, and she has become the seven-year-old leader of the gang paid to grace Dhimbala with her little dances. She used to be so opinionated, Jeet thinks, now she has learned how to smile. The few paise she earns keep her from starving. She will not suffer the same fate as her cousin-sister Sakina (not her real name), a girl who has gone mute since she was taken in multiple orifices by the men of Amritsar and Napurthala, in the chaos of the storm.

. . .

The new guard does not take much notice of the basti dwellers. No one brings him tea. All the boys can find out is this: he reports to "Jivan Sahib." This arrests Jeet. His energy sinks inside him and his spirits become low. The fever has not fully left him. When it rises, there is a new central character in his visions: Jivan. Jivan, sitting in his place at dinner, at his father's right hand. Jivan, laughing with Gargi and Radha. Jivan, drinking Cristal at an art auction in Delhi. Jivan, in the British Museum—in the Treasures of Kashmir gallery, picking out pieces for the Company Srinagar hotel. Finally, the one that makes him want to scream: Jivan and Vik, lovers. Jeet rolls himself a bidi; he climbs up the rubbish pit and sits, smoking as the night passes. So what if Jivan prefers women? So what if he and Vik have never met, and probably never will? Vik is still there, in Delhi. Probably, he is progressing with his life. Probably, he has hooked up with some writer-type who is fully out and knows everyone, who has a scene at a few city jazz clubs and never wears a tie— the kind of man, Jeet thinks, anyone would love and want to serve, who anyone would fuck with respect.

Jeet wakes before dawn in the settled stench of the basti, a starving pup pressed against him for warmth. He strokes the shivering body. The wet snout nuzzles at him. He pushes the beast away, and climbs down to the square to begin the day again.

Each day has taken on a new rhythm. Jeet wakes and sweeps his hovel; he sprinkles water on the dust. He makes his way to the field on the far side of the basti; he takes his turn to squat and shit with his phone before he goes to the square to wash his body at the pumps. *Man can get used to anything, as long as there is routine.* He returns to the ninth-circle shrine to say his prayers. He stirs his pot over a low fire, waiting for his mash to cook. Then goes to the square for morning Yoga, to collect water and oversee its distribution. Every day at 9 a.m., on the dhaba TV, Bapuji's speeches are broadcast from across the country; today he is at a rally in Maharashtra, an image of Gandhiji and one of Lord Ram on the backdrop behind him. From the camera angle it looks like thousands of people have gathered there.

—Then you tell me, who is the chor and who is the Saint? Bapuji asks. Dress a dog in a sari and teach it to nod—Madam Kuti is running the Company and who can tell, indeed? None of us should be punished for this state of affairs. Who is your master? Clean your own houses. Look at your daughters. Ask yourselves, choli ke peeche kya hai? Then check beneath their lehenga skirts. Find what stinks there. Filth. I am India. I am you, I am you, I am you, you, you—he jabs his finger through the screen.

Feroze Shah brings Rudra a cup of masala chai.

—What did he say, before this? Jeet asks.

—He talked sense, Shah shrugs. As all husbands know, if there is corruption, it is because women promise so much, and men will do anything for them.

—Gargi Madam, did he mention her?

—He said, "A mouse feeds the cat, the cat feeds the dogs, the big fish eat the small fish. This is the nature of the world." He has seen into our hearts; he knows our lives, says Shah. Rudra bhai, you were close to him. Is it not the case that he changes the common man's life for good?

Bapuji's words lubricate the basti from the Amritsar side to the Napurthala Palace. Slowly, the circles begin to move. Napurthali men of the sixth come with stones to the Amritsar side. They start pelting the Muslims in the fifth, shouting they must relocate to the far curve of the seventh or come work to clear the heaviest stones from the old Palace site. The Muslims in the fifth displace the castes of the ninth, they flood the Amritsar side, causing the circles to turn the other way. They plan to use the debris to build a wall between the circles, and the left-over rubble to fortify their dwellings. *"Build the wall, build the wall"* becomes the first-circle song.

The Amritsar-side boys from all circles come to Rudra under his tree; they demand he replace his made-up stories with Bapuji's latest sayings. They don't want imaginary worlds, they want to recite instead. The key dates of the Company. Arthasastra (abridged and updated). And, of course, the Manusmṛti. Jeet gives it to them. He gives it to them in Sanskrit for the schooled ones, Hindi for the rest, Napurthali for the boys who need basic letters first.

The classes grow. Boys he has never seen begin to join in. Jeet divides them by fathers, faith and basti circle, blurring the difference between Amritsar-side and Napurthala-side boys in favour of caste and sect, something more natural. He sets each group tests for a tournament he plans at the end of each week. He tasks them all to compete in Yoga poses and to sing the national anthem before doing eka hasta bhujasana in the dirt.

Then Jeet orbits the lanes with a select crew of boys, a stick in each hand, advising the elder ones to divide up the watch, to ensure every last basti female obeys a curfew of 6 p.m., that they always wear salwar kameez and do not come out when bleeding (even in their own hovels). Jeet oversees the plans of a rival boy's group, headed by the son of the marble wala in the second circle; they have heard his whispered sug-gestion to bring the city cows into Dhimbala square, designating the new Company Amritsar wall a place to tether them. They plan to care for them and gather their dung for cooking, just as they once did with Haathi the elephant. Some of the boys form a gang to pelt the Christian moonshine makers with wet rags tied around stones; Jeet orders rein-forcements from the resettled Muslim kids to help them tie their rocks more tightly and to admonish those who do not join in. The Katarias do not interfere as Rudra walks the circles, chanting his mantras with his boys. The Watch, they call themselves. Counting steps and hours and changing guard at Madam's bell, which (for her own protection) she allows them to use. Dhimbala is one-half naked, one-half mad. Rudra will keep it true to his vision of civilisation. The highest.

By the last week of September, Bapuji has been fasting for almost three weeks, devouring the headlines state by state. On the dhaba TV, his sup-porters appeal for the end of Company market domination, a return to a time when local traders were kings of their own affairs. Jeet watches this as—in the cold evenings, on the street corners all over the city—nightwatchmen huddle, sticks trying to spark. The days get shorter. A curtain falls: a yellow smog that scours the eyes. Oil lamps are lit across the basti. The fumes burn the slum dwellers' lungs.

One afternoon, Feroze Shah flicks through the TV channels and finds Gargi on FemmeIndiaTV (590, Star Plus syndicate). Jeet sips his tea. He watches her on the dhaba screen. She has aged; even through her smile Jeet can see new lines set around her mouth and eyes. She has cut her hair; it makes her look tired. The grey streak at her left temple has gone undyed for the first time. God, has she no image consciousness? Jeet is almost insulted by how old she looks. She's in saris—is that homespun? Each time, she appears wearing heavier and heavier jewellery. Her pearl earrings sit, two extra eyeballs on each side of her head. Gargi! Jeet remembers her fat tears on her fat cheeks; he wasted his youth trying to teach her beauty, she had a tendency to think that she always knew best.

It is not just the way she looks that offends. Uppal is always pictured in the background, nodding and smiling at every line Gargi says as if he has primed her for it. It's the news reports too. How she has renamed all the Company women with Western names; how she refuses to negotiate with any of the labour unions; how each of her hotels, each mall, each hospital has been built by workers brought in from out of state—because that way they don't have their traditional support systems, they don't know their rights. They are made to work without helmets, without shoes, without proper hours. And also how many have died, or were never compensated for their labours—how could she let all this become news?

Scenes of utter normalcy now make headlines. Here is one, of the Company brick kilns in Chattisgarh: men, women and children barefoot and covered in bright red dust working for less than eight rupees a day. The metro building sites where women crouch, breaking stones with their hammers, scaling scaffolding made of bamboo while the yellow, metal maws of Chinese diggers gorge on the land around them. Yesterday's newspapers announce: *No hard hats! No shoes! No high-vis safetywear!* These—against pictures of the rearing, seven-star splendour that is the Company Kashmir, being built while Bapuji is fasting. And on the back pages—ads for the winter season there. *And God*, thinks Jeet—*to go to the mountains, to the white quiet, white pool—just to swim in it.* Then Rudra shuts this thought away.

The newsreaders call Gargi *Devi*, for she never cracks. There she is, inscrutable, always smiling, speaking in considered tones about how she only became aware of the problems when she was given trust of the Company by her own father, just three months ago. How she has always believed in Bapuji, no matter what he did.

—How could a woman running her father's vast household and taking care of human lives across such a big company, be aware, let alone party to, such terrible abuses in other offices of the Company? This is what Gargi asks. And how could my dear simple sister Radha—who has never done more than support our father, who is known for her tender nature—be party to such intricate corruption? All I do is a matter of Company izzat. I have the ultimate respect for my father. She begins and ends every interview like this.

Rudra wants to gather up the basti shit and smear it in her face. The men in the dhaba jeer at her, even the drunks in the ninth start spitting her name. Few reports mention that under Gargi, the Kashmir hotel is the first eco-palace in the world—powered by solar energy, sustainable laundry, all furniture made of repurposed bamboo. Instead, the better magazines run exposés: *Cash for contracts! MPs Eashun Sahib, Vijay Sahib, Priyam Sahib under pressure to resign! Did they gift state building contracts to Bubu Balraj?* Government secretaries are named and three state ministers: transport, home and Bandha Pradesh. A roll call begins: those who made sure Bubu got the contracts to build malls in the megacities; who looked away as Bubu paid over the odds; who submitted budgets of four times what each state project would cost. Even the basti boys who once begged Rudra for stories of the fine, fine life he was last born to know that there isn't a light bulb on earth that costs three thousand rupees.

The mornings are brutal. Jeet crouches in the shitting field; he cradles his simple phone and rocks with it; he hums to himself, to block the sense of his bowels emptying. How has he got used to doing this? So used to it as if he was born this way and returned to the origins. Something about that thought makes his muscles clench and his calves shiver—he almost drops the phone. He scrolls through the spam messages in the INBOX folder, reading about offers for sure-fire lottery wins and big-breasted girls with wet wet * takeaway Punjabi desi khaana just text BALTI. He hums, warming his voice before class with the boys. Until one cold morning the phone vibrates gently in his hand. He stares at it—around him the other men's phones are doing the same—but still they don't look over at each other, even though what they have read has them all finishing up, on their feet, washing, wiping, pulling:

What, do you want to remain in the filth of corruption?
Are you a citizen of Bharat or a slave of the India Company?
Time to stand up! Time to walk! Time to run for Chandigarh,
    and Delhi—where SRI DEVRAJ BAPUJI is waiting to join
    hands!

Come join the Everyday People! Fight against the disease that
blights us!
Pickup is coming. Txt your basti ki naam to 76877. Await your
bus!

Jeet makes for the square, where the men of Dhimbala, the Amrit-saris, even the Napurthalis (tattooed and not), and many he does not know, who have no history, are gathering.

—What is happening? Jeet says to the nearest man.

The general murmurings amount to this: that Devraj has called to those who gave him succour three weeks ago, during the great storm. He is sending buses in the next one hour to bring them to Chandigarh to join his cause. They must be ready at the Napurthala Gate.

The news sweeps through the square, sand on the wind. The people stream back through the Amritsar Gate in the opposite direction of flood water. Around the pit, around the lanes, to the designated place.

There are six buses—some missing windows, some with missing seats, some that have no doors. All driven by local men. Each passenger is given a plastic cup of water with a pierce-able film and a pointed straw. A picture of Ranjit and one of Devraj hang garlanded over the driver's wheel. This knowledge—that even his father is working against the girls, against even Radha—seeps into Jeet. He has a sudden longing to see the old man's face, to see if he can't fix things again. To see if, after all, there might not be some way they could be honest with each other. Just to see.

Four hours or five. The bus rattles down the highway. The women sit at the back with the children, the men are at the front. The driver stops, to hand out foil packets with a cartoon picture of a long-armed monkey in a cap, eating peanuts and grinning. Jeet takes a window seat in the third bus. It has been years since he last went to Chandigarh. Built by a Frenchman to a socialist dream. A modern grid city realised in concrete the Company had not won the right to pour. Jeet has never cared much for the ways it picked and chose its modernity with accessories from the old Mughal city at Fatehpur Sikri, as if there was no other tradition to reference. And how will the people of Dhimbala fare in a grid system?

For Jeet the city has never been about streets; instead it is all about discrete places linked by doing time in the car. The best bar in which to find a dirty martini, the best quiet, shadowed beauty spot in Lodhi gardens in the mornings. These places to him were (alongside the best bakeries and coffee shops and certain tailors with roof gardens in the block markets of Greater Kailash) what a city is made of. Jeet did not know how to walk in Chandigarh, he found its avenues too exposed.

The bus rattles through the suburbs and reaches the caged streets, turning right and right. Stopping. No idea where exactly—but from the bus it seems over three thousand people have gathered. A sea of banners painted with slogans: *Quit Corruption, Company Quit!*

Rudra slips through bodies to get to the front. He can sense Ranjit's hand everywhere—money has been spent—the people have no chairs but there is a dais with a table draped in white, there are speakers for Bapuji's voice. The PA system plays the national anthem; the mothers calm their children with nursery rhymes. Many are not basti dwellers; they have scooters and cars; their children have nannies, private tuition, badminton lessons and plans for month-long weddings bigger than this gathering. Would any of them share out what they have equally with the people of Dhimbala? Join hands, actually touch? Or marry their daughters to the sons of that place? Of course not. *And nor should they,* he thinks. Dharma does not ask this of them; all dharma asks is that they fulfil their own destiny, as it is written.

Bapuji seems small on the dais in his vest, dhoti and cap. Behind him is a vast picture of a lotus flower, a tiger, one of Gandhiji and one of Subash Chandra Bose. To his left are twenty-five young men dressed as Bapuji. Who stands at a lectern, the bright orange of his scarf a beacon to Jeet over the heads of the crowd.

Bapuji points his finger at the sky. A hush falls. There is no breeze; even the clouds seem stuck in place. This is not the storm-tossed Dhimbala refugee, with his sudden rage. This is Bapuji, backed by his twenty-five young men; he smiles as he points his finger, points it, up, up! He opens his mouth—Jeet takes a deep breath, as if he, not Bapuji, is about to speak—then, as if reciting something he learned for this moment, Bapuji says,

—What about you, the people? We deserve freedom. We demand answers from Gargi Madam. When can we expect them? Time to cut the culprit of corruption, creator of poverty, causer of displacement, builder of unsafe houses, trafficking in Kashmir for love of money, breaker of laws—The Company.

A cheer sweeps back through the crowd. Forgiving Bapuji, founder of the Company, shifting the blame to his daughters. But drugs and violence and hotels must coexist, Jeet knows, Bubu knows, Radha and Gargi know—this is how their elders taught them to maintain *the delicate balance of life in the forest*—and now Bapuji wants to overturn it.

Jeet could tell them. He knows, he knows—that Bapuji is speaking the truth. He has worked the drug route, seen the gun stores; he knows every back lane in Srinagar; every houseboat secret deal. Terror holds within itself the promise of a prosperous future. He wants to stick his hand up and shout, *I know!* as if he is the best boy in the class.

He looks at the dais—one of the young men is standing there in Bapuji's place (it could have been Jeet: if he had stayed that night, he would have had every single one of these people eating from his hand).

—The Company was begun by Bapuji to thrive within India's borders. Decades have passed since Bapuji gave his daughters every opportunity that any loving father would. Yet they have been siphoning off money from the businesses, paying off with gifts and bribes, trading on their father's name. Are any of you shareholders?

—Us! Company Bricks Division! A group of Sardarjis in front of Jeet shout.

—Yes, many of you are, Bapuji's man says. Check that your bonds are not being stretched to breaking. The love between fathers and daughters, Company and customers, is sacred as the farmer's for our beloved prithvi. This is one of the reasons why Bapuji is here today: more than even his own family, he loves you. He demands the government investigate his daughters, to end their stranglehold on democratic India.

A woman in white jeans and a pale, woven shirt is standing near Jeet, her arms hooked around her small daughter. A Munni lookalike, but for her fairer skin. The child has delicate silver clips shaped into butterfly wings in her hair; they flutter as her mother, hands on her shoulders, rocks her side to side.

—How bad those girls must be to make Bapuji hate them so, the mother says to her daughter. See what happens when you misbehave?

Around them a sudden cheer rises. Jeet looks to the dais; Bapuji is shaking his joined hands at the crowd, including all of them in his grip. He releases, and points at the sky again as he walks off with his men.

See, Rudra? thinks Jeet. *What a man can do to inspire, with a pointing finger and a mastery of words!*

The last of Bapuji's men stays behind, waiting for silence. The space behind him looks desolate now, littered with half-drunk bottles of water and empty chairs.

—Until the government takes action against the Company, and removes those ministers who have enhanced and benefited from its bad deeds, not one word more will come from Bapuji's mouth. He has taken a vow of silence and will drink only water straight from the tap, purified by nothing more than fire.

—Devraj Bapuji zindabad! shouts Jeet. Jumping, jubilant, he punches the air with the others around him—and in the jostling crowd takes a moment to pick himself a BlackBerry from a turbaned businessman's backpocket. Phone upgrade toh karna hai, no? *Devraj Bapuji zindabad!*

—Devraj Bapuji Zindabad!

The crowd is joyous around him. *Company Cut-off!* they shout.

That is all. Bapuji's man makes his way off the stage, his arms in the air, embracing the applause, or perhaps surrendering to whatever will come next.

Jeet boards the bus with his new BlackBerry, ready for the long journey home. What a thing it is to hold the life of Prem Singh in his hand. He has Facebook, Twitter, WhatsApp, hundreds of pics of Prem's lovely wife, his three studious little girls and the Punjabi Aunty XXX app. He has 3G. And an Instagram full of cars and bars and watches and bowls of homemade daal garnished with half a boiled egg.

Jeet feels breathless as he scrolls through Prem's Twitter feed. He loses hours as he stares at the phone—as #*CompanyCutoff!* begins to trend. He checks @MrGee, which he loves, but there is nothing, nothing, nothing about the rally. Around him, children doze, clutching their new toys. The women, sitting together at the back, crunch roasted chana and pick over a plan: they will order the men to go and occupy the Company Napurthala grounds, to work on the gardens and restore the building—payment to be forwarded to time of completion—for has not Bapuji promised rewards to all who support his cause? Yes!

Jeet only half listens to the chatter, the road noise. What would Samir say if he could see this beautiful device, given as if by Bapuji himself? Rudra would give Samir the old phone, and then they could call each other. Jeet holds the smooth black plastic to his forehead. He finds his eyes are wet.

As they pull up at the Napurthala Gate, Jeet checks through the accounts one last time. A new post on Facebook—Prem Singh offering a reward of Rs 1000 to have the phone back—a new tweet from his account says—*#CompanyQuit! And my phone back too*—Jeet checks @MrGee again—all there is to read is a cynical tweet about the rally, Bapuji's pointing finger, girls and skirt lengths. *Shame*, Jeet thinks, clearly @MrGee wasn't there.

That night the moon is obscured by smoke. Jeet keeps the phone tied in his putta, next to his head. He cannot sleep. He spends some time scavenging on the dump, looking for implements for his fighting boys.

Madam's bell begins to ring. A group of boys come running from the first circles, down the basti's boards, screaming about an eyeless demon making its way to the fourth. They are followed by waves of sound as if the earth's heart is being ripped out and emptied onto the dump, raising sleepers from their shacks; Rudra scrabbles into the fourth circle, the smog is so thick, he thinks the sound is coming for him. He follows the oil lamps to Madam's courtyard, where one electric light bulb hangs suspended over a group of men: bandwale, hijras, boys, have gathered around something in the yard. When they see Rudra, they let him through.

A figure is at the centre; its shirttails hang loose over the rolls of its belly, it has soiled itself. What is left of its face is wrapped in blood-soaked rags. A man, blinded—a Company guard beside him. A two-headed beast.

The prostitutes whistle and call from their balconies. The blind man's hands grope towards Madam, who is bringing more light outside. She stands in the centre of the group—Jeet can see—he *knows* those shoulders, that head. From the back—he knows the man—he moves around him, reaches forwards and grasps at him. His stomach heaves. *Ranjit.* He opens his mouth, and to stop himself laughing he begins to chant:

—Om, Om, Om.

Ranjit scrabbles for the sound. Jeet kneels; he finds his cheeks and ears being pinched and pulled, his dark beard yanked. Around him, voices demand to know what has happened—who this man is, who has hurt him, who? Chanting leaves Jeet's body shaking—Ranjit does not know him. He wants to say, *I'm here.*

Then a group of Madam's women push into the centre of the circle, surrounding Jeet, his father and the guard.

—It is our duty to take care of the blind, says one. Half her face is covered in a burn; the rest is obscured by her chunni.

Ranjit makes a sound. A whimper. He holds one arm out to keep them away, the other on the bandage over his eyes.

—Take him to old Mumtaz, she will heal him, says another girl, pushing the first aside. She also has burns, Jeet sees—from chin to neck-line, as if the acid had dripped into her mouth and spilled from there down her throat. The gathered men are staring at the women, at Ranjit—all of them caught under the light.

—Back off. This from the Company guard; his tone carries a warn-ing, and he raises a hand up against the women.

Jeet can see the guard's face. It seems streaked with blood, his shirt is missing. He realises it was used to make the strips covering Ranjit's eyes.

—Put on curd and ghee, or egg whites, says a whore; her two small children hang around her neck like mufflers.

—Eggs? Are you crazy? Who has eggs to waste right now? shouts a band wala (the French horn, or is it the cymbal?).

Now Rudra is pushed this way and that; he falls back, someone steps on his hands; if he gets close to Ranjit again, he must speak, he must tell him the truth, he thinks—but then the whole basti will know that for all these weeks he has lied. Sick to his eyes, his throat dry, he lets the men push past him, listens to them dispute what to do.

—He cannot stay here; more trouble for us.

—We already have too many blind—and this one is not even young!

—Hospital—take him to the hospital.

—Are you stupid? Do you want to bring the police down on your head?

—What is your name, old man?

—Chup! snaps the Company guard. The men draw breath. Who are you talking to? This is Ranjit Sahib, who owns your sorry skin!

The babble stops. Madam shakes her head from side to side. The torch bobs in her hand. Shadows splinter the smog and Rudra's laughter spurts up in him again: the men haven't even recognised Ranjit. *Lord Krishna*, Jeet thinks, *has a wry sense of humour.*

The men and the girls, now silent, stare. For the second time Bhagwan has brought a Babu here: a man with so much wealth. This one, their own Sarkar, is weeping blood in front of them. Jeet looks up: the younger girls shrink back on their balconies, awed, fearful.

Should he speak?

—Ayo! Madam shouts.

Two girls bring more lanterns from inside the brothel; three carry out a low cane chair, they guide Ranjit to sit. The men watch as Madam herself goes back inside; she brings a bowl of warm water, she kneels next to Ranjit in the dirt. As if she does this often, she dips the corner of her dupatta in it and gently wipes Ranjit's pulped face.

—I had a son! Ranjit moans. He left me to this—may his punishment be to see what he has done.

Rudra turns hot with grief and rage. He squeezes his own cheeks; his breath melts into the fog.

—Who did this thing? a basti man asks loudly.

—I tried to help, the Company man says from behind Ranjit's chair. I tried to intervene. My dear friend Ramchand also did, now he is dead.

Ramchand, Radha Madam, Ranjit Sahib, Bapuji—the names pour from the guard over Ranjit's head; Ranjit begins to wail again and Madam soothes him. Jeet can only hear snatches—tiny piercings on his skin. Smoke rises from the dung burning in the brazier; it chokes the Company man, he coughs. Then he tells them more: he tells them to look at Ranjit Sahib's bandaged eyes, to look at his own chest, in a singlet under his jacket on this cold night.

—My own shirt, I tore, he says. I bound Ranjitji's head. He wipes his face with his hand. It would have been just one eye. But Radha Madam demanded "the other one too." As if selecting bangles for her wrists.

The man coughs again, he looks around at them all.

—And now Bubu Sahib is dead. I know, says the guard. I killed him.

Jeet feels the Dhimbala men take a few steps back. They stare at the guard; a fresh sense of fear hangs suspended in the fog. Then, a spitting out of something—rage, excitement? Jeet feels it in their bodies, their tone. The shouts begin: *Burn the Company Amritsar!* The replies come: *We should not!* A whore calls down from her balcony, *Hey you! Why are you trying to be Amir Khan?*

—Someone should take Ranjitji to the hospital, the Company man says. Or to the police station, and leave him there.

—Would you? says Madam. No. And neither will any of us. The people of this basti do not need town justice. We do not go voluntarily to them.

Rudra remembers Samir telling him stories of those places: a cousin who suffered a near-fatal beating for the smallest of crimes (the stoning of the CCTV camera, the cutting of its wires). There were rumours of cattle prods and electrodes. He drops to his knees at his father's side again. The broken body is trembling; somehow, through his bandages, Ranjit is weeping. His pains so visible, Jeet thinks of the night he crawled through wire to escape the Farm. Of that life, now absolutely gone.

—Quiet, quiet, Madam shouts. She flicks her shawl around herself; her bangles chime up her arms, glass bangles, the kind brides give to their women. The sound reaches the men's ears. Look at them, how it calms them all. Every man here—except Jeet.

—He should go to Delhi, to the campaign. He should go to Bapuji, the only one who can protect him, Madam says.

The men stay silent.

—Yes. Let him go to Delhi, to Bapuji, says the Company man.

The men around Jeet murmur. *Yes.*

—We have a bed here, Madam says. Mumtaz can come tend Ranjitji among my women, and he can rest until he can walk. He is not the first blind man she, or any of us, has known. Any dissenters? Any of you think Lord Ranjit Singh should not enter into our house? She laughs. Are you willing to take him in?

She looks around at them; her lamp casts her face half light, half dark. She waits.

—Good, she says. Now you. Rudra the Naph. She pulls a small drawstring purse out of her sari blouse. From inside, she picks two notes; she looks around the men, all of them Amritsaris, she elbows them out of the way, she shows the notes to Rudra—a ten and a five.

—Go to Mumtaz, she says. Tell her to come back if she wants this; bring her if you want a share too. The rest of you, back to your beds. Not a word about this to the Katarias, or anyone outside, until we get Ranjitji out of Dhimbala to Bapuji.

The men in the courtyard watch while Madam and her girls help Ranjit inside. Then, arms around the guard, they lead him towards the ninth circle, to tell them more, to drink.

The dung-smoke fucks the smog and births a sickening pall, picked up by the wind and carried over the basti that night. The rats squeal as Rudra makes his way through the lanes, around the pit where Samir's mother's body still waits to be recovered; the municipal authorities will not allow the Jhimbas time off for this task for ten more days. The woman is already dead. *What does it matter?* thinks Jeet. Ranjit has been blinded by Radha, the silly girl whose clothes he always thought so *try-hard;* who he, Jeet, used to tease to tears for her matching purses and earrings. He stops to be sick, now, not from fever returning, but the sight of his father's face, his body. Radha did this, with a stick in her hand. What was she wearing? Her signet ring. Perhaps Bubu joined in. Bubu, who is dead. *Where is Gargi?* Jeet thinks, as he slips through the lanes. A few dogs run beside him before turning off to follow some other scent. He passes his own hovel, then the Naph shrine. Feeling his way, trying not to be sick again, he reaches Mumtaz.

He knocks gently on her shutter. He waits. It opens a crack. He gives her Madam's message. The shutter closes again. He waits. A minute in the dark. Mumtaz comes out of her hut with her bundle, she gestures to him to follow her. Gaps seem to open up where there were none before; she turns between the circles, winding the lanes around her feet instead of obeying their logic. They reach the fourth when Jeet thinks they should only be in the seventh. They come out flush to the brothel.

Madam is waiting, smoking her bidi in the courtyard. She gives Rudra the five rupees and the end of her smoke. She takes Mumtaz inside.

Smoke the bidi, Rudra, stay by the smouldering brazier. Just as fire is obscured by smoke—he can see no stars. The rats scuttle, their claws on the tin roofs scratching his nerves. He waits, shivering in the doorway almost until dawn. He is dry, he has lost the need for water or for food. He sleeps until the door opens. Mumtaz steps over him, looks down at him, and pushes him gently with her foot. *Go inside.*

· · ·

Rudra expects the inside to be pink with drapes, incense and candles, to smell of disinfectant and fish. The next scenes should be hallucinatory—women and singing, curved flesh, long hair, whispering. The bell has not rung for customers tonight—yet he expects to see men, watching, touching. But inside he passes small cells, each doorway covered with a thick crewel-work curtain (birds in branches, singing). Each cell is small, he thinks, there would only be space for a single bed and perhaps a cupboard, a mirror, in there.

Madam unlocks her room—a corner space, laid with a carpet—Jeet cannot remember the last time he walked on such a thing. In a corner is a cracked sink. A bucket of water lies next to it, a tin bowl floating on top. Madam gestures to Rudra to wash his hands. Then she unlocks an inner door and takes him to Ranjit.

Mumtaz has cleaned his eyes and applied herbs and fresh bandages. She has left pain balm, the sharp colour and scent of lemons. A sleeping drought, made of who knows what. Now Ranjit seems to be dreaming, muttering in his sleep. Jeet leans over him, without touching him.

—What's he saying? Abbaji, what are you dreaming? he says.

—Jammu and Kashmir, Madam says. Amarnath.

Ranjit hears her; he seems to wake. He raises a hand a little. Jeet bends low, ears to lips.

—Let me go there again, and climb the mountain, Ranjit whispers. I need to feel God's healing breath in the land of the lotus root. Let me be led to Amarnath by one who has no fear of death. What does anyone care when we die? He falls silent.

—All night he has been raving, says Madam. A Sikh prince begging for Hindu blessings moonlighting in a whore's bed. What a moment! Weren't you heading to Amarnath, Rudra, Naph Sage, traveller, when the charms of our basti stopped you in your tracks?

She grins at him.

—Poor Rudra, she says. Poor Samir.

He ignores this. He looks down at his father.

—What should I do?

—I always thought you had such smooth skin, Rudra, for a traveller. Such clean hands, Madam says. So refined. Someone has to take him from here. Someone who can pass easily outside with him and get him to

Bapuji. I've heard the stories you tell the boys. Only you remember the way through the city. And were you not blessed to be Bapuji's pet only three weeks ago?

Jeet wants to stop her voice. This room is so sterile; there is nothing soft about its brick walls, its concrete floor. The carpet is outside, waiting for him. He remembers seeing Ranjit's arm around Jivan. His father is now shivering, silent. His eyes are bandaged. Jeet knows that Rudra's time is almost up. Madam is right: he must face it—love, gullibility, rage.

A day later, the Company man comes back to the brothel. He waits in the courtyard. When Rudra comes out, he gives him 2000 rupees in two slim bricks of 100s. He says in a week, when Ranjit has recovered enough to be moved, he should bring him to the Napurthala Gate, where Amrit, his second wife's nephew, will meet them with a car. He gives Jeet a cloth bag; inside is a kurta pyjama for Ranjit. A Company uniform: shirt, pant, cap, which is meant for Rudra.

—There, he says. Naph or no, the nights are cold. Keep warm in the cloth of the Company, even as you follow its hero to God.

Jeet holds the money. How fresh it smells. How solid it seems.

—Thank you, he says. The English words come with difficulty, almost through tears.

A day and a night passes; days and three more nights. Mumtaz comes and goes. Jeet sits with his father after he has finished his rounds in the basti. His boys circle the lanes, ensuring that everyone is inside before dusk, that nobody is gossiping about Ranjit, or what anyone saw. Their recitations continue; their bodies strong with daily Yoga. The dhaba TV churns out news of the campaign: in Delhi, Bapuji has set up at Ramlila Maidan. He is still fasting. No drop has passed his lips. On the fifth day, they hear he has been arrested, put into Tihar Jail. A crowd has gathered outside, demanding the government release him. In Kashmir, the Company hotel is almost finished. And Gargi and Radha? No comment.

Madam hardly speaks to Jeet as she brings food and water to Ranjit's rooms. He absents himself while she feeds Ranjit and cleans him. She has told her girls to keep as quiet as possible, even as they go about their business. Jeet can still hear the men, coming for them.

So can Ranjit.

Sometimes, he moans—*Radha!*

. . .

In the dawn of the seventh day, Rudra washes in the square. He wraps his Shahtoosh, and then his bright cloth around his legs and ties it. On top, the Company jacket and cap. He does not even think anymore about mirrors. Or wish for them, at all. He combs his beard with his fingers, he stands under the neem tree, his hand pressed against the bark.

The guard box is empty. The dhaba shutters are closed. For the last time, he goes through the Amritsar Gate and walks the circles of Dhimbala until he gets to the fourth.

He goes into the brothel to collect Ranjit. Madam is waiting with him at the door; she has dressed him in white and wrapped him in a duncoloured quilt. Jeet thinks his father looks like a chaukidar. So, they go through the deeper lanes, the image of a gatekeeper and a Saint.

It is cold before sunrise. He thinks they are not followed, though enough people see them go. Except for the dawn patrol of Little Amar, Motu and a few of their friends, the basti boys are all sleeping. At the Napurthala Gate, an old, white Ambassador car is waiting, a young man leaning against the bonnet. Jeet does not know this person, but the car is familiar—it is from the Company Amritsar tourist fleet; they hire it out for wedding nostalgia. How shocking to see it here—but why? After all he has seen, why does this old relic seem strange?

The driver, Amrit, is short. He wears his bomber jacket and jeans, his white T-shirt, as if revealing new buys from the mall; he has a way of flicking his wrist out that shows off his watch—a Timex with a thick silver bracelet. He has a bowl cut over a moon face and a gap-toothed smile; *cute,* Jeet thinks, then realises the boy has a habit of chewing chicklets as he talks.

At least Amrit has brought five one-litre bottles of water and thirty homemade mooli paranthe in a round, steel tin.

—Just as a snack, he says. He chews his gum and starts the car. He tells them the journey should take seven hours, according to MapmyIndia. He has never used the app before—has downloaded it just for today.

The basti recedes. Jeet holds his father's head cradled in his lap, he is dabbing at the tears that trickle every now and then from under the bandages

Mumtaz applied. Jeet is wearing a borrowed, too-big Company uniform; it keeps him warm—he feels warm for the first time in weeks. He opens a bottle of water. He drinks slowly, carefully. He is aware of the money in his pocket.

—Amrit, take the back routes, he says. Find us some village for our first meal of the morning.

They cut off the highway.

Jeet has his Prem BlackBerry; Amrit has his Samsung Galaxy—from these, they learn that in Delhi, Bapuji has been released from Tihar Jail. A crowd has gathered on the streets outside, lining the route to Ramlila Maidan where a vast tent is waiting to receive him, where thousands have gathered to see him. He will appear, it is promised, still keeping his fast and his tongue.

Ranjit drifts in and out of sleep. For an hour that morning Jeet, too, closes his eyes to the sound of chewing gum and the road. Then Ranjit screams. His arms come up, trying to claw at Jeet's face; Amrit swerves, just missing a boy who is driving an old woman sitting sideways on a motorbike. Her sari catches in the wind, sending ripples across her body. Amrit honks his horn. He rights the wheel.

—All good in the back? he says.

—All good, says Jeet. Next village, we stop.

Ranjit seems calm again. In his white kurta, his bandaged face, it is hard for Jeet to remember that so many women have sat on his lap. So many have stroked his beard.

—What is your name? Ranjit whispers to Jeet. I will call you *Yogi*, for I know you are my guide.

Ranjit seems to think that they're driving north. He talks about the days he spent taking tea before going hunting through palace gardens. Sometimes he seems more awake, giving Jeet and Amrit a masterclass in the true history of the Company and its spoils. So they learn that the child-sized, custom-made, automated, open-top, four-seater Mercedes Jeet was gifted for his sixth birthday (complete with Company walnut interiors, the Company shield replacing the Mercedes badge in the centre of the wheel) was bought with the profit from high-interest loans, granted for the cultivating of land for cash crops in Punjab. Jeet and Gargi played Mummy–Daddy in the front of that toy, driving Jivan and Radha around in the back, making them stop for pee-pee or picnics on the Farm grounds: lamb patties and Company Cola. Aged eighteen,

Jeet's birthday gift was the life-sized version: a white soft-top and matching 4×4 with customised interiors and the number plate JIT. Bought, Ranjit laughs, his head lolling on Jeet's thigh, with interest paid by farmers through Company part-owned banks across the backward states. How lucid Ranjit seems in these memories. Each one more familiar than his own son's hands on his face. Jeet holds his palms above his father, batting the one insistent car fly away.

As Amrit takes the back roads, with flat fields and dirt tracks running alongside, Ranjit begins to hum old freedom songs. Jeet claps his hands over his mouth, feeling his beard prick him. He tries not to tell his father to stop. Instead he asks for the radio—and gets Punjabi love songs, songs from Bollywood hits and weepies. Sometimes, even Madonna.

They drive for an hour or more. Then stop for breakfast at a small dhaba on a back road next to a tyre garage. Posters of Bapuji's face, caught mid-speech, mouth open, eyes squinting, his finger pointing upwards, are plastered across a square of wall. Twenty or thirty Bapujis, each laid over the other, so Jeet has to piece together the saying:

> *Don but such apparel as will cause the cold to flee.*
> *Eat but so much food as will cause hunger to cease.*
> *O Mind! Devote thyself to discernment of the Self and of the*
>   *Supreme,*
> *And recognise thy body as but food for forest crows.*
> *JOIN THE RAMLILA GATHERING—TEXT 88676 FOR*
>   *MORE*

Jeet looks at his own strange attire. At his father, all in white. He thinks about where they are going. Can he arrive in Delhi, like this? Hours have passed; already the basti seems so far from here, childhood seems nearer. Amrit buys them hot tea, he places the cups on the ground so he can help Jeet pull Ranjit upright; then drags a red plastic chair to the car so Rudra can sit by the open door, and feed small bites of cold parantha, watching his blind father lick his lips, and sigh.

—Here is Ranjit Singh, the living evidence that God is great. You will not age if you keep your wits in service to your country. Are there any gulab jamun here?

Amrit and Jeet look at each other, then Amrit shakes his head. He goes for a smoke with his phone, standing under the posters of Bapuji, again, again, again.

On the road again, Ranjit strokes Jeet's arm. His voice turns melancholy as he tells stories Jeet has heard four hundred times before.

—*But listen,* says Ranjit. We are travelling—stories are for retelling—

Jeet keeps quiet. He thinks that it might help Ranjit to stay alert, alive even, if he recalls meeting ambassadors and other dignitaries: Bush, Blair, Idi Amin (who Amrit has never heard of). Mrs. Gandhi nos. 1 and 2, shaking them all by the hand while giving and receiving gifts passed down to one of the divisions or another. None of which were ever accounted for; some were re-gifted to certain friends—a member of the Hundred perhaps, who was destined to shortly join the Company anyway. No tax levied for them.

—This is not corruption, Amrit says, raising his hands from the steering wheel. Rudra bhai, this is the way of the world. A great business was built.

—But we must move on, says Jeet. The way Gargi and Radha are conducting now—you must understand that it cannot continue—that is what Bapuji's campaign is about. This is not the India I imagine. Did you know that Christians believe that by repenting, a man can be reborn in this life?

Amrit did not know this. All he knows about that faith is that when they gather in their churches everybody sings, not only those trained to recite their holy book.

—And is it true, Rudra bhai, that they also eat God's body and drink his blood? And actually marry their girls to God before they even bleed?

Jeet does not answer; he is listening to Ranjit's breathing. Outside, somewhere, the fields are burning. It is the end of the harvest. Black smoke rises in plumes—five, six, seven of them, against the white sky. A dry, choking taste of roasting wheat penetrates the car, making Jeet's eyes water, making Amrit cough.

Shame stacks up—cards in a poker hand as Ranjit keeps on talking. Revealing the how, the when, the where, the jack, the ace, the king.

Jeet could tell his father who he is. He could shout at him —*Why don't you know? Are you fucking with me, Dad? Are you? Are you?* Silence has become a habit too precious to remove.

Ranjit's face feels burning hot. He tries to turn on one side then another, but the back of the car is no place for this. He sighs: *Sita.*

Jeet leans over him.

—Shh.

Lying on his back with his knees bent, feet pressed against the door, Ranjit sleeps.

They stop in a small market, three or four stalls arranged around a roundabout, for a lunch of chana bhature and gulab jamun mashed into its own juice. They share a long table where men look at them—a Sanyassi dressed as a Company guard, a stocky driver with his thick Timex, ek andha who should be resting in a bed. Jeet tells them he is taking Ranjit to Delhi and to Bapuji. Ranjit hears him: he bangs his spoon on the wooden table.

—You are no one, you do not know our way. We will go to Chennai, we will take the Company tunnel, though it is not yet built—we will go to Srinagar and from there to Amarnath, where I will make the ultimate sacrifice, he says. His voice breaks.

Amarnath—everyone at the table knows it is too late in the year for this. No one protests.

—Rudra, Ranjit says, will you accompany me to the Rishi Bhumi? To the holy shrine? From there, you will see the sacrifice I will make. I will go from that place, to make amends for this life.

—I will come, Rudra says.

He watches the faces around the long tables—their smiles as he comforts Ranjit—as his father grips his fingers so tightly, he almost loses feeling.

Jeet raises their joined hands above the steaming bowl of channa. The warmth of the dhaba washes over him.

But Ranjit is not used to the food from the street. As the day falls into afternoon, they have to pull in at least two times an hour. Jeet has to help Ranjit to the roadside toilets, where even the sweepers waiting outside say *chi chi* under their breaths at the mess he makes. Once or twice Jeet feels wistful for the open basti field, the sky. In the car again, he soothes Ranjit, chanting the Gyatri Mantra, then singing the chorus to "Dum Maro Dum" in Rudra's high voice: *Hare Krishna Hare Ram, Hare Krishna Hare Ram, Hare Krishna Hare Ram.* He amuses himself by doing both: the ask and the response. When evening begins to fall, he switches to "Aaj ki Raat"; he knows this film song will keep Ranjit's blood up. *Aana hai kya? Hona hai kya?* What will be, will be. Ranjit has a sudden desire to sit up. Face outwards. Though he cannot see anything, he claps time.

Twenty kilometres outside Kurukshetra—a town Jeet has always wanted to go to but never has, for fear of being disappointed by its banality—they stop again for sweet chai. The night market is beginning; girls in jeans and bindis and sweaters and bangles, all clutching their binders, arrive in twos and threes to walk the strip, to text each other, to stop and meet outside the sari emporiums, though they do not go in. Young couples and small families stop for frozen yoghurt, it is almost November—Diwali is coming; fireworks are on sale outside almost every store—while on street corners groups of boys meet to smoke and stand around. Bollywood serenades the street with tunes Jeet doesn't recognise from films he does not know. It is so long since he passed through this world. It almost seems too bright, too full of young people, all shopping, all talking—not seeing that here again, on every post and bin and shop front, is Bapuji's face and finger, pointing them to Delhi.

Jeet imagines himself standing, now, on the roof of the car, shouting. *I am here to tell you it is time to renounce your old lives, to follow in Bapuji's example! Join his sacred fight. We must take our protest from Delhi, where Bapuji is sitting in silent fast from lying words, to Srinagar, the paradise on earth which belongs to us. It is time to take a stand and join Team Devraj!*

They would all join in with applause. It would be as the Chandigarh rally, when Bapuji inspired every person to cheer for him.

Instead, Jeet sips his tea. At the newsstand he picks up a copy of *The Economic Times;* it has a cover on Surendraji, "Mr. Gargi," who is now acting CEO of the Company board. He is quoted as saying, "After the first crore, one stops counting." He has never been involved in corruption, has not taken any part in the business so far: this is well-known. Jeet flips through the *Times of India* for more; he finds that Surendra has also finally made it as author of the *Speaking Tree:* "Potting the Hole: The Purpose of Dharma in Business."

Jeet reads the column in the cold air, tasting, with vicious guilt, his own satisfaction that Surendra's point about dharma is actually quite crude. Surendra is only being published here to steady the Company share price. Flicking back automatically to check out the Page Three people, he finds instead a picture story of Bubu's funeral. He looks up to see a bank of TV screens in a SONY store showing late-breaking news—an insert of Amrit's uncle, the Company guard, an iPhone video of him being arrested for Bubu's murder earlier today. Jeet checks his Black-Berry: Twitter has the story—and more. Alone in his cell, Jeet learns, the Company guard beat himself badly, perhaps to show his remorse. Then he took his own life with a leather belt he was wearing, which happened to be just the right length.

In the car, Amrit is silent, his jaw clenched. He grips the wheel. His phone is on the seat beside him. Ranjit is sleeping on the backseat.

—Move over, Jeet says. I will drive.

How strange it is that eyes, hands, arms and feet remember how to indicate, clutch, accelerate, check rearview, shift stick, change lanes. Amrit stays quiet, sometimes looking out of the window, sometimes texting. Jeet wants to tell him not to mourn; his uncle, the guard, was a martyr and a hero, who has sent Amrit to Delhi to join the highest cause.

But Ranjit is sleeping and Jeet has not driven a car for so many months; this old model has a sticky clutch. So he keeps quiet and watches the road, letting Amrit's silence fill him.

The highway widens into seven, then eight, then nine lanes. Jeet swings the car through narrow gaps between scooters, taxis, jeeps, estates. They pass an elephant lumbering towards some groom's baraat, a trumpet player in a tinsel waistcoat squatting on its neck.

—When will we reach, Sita? When will we reach? Amarnath! Lord Shiv, to you I am bound. I want to touch the lingha that waxes and wanes. So sighs Ranjit.

Although Jeet is driving, he can't bear to look as the road becomes more and more familiar. Here are the Wedding Farms where at least four brides' fathers will be hiring space for their betiyan tonight. There are the stone slab outlets; then the low houses, the shuttered markets. The streets seem free compared to the gridlock in the daytime. Jeet speeds around the ring road as if taking mountain passes with a wish to die. Ranjit begins to snore, comforted by the swerving car. *Stay still, old man,* Jeet thinks. *Dream that we are about to enter the blasted heart of the mountains.*

The air gets thicker. The yellow smog they left in Dhimbala has beaten them to this place. It muffles all noise; it almost blocks any view of the road. Jeet passes over flyovers and under the metro highlines, ignoring the sleeping enclaves and high-rise blocks; the city comes towards him, low at first, then more and more vertical, dizzying—how he used to be proud of every inch of concrete and glass, as if he had made it himself. Now he feels the road to be an old friend he has outgrown—there is nothing here he cannot face—he has been driving this route since he was sixteen years old. He moves the little car through and around; the metro stations are lit above them, strange portals of night. He gets lost around Satyagraha Marg, takes a right, a right, and a right, and a sharp right—then realises he is quite near old Delhi Gate. He cannot reach the centre; the car is surrounded by people walking in ones and twos, fives, tens and groups of twenty, carrying torches and tricolour flags. A river of boys, men and women—more than Napurthala or Chandigarh—moving through the smog towards Ramlila Maidan. Where Bapuji is holding fast.

Jeet stops at the side road. He tries to wake Ranjit and help him up.

—Have we reached? When will we reach? asks Ranjit; he is hardly able to stand alone.

—We still have some way to go, Jeet says. At least we have so many others to keep us warm! So many pilgrims have gathered to march— there must be five or ten thousand people here—the biggest crowd we have seen. Everywhere, against the night, saffron, white and green flags are waving, the centre wheel spinning in the wind. A group is coming towards us, singing.

Jeet's breath fogs in front of him; he is glad of the Company jacket, the remains of Bapuji's Shahtoosh underneath his Yogi's wrapping. He feels himself a thin spike amongst the Puffa-protected youth. Some have Bapuji masks on—some have painted their faces with flags—some are carrying *Sita Devi* banners with pictures of Sita with Bapuji from months ago—and most have Gandhi caps. Sita Devi! None of them take any notice of Jeet. A young man walking near to them veers away, as if their smell, even in the smog, is of Dhimbala.

This, after the whole long day that began on a Tuesday night so many months ago, makes him want to shout.

I am here.

—I can't feel any hill at all, says Ranjit. Have we reached?

—Almost, Jeet tells him, right into his ear. Stay close to me.

He looks back for a landmark—the car is parked sideways, like a dash, next to a Company billboard for a new eco-car. Jeet supports Ranjit—it is difficult—Amrit is on the other side, quiet, withdrawn—Jeet feels as if he is carrying both of them. He looks around at the flashes of Burberry lining, Ralph Lauren fur, at the Zara, Mango, Marks and Spencer, Woodlands, Kim & Kareena; the soldiers of India's newest civilisation are on the march, mixing with those from the outskirts of the city, the towns and villages Jeet and Amrit have just passed through.

Here are the people of the new model army. Jeet wants to gather them to himself. There are no airplanes here, no trains or cars. Not even a bicycle can pass. Jeet has lived to see it: when, finally, the people go with their feet. Some waving flags, others hoisting their homemade banners. *Now is the time,* he thinks, *when every person must choose. Whose world will it be? Jeet's or Sita's? Will the people want an heiress girl or a self-styled warrior of dharma? A man who has survived every circle of this earth to rise, here, now? Or a woman with nothing but her name?* He tries to make out individual faces, but the night limits his vision: all he can see is labels, clothes.

Watching Bapuji, Jeet has learned: flatter the people—they demand it. Show them purity to mask decay. Observe the rituals and call it freedom. Offer them riches blessed by God. Money, health, happiness, individual, family, nation—what more is there in this life?

Jeet will build an ancient tribe of modern men, in thrall to all he can promise. He will harness their sadness and their rage. He will put them to work in the service of God and country. He shoulders his father. Around him the people are feeling their way through the smog. *If a man is blind, he can be led,* Jeet thinks. He stores this knowledge inside himself to use one day, when the time comes. In Kashmir.

Faces loom out of the darkness: half brown, half in white masks; those without use their scarves against the smog. Everywhere Jeet sees police on their mobiles, and private security in checked shirts and jackets, headsets and walkie-talkies, sniffer dogs. There is a smell of onions and frying—somewhere food is being made to feed these thousands.

They push forwards into the rally grounds, following the lights. An ocean of bodies sits quietly facing a stage, empty except for the table swathed in white, a microphone on a stand and the backdrop—two huge pictures, one of Gandhiji and one of Bapuji, wrapped in white with a string of marigolds around his neck.

—Have we reached Amarnath? How can that be? says Ranjit. I can smell pakora, I feel quite warm. I can sense there are people—but why is nobody moving?

—No—not Amarnath, Jeet says. He presses his eyes into their sockets until bright saffron garlands bloom behind his lids. Then he gives in. Can't you feel the sweet high mountain winds on your face? Thand toh lagni chahyie.

—No, really, it smells of potatoes.

—Imagine you are in the fresh mountain air, Jeet says. He nods Amrit permission to let go of Ranjit. Then he walks his father slowly around the outside of the tent.

—There is thick smog everywhere, he says. The ice is all around.

—Yes! But how poetic your voice sounds now, almost as if you have been educated, says Ranjit.

—No, not at all. You are imagining it. I am exactly the same, only with a better jacket, which your kindness has given me.

—Do not argue with me; I hear what I hear.

They reach the front, where, despite the security Jeet has seen, the bamboo barriers are easy to slip through. There is a ramp leading up to the stage. They climb it together. Rudra the Naph in his saffron cloth wrap, his sandalwood mala, his black beard hiding his face. Ranjit in his dun shawl and white cap.

—Old man, dear sir, Jeet says. The high slopes of the Kashmiri mountains rise around us. The snow line. The black, jagged rocks. The ice bridge, where, if you walk in spring, you will fall through a crevice so deep your body will petrify there. We cannot reach the ice of Amarnath, we are lucky to have made it this far in such cold. We have driven through walls of solid white. The road is about to close behind us. And if only you could see how majestic the mountains are! It is midday. Can't you feel the pure light reflecting off the hill? Can't you perceive it behind your poor eyes? I can see, when I look down, the tops of the eagles' wings, swooping below us, chasing sparrows small as mice. I can hear the saffron pickers singing while they bend to their tireless work. Listen!

He helps Ranjit up the slope onto the stage, he sings into his father's ear,

—*How pink is saffron's colour, Collecting it into heaps we are bathed in sweat, soon too soon, it will be humid in the city. Enjoy its glorious view, O Samad! How pink is saffron's colour!* It's wonderful! Sir, there is a boy carrying stones on his head trying to clear a path for the pilgrims. What a job! He is an ant carrying a crumb to its hole. The donkey boys are down where we began, trying to get a fare for their raat ka khaana and there are pilgrims climbing up, carrying their bundles as topknots. Men and women, all of us climbing, climbing—Hai Ram, but the height, the distance down, I'll feel dizzy! I cannot look down from such heights or I will fall.

—Move and let me stand where you are, says Ranjit. In a wavering voice, he begins to sing.

Om bhur bhuvah svaha

Tat savitur varenyam—

Then he tumbles forwards, flat onto the stage.

—Hey Uncle, what happened? You fell!

Jeet kneels. He shakes Ranjit, sitting him up.

—Did you slip? Who was with you? Can you stand? Hup, hup, that's right. That's right.

—I can't see, says his father. Ek admi mere saath tha . . . ek basti wala.

—You are lucky, Uncleji, God has blessed you today. Now do you see? You're in Delhi with Bapuji, at Ramlila Maidan.

His voice gentle, his arm around his father, Jeet leads him back, into the masses.

—Ladies and gentlemen, we welcome Bapuji! one of the men onstage shouts into the mic. Feedback screams around the tent; with a shock, Jeet sees Kritik Sahib—and with him, Bapuji. In a clean white kurta, a garland of marigolds tied in a circlet around his old head, instead of his neck where it should be.

—What is happening? says Ranjit.

As one, the crowd stands. It begins its cheer—Mar! Mar! which rises, rises until Jeet wants to leave Ranjit and jump back onto the stage, to shout—*I'm here, I'm Jeet, and Rudra, your boy!* But no one would hear. He is too far now from the day when Rudra was led by the hand through the welcoming crowds at Napurthala.

On the screen above the stage, Bapuji's face is in close-up: he looks truly unwell. His eyes shift here and there, his skin is sallow. *It must be true, then,* Jeet thinks, *he has refused to eat anything for weeks.* Now one of his Hundred steps forwards with a microphone. He announces that *he* will address the crowd with something Bapuji wrote while inside Tihar Jail.

Rudra steps back—he thinks he knows this spokesman, his father is a high-ranking civil servant. Jeet thinks he may have even taught this guy's sister how to kneel (and apply the correct pressure, depth and movement for maximum satisfaction, a service to her future husband, of course). Under Jeet's trousers the Shahtoosh chafes him: he wants to change for Bapuji. In Bapuji's smile, in his gaze over their heads, Jeet sees Gargi when she needs something she cannot ask directly for. He waits. Ranjit also waits, his face so wrinkled, as if he has been held underwater for too long. Camera crews, radio, newspaper journalists—is that *Ashutosh?* Mobile phones—everyone is waiting. The Company owns shares in all networks, Jeet thinks. *How much money will Gargi make tonight while her father is here?* Feedback screams around the stadium. Bapuji, who has not spoken for a week or more, opens his mouth. He points at the crowd. He laughs.

—Mice! Has anyone brought a cat?

—Is that Devraj? My old friend? says Ranjit to the air.

Bapuji clears his throat; his face turns serious, and he ignores all the men behind him onstage still jostling each other. One of them, in a police uniform, is speaking into his phone.

—So many of you have come to see me. So many of you have stood up and asked me to help you solve the problems in your lives. Don't blame yourself, young man, if your wife is a cheat. Everyone in the world fornicates—this is nature. Mice and elephants, all do the same. What do you say?

The crowd roars, *Bapuji!*

Five thousand voices, business types to fresh college girls and boys— the everyday people he has come to know—all cry:

—Mar! Mar! Mar! Mar! Mar! Mar! Mar! Corruption, Mar!

The stage lights flame and die: an energy surge and blackout. Thousands of mobile phones are held up. In this forest of luminous fruit, the chant possesses Rudra; he may never need food or water again, so what? From the first Napurthala rally, to Chandigarh, to the basti boys, looking to him for guidance—to this, all of this, eyes watching him, hands clapping him—he is soaring, his senses stretched as if flesh has no matter, so beautiful, so dark and so light.

Then a rush of dark shapes; the cries turn to screams. People fall over each other across the grounds, pushing over him, pushing Ranjit. Police shout back—Arrest! Arrest! They storm through the tent, picking people up, kicking them aside. The crowd splits and falls, running in all directions. The stage is all confusion.

—Ranjitji, we must go, Rudra says, pulling his father backwards, thinking *where can we go?* He almost has to carry Ranjit through the smoke and dark; he feels stones pelting around him and starts to weep—white smoke mixes into the smog—tear gas. He must get out, for Ranjit's eyes.

—*Me, mine, mine;* Ranjit moans. Then, somehow, they stumble out of the Maidan. Swept along with people trying to escape, they reach the road; the car is still there under the Company sign. Amrit? They cannot wait. Jeet buckles Ranjit into the back of the car. He takes the wheel. Reverses through the crowd—then they are clear—they fly across the city. Jeet breaks free of the old town; he crosses India Gate, all the way back, around the dividing, ruled streets and endless circles of the Imperial city. *Welcome home,* say the empty avenues—then, past the townhouses of the Princely States, the vast gated bungalows with their secrets kept safely in cupboards—he is home! Jeet's foot presses down on the accelerator as hard as he did when he was younger; he races the lights down and down, around the flyover where silver balloon sculptures rise from the traffic island as if celebrating this return. Past Aurobindo and INA, follow the yellow line under the ground, until he reaches Qutb Minar, and from there to the white maze of walls, the bumpy track that is never fixed. Slow, slow, turn, and turn, and turn—to the Farm.

At the gates Jeet slides his window down, enough to show his eyes. He clears his throat, a driver on his best deference.

—Come to deliver a gift to the hosts. Koi hai? he says.

—Nahinji. Surendraji is in Mumbai, Radha and Gargi Madam have gone to the north. Jivan Sir is with them.

—I have brought Ranjit Sahib, he says.

—Where are we? says Ranjit.

At his voice, the chaukidar takes a step back. *O!* he says. Grins. Then, the gates swing open.

Rudra takes the perimeter road to his father's cabana. They pass no one; the smog has settled low over the ground and the car lights bounce off it, casting every tree and shrub into a many-fingered demon. Why does he expect to see the whole place ransacked? The grass is neatly trimmed. The little flowers in pots and tubs are freshly watered. Over there a piece he had forgotten—a red sandstone sculpture from fifth-century Uttar Pradesh, the boar avatar of Vishnu, rescuing the Earth in the form of a sunken woman, lost at the bottom of the sea—still presides over a pristine, lunar strangeness.

He settles Ranjit on the outside porch. It is swept, the glass-topped table empty but for a crystal ashtray holding a box of Company matches, contents waiting to burn. Inside, the rich smell of leather polish and dried roses soothes him, and he thinks of the food he will order, the drinks he can drink again. The soft bed is waiting: in an hour he could be clean, be full, be asleep. The nightmare almost over, his season in hell. He opens the second bedroom cupboard. Finds a wool suit and a linen one, looped with a striped collegiate tie, hanging in dry-cleaner's bags.

He prowls up and down, not speaking; he stands for a moment in the dark-panelled lounge, turning on the television, catching a Star Plus serial, switch, an ad for a skin-lightening face cream, switch, a new type of refrigerator complete with happy Bibi, *keeping the goods fresh for longer,* switch, a new kind of paint for the outside of the house, that keeps *itself* clean, switch, some kids in Benetton brights, jumping fully clothed off a pier into the sea, to the slogan, *Inko InCo pasand hai! Fun! Fun! Fun! Fun! Fun!*

Inhe, Jeet thinks; FFS; even the slogan is corrupt—the first word should be *Inhe.* He switches again: to a Hollywood film about the end of the world. The Statue of Liberty is submerged in water and only her torch is visible. The President of the United States is being taken to safety. It takes Jeet a moment—then he realises—the movie has been dubbed into Hindi, the white men are speaking brown. He switches again— NDTV—there it is: the end of the rally. The police are using sticks to push back the crowd. There have been reports of tear gas: a college girl is crying as she supports her friend from the grounds. Bapuji himself has gone. It is believed his youngest daughter, Sita, was with him. The Company concerns are at an all-time low; the state must answer for this outrage. Who sent the police? Who is running the Company? Is this any way to operate when the Kashmir hotel is at stake? Jeet waits for the screen to go dark—for someone to realise the cameras have gone too far (does the whole country need to see this?). The reporter is called Nina; she's a standard pretty girl, Jeet thinks, wearing glasses and a Nehru collared shirt. She says,

—What is really going on here? India has a right to know.

—*Mar! Mar! Mar!* the crowd's demand echoes.

Still holding the remote, Jeet goes back outside to his father. A golf cart is pulling up across the green. The driver jumps out, starts towards them.

Jeet's heartbeat slows then speeds up. He steps back, into the shadowed doorway to the house, feels a rushing in his ears, a sandstorm memory. By the neat jacket and rimmed glasses, by the unassuming posture, he knows who this is: Uppal.

—Aré wah! Uppal says, his hands up as if praising God. So the chaukidar did not lie. Here you are, Ranjit, you mad old man, why have you come back here? Don't you know there is a bounty on your head?

He is at the porch stairs; he stands, grinning, waiting for Ranjit to answer.

—All this time, Uppal says, we have been looking for you, while Radha Madam has been left a widow. You should die just for that.

—Bhaiyya! My friend! shouts Ranjit.

Jeet cannot move. Caught by the memory of evenings under the neem tree, listening to the boys and their questions. The sound of the rally coming from inside—Mar! Mar! And Uppal on the dhaba TV, always smiling, speaking for Gargi as if he were her *father*.

—Who are you, meri bhen ki lodi?

Jeet watches Uppal—knowing that his eyes will only see a Sage in orange robes and secondhand Company jacket, a beard that covers a face.

—Why is this holy man here with you, Ranjit? Are you seeking spiritual guidance after all you have done? Do you realise he is only here to get some reward? And you, he says to Jeet. There is a prize for someone to hurt—are you ready to forfeit?

Uppal reaches inside his jacket, Jeet steps forwards into the light. He sees Uppal's mouth drop, his head go back.

—You, he says. Returned?

Something happened next—so quickly—something was glinting in Uppal's hand—Rudra saw something glinting—a blade—maybe the kind one uses to gut fish—and he thought: *If Rudra dies now, on this night, there will be no one to witness his passing, or care.*

—*Aré bhai sahib,* Jeet chattered. He heard himself high-pitched, strange. *Na maro, main aapko haath jod ke bolta hoon. Aré bhaiyya, joke mut karo, mujhko pata hai aap aise nahi kur sakte, yahan anja karo, mut ao, na, mut ao,* keep out, no entry, sir. Also something about mercy—yes—he begged Uppal for mercy. His throat dry, limbs shivering, blood surging, he picked up the ashtray and brought it down hard on the corner of the glass table. It was stronger than it looked—the surface held, the ashtray splintered and Jeet had a ragged-edged scythe made of glass. *What does it take to kill a man?* Behind him, Ranjit was shouting, the sound rushed through Jeet right to his burning eyes. He launched himself at Uppal, twisted his free arm, grappled him to the ground—as he used to when he was a boy and Jivan was the chiru and their father would shout,

—*Kill! Kill!*

Uppal screamed.

Rudra leaned all his weight in, bending Uppal's head back, finding the tender part of his throat, his windpipe an apple core. Then his arm tensed—Uppal's eyes bulged as he struggled but he could not escape the deadlock of knees on chest on arms, hands on head, head bent back, neck exposed and begging. Jeet straddled the panting man, seeing a tongue, teeth, the dark cavern of the voice, then he ripped across skin in a deep gash. There was warm, thick redness. Uppal's screams ended on a gurgle as his muscles and gristle split under the pretty shard in a red, red smile. The blood gushed out all over the grass, soaking Rudra's hands, his knees. Uppal shuddered, went still. His face washed by tears. Whose tears? Falling from Rudra's eyes onto skin stretched over bone, grinning in surprise that death could come so quickly, that hands could work in this way to clean the world of those who should not be in it.

—Has he gone? shouted Ranjit.

If you could only see, Jeet thought. *What your son can do.*

He kicked the body. Its mouth gaped at him. He slipped his arm into Uppal's jacket and found that his hand was clutching a silver phone: he pocketed it.

Then he dragged the body to the side of the house. Blood, a thin red carpet trailing behind them. The smell of the pine forest just beyond the road. Mixing with the taste of sweat. Uppal was heavy for a small man, and for the first time ever refused to cooperate. How accommodating he was alive—in death, he flopped this way and that. His blood escaped from his body to the earth. Jeet got to the back door of the bungalow and paused at the washing step. The body was warm: he was grateful for it. Then he bumped it down the stairs to the basement, its feet twisting, its hair tangling in his beard. Jeet swallowed some, he couldn't help it. Defiled, he propped the body amongst the filing cabinets and shut the basement door.

Killing is a natural part of war. Killing in sacrifice is not murder. Jeet stands in the bathroom, red from collar to heels. For the first time in his life he comprehends the sacrifice of appadharma, all conduct that must be undertaken in times of great crises. He turns on the shower, the water is bright orange; it washes his feet.

From his father's mirrored cabinet he takes a gold phial; he rubs a mix of pure jasmine and rose oil into his skin. His bones are near the surface, his muscles have hardened. He takes scissors, then a razor to his own head and face. Curls of hair drop onto the floor, into the sink. Jeet reveals himself anew.

Savour his eyes and mouth and nose. Savour the clean lines of bones. Savour the rush in his blood, the ache, signalling something he has not allowed himself to feel for months.

The things he left behind are here in his father's cupboard. A silver kurta he cannot believe was ever his. His jeans. Washed, pressed, put away. He takes a T-shirt from Ranjit's drawer, he wears his jeans. He cannot fit his feet into his black sliders anymore, so keeps his basti chappals, with socks. Here is his own phone: *his phone!* His wallet, full of cards. He packs a small bag with as much money as he can find in the house. He keeps the Company cap, and wears it to shadow his face.

Outside, Ranjit is slumped in his chair. From shards of glass Jeet picks out the matches; he uses them to burn the remnants of Bapuji's Shahtoosh. Phut! It is gone. So do truly pure substances burn.

Where can he take his father? There is only one place where no one will think to look for Ranjit, where no one will take notice of his moans. A set of rooms above a butcher's shop, where all that mattered was two young men together, bound by the names they chose. There, Jeet believed he would never grow old, nor die. There was love, a bed, and happy ever after, and the only person Jeet has ever trusted. He will take his father back to Old Delhi with half the bag of cash. Money, faith, happiness. He will leave Ranjit with Vik.

—— • ——

TIHAR JAIL? Is that where you thought I was?

O no, that was Kritik's idea—he set it up for media report only. We did this for the cause, and as we gathered voices across the land, and as we gathered feet marching for us, people came to us. How to incentivise them? From all walks of life? This takes skill and strategy. Storytelling helps. We gathered a hundred, and another hundred, and another, and every hundred gave another hundred, mobilising towns and cities, sweeping us back into consciousness, reborn.

We fasted and kept silent for purity of heart, thought, word and deed. For India, beloved country, we urged the crowds, keep your legs closed, mouth open, hand to mouth, eyes shut, receive the word through the orifice that cannot be blocked.

Stories are a prison as much as a release.

We gathered backstage at Ramlila Maidan and we waited for our cue. I had not spoken for days. And nor had I taken a drop. Of comfort, water, finger chips or sauce. For every grain of rice has my name on it.

Fast girls, fast cars, fast times. Faster, faster through the years, tear through the pages to the end.

Fast.

The only thing I lost is weight. The definition of corruption? Money into goods, services into pleasure, bodies into her bodies, his bodies, their bodies all bathed in their value on this earth. Pay to escape, to remain. Is it all not so fleeting? We are all at the mercy of other tongues. Living our lives in translation. I am India, I told them. I am you.

. . .

Burning ashes float on the wind. Red hot, scorching the night. Huff and puff and burn. When the wind changes, burn the books for warmth.

Excuse me. Mr. Stinku, is that you? Can you see me?

The river at the back used to run fresh and fast. Five storeys falling down in this house—each panel, each joist was once carved and settled gracefully in its place.

In the basement a bitch has given birth to a party of pups. Yip-yip! She growls, to keep us off them. We may hunt with them, or hunt them, see if we don't! And see how she growls! They are safe. We are all safe here. We are watched over by this lovely angel with pretty brown feet, turning above our heads.

I heard they threw the bodies of the Pandits and all the ones they wanted to hide into the Jhelum. I heard that some got eaten. No. This must be a lie. But see, they were the ruling class. And now, their school-houses are broken, their stories are kindling. That is the way of this world. So it keeps turning.

Since then there has been torture and death. Whole Temples devoted to this, in the name of the mother, Mama 2. I dwell on this? We all do. Profit on it, to survive.

Before the end must come we shall have to dance. And offer some comfort, in the form of Sita. Kind hands, gentle eyes, yesterday. Under the forget-me-not sky.

Tonight, Diwali night, there will be fireworks. A new Company citadel will open up its doors. The brightest-lit, most hidden of houses between north and state. In the Kashmir Corridor, the weapons to blind are cocked.

Prepare to be amazed.

Silence to the people!

V

—.—

SITA

i

And all of them are still waiting for her to say *sorry*. Sita lights her cigarette. Inhale. Exhale. She will not say where she has been all summer—
there are other stories to tell. She will not tell them that she can now say
"lost" in the Tamil. Ilantu. And write this word in curling script: its first
letter looks like a woman sitting cross-legged, her dupatta cast over her.
Ilantu. She does not know the word in Kashmiri, but has learned to say
this, at least:

—Vakhet kyaah aav?

It has been a week since she came here. To Srinagar, city of her father-
desires and mother-dreams. Driving through the night, straight from the
protest in Delhi to Jammu, then resting in Jammu for a day and most
of one more night before moving on to Srinagar. Kritik Uncle in the
passenger seat, dressed as if he just came from the village: a turban tied
to obscure most of his face. Sita in the back with Papa. He slept, mouth
open, his head against the seatbelt.

They reached the city as dawn rose. The light was pale gold, and as
they drove down the boulevards the chinar trees shed leaves on them as if
they were the winners of some game-show final. The city was still, shuttered. Sita caught her first glimpse of the lake, so serene. On every side
the mountains rose. They astonished her.

Kritik Uncle says the safe house is owned by a friend of her father's. It is a
concrete box, newly built, turning its grey shoulder to the old town. She

asks about it—she knows her father cannot legally own land here; nor can she, or her sisters—she knows her mother's childhood home is still standing, somewhere in the old town—she does not understand how the hotel has been allowed to blur the lines of Article 370, which tries to keep everyone a part of its control. She knows the law on paper—and so, she knows the Company hotel should not exist. She asks, as loudly as she can:

—Why are we even here?

Kritik Uncle does not reply. He begs her to keep quiet for her father's sake. They are in Srinagar for her, for him, for the campaign. Opening night is coming. He's planning something. What?

For now, the safe house. Five rooms on each of the three floors. Most are unoccupied. Each room dark, unpainted concrete, bare light bulbs. Unadorned walls, doors to ante-rooms, doors to bedrooms, inner doors to bathrooms. All of them stark, barely furnished. She has a set for herself.

A bedroom, her own bathroom has two inner doors, connecting her resting place to Papa's. All of the rooms have such small windows.

When they reached Srinagar, a male nurse was waiting. The house also had a cook, a potwasher and a bearer. They insisted Sita undress her Papa herself. Since then, every day, she has had to see him almost naked. Underneath his kurta are two surprisingly pointed breasts, crowned by mahogany nipples, puckered lips always waiting to be kissed. His bones are a visible cage keeping his heart in place. Trying not to look at his body, she sees instead a crumpled map. She does not want to read it, but she has to. Now the tributaries of his veins swell blue beneath his skin then fade as if running dry. His hand trembles when he gestures for her to come close. She has seen his wasted muscles; he makes sucking noises as if kissing her doggies, they used to yip-yip around him. Then he stares up, for applause. She smiles at him—but he becomes uncertain. He stretches his hand out to her: his fingertips are splitting open in sharp, vertical cuts. The nurse says he is exhausted, that all he needs is time.

Papa's room is the same as most of the others in this house. Empty except for thick, handwoven carpets laid wall to wall. The only real furniture is an interloper: a steel hospital bed-chair, its sidebars and straps keeping him safe. Sita thinks he should be in rural England being nursed by aristocratic girls with names like Abby (for shelter), Florence (like the bulbul) or Megan (her skin pale as flushed pearls). Better he go to Switzerland or Dubai and rest at some hushed private clinic, where cutting-edge medicine would restore him. But to leave India right now would look bad: Bapuji needs to be here, in Srinagar, for the opening of his hotel. *My protests*—Sita thinks—*the streets*—*my plans.* Campaign ke liye, yahin rehna hain, Kritik Uncle says.

So. Here is the bed-chair, and Papa. Sita's hands learn to administer, her voice to soothe, her ducts to produce tears.

Papa is just a man, lying, spent. When he sits to eat, he stretches hairless, skinny arms, palms pink and empty across his knees. Waiting for her to feed him. With what?

His body is bony yet his flesh is heavy. When Sita tries to turn him, he grabs at the ends of her dupatta, forcing her spine to curve backwards. When she takes his weight, her muscles scream. Kissing him feels as if she is kissing herself. The texture of his skin seems to become hers when he grips her: her own hands have aged sixty years. He smells sweet—the way baby monkeys do after milk. His head nods towards her breasts, and she wants to run, to bite, to kick, to do anything other than be gentle and smile. Outside, she knows, there are little birds, punk-haired and brown-breasted. They come chasing, whistling through the trees, and land on her window sometimes. She wonders if her grandmother sees them, hanging out of the balcony of her sickroom in Napurthala.

Kritik Uncle has been coming and going from this safe house, for all of these months. Keeping an eye, he says, on the progress of the hotel. Papa's followers from Delhi, from Jammu, from Srinagar itself, come and go. Most are men she has not met before now. They either try not to look at her, or gape at her like cows, without the intelligence. She has attempted to speak to them—hello, please, thank you—but they are listening for her to say—what?

In Papa's safe house, there are no books. All Sita has with her is her Tamil–English dictionary, bought in the summer and carried all this way. Between its leaves she has pressed seedlings. When she sits with the dictionary, no one disturbs her. For an hour or two each day she can be lost in its roots, branches, leaves.

Lost. Definitions and Meaning of ilantu—in English—
Adjective
- not caught with the senses or the mind
- unable to function; without help
- no longer in your possession or control; unable to be found or recovered

Examples:
· lost friends
· his lost book
· spiritually or physically doomed or destroyed
Examples:
· a lost generation
· the lost platoon
· not gained or won
Examples:
· a lost prize
· having lost your bearings; confused as to time or place or personal identity
Example:
· perplexed by many conflicting situations or statements; filled with bewilderment
Examples:
· bewildered and confused
· a cloudy and confounded philosopher
· incapable of being recovered or regained
Example:
· lost in thought
Noun
· people who are destined to die soon

Ilantu. In her daydreams she is dressed in shorts and a T-shirt, roaming the ancient kingdom of Polonnaruwa, sleeping in a tent and rising each morning to find she is sharing her bedroll with bald-headed macaques. Nervous and trembling in the day, at night they creep under her canvas to find warmth against her skin. They blink at her with reptilian eyes from the beginning of the world. They leave her a gift of poop and pee-pee. They have adopted her while she works to keep them safe.

Inhale. Exhale. *For the eco-warrior-Indian-daughter, there is no such thing as a Duty Free smoke.* She stubs out the cigarette; ash falls on the pages of the dictionary, she wipes it. Burned paper absorbs back into itself. She marks the page with the pressed, dried seed-pod of a *Hopea cordifolia.* Endangered, almost extinct. She closes the book. One day she will return.

. . .

She wants to go outside. Just at the end of the street the beautiful morning is waiting—a hopscotch of warm and chill. Sita cranes her neck—she can almost feel the market bustle, taste freshly baked moons of girda and lavasa. The hot bread smell reminds her of Cambridge on winter mornings, coffee and a Fitzbillies Chelsea bun. Spinning down King's Parade on her bicycle after nights spent studying or drinking or debating, climbing Castle Hill to watch the sun rise over the town. It was a small hill, but it was something. Up she would climb, and stand, then run down. The whorl of bread, currants and sugar was her climber's prize.

She breathes on the glass and writes her name: Sita. She watches a woman in a black chadar go along the street; her small daughter in hijab and smart school kilt and blazer skips next to her. The two are holding hands, talking, maybe about school—What will she learn in class today? The little girl looks up at her mother, she says something and they laugh, then the two turn the corner and disappear.

All her life, her sisters have told her of times they spent in Srinagar. Radha liked to talk about her first sight of snow. How she had to hold Gargi's hand because Nanu told her to, when all she wanted to do was run and slide and tumble, to dig like an arctic doggy, right down past the cold. Radha would climb into her bed, show Sita how the little pups made their lairs in winter. *Radha loves her bed so much she should marry it*—this is how they used to tease her. Gargi's memories were of studying in the library of the Grand Palace, while Papa and Ranjit Uncle worked to make deals. The smell of their cigars. That is the kind of thing Gargi remembers. It would have been 1984.

Papa always told her the city belonged to her, and he would make sure she got it. She let him talk until she could not hear him anymore. At college, she read every India book and article and blog, every passionate report and counter-report from the archives of the world's media, its NGOs. She watched vlogs of activists and of patriots, collected blogs of triumph and of resistance, ordered books of the dead by poets and playwrights, journalists and peers whose words have left her weeping—lines of black-and-white mourning blurred until they seemed to be waving to her.

In 2010, when military curfew shut Srinagar down, when one hundred protesting teenagers were shot by Indian soldiers, Sita was safe in Cambridge. She organised student seminars, she invited speakers, she wrote to journalists, she excavated, debated and discussed her own mother's history—had plans to visit her mother's people, still in camps in Jammu. People, camps, cities—these things existed for her in the space between words and life. She held film screenings and put up posters of every movie made in Srinagar since her parents met. The anti-Muslim films starring Indian army heroes, the gangster flicks of local resistance. The independent men with their movie cameras: screening their lives for a festival world. The disappearing sons and the heartbroken women; even the bittersweet lovers of *Kabhi Kabhi*. Feeling Gargi's hand smoothing her hair as she watched that one in the dark. Transfixed by the land behind the actors—lush and green, hiding so much sorrow, no cause, no cause. And realised it was not enough. And tried telling herself this was not all in her hands.

Somewhere in this city right now—she has read—an Indian director with a passionate mind is scouting locations, for the first film to be shot here in years. She wonders, if she met him, what story he would tell her. Would he ask, as someone always did in her sparsely attended seminars—in the lectures she organised—why her father, a man so dedicated to his nation that they call him Mr. India in the West, was opening a hotel here at all? What would she answer? *I don't know.* Maybe this director would want to talk with her, as no one else did, about her mental state, about the state-sanctioned rapes of women and girls, the blinding of boys and men with pellet guns and rubber bullets. Maybe he would ask her to answer with her body for Papa's hubris, for her sisters' myopic obedience to him.

She longs to explore. She knows she should not be here. Kritik Uncle says she is free to go out, but so far it has been "discouraged." She wants to find her mother's house—and, no matter what Kritik Uncle says they have done, see her sisters again.

A week since she arrived. On the first morning she sat with Kritik Uncle and they were served kahwa, rich with cinnamon and saffron, in china mugs painted with English flowers, wild irises, yellow gorse. A selection-plate of Parle biscuits was offered and accepted. Sita poured the tea, Kritik Uncle took a biscuit; he told her that over the summer, while she was gone, power had turned Gargi's head.

—Now she is playing at directing the Company. Sorry, the India Company. What arrogance!

Kritik Uncle snapped the biscuit. He ate half, then half, brushing the crumbs from his mouth. He said that though Gargi herself tried to delay the transfer of shares Ranjit Uncle wanted to gift Sita, it was an issue likely to drag on, to remain disputed in court for years. It would be the thorn in the Company's side. He wanted to try to re*solve* it, he said. By presenting Sita and Bapuji to her sisters on opening night, with everybody there.

He called her "Sita beti." He said that she should have more power than Gargi. He took another biscuit; this one he soaked into his tea.

—And Radha? she had asked.

He sucked on the biscuit and called Radha a *junglee. Chi chi chi chi chi.* Now—Kritik Uncle said—she is eating all night, sleeping until noon. Cutting up her suite. Refusing to travel without at least twenty-five security men for the shortest of excursions, sometimes demanding even more. He said that he was not surprised—because, as everyone knows, there was always hysteria on her mother's side.

As if this could not be any worse, he told Sita (and though she already knows, it shocks her to hear it):

—*Your Bubu Jiju is dead.*

Bubu! Sita liked him best of her two brothers-in-law. She thought he was an asshat (his own word)—but for every cigarette he stole from her, he let her smoke one of his. He teased her about her idealism but she always felt he respected her for not toeing the family line. Poor Bubu. He didn't deserve what happened.

As if he could sense he was losing her, Kritik Uncle had said,

—Do you know Bubu and Radha almost killed a man of mine, by letting him burn in the sun? Then, your father was made to feel so unwelcome, they forced him to brave the great storm. Now look. He is as broken as the Napurthala Palace.

—I want to see my sisters, she said. Kritik Uncle, you promised once we got here, we would go to them.

He promised that as soon as the moment was right, they would go—drive through the city and up the winding road, new-built for this exact purpose, to the gates of the new hotel. She had to trust him, he said. She must wait.

She asked Kritik Uncle about Jeet Bahiya. He had told her instead about Ranjit Uncle's illegitimate son, Jivan Singh, who had come home from America and—here Kritik Uncle stopped and cleared his throat, once, twice, again—was now taking care of Radha, all the while becoming indispensable to Gargi—closer to her than that kameena Uppal ever got. He said:

—And do not even question me about Ranjit. Blinded. By your sister's nails. Gone.

Hiding her shock, Sita asked, *Where is he? Where is Jeet?*

There were no more biscuits on the plate. Kritik had looked at her, shaken his head.

—*I don't know,* he said.

He has no idea where Jeet is. This, after all, makes her believe that every other story he has told her is true.

She paces her room in the safe house. She thinks of Gargi doing the same in Delhi, never able to share her feelings. Always so critical. Dressing Sita in pink when she begged for purple, blue, yellow—anything else. Always talking about her achievements loudly, in public, while pushing her out, out and away from the family, into the world, sometimes so emphatically it felt as if her sister didn't really want her around. And Radha, who taught Sita to smoke and to shave, who peeled a banana behind Nanu's back and used it to demonstrate the difference between blowjobs and handjobs and the texture of sperm, which she made by squeezing the banana into mush, when Sita was thirteen. Radha—her sharp, silly jokes and her kuch-puch words, her MrGee Twitter (which she thinks no one knows about)—neither of her sisters ever mentioned Jivan, in all the years of growth.

Sita locks all of her inner doors. By herself in her bedroom, she smokes. There are only five cigarettes left in the carton. She will go out today and buy more, in an English accent, to help her courage. As she inhales, her lower muscles spasm. Another thought occurs—she has brought no tampons. Perfect. She does not know the city, but Kritik Uncle cannot stop her from going to buy supplies. There are no women to ask. Even the food is prepared by Kritik Uncle's men: daal, chawal, mutton, paneer. Not much else alongside.

Scratch-scratch on the outside of her door. She stubs her cigarette, she smoothes her kameez, adjusts her dupatta: smile-smile. Hasn't she seen Radha do this every day, for all her growing-up years? Looking the part is just one of Sita's new survival skills, her sisters would be proud.

She opens the door.

—Yes, Kritik Uncle?

Here he is, in a heavy wool pheran, down to his ankles. A putti still tied around his face. She understands the warm covering but not his headgear: he says that he wants to blend into the streets. As if he can assume the habits of this city. It is a lie, she thinks. He should not do it.

—Any news? she says.

He smiles his "sorry" smile. She thinks—*You are not sorry. Why didn't you stop this? It was in your hands. You could have stopped it all and you didn't.* She thinks that pride, which he calls plainness, is his crime.

—I brought you apricots. Look!

From his pocket he produces a small bag of dried fruits. Fat, gold with the promise of the outside world. She takes it. The apricots are hard, wrinkled. Her other hand goes to her throat, pressing lightly on the ridges under her skin.

—Kritik Uncle, she says. Thank you so much for helping Papa. I don't know what he would do without you. What I would do.

She takes his empty hand, leans forwards and adds a kiss on his cheek, to punctuate.

—Of course, beti, of course. This is nothing. You are my daughter too, no? Isn't it enough for me that you have come home?

She turns away from him to put the apricots into her bag. She gathers her useless phone, her laptop, her dictionary and diaries. She has no connection here, there is an e-curfew, state-wide, it seems. She must go, find an internet café—a bookstore—there are some, she knows, she has read about them. In her notebooks are lists of names, email IDs—all the student protestors she left in Delhi. They read now like a wish list of lives she might have had: her hopes are with them.

—What are you doing? he says.

—Kritik Uncle, when can we go to see Gargi and Radha? she says.

—Tell me what is the matter. Are you feeling scared? Is someone bothering you?

He clears his throat three times.

Keeping her voice light, she says,

—You should go change, Uncle, I can't look at you like this. What are you wearing? Please, go and make yourself fresh, wear your proper suit. Then we can talk more. I don't want to imagine what you have been doing dressed like this. Please change, and come back as yourself.

—My dear Sita. What is upsetting you? He clears his throat and bows his head to one side.

—Kritik Uncle, I need to go out. I have to buy some women's supplies.

He comes to her; he takes her shoulders in his hands. They are standing by the bed; the window is behind him, the bright blue day.

—Be careful, Sita. Troubles are on hold right now, but you can't just go out and about. For you especially, it is not safe. Tell me what you need. I will procure it.

She raises her arms to adjust her dupatta; he has to let her go.

—No. I'll wear my shades and take my backpack. I look like a tourist anyway. You've always said yourself that tourists here are safe. If they aren't, why are we fighting so hard for the hotel?

—Sita. You are the daughter of a high-profile VIP. There are wounds here that you do not understand.

—I won't go to the old town, if that is what concerns you. But I will go out. I will be back before Papa wakes up.

Kritik Uncle says he does not mean danger on the streets.

—Must I spell it out? I have not told you all that your sisters have done, if only to protect you, my dear. But they won't hesitate to do— such things! If they know we are here. So. Let us go and do the puja, and see if we can wake Bapuji up.

—Kritik Uncle. Just send me in a taxi to Lal Chowk, then I'll walk and do my shopping. I will be careful. No one will see me, I promise. If you send someone to follow me, I'll be very upset. It's that time—I need supplies.

He smiles, and considers her for a moment, then shrugs. He steps back, allowing her to pass. The doorway is there, he gestures to it. He lets her go.

. . .

She almost skips. She didn't expect him to give in so easily! Before she leaves, she checks on Papa. His ravaged face: mouth open, saliva collecting at the corners, beloved eyes shut. The cheeks she has kissed so often, now sucked into themselves. He has slept as if waiting for some magic to wake him. He has not been fevered, only confused. Exhaustion, says the nurse. Respiratory infection. The pressures of the campaign, his fast, all of it has weakened his immune system. Only rest, and Sita, can heal him.

She strokes his forehead. She swallows her sorrow and reminds herself that life is sacrificed in a blaze of red and gold each autumn; then spring comes again. It is bound to happen, nature makes it so.

The taxi stops on the corner of Lal Chowk, the heart of commerce in Srinagar. Sita knows this place from her reading, her films—she tries not to scrabble at the car door to get to it. *Take it slowly; cover your head for Kritik Uncle's sake.* Then, she greets the city. The rush-hour people, normal people, so many young people, perhaps artists or accountants and shoppers and secretaries, leaving their buildings. They take no notice of her; they brush past her. She is swept up by their movement, by the sounds of love songs drifting out from the music store, by the ones of boys and the twos of lovers and threes of families, all sharing the street. Light bleeds over the concrete malls. There is a thick, sweet smell of roasting chestnuts. The sellers look up, offering her paper cones full of their dark treasure. She sees the faces of young men, their skin lined beyond their years, their eyes hooded, the sudden smiles and shouts they give each other as they greet friends in passing. No one is following her here.

Behind the shop windows on a tree-lined street, there are white plastic bodies draped in shawls and scarves. A leather shop has bags and belts that she loves—she will come back tomorrow. There is a shop selling spices; packets of saffron are on display in the windows. Everywhere bright apples are stacked in carts and outside stalls—deep red, russet, speckled gold. Another place sells pure honey, in hundreds of jars from Kashmiri bees. Amongst the liquid gold she browses the flavours, tasting each sample from a small stick. Papa will love this one: made by local women, scented with kesar and gulab.

She crosses the road, towards a Punjabi restaurant where the smells of ghee-soaked naan and tandoor spices are losing to the stench from the stagnant drains. She feels something brush at her, hears a sound: a woman crouches on the pavement, her blackened hands reaching out. All five of her fingers are missing and her elbow has been broken into a new shape. Her face could only have been burned; half of it is puckered—the eyes are bruised, the throat is ringed in marks as if from a wire. She is draped in rags, so loose on her skeleton that her breastbone is visible. Her breasts and nipples are like Papa's. Sita recoils, she cannot stop herself; the scarred woman shuffles along, trying to tell her something. There is a picture of a young man on a cord around her neck. Around her the car horns blaze.

Almost running, Sita ducks down a side street—a dead end. She climbs the steps and finds herself at a small park, a stamp of grass fenced with rusted wrought iron. The Jhelum is here: sludge-brown and weed-strewn. People come here to walk, to sit as if it were a holiday, and they have come to taste the air. The benches are occupied by young men, robbed of any more to do in the late afternoon than argue or reminisce, or watch the birds swoop over the water.

She watches shikaras slide past. She is trying to see the city for itself. But her films—her books—and the feeling again, strange, soothing—it could almost be Cambridge—with students punting down the river past the deep wine cellars of John's and King's and Queens'. The golden light flickers off the water, the colour of her last year in college, when all she had to worry about was bagging a seat under Nehru's bust in the college library (good luck while she crammed for her finals). The need to smoke makes her dizzy and brings the river towards her; it swings away again, back to its brooding meander.

Sita is lost in the life created. The city is crumbling, pockmarked and ruined, neon lights illuminate the shop fronts while posters of boys' faces are put up—there, on that wall, so many old posters—and women search the decades for their missing and their dead. Under the kangri smoke, the smiles, the sharp tang of a people who are always on their guard. She still does not understand why Papa and Kritik Uncle want this hotel so much. *Go India, Go back!* She has seen the graffiti carved into the trees.

How was the hotel approved? Who allowed it? Who agreed? She knows Kritik Uncle will never tell her the full story. He would say that is something that nobody, not even a spy, can ever really know.

A group of young men walk by. Tourists, like her. One in a crimson hoodie and jeans. He's tall, she thinks. Good-looking. The thought surprises her. The other boys hang back a little, except one—almost as tall as the hooded guy, with ears like handles on each side of his head. She tries not to smile at them. But it feels good, for a second, to imagine meeting a stranger, falling into some kind of flirtation. For most of her "friends" in Delhi, that is the romance of Srinagar. The boys pass behind her, and carry on down the bund. The one with the ears looks back briefly—almost, she thinks, as if he is going to raise his hand and salute.

She leans forwards over the railings, looking down the river towards the Zero Bridge. A few houseboats bob gently as the call to prayer crackles across the water, raising the birds, so many birds, all the different birds she cannot identify, circling over her head like an aarti blessing, disappearing into the clouds. It is nearly sunset, the temperature is dropping. She can taste the winter on its way.

The sun has set, leaving smoky grey dusk. Sita clutches her coat, wishing for a pheran and a kangri to keep her warm now the light has gone. She retraces her steps, wondering if her mother ever walked here. She has been warned that wild dogs plague these streets. She ducks into an old convenience store, stocked with old packets of hair dye and skin lightener; strange '70s models with blond hair and blue eyes stare out at her from the shelves. She cannot see any kind of tampon. Instead, she points to the highest shelf, above the shop boy's head. He climbs up a ladder and throws onto the counter an imported packet of twenty-four pads: Stayfree.

She takes a taxi back to the safe house. Every house on the street looks the same—grey, new-built concrete, with no detailing. And on the corner—a young man getting out of a jeep—unlocking his own front door. It is him. He has the same head, the same ears as that boy she saw earlier. *One of Kritik Uncle's,* she sighs. *No wonder he let her go out.*

She counts the five paces from the gate to the door. As she steps into the hallway, she listens for movement. Kritik Uncle appears from the kitchen, still wearing his pheran, the turban obscuring his face.

—Sita? Enjoyed your walking? Good. Come. We are all waiting for you upstairs.

—Is Papa awake?

—You should be the first thing he sees when he opens his eyes.

This is what Kritik Uncle always says, every single day. He means to charm her, she thinks. When she goes to Papa, he does seem pleased to see her sometimes. More often, he does not. Some days he does not recognise her at all, and calls her "Nanu."

—Let's see what the doctor says. Did you contact him?

—Our local nurse is here. He at least has been watching your Papa non-stop.

Her confidence shrivels at the cold in Kritik Uncle's voice. Everything about him makes her feel ten years old again. Bookless, under-travelled, dependent on Gargi for every permission to speak, laugh, skip.

—Let's go and do the puja, he says.

He follows Sita up the narrow stairs. More concrete, more grey walls. The skylight casts squares of blue on them. Sita pulls her dupatta over her head and crosses it around her neck. Perhaps the ends flick Kritik Uncle; if they do, he doesn't comment.

The ante-room is a grey box, the carpet a dull brown. A sheet has been laid over it. The men—there are fifteen here, at least—should be in business suits, but they are all in kurtas, in pherans, in jeans and jumpers. For all these years, they have had no work except spying for Kritik Uncle, with skills they learned from constantly being watched. Now they sit, saying nothing to her at all—but all wondering where she has been, who with, doing what-all. In the centre of their circle, a pundit, naked to the waist, his red beads dark blood blisters against his skin, sits in front of a foil-covered brazier, waiting to begin the prayers.

Sita pulls her slipping chunni over her head again, and sits cross-legged next to the pundit. A spoonful of dirt, a match—the flames hiss and rise. She stares into them. What did Ranjit Uncle do to Radha? How did Bubu Jiju die? Where is Jeet Bahiya? Why hasn't Gargi even tried to fix this? Why hasn't Kritik Uncle? No one will tell her anything—only that her sisters let her father go wandering in Dhimbala basti in a storm.

—Om, shanti, shanti Om, she prays with the group.

Don't die, Daddy. Come back. Please, she thinks. *Don't leave me alone with these men. I promise I will never leave again.*

The door to the inner room opens. The nurse comes out. He is a middle-aged man, with bony hands clasped across his pheran. His clean-shaven face is expressionless.

—How is Bapuji? Sita says.

—Ma'am, he is sleeping.

Above the makeshift mandir hangs a black-and-white photograph of Papa as a dashing young man with full, dark hair, a forehead with no lines. A marigold garland adorns the frame, as if he is already dead. She swallows, needing water, trying to stop her tears from choking her as they rise, betraying her as they fall. Grief roars in her ears.

—Hai Bhagwan, merciful and compassionate! she prays. Joh toota hai, usse sahi karo. Papa ko bachcha mat banao, bring him back from where he has wandered, bring him back to me.

She gets up and picks her way forwards through the seated worshippers to the inner door. The nurse holds it open; she hesitates then feels him gently pushing her. The sensation of his hand makes her want to scream.

—Come, Madam, come. Don't be scared, I am sure he is calm now.

Does the nurse think her disgust, her rage, is against Papa?

—Paas aajao, he says. Let him see you when he wakes.

The music stops. The whole room is watching through the open door. Papa is in the bed-chair, wrapped in woollen blankets. His gaunt face the only part visible. *Sita. Bend your head, lick your lips, touch them lightly to your Papa's.* This is what the men outside expect of her. She kisses Papa's forehead. The smell of jasmine and, underneath, a stench that proves he has been dressed but not washed. Can a job never be done right? Or is this also her task to complete?

—My dear Papa. Sabh kuch theek ho jayega.

—Yes, says the nurse. Kiss, and make it all better.

Sita ignores him.

—Papa, what were you doing in the basti? Who sent you there?

She sweeps her hand along his forehead, smoothing the white hair down.

—Sita Rani!

It is Kritik Uncle; he is standing behind her, a fraction too close.

A whispering sound swells and she realises again what Radha has always tried to teach her. Giving the appropriate performance takes skill. Encore.

—How could Gargi and Radha have done this? she says.

—Actually, seriously, says the nurse.

—These white hairs, these poor wrinkles.

—Of course, she is right, this is the story, Kritik Uncle says.

—Should such a man have tackled poverty and filth alone in the slums? Sita says. This time she does address the nurse; he only replies,

—Nahin, beti, do not talk about that time.

—Did you face the thunder and lightning all alone on that terrible night, like the hero that you are? You could have been struck, or hurt, and no one was there to help you.

This, they like better. None of them realise she means them to.

For good measure and to make sure she does not speak one word of how she really feels, she decides to act out what they expect of her, Bollywood style. The tearful death scenes of grand old men watched over by hand-wringing daughters, mourners, brave sons, all weeping and wailing. She drops into Hindi, says *Dada*—to them it will sound more poignant.

—Aap kaise chale gaye, itne gandh mein, in filth, with those pigs and donkeys in Dhimbala, haan? Chi, chi, Dada, forced to wade through mitti and shit in such heavy rain, as if the sky was weeping, Papa, weeping on your head! It is a miracle you are still with us, that your mind has stayed so strong. This is the power you have, Dada, please, wake up! Wake up!

Hands try to restrain her from throwing herself onto his body—or are they pushing her forwards? All the while she is thinking—let me go. This is not my voice, not me, not me, not me, not me, not me—so many times that she cannot tell what is real anymore, whether the acting is a lie or the lie is an act, so maybe she meant everything she said, or maybe she did not.

—*Sita Ma'am, be calm.*

—*Sita Madam, be quiet.*

—*Sita Madam, sing to him.*

Do the people around Gargi constantly tell her how to behave? Is she forced to fight with everyone she speaks to?

—Papaji? Are you there?

There is a groan. Sita is almost pushed out of the way. With Kritik Uncle, she heaves; she props the back of the bed up, swinging the last third down so her father's feet dangle, naked, a few inches from the floor.

—What!

He comes awake in a roaring stink of breath. His arms push the blankets; they claw the air towards her. Sita tries not to move or wince. He starts to speak in mid-sentence, as if he has been talking for hours and they have not been able to hear.

—Aré maya, what is this? Yes? No?

He looks around at them, one to the next to the next.

Sita takes his arms, she tries to fold them back into the blankets. He keeps escaping her, slapping the sides of the bed, then reaching up towards her again. She tries to tell him who she is; she asks him how he is feeling. He looks at her, then around. The men from the havan are filling the doorway, watching her in Papa's room, listening to him ask what he has done that his dharma keeps him here. And begs that this time—this turn—he finds some peace. He looks at them as if they are his gaolers and he is pleading innocent.

She has never seen his face like this. She was expecting confusion, yes—but perhaps, also, sweetness. The way he used to be after eating a delicious hot halwa spiked with almonds. Instead he looks wide-awake. Cunning, even; calculating. Tricksy.

—Papa, can you stand?

—This world? he says. He looks around.

—How it binds, he exclaims. What visions it gives!

His eyes challenge the room to reply. Then he focuses: Sita. His face softens. He reaches out and strokes her cheek. The split skin of his fingertips scratches her lightly. His voice is soft.

—Who does not know such a beautiful hoor? Where did you die, that you are come here?

The men move forwards, filling the room; they gather around the bed. Sita is crushed as they try to touch her father's hand, his feet, his hair.

—We should leave him, he needs rest, Sita says. No one listens. Kritik Uncle? she says. Tell them.

—No, no, he is awake, says the nurse.

—He is fine, he will speak, says one of the men.

—Let him speak, says another. Don't speak until he speaks—

The words flip and list over each other: he is right as rain, he is a hero, he is Devraj, he will speak.

—Main kahan hoon? Hum kahan hain? Is it morning? Get up! Get up! Or am I still dreaming? This is not my body. See this hand? Not mine. This is my daughter's leg!

Papaji pinches his own thigh. The skin turns red. He roars.

Sita does the only thing she can. She bends, feeling the crowd around her step back. One man after another gets out his mobile phone. *Why?* They point at her. —*Are they?* Ah. Ready to record this classic moment. Sita stretches forwards, her chuni slipping down her arm. In a gesture she has not made since Gargi had to bribe her with ladoos, she reaches out her hand with a clink of gold bangles, to touch her father's feet.

—Ram Ram, Papaji. Ram Ram.

Tears begin to slide down her cheeks. Her father shifts, almost falling, the covers crumple in front of her; he is reaching, trying to touch her feet in return.

—Papa! She catches him in her arms.

He lets her take his weight. She must use her whole body to raise him and ease him back into the chair. It is difficult—he wants to know why she has brought him here, he accuses her of having no respect, of dressing him in borrowed clothes. She struggles to calm him, aware that no one is helping her. He points over her shoulder at Kritik Uncle, demanding to know who he is.

—You're in rags, he says. I don't like this thing. And you! (He looks at Sita.) Don't cry, your tears will wet my feet. I hate to have wet feet. Wife of a Raksha! Didn't you go to Sri Lanka? Are your sisters here too? I will never forgive them.

—Never, never, she agrees.

(Let all here understand he is never going to be well.)

—So, make it quick, I am a chicken ready for the chop. Chop chop.

Papa sits back in the chair and closes his eyes.

—We are in Srinagar, Papa, Sita says.

She strokes his hair, she reaches out to take his hand.

—We are in a safe house, a nice new house. And on the hill, the new Company Kashmir hotel is looking so beautiful, waiting for you. Everyone is waiting for you.

—Natak mat karo. I deserve more.

A shaky laugh escapes Sita. Even like this, Papa knows her. She is ready with her most witty retort when the nurse clears his throat behind her. He reaches an arm across her towards Papaji, forcing her to step aside.

—Sita Madam, he says. Don't speak about the past now, or Bapuji will only get mad again. He should not be reminded of all he has lost, but made to stay calm and quiet.

If Radha were here, a raise of one eyebrow and a cutting remark, a flick of her hair and a sharp turn of shoulder would shame them all into obeying. If Gargi were here, they would not even dare to open their mouths.

—See if he will sleep some more, and tell him he should rest, the nurse says.

—Will you come and walk with me Papa? she says.

She moves away from the nurse.

—I will walk, agar tum walk karogi, lekin dheere, her Papa says.

The nurse shakes his head. He retreats back to the wall, arms crossed over his chest.

She helps Papa to get onto his feet. No one comes forwards to help. Over her shoulder Kritik Uncle and the rest of the men are talking, fussing, she thinks—waiting for her to show her mind.

—Kritik Uncle, she says, in a voice like Gargi's. Send your spies to see what my sisters are up to. I want a full report. How dare they do this? They must be reckoned with. And get all these men out of here: I want to be alone with Papa. One of you tell the cook that for this evening, tari wala chicken, chawal, moong ki daal. Papa needs solid food. Make sure the curd is fresh. In the next few days we want to eat a wazwan, all sixteen courses: the cook should slaughter the lambs.

Kritik Uncle inclines his head, as if he always knew she could give orders like this. With a small smile he calls her *dear* and says that he will do everything she wishes; also that she must fight the good fight.

Before she has time to think about that, he leaves, and the followers go with him.

Now alone, now. Sita helps Papa out of the chair. He seems so fragile, on the surface so sweet-smelling—almond oil from his nurse's hands. Shall she walk him, up and down the room? She knows invalids need exercise. The world shrunken to country—to state—to house—to room—to body—taking these small steps. And she wants to comfort him, but all she can think of is a story that was told to Gargi by their mother, who learned it from her mother and so on, going back, right to the beginning. Gargi told it to Radha and Jeet—and whichever of them was there to tuck Sita in told it to her, over and over again—the story of the farmer's wife and the honeybee, in words as near to the original as they could remember.

Papa leans on her neck and arm. She takes small, close steps with him across the carpeted room.

It begins with the farmer's wife, who has fled from her home to the forest.

—And why had she done this?

Sita asks Papa the question, waits, then tells him: the village headman was a tyrant. The farmer's wife met a honeybee, who asked why she had fled, and when she heard the answer, replied that she too had been tyrannised.

—The two lamented, Sita says, each sorrowing for the other. The honeybee said they should fall at God's feet, and make their prayers to Him.

Here Papa pauses to catch his breath. He does not look at Sita. His face is turned to the concrete wall. Sita presses his arm, presses him onwards. She voices the story's refrain:

—Lo, I am thy honeybee, a poor winged creature of the forest.

Papa looks as if he wants to hear more. Now comes the part about the honeybee, who went from hill to hill to collect her flower-nectar, becoming possessed of many children. Sita floats her spare hand like the bee, she clenches her fist, to tell of how a bear came to crush the bee—may ruin seize that ruthless bear, for it was he that drove me to the forests! He destroyed my little ones! Then the farmer's wife asked the bee why God sent no pity to her, only to get this reply—

—Lo, I am thy honeybee, a poor winged creature of the forest.

If Papa trembles and begins to sigh, Sita thinks it is because he is beginning to let the words seep down inside, to smooth the stiffness of his joints. She carries on with the story, helping him to take small steps, matching her pace to his. But now comes the part she used to hide under the covers for, while Gargi made her scary face, or Radha tickled her until she cried, or Jeet gave his clever smile and twisted his limbs into toes-up-your-nose. This is the part where the bee tells the farmer's wife how she fled from the forest, pursued by a bear, how she alighted at the farmer's house and was promised peace and comfort.

—Nothing so bad in that, Papa, no? she says.

No. He nods, sweetly, waiting for the rest. Sita must keep walking, keep telling—see, said the honeybee, what the farmer did: he made a hive for me to abide in, and rubbed it over with fresh butter. It became a prison of death for me. With a sickle he cut off my honeycombs and was cursed with the guilt of countless murders. But, said the bee, it was my fate that brought me to the farmer's house, and that fate was humiliation.

Now Sita cannot ignore Papa's trembling. She knows he might break down. But what about the poor, flightless honeybee? She must continue with the next part—where the honeybee asks the farmer's wife to share what happened to her. The farmer's wife speaks strange words, a spell that Sita has never deciphered. She loved instead to savour their strangeness, to feel the privilege of not having to understand.

—Each soul must dree its weird: endure, submit, practice and perpetrate its own strange destiny. There is a place below to which we must descend. Lo, I am a farmer's wife! We came not to this world as an abiding place.

Papaji pauses by the small window. He grips Sita's arm.

—Have you seen your grandfather's land, in the meadows of the Valley? Flowers and bees. Burned, gone, he says.

Sita tries to look outside with him but the angle is wrong. They begin to walk back towards the bed-chair, and Sita takes up the story, speaking as the farmer's wife, telling of the spring. Spring—when the tax gatherers came to the farmers to fill their bellies, and trap the farmers as if in a net. In the autumn the tax gatherers forgot all their kindness. They came and beat the farmers.

—The farmers! says Papaji. He starts and then seems to stumble. The look he gives Sita almost stops her words, but she continues, softly:

—Lo, I am thy farmer's wife. We came not to this world as an abiding place.

Now she must tell of how the farmer's wife managed, by sowing crops in the welcoming earth, which sprung up and ripened. She collected and piled them on the threshing floor, hundreds of kharawars in weight. She went around from village to village. And in each one the headman and the accountant came to weigh the goods. Each time, she lamented:

—Lo, I am thy farmer's wife. We came not to this world as an abiding place.

—Enough, Papa says. Khatam.

—Just one part more, she says. How can she finish now? The end of the story is the hardest to tell, but she would never sleep until it was done. This is the part where the poor and needy came as beggars, holding out their lap cloths to the farmer's wife. And she filled and filled their skirts, believing that in doing so she was giving them the assurance of salvation while securing her own rewards in heaven.

—Lo, I am thy farmer's wife. We came not to this world as an abiding place.

This is how it ends. Papa seems to have lost his fight. Sita lowers him into his chair. She stands and watches him hide his face, and weep. The darkness is gradual, soft, it smudges the room's shapes. She sits on the floor cross-legged; she rests against Papa's leg. She can feel his bones, where before she could not.

—Good girl, he says. Thank you.

He puts his hand on her head. She closes her eyes, feeling the weight of it. He strokes her hair. His hand makes a whispering sound: yes, yes, yes, yes, yes.

The next two days pass with strange monotony. November mists fall around the house and do not lift, except for a few hours around noon. The cold invades through every crack in the concrete and wood. Sita has been furnished with a kangri, she takes to nursing it, a mother with a fevered child. A bell chimes: Papa is calling her. How she loves him every morning and hates him by bedtime. Sometimes she does want to be skiing down the mountains in reflective goggles and a fur-lined ski-suit, going faster than anyone else. Coming to the end in a plume of fresh snow, needing nothing and nobody to know her. Could she live as Sita Devraj, with all her pearls and diamonds?

Lost tourists pass her window in lemon and fuchsia fleece jackets like fantastic dip-dyed sheep. They wear brand-new Adidas and Nike; the pigtailed bachche have Barbie backpacks and high-waisted jeans. Across the hilltops lights from the Oberoi, the Lalit, the India Company Srinagar hotels wink at each other. Her sisters are probably there already, eating snacks, drinking first-flush Assam and whispering bad things about new money. They think she is an ungrateful girl who left them over nothing. She does not need anyone to tell her she has been a bad daughter. She knows. That is why she has come back—and why she stays.

Sita walks to the end of the street after lunch, wondering about those boys in the corner house. She loiters. If she takes a step, will a door open behind her? No sound comes; it is just a cold, fresh autumn day—a day like the next, and the next. She wants to hear the stories of the people of this place, she doesn't know how to ask. She takes a taxi to the jetties in the afternoons, and buys herself solitary shikara rides across the Dal. The boats bear her gently through the backwaters, until they reach the ghost town.

She cannot speak of what happened here. The wooden houses are charred wrecks, the corrugated roofs held down with bricks. There was once grandeur—she can see it in the lattices and stonework, the skeletons of turrets, oversized birdcages swinging in the sky. Here she could get out, and search for the house where her grandfather lived—where they died. She wouldn't know it, if she saw it. Every place is rotting, and sweet, stray dogs have taken over; sometimes they come to the steps by the river and watch her, as if she is the vision, not them.

Now a small child waves at her from the crumbling steps. Sita catches the eye of a woman with bare feet, waiting until she passes to empty her slops and pull her child back into the broken house.

The English newspaper announces that across the Zero Bridge, banners have appeared proclaiming "Happy Diwali!" This is the first time in so many years that the festival will be celebrated in the streets. It will fall on a Wednesday, and that is auspicious for businessmen. People will decorate the Hanuman Temple with flowers, and diyas with four wicks for luck, and adorn all statues of Kali, goddess of time and of change. For is she not also redeemer of the universe? It is time they had fireworks of the best kind in this city.

But the local newspapers report on the hotel, voicing the anger that many local people feel. Some say there is risk of unrest—extra military and police will be deployed in the city. Some say a curfew will be imposed—there will be no Diwali or any going out while the opening of the hotel goes on—that the people of the city have suffered enough of such lockdowns.

A few interviewees say they think money is good, however it comes to the Valley.

Under every skin Sita sees here, there is a history of violence. She wanders through the daily city, trying, trying to read it.

In the evenings when the birds become a thousand-piece orchestra tuning in the sky, she wraps herself in a quilt and takes her notebook to the garden. The house is unadorned, but someone has planted outside. Palms mix with pine trees that frame the sloping grass, shedding needles and filling the air with their scent. She wonders if she will still be here in late winter, when the dark purple shrubs will trumpet tiny pink flowers. *Himalayan fingerprints,* called so for their fleshy petals—she cannot remember their real name.

She curls in a plastic chair, sipping lemon tea. Kritik Uncle appears from the gloom around the house; a man carries his chair, another his shawl, another waits to take his order for snacks. He sits next to her, the shawl on his knees. When the snacks arrive—fresh fried finger chips, salt-and-peppered in a plastic bowl—they come with imli chutney and homemade ketchup.

—The taste of pre-'91, Kritik Uncle says, dipping a chip in tomato sauce. See how far we have come? Remember the first time we bought shares in Heinz to use in the hotels? What days.

Sita was two years old in 1991. Maybe Kritik Uncle thinks he is talking to Gargi, those lessons he used to give her on Company history loop-looping in his brain. As he sits with her, the night becomes charged instead of gentle, the palm silhouettes go from sprouting hair tops to fingers grabbing the clouds.

—You like this garden? Kritik Uncle asks her. You know, tulips bloom in the Mughal gardens: Shalimar, Nishat—I'll take you in spring.

Online, she has seen pictures of the tulips pouting in so many hopeful rows. On Sundays, she imagines, families come and picnic, and dress for photographs in traditional costumes, and children splash in the stone sluices that frame each patch of grass.

—In the summer, says Kritik Uncle. Then you will see. How so many shikaras might glide along the lake. Floating toy shops, floating shoe stalls—so many people come for honeymoon; so many come with families. Bapuji always understood, domestic tourism is our biggest opportunity. People want to experience this thing, some remember it from years back and want to see again with their own eyes. Do you know how much the industry has boomed here in the last five years? Four million people come for Amarnath pilgrimage alone. Not from your strata, but why not? Why shouldn't everyone enjoy this thing? We will offer a package to get the right class here only. Vision, Sita beti, and belief. This is what you need. Just imagine the fun to be had! We should be right at the front of this thing.

He takes a samosa, dips it in tomato sauce, bites off the corner.

—What you mean is that India has grown a big fat middle while the people of this state have struggled under sanctions, Sita says.

—Such a sweet girl! he says.

He finishes the samosa and his hand and chin twist upwards like a novice poet about to recite. He stares into the shadowed garden as if he can hear a beautiful qawwal.

—You will come and develop the Company here, and everyone will thank you. First the faithful Company customers will come, searching for novelty, for skiing, to see saffron picking, and tour inside our shawl weavers' homes. We will build a private gondola swinging high into the mountains, to avoid the riffraff queuing at Gulmarg; the lame packhorses at Pahalgam. Then those that follow our story will come, wanting to be seen in the same places, and so on, and so forth. The thrill of it will be this place. So life continues.

Sita thinks of the woman with the picture of a boy around her neck. The young men: sitting on the benches by the river in the late afternoon. All the things simply seeing cannot show.

—Do you know how much produce this place can yield? he asks. How much we can benefit from free trade? The land is so fertile; we will sprout money. The West of the East, this place could be. And now is the time for us to come make it good. We will occupy the people with tourism. So what if the old laws prohibit? Time to sweep it away. And you will manage it all.

He talks and talks. There will be daisies and lotus flowers everywhere in spring. There are passionflowers in the summer, and right now, apples—so many apples fallen on the grass, slowly rotting into the earth.

A man slides through the garden to them, bringing a candle and another shawl, which she takes before they can tell her she needs it. Behind him stands another man in a dull-coloured pheran. Kritik Uncle says,

—Chalo, Isa. Report.

—Sir, Gargi and Radha Madam are not leaving the hotel.

—And?

—Sir, Fortress America ban gaya hain. No one can currently get into the hotel grounds without a pass, we must hand it back when we leave. A respectable man who runs a mid-ranger guesthouse in the Rajbagh area is supplying these passes. His family is being monitored to see what he might require in exchange for making a deal.

—Good. Next?

More men materialise. Four of them—waiting for Kritik Uncle's attention. Sita feels the cold seeping through the layers of her shawls to her skin, veins, muscles; to her bones. They report the details of the hotel opening, now just days away.

—Itne phool! At least five thousand stems are being arranged. Extra power generators have been ordered to keep electricity constant. And servants thought Kashmiri outfits would be called for but Gargi Madam has ordered tailors in Delhi to stitch to some Western design.

Sita has seen the layouts. There will be an Empire Room, complete with maps and globes and a telescope; old charts and trade documents, a signed print of the Napurthala Instrument of Accession on the walls. There will be a ballroom, a boating lake, a business centre and an outdoor stage, for travelling players to come.

—What about khaana? asks Kritik Uncle. What are the plans for that?

—There will be wazwan. Sixty-four courses. At least fifty lambs are waiting in pens in the old town. They will be killed and cooked in the traditional ways and with some variations also. I believe Western food has been ordered and I have good information Gargi Madam has asked for fish to come from Goa. A chef has come from Japan also. He has brought his own knives.

—What provision has been made for the slaughter?

Sita looks up, she tries to see the first stars. Last year, even before the building was finished, she let Gargi persuade her to help plan a farm on the terraces above the hotel. Reluctantly she did it, as if growing their own fruits and vegetables would make any difference.

—Sir, in the area behind the orchards there is a concrete cooking-ground with at least five brick ovens, it will all happen there.

So: The streets of Srinagar will wash with blood. The citizens of Srinagar will be locked out of the celebrations, unless they are serving the hotel.

—See, Sita beti? Kritik says, after the men have gone. Details are the most important part of planning any assault.

She stays up late huddled in her shawls in the garden. The moonlight catches the bare branches; they shine like silver hairs tangled in the dark.

The next day she escapes the safe house, the boys on the corner, for the busy avenues again. Some of the shops have Diwali sweets and cards. The window displays are sets of necklace–bangles–rings and golden tik-kas to anoint a bride. Sita walks quickly past the mall, the street-corner dhaba, crowded with young men and old, sipping tea. She cuts through the tourist complex towards the river, wondering if Kritik Uncle would dare set a watch to follow her. Today, she will bore whoever it is, with her solitary tour.

She chooses a shikara, its posts twined with plastic forget-me-nots and stuck with cheerful toy birds. The deep seat is covered in rugs. She climbs in and sits carefully, not wanting to look a fool. The boatman waits for a moment, to see if more customers will come. A family join her—a mother, a small boy, and an older woman. They greet her with smiles, but at first they talk only amongst themselves.

—Sit, Madams, sit, says the boatman, and his pleasure makes her laugh; the sound echoes over the lake, startling a long-legged bird. It rises, shockingly white against the silver water, wingspan wide as it skims the surface and disappears into the reeds.

Standing on the stern, the boatman lights a cigarette and steers towards the tributaries of the lake, into the wild grasses and the reeds, away from the other tourists. Sita inhales his smoke, tasting the dankness of water and air. They float along narrow canals. There are the vegetable gardens, called Rad in Kashmiri; there is a sign for a wild honey shop, closed in winter, and a boatyard where a man wrapped up against the cold is stripping logs to reveal their tender, pale flesh. Through the unpaned windows she catches glimpses of weavers, spinners, stitch-makers singing to relentless clack-clack.

In the backwaters her boat passes bright green patches where detergents and fertilisers and sewage have caused phytoplankton to bloom. Under the lotus leaves native to this lake, Sita knows there are roots stretching into the water, stronger and thicker than metres of rope. When lotus roots are sliced, they reveal rhizomes; they resemble English lace. One of the few flowers that can regulate their own temperature, like warm-blooded animals, like humans.

She wants to stop, to collect some samples of the plants and the water, but feels she cannot ask the boatman; she does not want to draw attention to herself. Here, almost in the centre of the lake, she feels even more conspicuous.

The boat takes a turn into another tributary. Shikaras loaded with groceries sidle through the water to her. She ignores the packets of custard creams and Scottish shortbread, the tubes of Pringles crisps. Instead, she barters for blood-red chillies like dried-up organs, and maroon wisps of saffron sold by weight. She buys cardamom, cinnamon, cumin, turmeric; flavours for food she might one day try and prepare—maybe when they get back to Delhi, she will get her own place, alone. She will hold campaign meetings, and cook for herself. The dishes will begin with this hoard of spices. No one else chose them, no one else gave them and no one, but her, thought she should have them.

When she gets back to her street, the house on the corner where the boys live seems closed. In the safe house, she hides her treasure in her underwear drawer.

The morning of Diwali, before she is meant to greet her sisters, Kritik Uncle has a box for her, which he insists she open. Inside layers of tissue is a calf-length pashmina kameez in a bright, happy red. To wear with it: a matching red shawl embroidered with black paisleys, long enough to skip with. She puts them on in the bathroom, hooking the shawl around her neck, over her head, a hood. And despite herself she is entranced; it's as if the spinner, the weaver, the ironer, the right-handed cutter have all left their meditations in it, for her. Kritik Uncle has forgotten to give her a salwar, so she has to wear the kameez over her jeans. Anyway, it is so long that no one will look at her ankles, her feet.

—Thank you, Kritik Uncle, she says. She kisses him.

—Happy Diwali, Sita beti.

Now Kritik Uncle says she is ready to meet those who are here to help her. Wrapped so warm, she gets into the car with him. She watches his face as they pass the house on the corner—he does not flick his eyes to it, nor does he turn away. She looks out of the window, trying to get a sense of the whole city—past the prison, the hospital, a cinema. Sandbags are piled against the door, the windows are boarded shut. Barbed wire scrolls around thick-fleshed soldiers; they stand to attention at the checkpoints, cradling their guns. Despite them there is a sense of something in the air—or maybe that is just her own excitement. Tonight she will see her sisters. Even while the graffiti'd walls still cry—*Azad Kashmir.*

The car skirts the lake—it is forty-five minutes or more before they turn off a dirt track behind a low white building, and stop at the gates to a children's play park. It runs down to silvering water, where three or four tourist houseboats are stationed.

—Where are we, Kritik Uncle?

—Nagin Lake. See over there? Zabarwan mountain. Come.

One foot in front of the other, she follows Kritik Uncle across the park towards the water's edge. There are no children on the swings or slide; the roundabout is still. A blue flash catches her; a bird skims the water's surface for a few beats and vanishes. A kingfisher.

A young man in a pheran with a small, trimmed beard gets up from a bench to meet them. He clasps Kritik Uncle's hands and receives an arm around the shoulder.

—As salaam alaikum, he says.

—Wa alaikum salaam, says Kritik Uncle.

They bow to each other.

—Imran is the son of one of our best friends in Srinagar, Sita, Kritik Uncle says. His father has given us the safe house here, and all the men looking after us. He is a great supporter of your Papa.

—Thank you, we are so well looked after, she says.

Imran's prayer cap is pinned to his hair with the same grips Gargi used to force on her. He leads them across a gangplank to a houseboat door; they must hop like chickens to remove their shoes. Through the houseboat they walk, single file towards the narrow, arched front room. Polished walnut furniture; the carpet is thick underfoot, baking in the warmth from a small fan heater that growls quietly in the corner. A short old man in a pheran, a prayer cap on his head. His beard is the colour of Sita's pashmina.

—Kritik Sahib! How are you?

—What can I tell you, Maulana Sahib? Today is the day of celebration.

—The Princess shall go to the ball, no?

The old man looks at Sita.

—What a beautiful outfit, he says. He shows her his open palms. Sita. My dear, I greet you as my own daughter. Come, please, my home is your home. I wish you a Happy Diwali. He joins his hands and bows.

Behind him, an arched window frames the lake, the mountains. Behind Sita, Imran, the walnut furniture, the children's park.

The Maulana's palms are so big, she thinks. The walls of the room are covered in crewel-worked cloth: vines, birds of paradise. It's the same on the chair covers, the curtains, the cushions and bolsters, a stitched forest of patterns repeating.

She swallows and answers as she should; as if she has known him all her life.

—Thank you, Uncle. My Papaji is recovering, slowly.

His eyes peer at her from behind rimless glasses; she tries to look at him steadily.

Sita, she thinks. *Stay calm.*

There is a framed picture of the Maulana with George H. W. Bush. And see the awards from TripAdvisor, and the India Tourist Board, also hanging there? There is an open visitors' book on a low table, a pen lying next to it. Should she sign? So someone might know she was here?

Imran comes with a tea tray. A flask and three glasses that seem too fragile to take heat. Sita accepts one filled with pink tea.

—You have tried our noon chai before? Saffron goes so well in milk, our own recipe here, the Maulana says.

—Yes, Uncle. It's delicious.

—Maulana Umer owns many of these beautiful boats, Kritik Uncle says. And so much of the land in this state. He will help us resolve all troubles with your sisters. Any problems, you can contact him.

—Thank you, Umer Sahib, for all your help, Sita says. But Kritik Uncle knows, I don't want to fight my sisters. The campaign we started is about more than my family—it's about changing the way people think, you know? My father promised me this.

—And did you know I am one of your father's oldest friends? All this. Umer Sahib waves his hand at the furnishings. I owe him all of this. Your father has always understood that wealth creation knows no borders. That is the cure for the sickness in Srinagar. All through these years of conflict and hardship he has helped us invest, so we have helped him, and so we have not starved, and some of us have prospered.

—What do you mean? she asks.

She sips her tea. Her eyes smart with the heat of it, the salt.

—Ah, Sita, this is not for you to worry about. Just know that whatever you need, I can arrange for you, says Maulana Umer.

—What about my sisters?

—Why not let the future take care of itself? My dear, we will make sure you get what is rightfully yours.

—But what do you mean? she asks again.

Kritik Uncle reaches a hand out to take his tea. How dark his skin is! Her own is pale. Her mother's skin.

—Without Maulana Sahib's support, all of Srinagar would have risen up against the hotel. Gargi's tactics did not help—bringing workers from outside states, contracting foreign architects and so on.

—But, Kritik Uncle, the Company has always done this, she says.

—Be that as it may. Local people—after years of war, of course they have wanted to protest this development, since the project began. I know you want to support them, no, Sita beti? So, we will. One cannot create paradise without maintaining hell. Need is a powerful motivator.

—But, Kritik Uncle, she says. Bapuji—and Gargi—

—How soft she is, Maulana Umer says. We have to toughen her up. Does she know the bottom line?

—The what? says Sita.

—Our streets may have been decimated by the years, he says. But we have such beautiful halls in Kashmir, beautiful rooms and corridors. Particularly beautiful are the corridors of your new hotel. Ask Kritik Uncle to show you their treasures sometime. Or even better, your dear widowed sister, Radha.

She sips her tea—sweet, bitter, bitter—she has no real idea what he is talking about. A fist squeezes her insides; look at Kritik Uncle, look at Maulana Umer—look, look, steadily. She realises that for all the books she has read, she has never quite believed in the terror of this world. She knows it exists, she thought she knew how it worked. But she has never actually seen it.

Here it is.

Kritik Uncle, and this man, talking in riddles about Kashmir, corridors, "her" hotel, treasure that will bring her power to wield.

Outside, the waters of the lake are silver, and still.

She does not belong in this world. She lives with spreading plants and strange fruits in a country these men cannot imagine.

—Chalo, Sita, you should get back, says Kritik Uncle. Your Papa will be needing you. Go, take the car and I will follow. Tonight is the opening. We must prepare.

She rises. Her blood is telling her to run, her head to stay and force answers. Her heart wants Gargi and Radha: her hands need to hold theirs.

—•—

WHEN SITA CAME HOME she talked about her sisters—but she came back to be with me. She watched me as if I might escape her. What did she think, that I was a cat or a cockroach? She watched me watch the pigeons on the ledge. Little birds, what a life. Eat some food, fly around, have some sex, what else? They told me this is Kashmir and we came here for my honour. They said I was a great man. But they didn't know this one secret—I am not too great to die. Ha! I thought. They will never let me die.

They will build statues to me—I will be a bird, and come and sit on my own shoulder, and shit on my own stone head. Who will clean me? Sita will. Goddess of rain and tears. Water to fill the cracks in this earth.

In the recent mornings I heard her singing, fighting with the birds. I wondered why she could not understand: this disturbed me.

I want tea. There are only dogs here. Don't think I do not recognise them. Here. Here doggy doggy, kuch khaoge kya? No, they are resting. Their pups are suckling. They are the Lords and Ladies of this shit heap. Why can I see the sky above the angel's head? Why does she not speak? This is the house where I wooed my wife. Where I began the Company's finest trade. Come, sit. And we will refine it.

OK, come sit, do not dance. Be soft. See? Much better. Sleep, baby, sleep. I pushed her down to my lap, I petted her head. The night will be over and the sun will warm. This is not the first time I have lost a night dreaming over Sita.

Sit, and I will tell you a tale.

> The King of Beasts, full of energy,
> Dwells in the woods, solitary
> Without emblems of royalty;
> Unlearned, untrained in polity,
> His superior strength gives him sovereignty;
> He rules, crowned simply by the words, Oh King! Hail. Oh King!
> Meat of tuskers moving slow, majestic,
> Drops of rut trickling, he relishes most;
> But if his favourite food comes not his way,
> Still you'll never catch a lion eating hay.

We can wait until the auspicious moment. We can wait.

WHEN SITA GETS BACK, the nurse meets her; behind him, the safe house is in uproar. Roar! A panic so fierce it could crack the walls.

—Where is Kritik Sahib? he says.

—Why? What has happened?

Papa is missing. *Missing*—when these men did not even expect him to be able to stand up alone. She leans against the door, watching them, on their phones, putting on their shoes, pushing each other around, each accusing the other.

—Where has he gone?

—You were supposed to be with him, are you blaming me?

—He said he wanted to go outside, I brought him to the courtyard, I went for a piss, how could I stop him, who am I to tell him?

On and on—

—Stop! she says.

For the first time, they obey her.

—I'll go find him. Stay here, all of you, or you will feel Kritik Uncle's rage. This is your fault. Stay. I'll go alone.

LET US TAKE A WANDER in the city of youth all the way back to the cradle. In the early days, red coats and white skins, skirts on boats for romancing. The wind changed and the red coats left chameleons of many shades, the people in between. We rode our motorbikes in autumn, under the shedding chinar trees, dreams of being crorepatis never far from our minds. We feasted on wazwan, all thirty-two courses, lamb skewered, lamb beaten, lamb marinated. Lamb balls, lamb eyes and testicles in sauce. Lamb brains, with curd and fresh ground spices. Lamb liver so tender and rich in iron for strength in the fight to come, lamb innards in sweet milk gravy. We add a chicken, cooked whole and cut. Into two halves. Serve with green spinach for the two shades of cloth— the flag and the uniform. We played both sides and ate both halves and paid for what we ate and got good returns. Ours is not the business of war or land, but money.

Back to the city and the golden days. Across the whole country, the youth are resourceful. All should come here and settle and claim their due. For this I have built the Company.

I chose the site as a young man. On the hills overlooking the city. Began a stone quarry with blast dynamite. Glass houses were built into the plans.

My favourite part of this city is the market.

. . .

I want to find that market, for my wife enjoys pink tea.

I trade promises for air and buy what I like. This is what my Company is built on—between you and me.

What have I left? A walnut shell cracked open. We came not to this world as an abiding place.

I ran until I reached the Temple, I went to seek the Pandit's blessing, I wanted to hide in stories and on the stage. I am everywhere, can you find me in your mouth and your memories? Come seek, come seek! I am here.

And do not scream for I will scream louder, and drown your voice in the syrup of mine—just watch, just wait, just come find me.

Come on, little bee, fly home.

·

SHE RUNS TO THE END of the road. She bangs on the door of the house
on the corner. When the young man opens it, he looks shocked; as if he
is face to face with someone he's only ever seen in a film.

—I know you are Kritik's men, watching for my safety, she says.

The young man nods. *What big ears he has.*

—Did you see my father leave? He's gone—he's gone! I have to find
him, she says.

—Don't worry, he says. He gives a high-pitched laugh. He steps
towards her. We were watching. Your father also came banging on our
door. He demanded we take him to the Pandit Temple. In the old town.
Come, we will follow him there.

In the streets the sound of firecrackers. The cold is electric, so many
families, so many children are out; all walking towards the river and the
Zero Bridge. Sita should be with Gargi and Radha, writing her name
with a sparkler, admiring each other's new clothes. *Papa, where are you?*
There are candles in the windows, and people are going from house to
house. Tonight there is no curfew; only the road to the new hotel will be
closed, keeping the people locked in their own circles. Sita follows the
young man, he tells her his name is Punj; they keep walking, towards the
parts of the city she has not yet been to. She looks up. In a high window
lit by a naked bulb, a man is bent over, stitching onto a cashmere shawl.
It was probably commissioned by Bubu himself—it will be delivered to

Radha soon. She wraps herself close in her own red shawl; the man at the window has paused in his work. He smiles down at her. He has no teeth and his face is more lined than Papa's. He points at her and seems to offer her the shawl, nodding, rubbing the fabric between his fingers to show her its value.

Behind her, a motorbike carrying two boys swerves and misses her. People are spilling from their prayers, brushing past her, knocking her, they go into grocers' and butchers' shops to buy for their evening meals. She feels she's being watched: Is it because she is the only woman not wearing a hijab? No—there are some women in salwar kameez and shawls, heads uncovered. No one is looking at her. *Sita,* she thinks. *Stop.*

—Stop, she says. Punj, stop. Where are we going?

—To the Temple, no?

He grins at her. A tour guide trying to stay calm, to hurry up the difficult customer without seeming to.

—Wait. I have to—just give me one minute.

She slinks into a general store and walks the aisles, trying to keep breathing. Old tins of condensed milk and custard powder, bags of dry spices and sacks of flour. Uncle Chipps—a brand she has not seen since she was a child.

She waits; two minutes, three. She picks at her nails, wondering if Kritik Uncle has come back to the safe house—if he is looking for her and Papa. Outside she can see Punj, talking on his phone.

She goes back without buying anything.

—Who are you talking to? she says. Across the street a broken neon sign flashes—*GYM, BODY-BUILDING, BOXING.*

Punj gestures behind her.

A group of young men is coming down the street—with them, the good-looking one in the crimson hoodie. She saw him that first time she went out. When she stood by the Jhelum worrying about buying cigarettes, as if she had nothing else to care about at all.

What long eyelashes he has, she thinks.

—I know you, she falters. You look like people I know.

—Jivan, he smiles. Great to finally meet you. Again. He laughs. It's been fifteen years.

Her body feels as if it is waking up after a hundred years of sleep. She straightens her shoulders. *Jivan*. She looks around, behind—his boys are grouped in a loose circle. Not friends. Security.

Jivan takes her hand. She is so surprised, she does not move. She feels how warm his fingers are, feels the cold in her own even more.

—Don't worry. I know where your dad is, he says. Gargi sent me. She just wanted to make sure he was OK. She wants to see you both.

—Gargi?

—Come with me, he says. He is still holding her hand. Your dad's at the shrine. We'll go get him, then go up to the hotel. It's going to be OK.

She thinks of Kritik Uncle, the danger on the boat, repeats to herself: *Jivan is from my sisters, he knows where Papa is, it's going to be OK.*

Jivan presses his hand lightly into the small of Sita's back. She doesn't understand why this small gesture soothes her. She lets him take the lead—she follows him and Punj and the other boys through the winding streets. As they go, the roads become more and more empty—of people, of any noise. The houses tumble to sticks. How common she must look in her bright red kameez, amongst their jackets and jeans. The thought nags at her and is lost; around every corner she thinks she sees her father's head, his collar, his shoulders—she can almost hear his laugh. She senses the river is to her right, but then they loop back into a maze of dark, narrow streets, broken brick walls, wooden houses burned to black, the road potholed, raw, she knows what happened here—but not how to grieve. She is twenty years too late.

They reach the water, and stop.

—The Pandit Temple is nearby to here, Punj says.

Sita looks over the edge. The river is luminous. Phytoplankton. The sky slides into the blue as if it cannot help itself. They have stepped through a door between the city and this place, and come to a world only trespassers find. She looks at Jivan, feels his quick smile. He nods ahead, to where Punj has paused by a flight of wooden steps; he is removing his shoes. Perched over the stagnant water is a small hut on stilts; one of the men climbs the stairs to open the hatch door. He speaks—it does not sound like Kashmiri, or Arabic or Hindi or Urdu or any tongue she knows. How funny—the place is dirty and abandoned, but here she is, surrounded by boys doing things for her. It is normal beyond reason in this strange place.

She climbs up the steps. An old woman sits in a low chair, dressed in a deep black robe. Her eyes don't seem to blink.

—Is my father here? Sita asks.

—No. I just thought you might like this original slice of Kashmiri life. Isn't her hut tidy? Are you hungry? Look, she has a dish of Kashmiri apples. She has her television too, says Punj.

He is right. In the corner of the spotless hut the television is covered with a crocheted cloth. On top stands a bowl full of deep-red apples. Highly polished, reflective.

—You want a photo? he asks.

—What? No. Sita cranes her neck, so hard and quick that it feels as though it's bending in half, almost breaking as she looks for Jivan.

—What's up? He is still there. Jivan. He climbs up the ladder. His hands stretch out either side, holding her in the doorframe.

—Where's my dad? she says.

He looks at her. Everything seems to turn around her. The terror she felt on the boat returns, full-grown.

Jivan. Punj. They are not here to help her. Is this Gargi? Has Radha sent them? *Sita,* she thinks. *What have you done?*

Punj comes to stand full frontal to Jivan, hands on his shoulders as if they are going to kiss. She turns but there is only the stagnant river and another guy behind her and the old woman grinning in her shack. She pushes through the group; before they realise what is happening, she begins to run.

She goes blindly, turning left and right; a forest of broken houses springs up, she is lost. When she can she picks up stones and pelts them behind her. But there is Papaji, there, just ahead—a flash, a laugh, he is there, playing hide-and-seek like she did with her sisters, with Jeet Bahiya and another younger boy—was it him? Was it Jivan? She turns, and turns, and turns: she reaches a dead end. In front of her, steps lead down to a small courtyard, blocked off by a high pink wall. She can make out the Om. The Pandit Temple. Her mother's religion. Her father is there, staring down from the balcony, a fresh red tikka on his forehead.

—Sita! he calls.

—Shall we go get him? Jivan is beside her, offering his arm. She does not take it. She tries to keep walking past him but he grabs her.

—What are you doing? she says.

—This is Srinagar, Jivan says. You know that.

He shrugs. It changes his face. His expression is so cold that she cannot look away.

—Didn't old Kritik tell you not to talk to strangers, and not to go out all alone? he says.

He hands her to Punj, who grips her arm. She tries to free herself; he uses both hands, pulling her backwards so she almost falls. They watch Jivan trot up the steps into the mandir. He bends for a moment, out of sight. Then reappears with Papa; someone has draped a long mala around his neck and he is throwing nuts, one after the other into his mouth. It is a trick, she remembers, Bubu once taught him. He's smiling as if this is the best game he has ever played. He follows Jivan, with no coercion, no force at all, down to where she is held.

—Papa, she says. Please.

—Punj, Jivan says. Take them to the house. Be careful with Sita Madam, treat her with respect, he smiles.

The word "Madam" sounds so strange on his lips. Shock follows; clarity—a hood being ripped from her head. *See what happens to all wilful girls?*

She tries to get free of Punj; he grips her.

—Papa, she says. Let's go back to the safe house?

Punj and Jivan shake their heads. Papa only shrugs. She looks from each to each: she wants her sisters—one to soothe her, the other to make her laugh. Was there ever a time they were happy?

Not since they were all young.

—Shall we go and see Gargi and Radha? she says.

Jivan laughs, a hollow sound. But they would stop this, if they could see her. She will say she is sorry and warn them about Kritik Uncle and Maulana Umer. She could trade that, couldn't she? That could be of value.

—Nahin, nahin, nahin, nahin, Papa says. Why should we?

He gestures to the broken houses, lilting either side. The sky crisscrossed with telephone wires, sagging into the lanes. He halts, forcing them all to stop with him. He licks his finger and points it in the air.

—Wherever this good young man will take us, let's go there. He's well-dressed and handsome, and I am sure does his best. No, don't cry. Birds sing in the bird tower, such pretty birds. Do you know what happened to them? Let's go see. We can play get-your-feet-in-the-others'-face, isn't that you girls' favourite game? Tumbling about like circus clowns, topsy-turvy always.

She is limp and heavy: like stone. The birds in the bird tower? There is no tower here. Darkness is falling—a curtain over the river, the old town. It is almost night and the birds are gone. What will you do, Sita, to save yourself? Will you stop at nothing?

She walks, Punj on one side, Papa on the other. They do not touch her; there are no hands on her but their bodies are so solid—the old man, the young—there may as well be fingers digging into her arms, tenderising her skin. Papa almost skips, though, Papa seems so happy—she has never seen him like this—feverish with energy. This is what silences her.

—You, sir, you! Do you have a pack of cards? He sings over Sita's head. We will shuffle the deck to let the joker decide who we will allow to see us and who not, and where we will make our investments and who we can help with a gift of our money.

And:

—We can laugh at the bhainjis in their spun-gold saris, the bullocks in bindis; these must be accommodated, no?

And:

—Come, Sita, no, do not shiver and sniff like a cold, sick, silly girl. We can recite shlokas from the epics if you do not want to gamble, we can talk as if we are Vishnu and Lakshmi spinning the wheel for the wealth of this world. Come, Sita, it is time to go.

Where?

They take her and move her through narrow streets, her tears spill onto her toosh.

—Sssh, sssh, don't cry now, hmm? Devraj ki beti roti nahin hai.

Papa puts his arms, like steel, around her.

—Ro mat, meri beti, ro mat, he says. Around your head the aarti will circle, and shanti will come, and Bhagwan himself will praise you. We will play at being twins, dancing, talking, laughing over minds, in rivers. Let us move to Mumbai, or to the south and open up a pickle factory. Don't cry, it will make you look old. There is plenty of time for that! Before you fade, we will see them all starve on their own greed.

The men move. They might be nothing more than a clutch of brothers and a girl.

—Wait! They stop. Jivan whispers something to Punj.

—Aré, Jivan Sahib, says Punj, putting his arm round Sita's shoulders. Men have done worse to survive in this paradise.

Papa giggles. They move on at a trot. All of her care has given him this new, skittish life. Sita has that sense again—that before this moment, she did not understand even the simplest things about the world. Still. She does not pull away.

—•—

WE WERE BROUGHT TO THIS: the house of my father-in-law, and after that there was nothing to do except play. We raced through it together, Sita and I. And Punj followed us, pounding up the old stairs after us. I knew the way.

Through this old roof, rain, snow, spring ivy and summer pollen sweep through, year after year after year after year after year. This place was a haven for dakoits. In the conflict. After they murdered their prey. After they all fled. Ha! See how the kitchen still works, even though the commode looks out to the naked street. We have no fresh water to wash or to drink. There is only moonshine. This is just a bare room with broken floorboards and king of the castle dogs on the rising sand pile outside.

She would not play, so I slapped her to stop her crying. Silly girl. Chup! She should listen to her father. She stopped crying, good girl, good girl, and her shawl was so fine, so fine, a beautiful pashmina. Just like her mother. I am not, she said. She did not understand. She said I didn't know her, and she didn't understand. I am her. Mine until married. She said she never wants to be married. Hasn't she been all this time with a man she did not marry? Wound without end. She didn't understand; she was just a child.

Take her, I said.

. . .

Punj thought her beautiful, I could tell. He lifted her like a bridegroom but she struggled like a cat. What claws! No, no, Sita, I said, do not struggle. Punj just wants to help you fly and he is right, she is a beautiful bird. See how she spreads! Do not let her squawk!

I sleep. I wake and she is gone. The mosque is making an infernal noise. Shut up! She thought we were going to the safe house. Poor silly one. She has always been so sweet. A sweet girl. She is my sweet girl. Sweetie pie. A very trusting girl. Never questioning me. Always caring, caring. Sita. But she has this bad habit of disappearing. Hide-and-seeking. Where are you? See? She does not want to be found. But I will find her. And when I do, she will sing. Remember the birds in the tower at the Farm? Such pretty birds they were. Sita! Lovely Sita! Sita Savitri? Where are you?

I hate the way she never answered, always muttering to herself under her breath. As if I did not know what she was saying.

From here I can see apples on the tree, and the world is turning, turning. From here I can see all the lights of the new Company, twinkling for me, and the world is turning, turning. From here I could be the sweet honeybee, and the world is turning, turning.

I returned her to my embrace. Her body was so tired. She refused to speak. One hand on her breast.

No? Sing! No? She wouldn't sing. Nor would she comfort. She will burn it all to the ground with her eyes. She will do her will, like a goddess of death. She said,
  —*I will return. And when I do, I will change the face of this earth.*

I shook her until her teeth rattled. I removed her jeans. There was blood on her legs. No water to wash. Her hair was matted with dirt and bird shit.

Shh, I whispered, stroking her there. We came not to this world as an abiding place.

. . .

The games began again. She struggled!

Punj held her down.

I hitched her shawl around the beam and tied a clever knot. The thing will hold, it is strong as Company steel. The other end around her neck. Such fine work, the finest!

We pulled. When I was a young man, I rode, and swam, and ran and lifted weights, all through my business years. When Sita was a little girl, the shooting parties, the polo matches, all this I could still do.

Do we ever know, really, what we can do? Not until it is done, my friends, not until it is done. Hoist to song.

> *Swift the current, dark the light*
> *Ya illa, la-illa*
> *Stars above our guide and light*
> *Kraliar, baliar!*
> *All together on the rope,*
> *Ya Pir-Dust Gir*
> *In our sinews lies our hope*
> *Khaliko, Malik-ko!*

How the world turns and brings us to these things. Such a pretty being, Sita: looped around the neck in the safe circle of her shawl. Heave! Dangle dangle.

There. It is done. Tie the knot! Circle the fire! See how she dances in the breeze? She looked so pretty, like a beautiful chandelier: diamonds and pearl drops. What do you see, my angel? The world. She rasps, hands at her throat. Her voice is faint. Ilantu. Turning, turning.

Just bring me a lotus-stem salad; let me fall into reverie.

Her head snapped sideways and she looked down at me, wide-eyed, bulging tongue. Breasts drooping, legs bare, mouth gaping, no sound. And then, finally, she danced. See her pretty feet, fanning the flames, now the fire is spreading.

.   .   .

Punj started to laugh. He looked up her red kameez. I pushed him and he fell straight through the broken floor, where the woodworm had eaten a hole. The size of a pit. He landed on his back, surprised. He disturbed the dogs.

Sita gazes down, turning.
    Speak! She cannot speak, now.

The fire; what is that noise? Crack and fall—the wooden house is falling down—hear the dog chorus—howl, howl, howl, howl.

VI

WE THAT ARE YOUNG

i

Stay loose, Jivan. Chill, Jivan. The trick is to roll the dice as if any out-come is the one you want, whatever numbers you get. Whatever you have done you just keep going. There are so many old sores here, they're not going to come back like some Foreign Return—ha ha—a tax on his actions, no a lag-haan, Hindi lessons, see? He hasn't met a word yet that cannot be broken into bite-sized biscuits . . . anything can be made to look filmic or tragic and anyone can sound like a fool.

Jivan once read somewhere that money is a suicide note—it can play murderer too, and no one is coming up the long drive behind him, no one can tell the difference between a smile and a rictus face. He tries not to think as he walks toward the hotel. There has got to be a hundred, a thousand, ten thousand, a hundred thousand, five lakh, twenty lakhs, thirty crores of candles burning inside clay pots, moulding the light into petals, birds of paradise, curved moons.

Jesus, can Sita still see the moon?

It's a cold clear night above the old city of Srinagar; the mountains are sparkling behind the hotel. The mornings here are spiced like the taste of coffee and pretzels in Boston in winter, thick salty dough twisted into lovers' knots. Jivan never properly appreciated them, nor the fresh college girls with their apple-scented shampoo, thrift-store scarves and beaten-leather book bags bought for less than fifty dollars apiece. Straight off the river the crew team came, jogging over fall leaves, late for their seminars in banking and law. Rushing in the evenings down the straight roads, the

street lights casting pots of gold on the ground at regular intervals, leading to a keg party with some simple theme like *Mad Men* or the sixties.

When this night is over, Jivan thinks, he is going to take a break, go
back to Boston, check it's all still there.

Jivan stands to one side of the glittering lobby. A river of gilded men
and women flows past him. Their talk breaks over him; it makes the
space feel too small. He pushes off and up the staircase. Its steps are wide
and long; it curves up the side of the wall. The kind of staircase you only
see in Disney movies—*Cinderella,* no, *Aladdin* or whatever that one with
the foreign princesses is.

—See this, the cost of this. See even this: so much more than this?
The chatter goes. —Have you stayed in Company Mumbai? —No only
Delhi and Goa but this is better even, better? Best in the world . . . —But
don't you think that Gargi should not have done all this right now? —Is
Bapuji even here? —Radha is after all in mourning still. —What is happening in the Delhi protests, do you know? —It looks so bad. —Friends,
what does it matter? We are here, we should enjoy.

No one is talking about Sita.

Brown skin glitters under golden lights and dark hair is piled high.
The saris, the smells, the slippery sound of women's bangles blur together.
Some have tried for Gargi's elegance and come off plain, some have overdone it in the jewellery store and salon. Some look like time-travellers
from the 1980s, dated like the décor in the local restaurants by the lake.
Girls dressed like frontier robbers stalk through the party, their cross-
body holsters loaded with India Company shots. The waiting staff have
been culled from the best of the hotels across the country; they are trained
not to stare, not to hang around the guests, not to insist, non-stop—

Mozzarella ball? Seekh kebab? Spiced corn fritter? Tonight the new
India Company makes its debut on the napkins and the uniforms, on
the newly laid silk rugs.

Jivan watches from the turn of the stairs as Company guards screen
for bombs and weapons. His own boys, selected from local neighbour-
hoods, have been trained by him to mingle with the crowds, tapping the
industrialists and the politicians, trailing the journalists (though Barun J.
Bharat, who RSVP'd *yes,* hasn't yet shown). Making sure the drugs are
discreet, are ready when required. That the carefully planned tours of the
hotel and grounds stick to the route, and no one ventures into the private
wing. Jivan respects these Srinagar boys. He knows they have lost friends,

brothers, fathers. But in the four weeks he has been here, getting this place ready, he has never heard them complain or say one word about anything but work. All of them use English—he has banned them from speaking their own tongues; it was his first rule of order.

He takes a whisky from one of the turbaned waiters. Dude has a dropkick moustache. He knocks it back, takes another, keeps moving. The Sari Army smile at him, so handsome, so polished. Of course they think they know him, they have met each other at such and such's house—that party—that wedding, of course.

—Helloji, how are you?

He nods back at them. Then mixes hysteria with a twist of lime and washes it down with tequila at the long glass bar. Tastes bitter, like metal, like blood.

In the poker room, the dice roll, ones and fives and eights. The chips stack up on the baize tables, models of the half-built Bubu towers Radha has been left to play with. Where is she? Well, she's been puking all day; she is still in her room. A few of the more experienced Company PRs are working the party in her place, introducing Bollywood to bankers, state and private; property developers to governments, national and regional, letting a select few know what kind of gift might buy them a personal audience with Gargi when the time comes.

Jivan loads a small plate with ladoos. Outside Radha's suite, her women—one called Sheila, the other, he thinks, Rachel—stand guard at her door. They are dressed in one-shouldered tops and dark leather trousers; their hair has been teased and sprayed into someone's idea of punk, their faces powdered almost white. Their lips are painted the kind of red that makes whatever it touches look wounded. They say Madam is too sick for him to see her. He hands them the ladoos; they smile and let him pass.

Now, since when does Radha have such a thing for scented candles? She has to have at least five burning at any given time. She has developed this obsession with lavender: everything has to be purple and smell, Jivan thinks, like a gift shop. He gives a quick salute to a painting of Bubu brought up from Delhi; he is dressed like the Emperor Akbar, leaning on his sword. Bubu doesn't look down at him but straight out into the private garden, planted with brutal steel sculptures that loom at the windows: alien skeletons of the industrial modern.

Radha's sari for this evening, deep purple, shot through with gold thread, is stiff on its hanger, waiting to be unfurled. Radha's sandals—gold, delicate—are standing to attention by her dressing table. *Where is Radha?* Curled in the middle of her four-poster; Jivan has to fight swathes of silk and chiffon to find her. She is wearing jogging pants and his crimson Harvard sweatshirt. She smells too sweet; of Company perfume, and puke.

—How are you? he says.

—Jivan. You came.

He smiles at her; her eyes and skin are glazed. He could take her down to the Egyptian lobby and display her in a cabinet. But this is not gold, it is the sheen of the sickroom. He shudders.

—You have to come down, Rads. You're missing the party. I need you to come. Look, your lovely sari is waiting for you over there—Sheila is outside, to help you.

—Is Gargi downstairs?

—I haven't seen her yet, and I don't know anyone. I don't know if Surendra is giving the opening speech or Gargi is. See? I can't cope without you.

—Ask Gargi, Radha says. She curls away from him; her hair covers her face.

—Raddy, don't be like that.

She rolls back to face him. Her face is going grey; she is clearly sick, not fronting. She looks almost like a little girl, when he used to make her dens with cushions to hide in. In those soft places, no one could hear her cry.

—You know what Uppal told me? That you and her—on the way back from Amritsar, that night of Bubu and Ranjit Uncle—

—Shh, he says. Why are you thinking about that now? No one has seen Uppal for weeks. The guy doesn't even have the courtesy to show up for work anymore.

Radha's hair is sticking to her scalp. Jivan strokes it back with a finger. He tries not to look at her too closely. The room is tiled with lavender and turquoise mosaics, as if she took a pair of scissors to these walls too, and then ordered some poor slave to piece it all back together.

—Don't you think it's too, too sad? she says. Everyone is leaving us. Sita, Kritik Uncle. Jeet. Bubu, Ranjit Uncle, Uppal. My dad. So sad.

She sniffs and tries to pull herself onto his lap, up his body, get her arms around his neck. Now he has to hold her. She is so thin in the waist, and so heavy around the breasts, the hips. Much more so than she was in Amritsar. Too many Kashmiri sweets, he thinks. Isn't it?

—Radha, he says. How long have you been feeling sick for? What are you taking? Answer me.

He pushes her away.

—You aren't leaving, are you? She reaches for him; her pupils are tiny black pinpricks.

—Get up. Wash yourself. I'll check in with Gargi for a doctor. I'll bring you some food.

—Feed me like a baby, she says.

She pulls her knees up to her chest, locking them to her belly. She rocks from side to side, smiling at him through sleep-crusted eyes. Her face is smudged pink all over, as if she has used too much blush. It should be grotesque but there is something about the way she is curled on the lavender sheets: she is still a pretty Radha.

—Sure, I'll feed you, whatever you want, he says. I might be an hour.

—Would you feed Gargi? she asks.

—Stop it, Radha, or I'll just leave.

Now she rolls onto her stomach, her face in the pillow. Her sweatpants are filthy.

—Do you love her? she says, muffled.

—Of course.

He moves himself off the bed; it's like swimming through lavender sludge.

Radha kneels up, wiping her hair off her face again, and again, even when she does not need to.

—Would you have sex with her? Do you think about it? I can't believe you'd find her sexy—as if she even knows what the word means.

—Enough, he says. It's insulting. She's your Didi, or did you forget?

She flops back into the bed, a dark-skinned Rapunzel with burned black hair. She starts to hum to herself; she says:

—Did you know that in the first trimester, pregnant women like anything pink if they are going to have a girl, anything blue for a boy?

—What did you say?

—Nothing.

She lies there, grinning at him. Hums the opening bars of "Lavender's Blue."

—I have to go, he says. I'll see you later.

He forces himself to bend, brush his lips over her forehead. She tastes like a pillar of salt.

Back downstairs he loops around, Radha's words in his head. He checks his phone: no message from Punj. He looks for Gargi in the Napurthala Room, where gift-wrapped girls and festooned matrons are comparing notes on each other's children. She is not in the English pub that Radha insisted on; it's full of Bubu 2.0s, all in black tie, smoking cigars, drinking whisky sours. In the Orchid Room, where plants on polished walnut tables droop purple, white and yellow labia over their own reflections, Jivan eavesdrops on couples talking about everything but sex. He asks the security where Gargi is. Have they seen her? No? Have they met her tonight? Every one of them nods—she cares about me, they seem to be saying, she cares about my uniform and whether it fits. She knows I have a sick daughter, she sent Diwali clothes to my wife.

No—that's her way of protecting her investments, Jivan wants to tell them. Gargi only cares about work. She doesn't love you, or your family, and she doesn't love your children. How could she? She doesn't have it in her.

In the Modernists' Room—painted stark white, with a band of dark colour around its walls—Jivan pauses. He stands under spotlights, turning through the pages of hardback art books arranged on one of the tables. He does not recognise the artists' names. Husain. Reddy. Sher-Gil.

Gargi—on that drive from Amritsar to Delhi, the night that his dad was blinded and Bubu died. Radha won't talk about what happened. Still. Jivan was with Gargi in the back of the SUV; Uppal was in the front (where is he, really?). None of them aware of the chaos they left behind. Poor old Bubu must have croaked somewhere around the time they crossed the state line out of Punjab.

They did not know. They were still shocked at Ranjit's betrayal. He remembers that Gargi cried in the car, about Sita. She said she felt every day was forcing her to steel. He listened until she stopped, and said,

—*Sorry.*

They had a car picnic of beers and spiced fruit salad, eaten from a tiffin box. There were chicken kebabs and minted yoghurt dip—he remembers this because they laughed about getting it on their fingers and licking it off. When they finished the beer, they drank French red wine shared straight from the bottle. Parts of the country he never wanted to know flashed by in the dark. Gargi cried again; she said Sita had always been self-centred—that maybe it was a generational thing. She said Sita had a death wish, that if she came back, all the plays would end. *And if she didn't?*

Gargi fell asleep, her sandals kicked off, her feet pushing against Jivan's leg. Her heels were surprisingly dry—the skin cracked, as if she walked around barefoot in the dirt all day.

She woke up around dawn, surprised by her phone's cheerful buzz.

—Aw, sod off, she said. Then she looked at Jivan's face, and laughed. Only Amritsar. Probably to see if we reached.

If she had answered the phone, they would have learned that Ranjit had gone blind and gone missing, that Bubu had *expired,* as Uppal told him later (as if Bubu was a library book, not a man). And that Radha was locked in her suite making the kind of noises an animal might as it dies. Instead, Gargi reached forward to the passenger seat and shook Uppal awake. They pulled over, they got out of the car, to stretch and drink coffee with petit fours: high tea on the highway. A few cars passed and beeped; otherwise it was just the tarmac, pasted flat to the earth, desert stretching out either side. Leading toward a sunrise the exact same pink, he thought, as the five-dollar bill in Monopoly.

—Jivan, Gargi had said. Do you want to get married one day?

Sure, why not? This is what he had thought. *If you lose your husband and change your mind about having kids.*

She looked at her wedding ring. He remembers this because her family signet ring was nested on top.

—Just got to find the right girl, he said.

Gargi smiled, full wattage.

—Should I start looking in the Sunday classifieds? Telling the Aunties I know a suitable boy? Foreign Return, MBA, rising salary, seeks fair-skinned beauty from good business or Brahmin family, appreciation of Abercrombie and a taste for single malt. Sound right?

Trucks roared past, whipping grit into their eyes. He told her he didn't have so many demands. The sun was racing into the sky, glaring red as if trying to warn them to get back into the car, keep on! Toward the city and its marching crowds. He told her he wanted something more simple: just wanted to be happy, that's all.

Gargi teased him. She said the girl would have to be quite pretty— but not too much—she wouldn't choose one from skinnybitchland. She laughed again at the look on his face when she said that. Then she twisted her hands, then picked up a petit four and placed it back down. Her nails were painted bright coral. He thought about Radha, slippery and firm in the afternoons when she sucked him. Her hair so long. Sometimes he wants to wind it round her neck and pull it tight.

Gargi had said, without looking at him,

—Do I seem happy to you?

The day was firming its claim. He took a piss, then got back into the car with her. They had to slow to make way for a parade of cows—lean in the ribs but with big, low bellies. Unseeing as they clopped past, tails swishing, assholes dark and stained. The boy riding them had a home-made whip and bare feet; he balanced on the back of a cow, performing for the long grass waving at the side of the road. He asked Gargi if she was lonely and she told him no, that she loved being at the helm of the Company. *Yes,* she had said, *I love it.*

— Just, since you've been in Amritsar, I've had so much on my mind. Work, accounts, how to be good. You make me think.

—What? he asked, and looked out of the window. A hand-painted sign flashed by—*Freeway Toll Coming Soon.*

—Jivan, she said.

The city was rising all around them in squats and slums and drunken towers. They passed wedding grounds being assembled; Taj Mahal façades and the desert behind.

—Jivan, she had said again. She stroked her palm down his face.

He looked at the lines in her face, around her eyes. He wanted to sink into her belly and feast on her softness and power. Could he really do this? Looking into her face, he imagined: divorce from Surendra, remarriage. Could he actually become head of the Company? And have Gargi, who anticipates everything he's ever needed, as his wife? Mother to two (or maybe three?) pure Indian children who would grow up to inherit so much? Two would be enough. A boy and a girl. Jivan Junior. Jivanka.

—You know, he said. You'd be a great mom.

She looked at him and shook her head.

—No. Then: You know I've never experienced a really good fuck?

He, who never shows surprise, wanted to raise his fist and stop her mouth.

They left the freeway, heading down the dirt tracks toward the maze. Their hands separated as the car bumped over the potholes. They turned into the Farmhouse drive and Gargi sat up straight. Just like that, Jivan's bright vision faded. She looked older. Despite the air-conditioning in the car, she was sweating.

It was late August, or was it early September? All the flowers had been replaced with grass and there were no peacocks to greet them. Surendra's Mercedes was parked in front of the Farmhouse. Before Jivan could say anything else, Uppal was jumping out to open Gargi's door.

—Welcome home, Gargi Madam, Uppal said.

Jivan stayed in the car, in the debris of their journey. He watched Gargi go inside. He thought about calling Bubu, but didn't. After five minutes or so, Gargi came back out. She opened the door and said she was sorry, Surendra was having some kind of fit.

—You better not come in. Go to Ranjit's bungalow. Freshen up, then meet me in the office downtown. Call Bubu in a couple of hours, tell him to keep an eye on Radha, please? Not too many wild parties. We just don't know what's coming up.

—Will you be OK?

—Of course, she said.

She looked back at the house.

—I just have to go and press Surendra's feet for a while. Listen to his latest attempt at writing for the *Speaking Tree*. But, Jivan—she said (and this is the moment he cannot let go of)—you know whatever you want, I'll do my best to give you.

She started toward him. They were face to face, the car window in between. His vision flared again. The idea that Surendra never existed, that he could marry Gargi and the Company and the Farm—and the mines and the cement and the cars and parts and all the hotels. All that land—which means so much money, for him, for Jivan and Jivanka, for the children down the ages.

He went to the bungalow. He washed and ate. He went to the Delhi office—but she didn't come. Nor did she text him—not even one coy little kissy face smiley. Then, Uppal himself came to tell him what Bubu had done. That Radha had been widowed—his father was missing—that he had to go back to Amritsar.

Since then Gargi has been in Delhi, he has been in the north. Four weeks working with Punj in Amritsar and Srinagar, all toward this night. They walked the city. They made recruits and began a watch. Jivan knew when Sita had arrived—with Kritik, of all people, and Devraj. He did not share this information with Gargi, or Surendra or Radha. Instead he took it slowly; he wanted to get to know her. He sat in a coffee place near her safe house, drinking bitter cups of black, waiting for her to come out alone. He watched her go on endless boat-rides, wondering what she was planning. Would she want to continue the campaign? For her, he thought, it would not be about boycotting the Company—she would probably want to take her place in it, with all of Ranjit's shares. She might want to break the whole thing into pieces and offer the parts to the People. In the badly recorded films he has watched of her, she stands in wood-panelled rooms in England, going on and on about changing the lives of the bottom rung. The pieces were in place, she said, the public marches were only the beginning. So many others wanted a new way forward. They believed they had a duty to speak up. And such causes! The environment, labour laws, child marriage. There was even a debate where she told the floor that the prohibited practice of dowry still led to women being sold as slaves across India. That rape within marriage was not classed as a crime. *Sure,* he said to the screen, *Satyamev Jayate.* He watched her as she talked. The things she said, the people she wanted to help, whom she felt she really could make a difference to—it made him nostalgic again, for Iris and the old American life.

What would happen if Sita never came back? Idly, he wondered.

Tonight, he wanted to talk to Gargi. He was going to tell her his dreams. But Radha—so thin around the waist—so thick in the hips—and now sick . . . O.

He stares at the walls of the Modernists' Room, the dark band of colour. It is actually a mural—a rusted, earth-coloured background. Over there, a yellow horse rears behind a faceless woman. Her angular body is wrapped in white bandages around the breasts, she cradles a long-necked, fat-bottomed instrument. Her black hair streams behind her, and over there, in a corner, the blanched ribs of a cow are etched on the canvas. In the centre, a Mother Teresa headdress, white with blue stripes, floats with no face. And low in one corner, a yellow-skinned baby holds out its arms to the void.

—Gargi Madam, here, please, look this way!

The camera flashes. Gargi poses on the stairs and feels the glitter and chatter, the wine and music, a column of gold under her feet. People have come here. People have been seduced here. By Gargi Ma. This new skill was learned as the panic began for her, late at night. As the Company went into a freefall, a kind of spin she once thought only happened in movies, where the plane is going down, nose first, and begins to roll, beating the clouds like a ceiling fan does the air. Sweet words, eye-fluttering persuasion. *Transferable skills.* She used to do this only to flatter Bapuji; now these attitudes wait in her office each morning, to help her through the day. They work. The panic recedes, the evidence is every-where around her. She is the seductress and each of her guests is in love.

The seductress is a strange goddess. A seven-headed Rakshas, with a different instrument of persuasion in each of its uncountable hands. When the fact of Radha and Jivan presented itself to Gargi, she set that demon to work. Tonight, among the celebrations, she will see what returns will come.

No one told Gargi. She simply became aware, after her sister cried herself to sleep for the nth time since Bubu died—which was when, if she thinks about it, her own, silvering panic began—that there was an edge of something euphoric undercutting her sister's terrible grief. Radha wants new clothes, a spa weekend in Dubai. She will not work; instead she spends hours doing Yoga or playing craps against herself using a pair of pearl dice (which, Gargi is almost sure, used to belong to Bubu, or were they Ranjit Uncle's?). Instead of partying or talking, Radha now spends nights in her Amritsar room, alone, Pinteresting pictures of strange and ever-more-extravagant cakes she says she will order for her staff to distribute to the poor.

When she was young, Radha used to love going on the water. Since they arrived in Srinagar—she has told Gargi over and over—she is afraid that if she even rides in a pleasure boat on the hotel lake, she will fall in, she will drown. All she wants is to be told stories; stories from their mother, stories, stories, stories until she falls asleep. When Radha wakes up in the night, she screams that the walls are mocking her. She will only allow Jivan to come to her. He stays until she can sleep again.

In the mornings Radha is docile, as she used to be when she ate something sugary-tasty or had a good massage from their Lottie. Over time her body gets leaner but plumper, her hair sleeker, her face more rested. She begins to look as fresh as a new doll. She telephones the couture houses in Mumbai and Delhi and has the designers send trunks of clothes. She orders evening gowns and winter coats, as if planning her wedding trousseau.

With a growing sense of outrage (a word she learned from Surendra—and which he only uses for her and her sisters), Gargi realises that Radha is very much in love. As Gargi works to complete negotiations, orders, budgets, and tries to make a profit on the hotel opening instead of losing everything there is left, Radha floats around the high-security grounds. Wrapped in a muffler, she strokes the flowers and talks to the birds, before disappearing for daily afternoon naps.

Gargi's need to keep busy both powers and exhausts her. Left to manage Bubu's side of the business, she begins to sluice the best parts to her own name. Outrage feeds on grief, she finds. Though the grief is not for Bubu. In the early mornings, before anyone can call her, she dresses in clothes no one would recognise, and slips down the hill in an auto—into the city, to walk.

She walks through the party, watching Radha's friends. What does it feel like to be so thin, so polished, so ripe that no matter what clothes you put on your body, your body is the only thing men see? What does it feel like to have the kind of conviction that no matter what you wear, your eyes seem to shine with everything you know you are owed from life?

These girls never preen; they are too confident for that. They stand next to the pyramids of ladoos, of burfi, chocolate brownies and bite-sized sushi rolls. They do not eat a single thing.

First, they drink and smoke on the terrace—and stub the butts out on her inlaid floor. Then there will be drugs, discreetly. There are pockets of time when none of the girls can be seen, and she knows they have left as a flock of geese seeks warm weather; the rooms of the party are only a resting post between bathroom highs. Only later, past midnight, they might eat, picking at every tender shred of lamb, every juicy lychee, every bowl of rose syrup jalebi and lavender ice cream her new Srinagar kitchen can produce. Washed down with her champagne, taxed per bottle as import.

The Company must recover. They have not steadied since Barun J. Bharat—on a tip-off from Twitter's MrGee—asked Bapuji for *the truth* about a servant who died from a beating at the Farm. Barun said he had photographs. How, he asked, could a campaigner such as Devraj Bapuji call for equality without answering this charge?

—Gargi begged me to respond, Bapuji said. She told me—What is the nature of village justice? It is brutality.

After that, her reputation took a beating that even the dead man might have sympathised with. And though he broke the story, Barun did not correct it, or report that the servant's widow was given a proper pension: five thousand rupees a month. And had a house bought in her village and jobs for her three nephews on some part of the site that will be the India Company's Odisha sand mine, if tonight goes well. The woman's daughters' dowries are fixed also.

Every day has brought some fresh fight. There are charges that include corruption, money laundering, major defaulting on unsecured loans from state banks (to fund, mostly, the eco-car); fraud, tax evasion, theft. The Company has broken labour, development and transport laws that no one, particularly the national government, has ever before given two hoots about (no, Gargi corrects her own pitiable naïvity—a shit about). These accusations must be made to disappear. After the Delhi protest, the proposals for an anti-corruption bill are stalled and might be persuaded to die; of this, Gargi can only feel guiltily glad. The guilt stopped with the most astonishing news of all: that Gargi Devraj Grover is being charged by the state of Napurthala under the Maintenance and Welfare of Parents and Senior Citizens Bill, 2007—which carries, as her vakil has informed her, a five-thousand-rupee fine (plus tax, the Company mani-pedi costs more) and a jail term of three months. This, if Bapuji and Sita can prove that Gargi has neglected to look after her father as a daughter should. The column inches have been harder and longer on this than any other charge made against the Company to date.

This is how the people lick the foam from a cappuccino that—if it wasn't for Gargi—they wouldn't even be able to beg for in India. She cannot bring herself to pay the fine. She would rather go sing in jail.

In the mornings she wanders in the city, and all of these thoughts fall away. She notices instead the gap between the white models in the shop windows and the real women of this place—how, after years of coming and going here, she sees more and more are wearing chadors, head to floor. Her own artisans—the box-makers—all confirm this. They work in one house, a different floor for whittling, a different room for sanding, another for base coat (the middle floor, with the most light, given over to hand-painting the lovely patterns before varnishing takes place under the eaves). As she sits with them, watching their rhythmic work, they tell her their sons are leaving for Aligarh and Delhi; also that their ways are being lost between the Sunnis and the Hindus tearing the state between them. The shawl men say the same. Some mornings she goes to the home of the embroiderers she knows, and drinks sheer chai. She watches them stitch leaves and flowers, pink roses primped with white, knowing a year or more will go by until the piece is finished. Sometimes their young sons come sit and stare at her. They tell her what they are studying and she brings them iPods and earphones; she sees them try to hide their pleasure from their fathers—stitching, stitching. Where will these boys be in two years, in five?

Gargi goes to a particular market. She is there as it opens for the morning—the one around the bridge, at the junction of lake and road. She watches the men unload their wooden cages of chickens, scrawny-looking, stacked on top of each other, miserable as forgotten old men. They don't raise a squawk when the traders pick them out one by one to cleave off their heads. Chop chop. She buys slices of paneer cut from a fresh, soggy moon of the stuff, she sprinkles a sachet of Company sugar on it, and eats it straight from the paper bag. Never mind the flies. Always, she is back at her desk in the hotel before the first business of the day. Thinking about Radha, and Jivan.

It is morning, the day before the party. Gargi feels an answer come to her just as the muezzin heralds the dawn and calls the faithful to prayer. She is alone in her suite, counting her breaths. Tomorrow, the New India Company will open the heavy, handmade doors of its most desirable address. A 360-room hotel, with panopticon views. Screening rooms on the VIP floors. A martini bar carved out of ice. Several landings for women travelling alone, served only by female staff until the hour of 9 p.m. (none of them would work beyond that). A dumpling restaurant with an antique Buddhist bell (sourced by Jeet all the way from Tibet). In the grounds, a tower that seems to hang suspended over a private lake. All of Srinagar below. The Rani Suite.

Gargi hears the summons to prayer echo across the city, and thinks: Jivan. Radha.

In the bathroom she pulls at the dark circles under her eyes; she picks at the blemishes her dermatologist has not been able to eradicate. A few hairs coming from her chin must be removed before tomorrow. She washes her face. *Shameless,* Surendra called her. *Worse than a whore, a sexless woman, the kind no one would even rape.* That morning, after the night Bubu died, when Jivan and she reached Delhi, Surendra was waiting, outraged—of course—that she had let Bapuji leave Amritsar and take his chances in the storm.

Then Uppal (where is he?) came to tell them about Ranjit, and Bubu. She stood on the verandah in the clothes she had worn since the night before. She felt cold all over although it was almost noon.

How—Surendra wanted to know—*did Bubu, a man, a leader of the family, allow you and Radha to behave so badly?*

Surendra said that she and Radha could not run the Company alone. He said it was out of the question: they must apologise to Bapuji; they must take care of Ranjitji; they must get Sita back.

—Shut up, Surendra, she said. Then wanted to laugh at his gaping fish mouth.

She could tell him what his life is built on—and watch him run crying, calling for his Mama to give milk. She knows he does not care about Bapuji, and even less about her. He cares about how things look and what people say. He is so stupid that he does not realise: Sita is going to come back for her part. Then Surendra will smile at her and try to appease her, while whining to the pundit about his fate and raging in private about her lack of respect.

She realised then that nothing about Sita makes sense to Surendra, or Bubu, or Bapuji. She hoped, fiercely, that Sita would come back and show them what women can really be. She hoped Sita had taken a lover, found more pleasure with him than she, Gargi, ever did in the marriage bed. *With Surendra for a husband,* she thought, *who needs eunuchs?* She said this to him, out loud—and sounded to herself like a peacock screeching. Then she remembered that all the peacocks are dead.

Me, and mine, and the Company.
Me, and mine and the Company.
Me and mine and the Company.
Me and mine and the Company.
Me and mine and the Company.

She sang this under her breath. It kept her standing against him. Never has she spoken what she really feels, or wants to say. Out, rage!—it's a drug. A truth drug! Laughter bubbled up in her and she had to put her hands over her mouth to actually stop it from escaping. It came out as a croak—as if Surendra had cursed her to become a fat frog. A Frog Princess in need of kissing. She liked it. She decided that she would find a Prince brave enough to do it.

The day before the opening night Gargi dresses in her old clothes; she makes her way into the city. In the market the sellers nod to her now; they have seen her face for three weeks almost—a middle-aged, middle-class Indian woman in a dun-coloured shawl with no children attached to her, a crone and some money to spend (that's all they are interested in). She passes the chickens. She does not stop for paneer. Hunger has her looking for something else. The market climbs a steep hill and she follows it until she reaches the apple sellers. In her youth she and Radha were brought rare, late Ambris from the orchards around Shopian and the villages of Anantnag at this time of year—deep, blush-red apples, medium-sized and polished, with an aroma that could fill a room. They ate slice after slice of them, year after year, until the American apple became the more popular. Gargi is looking for a perfect Ambri, to gift to Radha today.

She is back in her room by 9 a.m. She showers and dresses carefully. White, her new favourite colour. The apple so stark against her reflection, her dun-coloured shawl. In the bathroom cabinet she searches through her medicine box, until she finds what she is looking for. A liquid laxative which Jeet used to give her before parties, to help her lose weight. The stuff is ayurvedic, it scours the insides; two drops can keep a woman in her room for twenty-four hours. Using the medicine-pack syringe, Gargi injects half the bottle into the apple's flesh.

—What's up, Big Sis? Radha opens the door and squinnys at her. Gargs, you're looking tired.

Gargi smiles at Radha, in her vest and loose silk pants; even unwashed she is so lovely. She smells of fat and soap—the whole room does, Gargi thinks. That intricate French furniture. The lilac walls. That terrible picture of Bubu. On the dining table dishes are laid; there is a plate of half-eaten food—Radha is having a breakfast of khichdi and lamb chops. The rest of the suite, bedroom, bathroom, open-plan living area, is pristine—every surface polished, each cushion standing on point.

—I'm exhausted with so much going on, Gargi says. I can't wait for this thing to be over. And just go back to everyday work.

—Are you crazy? Radha spins around in a circle, she collapses on her chaise longue, her hands resting on her stomach. She drums it, gently.

—Tomorrow is going to be awesome! We're going to party all night. @MrGee says we shouldn't be opening hotels while the people are suffering here but what does he know? No one hearted that tweet. Radha hugs a cushion. Everyone is going to love you, Didi, just like I do. Come here, come sit down. Want to have gulab jamun? Ice cream? Sheila! Radha calls to her new companion. A confident girl; Gargi has instructed her to sleep in an ante-room, and not to leave Radha alone.

—No, no, Gargi says. I don't want to eat. But look what I brought you.

Now is the time, now.

—An Ambri! says Radha.

—I went to the market this morning and I found it for you myself. Remember how we used to love these?

—Gargi!

Radha takes the apple. She kisses it and rubs it. She takes a large bite.

Gargi wanders to the windows, as if she wants to look at the sculptures outside. She thinks of Jivan, of tomorrow night—and the party—and hears herself say,

—Do you want to try out the medium with me? He's waiting downstairs.

—He's here? Radha eats some more apple. She nods. Let's get him up. Are you sure you won't have something? Sheila! Get me that champagne open, and bring the Lalique flutes. And bring my Kashmiri medicine, you know which the box is?

—Hanji, Radha Madam, party shuru ho rahi hai? Sheila comes in from Radha's bedroom, carrying a sandalwood box, intricately carved. She gives Radha and Gargi a wild look as if they are her friends or sisters.

Rude girl, thinks Gargi. Radha shouldn't encourage her.

Sheila steps to one side, but Gargi can feel her, watching them.

—Let me introduce you to my lovely little golden box of Kashmiri medicine, Radha says. Gifted to me by the two dearly departed men from my life. My darling Bubu, and Ranjit Uncle, one of whom got this for me when I got married and took up my post as head of PR, the other has been filling it ever since. So thoughtful! You know, Ranjit Uncle even arranged a special delivery for the party, and it came, addressed to him only, as if he didn't intend to share. Never mind. I am sure he would want us to have it. Radha gnaws on the apple; she is almost at the core.

What is it about Radha that so seduces? If Gargi can answer this question, she thinks she will feel the kind of youth that her sister wears as carelessly as that silk strap, which falls off her shoulder as if in awe of her skin. She wants to belong, like that strap to the body it clings to— she does not always want to be the one who pulls herself up, Ma Gargiji. She imagines herself at the party. Tomorrow, when Radha will lie like a peanut shell in the bed, Gargi will be herself, and Radha, and Sita—all at once. She will go in search of Jivan.

—Drugs? Now? Gargi says. It's 10 a.m.

—Don't freak out. Think of it as a painkiller. It comes straight through from Afghanistan. Radha laughs, and rolls her eyes. *Chill out, Big Sis.* Soaked in the strands of the cloth coming in from Pakistan. Woven into the rugs, Bubu's own designs—hero of mine.

Radha bites the apple. Chews, swallows, grins. *She is eating the apple,* thinks Gargi. *Stop! No. Good.*

—Do you really think there is anything I don't know about the Company? she says. How do you think we paid for your wedding?

—Sure, Gargi, Radha says. But did you know that Ranjit Uncle kept back a special little stash of the very finest all for himself and Kritik Uncle—and even Daddy took some, every now and then?

—The public will never believe it. Can you get Barun?

—Aré, stop working for one second, Gargi. Come on. And didn't you hear that Barun quit his newspaper job? Some sex scandal. He's gone to the UK, to write a fiction.

—O, says Gargi.

—Never mind. It's time you took your first ride. It's going to be wild.

—The medium is here, Gargi says. Finish your apple. We can save this for tomorrow. OK?

—OK. But you have to promise you will do this with me. For once, we'll party together.

Radha chews the apple down to the core. All that remains is the stick.

—I promise, Gargi says.

They wait together for the medium. Radha orders the curtains to be closed against the sun, blocking out the long shadows cast by the Western garden across her tiled floor. They lie on cushions on the Kashmiri carpet. Gargi strokes it, remembering how she ordered it when Radha got married. It is silk. The colour of a lake in winter, woven with fine shapes of rare animals, somewhere among them a precious white tiger cub, the palest the world has seen. It was her personal wedding gift for Radha and Bubu. It is sweet, after all, that Radha wants it here. Yes, she seems to be in a very sweet mood today.

Radha folds herself up so her head is resting on her feet. Like a little cat, the pet she always wanted when Bapuji insisted they should have only dogs.

—You're like a small dog, Gargi says affectionately.

—Sing me a song, Gargi Didi. You've got such a great voice.

Such a sweet mood. She strokes her sister's hair.

—What do you want to hear?

—I don't know. Anything. Something silly.

—Umm. God. Radha, I haven't sung to you since you were a little girl.

—I want it, though. Please?

—*Matchmaker, matchmaker, make me a match . . .*

—No! Not that one.

—So what do you want me to sing?

—Something Kashmiri. Tell me the honeybee tale.

—OK. But not now. The medium is coming. Are you ready?

—Ready! Radha stretches full length, flashing her stomach. Curved, Gargi thinks, with a little bloat. Then she curls back on the cushions.

—I'm ready, she says again.

We came not to this world as an abiding place.

Later, they went to the medium—for Radha, the story was clear.

That she must take more care, and also go on a journey with all of her precious baggage. To a place with mountains like this, but far away from here. Switzerland? Perhaps. Otherwise your beauty will turn to dust.

What does this mean for Radha? Will she ever be loved again? The medium, primed for this question, tells Radha that she should not be filling her head and her body with such thoughts, for they would make her old before her time. No—she should keep her head down, agar Jivan ko sudhaarna hai. To live up to her husband's legacy, she should go and have a period of solitary reflection, of meditation. Then come back, and take her place in the business.

For Gargi, the medium holds few surprises. He says she loves her sisters, yes, but she has sacrificed her youth to them. The celestial stars of Modo and Mahu govern their behaviour and these two themselves have nothing in common. But everything they have must be shared. Then, using a star chart from his laptop computer and the coordinates of their births, he shows her that she and Radha are also Gemini-starred twins, born separately because of a cosmic mistake on their mother's part and the strength of their father's desire. This has caused a critical tension between them. They should love each other as two parts of a whole. One is ambitious and the other is beautiful. A crucial third of their hearts is missing. To make sure of health and wealth and prosperity, they have to get this back.

—I can see you want, he says, to be young, and have all of life again.

How true, Gargi thinks. And then, *What nonsense. Everyone knows my story, a child could tell these things.*

She does not want to go back. She wants Jivan, just for this one night.

When the sickness begins, Radha does not scream for Jivan. Instead she sends for—who else? Gargi, the only person she can talk to about loose motions. Once every fifteen minutes and nothing will stay inside. Gargi soothes her and gives her warm milk, laced with a little more laxative.

She walks through the party, greeting people, smiling. She makes sure the Polaroid photographer with his vintage camera captures the many important men who are only too happy to stand with their arm around her. They still call her "Gargi beti." She smiles, and the photographer flaps the picture in her face till her image reveals itself.

—Wah! Gargi Madam with the world at her feet, he says.

She takes the snap and orders a vodka-shot girl to follow her while she knocks back every tiny rejection, betrayal, every hurt, every minute and second of loneliness she has ever felt.

Then she returns to Radha's rooms. The Kashmiri box is fetched. Radha demonstrates what to do with a quick sharp sniff. She grins but she looks truly ill. She is splayed on the bed. Wearing a pair of Donald Duck boxer shorts and a white singlet that are far too big for her. She refuses water but asks for champagne, which is given. Jivan has been already; he has promised to return with food, Radha says. She does not want it, though. To want food would mean she is well enough to stand. She wants to stand but the floor seems so far away. The ceiling is telling her to stay in the bed, the bedsheets want to strangle her. Her eyes feel heavy, as if her kohl has weight. Radha says she has been sick so many times, how can she still have organs inside her? She is not sure that Jivan will come back.

—Gargi, she says, eyes glittering. Help. There is going to be a baby.

There is a storm in Gargi's head. She watches as her sister lies back, eyes glazed, her fingers drumming on her belly.

—Bubu's or Jivan's, what does it matter? Radha says. I gave Jivan my ring. He's going to marry me.

Gargi grips the Kashmiri box. She traces its carvings and wants to believe Radha is lying. But there it is. So clear to see, now that she has been told.

For the first time in her life, Gargi copies her sister. A bend of the head, a quick inhale. Her eyes begin to water. The storm turns to sand through her veins. The cold outside frosts the windows, freezes her smile, her skin. A child. Radha starts to hum. *A tune you know, Gargi, you should recognise.*

—In the summer, Radha says— (her eyes closing, her arms drifting as if she is conducting a silent orchestra) —all the birds will return to the lake. What shall the baby be called?

Gargi backs off the bed. She smiles at her sister; she spins—she cannot stop herself—out of the room, as quickly as she can.

—Doctor Sahib ko bulao, she tells Sheila. Right now. Radha Madam needs help.

Gargi cannot go to Jivan. She cannot return to the party. If you falter on these shining steps, you will fall. There are fireworks behind her eyes and she has misplaced her tongue.

What have I done?

She wanders around her kingdom, seeing it as if for the first time. Terror here, and there, in corners, in rooms. Then, lovely kingdom! Beautiful night! Built on concrete foundations deep as the pit of Dhimbala. Gargi goes outside, down the terraced gardens; silver cold and clear. She sees the yews, waiting to be sculpted, the crates of tulip bulbs waiting to be planted. She slips over the grass, down the terraces, towards the small forest that rings her new lake. The last of the trees that were here before the land was cleared for the hotel to rise. *Pinus roxburghii,* for the man they called the founding father of Indian botany. Interloper. Thief. Such strange thoughts she is having! Radha cannot see this moon. Radha—she should go back. She cannot go back. She goes on. The moon is so bright; so full. The party recedes behind her. The lights from the hotel retreat; the stars reach down to her instead. *Radha is having a baby. Radha is sick, so sick that she cannot hold any food down, or water.*

What does it mean to kill a child?

Gargi reaches the tower. The old chandelier, brought in from the Farm, swings down through the centre. She climbs the stairs. At the top is the Rani Suite. No, she will not lie down. She opens the balcony doors. Wooden slats beneath her feet; a concrete balustrade just thick enough to stand on; low enough to lean over. Above Gargi's head, a vast ebony sky inlaid with tiny stars. Below is a body of silver water, as if one of those diamonds has slipped from the sky and melted. There is no breeze up here; it is so cold. Running down the hillside, the city offers pinpricks of electric light. That stop around a black hole cut out of the earth.

—That's the lake, a voice says.

She turns, feels weightless. Jeet.

Months dissolve. He looks real (but thinner). He is all in black. His eyes are hollow and his lips so red. She bends and grips his arms (they are more bony than before). She feels that if she does not touch him—she cannot banish him, she will float away. She tightens her hold.

—I've done something, she says.

To touch him is to be possessed by childhood games and teenage secrets, the terrors of getting older soothed because they are together. She wants to slap him and demand to know where he has been.

—I've hurt Radha.

She hangs her head. Jeet's hands on her arms look aged; the knuckles are scarred, the nails short and unshined. He opens his palm. She places her hand in his.

—I am in love with Jivan, she says.

Jeet laughs.

—Do you know what he has done to your sister?

She stares at him. His face is definitely thinner and his eyebrows have fallen out.

No, she thinks, what has he done? This can't be a vision. Isn't it true that visions don't chit-chat? They don't wear pocket handkerchiefs that match their buttons. Gargi frowns. Behind Jeet's head the stars seem to shift; she knows she cannot trust her own eyes. Panic chokes her.

—We have to go back. Radha needs help.

—Not Radha. Did you know Sita is in the old town?

Thinking of Radha, she does not hear this. Wait. Visions do not mock or make up stories. Do they? Isn't that—in fact—all they do?

—Sita? Where is she, Jeet? I have to see her.

—You can't. She's down there.

He sweeps his hand across Gargi's forehead, the short brush of her hair. His fingers are not cold, even though the night is so clear and she is shivering. The city seems so calm from here, patches of dark, pinpricks of light. And far down there, by the silver river, someone is holding a Diwali party. Gargi can see something: the streets are on fire. All of her life, hollow in her throat.

—Jeet, she says. It's so beautiful. I want to see it better.

—Come. I'll help you. His hand grips her waist. She lifts her sari and he pushes her up, onto the balustrade. She looks down on the hotel gardens, the shimmering lake, the city in the Valley. That beauty, all ablaze. She puts her hand on Jeet's head to steady herself. He takes it, stands on tiptoe and kisses her palm.

—Sita is down there, Jeet says. A fire started in the old town, Gargi. She is at your mother's old house—don't you want to go to her? Help. She needs your help.

A sound rises on the wind, strange sirens wailing somewhere in the city below. *Sita!* Gargi thinks of her sisters standing tall around a table. She wants to be with them. She must help Sita. She trembles on the ledge. She thinks of her mother running somewhere through these streets. She shifts her feet a little forward. The lake is so silvery tonight. Sita! Her body could be light, lighter than a wisp of a shawl. *To be young and have all my life again.* Sita and Radha and her mother are waiting. She reaches her hands towards the city on fire. *All creatures rush to their destruction like flakes of snow, so joyous as they*— She steps into the air.

iii

Fireworks break the dark. Sparks draw crazy patterns, below in the grounds the people look up to wonder at the pop and shower of pink and blue and gold. Above them, in an old-fashioned library, Kritik sits at the end of the table. Weeping. *Papapapapapapapapapapa.*

Jeet. Holder of a fair share in the Company thanks to his dear father. Jeet swirls his whisky and watches Kritik cry. And here is Surendra, Gargi's poor husband, aghast with all around him. His wife—her sisters—the fact of Jeet. He looks ill, Jeet thinks, as if he wants to run.

Surendra places a hand on Kritik's shoulder. The fireworks fizz and whistle outside. Midnight is coming. Announcements have to be made, Surendra knows this. Watching, Jeet realises that both men are shaking.

Jeet wants to laugh (but doesn't). Surendra cannot lead the Company any more than a slug could win a race against a fly. Gargi used to do an impression of him in bed, pawing at her. Mew! Mew! Mew!

All those nights in Dhimbala. He fought so hard to stay away from this world. Kritik looks up—his hair is white, and nearly all gone. His eyes have dark circles below them. *What is the matter, Uncleji?* Jeet thinks. *Is it so impossible for you to understand how, of all the five, it is Jeet who is left at the end?*

—A fire across the old town, Kritik says. I could not reach them in time. Devraj, my dear. He is gone. Sita with him—I could not even get close.

Probably the news will be out already, the whispers rushing from the butlers to the waiters to the bartenders to the cooks to the potwashers to the sweepers to the children in their beds across the city. The myth will be made before the peacocks in the garden can raise one squawk.

—Kritik Uncle, your words are never false, Jeet says. Perhaps your nature sent them out into the night—has allowed this tragedy to happen.

—Ask your brother what he allows, Kritik says. He thumps the table. I should have stayed with Devraj. Sita would not listen.

Jeet looks at the monitors. Jivan appears, disappears, appears again, walking through each room, looking for something in a black-and-white world, littered with repro things.

Surendra clears his throat; he tips his glass so the whisky trembles at the edge and almost spills.

—What is your advice, Jeet? he says. At least you and I are cut from the same spiritual cloth.

Jeet tries to imagine Surendra in the basti, with the rats. On the monitors, Jivan has reached the soft drapes and overblown vases of the ladies' wing. Jeet watches his half brother walk the corridors: turning, retracing, double-backing.

—The first thing we must do is to announce that I am joining the board, Jeet says. Then we can mourn appropriately. Tonight is Diwali. We should conduct the Lakshmi puja.

—You are correct, says Kritik. But I am handcuffed to death. I will climb to Amarnath, though it is late in the year. God knows how I will go to ground, then continue from that point.

—Kritik Sahib, Jeet says. Please. Whatever you need from me I will give you—and if you must go, I understand.

This is all—the old man slips from the room, he shuts the door quietly after himself. Jeet monitors him as he goes down the stairs and off the screen. He stays to watch Jivan; he is standing, a tiny black-and-white figure, in Radha's suite. A maid is crying as she strips the bed. The room is full of Company security. A nurse is there, making notes in a book. A tiger-haired girl in a one-shoulder top pushes herself into Jivan's arms. He holds her, then lets her go. He drops into a Louis XV chair and picks up a plate of small sweets or savouries: Who knows? He eats them slowly, one by one. Where is Radha? Gone. Jeet was there, standing in the corridor when she was taken away.

—Devraj, Kritik, Ranjit, Surendra says. We can only hope to resemble.

Jeet hears the fireworks ricochet outside. He feels lit by the shower of manufactured stars. He surveys the room. There are so many books here—how did they get here? Where did they come from? Who will write of Jeet Singh, whose dharma brought him to this place? In the vast mirror hanging over the fire, his own reflection is blurred. He is not Jeet, favourite son of Bapuji, not Rudra the tea seller, cow worshipper, Yogi, teacher of basti boys. Not Jeet returned. Someone new stares back at him, a fierce Hanuman, waiting.

For a moment he sees the library, the books destroyed, the walls covered in blood. His family: all dead. His friends lost to his enemies. Vik is the ruler of a vast palace, then another and another, each one built to show the people what greatness might be. He sees hotels, paradise gardens, the jet. The emerald green of golf courses, the gleaming bodies of Bapuji's cars, the Company Goa, Delhi, Mumbai. Amritsar and Napurthala. Kashmir. Corridors all leading back to this room.

He sees Dhimbala, razes it to the ground.

Now come the screams of the women in the night, a fire burning. Then a vast cool vision, a block of pure marble in a landscaped garden, rises where Dhimbala once was. Jeet will rename every gully. He will build his Temples and his voice will rise—remember the cheers at the Company campaigns? For every one of Sita's fragile army, there are thousands upon thousands waiting for him. It is too bright, too brilliant to look.

He thinks he will never live to the grand age of spent wisdom and withering decay. The blind age. It is his dharma to leave a legacy so strong that none will be able to erase it. A wife will not be needed: if she is, a female will be found. And he will reverse the laws that promote his sick desire. Here is the next incarnation of Jeet, reborn a pure leader of men.

—Jeet, Surendra says. You and I will always speak truth to each other, no? The times charge us to do so.

Outside the fireworks yield to qawwali, sung by a troupe of world-famous players, a family of five sons. Their voices rasp and rub against each other's, floating through the window, entreating the night to remain.

Jeet raises his glass, and drinks.

—Come, he says. Let us go down. It is time to begin.

Acknowledgements

This book would not be without the following people's brilliance, generosity, support—

and love. Ben Crowe.

Aubrey and Patricia Crowe. Dan Crowe and Emily Evans. Pria Doogan. Asha and Raj Kubba. Neelam Taneja.

Sam Jordison, Eloise Millar and all at Galley Beggar Press.

Sonny Mehta and all at Alfred A. Knopf.

Gitanjali Kumar. Kristen Harrison. So Mayer.

My deepest thanks indeed are due to—

Mary Campbell. Christie Carson. Andrew Dickson. Maureen Freely. Gatehouse Press. Sophie Gilmartin. David Godwin and all at DGA. Sam Hall. Robert Hampson. Imtiaz. Sujata Khanna. Susanna Lea and all at SLA. Matt Lingley. Juliet Mitchell. Andrew Motion. Deana Rankin. Carol Rutter. Kiernan Ryan. SF Said. David Schalkwyk. Tani Vadehra Singh. Anna South. Ashish and Pooja Taneja. Simon Trewin. Poonam Trivedi. Nilita Vachani. Amit, Amol and Aseem Vadehra. Eley Williams.

ACKNOWLEDGEMENTS

. . .

All of the contributors to *Visual Verse.*
    And so many friends, survivors on the journey.

I am grateful to Arvind Krishna Mehrotra for permitting me to use his translations of Kabir as epigraph and on page 252, and scattered in lines throughout.

Somitra Ganguly translated the ghazal on pages 172–73.

The fable on page 436 is abridged and reprinted with kind permission of Tilottama Rajan from the Penguin Classics edition of the *Pancatantra,* translated by Chandra Rajan (1993, p. 13).

The first draft of this book was made possible with the award of the Reid Scholarship (2010–2013) at Royal Holloway, University of London. It was finished alongside academic work at Queen Mary University of London and Warwick University (2014–2016), and with the support of the fellowship at Jesus College, Cambridge University, and a Leverhulme Early Career Research Fellowship, held at Warwick University (2017–2019).

A NOTE ON THE TYPE

This book was set in Adobe Garamond. Designed for the Adobe Corporation by Robert Slimbach, the fonts are based on types first cut by Claude Garamond (ca. 1480–1561). Garamond was a pupil of Geoffroy Tory and is believed to have followed the Venetian models, although he introduced a number of important differences, and it is to him that we owe the letter we now know as "old style."

Composed by North Market Street Graphics,
Lancaster, Pennsylvania
Printed and bound by Berryville Graphics,
Berryville, Virginia
Designed by Soonyoung Kwon